KINDRED SPIRITS MYSTERIES

Volume One: Books 1-5

The Secret of Misthaven Light

Bridging the Heart

The Curse at White Pines

The Last Act

I'll Be Home for Christmas

BETH CONNOR

The Secret of Misthaven Light

KINDRED SPIRITS MYSTERIES

BETH CONNOR

WOLF GROVE MEDIA, LLC

Contents

CHAPTER ONE

In the Depths of Dreams

Ella Hayes found herself on the cusp of a world suspended between reality and fantasy. Before her, the beacon of a distant lighthouse cut through the night, a solitary pulse in the vast expanse of shadow and light. This rhythmic glow, like the heartbeat of the sea, seemed to whisper secrets carried on the wind meant only for her.

Moonlight wove through her chestnut hair, casting silver highlights that danced across her features. Her hazel eyes mirrored the wild spirit, reflecting its fierce beauty. She stood far from the familiar walls of her apartment and was drawn to the beacon's light. It flashed, and her heart kept time with its pulse.

The island itself emerged from the mist, a silhouette of rugged cliffs. It was an untamed land, with a solitary dwelling nearby the lighthouse. This was a place wrapped in the legends of those who had walked its shores before—echoes of laughter, whispers of sorrow, and love lost to time.

As she watched, a figure appeared from the shadows, a silent sentinel emerging from the night's embrace. His presence was a mystery, his features blurred, as if he were a spirit conjured from the island's soul. Ella felt a whirlwind of emotions stir. He was a whisper against the sea's roar, a curiosity that reached beyond the confines of her solitary life.

This was not the first time she had had this dream. Their fleeting encounters, veiled in twilight, wove a tapestry of intrigue and promises, pulling her heart toward a story waiting to be discovered and an island shrouded in secrets.

Dawn broke and Ella stirred from slumber, the remnants of her dream clinging like a second skin. It was in these dreams she wished to remain, for within their embrace, she felt a vibrancy, a life far removed from the waking world's dull hues. Here, in reality, a sense of isolation enveloped her, a stark emptiness that no sunlight could dispel. How she yearned to dwell where her dreams lent color to existence and she was never alone.

The days became a whirlwind of thoughts about the man and the mysterious lighthouse haunting her dreams. Life settled into a rhythm of eat, sleep, paint, repeat. Yet with each stroke of her brush, her obsession with the man and the unknown location grew, consuming her. Her apartment transformed into a chaotic collection of canvases and sketches, all depicting scenes from a place she'd never visited, and a man she'd never seen. She wondered if he was real, or just a figment of her overactive imagination? Each day, she delved deeper into this passion, her soul ablaze with the need to solve the mystery that intertwined her dreams and waking life.

One morning, as Ella was immersed in the swirls of paint on her canvas, a sudden knock at the door snapped her back to the present. A wave of annoyance swept over her. She treasured the quiet cocoon of her studio, her refuge from the outside world, and was annoyed at the interruption. Yet, as she made her way to the door, her heart ached with a twinge of loneliness, a reminder of her recent loss.

Her parents, who had not survived an awful car accident, had been the anchors in her otherwise solitary existence. They had always breezed through the walls she had built around herself, offering unconditional love and understanding. Her father's gentle humor and her mother's nurturing presence had been a balm to her introverted soul. Their sudden absence in her life left a void no amount of painting could fill.

As she reached the door, memories flooded her thoughts - the way they had always encouraged her art, their smiles as they admired each new piece, and the comfort of their quiet support. Their passing, though it had been a few months, still felt raw, the wound fresh as if it were just yesterday.

With a heavy heart, Ella opened the door, half-expecting to see their familiar, loving faces, only to be greeted by an outside world that seemed so distant now. She missed their gentle intrusion, the way they could turn her solitary space into a home filled with laughter and warmth.

Instead, she found Tanya. Ella always considered her neighbor Tanya more of an obligatory acquaintance than a friend. The older woman loved cats a little too much, and had a habit of imposing her presence on Ella. Still, Tanya's interruptions, though inconvenient, were never unpleasant.

"Hey, sweetie," Tanya greeted her with a sympathetic smile. "I haven't seen you a lot since, well... Just checking in."

Ella managed a faint response. "I'm fine. Just caught up in a new project."

Without waiting for an invitation, Tanya stepped in, her eyes drawn to the canvases. "Oh, honey, these are beautiful. What is this place?"

"Please don't... they're not ready yet." Ella moved to shield her work.

But Tanya, undaunted, continued to peruse the room. "You're looking thin, dear. I'll bring you some lunch later, okay?"

Ella nodded and acknowledged Tanya's impending return, her eyes following Tanya as the woman paused in front of the painting of her dream lighthouse.

"This scene, it has the feel of the East Coast, maybe Maine." Tanya mused, "Did you know many lighthouses there are rumored to be haunted?"

A spark of interest flickered in Ella. "Maine, you say?"

Tanya nodded, a small smile playing on her lips. "Yes, Maine. I've got a book about its lighthouses. I'll bring it along with your lunch."

Ella's response was measured, a careful balance to mask her growing excitement. "That would be nice." Her eyes betrayed a hint of the enthusiasm she was trying to contain. The notion that her recurring dream could be linked to an actual place sent a ripple of anticipation through her.

As Tanya disappeared to fetch the book and lunch, Ella's mind danced with images of rugged coasts and spectral lighthouses, wondering if the answers she sought lay within their storied walls.

Ella returned to her canvas. The brush danced across the surface with a life of its own. She was lost in the swirls of color that brought the scene to life, capturing the rugged beauty of a lighthouse perched on a cliff. It stood tall against the backdrop of a tumultuous sea, its beacon a solitary point of light in the encroaching twilight. Ella's strokes were deliberate, each one adding depth and emotion to the painting, the scene unfolding under her skilled hands as if by magic. Just then, the tranquility was shattered by the door swinging open.

"I'm back!" Tanya breezed in. Clutched in her hands were two mugs, the steam wafting from them carrying the rich scent of chowder. "Thought we'd stick with the lighthouse theme," she declared, a grin spreading across her face.

Ella's lips tightened. She hadn't expected sitting down with Tanya. Yet, the gesture softened her resolve. With a nod, she settled in at the table.

Tanya set the soup down before taking a seat. The book of lighthouses she placed on the table seemed to bridge the space between them.

Curiosity piqued, Ella reached for the book, her fingers tracing the title, "Shadows on the Shore: Unveiling Maine's Haunted Lighthouses and Their Forgotten Tales." As she flipped through the pages, a strange affinity for the tales and images of those remote sentinels washed over her. One story, in particular, captured her imagination—*the Curse of Misthaven Light.* The image if the lighthouse with the small dwelling next to it felt like a memory, as though she could wander its halls and climb its tower with her eyes closed.

This was it. The place in her dreams! She devoured the words, each syllable a morsel feeding her curiosity. The passage was brief, a mere whisper of lore about the Misthaven Light on a small island, nestled just off the shores of Bar Harbor, Maine. It teased at the notion of a curse, yet withheld the why.

Bar Harbor... With a sudden clarity, Ella realized her dream lighthouse was real! Her excitement was palpable, yet she held a part of it back, aware of Tanya's curiousity. "This lighthouse that looks like the one I painted, it's in Bar Harbor," she remarked, more to herself than to Tanya, her finger tracing the image of the lighthouse on the page.

"Oh?" Tanya picked up on Ella's interest, her tone casual. "Sounds intriguing. What's so special about this one?"

"It's... It's just different. There's a story here, something...unresolved."

"I love a good mystery, and you seem quite taken by it." Tanya smiled. "Keep the book. I have too much stuff."

"Thanks." Ella replied the gratitude clear in her face.

As Tanya's attention returned to her soup, Ella's thoughts were miles away, with Misthaven Light's steadfast beam and the mysterious man. They urged her to look beyond her life in Sacramento and to explore the connection tying them together.

Night after night, she was left with a maze of questions, but Ella sensed that understanding her link to the distant lighthouse and the figure was crucial to solving this mystery. In her dreams, the man was like a song on repeat, always there but forever blurred and elusive, shrouded in mist. His face was indistinct, but his lips moved as though he were trying to tell her something.

"Find me," he seemed to whisper.

One morning, Ella opened her laptop and searched for Bar Harbor, Maine, and Misthaven Island. A real estate listing caught her eye, sparking the beginnings of a daring plan. With her parents gone, she found herself untethered and questioning what held her in California.

This realization struck her with the force of a lightning bolt. The inheritance left by her parents was the key to a new chapter waiting to be written. With a clarity that surprised even herself, Ella chased her dreams to the rugged coast of Maine.

Maybe, just maybe, in the embrace of Misthaven Island's lighthouse, she would uncover the secrets that seemed to beckon her. This choice, fueled by curiosity, yearning, and perhaps a touch of fate, signaled the start of Ella's quest for self-discovery and the deep connection she felt with a place she had yet to see.

As soon as she embraced her decision, her life transformed with remarkable swiftness. She took a leap of faith, purchasing the cozy, furnished cottage in Bar Harbor without seeing it in person. The timing aligned with the end of her apartment lease, propelling her forward on her journey with a seamless transition.

In preparing for her move, Ella realized the simplicity of her needs. The essentials were her art supplies — the lifeblood of her creative spirit—and a modest selection of clothing for a few weeks. These were the tools and comforts that would accompany her into this new phase. Everything else she sold.

On the day of her move, she lingered for a moment in the doorway of her apartment, soaking in its familiar embrace for the last time. The cozy space was steeped in the sweet scent of dried lavender from the windowsill, intertwined with the comforting smell of oil paints and well-used canvas. Every corner, every shadow of the room, seemed to hold echoes of joy and sorrow from her past life.

Tanya spotted Ella surrounded by boxes. "So this is it?" Tanya asked.

"Yes, off to Bar Harbor, Maine," Ella responded.

"That's quite the journey. Ill miss you kiddo."

Ella's fingers played with the frayed edge of a cardboard box, her attention caught between the silent object and the unspoken words hanging in the air with Tanya. She chose silence, unsure of what to say next.

Tanya's eyes, much like those of her feline companions, reflected a deep understanding, an empathy that went beyond mere words. "Sometimes, our soul yearns for a new horizon, a change in scenery to stir our creativity," Tanya said. "Bar Harbor sounds like a place straight out of a dream. I hope you find what you're seeking."

In Tanya's words, Ella found a surprising comfort and an unexpected validation of her quest. As she turned to leave, she carried with her Tanya's understanding, a reminder that connections *could* be formed and cherished.

On her arrival in Bar Harbor, the sharp salty breeze and the distant crash of waves greeted Ella. The town unfolded before her like a scene from a storybook, with its cobblestone pathways, quaint cottages, and the endless dance of light upon the sea merging with the horizon.

Her new home was a portrait of New England's charm. Perched on a gentle hill, it boasted breathtaking views of the bay and the distant lighthouse. The cottage, with its weathered shingles, whispered tales of yesteryear. Roses and ivy graced its stone base, infusing vitality into its storied exterior.

Stepping inside, the cottage's warmth enveloped her—a living room, cozy and inviting, hosted a stone fireplace marked by the laughter of fires long past. Above, wooden beams cradled the ceiling, and the light danced on the polished hardwood floors.

To the left, was a kitchen painted in hues of the sea. The countertops were worn smooth by time and a porcelain sink overlooking a garden lush with wildflowers and herbs. A staircase led her to the bedroom that was furnished with a four-poster bed, cloaked in white muslin. It beckoned with the promise of rest, while a modest table stood ready for her sketches and blooms.

It was the three-season room, filled with natural light and offering an expansive view, that became her favored retreat—a perfect studio for her art. The wide windows not only provided a breathtaking panorama but also infused the space with energy. Here, Ella felt a deep connection to the surrounding landscape, which fueled her creativity and transformed the room into a sanctuary where her visions could take flight.

Living in the cottage was like becoming a strand in the fabric of a beloved tapestry. Every day brought new marvels, and the occasional nod from a neighbor while passing by hinted at the interconnectedness of this coastal community.

One bustling day at the local market, Ella found herself among a dance of sights and sounds. Fishermen announced their catch, bakers tempted with sweet pastries, and craftspeople displayed their labors of love. As she wandered the streets, a stall adorned with delicate seashell necklaces caught her eye.

Captivated by the craftsmanship, Ella complimented their beauty. The vendor, an older woman whose face was mapped with smile lines, responded. "They're pieces of Bar Harbor itself, dear. Each one holds a chapter of our seaside lore."

Ella was intrigued. She chose a necklace that seemed to whisper of the ocean's mysteries and asked, "Could you tell me the story behind this one?"

The woman began, "Ah, this one is a whispering shell. Legend has it that if two people each tell their deepest desires into it and then release it back to the sea together, the tides will carry their wishes to the heart of the ocean."

After hearing this, Ella felt a spark of wonder. That such a simple act could intertwine destinies intrigued her. While the tale seemed more like a charming fable than reality, it stirred within her a curious blend of hope and whimsy.

"I'll take it." Ella said.

As she reached for her wallet, a sudden jostle from a passerby sent a cascade of coins clattering to the ground. Flustered and a bit embarrassed, she knelt to gather them, her cheeks warming with a flush of awkwardness.

Just then, she was joined by a man who seemed to personify the essence Bar Harbor. His sandy hair shimmered with hints of gold in the morning light and his eyes were as deep and varied as the ocean.

"Let me help you with that," he offered, his voice a comforting melody of warmth and concern.

Their fingers brushed as he handed her the scattered coins, sending a surprising jolt of connection through Ella. It was as if a circuit had been completed, a current of unspoken understanding flowing between them.

"First time at the market?" he asked, a twinkle in his eyes.

Ella, still gathering her composure, managed a response. "Not my first market, just... not usually this clumsy." She could feel her face burning, hoping her embarrassment wasn't as obvious as it felt.

His smile was like a lighthouse beam cutting through a foggy harbor—bright, welcoming, and tinged with mischief. "It happens to the best of us. I'm Benjamin. Welcome to Bar Harbor," he introduced himself, offering a handshake.

"Ella," she managed, her voice barely above a whisper, betraying her nervousness.

Benjamin paused, as if expecting something more, but noticing her hesitation, he shifted to a softer tone. "If you're looking for tips about the area or just fancy a chat, I'm around."

After a moment that felt suspended in time, she found an opening to withdraw. "Thank you, Benjamin. I might take you up on that," she said, her voice steadier now, though her heart still skipped erratically.

With a small, understanding smile, Benjamin stepped aside, giving her the room she seemed to need. Ella turned towards the stall with a sense of relief and exchanged the money for the necklace. When she glanced back, hoping for a last nod or maybe to memorize his face for her sketches, Benjamin had vanished into the crowd. The space where he stood was now just an empty patch of cobblestone.

That evening, nestled in the snug embrace of an old armchair within her new cottage, Ella mulled over the day's encounters. The memory of meeting Benjamin brought a gentle warmth to her cheeks. His friendly chatter and observant eyes had offered a moment of comfort in the unknown landscape of Bar Harbor.

"Should I have asked for his number?" she mused to the room's stillness, her reflection in the window mirroring a shy smile. The idea of reaching out first was foreign to her, especially given the fleeting nature of their meeting.

As darkness enfolded the town, Ella's thoughts buzzed with a cocktail of emotions — excitement, hesitation, a budding sense of adventure, and regret for not doing more. She sighed, accepting her reluctance to act. Yet, the spark of curiosity about Benjamin and what he represented — a potential new bond — lingered.

She resigned herself to whatever might come, she trusted that if their paths were meant to cross again, they would. For now, she turned her focus to the adventures awaiting in her dreams.

Chapter Two

A Fresh Start

In the quaint pulse of Bar Harbor, Ella discovered herself seamlessly woven into the fabric of its existence.

The once alien landscapes now brimmed with inclusion and camaraderie. As she meandered through the cozy, narrow lanes, she felt a newfound happiness.

The inhabitants of this locale extended a welcome toward her that was devoid of any pretense. They embraced her as if she had always been a part of their close-knit community. It was in these simple, unassuming interactions—laughing together over steaming cups of coffee, exchanging knowing glances during the everyday hustle—that Ella discovered her niche.

In the crisp embrace of morning, bathed in the golden hues of the sun, Ella found herself drawn to the bustling activity at the dock. Here, in the salty air and the creaking of boats, seasoned fishermen prepared for their day. It was during one of these early walks that Ella, driven by a blend of curiosity and the thrill of adventure, broached the subject of a voyage to Misthaven Island. However, the captain, his gaze as weathered as the decks he trod upon, offered a gentle but firm refusal. "I'm afraid that's not possible, miss. The island's off-limits."

This refusal left Ella disappointed. The captain's words had a finality that discouraged further inquiry. Why was Misthaven Island enveloped in such secrecy? What mysteries did it hold that made it forbidden to outsiders? Despite the flurry of questions dancing through her mind, she felt unease—a hesitancy to probe deeper. She wasn't comfortable enough in these new surroundings to challenge the boundaries. This unspoken barrier cast a shadow of melancholy over her spirit, yet it also sowed the seeds of a deeper intrigue about the island and its untold stories.

Despite this setback, the village itself seemed to cradle her spirits in its embrace. A visit to the market saw Martha, the kind owner of a local bakery, with her hands cloaked in flour. Her eyes gleamed as she encouraged Ella to sample her homemade blueberry jam. This gesture showed the genuine web of relationships that Ella was forming within this community.

As Ella savored the delicious jam spread on a freshly baked biscuit, she found the courage to broach the topic of Misthaven Island, speaking through bites of her snack. Martha, with a twinkle of amusement in her eye, waited for Ella to finish her treat before responding. In a low, almost secretive tone, she said, "Oh, bad things always seem to happen there—too many people have been hurt, and it's fallen into disrepair. The authorities keep it off limits, but we all whisper that it's because of the curse."

"Cursed?" Ella echoed, her curiosity piqued even though she had come across this detail in her reading.

"Yes," Martha continued, leaning in closer. "Legend says that a long time ago, a sea captain's crew mutinied, leaving him stranded on the island before there was even a lighthouse. He perished from exposure, only miles from his own doorstep."

"Oh, wow," Ella responded, her interest deepening.

"But wait—it gets even more grim. The leader of the mutineers came back to Bar Harbor, and he claimed the captain's betrothed for himself. They were married soon after!"

Ella, intrigued and unsettled by the tales swirling around Misthaven Island, decided it was time to shift the conversation away from its eerie history. "I'll take a jar of this jam, and some bread, please," she said, eager to bring a piece of this warm community spirit back to her cottage. Martha, with a knowing smile, packaged up the jam and a loaf, her hands skilled and quick from years of practice.

As Ella handed over the payment, she felt a sense of connection to this little town. With her purchase in hand, she thanked Martha for both the food and the conversation.

As the day unfolded, Ella decided not to go home. Instead, she secured her recent purchases in her bag. The bread and jam, more than just food, now represented her connection to Bar Harbor's rich narrative, and its welcoming community. Despite the haunting stories that lingered like fog over Misthaven Island, Ella felt a reassuring sense of purpose and place here. Her steps meandered through the town's historic heart.

As she wandered, Bar Harbor unfurled itself like a well-loved book. Each street and building became a paragraph in its ongoing story. The cobblestones underfoot and the venerable facades around her whispered tales of days long past. This journey of discovery brought her to the doorstep of the town library. Ella found solace among stories and facts. The musty aroma of old books enveloped her in a comforting embrace. It was in this refuge, nestled among the chronicles of history, that Ella's solitude was shattered.

The unexpected sight of Benjamin, the man from the market, caused her heart to skip a beat. As he delved into the book with the focus of a detective on a case sent her heart into a frenzy, she couldn't help but state. Memories of their last encounter prompted an instant reaction. Ella, determined to avoid a repeat performance, morphed into an amateur spy attempting to navigate the maze of bookshelves with the grace of a gazelle. Unfortunately, her grace was more like that of a newborn deer on a slippery floor. This resulted in a less than graceful shuffle behind a stack of books as Benjamin looked up from his reading.

Her covert operation reached its peak when Benjamin, perhaps sensing a disturbance in the force or simply needing more books, stood up and stretched. Ella, in a moment of panic, executed a swift dive behind the nearest bookshelf, knocking a few books off in her haste, her heart racing like she'd just run a marathon.

The librarian, having witnessed the whole spectacle, approached. "Everything alright here?" she asked, her eyes twinkling as she glanced from the scattered books to Ella's mortified expression.

"Oh, yes, just, um, researching...gravity!" Ella blurted out. "And lighthouses," she added.

The librarian, struggling to maintain her professional demeanor, couldn't help but let out a gentle laugh. "Well, it seems you're quite the multi-tasker. Let me help you with these," she said, bending down to pick up the books. With a conspiratorial lean closer, she whispered, "You know, Benjamin is a great guy, and single. No need to hide from him. I would be happy to introduce you."

Ella, now a brilliant shade of red, could only shake her head, her voice having taken an impromptu vacation.

"You let me know if you change your mind." The librarian winked.

As Benjamin left the area, Ella dared to peek from her hiding spot.

When she was sure Benjamin was long gone, she stepped outside. The day's escapades replayed in her mind, painting a smile on her lips. Bar Harbor turned even the most mundane days into chapters of a personal novel. It had once again left her heart fluttering with anticipation for adventures—and perhaps more encounters with Benjamin (at a safe distance)—tomorrow might bring.

In the weeks to follow, Ella's seaside cottage became more than a home. It was a canvas for her story, each room echoing with the potential for new tales. The whispers of history and the call of the ocean through its windows set a rhythm to her life, inspiring her transformation. She carved out a nook with an ocean view, making it a haven for reading and reflection, adorned with a vintage armchair and books on local lore, in particular, lighthouses.

The process of turning the cottage into a place that reflected her soul was a journey of love, blending pictures and family treasures with quirky market finds.

Sunlight and shadows played across rooms lined with handcrafted rugs and sheer curtains, crafting a serene setting.

Her studio, bathed in natural light and overlooking the sea, became the heart of her artistic exploration. Amidst paints, brushes, and turpentine, Ella found her voice. The sea and sky fueled her creativity, guiding her brushstrokes to capture the essence of Bar Harbor and Misthaven Island. Her lighthouse, once just a motif, became a symbol of her journey—both as an artist finding her path and as a soul connected to the coastal landscape that embraced her.

Ella's art led to a partnership with a local shop catering to tourists. They featured her lighthouse designs on postcards, blending Ella's vision with the community's charm. This collaboration extended her art beyond her studio, turning her creations into mementos that connected visitors with Maine landscapes. Through these postcards, her work wove itself into the fabric of the community, becoming a shared piece of the region's essence and heritage.

Amid Ella's creative renaissance, the mystery man continued to visit her dreams. He stirred a whirlwind of emotions she couldn't quite grasp. She resisted the urge to capture his image on canvas, instead pouring her feelings into her depictions of the lighthouse, making it a silent testament to the mysteries of her heart.

A revealing dream soon offered a clearer vision of this man. As the lines between her dreams and reality blurred more and more, Ella found herself in a dance of anticipation. Each night's sleep was a portal to further intimacy with this presence.

Compelled to unravel the mystery of this faceless man, Ella's days were consumed by her art, her talent blossoming. Yet, as dusk fell, she yearned for the dream world, for another encounter with the man who had become an indelible part of her soul.

Questions haunted Ella. Was she crafting a fantasy so vivid it overshadowed reality? Her quest for answers drove her deep into Bar Harbor's history, sifting through old books and faded photographs, desperate for a clue to the dream man's identity. Was it possible he was more than just a figment of her imagination? Did his story intertwine with the lore of the town itself?

Her art reflected this inner turmoil. Once tranquil, seascapes now churned with stormy emotions, her lighthouses standing as beacons of a desperate search, their light cutting through the dark mysteries of the sea. Ella stood at a crossroads, torn between the allure of her nighttime visitor and the grounding pull of the tangible world around her. As she navigated this twilight of doubt and discovery, the town of Bar Harbor became the backdrop for a journey.

Ella hadn't seen Benjamin again since the incident at the library incident. Maybe he is a tourist passing through? Yet, the librarian had vouched for his character, describing him as a "great guy." She wouldn't have spoken so confidently without knowing him. The discomfort from their last meeting lingered, a persistent fog of awkwardness that served as a barrier preventing her from searching for him. Ella couldn't help but mourn the loss of what might have been—a potential connection that was severed before it could flourish. Perhaps she had let a rare chance slip through her fingers. There had been something real between them, a spark of possibility that hadn't been given the chance to ignite.

The burden she carried wasn't solely because of unresolved feelings. Guilt gnawed at her for allowing the memory of a real man to fade, overshadowed by a figure from her dreams. These fantasies infiltrated her waking hours, casting a shadow that dwarfed the fleeting moments she had shared with Benjamin.

The man from her dreams seemed to fill the spaces Benjamin left behind, offering an allure that was intoxicating. This dream visitor, with no name and a face that eluded clarity, became a fixture in her nights, stirring a longing for something indefinable. His presence was a constant reminder of the unknown, a challenge to the boundaries of Ella's reality. As each night unfolded into day, the line between the dream world and her waking life blurred, leaving her to wonder if the emotions he evoked were as real as they felt, or the echo of her own desires projected onto the canvas of her dreams.

Caught in duality, Ella navigated her days with a sense of disquiet. Her art became an outlet for the sea of emotions. This internal struggle, set against the backdrop of Bar Harbor's beauty, painted a poignant picture of longing and introspection, a soul searching for answers in a world where the line between reality and fantasy was ever wavering.

Nights found Ella nestled in her reading nook, adrift in historical documents and town archives, searching for any clue that might anchor her dream visitor to Bar Harbor's past. Was he a sailor whose life was woven into the fabric of the town? An ancient keeper of the lighthouse? Or her own longing?

In her quieter moments, Ella wrestled with seeking therapy, questioning whether her mind had crafted an imaginary companion to occupy the silent, empty spaces that had grown in her life. The death of her parents had left her adrift, and the mysterious dream man had not appeared until after that devastating loss. Was this a sign of her psyche fracturing under grief? Could her decision to pack up and leave, chasing the phantom comforts of a dream, be evidence of her unraveling? She harbored regrets, wondering if her actions were a flight from reality rather than a step toward healing.

Yet, every time she considered distancing herself from these nighttime escapades, the undeniable pull of the dream man beckoned her back into his arms. His presence felt real. The thought of losing this connection terrified her more than the prospect of facing her mental state. It was a complex dance of desire and denial, where the fear of confronting her loss mingled with the fear of losing the one source of comfort she had come to rely on.

Ella's existence was a mosaic of dreams and waking moments. It was hard to distinguish between the two. Somewhere within this maze lay the truth she yearned to uncover.

The man's face became more distinct. His eyes held deep, untold stories, and his well-defined jawline added to his allure. He appeared to mouth words to her, but she couldn't make them out. She remembered the night when she first saw his features. This made her dreams feel almost touchable, as though she could feel his warmth and touch, as vivid as the sea breeze caressing her skin.

With each morning, the essence of those dreams lingered around Ella like a perfume pervading her waking hours. Her studio, quiet and observant, bore witness to the emotional whirlwind within her. Her canvases came alive with vibrant, passionate hues—fiery reds and deep blues painted with bold, enthusiastic strokes, each one more expressive than the last.

Caught in a wave of inspiration, Ella felt a resolve take hold. She faced the mysterious figure from her dreams through her art, her true domain. With charcoal in hand, she aimed to capture his image—the intense look in his eyes, the slight smirk on his lips, and the precise contours of his face. Through her artwork, she hoped to grasp his essence, to calm the storm he stirred within her, and to find the clarity she sought.

Positioned in front of her blank canvas, Ella aimed to immortalize the man who invaded her dreams and daydreams. He had become a constant in the tumult of her emotions and stability in her inner turmoil.

The image expanded into an infinite landscape in her imagination.. She pictured the man, with the life and emotions etched in the shadows and light of his gray eyes—eyes that had beheld incredible sights and braved fierce challenges with resilience. His skin told stories of sunlit days and contrasted the darkness of his hair. A weathered tricorn hat sat atop his head, symbolizing the adventures and tales he carried with him.

With this vivid image in her mind, Ella's hand moved, guided by both certainty and skill. The charcoal became a tool of her intent, outlining the powerful jaw, the flow of his hair, and the unique traits that seemed to tell of ancient lore. Her lines awakened the depth in his gaze, so intense it felt as though he was there, looking back at her, their connection bridging worlds through the power of her artistry.

The Historians Tale

Ella was on the edge of a defining moment, but sharing her research felt as intimate as divulging a secret crush. Despite the trepidation, she recognized the need for help, as her solo efforts to decode her perplexing dreams had reached an impasse. She caught her reflection in a puddle, wondering if her anxiety was as apparent as it felt. A quick adjustment of a stray lock of hair and a glance at her slightly flushed cheeks confirmed her suspicion that her usual calm demeanor was betrayed by a look of concern. "Come on, Ella, you've got this," she whispered to herself, trying to drum up some courage.

Upon entering the library, Ella was struck by a wave of self-consciousness. It felt as though the patrons had a supernatural ability to peer into her soul, witnessing her inner turmoil and the vivid dreams that haunted her nights. Her heart thumped so loudly she was convinced it could be heard across the room.

The librarian offered a small sense of familiarity in the sea of uncertainty. After remembering the librarian's previous acts of kindness, Ella approached the desk with a mixture of hope and nerves. "Excuse me," she began, her voice shaky, "I'm looking for information on the history of Misthaven Light. Could you help me?"

The librarian glanced up, her expression shifting to one of intrigue. "Today might just be your lucky day," she said with a secret smile. "Our very own expert on Misthaven Light is here in the library at this moment!"

Ella's stomach churned with dread at the thought of discussing her research so directly, and did not trust the woman's smile.

Leading the way, the librarian navigated through the library's maze of bookshelves, with Ella trailing behind, her mind buzzing with questions and concerns. How would this expert react to her questions?

They stopped in a secluded corner, and Ella's heart skipped a beat. In front of her, buried under a pile of books, was Benjamin. For a moment, Ella's mind raced with panic. It was one thing to face an expert, but confronting Benjamin, with all her unspoken feelings tangled up in the mix, felt like a twist of fate designed to test her resolve to its limits.

"Benjamin," the librarian called out, "this young lady has questions about the lighthouse."

He looked up, his deep blue eyes locking onto Ella's. To her surprise, there wasn't a trace of judgment in his gaze, only curiosity. She forced herself to regain composure and take a deep breath. The past was behind them.

As Ella blurted out a quick "Hello." Benjamin's fingers fidgeted with the edge of the book in front of him, betraying a nervous energy she hadn't noticed before.

"Well," he began, clearing his throat more times than was necessary, "I, uh, must say that our previous encounter was...interesting, right?" He chuckled, a little too loud, a blush creeping up his neck. "And, um, I totally forgot to ask for your number. It's not a usual oversight for someone who's supposed to pay attention to details."

Ella smiled, her own cheeks warming. "It's okay. I did not plan to bump into... well, anyone that day."

His fingers halted their dance with the book's edge. "And yet, here we are. What drew you to the lighthouse's story?"

She hesitated, picking at the corner of the book she held, searching for words that wouldn't sound too foolish. "I've been seeing... patterns in old paintings I've come across. The lighthouse keeps appearing, and I wanted to learn more. To see if there's a connection."

He regarded her with thoughtful eyes, a slow smile forming. "Misthaven Light has so many tales attached to it. I've always found it fascinating."

There was a silence, filled with the rustling of pages and distant murmurs of other library-goers. Both seemed unsure of how to bridge the gap that their shared awkwardness had created.

Finally, Benjamin ventured, "You know, discussing history in hushed library tones isn't ideal. Would you consider a coffee? Somewhere we can...talk?" He grimaced, his face turning red.

Ella grinned, finding his discomfort a relief. At least she wasn't the only one. "I think a coffee chat about lighthouses sounds just right."

Benjamin chuckled, his eyes lighting up. "Perfect. I'll pick up some books and papers from my place, and then let's meet at The Harbor Brew in about thirty minutes."

The Harbor Brew was a small cafe that served as both a coffee shop and a brewery. Ella was charmed by the clever wordplay in its name. While waiting for Benjamin, she browsed the posters on the community board. The place was alive with events, from art exhibitions to poetry readings and live music by local bands. She made a mental note to return one evening.

Within minutes, she noticed Benjamin tucked away in a corner, surrounded by a collection of papers and old books. He had been observing her as she explored, causing her cheeks to flush with a bright red as she caught his gaze. Ella approached him and was met with the sparkle of his blue eyes.

"Ready to dive deep into the history of Misthaven?" he asked.

Ella nodded, brushing a strand of her brown hair behind an ear. "I can't wait."

Benjamin adjusted his glasses. "Long before the lighthouse became the beacon of Misthaven Island, the area was infamous for its treacherous waters and cruel tales. One such tale is haunting."

Ella leaned in, her eyes wide with anticipation.

"There was a sailor, Captain Elias, known for his bravery and nobility. He was in love with a woman named Clara, a beauty who held the heart of many a man in Bar Harbor, but she only had eyes for Elias. That is until a treacherous first mate, Blackwood, took matters into his own hands."

Benjamin paused, letting his story sink in. "On a fateful night, Blackwood marooned Elias on the desolate Misthaven Island, leaving him at the mercy of the elements, with no hope of escape. With Elias out of the picture, Blackwood returned to Bar Harbor, weaving a tale of Elias's heroic death. Grief-stricken, Clara found solace in Blackwood's arms, unaware of his betrayal."

Ella's eyes welled up, the cruelty of the tale striking a chord within her. "That's devastating."

"It gets darker," Benjamin murmured. "Blackwood, realizing the strategic location of the island, spearheaded the construction of the lighthouse, becoming its very first keeper. He married Clara, and they lived on the island, forever shadowed by Elias's anguished spirit."

Ella shivered. "So, Captain Elias haunts Misthaven Island?"

Benjamin nodded. "Many claim to have heard his mournful cries on stormy nights, a chilling reminder of a love betrayed. The lighthouse stands, not just as a beacon for ships, but as a testament to love that was snatched away."

Benjamin looked pensive for a moment, swirling the coffee in his mug. The afternoon sunlight streamed through the coffee shop's windows, casting long shadows on the table, reflecting the somber mood.

"But the island's tragedies didn't end with Elias," he began with a solemn tone. "The curse of Misthaven Island, as some locals believe, continued with the next generation. Blackwood and Clara had a daughter, Isabella, as radiant as the dawn and kind-hearted. Many sought her hand, but it was Captain Nathaniel Hawthorne who won her heart."

Benjamin continued, "However, just when happiness might grace Misthaven Island once again, fate intervened. They found Isabella dead at the base of the cliffs surrounding the lighthouse. The whole town mourned the young beauty, and rumors spread like wildfire."

Ella's eyes shone with anticipation. "What rumors?" she whispered.

"There were whispers of a love triangle. While Isabella was set to marry Nathaniel, there was another who was infatuated with her, a man named Samuel. Some say..." Benjamin hesitated, weighing his words, "Samuel had feelings for Isabella that went unrequited."

Benjamin looked down, his fingers tracing the wood grain of the table. "Both Nathaniel and Samuel were accused of Isabella's murder at different points in time. The town was divided. Some believed that Nathaniel, out of jealousy, had killed Isabella, suspecting her of having feelings for Samuel. Others thought that Samuel, in a fit of rage and passion, might have committed the crime. But nothing concrete ever came to light. No evidence, no witnesses. Only an island haunted by the echoes of a love torn apart by fate."

Ella was lost in thought, digesting the heavy tale. The tragedies of Misthaven Island were more profound and tangled than she had ever imagined. "And what became of Nathaniel and Samuel after that?" She wondered out loud.

Benjamin sighed. "Nathaniel took over the lighthouse, a shadow of the man he once was. Some say he would stand on the cliff that Isabella fell from searching for her memory or spirit. As for Samuel, he became a recluse, shutting himself away from the world, drowning in his sorrows in alcohol."

Ella felt a growing trepidation. She cast a hesitant glance at Benjamin. The stories intertwined with the puzzle of her dreams. After steadying herself, she asked, "Benjamin, do you have any pictures of these people? Elias, Blackwood, Nathaniel, Isabella, Samuel?"

Benjamin paused, deep in thought. After what felt like an eternity to Ella, he reached into his leather satchel and pulled out an old yellowed newspaper article that had been laminated to keep it from crumbling away. A grainy image of a handsome man with an intense gaze appeared. The headline read: "Mysterious Death associated with Captain Nathaniel Hawthorne."

Ella's heart skipped a beat as she took in the image. It was him. The man from her dreams. But how? Why? The fabric of her understanding seemed to come apart at the seams.

Besides the newspaper article, a corner of a drawing peeked out. Ella's eyes darted toward it. "What's that?" she asked, pointing to the hidden photograph.

Benjamin tucked the picture away, a shade of unease crossing his face. "Oh, it's nothing," he replied, a little too quickly.

Ella's instincts tingled with curiosity. The energy shifted, and she could tell he was holding back. She wanted to press further, but decided not to. Perhaps it was a part of the story Benjamin wasn't ready to share. Or perhaps it was something else.

Ella's gaze wandered to the window, where a distant view of the water hinted at the forbidden contours of Misthaven Island. "I wish I could visit Misthaven Island," she began, "to feel its stories beneath my feet. But, of course, it's closed to the public."

Benjamin adjusted his glasses, an unreadable look in his blue eyes. He hesitated, as if measuring his words. "You know, there might be a way."

She looked at him. "What do you mean?"

"Next month," Benjamin began, choosing each word with care, "A group has asked me to collaborate with a paranormal investigation for a television show. They want me to provide historical context and background, and they've secured special permission to be on the island."

Ella's heart raced at the possibilities, the chance to be where her dreams and the stories converged.

"And," he continued, looking into her eyes, "perhaps you could join me... as my assistant?"

For a moment, the offer hung in the air between them, charged with potential. Without a second thought, Ella responded, the excitement clear in her voice. "Yes! Absolutely, I'd love to!"

Benjamin smiled, relieved by her immediate acceptance. "I should warn you, the team is quite... eclectic. There are a couple of investigators with some intriguing gadgets and methods. But the most interesting among them is a woman who is a psychic medium. She has a gift for communicating with the other side."

Ella leaned in, her intrigue deepening. "This sounds more fascinating by the minute. And maybe we might uncover some truths behind the stories, legends."

Time had a funny way of slipping away when engrossed in tales and the company of a kindred spirit. As the ambiance of the coffee shop had become more intimate with the dimming light, the voice of the server interrupted their historical odyssey.

"Sorry to interrupt. We'll be closing up for the afternoon in about 15 minutes." The young woman said. "But, we open again at 5!"

Both Ella and Benjamin looked around, surprised at the near-empty shop. They hadn't even noticed the dwindling crowd.

"I can't believe how fast the time has flown," Ella said.

"Neither can I. It's not every day you get so lost in history that you forget the present." Benjamin replied. "Well, that not true... that happens daily for me."

As they began gathering their things, the connection between them remained, and their conversation shifted from the stories of the past to their plans for the future.

Benjamin cleared his throat, a touch of nervousness clear as he adjusted his glasses. "Ella," he began, the blush in his cheeks making his deep blue eyes appear even more vivid, "today has been... unexpected and delightful. I've cherished our conversation."

Ella's heart skipped a beat, the sincerity in his words warming her from the inside. "I felt the same, Benjamin. It's been a while since I've had such a great conversation."

There was a brief pause, a moment where possibilities hovered in the air between them. Finally, with a smile that hinted at both hope and hesitancy, Benjamin ventured, "Would you be interested in continuing our discussions over dinner sometime? Perhaps explore more tales, or just... get to know each other better?"

Surprised, Ella met his gaze, her eyes reflecting her genuine interest. "I would love that," she replied, the corners of her mouth tugging into a soft smile.

Benjamin's relief was clear as he produced a card from his pocket. "At least this time, I remembered to give you my number," he grinned.

Ella's fingers closed around the card, her gaze landing on the embossed lettering: **Benjamin Hartley, Historical Researcher & Archivist.**

She laughed. "I'm glad you did."

Their farewells were filled with promise as Ella stepped into the dusky evening, clutching the card close.

When she returned home, her mind was filled with the captivating stories shared by Benjamin. The cottage seemed to echo with the remnants of their conversation, the aroma of coffee still clinging to her clothes. She hung her jacket, the smile from their meeting still dancing on her lips.

Her gaze wandered over to the easel that held the charcoal image of the faceless man from her dreams. She approached the drawing, her fingers grazing the rough texture of the paper. With a faint sigh, she dared to do what she had been avoiding—she gave the faceless man a name.

"Nathaniel," she whispered, the name hanging in the air, somehow fitting with the image before her. She studied the figure, the rugged outline of his form familiar, yet alien, in the soft lamplight.

After shaking herself out of her reverie, Ella moved to her bedroom, readying herself for sleep. As she brushed her hair, her thoughts drifted back to Benjamin. His bright smile, animated expressions, and the warmth he exuded all painted a picture of a man she was drawn to. His words, laden with passion and genuine interest, still echoed in her ears, and the historian's tales still sparked her imagination.

The fluttering feeling in her stomach, whenever she thought of Benjamin, confused her. He differed from Nathaniel—less intense, less mysterious—yet she found his kind-hearted nature and enthusiastic spirit compelling. His presence offered a companionship she hadn't realized she'd been missing. It felt pleasant, comfortable—different from the strange allure of her dream companion.

Ella was torn between the two worlds. Benjamin, with his tangible presence and affable charm, made her laugh and feel at ease. Yet Nathaniel, a figure that lived in her dreams, stirred within her an insatiable curiosity and an inexplicable connection that left her yearning for more.

"Quite the predicament," she mused to herself, letting out a soft laugh. She took one last look at the charcoal sketch, her finger tracing the outline of Nathaniel's face before she turned off the lights. She nestled into the soft embrace of her bed, anticipating the next dream, and closed her eyes.

As she drifted off, her thoughts wavered between Benjamin and Nathaniel. She was unsure of what the morning would bring, but for now, she allowed herself to be swept away into the realm of sleep, where the lighthouse stood tall, and Nathaniel waited.

CHAPTER FOUR

Shadows of the Past

The night was cloaked in an eerie stillness, an expectant hush that echoed in the silence of Ella's seaside cottage. She lay in her bed, wrapped up in the cocoon of her blankets, thoughts swirling around in her head. The stories Benjamin had shared with her played on a loop in her mind. The tragedy, the romance, the betrayal—it all seemed so vivid, like a movie playing before her eyes.

She couldn't shake off how closely intertwined her dreams were with Benjamin's tales. The stories of Elias, Blackwood, Captain Nathaniel Hawthorne, and the ill-fated Isabella sounded familiar, as if they were fragments of memories long buried.

As she mulled over the story's details, Ella found her thoughts drifting to Benjamin himself. His infectious enthusiasm for history, the spark in his eyes when he spoke, and the gentle, tentative way he had reached out to her. There was a magnetic pull towards him she couldn't deny, even if she tried. The idea of exploring whatever connection they had further was exhilarating.

A sudden chill jolted her back to reality. The curtains fluttered despite the windows being shut. An uneasy feeling settled in the pit of her stomach, as though she wasn't alone.

She sat up, scanning her room. Everything appeared normal. The familiar furniture, the pictures on her walls. And yet, something felt amiss.

There it was again, that coldness. A soft whisper, almost imperceptible, it danced on the edges of her hearing. Ella held her breath, straining her ears. The whispering drew closer and yet remained out of reach.

She nudged the blanket aside, the cool air of the room enveloping her as she swung her legs out of bed. With a sense of purpose, she moved towards the wall, her steps silent against the floor. Her fingertips brushed against the switch. The click resonated, a sharp and clear interruption to the quiet of the room.

Light flooded the room, harsh and unforgiving, banishing shadows to the furthest reaches of her space. Ella squinted against the sudden brightness, her eyes taking a moment to adjust. She had hoped the light would be her ally and chase away the creeping dread that had settled in her bones. The whispering persisted, a sinister sound from nowhere and everywhere. A crescendo of murmurs seemed to press against her, demanding attention, before it retreated as abruptly as it had come.

The silence that followed was oppressive, a heavy cloak that threatened to smother her newfound courage. Ella stood in the aftermath, her breath quick in the bright room, the uneasiness lingering like an unpleasant aftertaste.

She tried to dismiss it as a product of her overactive imagination, fueled by the haunting tales and the mysteries of the past. Yet, she couldn't get rid of the feeling.

After turning off the light, Ella tiptoed back to her bed, the darkness enveloping the room once more, but feeling a tad less menacing than before. She slipped under the covers, pulling them up to her chin. She nestled into her pillow and closed her eyes, focusing on the rhythm of her breathing. Inhale. Exhale. Each breath was a deliberate step away from the edge of her earlier anxiety, guiding her towards a tranquil state of mind.

As her body relaxed, she felt herself drifting. The transition was gentle, a seamless slipping away from the tangible world into the realm of sleep. And there, in the embrace of slumber, her dreams awaited—different this time.

Gone was the usual fog that shrouded her dreams, replaced by a clarity that felt almost tangible. It was as if a veil had indeed been lifted, revealing a dreamscape rich with detail and depth. Colors were more vibrant, the sounds more distinct.

This new world beckoned, promising discoveries and adventures that felt real, each moment unfolding with the potent magic of the unseen and the untold.

The familiar setting of the lighthouse emerged, but with a new intensity. Everything was so much more tangible. And then there was him - Nathaniel, his name rolling off her tongue like a well-kept secret, as if it breathed life into the shadowy figure.

He was no longer just a faceless entity. He had a name. His striking features were sharply defined, his deep-set eyes reflecting a whirlwind of emotions. There was a marked change in his demeanor. An intensity that was startling overshadowed his usual calm and intriguing nature.

Ella's breath quickened as the pull between her and Nathaniel grew stronger. The space around seemed to shrink. The warmth coming from Nathaniel felt so real, a heady blend of musk and the salty tang of the sea. As their bodies met, the thin fabric of their clothes barely served as a barrier, doing little to shield them from the current that zipped and buzzed at their touch. The sensation was intoxicating.

What frightened Ella the most was not the strength of her feelings, but the lack of control she felt over them. They surged forth like a tidal wave, washing over her, leaving her breathless and desperate for more. This Ella was unfamiliar - not the one who always had control. No, this was someone else, someone who yearned and ached in ways she never thought possible.

"Nathaniel..." Ella's voice shook, a delicate thread of sound in the storm. She sought clarity and understanding in this whirlwind of emotion. But the dream offered no answers. The mystery of Nathaniel deepened, his presence a tantalizing puzzle that left her yearning for more, even as she feared the intensity of her own desires.

The face of Nathaniel in her dreams began to shift and merge. His visage melded into the softer, kinder features of Benjamin. The reassuring warmth of his smile, the depth of his brown eyes that always seemed to hold a secret, and the gentle cadence of his voice that made her feel cherished all intertwined with her heightened emotions.

Torn between the world of dreams and reality, Ella grappled with the difference between the two men. Nathaniel, the embodiment of desires, felt as real as the sheets she lay upon. And then there was Benjamin, the thoughtful historian who had awakened something different within her — a budding affection, a comforting connection. The lines between the men blurred, leaving her in a sea of emotion, wondering where one feeling ended and the other began.

As the first rays of the morning sun peeked into her bedroom, Ella gathered herself. The remnants of her dream lingered at the edges of her consciousness. She pushed these sensations aside, focusing on the day ahead. It had been a roller coaster of a night, her emotions swinging from fear to fascination, leaving her feeling more exhausted than rested.

With a sigh, she rose from her bed. Her body moved on autopilot, carrying her to the kitchen, where she set about making herself a much-needed pot of coffee. The rich aroma of the brewing coffee filled the air, a comforting ritual that promised a semblance of normalcy.

As she waited for her coffee to finish, she made her way to the bathroom. The mirror revealed the toll the night had taken on her. Dark circles under her eyes stood out against her pale skin, highlighting her restless night. With a heavy sigh, she traced the shadows beneath her eyes with a fingertip, feeling the evidence of her exhaustion.

Despite the weariness that pulled at her, Ella knew the day wouldn't pause for her to catch up. She grabbed her toothbrush, applying a stripe of toothpaste with a practiced motion, and swiped the brush over her teeth. She felt a slight jolt of alertness, a minor victory against the fatigue that draped over her like a heavy cloak.

When she returned to the kitchen and poured the hot coffee into her mug, she took a moment to let the warmth from the cup seep into her hands. The exhaustion was not just a physical tiredness but a deep, mental fatigue from the emotional ups and downs of her journey. She wanted to go back to bed. However, duty called, and with her coffee in hand, she grabbed the stack of watercolors she had planned to bring to the gift shop.

Mr. Elsnore, the show owner, had not arrived yet, so she handed them to the young cashier. She and Mr. Elsnore had agreed that he would select a couple for the postcards to be printed, and then frame and sell the rest on consignment. This arrangement, she realized, marked a significant milestone for her in Bar Harbor. It went beyond a mere transaction. It felt like a sign of acceptance, a recognition of her talent and contribution to the local culture. Slowly but surely, she was feeling like she had a place in this town.

She wasn't quite ready to head home just yet, so she took a detour and stopped by the local grocery store. The familiar jingle of the door chime greeted her as she stepped inside, the cool air from the air conditioning a welcome relief against her skin. As she wandered through the aisles, she enjoyed the simple pleasure of browsing the shelves, admiring the array of fresh produce and local delicacies.

She found herself lost in a daydream as she stared at the aisle of fruits, her fingers tracing the texture of an apple.

"Rough night, dear?" Mrs. Potter, the elderly clerk, broke through Ella's reverie with a knowing smile. The small community of Bar Harbor was more like an extended family, their warmth and friendliness so different from the she had been used to in Sacramento.

Ella offered a sheepish smile. "You could say that, Mrs. Potter."

"Ah, well. We all have those, don't we?" The older woman's eyes held a soft gleam.

Ella spent the rest of the day running her errands, the mundane tasks providing a much-needed distraction. Yet, the undercurrent of her thoughts, of her perplexing emotions, was omnipresent. Benjamin's smile, Nathaniel's touch, the burgeoning friendships - all of it was reshaping her existence in ways she had never expected.

As evening fell, Ella was back in her studio. Brush in hand, she stared at the blank canvas, her mind teetering between the world of dreams and the world of reality. She was an artist, lost in her own creation, the colors of her life now reflecting the hues of the mystery man and the historian alike.

The sudden, sharp trill of her phone jolted Ella from her thoughts, piercing the quiet of the cottage. Benjamin's name flashed on the screen. With a quickening pulse, a blend of excitement and nervous anticipation surged through her as she hurried to answer the call.

"Hello?" she managed.

"Ella, it's Benjamin," his voice flowed through the line, warm and familiar.

"Hi, Benjamin," she responded, her grip tightening around the phone.

"I was wondering if you'd like to join me for dinner tomorrow. At Le Petit Bistro, perhaps?" Benjamin's invitation was formal, almost old-fashioned.

Her heart skipped a beat. Prior to this, she had never experienced a proper date. Her experience with relationships was a few casual boyfriends in high school.

"Yes, I'd like that," she said, her voice steady despite the pounding of her heart.

"Great, I'll pick you up around seven?" he suggested, his tone filled with anticipation.

"Sure, Benjamin. Seven sounds perfect," she agreed.

After ending the call, Ella stared at the phone in her hand, her mind cycling through every word of their conversation. Tomorrow, she would be on a date. With Benjamin. The thought alone was enough to paint a smile across her face, her cheeks warming at the mere idea.

Her heart danced with a mix of emotions, a nervous excitement that felt both foreign and thrilling. The reality of stepping into this new experience with Benjamin filled her with a sense of anticipation, each heartbeat echoing her nervousness.

She couldn't help but feel a flutter of anxiety at the prospect of tomorrow. What to wear, what to say, how to act—questions swirled in her head, each one feeding her apprehension. Yet, beneath the layers of nervousness, there was a current of joy. The opportunity to explore this budding connection with Benjamin.

A chill night breeze rustled through Ella's bedroom, pulling her into a slumber that turned into another dream. The familiar scenery of the lighthouse on Misthaven Island welcomed her, the towering structure casting an ominous shadow under the moonlit sky.

Although last night's dream was intense, Nathaniel had always been a source of solace for her. The lighthouse, a constant companion in her dreams, never evoked fear. Yet, tonight, as she moved through the familiar setting, she was struck by a realization: Nathaniel was gone.

His absence left a void that resonated with her deepest fears. Could her feelings for Benjamin have driven him away? She roamed the lighthouse, peering into every nook, her calls only answered by the chilling echo of her voice against the stark stone walls. Warmth was replaced by a cold draft of uncertainty, casting an ominous shadow over her heart.

The dream's nature shifted. The sea turned tumultuous, its angry waves clashing with the shore. A storm broke the night's calm, lightning slashing the dark sky, painting the lighthouse in a threatening light. The curiosity that usually filled her dreams was now overshadowed by fear.

Compelled by an unseen force, Ella found herself on the cliff's edge, overlooking the raging waters below. Despite her inner pleas to retreat, her legs carried her closer to the abyss, her sense of safety unraveling with each step. Panic surged as the cliff's edge loomed closer. Was she being drawn to her own end?

Then, an unexpected hand brushed against her back, like a whisper against her skin. Whirling around, her heart caught between hope and dread, she half-expected, half-wished for Nathaniel. Instead, a stranger stood before her, his gaze filled with an intense loathing. The malice in his eyes plunged her into a fear far deeper than the unsettling dream itself, turning the experience from disturbing to terrifying.

She was jolted awake and sat up in bed, her heart pounding in her chest. The horror of the dream causing a shiver to run down her spine. Her skin was slick with cold sweat, and her breaths came out in short, ragged gasps. It was just a dream; she reminded herself, but the lingering sense of dread felt all too real.

As she calmed her racing heart, a thought occurred to her. She *had* to see the lighthouse. The need was inexplicable, yet compelling. She wanted to stand on the actual grounds, touch the real bricks, and maybe, just maybe, it would bring some clarity to the chaotic storm her dreams had conjured. This ghost-hunting adventure couldn't come soon enough!

CHAPTER FIVE

The Date

As the day turned to dusk, Ella found solace in her art. Her brushstrokes whispered of inner turmoil, yet offered calm to her nerves. Tonight's date with Benjamin wasn't just any evening. It was a step into vulnerability, a dance with the possibility of something new.

Her studio was a sanctuary where her creations whispered the secrets of her soul. As she cleaned her brushes and capped her paint tubes, a wave of satisfaction washed over her. She was surrounded by the evidence of her day's passion, the visible rhythm of her heart's labor. It was here, among her artwork, that she felt most herself, unguarded and true.

Among her pieces, the charcoal sketch of Nathaniel held an allure. She had rendered him with such precision and depth that it felt as if she had breathed a part of herself into the drawing. His eyes, deep pools of mystery, held stories untold. For a moment, Ella was lost in the gaze of this figure from another era, wondering about the life he might have led.

The sudden realization of that time had flown by snapped her out of her daydream. A quick look at the clock sent a jolt of surprise. It was later than she thought. Benjamin would arrive and she was still in her art-stained clothes.

Nerves fluttered in her stomach. As Ella moved to her bedroom, self-doubt pressed on her shoulders. Could she embody the woman she aspired to be? She wanted to radiate confidence, exude kindness, showcase her intellect, and share her sense of humor.

She rummaged through her wardrobe, searching for an outfit that could speak of effortless grace yet comfort her simmering nerves. Her fingers brushed against the soft fabric of a sundress, and she paused. This dress complimented her body and promised a whisper of elegance. It was perfect.

Ella faced the mirror, seeking reassurance in her reflection. The dress hugged her curves, showing the artist consumed by her craft and the woman stepping into a life-changing evening. Beneath the surface, her doubts lingered—was she enough? Ella allowed herself a moment of admiration. The warmth in her eyes reflected depth, while her hair cascaded around her shoulders like a veil of strength.

Yet, as she readied herself, the memory of Nathaniel's touch in a dream lingered, a ghostly caress that sent a shiver through her. It was a reminder of the complexities of the heart, the way it could hold on to a dream with the same fervor as a living person.

The soft rap at her door announced Benjamin's arrival. Ella, in a flurry of motions, fastened her sandals and tucked a stray strand of hair behind her ear. With a deep, steadying breath that did little to calm her fluttering heart, she made her way to the door. A quick glance in the mirror revealed a woman tinged with hopeful anticipation.

Opening the door, Ella was greeted by Benjamin's smile and eyes of such a striking blue that they lit up her spirits. "You look beautiful," he said, his voice carrying a sincerity that seemed to reach straight into her heart.

"You too," she replied. Realizing her response might have sounded too reciprocal for a compliment about beauty, she added, "Well, handsome, I mean." Pausing and blushing as the words tumbled out, she added, "Although men can be beautiful too." Her attempt to correct herself only deepened the embarrassment.

He reached out to her, his gesture so chivalrous it seemed to echo from a bygone era of knights and fair maidens. With a small, appreciative smile, Ella placed her hand on his arm, finding an unexpected anchor in his steady presence.

Together, they stepped into the cool evening air and the world around them faded into the backdrop.

As they approached his car, Benjamin continued his role as a gallant escort. With a playful and somewhat exaggerated flourish, he opened the passenger door for her. This grand gesture brought a light laugh from Ella.

She settled into the passenger seat, sneaking a glance at Benjamin's smile just as he secured the door with a soft click. This thoughtful gesture sparkled with an unexpected depth. In that moment, their connection deepened, hinting at a budding camaraderie and shared excitement for the evening.

Their destination 'Le Petit Bistro', was a charming little restaurant that carried the aroma of authentic French cuisine right out onto the sidewalk. The subtle smell of roasting garlic and fresh pastries wafted through the air, making Ella's stomach growl in anticipation. The ambiance and soft melodies playing in the background set the mood for a wonderful evening.

Once seated at a cozy corner table in the corner, Benjamin couldn't contain his enthusiasm. He extracted an old leather-bound folder from his bag. "I thought you might enjoy these," he said, his eyes alight with excitement as he presented Ella with historical documents about the lighthouse and its keepers.

Ella was surprised. This evening was supposed to be a date, yet here they were, about to dive into history again. But seeing the genuine eagerness in Benjamin's expression, it was impossible not to be drawn in. His passion for the past was infectious, and she found herself eager to explore the stories he was so keen to share. After all, this was the reason she moved to Bar Harbor. There was something charming about uncovering secrets of the past with the most handsome guide by her side.

As Ella leaned in over the documents, the server approached with a pitcher of water. In a moment of clumsy timing, the man stumbled, nearly dousing the precious papers. In a panic, both Ella and Benjamin lunged forward, their hands brushing and lingering for a moment longer than necessary. They shared a relieved laugh at the near-disaster averted.

Ella's fingers then resumed their exploration of the documents' brittle pages, now even more aware of Benjamin's close presence. The archaic script and the pages' time-worn paper seemed to whisper tales of perseverance, mystery, and the intimate lives of those who had kept the lighthouse beacon burning. As the server, now more cautious, quietly filled their glasses and left them to their exploration, the history of the lighthouse keepers unfolded before them, drawing them deeper into the intrigue of the past—and each other.

Then, a particular image caught her eye. The sepia tones of the photograph didn't do justice to the striking young woman it showcased—Isabella, one of the lighthouse keeper's daughter. Ella's heart stuttered, her fingers trembling as she took in the image. Every line, every curve of Isabella's face mirrored her own. From the tilt of her chin to the intensity of her gaze, the parallels were unsettling. It felt as if she was staring at her own reflection, albeit from a time long past. Could it be a mere coincidence, or was there a deeper connection binding her to this mysterious lighthouse family?

Her introspection was interrupted by Benjamin's voice. "Doesn't she look like you?" He leaned closer, his eyes darting between Ella and the photograph, a playful smile playing on his lips.

She hesitated, still reeling from the discovery. "It's...uncanny," she murmured, trying to steady her voice. "I can't explain it, but it feels like more than just a resemblance."

Benjamin studied her for a moment. "Perhaps there's a story there," he mused, "one that's waiting to be uncovered." And as he spoke, Ella couldn't help but wonder if the story would be more personal than she had ever imagined.

Just then, the server arrived, poised with pen and pad, eager to capture their dinner choices. "I'll have the Soupe à l'oignon" Ella declared in her best French accent. Benjamin, with a nod of approval, chose the Coq au Vin.

"I have more information on Isabella, but maybe we should wait until after we've eaten," Benjamin suggested, his eyes flicking to the clumsy server before he cracked a grin.

"That sounds intriguing," Ella replied. "After the food, it is!"

As they awaited their meal, Benjamin offered a slice of bread across the table. "Try this with the olive oil," he encouraged.

Ella smiled as she took the bread and dipped it into the olive oil. She savored the crisp exterior yielding to a soft, airy interior, each bite a perfect blend of rustic simplicity and comforting warmth. This simple exchange, over a piece of bread, felt like an intimate dance of flavors and laughter.

Their food arrived, steaming and fragrant, and as they ate, the conversation flowed as freely as the wine. Ella, stirring her soup, hesitated for a moment before sharing, "My parents...they passed away recently." Her voice was soft, tinged with the pain of their memory.

Benjamin paused, his fork mid-air. "I'm so sorry, Ella," he said, his tone sincere. "I can't imagine what that must have been like for you." His eyes held a depth of empathy that made Ella's heart swell.

The conversation shifted as Benjamin shared his own story. "Growing up here, my family's history was always a part of me. It's like the town and the lighthouse are part of our DNA." He chuckled, a sound full of warmth. "Sounds cheesy, I know."

Ella smiled, shaking her head. "No, it's wonderful to have roots like that. To know where you come from. I've always wondered about my background. I was adopted, so my genetic history is a mystery to me."

Their meal progressed, with laughter and shared stories filling the gaps between bites. As they discussed the lighthouse and its keepers, their interest in the past seemed to pull them even closer.

As the evening drew to a close, the remnants of their feast were whisked away and the last sips of wine were savored. They found themselves engrossed in the lighthouse's lore. The tales, rich with history and mystery, seemed to weave around them, pulling them closer in a shared bubble of curiosity and excitement.

"Thanks for sharing this with me," Ella said, her eyes meeting Benjamin's across the table. "I've never met anyone who brings history to life quite like you do."

Benjamin's response was a smile that seemed to glow in the dim light of the restaurant. "And I've never met anyone as willing to jump into these stories with both feet. It's been a fantastic evening."

Pausing, Benjamin seemed to consider something for a moment before adding, "You know, we never got to the documents about Isabella, and I'd love to show you. How about we plan another day to dive into it? Maybe somewhere we can spread out the documents without fear of water attacks," he joked, recalling their earlier mishap with the server.

Ella's face lit up at the suggestion, the prospect of continuing their adventure sparking visible excitement. "I'd like that," she agreed, enthusiasm coloring her voice. "It sounds like a perfect plan for our next date."

As the words left her mouth, Ella felt a sudden rush of embarrassment for being so forward. Her cheeks flushed a deeper shade, and she glanced down, fearing she might have overstepped. But when she looked up again, the warmth in Benjamin's expression melted away any doubt.

"I'm really glad you think so," Benjamin responded, his excitement matching hers. "There's something special about sharing these discoveries with someone who appreciates them as much as I do." His voice carried a note of genuine appreciation, clarifying that the prospect of a second date was as thrilling for him as it was for her.

Ella's initial embarrassment turned into a shared anticipation. "Then it's settled," she said, her smile returning as she felt a wave of relief and happiness. "I can't wait to dive deeper into the history of Isabella and see what other secrets we can uncover."

They gathered their belongings and stepped outside. The chill of the night air was a contrast to the warmth they'd left behind, making Ella wrapped her arms around herself, suppressing the shivers. Benjamin noticed and offered his arm, a gesture she accepted with a shy smile. The walk to his car was short but filled with a comfortable silence that spoke volumes of the ease developing between them.

Again, Benjamin held the passenger door open for Ella, and she settled into the seat. "Thank you, Benjamin. This evening has been...more than I expected."

"The pleasure was all mine," Benjamin replied as he started the car. The drive to her home was smooth, yet charged with an unspoken anticipation. Every stoplight seemed to prolong the inevitable end of their evening, and each glance they exchanged was tinged with a sweet awkwardness, neither quite ready to part ways.

As they arrived at her home, the car engine's soft purring ceased. Ella lingered for a moment, her hand resting on the door handle, hesitating.

"Would you... like to come in?" Ella blurted out, her heart racing. "I mean, we could take a first look at the documents tonight. No time like the present, right?" Her words stumbled into the silence, her tone lifting at the end of the sentence hanging a question in the air. She bit her lip.

Benjamin's eyebrows rose in surprise, but his response was eager. "I'd like that," he said. "Only if you're sure, though."

"I am," Ella affirmed, stepping out of the car and leading the way to her front door. Inside, she flicked on the lights, casting a warm glow over the living room. Her home added an extra layer to their dynamic, and she didn't quite know how to act. She had never taken anyone home before.

As Benjamin entered, he removed his shoes, showing a respect for her space that Ella appreciated. She led him to the dining table where they spread out the documents.

"This document," Benjamin began, "contains the personal musings and thoughts of Isabella."

Ella's gaze met his, a thousand questions dancing in her eyes. "What did she write?" she whispered, her fingers running over the elegant cursive.

Benjamin leaned closer, his voice taking on a hushed, storytelling quality. "Isabella often wrote about her life by the sea, the ever-changing moods of the ocean, and her deep love for the lighthouse, which she considered a constant companion. But most poignantly, she chronicled her whirlwind romance with Captain Nathaniel. It was, by her accounts, an all-consuming love, filled with stolen moments by the shoreline, secret rendezvous under the moonlight, and dreams of a future together."

Ella's heart raced as he recounted Isabella's tales. She could almost feel the salt-laden breeze on her face and hear the rhythmic lapping of the waves against the shore.

Reaching into his bag, Benjamin unveiled an old photograph. The sight stole Ella's breath. The image showcased a marriage announcement with Isabella and Captain Nathaniel poised by the lighthouse. Their expressions spoke of love deep and undeniable. Isabella's beauty was familiar, while Captain Nathaniel bore an uncanny resemblance to the man who had occupied Ella's dreams.

The surrounding atmosphere grew thick. Ella's fingers trembled as she traced the contours of the faces in the photograph. "It's as if...as if I'm looking at reflections from another time," she articulated. "Their love story...it feels personal."

Together, they leaned over the papers, their heads occasionally bumping as they pointed out details and shared theories. The initial awkwardness of inviting him into her home faded as they delved into their shared passion.

Benjamin's eyes bore into Ella's, a shadow of uncertainty passing over his features. "It's strange," he began, his voice a touch strained, "how the past can have such a grip on the present. One would think Captain Nathaniel's presence is so strong that it might overshadow those who are here, in the now." His eyes darted to the photograph and then back to her.

Ella caught the hint of jealousy in Benjamin's voice and found it strange. An uncomfortable knot tightened in her stomach. As her dreams with Nathaniel pressed on her mind, she made a silent resolution to keep those dreams to herself. Sharing them with Benjamin would only complicate things. She offered him a reassuring smile, trying to lighten the atmosphere. "The past is fascinating, but it's the present that matters," she said, hoping to steer the conversation to safer waters. "May I look at Isabella's diary?"

Surprised, Benjamin blinked a few times before responding with an enthusiastic, "Of course!" He handed her the aged journal, its pages yellowed with time, bearing the silent witness of a bygone era.

As Ella opened the diary, the first thing that struck her was Isabella's elegant handwriting, flowing across the pages like waves. It wasn't long before she stumbled upon entries detailing her friendship with Samuel, described as a steadfast companion and a bridge to the most pivotal encounter of her life—meeting Nathaniel. Isabella wrote of Samuel with affection and gratitude, crediting him for introducing her to a soul whose presence would redefine her existence.

The diary entries became poetic as Isabella chronicled her growing affection for Nathaniel. She detailed their shared moments, the conversations that seemed to stretch into infinity, and the comfort she found in his presence. It was clear through her words that what started as a friendship blossomed into love.

One entry, in particular, caught Ella's eye—a page adorned with a delicate sketch of Nathaniel. The lines were tender, yet captured an unmistakable likeness. His gaze seemed to leap off the page. It was clear Isabella not only possessed a keen eye for detail but also an artist's soul. "Oh, she was an artist, too. This gets stranger by the minute!" Ella exclaimed.

Ella turned the page to find more sketches—candid moments of Nathaniel and Samuel, the lighthouse in the distance, the wild sea—all brought to life by Isabella's skilled hand. Her words danced around her sketches, a visual diary that intertwined with her written thoughts, offering a window into her heart's deepest chambers.

Isabella's descriptions of Nathaniel were not just of his physical appearance, but of that made him who he was—the strength in his convictions, the warmth of his smile, and the depth of his understanding. It was as though, through her art and words, Isabella was trying to capture the very soul of the man she loved.

Amid the sketches and heartfelt entries, Ella found a note about Samuel's changing demeanor over time, a subtle shift that Isabella seemed to ponder with a mix of confusion and concern. Samuel's introduction of Nathaniel to Isabella, a gesture of friendship, had given rise to a complex web of emotions, leaving Isabella torn between her loyalty to Samuel and her love for Nathaniel.

Ella closed the diary, her mind racing with thoughts. The parallels between her own experiences and Isabella's story were uncanny. The night stretched on, the documents between them a bridge to understanding not only the history they were unraveling but also each other.

Benjamin's gaze turned somber, a fleeting shadow crossing his face as he handled the worn photo of Isabella and Captain Nathaniel. "Isabella's death is the aspect of history most avoid," he remarked.

A shiver trailed down Ella's spine. Intrigued, she leaned in closer. Benjamin's voice grew softer, and Ella, eager to hear more, squeezed his hand in encouragement.

"When she was found," he began, pausing for a breath, "her friend Samuel had been to visit her on the island that day. According to court documents, Samuel claimed he was there to inform her of Nathaniel's supposed demise at sea. Samuel believed she leaped to her death. Yet Nathaniel hadn't perished, and there was no evidence that anyone had relayed such news to Samuel. Still, he insisted someone had told him."

Ella's heart tightened, sensing the sorrow that would shadow the beautiful love story she had imagined. "You mentioned this briefly at the coffee shop... but how did they find her?"

Benjamin sighed, his eyes drifting to a distant point. "Legend has it, she was found at the cliff's base, near her lighthouse. Life ebbed away in a tide pool. That's when the rumors swirled, especially since Samuel's visit coincided with Nathaniel's unexpected early return home. Nathaniel had hoped to surprise her. He was there when they discovered her body."

As Benjamin hesitated, Ella probed, "What rumors?"

"People started accusing Captain Nathaniel of pushing her, and that he suspected her of infidelity with Samuel," he revealed.

"But he was innocent, right?" Ella felt a chill as she recalled the face from her dream.

Benjamin nodded. "Yes, he was cleared, but the damage to his reputation was beyond repair. The dual blow of losing Isabella and facing baseless accusations shattered him. He retreated to the life of solitude in the lighthouse, which had belonged to Isabella's family, vowing never to marry."

Ella paused, processing the story, her thoughts in turmoil. Benjamin's hand hovered over his briefcase, then withdrew. "The other man in this story—Samuel," he added, voice tinged with reluctance.

"Samuel," Ella repeated, prompting him to continue.

"He was Isabella's closest confidante and friend, son to a wealthy merchant. Their families had envisioned a union through their marriage. Yet, Isabella's heart was with Nathaniel, and Samuel..." Benjamin's voice faltered, a storm of unspoken words in his eyes. "Despite being portrayed as merely a friend in their letters, rumors abounded. Some suggested his unrequited love for Isabella led him to extreme actions, while others believed his jealousy was not for Isabella's affection, but stemmed from a rivalry with Nathaniel."

Ella's eyes widened, the implications dawning on her. "Oh no," she breathed out. "And we might never uncover what really happened."

A heavy silence enveloped them. Ella's mind raced, the parallels between her dreams and the recounted history unsettling her. Benjamin's look was distant, lost in thought, and sensing the mood, Ella sought to lighten the atmosphere. She cleared her throat, shifting the topic. "So, any childhood stories you've yet to share?" she ventured with a light chuckle, hoping to dispel the somber air.

Benjamin's smile returned, a spark of mischief in his eyes. "Well, there was the summer I attempted to build a treehouse with my cousins. Let's just say it didn't quite go as planned."

Their conversation veered into tales of youthful endeavors, laughter mingling with the nostalgia of past innocence and boldness. Their mutual love for history and the arts shone through in stories of school, college, and career paths. Ella found herself drawn to Benjamin's sincerity and warmth.

The night wore on, and Ella mused, "You know, I'm really excited to visit Misthaven Island."

Benjamin paused, collecting his thoughts. "Actually," he began, "I've been coordinating with a psychic named Ashlyn. She's helped with my research before. And is part of the team we will join,"

"I can give you her number," he offered, his phone already in hand. "She is great at pointing you in the right direction for research."

With a gentle tap on the screen button, he sent the psychic's contact to Ella. Their eyes locked, and in that moment, the space between them seemed to dissolve, drawn together by an unseen force. Benjamin closed the distance, their lips meeting in a soft kiss. This stirred something new in Ella, a longing connected to the mysteries they were diving into together. They hesitated to break apart, grinning, excited by their shared moment.

The spell was broken by an unexpected sound—a loud thump, like a door slammed by an unseen force, sending a ripple of tension through the room. Ella's pulse quickened. "Did you hear that?" she murmured.

Upon hearing the unexpected noise, Benjamin stepped back, prepared to confront whatever was behind it. Ella's mind raced with possibilities. Fear gripped her—could it be an intruder? Crime in Bar Harbor seemed to be non-existent.

Then, as she tried to rationalize, wondering if perhaps an animal had somehow found its way inside. But her thoughts spiraled, and she landed on a more supernatural explanation. Could the ghostly tales be real? Was it Nathaniel's spirit? And if so, was this a sign of his discontent, or even jealousy?

After Benjamin had reassured Ella that the disturbance was likely nothing more than the wind, a subtle change washed over the room. Despite the scare, practical concerns surfaced. "Ella... I should go," he admitted, the reality of tomorrow's obligations looming.

Ella, caught between the warmth of the moment and the impending return to normalcy, watched Benjamin gather his belongings. When he paused, the space between them charged with unspoken words, he leaned in, sealing their evening with another kiss—a soft, lingering connection that spoke of promises yet to be kept. "I'll fill you in on the lighthouse trip soon, okay?" he whispered.

In response, Ella's heart fluttered. "Thank you," she managed, her smile bittersweet.

As the door clicked shut behind him, Ella was adrift in the quiet house, echoes of their evening together lingering like a half-remembered melody. New possibilities with Benjamin danced through her mind, each thought a step into uncharted territory, thrilling and daunting in equal measure. Yet, in the wake of his departure, an unexpected void spread.

Retreating to her room, Ella felt a tangled web of dreams and reality. Nathaniel in her dreams, once a constant, now jostled for space with the very tangible memories of Benjamin. Their images combined and shifted in her mind's eye, the ghostly allure of Nathaniel intertwining with the warmth of Benjamin's smile.

Lying in the quiet of her room, Ella grappled with the duality of her feelings. The prospect of Nathaniel being more than a figment of her imagination loomed large, casting a shadow over her budding relationship with Benjamin. Could she navigate the waters of a new romance while in love with to a ghost?

As Ella surrendered to sleep, the beacon of the lighthouse guided her through the murky waters of her emotions. Tonight, the questions could wait as she found herself lost in the fog of dreams, where both Nathaniel and Benjamin awaited.

CHAPTER SIX

A Heart Unseen

Ella's bedroom was wrapped in quiet, pierced only by the distant, gentle lapping of waves. Morning light seeped through her curtains, casting playful shadows across her walls. As fragments of her dream lingered, a profound sadness washed over her.

Nathaniel, with his deep, yearning eyes, felt more tangible than ever. He reached out across time and space. His eyes, brimming with a timeless sorrow, drew her in, even if they were anchored in a far-off past.

Wrapped in her tangled sheets, Ella could still sense his stare. The emotions that surged within her felt overwhelmingly real. They threatened to overshadow the fledgling feelings she harbored for Benjamin.

The idea of therapy crossed her mind once more. It didn't seem like such a bad idea, especially with the unresolved grief from her parents' passing still hanging over her. But discussing her dream-induced infatuation? She wasn't ready for Nathaniel to fade into oblivion. He called to her in a way she couldn't ignore.

Then she remembered Benjamin's suggestion to consult Ashlyn Alden, a psychic. Her phone lay within easy reach on the bedside table. Benjamin had already spoken to Ashlyn about her situation. Torn, Ella pondered over her next move. She sought answers, yet how could she tell such intimate dreams to a stranger? Moreover, this stranger was Benjamin's friend.

She pictured herself on the phone, her voice breaking as she tried to articulate her dreams to Ashlyn. Heat crept into her cheeks at the thought. Would Ashlyn dismiss her as just another lovesick ghost hunter, reading too much into her nighttime fantasies? And if Ashlyn believed her, would she end up discussing it with Benjamin? This possibility made Ella even more hesitant.

She put the phone, deciding not to call—at least not yet. But as the morning glow intensified, filling her room with light and dispelling the shadows, Ella felt herself unraveling.

The weather over Bar Harbor had draped itself in a cloak of dreariness for days, the persistent drizzle and fog that seemed to seep into the bones and the hearts of its inhabitants. Within the cozy confines of Ella's living room, she and Benjamin found solace from the grey skies, surrounded by history.

Benjamin opened a folder he had prepared for the ghost hunting expedition, revealing the faded images of those whose stories were intertwined with the island's lore. "Let's start with Captain Elias Thornton," he began, pointing to an image of a man whose gaze was as deep as the ocean he had once mastered. "Thornton was born in 1823 and became a legend on the seas. However, his story took a tragic turn when he was lost in the very waters he loved. It's said his spirit still wanders the shores of Misthaven Island, perhaps unable to leave the love he left behind."

Ella, drawn into the tale, leaned in. "And that love would be Clara?" she ventured, her voice a soft echo in the room filled with the sound of rain against the windows.

"Yes, that's where the story becomes even more entangled," Benjamin replied, shifting to another photograph, and practicing for his camera time. "Thornton was betrothed to a woman named Clara, who had a remarkable spirit and beauty, but fate had other plans. All too soon after Thornton's death, she found solace and eventually love with Armand Blackwood."

"Blackwood?" Ella's brow furrowed. "Was the man that marooned Elias Thornton, right?"

"Exactly," Benjamin confirmed, revealing a portrait of Armand Blackwood, a man whose eyes carried deep secrets. "Armand and Clara married and had one daughter, Isabella. This island was their world, and the lighthouse was their beacon. But it was also the setting for a love story that would echo through the ages."

He then turned to a delicate, age-worn picture of Isabella Blackwood. It was still strange to Ella how much this woman resembled her. "Isabella grew up in the lighthouse's shadow, nurtured by the loving, vigilant care of her parents. Both her mother, Clara, and her father played pivotal roles in her upbringing, ensuring she was well-loved and protected. However, tragedy struck early when Clara passed away, leaving a young Isabella to navigate the world with only her father's guidance. Despite this loss, her spirit remained unbroken, and her life took a poignant turn when Nathaniel Hawthorne entered her life, capturing her heart with a story all their own."

Ella traced her finger over Isabella's image. "So, Hawthorne and Isabella were the true loves of this tale," she murmured, lost in thought.

"Yes, but as with all the great tales, tragedy was never far behind. Their union, destined for happiness, was cut short by circumstances beyond their control. Isabella's untimely death. Now, it's as if Misthaven itself holds their memories, whispering their names with every gust of wind and crash of wave against the shore."

"That sounded amazing. The camera is going to love you!" She paused. "do you know why we are reaching out to them?" Ella asked, her voice barely above the crackle of the fireplace.

Benjamin closed the folder, his eyes meeting Ella's. "Their stories are unresolved, their spirits restless. By connecting with them, we not only uncover the mysteries of the past, but perhaps bring peace to those who have been silent for too long."

As the rain intensified outside, blurring the world into a monochrome of grey, Ella felt the magnitude of their task deepen. Within the safety of her living room, she and Benjamin were not chasing shadows for a ghost hunter's project. They were threading through the fabric of history itself.

Ella pondered the intertwining tales of Nathaniel, Isabella, Elias, and the others whose spirits still whispered through the island. She realized this endeavor transcended the more than uncovering ghostly tales. It mirrored her own search for answers, a journey through her personal labyrinth of questions and curiosities about the past.

In pursuing understanding these long-gone lives, Ella realized she might also illuminate the darker corners of her own story. The project offered a unique lens through which to view her own mysteries. Perhaps this journey might hold keys to unlocking parts of her own history and identity.

Ella and Benjamin found themselves caught in a whirlwind of preparation, their days filled with a sense of anticipation for the investigation. Beneath the surface, the undercurrents of a budding romance wove through their interactions. Yet, as much as Benjamin inhabited her waking thoughts, Nathaniel still haunted Ella's dreams.

One evening, as they sat side by side on Ella's porch, watching the soft glow of twilight, Benjamin's hand found Ella's. The warmth of his touch spiraled up her arm. "You seem distant," he noted.

Ella hesitated, caught between the desire to share her dreams and the fear of what revealing them might entail. She opted for half-truths. "Just lost in thought," she murmured, her gaze fixed on the fading light.

The moment of evasion cast a shadow over Benjamin's features. However, their conversation was halted by the ring of his phone. "It's Ashlyn. I need to take this," he excused himself, stepping away with a glance that left Ella feeling isolated.

From her vantage point, Ella watched him, noting the ease and animation that flowed into his conversation with Ashlyn. A pang of jealousy, sharp and unexpected, pierced through her, leaving her unsettled and questioning the intensity of her feelings. Why did this glimpse into Benjamin's world, shared with someone else, stir such a storm within her?

Ella turned her attention back to the horizon, seeking solace in the evening's beauty. She let the moment—a whisper of the sea, the chirping of the crickets, and the caress of the breeze—enfold her. If nothing else the it dispelled the unwelcome surge of jealousy.

When Benjamin ended the call and returned, the atmosphere between them felt changed. The earlier warmth seemed to have dulled, replaced by a quiet tension. Both seemed lost in their own worlds, the chasm of unspoken thoughts and feelings creating a distance that wasn't there before.

Benjamin cleared his throat, breaking the silence that had settled between them. "I should go," he said, avoiding direct eye contact.

Ella nodded, unspoken words between them pressing down on her chest. "Can I keep the files for tonight?" she asked, gesturing to the pile of documents they had been going through earlier. She hoped to lose herself in the work, to quiet the turmoil of her emotions.

Benjamin hesitated, his gaze flitting between the files and then back to Ella. "I... yes, of course," he replied, though reluctance tinged his voice. "Just take care of them, okay? They're quite valuable."

Ella offered a small smile. "I promise. I'll keep them safe."

They exchanged a few more words. A formal veneer of politeness amid the strange tension. As the door closed behind Benjamin, Ella was left with the files, and the haunting image of Nathaniel, whose presence in her dreams, added layers of complexity to her emotions.

Ella seized the moment to delve into a treasure she had been yearning to explore in private: Isabella's journal. The personal artifact, a window into the life of her counterpart from the 1800s, was nothing short of astonishing. The leather-bound journal, its pages yellowed with age, lay in her hands like a delicate piece of history, eager to unveil its secrets.

Ella's fingers traced the edges of the journal's pages, now more familiar to her touch, as she settled into the armchair. This time, however, she bypassed the early entries she had already poured over. Instead, she went to a series of delicate sketches nestled between the written accounts—a gallery of Nathaniel's visage captured in Isabella's hand. These drawings were intimate and revealing, each stroke of the pencil whispering secrets of love.

As she delved deeper, the journal told of Isabella's life in a way that was less about the words on the page and more about the emotions. Isabella's unease and the sense of being watched by something unseen were now familiar tales to Ella. Yet, setting, with the soft hum of the sea beyond, she found herself enveloped in the warmth of Isabella's more personal revelations (and encounters) Nathaniel.

Ella blushed as she pored over entries nestled between sketches of Nathaniel in Isabella's journal. These sections were full of Isabella's feelings, portraying a side of the past Ella had never imagined. She had always pictured women of that era as reserved and devout, their lives laced within the confines of propriety. Yet here was Isabella, expressing a passion and depth of feeling that was surprising.

More intriguing were the hints of their closeness, the intimacies shared in the quiet moments away from prying eyes. These were not the escapades of romance novels, but hinted at a depth of relationship Ella hadn't expected.

Isabella's yearning during Nathaniel's absences was obvious. Yet, even in these moments of vulnerability, there was a strength in her longing, a candid acknowledgment of desire and affection that made Ella's cheeks warm with a mix of embarrassment.

Through these revelations, Ella discovered a connection to Isabella. She realized the past was not a world of restraint and repression, but was as vivid and full of emotion as her own. Isabella's expressions of love painted a portrait of a woman bold in her emotional honesty, challenging Ella's preconceptions and inviting her to view the past through a new lens.

That night, Ella's bed felt vast and empty. As she closed her eyes, Nathaniel's image greeted her, his gaze fervent yet veiled with a melancholy she couldn't decipher. There seemed to be an air of distance, a chasm growing between them.

This growing rift in her dreams mirrored the distance that had crept into her waking world with Benjamin. Just as Nathaniel's image receded into subconscious, the warmth and immediacy of her connection with Benjamin seemed to ebb away, leaving her adrift in both worlds—each filled with its own brand of silence and yearning.

Within the dream, Nathaniel cradled her cheek, his touch both a sanctuary and a promise. The fervor in these moments eclipsed any physical connection she'd felt with Benjamin. It felt like Nathaniel entrusted her with his being.

But with every tender touch, Ella sensed Nathaniel's presence diminishing. Where he once stood commanding, he was fading into the background. His figure dimming, like an old photograph losing its contrast. It was as if he was receding into the foggy recesses of her mind, retreating to that shadowy corner where he first materialized.

The next morning, Ella rose with the first light, her dreams still clinging to her. She had slipped out of bed, opting for a quick change into a pair of underwear and throwing on an oversized t-shirt rather than a full outfit. Her studio always called to her, especially when emotions ran high. It was her sanctuary. Here, surrounded by the hush of morning and the familiar scent of paint and charcoal, her thoughts flowed onto the canvas. The portrait she now drew with such fervor was that of Nathaniel.

Engrossed in her art, the sudden creak of the studio door jolted Ella from her introspection. The sight of Benjamin caught her off guard, especially given her scant attire. Benjamin's eyes, however, held no judgment but an unspoken apology. In his hand, a bouquet seemed like a peace offering, a gesture to mend the rift that had grown between them.

"You scared me," she whispered, her previous discomfort forgotten. "I wasn't expecting you."

He grinned, yet as his gaze fell upon the portrait, there was a flash of intensity. "The captain from the lighthouse photographs?" he inquired, voice strained.

Ella felt a mix of pride and unease. "I felt inspired," she said, trying to deflect from the tension that filled the space between them. His eyes darkened, and a silence settled. Hoping to dissipate the heaviness, she suggested, "Let's go to the living room?"

As they moved, Ella sensed a shift in Benjamin. His arm wrapped around her, pulling her close. His touch, usually comforting, felt possessive now.

Benjamin's grip tightened on Ella as he spun her around and pushed her forward.

"Benjamin..." she began

"You're mine," he rasped into her ear, his voice dark and edged with dominance. "Only mine."

Ella's heart raced as the words filled her head and the hairs on the back of her neck stood on end. *Does he somehow know about Nathaniel?* It felt impossible, but the grip of his hands told another story. The need to confront this unexpected side of Benjamin became overwhelming.

She twisted and found herself face-to-face with him. His eyes were tempestuous and black with intensity. Their depth held a swirling mix of emotions she couldn't decode, but what was unmistakable was the raw desire and urgency. The intensity felt misplaced, too abrupt. This wasn't the Benjamin she knew.

He twitched, as though snapping back to the man she knew. Benjamin's confusion was apparent in his clear blue eyes. Ella tugged at the hem of her t-shirt, trying to cover herself.

"Yes, Benjamin, you're the only one. But..." Ella's voice wavered.

The moment bore down on him. "Ella, I... I can't recall... I'm so sorry." He paused, regret in his gaze. "I don't understand what just took over."

The distance between them grew as he shuffled, awkward and disheveled, towards the door. "Maybe I should go," he whispered, his voice thick with mixed emotions.

"No, Benjamin, wait," she called out with a half-hearted attempt to keep him from leaving, but he was already through the door.

From her vantage point, she watched him take out his phone and start dialing. Could he be calling Ashlyn? The mere thought added a sting to the tumult of emotions swirling within her. Was she the one he'd sought now? The idea sent Ella's thoughts into a tailspin.

Now by herself, she slumped onto the couch. Images of Benjamin clouded her thoughts—his strange eyes and the firm grip of his hands.

As Ella sat near the open window, a sudden breeze teased the curtains, bringing an unexpected chill to what had been a balmy evening. Yet, it wasn't the cool air that caught her breath, but an unseen, icy caress along her arm.

Then, as if called forth from the pages of her own thoughts, a colder, more distinct touch brushed across her face. In that moment, Ella realized Nathaniel was there before her, not a figment of her imagination, but as a ghost made manifest. His presence, ethereal yet real, brought not fear but a deep sense of peace, as if he were protecting her.

But as quickly as he appeared, Nathaniel's form faded and dissolved into the ether. Ella pondered the visitation in the silent room.

Later, as she settled into bed, Ella's mind drifted back to Benjamin. The events of the day, especially the unexpected side of Benjamin, replayed in her thoughts. It was a fleeting glimpse of something intense, a hint of vulnerability, contrasting with the familiar, comforting steadiness she knew. She wanted to clear the air between them, yet found her thoughts returning to Nathaniel.

The dream realm soon beckoned, drawing her into its mist-shrouded embrace. Nathaniel was there once more, his visage full of of pain and indignation. His attempt to speak, to bridge the silence that enveloped them, was futile.

His eyes clouded with hurt and a glint of anger that she did not understand, and his lips moved, trying to form words.

As their eyes met, a transformation occurred. The hardness in Nathaniel's expression gave way to a profound sadness, his demeanor softening as he reached out to Ella with a tenderness that spoke volumes. The ghostly tension that had flared between them dissolved, leaving only the gentle touch of his hands on her face, a touch that evoked memories of the Nathaniel she held dear in her heart. They stood there, locked in a silent embrace, and Ella felt a pang of longing so intense it was almost painful. She wished, more than ever, that he could be real, that she could hear his voice, feel his warmth, and be enveloped in the certainty of his love. But the dream, like all dreams, was fleeting, and as dawn approached, she felt him slip away, leaving her yearning for the next time they would meet in this realm.

CHAPTER SEVEN

A Dark Spirit Revealed

Ella steered her car through the tree-canopied streets, drawing closer to Benjamin's apartment. Her hands were firm on the steering wheel, the peculiar incident at her cottage still weighing on her mind. She hoped to find some clarity, or at least prove to herself she was just imagining things.

With every step closer to his door, Ella fought the urge to turn and flee. How would she even begin the conversation? Her knock was tentative, and a brief silence lingered before the door swung open, revealing Benjamin. His warm, inviting grin—so normal—melted away the uncertainty that had enveloped Ella.

"Ella," he greeted. "What a surprise."

She smiled. "I hope it's a good time?"

"Always," he assured, stepping aside.

His home was a sanctuary, steeped in history and mystery. An alcove in one corner was adorned with relics from yesteryear and towering stacks of books. Scattered across the desk, evidence of his recent endeavors lay in the clutter.

They sat on the couch not speaking, until Benjamin offered, "Tea? Coffee?"

"Coffee, please," Ella responded.

As Benjamin retreated to the kitchen, the gentle clink of cups and the shuffle of his movements provided a soothing backdrop to Ella's thoughts. The air filled with the rich, earthy aroma of coffee, drifting through the space and coaxing a sense of calm anticipation.

When he returned, Benjamin handed her a mug and looked at her. "To what do I owe this visit?"

Ella exhaled, clutching the mug for warmth and courage. "I've been replaying the events at my cottage... and I thought we should talk. Try to make sense of it all."

The atmosphere shifted. An eerie coldness spread through the room, making Ella's skin prickle with goosebumps. The comforting warmth seemed to dissipate almost instantly, and the curtains fluttered despite the closed windows. Meanwhile, a faint whisper seemed to dance at the edge of her hearing.

Benjamin's expression became serious. "What happened? I don't understand."

"The other day at my place."

The air in the room grew heavier as the temperature continued to drop. Benjamin's body seemed to stiffen, his posture altering. His relaxed demeanor vanished, replaced by a rigidity that was foreign to his nature. For a split second, his eyes glazed over before darkening to an almost black hue, losing their usual warmth.

His breathing slowed, every exhale more pronounced than the last, filling the room with tension. Ella watched with growing apprehension as his fingers tightened around his mug.

When he finally spoke, his voice was deeper, laced with a strange undertone. "You didn't like that? Your body said otherwise." The aggression in his words, so unlike the Benjamin she knew, sent an icy shiver down Ella's spine. It was as though something else, some darker force, had taken residence in him.

The room grew charged with a tension that Ella could almost touch. She hesitated, her thoughts racing as she tried to piece together the puzzle of Benjamin's behavior. "I... I was taken aback. It wasn't the Benjamin I knew. It was...intense, so unlike you."

His eyes seemed distant. There was a fleeting glimmer of recognition of the kind-hearted man she knew, but it was clouded by darkness. "Are you scared of me now, Ella?"

Ella swallowed her fear. "No, I'm not scared. Just...worried. That wasn't you, Benjamin. The connection we share has always been genuine, deep. But that night... it felt... different..."

The shadow in Benjamin's eyes lifted, replaced by genuine confusion. "I...I don't understand it either. Ever since that night at the cottage, it's as if I'm being pulled in two directions. There's a force, a pressure that sometimes takes over."

Ella, despite her instincts screaming at her to run, leaned forward, her hand finding his. "That's what terrifies me. It wasn't just aggression. It felt... possessed, like you weren't in control."

His gaze flickered with defiance and fear. "What are you saying, Ella? That I'm haunted? That some spirit has control over me?"

She inhaled, steadying herself. "I don't know, but I can't deny what I felt, what I saw. Something changed in you, and it just happened again."

Benjamin's face crumpled, realization sinking in. "I... I never want to be a threat to you, Ella. If I ever scared you, I'm sorry. You should go."

Her eyes locked with his. "We're going to figure this out, okay? It's like our paths are caught up in... I don't know, some sort of history? There's something pulling us together. We've got to deal with it before it overwhelms us."

As her words hung in the air, a shift occurred in Benjamin again. It was as though the room had taken a breath. The warmth in Benjamin's apartment was gone. Comforting sounds of day now distant, muffled echoes, filtered through water. It was as if the surrounding space had contracted and the walls inched inward in a suffocating embrace.

Benjamin's voice cut through the silence, alien and dark. "Why so scared?" he murmured, his tone chilling, his smile a sinister smirk. "Don't you crave the closeness, the deep heart of our bond?"

Before Ella could react, Benjamin's aggression became physical, pushing her onto the couch with surprising speed. Despite the cushioning, the force left her breathless, feeling his icy presence against her warmth.

The change in his eyes unsettled her. This was not Benjamin. Her heart raced with a mix of confusion and fear. She attempted to free herself, but his presence was overpowering, a stark reminder of the unexpected turn their encounter had taken.

"You can't ignore this," he whispered. His words left her feeling exposed.

Tears brimmed in Ella's eyes. She wanted to call out, but her voice seemed lost, choked by the knot of fear in her throat. Just when despair seemed to take hold, the room's energy shifted again.

The flickering lights waged a war against the encroaching darkness, while outside, the wind rose in a protective crescendo. A gust burst through the room, sending papers into a chaotic dance. A glowing figure emerged, standing as a beacon of hope.

It was Nathaniel.

The spirit glowed with a pale light. His eyes filled with determination and anguish. They were fixed on Benjamin. Without uttering a word, Nathaniel raised his arms, creating an impenetrable barrier that shielded Ella. The room crackled with electric tension as the two forces — one dark and menacing, the other protective and radiant — clashed.

Benjamin, or the entity controlling him, let out a guttural roar of frustration. "She is mine—they are all mine," the entity declared.

Nathaniel, unshaken, countered with a calm authority that filled the charged air. "She rests under my protection."

As the standoff continued, Ella, fueled by adrenaline and sheer willpower, broke free from the grip of fear. She made a beeline for the door, sparing one last glance at the scene playing out behind her.

Outside, the air wrapped around her, slicing through the terror that clouded her thoughts. She hurried to her car, the ground beneath her feet blurring as she moved. With her heart hammering against her ribs, she started the engine and sped away from Benjamin's apartment. Tears streamed down her face, not from fear, but also from the crushing realization that she had left Benjamin alone to deal with whatever that was.

As she arrived back home, the night's events pressing upon her and she collected her thoughts. Just then, her phone buzzed with a text from Benjamin: *Where did you go?*

Had to get home, she replied. At least she knew he was safe and unaware of the night's ordeal. Clearly, she was the catalyst for something inexplicable.

She knew she couldn't put this call off any longer.

Ashlyn Alden

Ella had been reluctant to make the call, yet desperation drove her to act. After a moment of clumsiness with her phone, she dialed the number, her breath held in suspense as it rang.

A breathy voice answered. "Hello, this is Ashlyn."

"Hello... My name is Ella," she began. "Benjamin Hartley gave me your number. I'm not sure if he mentioned me, but... I need your help."

A soft sigh came from the other end. "Ah, Ella. I was wondering when you'd call. Benjamin has spoken of you. What's happened?"

Ella recounted the evening's events, along with the other unsettling experiences she'd faced in recent times. She even mentioned her dreams, but not in much detail.

Ashlyn listened, pausing Ella to ask a question. "Ella, in these visions or dreams, do you feel you're watching or actively living them?"

"It feels... real. Like I'm there, experiencing everything," Ella admitted.

"And Benjamin's behavior, does it change suddenly or over time?"

"It's sudden, usually during emotional moments or when discussing these... incidents," Ella whispered.

Ashlyn was silent for a moment, processing. "Ella, more is going on than meets the eye. I believe you're caught in something much larger than you realize. And while I'm cautious about sharing others' personal matters, I think you should know I've been working with Benjamin, helping him understand certain... abilities."

Ella's brow furrowed in confusion. "Abilities?"

"It's not my place to go into details," Ashlyn replied. "However, it's fortunate timing that I'm in town for the paranormal investigation. How about we meet tomorrow at the museum on West Street? Does 11 work for you? There's something there I believe you should see."

Relief flooded Ella. "Thank you, Ashlyn. I'll be there tomorrow, at 11."

The call ended, and though Ella was filled with unease, she felt a spark of hope. Whatever was unfolding, she would not face it alone.

* * *

The world of dreams has a unique way of distorting time and space, making the unbelievable seem ordinary, and bringing the distant close. That night, as Ella's consciousness sank into the gentle embrace of sleep, she found herself again in the realm where the spectral and the living coalesced.

The familiar sound of waves crashing against rocks greeted her, and when she opened her eyes, she stood at the very peak of the Misthaven lighthouse. The ambiance was surreal. An otherworldly glow enveloped the space, bathing everything in a silvery light that seemed to emanate from the moon.

Standing before her was Nathaniel. He appeared more tangible than ever, his form no longer the fleeting, translucent apparition she'd grown accustomed to. The very air around him pulsed with energy, making the space between them feel charged.

They gravitated toward each other, the pull between them undeniable. As they came face to face, their fingers brushing, a rush of emotions surged through Ella. Memories, not her own sensations, feelings, and glimpses of a time long past, played out before her eyes.

The dream felt more like a journey through time than random images. Ella was adrift in a sea of memories, each wave crashing against the shore of her consciousness with the vividness of a lived moment. She was a little girl again, her laughter echoing against the sturdy walls of the lighthouse that had been her childhood sanctuary. The dream painted her younger self with a palette in hand, strokes of vibrant colors blending into forms and shapes on canvas.

The scene shifted, and there she was, looking up into her mother's eyes—eyes that sparkled with life and love, a memory untouched by the shadow of death. Her father's voice, a firm reprimand, cautioned her each time she spoke of the ghostly figures that only she could see.

Then, a younger Nathaniel appeared before her, his presence igniting a spark that illuminated her soul. It was love at first sight, a moment of profound connection that defied words, as if their souls recognized each other from lifetimes past.

As the dream wove these memories together, the distinction between observer and participant blurred. At first, Ella watched these moments unfold as if she were a spectator in her own life, but the dream enveloped her. The barrier between herself and the young girl in the memory dissipating until they became the same.

She questioned the origins of these memories. Were they hers, or did they belong to Isabella? The dream shifted between past and present, weaving Ella's emotions and experiences with those of a life that might once have been hers, leaving her to wonder at the interconnection of souls and the timeless nature of love and loss.

As dawn's early light made itself known, a shift occurred to Nathaniel. His playful tenderness was replaced by an urgency that gripped Ella's attention. He tried to communicate, his eyes darting with distress and a desperate need to convey something vital. With every attempt to speak, his voice seemed choked, stifled by an unseen force.

Nathaniel didn't need words to convey his warning. His anxious demeanor spoke volumes. Ella's mind was awash with unsettling images. Cautionary flashes appeared in front of her and the dark outline of a spirit seemed to seethe with rage. Nathaniel's message was crystal clear—beware of the angry ghost lurking ahead.

The fabric of their shared dream unraveled, drawing them back towards the stark light of reality. Nathaniel's figure stretched out, a desperate attempt to bridge the growing gap between them. In a silent whisper, he mouthed a name: "Isabella." The echo of that name lingered, a presence in the room, unveiling the painful truth that perhaps Ella wasn't the focus of his desires, but a shadow of his long-lost love.

Now fully awakened, Ella's heart ached with emotions—the beauty of their dream entangled with the sharpness of Nathaniel's whisper. Caught in a whirlwind of feelings, she navigated the blurred lines where past dreams and present realities converge.

Ella pulled her knees to her chest, wrapping her arms around them for comfort. She felt alone. Nathaniel's heart belonged to someone else, and Benjamin was under the control of something evil. The thought left her adrift.

She held onto the hope that her meeting with Ashlyn tomorrow might shed some light on these dark circumstances. Answers were what she needed, and perhaps Ashlyn could provide them. It was a slim hope, but it was all she had to cling to during her confusion and fear.

Chapter Eight

A Twist in the Tale

In the halls of the local museum, the air was thick with anticipation. The sleepy coastal town buzzed with whispers, its heartbeat quickened by the promise of recognition from the upcoming episode of the ghost hunter show. The town council, in a stroke of inspiration, had seized upon this opportunity, curating a new exhibit that delved into the area's haunted legacy. It was a clever ruse, designed to entice tourists and ghost enthusiasts alike to their quiet shores.

Ella wandered among the exhibits, reading the captions and taking it all in. Each display was a portal to the past, arranged with relics that whispered of forgotten lives. She could see Benjamin's hand in some displays and wondered if he had worked on them. There were diaries frayed at the edges, photographs faded with time, and objects that once held meaning in the hands of their original owners.

The lighting in the room was a deliberate choice, casting a warm, amber glow that seemed to pull the shadows back just enough to illuminate the treasures of yesteryear. Around her, the murmurs of other visitors floated, full of excitement and speculation about the ghost hunter show and the secrets it promised to unveil.

Drawn as if by a magnet, Ella stood before a display that called to her very soul. It featured Misthaven Light. Among the artifacts, a photograph captured her gaze and held it fast. It depicted two men, standing side by side with an air of camaraderie and solemn duty. One figure was Nathaniel, and the man beside him bore a striking resemblance to someone she knew all too well—Benjamin.

The shock of the recognition rooted her to the spot, her thoughts raced as she absorbed the revelation. The elegant script on the caption of the date etching itself into her memory: "Lighthouse Keeper Nathaniel and friend, Samuel Hartley, 1879" A surge of unease washed over her. Benjamin had never mentioned that Samuel's surname was Hartley, too—and now this. Samuel looked JUST like Benjamin. The resemblance was unsettling.

Implications of the photograph spiraled through her mind, intertwining with the hauntings and Benjamin's strange behavior. Was it Samuel that possessed him? It was as if the past refused to remain silent, each piece of the puzzle falling into place with an almost audible click. Ella knew that the mysteries of the lighthouse—and the connections between Nathaniel, Isabella, and now Samuel and Benjamin,—were far from resolved.

As she stood there, a deeper discomfort settled, stemming from how much she herself looked like Isabella. What if Samuel had been Isabella's killer? Was history fated to repeat itself, casting her and Benjamin in their tragic roles? This personal connection to the lore felt too close, making her skin crawl.

The secrets buried in the town's history were dragging her deeper into a story she had not expected. Despite the discomfort and the growing fear, Ella felt an irresistible pull towards uncovering these hidden truths. The past, with its ghostly whispers and unresolved mysteries, beckoned, and she found herself powerless to resist its call.

A hushed voice behind her remarked, "Ah, you've noticed Samuel, haven't you?"

Startled, Ella whirled around to find herself face-to-face with a captivating woman. Raven-black hair flowed down her back, framing pale blue eyes that sparkled with an otherworldly intensity—it was Ashlyn Alden. Dressed in flowing garments, with a crystal pendant adorning her neck, every detail of her appearance whispered of her deep ties to the mystical.

"Benjamin bears a striking resemblance to Samuel Hartley, his ancestor," Ashlyn continued, and extended a graceful hand towards a secluded bench. "Shall we?" she suggested.

As they headed toward the spot, their path took them past displays rich with the lighthouse lore.

"It's quite the collection, isn't it?" Ashlyn remarked.

"It is," Ella agreed, her gaze stopping on an old logbook. "Every piece seems to hold a story eager to leap off the page—or out of the shadows."

After reaching the bench, the two introduced themselves, the initial unfamiliarity melting away as they exchanged names and smiles. "I'm Ashlyn Alden," said the woman, her handshake firm yet inviting.

"Ella Hayes," Ella responded.

After the initial pleasantries and a mutual recognition that they were on the cusp of exploring the extraordinary, Ashlyn leaned closer. With a low voice, she confided, "Since starting the lighthouse project, Benjamin has been tormented by dreams. These dreams connect him with Samuel and Nathaniel, suggesting the past is trying to tell us something. Given Benjamin's undeveloped psychic potential, he's unusually open to these messages."

Ella paused, a hint of color rising to her cheeks. "These dreams... are they intimate?" she asked.

As she observed Ella with a lifted eyebrow, Ashlyn replied in a measured tone, "Those dreams are Benjamin's to disclose, should he wish to." Her response, diplomatic yet firm, hinted at the depth of Benjamin's experiences, leaving Ella to ponder his psychic connection.

Feeling somewhat rebuffed, Ella attempted to redirect the conversation, her curiosity pushing her forward. "What do you know about these people historically, beyond mere photographs and legends?"

Ashlyn delved into the historical records she had come across, most of which Ella and Benjamin had already discussed. "There was a woman named Isabella Blackwell, a close friend to Samuel and engaged to Nathaniel. Tragically, her life was cut short, and the circumstances of her death were controversial. Both

Nathaniel and Samuel were charged with her murder. While Nathaniel's alibi held — he was aboard a ship, far out at sea — Samuel's exoneration was largely attributed to his family's significant wealth and influence. The newspapers and gossip of the time believed Samuel's guilt, suggesting he might have taken drastic steps because of his unreciprocated feelings for Isabella."

"The Hartley family's wealth was legendary in the town, with roots that stretched back several generations. Originally making their fortune in shipping and trade, the Hartleys expanded their empire into various other ventures, ensuring that their coffers never ran dry. "

Ella's brows knitted in thought. "But that's just what people believed, isn't it? What do *you* see?" she couldn't help but probe deeper, seeking clarity from someone who could see beyond the veil of time.

Ashlyn took a moment, closing her eyes as if reaching into her psychic memories. "The impressions I've received are fluid and elusive. From what I've gathered, the relationship between Isabella and Samuel was one of genuine friendship. Pure, without romantic entanglement." She paused, her voice dropping a tad lower. "But Samuel... he had a different affection, one not for Isabella, but for Nathaniel. A love that was taboo in their era. It wasn't reciprocated, which might have been a source of pain for Samuel."

Ella's eyes widened in realization. "So the idea Samuel might have harmed Isabella out of jealousy could have been misconstrued?"

Ashlyn nodded. "At least in the way they suspected. But emotions, especially those suppressed and hidden, have a way of influencing events in ways we might not expect. We may never know what happened."

This revelation weighed on Ella. The interconnected lives of Isabella, Samuel, Nathaniel, and now, she and Benjamin, formed a web of history and emotion that was hard to disentangle. She felt sympathy for Samuel and a growing unease about the unresolved past that might haunt her present.

"It's important for me to know the specifics of the dreams you've had." Ashlyn's eyes met Ella's. "It might help us understand the connection better. Can you share them?"

Ella blushed, her fingers fidgeting with the hem of her shirt. "They're so... personal. Most of the time, it feels like it's just me and Nathaniel. We share these moments where emotions run so deep. But in the most recent dream, Nathaniel called me 'Isabella'. And that's when it hit me. Those feelings... they aren't really for me."

Ashlyns's brows furrowed. "That makes sense. You're channeling Isabella's memories, her emotions, her past. The bond you're feeling with Nathaniel in the dreams, it's the remnants of what Isabella felt for him."

"They started when I was on the other side of the country. How does that even work?" Ella took a shaky breath. "I didn't even know Misthaven Light existed."

"You may have your own latent abilities." Ashlyn pondered for a moment, the soft glow of the exhibit lighting casting shadows across her face. "Having an ancestor as a past life is quite rare, but it's not unheard of. It opens a unique channel for spiritual and emotional connections that can transcend time and space."

Ella nodded, absorbing Ashlyn's words. "Isabella isn't an ancestor, at least not that I'm aware of," she confessed. "But I suppose she could be. Without something like a DNA test, there's no way to know for sure." She sighed. "And really, whether she is or isn't doesn't change what's happening. This... connection, it's real, regardless of the reason."

Ashlyn leaned forward. "When exactly did you start having these dreams about Nathaniel?"

Ella thought back, trying to pinpoint the exact moment her nights became haunted by the past. "They started around late spring," she pursed her lips. "But I was on the other side of the country, which makes it even more bizarre. How does that even work?"

"That was around the time we first hired Benjamin to dig up history." Ashlyn nodded, a knowing look in her eyes. "It's clear that something has been stirred up. The timing of your dreams with Benjamin's research isn't a coincidence. It's as if the past is reaching out, using both of you as conduits to reconcile unfinished business."

Ella felt a chill run down her spine. The connection between her dreams and Benjamin's work was undeniable, and the thought that they might be part of something much larger than themselves was a bit terrifying, but also exhilarating.

"Am I safe?" Ella whispered.

Ashlyn leaned in, her tone taking on a more urgent note. "Benjamin confided in me he's been experiencing blackouts, moments when he doesn't remember his actions or what he's said. And sometimes, his personality... changes. It's unlike the Samuel I've seen in my impressions. Samuel's spirit is conflicted, but not malevolent. It's confusing and, frankly, I don't like being confused."

Ella's eyes widened in shock. "Why didn't he tell me?"

"He's terrified," Ashlyn responded. "And from my understanding, it seems Samuel's spirit is struggling within him."

Ella looked down at her hands and whispered, "I felt it, something dark and intense. But I also felt Benjamin, the real him, struggling beneath."

Ashlyn reached out, touching Ella's hand. "You're both caught in this drama from the past. And Ella," her voice dropped, "I *do* believe you have a latent psychic ability, too. You need to be careful."

Ella hesitated for a moment. "With all this happening, should Benjamin and I even go to Misthaven? Is it safe?"

"Under normal circumstances, I'd advise against it. However," Ashlyn sighed, "the connection you and Benjamin have with these spirits is undeniable. They won't let go until there's a resolution. And frankly, I believe the only way to uncover the truth and bring peace to these souls is to have both of you present on the island."

Ella's face drained of color. Ashlyns's words had hit her hard. "But that means..."

"Yes," Ashlyn interrupted, "it will be dangerous. You'll be diving into uncharted territories, confronting memories and emotions that have been suppressed for over a century."

Ashlyn's phone buzzed, breaking the intense atmosphere. She glanced at the message and sighed. "I need to meet with the show's team." She stood up, her flowing skirt rustling.

Ella hesitated for a moment, a trace of concern flickering in her eyes. "Ashlyn, do you think it's safe for me to be around Benjamin right now?" she asked, the question hanging in the air between them.

Ashlyn paused, considering Ella's question. "Given everything that's happening, it might be wise to keep your interactions in public places for the time being," she advised. "Until I have time to meet with the two of you together, we can't be too cautious. The energies at play here are complex, and we need to understand them better before we can make any definitive judgments about safety."

Ella nodded, reassurance washing over her despite the uncertainty of the situation. "Okay, I can do that. It's just... all of this is so overwhelming. I never imagined anything like this could happen."

"We will talk more, and I will make sure you are prepared. Trust your instincts. You'll get through this," Ashlyn reassured her, offering a comforting smile.

Ella managed a small smile in return. "Take care. We'll be in touch," she said, her voice steadier than before.

As Ashlyn's figure melded with the crowd and vanished from sight, the burden of their exchanged words settled upon Ella's shoulders. Caught in history, emotions, and otherworldly happenings, the true depth of their entanglement with spirits long gone was clear. The realization was overwhelming, casting a shadow over her understanding of the present and its ties to the past.

Ella inhaled, the cool air of the museum grounding her. She wandered through the remaining displays, trying to process everything. There were so many layers to unravel, so many truths hidden in the folds of time. The most pressing matter was Benjamin. Their experiences, his blackouts, the dreams — everything was intertwined. And the realization that he was vulnerable too only heightened her concern.

Her fingers hovered over her phone, hesitating for a moment. With a sigh, she dialed Benjamin's number. It rang twice before he picked up.

"Ella?" His voice was soft.

"Benjamin," she began, searching for the right words. "We need to talk."

There was a pause, and she could imagine him nodding on the other end. "Come over. We can—"

"No," she interrupted. Ashlyn had advised public places. "I'd feel better if we were somewhere public."

She could hear the hurt in his sigh. "Alright. How about the coffee shop? The one where we first met?"

Ella nodded, even though he couldn't see her. "That sounds perfect."

"Okay, see you there," he murmured, and with that, the call ended.

The bell above the door tinkled as Ella entered The Harbor Brew. The familiar scent of roasted coffee beans enveloped her, offering comfort. It was a setting she cherished, with the gentle hum of whispered conversations and the soft lighting lending a soothing aura. Their corner, with its worn-out leather seats, was occupied by Benjamin, who looked up when she approached.

His expression was a muddle of worry and relief when she mentioned Ashlyn. "You met with her?"

Ella nodded, settling across from him. "Yes, and before you get too worried, she didn't tell me any personal secrets you shared with her." She offered him a reassuring smile, though she could sense the tension radiating from him. "She respects privacy."

Benjamin ran a hand through his hair, looking relieved. "Thank you for telling me."

"Which brings me to my next point," she said. "We can't have secrets between us anymore. Not with everything that's going on."

He hesitated, eyes darting away from hers. He knew what she was talking about. "I found out about Samuel early in the research. The history, the tales... they all seemed to vilify him. They said he was responsible for Isabella's death.

When I saw you for the first time and noticed the resemblance to her, I was afraid how you'd react. Especially because the moment our paths crossed, it felt like fate. It felt as if our souls had known each other forever."

Silence hung in the airt. "You recognized me when we met?" Ella asked, surprised.

"From the very instant," he admitted. "It felt like destiny. I just... didn't want history to cloud the present."

She let out a deep sigh. "We need transparency, Benjamin, especially now. We have to face it." She leaned forward, her voice soft. "Tell me about your dreams."

His face flushed a deep shade of crimson, his eyes darting around as if looking for an escape. "I... I don't really think that's necessary. It's embarrassing."

"Remember what we agreed," Ella insisted, her gaze unwavering. "No secrets."

After taking a shaky breath, he began, "Fine. My dreams... they're not about my love for Isabella. They're about Captain Nathaniel." He paused, looking down at the table. "I dream about... desires for Nathaniel."

Ella's eyes widened, taken aback. "As in...?"

Benjamin's face turned even redder, the tips of his ears burning. "Yes. Intimate desires. I'm not gay. At least I never thought I was, but the feelings are so real. So intense. It's confusing."

Their voices had become whispers now, their conversation too intimate for the casual ear to hear.

Ella hesitated, jealousy in her voice. "Did Nathaniel return his affections?"

Benjamin shook his head, looking almost relieved to confirm Nathaniel's indifference. "No. Not in any of those dreams. But..."

Benjamin's eyes shifted away, uncomfortable. "But sometimes Nathaniel seemed to... blend into my regular dreams. And in those moments, there was also... you."

Ella's heart rate quickened. She could feel a warmth creeping up her cheeks, but she tried to keep her voice casual. "Me? As in Ella or...?"

"As Isabella at first," he clarified, his voice quiet. "And sometimes as... well, just you."

She recognized her own dreams in his words. "I had similar dreams, where I wasn't sure if I was myself or Isabella. But Nathaniel... he seemed very real, very present."

Benjamin looked at her with raised eyebrows. "What do you mean?"

She hesitated, her fingers playing with the rim of her coffee mug. "It's... it's hard to explain. Sometimes it felt like he was... reaching out to me, calling me."

Benjamin leaned forward, his voice gentle yet insistent. "Ella, you need to tell me everything, too."

She bit her lip, looking away. "I don't know if I can. It's just too personal."

He reached out, placing a hand over hers. "Remember, communication is a two-way street. You wanted transparency from me. I need the same from you."

Ella's fingers played with the necklace she was wearing. "In these dreams, it was often sunset at the lighthouse. The sky is painted in hues of orange and pink, the horizon a blend of the sea and the skies. Nathaniel would stand there, in his captain's uniform, looking out at the sea. And then, he'd turn to me... to Isabella, I mean, and there was always this deep longing in his eyes."

She paused, gathering her thoughts. "It wasn't just the surroundings, Benjamin. It was the emotions. They were so real. Sometimes he'd reach out, holding me close, and other times we would just stand side by side, lost in our own world. There was love there, a deep connection. But it was also tinged with sadness like there was always something unsaid between them."

Benjamin's jaw tightened as he listened, his fingers drumming on the table. There was a shadow in his eyes, one that spoke of jealousy and confusion, but he remained silent, letting Ella continue.

She sighed, "Sometimes the dreams got more—intimate."

As she gazed into Benjamin's eyes, she ventured further, "But it wasn't just about embodying Isabella's emotions. I felt them as my own. The depth of feeling, the bond, the yearning—it all seemed so tangible, as though Nathaniel and I shared a past."

An uneasy silence enveloped them. Benjamin's expression remained unreadable, yet the tightness in his posture betrayed his discomfort. "It's a lot to take in,

Ella," he confessed, his voice strained. "The idea of you—or Isabella—experiencing such intense connections, even in dreams... I almost feel jealous," he blushed.

Ella scanned their surroundings in the quaint coffee shop, ensuring their conversation remained private. The space around them felt cocooned, the soft murmur of patrons and the clinking of cups forming a serene backdrop.

"Could you share more about your dreams?" She asked as she leaned in.

Benjamin let out a sigh, his eyes flickering with hesitation before he spoke. "In one particular dream, which felt more like Samuel's wishes than actual events, we were in this small room, the ambiance heavy with anticipation. Samuel—I mean, I was there with Nathaniel, and the air was thick with unspoken tension."

He paused, collecting his thoughts. "There was a moment of hesitation, a look that conveyed so much without words. And suddenly, the distance between us vanished."

Carefully choosing his words, he continued, "It was a dream of seeking and finding comfort in each other's presence, a gentle, almost hesitant connection. We were navigating the complexities of our feelings, trying to understand them."

Ella, intrigued by the vulnerability in his admission, encouraged him, "It sounds like an experience."

"It was," Benjamin admitted, the complexity of his emotions clear. "It left me questioning and reflecting. I've experienced nothing like it."

Ella nodded. "I can imagine. It's all so interconnected, isn't it? Our dreams, the past... I think Ashlyn's insights could help us untangle some of this."

Benjamin looked thoughtful, his earlier tension easing. "I hope so. She seems to have a good understanding of these matters."

Ella leaned forward, her eyes sparkling. "I'm excited about the investigation. Not just for answers, but to see how all of this...," she gestured, encompassing their discussions, the dreams, and the psychic's guidance, "...fits together."

"Me too," Benjamin agreed. "And I'm glad we're doing this together. Whatever happens, it feels like we're on the right path to understanding the bigger picture."

Ella smiled.. "Exactly. And who knows? Maybe this will bring some closure to the spirits involved, too."

"Agreed." He chuckled.

As the conversation dwindled, a comfortable silence settled between Ella and Benjamin. They found the world around them fading into the background. It was one of those rare moments where words were unnecessary, where the connection between two people spoke volumes more than conversation ever could. Just as they were about to lean closer, a sudden buzz shattered the moment. Their phones vibrated in unison, pulling them back from the moment. With a shared smile, they reached for their devices.

It was a message from Ashlyn. *Investigation is on for tomorrow. Can we meet before boarding the boat? There are some things we need to go over.*

Let's meet at my place, Ella texted back, Benjamin nodding in approval as he peered over her shoulder.

See you both in the morning. Stay safe tonight. Ashlyn's last text read, a reminder of the seriousness beneath their excitement.

With a shared grin, they acknowledged the adventure that lay ahead.

"See you in the morning for the big reveal," Benjamin said.

"Can't wait," she responded, her voice full of resolve.

Then, with a promise of tomorrow's mysteries hanging in the air, they went their separate ways.

CHAPTER NINE

Between Two Worlds

Ashlyn arrived first, enveloped in the wave of mystery and otherworldliness that always seemed to swirl around her. Ella welcomed her at the door with a warm smile. "Coffee, tea?" she offered, leading her guest into the cozy kitchen.

"Tea, please," Ashlyn replied, her voice soft yet clear.

Ella busied herself with the tea, placing two mugs on the table before sitting down opposite Ashlyn. The atmosphere was filled with an anticipatory silence, the kind that precedes a storm of revelations.

"I wanted to get here early to prepare you for what I fear is unfolding with Benjamin," Ashlyn began, her gaze fixed on Ella with an intensity that felt almost palpable. "And perhaps to help you understand yourself better."

"I appreciate it," Ella replied. "I believe he's a good person, but the things happening have been quite frightening."

Ashlyn nodded, understanding the depth of Ella's concern. "My psychic abilities are strongest in the realm of retro cognition. I receive glimpses of events that have already happened, sometimes triggered by people, but most often by places with intense energy. Venturing to Misthaven Island will give me a clearer picture of what transpired. However, my visions are more akin to memories, colored by the emotions and perceptions of those who experienced them firsthand. In the end, it may be that one had to be there to grasp the full truth."

She continued, her voice gaining a note of passion as she spoke of her work with paranormal investigation groups. "Knowing the history, coupled with the emotions and perceptions surrounding a haunting, increases the likelihood of gathering tangible evidence—and yes, it makes for a good show. Some groups are committed to understanding the phenomena, while for others, it's more about the viewership."

"And where do you stand in all this?" Ella asked, curiosity piqued by Ashlyn's dedication.

Ashlyn laughed, a sound that seemed to echo around the room. "If I didn't need to eat, I'd do it for free. There's nothing more fulfilling than helping a kindred spirit, whether in life or death! The connection, the moment of under-standing and peace it can bring, is unparalleled. It's not just about the thrill of the investigation or the chase for evidence. It's about providing closure, answers, and sometimes, just the comfort of knowing one isn't alone in their experiences."

Ella listened, captivated by Ashlyn's words and the earnestness in her eyes. Ashlyn was driven by a deep-seated desire to aid both the living and the dead, a mission that went far beyond mere curiosity or the lure of the mysterious. In this moment, Ella felt hopeful, a sense that perhaps, with Ashlyn's help, they could unravel the mysteries that had been plaguing them and, in doing so, find a path to peace and understanding.

"So, where do Benjamin and I fit into all of this?" Ella asked, her brows fur-rowed in a mixture of concern and curiosity. Ashlyn's lips curved into a knowing, almost secretive smile.

"The force is strong in you," she quipped, her laughter lightening the moment with her playful reference. Seeing Ella's expectant look, she became serious again. "Honestly, it's rare to encounter two individuals so deeply intertwined with a haunting. And you, Ella, drawn all the way from the other side of the coun-try—it's as if the spirits themselves are clamoring for someone to unravel this mystery!"

Ella nodded, her mind racing with thoughts and possibilities. "Do you think Samuel was responsible? Do you believe he pushed Isabella?"

Ashlyn exhaled, her expression clouding over. "I can't say for certain. My visions only offer glimpses, fragments of the past. Samuel's presence is there, but the energies surrounding that moment are so muddled, so conflicting. It's as though he was battling within himself, possibly suffering from some kind of identity disorder. Yet, diagnosing a living person with such a condition is challenging enough in modern times, let alone speculating on the complex emotions of a spirit long passed."

Ella let out a soft sigh, her thoughts drifting to Benjamin. She was fond of him, but the idea of being close to someone mixed up with a dangerous spirit was daunting. "And Benjamin?" she asked, her voice barely above a whisper. "Do you think he'll be okay?"

Ashlyn's smile returned, this time imbued with a warmth and reassurance that touched Ella. "I believe so. I sense that once we reach the island and explore the actual scene of the haunting, I'll be able to help free him from his spectral stowaway."

Their intense discussion was interrupted by two soft raps at the door. Benjamin had arrived.

The sudden intrusion jolted Ella back to the present, her heart skipping a beat at the thought of facing Benjamin now, with all these swirling questions and fears. Yet Ashlyn's confident, reassuring presence gave her a glimmer of hope. Perhaps, together, they could confront the mysteries of the past and help Benjamin find peace.

As she rose to answer the door, Ella took a moment to steady her nerves, preparing herself for the uncertain journey ahead. The path to solving the mystery of the haunting, and understanding the roles they each played in it, was bound to be fraught with challenges. Yet, the prospect of uncovering the truth, and perhaps in doing so, bringing peace to restless spirits, filled her with a sense of purpose she hadn't realized she'd been seeking.

Benjamin's bright eyes sparked a flutter of butterflies in Ella's stomach—the good kind—as she welcomed him inside. "Hi," she greeted, her voice a soft whisper in the cozy room. "Do you want some coffee?"

He nodded, his gaze filled with a warmth that hinted at a longing for closeness, yet he hesitated as if unsure of the boundaries between them. "It's okay," she reassured him with a gentle smile, leaning in to give him a comforting hug. "I think we're safe here," she added, her laughter tinged with a nervous edge that betrayed her calm exterior.

As they gathered around the kitchen table, Ashlyn wasted no time diving into the heart of the matter. "I wanted to meet with you both first because I believe there's some heavy stuff entwined with this investigation. The crew and the other investigators are going to be all business, focusing more on capturing good shots and building a TV show than on the spirits' feelings. But from what I sense around you two, the impact of this investigation is going to hit you like a ton of bricks! You'll need to establish spiritual boundaries, or it could overwhelm you."

"How do we do that?" Benjamin asked. As a history student, the idea of history reaching out to communicate with him had left him unnerved.

Ashlyn offered a reassuring smile. "Think of yourself as a doctor or therapist. You need to set clear parameters with the spirits—define your 'office hours' and establish where these interactions can take place. Being on the island will present its challenges, but it also offers the best opportunity to set these limits. You can tell the spirits that you've come to their territory to engage with them, but they need to respect your boundaries. No more hitching a ride in your mind," she directed at Benjamin, then turning her attention to Ella, she added, "or in your dreams." Her gaze shifted back to Benjamin, seeking his understanding.

"Understood," Benjamin replied, a faint blush coloring his cheeks, showing his apprehension yet willingness to proceed.

Ella watched the exchange, a sense of solidarity building between them. Ashlyn's guidance provided a practical approach to navigating the uncharted waters of their investigation, offering a semblance of control over interactions that, until now, seemed beyond their grasp. Setting boundaries with the spirits, of treating their interactions as structured meetings, was comforting. It gave Ella and Benjamin a framework to protect themselves while delving into the mysteries that awaited them on the island.

Ashlyn outlined the plan, ensuring Ella and Benjamin understood each step. "We'll meet the crew at the docks," she began, her voice carrying a note of excitement. "The boat will take us to Misthaven Island, all above board with permission from the state. We'll all head over together."

"Once on the island," Ashlyn continued, "the camera crew will set up, taking advantage of the remaining daylight to capture shots of the island's scenic beauty. Benjamin, you'll be up first. As our historian, you'll be filmed detailing the history of the island and sharing the facts we know about its previous inhabitants—all the material you've already prepared."

Then, turning her attention to Ella, Ashlyn added with a wink, "There won't be much for you to do in that capacity, so you might find yourself taking on a variety of tasks. Most of the time, they don't bring along a historian's 'assistant,'" she teased, "so the director will probably put you to work wherever needed."

Ella and Benjamin absorbed the information, nodding along. Ella felt a surge of excitement. The anticipation was building, transforming her nerves into a buzzing excitement.

As they journeyed to the dock, Benjamin's car was enveloped in a contemplative silence, each passenger immersed in personal reflections. Sunshine bathed the day, casting a hopeful glow on their expedition. Upon arrival, they were greeted by the bustling crew, busy loading equipment. The atmosphere was serene, resembling a group gearing up for an afternoon cruise more than a team on the brink of unraveling the mysteries of a haunted island.

They watched the crew work. The professional manner in which they handled the gear and coordinated their efforts offered a reassuring glimpse into the forthcoming investigation's seriousness. Yet, the beautiful weather and the gentle lapping of the water against the dock lent an air of calm to the proceedings.

This was something significant, a chance to delve into the past and explore the untold stories of Misthaven Island. With Ashlyn's guidance, Benjamin's historical knowledge, and her own willingness to take on whatever role was needed, Ella was ready to face whatever the island had in store for them. The adventure was about to begin, and she couldn't wait to set sail into the unknown.

The salty sea breeze tousled Ella's hair as the motorboat bobbed on the waves. Misthaven Light, with its distinctive square tower piercing through the keeper's house, stood on the horizon.

Beside her, Benjamin leaned in, his warm breath mingling with the cool sea air. "It's even more mesmerizing up close, isn't it?" His voice held a note of wonder, his eyes reflecting the shimmering water.

Ella nodded, lost in the moment. "There's a sense of timelessness to it. Like it's been waiting just for us." Her fingers brushed against his, sending tingling currents up her arm.

Ashlyn, positioned at the front, shouted over the wind's hum. "This place holds many secrets. I feel them even now. It's eager to share its tales." She looked back at Ella and Benjamin, her piercing eyes softened. "And you two—be mindful of the living and the dead. This island can be quite... enchanting."

The boat's gentle sway, combined with the rhythmic lullaby of the lapping waves, brought them closer. Their shoulders touched, their shared anticipation building a bridge of intimacy. "Nervous?" Ella asked, her voice almost a whisper.

"A bit," Benjamin admitted, his fingers tracing hers. "But more excited. There's so much history here, and then there's... us."

The boat docked, its wooden planks creaking underfoot. As the team prepared for the shoot, the world seemed to pause, allowing Ella and Benjamin a moment suspended in time, the past and present intertwined under the watchful gaze of the lighthouse.

The team had a well-rehearsed rhythm, transitioning from the boat ride to preparing for the day's shoot and night's investigation. Their show, having aired multiple seasons, had garnered a loyal following. The blend of history, technology, and psychic insights made it a unique addition to the paranormal community.

Martin, the lead investigator, was tall and broad-shouldered. His dark hair was neatly combed, and a pair of round glasses perched on his nose gave him an academic appearance. Beside him was Travis, shorter but with an athletic build, exuding a quiet confidence. They had been friends long before the show's inception and their bond showed in the way they communicated—often without words.

While the duo conferred on the night's strategy, two camera operators, Naomi, a petite woman with pixie-cut blonde hair, and Raul, a burly man with a kind face, started setting up tripods and adjusting their lens angles. Lydia, the sound expert, tested her audio equipment, ensuring that every whisper, every EVP, would be captured.

Ashlyn, sensing Ella's curiosity, gestured at the infrared cameras being set up near the base of the lighthouse. "Those will help us see in the dark, and sometimes, they pick up figures or anomalies that the naked eye misses."

Ella, eyes wide, responded, "It's so fascinating. Do you need any help?"

Travis, overhearing, smiled. "Thanks for the offer, Ella, but we've got a system. Too many hands can sometimes make things tricky. But ask questions, and if you feel or see anything off, let us know."

Benjamin, already conversing with Martin about the island's history, nodded in agreement. "We're here to observe and assist when needed. Let the professionals do their job."

Once everything was set up, it was time for Benjamin to film the historical information.

Ella stood a little apart from the crew, her gaze fixed on Benjamin Hartley as he prepared to delve into the history of Misthaven Light. There was an air of earnest anticipation about her, her eyes betraying something deeper, something personal whenever they rested on Benjamin. The rustic backdrop of the lighthouse added a layer of intrigue to the scene, almost as if it were a silent character in their unfolding story.

As Benjamin began speaking, Ella couldn't help but admire the way his voice danced with excitement. "Early photographs of Misthaven Light reveal a basic square shape," he said, his scholarly enthusiasm infectious. Ella imagined the lighthouse as he described it: a unique, twelve-foot square brick tower emerging from a flat-roofed keeper's dwelling, its metal stairs mimicking the building's square form.

Her attention drifted as Martin interrupted Benjamin, asking him to emphasize the uniqueness of the structure. Ella smiled. She appreciated Benjamin's willingness to adapt, to make his wealth of knowledge accessible and engaging.

Benjamin cleared his throat and restarted, his voice now infused with a touch more drama. Ella found herself drawn in by his vivid storytelling, hanging on to every word about the lighthouse's construction and the early tragedies that befell the keeper's family.

When Benjamin described the ferocious gale of 1856, Ella could almost hear the howling winds and crashing waves, see the sea surging over the rock, sweeping away the fuel shed. His ability to bring history to life always amazed her, and today was no exception.

When Benjamin delved into the lighthouse's history, he spoke of the disturbing discovery made during its construction. "In 1854, as the foundation was being laid, workers unearthed human remains, an unsettling omen that delayed the project. Some say it was the body of a local captain, Elias Thorton, who had been lost to the sea," he revealed. Ella felt a shiver at the thought. The nature of these remains, shrouded in mystery, had been the subject of much speculation over the years.

He then recounted the tragedies that befell the lighthouse's first keeper, Armand Blackwood, and his family. "Armand's tenure was marked by sorrow from the outset. His infant son, born just a few weeks after they moved in, succumbed to unknown ailments, a devastating start to their life here." Ella felt a twinge of sadness, imagining the family's initial joy turning to mourning.

"The grief continued," Benjamin continued, "when Clara, Armand's wife, passed away in 1862, succumbing to a swift and merciless illness." His voice carried a note of sympathy that resonated with Ella. She pictured Clara, a figure of resilience turned frail by her untimely death.

Benjamin's narrative then took a darker turn as he spoke of Isabella's tragic end in 1875. "Isabella, their beloved daughter, met a tragic fate at just 19. She fell from the cliffs, her body claimed by the churning waters below." The sorrow in his tone was palpable, and Ella felt the family's tragedies as if they were her own.

"The death of Isabella broke Armand," Benjamin said. "He passed away a year later in 1876, some say of a broken heart, while others whispered of guilt. His death, like his daughter's, was shrouded in mystery and unresolved sorrow."

He then moved on to Nathaniel Hawthorn, Isabella's betrothed, and the next keeper. "Nathaniel, overcome by grief at the loss of his love, became a recluse, his life at the lighthouse marked by solitude until his untimely death in 1885, under circumstances that remain as mysterious as the island itself."

As Benjamin concluded, weaving together the threads of the lighthouse's history with the mystery of the curse, Ella felt a surge of admiration for him. His words hung in the air, a poignant reminder of the mysteries they were there to uncover.

The camera zoomed out, capturing the haunting beauty of the lighthouse against the darkening sky. Ella's thoughts lingered on Benjamin. His passion for history, his ability to animate the past, and the subtle warmth in his voice—all these qualities deepened the affection she felt for him.

Ella approached Benjamin as the crew took a brief respite, their equipment still poised for the night's paranormal investigation. The dying light of the day cast long shadows around Misthaven Light, adding an air of anticipation for the evening's activities.

"Benjamin," she said. "Your presentation was fantastic. You have a way of making the past come alive."

He turned toward her and blushed. "Thanks. I was nervous. I'm used to doing lectures for a bunch of stoic historians. I think these viewers are different."

His words hung in the air between them, mingling with the growing sense of mystery as the sky darkened. Around them, the crew was enjoying a well-deserved break, their laughter and chatter a contrast to the eerie quiet that surrounded the lighthouse.

"Speaking of tonight," Benjamin continued, lowering his voice to a whisper, "are you nervous? Think we'll encounter the ghosts of Misthaven Light?"

Ella cast a glance toward the lighthouse, now just a dark, brooding outline against the dimming sky. "I believe we might," she confessed, a note of uncertainty in her voice. "And I'm not sure whether that's thrilling or downright terrifying."

"I know what you mean," Benjamin responded, his hand reaching out to squeeze hers in a gesture of solidarity. He shivered, as if the cool air carried more than just the night's chill. "Whatever happens, tonight brings some kind of closure."

Hand in hand, they strolled towards the canopied area set up for the dinner break. Joining them was Ashlyn, whose quiet presence seemed to offer a comforting balance. The tingle of excitement mixed with apprehension within Ella grew stronger.

The dinner unfolded with lively chatter. Crew members exchanged theories and guesses about the potential encounters of the night. Despite the cheerful banter, an undercurrent of eager anticipation ran beneath it all. As darkness enveloped the area, the lighthouse stood silent and imposing, a guardian of history and secrets.

After the meal, as they prepared to resume the investigation, Ella noticed a distinct shift in the crew's mood. The earlier light-heartedness had now morphed into a focused determination as everyone geared up for the night's exploration. Catching her eye, Benjamin offered an encouraging nod, a silent message that they were in this together, whatever the night might reveal.

CHAPTER TEN

Memories in the Mist

Night descended upon them, shrouding the lighthouse and its surroundings in a cloak of mystery. The air was thick with anticipation, and the glow of lanterns and flashlights emanated from the lighthouse, casting long, haunting shadows across the team's path. As the equipment beeped to life and cameras started rolling, an energy wove through the group, binding them in shared purpose. They stood on the threshold of unveiling the hidden tales of Misthaven Light.

Ella leaned in, her voice a whisper. "Are you ready?"

Benjamin met her gaze. "As much as I can be." He paused, his expression softening. "How are you feeling?"

She hesitated for a beat, then confessed, "Terrified, excited, overwhelmed? Take your pick."

He chuckled. "Well, you're not alone in this. Remember that."

Just as she was about to respond, Trevor's voice cut through their conversation. "Alright, team, it's time!"

They turned, attention captured by Martin as he prepared for the opening segment. He cleared his throat, his voice resonating with a gravity that seemed to pull the night closer. "Tonight, on Ghostly Chronicles, we peer into the heart of Misthaven Light's past. This lighthouse, with its distinctive architecture, is a vessel of history and mystery alike."

With the introduction paving their way, the team ventured into the former abode of the lighthouse keepers. The moment Ella crossed the threshold, a sudden chill whispered across her skin, her body responding with an involuntary shiver.

It was Ashlyn who broke the silence. "To any spirits dwelling here, we seek your blessing to explore this place. We invite you to share your stories with us. To aid in our communication, we've arranged several tools throughout the grounds."

She gestured towards a table laden with an assortment of devices, each chosen with purpose. "This," she began, pointing to a small, box-like device, "is an EVP recorder. It can capture your voice, even if we can't hear you with our ears. Feel free to speak into it."

Next, she moved to a series of sensors spread across the room. "These are motion sensors and temperature gauges. Should you pass by them or affect the surrounding air, we'll know. It's a way for you to let us know of your presence without having to manifest."

Then Ashlyn showcased a modified radio, its static-filled airwaves slicing through the silence. "And this is a spirit box. It scans through radio frequencies rapidly, allowing you to form words or sentences. It's quite effective for real-time communication."

With the stage set, the atmosphere within the lighthouse keepers' residence thickened, charged with the energy of both the living and the ethereal. The team stood ready to bridge the gap between worlds while outside. Meanwhile, the soft murmur of the sea against the cliffs outside seemed to whisper secrets, urging them deeper into the mysteries of Misthaven Light.

The entire process turned out to be way less exciting than Ella had imagined. Once they had everything set, the night kinda just... slowed down. They ended up sitting around in a hush, the quiet that makes you aware of every little sound, like the creak of the old lighthouse floors or someone's stomach growling.

Every so often, the EMF meter would beep or flash, slicing through the boredom. Someone would toss out a comment like, "Oh, must be the wiring," or a hopeful, "Hey, maybe it's our ghostly host?" But after the first few times, even that lost its novelty.

The thrill of maybe, just maybe, catching a ghost on tape had morphed into a waiting game. A game of who could sit still the longest without checking their phone or, in Benjamin's case, becoming so quiet you'd almost forget he was there.

Ella tried to stay focused, but her mind kept drifting—until, out of nowhere, she'd get this tingle at the back of her neck. The air would feel different, cooler, maybe, or just... charged. Each time that happened, she'd snap to attention, scanning the room, half expecting to see someone standing in the corner. But then, nothing would happen, and the moment would pass, leaving her to wonder if it was all in her head.

As the night crawled on, with everyone sort of lost in their own world of boredom or quiet contemplation, Ella couldn't shake off the feeling that they weren't alone. Not in a spooky, there's-a-ghost-right-behind-you way, but more like a subtle nudge, a gentle hint that someone was just out of sight, watching.

During one of those quiet moments, Ella leaned towards Ashlyn. "I think Nathaniel is near. Like, really near." She didn't know if it was wishful thinking or something more, but now and then, she felt a presence similar to the intensity of her dreams.

Benjamin, still as a statue, gave nothing away. But Ella couldn't help but feel that, in his silence, he was sensing something too, maybe even more than the rest of them.

Ashlyn, with a look of deep focus shadowing her features, leaned in closer to the heart of their makeshift command center. Her hushed voice seemed to carry weight in the silence. "Nathaniel is here... I can feel him around us."

The team, caught in a moment of anticipation, adjusted their positions, ensuring the infrared cameras were angled to capture the unseen. Martin, with a nod, initiated the EVP (Electronic Voice Phenomenon) session with a steadiness in his voice. "Nathaniel, if you're among us, could you give us any sign of your presence?"

A moment passed, heavy with expectation, before Travis chimed in. "Nathaniel, if it's Isabella you wish to reach, do you have a message for her? Anything at all?"

The air within the room seemed to drop a few degrees, the only sounds filling the void being the mechanical hum of their equipment and the rhythmic, distant crash of waves against the cliffs. Question after question was posed, met with silence or the soft, ambiguous responses of their devices until Lydia, with a practiced motion, halted the recording to review the evidence they had collected.

Everyone leaned in, a collective breath held as the playback crackled to life, their ears tuned for the faintest hint of the otherworldly. And there it was, clear in the static after Travis's inquiry—a soft whisper that sent a shiver through the room. "Isabella."

The response was like a jolt, electrifying the stagnant air. Ella felt a chill creep down her spine as she sought Benjamin's hand for comfort. Misthaven Light, with its storied past and shadowed halls, was sharing its tale.

Throughout the night's vigil, Benjamin's presence had shifted, his usual attentiveness dimming into an uncharacteristic quietude. Ella couldn't help but notice the change. It hung between them, an invisible veil that had altered their dynamic.

As they moved from room to room, Benjamin trailed behind, his steps deliberate, almost hesitant. His gaze often drifted to distant corners, lingering on shadows that seemed no different to Ella. Yet, it was as if he saw something beyond the mundane, something that held his attention with an invisible grip.

Ella watched him, concern knitting her brow. At moments, he seemed to start at a sound only he could hear, his head tilting, as if straining to catch a noise carried on the air. His responses to her, when she reached out to him with a question or a comment, came slower, as if he were pulling his attention back from far away.

The decision to move closer to the spot where Isabella had fallen caused Ella to feel some unease. As the ghost hunting crew carried their equipment, the waning moon's light cast a haunting glow on the clifftop.

The moment Ella stepped outside, memories of Isabella's tragic fate washed over her. Her breath hitched, and a paralyzing fear gripped her. It felt as though she was being pulled towards the cliff's edge. She reached out to Benjamin again, but he had fallen behind.

Martin, sensing the intensity of the moment, took a deep breath and began addressing the camera. "Legend speaks of Isabella's tragic demise right here on this very cliff. A heartbroken soul, she plummeted to the waves below. Tonight, we hope to connect with her spirit, and perhaps bring solace to the lingering anguish that surrounds this spot."

Ashlyn closed her eyes, her fingertips touching the ground as if grounding herself. The team waited with bated breath as Martin called out, "Isabella, we come in peace, hoping to hear your story. Can you communicate with us?" When they listened back on the recorder, all they heard was silence.

Switching gears, Travis took a different approach. "Nathaniel, if you're here with us, could you give us a sign?" The reply was the same, just the gentle, melancholic touch of the breeze brushing against them.

The atmosphere felt heavier, as if the air itself was charged with a silent, watchful presence. Ashlyn broke through the growing tension, her voice brusque. "Stay sharp, everyone. There's something off here, a kind of dark presence among us."

"Maybe we should try the spirit box?" Lydia suggested, cutting through the unease with a practical solution. The idea was met with nods, and she set about preparing the device.

As the spirit box hummed to life, scanning through frequencies with a soft crackle, Travis proposed. "Let's attempt to reach out to Samuel. He was rumored to have murdered Isabella. Adding the headset might make it more direct."

All eyes shifted to Benjamin. Travis added, "Having a familial connection might just make our attempt more potent."

Benjamin hesitated before he agreed. "Okay, but if things get too intense, pull me out, promise?"

With the headphones set, Benjamin became a focal point of their circle, a bridge to the unseen, illuminated by the soft glow of the moon. Travis initiated the contact, "Samuel, if your spirit is with us, please communicate through Benjamin."

The night's stillness was punctuated by the static of the spirit box. Travis, his face illuminated by the glow of the equipment, continued his line of questioning, directing it towards Samuel. "Samuel, if you are here with us, please give us a sign. Why has this tragedy persisted over the years?"

Static buzzed with no answer.

Then Benjamin's voice, hollow yet clear, cut through, "The curse on the Blackwoods... forever." Ella felt a shift in her perception, as if reality was warping. The voices of the crew grew faint, their words echoing as though she was listening from underwater. A mysterious pull tugged at her, guiding her towards the cliff's edge. It was an involuntary lure, like a moth drawn to the flame.

Clarity flickered in and out. Benjamin's figure anchored these fleeting moments, his voice now distant and altered, laden with resentment. "Blackwood betrayed me... took everything... The curse shall never end." The others' voices turned into mere background noise, like flies buzzing, easy to ignore.

"How did Blackwood betray Samuel?..."

"It wasn't Samuel... It was Elias Thorton.."

"Those remains we found... Why didn't we connect the dots sooner?"

As the wind whipped through her hair and the salty scent of the sea intensified, Ella's awareness of her surroundings sharpened, alerting her to her position on the cliff. She noticed Benjamin's stiff posture, his gaze fixed on something distant, his voice echoing the pain and betrayal.

From afar, she heard Ashlyn's alarmed shout. Was it her name she was calling? "Ella!" It sounded urgent and worried.

But the call of the cliff was stronger, more insistent, urging her to come closer. A chill spread through her limbs, a sensation like icy fingers wrapping around her heart.

Somewhere, she registered Travis's horrified expression as he pieced together who they were communicating with. Martin was scrambling, papers rustling. But their actions were overshadowed by the compulsion, that undeniable urge leading her to the edge.

Flashes of Benjamin's face flitted through her consciousness—the same features, yet contorted.

A sudden warmth enveloped her wrist, breaking through the haze. Benjamin, or was it Elias, holding her back? Or perhaps trying to pull her further?

She tried to focus, to ground herself. But the world around her was spinning, a chaotic whirl of voices, sensations, and emotions. She was on the precipice, teetering between the past's pull and the present's desperate pleas.

She tried to summon words, but her voice wavered, caught by fear and uncertainty. "Benjamin? Is it you in there?"

His response was a murmur, words layered with bitterness. "Not entirely." His fingers clamped around her wrist, their icy touch cutting through her like a winter's chill.

Desperation surged through her. "Benjamin, fight it," she pleaded, seeking the familiar warmth in his eyes.

For a split second, agony played across his face, and in a voice quivering with effort, he uttered, "Ella... run."

Chapter Eleven

Whispers of the Future

Without thinking, she braced to run away from Benjamin, but he held tight. "She won't be leaving," came his venomous whisper, his breath now exuding a stench of rot.

Chills raced down Ella's spine. The atmosphere became suffocating, the cold pressing into her, making each breath a labor. She seized a fleeting burst of adrenaline, jerked her wrist free, and broke into a sprint, her heart pounding in tandem with her echoing footfalls. She dared not glance over her shoulder, but the prickling sensation told her he—or whatever had consumed him—would be close.

Ella's heartbeat thundered in her ears as she sped towards the cliff, the wind biting at her cheeks and tossing her hair into a chaotic dance. The silvery sheen of the moonlit path lit her way, the mischievous play of shadows threatening to trip her up at every step. Yet, she forged ahead.

The rhythmic crashing of the waves below crescendoed, calling out to her like a siren as she heard Benjamin's footsteps. They seemed distorted and out of place.

Just then, second set of steps and a voice cut through the night. It was Ashlyn, chasing them, her voice unwavering as she chanted a protection prayer. The words melded with the night, creating a shield. "By the light and the might, ward away the shadow's blight. Guard this soul, keep it whole, let the darkness take no toll."

Tears clouded Ella's vision, yet she didn't wipe them away. With each step, an inexplicable pull beckoned her closer to the cliff's edge, as if the land itself demanded her presence. She could no longer distinguish whether she was fleeing or being drawn to the precipice. Her body moved as if under the command of another. The sharp, briny scent of salt filled her nostrils, while the constant roar of the waves smashing against the cliff's base wove a haunting melody that seemed to both warm and welcome her.

But before she could reach safety, Benjamin overtook her. A chilling, iron-like grip clamped down on her shoulder. There he stood, his eyes devoid of any warmth blocking her path.

Just as despair was on the verge of engulfing Ella, a sudden comfort wrapped around her, piercing the icy dread. It was as if Nathaniel's spirit had materialized from the ether, his presence a hope in the darkness. He emerged beside her, his form coalescing from wisps of mist into a more solid figure, countering the malevolence emanating from the possessed Benjamin For a fleeting moment, time seemed to pause, the air charged with tension as the two forces—Nathaniel's spirit and the dark entity controlling Benjamin—engaged in a silent, metaphysical tug-of-war.

Benjamin's grip faltered under Nathaniel's influence, his fingers slackening as if the ghost's presence sapped the force of its power. Seizing the moment, Ella wrenched free, stumbling backwards. She drew in sharp, ragged gasps, her lungs burning for air after the terror-induced constriction.

As she regained her footing, Ella witnessed a spectacle that would forever alter her understanding of the world. Nathaniel, his visage glowing with light, stood firm against Benjamin, who appeared tormented, caught between his own consciousness and the dark will forcing its command upon him. Nathaniel's face was a mask of resolve, yet it bore a serene expression.

"Nathaniel?" Ella's voice was a whisper. The ghost turned towards her, his eyes conveying a depth of sorrow and determination. It was a look that spoke of battles fought in realms beyond her comprehension, of a love that transcended the boundaries of life and death.

"I'm here to protect you, Isabella," Nathaniel's voice resonated around her, a soothing balm. "But we must act with haste. He is not himself, and the darkness within him seeks to consume all it touches."

Ella's mind reeled at the name—Isabella. *I am not Isabella;* she thought. *Nathaniel never loved me.*

Ashlyn burst into the fray, her long coat trailing behind her like the wings of an avenging angel. "Ella!" she shouted, her voice breaking through the spectral standoff. Her outstretched hand was both an offer of safety and a desperate plea.

From the corner of her eye, Ella noticed the rest ghost hunting crew sprinting towards them, their faces full of fear and fascination. "Is this even real?" the cameraman yelled, his eyes darting between the two apparitions. "Is the camera catching this?" the other one shouted, adjusting the lens.

"Stay back!" Ella's voice cut through the air. "Stay away from him!"

Nathaniel and the spirit in Benjamin's body faced off. Their struggle was manifesting in the very fabric of the environment. The ground quivered beneath their feet, as if echoing their battle, while the sea mirrored their strife, waves crashing against the rocks below.

Ashlyn's voice rose above the chaos, clear and strong. Her hands moved, tracing symbols in the air as she began an incantation, a spell of separation.

"By the powers of the earth and sea, I command thee, release Benjamin and be free!"

Benjamin's body convulsed as if caught in a violent storm. His voice, echoing both the malice and his own terror, screamed out in agony. Ashlyn persisted, sweat beading on her forehead, her focus unwavering.

"Nathaniel, stand with us! Aid in this man's release and bring peace!"

Benjamin, with Ashlyn's guidance and the residual strength of Nathaniel's protective energy, fought against Elias. With a deafening scream, the entity was expelled from Benjamin's form, its shadowy essence clashing with Nathaniel in a blinding explosion of light. Before this, everyone had been certain the killer had been was Samuel, yet the truth unfurled most unexpectedly, revealing Elias Thornton as the true vessel for the malevolent presence.

The moment the spirit began its departure from Benjamin, the surroundings took on an eerie calm. It was as though the earth itself held its breath, anticipating the inevitable clash between Nathaniel and Elias. The sky, previously a clear canvas, morphed into a tumultuous sea of clouds. Cracks appeared, not with the sound of shattering glass but with the ominous silence of a world holding back its fury. From these fissures, a vortex of swirling energies emerged, commanding attention.

The sky above them opened, a vortex of swirling energies, with Nathaniel and Elias caught in its eye. Their bodies radiated, casting shadows that danced around them. They clashed above, ascending towards the heavens in a duel that seemed to defy the laws of nature itself.

This was no mere fight. It was a dance of destiny, a ballet of the damned. Each movement was charged, each strike a sentence in the story of their eternal struggle. Bolts of energy, raw and untamed, darted between them, illuminating the sky with their brilliance. Below, the world seemed to fade into insignificance, a mere backdrop to the cataclysm above.

When the brilliance faded, both Elias and Nathaniel were gone. The sky returned to its inky blackness, the stars twinkling as if they'd witnessed a legend unfold.

Benjamin, exhausted, collapsed to the ground, unconscious. Ashlyn, also spent from the ordeal, knelt by his side, placing her hand on his shoulder. The crew, their faces full of awe, moved closer, forgetting their equipment in the aftermath of the extraordinary events they had witnessed.

Ella felt a deep sorrow tightening around her heart, each beat sending ripples throughout her body. Nathaniel's fleeting image, now just a spectral memory in the sky, seemed to tug at her soul. Tears traced glistening paths down her cheeks. With each step she took, the sound of gravel underfoot echoed the sadness she carried.

"Is he... has Nathaniel left us?" Ella's voice trembled with emotion.

Ashlyn, drained by the night's events, looked up, following Ella's gaze toward the heavens. "In essence," she murmured, a note of sadness in her whisper. "I think what's left is an echo, a lingering vestige of his presence."

Her grief almost overwhelmed Ella, but then the sight of Benjamin, still on the ground, sparked a rush of concern within her. She hurried to his side, caressing his face in a gesture of comfort.

"Benjamin?" she whispered.

"He's going to be alright," Ashlyn said. "The ordeal of possession and its release has drained him, but he'll recover."

Ella responded with a nod, her arms encircling Benjamin.

Martin and Trevor approached, concern on their faces. It was Trevor who broke the silence. "Ash, I've been in this field for years, but I've never encountered anything this intense."

Ashlyn paused, as if absorbing the residual energy of their surroundings. "Love wields incredible power," she stated, glancing at the recovering Benjamin. "Our work here isn't finished. There are still many spirits eager to share their stories."

Martin inquired, ready to assist. "Should I gather the rest of the crew?"

Ella gave a nod of agreement, aware of their commitment to this journey. The crew had been accommodating, and it was only fair to include them. "Yes, but let's spare Benjamin the indignity of being filmed while he is passed out. He wouldn't appreciate that."

Martin chuckled in understanding and nodded in agreement.

In the shadow of the towering lighthouse, under the blanket of stars, Ashlyn gathered the group in a semi-circle on the rugged ground. The sea's roar provided a mournful soundtrack to the night's solemn proceedings. With only the moonlight, to illuminate their faces.

Ashlyn took a moment to address the circle, her voice calm and clear. "The spirits will speak through me tonight. I will not be conversing with them directly. If you have questions, or seek clarity on whom we're speaking with, you must ask. I'll be the vessel for their voices."

With the group's understanding, Ashlyn closed her eyes, her posture relaxed yet focused. A tense silence enveloped the gathering.

Soon, Ashlyn's demeanor changed, her facial expressions and posture reflecting someone else's presence. "I... I pushed her," a whisper carried by the wind filled the silence. "Isabella... it was an accident. Elias... he had taken hold of me. I would never harm her. She was like a sister to me, and her betrothed..." Ashlyn's voice trailed off, choked by unrequited love and despair. "I couldn't leave, not with this guilt."

"Who is this?" Ella asked.

Ashlyn, still under the influence of the spirit, replied, "Samuel."

The group absorbed Samuel's tragic confession, the air heavy with his centuries-old guilt.

"Can you find peace, knowing your remorse is acknowledged, and that we know you did not do it?" Benjamin ventured, his question directed at Samuel through Ashlyn.

The atmosphere shifted, a silent sign of Samuel's response, his spirit finding solace in the acknowledgment of his pain.

Ashlyn's expression changed again, softening as a fresh voice emerged. "I moved on too swiftly after Elias was lost to the sea," she expressed with a tone of sorrow and regret.

"Who are we speaking with now?" Martin asked, trying to piece together the historical puzzle.

"Clara. Marrying Blackwood was a mistake. I'm sorry, Elias," Ashlyn conveyed, the spirit of Clara seeking forgiveness through her confession.

As the evening progressed, Isabella and Nathaniel's spirits also found voice through Ashlyn, their words woven with the deep sorrow of a love and life unfulfilled. The group, now familiar with the process, asked questions, guiding the conversation to unearth the stories and sentiments of the lingering souls.

Beneath the canopy of stars, time seemed to stand still. With each spirit's confession and farewell, a sense of healing wove its way through the hearts of the living and the departed alike. The night air, once thick with untold stories and pent-up regrets, grew lighter, infused with whispers of forgiveness and the silent strength of closure.

It was as if the very essence of the lighthouse, witness to years of solitude and sorrow, now radiated a soft glow of reconciliation and peace. And then, as subtly as the night had embraced them in its shadowy fold, the first hints of dawn edged on the horizon. The transition was almost imperceptible at first, a gentle lightening of the sky that went unnoticed as the group lingered in the emotional aftermath of their spiritual journey. Yet, as the hues shifted from the deep indigo of night to the softer shades of morning, reality nudged its way back.

Around Ella, the crew moved in a daze, gathering equipment and exchanging murmured conversations. Their faces mirrored a melange of wonder, exhaustion, and profound relief.

Ashlyn, her voice hoarse from the evening's events, broke the pensive silence. "Never, in all my encounters with the supernatural, have I witnessed such an intense commingling of past and present." Her gaze rested on Ella, carrying a silent message of understanding. "The spirits tonight, Nathaniel above all, were drawn to the raw emotion tethering the past to the now."

Ella's gaze drifted towards the sea, each wave whispering ancient tales. A soft touch on her shoulder prompted her to turn. Benjamin stood there, his usual confidence dimmed by a hint of vulnerability. "I only remember bits and pieces of... you know, when I wasn't myself," he said, his voice shaking. "But the thought that I could've hurt you, even without meaning to, it's getting to me."

Ella slipped her fingers through his, offering comfort. "We were both caught up in it. I felt more like Isabella than myself, honestly." She nodded towards the lighthouse and suggested with a soft smile, "How about we grab some breakfast?"

It was then that she felt it. That all too familiar prickle at the nape of her neck. Turning, she stared at Nathaniel's waning silhouette, its translucence resembling the light of dawn. Their eyes met.

Benjamin stood next to her, squeezing her hand.

Nathaniel's voice, though faint, was unmistakable. "Isabella."

A surge of emotions threatened to break Ella. Tears blurred her vision as she reached out, hoping against hope to grasp the essence of a love lost in time. As the figure of Nathaniel dissolved, his smile left behind a silent adieu, etched forever into her soul.

They reconvened with the others beneath the breakfast canopy, where tables were laden with assorted pastries. But more crucial than the tempting array of baked goods was the coffee! Steaming pots promised to revive their spirits. This was an elixir that seemed more precious than gold in the soft light of the morning.

Ella traced the rim of her coffee mug, her mind a whirlpool of memories and emotions. Every time she closed her eyes, she saw Nathaniel, and faint whispers of 'Isabella' echoed in the wind. But the scent of warm toast and butter grounded her back to the present, to reality, to Benjamin.

Her gaze shifted to meet his. His eyes, while lit by the morning sun, bore exhaustion from the previous night. The unspoken bond, the shared experience, linked them in that moment. As the silence stretched, she ventured, "What happens now to the spirits we spoke to?"

Ashlyn answered, her voice softer than the rustle of leaves. "It's up to them. I felt both Samuel and Clara were at peace, and I believe they have moved on. As for Isabella, I still feel a whisper, same as Nathaniel. It's as if their souls still seek each other, even as echoes. They may never leave, but at least they are safe spirits."

Ella felt a pang in her heart. "Star-crossed lovers," she murmured. "Bound by fate, but forever separated."

Benjamin, sensing her melancholy, reached over, his warm hand enveloping hers. "Their tale is a good reminder," he began, "that we must seize the moments given to us and cherish those we share them with."

Ashlyn added, "Every soul has a tale, every echo a lament. They yearn to be remembered."

"Why do I feel this all so deeply?" Ella asked.

Ashlyn, looking thoughtful, replied. "Your experiences are bigger than just the echoes of trauma. Your dreams, these visions, are touched by something more. Psychic inclinations can be genetic."

Ella furrowed her brow, perplexed. "You really think Isabella is related to me?"

"Think of family lines as streams that carry echoes," Ashlyn explained. "These can be memories, emotions, or even talents. Your connection with Isabella could go much deeper than we thought. Perhaps she is an ancestor of yours. This bond, enhanced by your inherent psychic sensitivity, could be the reason your experiences seem so vivid."

Benjamin, looking bemused, chimed in, "So, what you're saying is, Ella's dreams could be ancestral memories?"

Ashlyn nodded, "Precisely, similar to your experiences with Samuel. They're reverberations from the past, touching Ella because of her psychic predisposition and potentially a familial connection."

Overwhelmed, Ella settled onto the ground. "That's a lot to process."

"It is," Ashlyn agreed, her smile warm. "But it's beautiful that you and Benjamin have found each other. You truly are kindred spirits."

Together, they sat in silent contemplation; the ocean stretching before them, its waves a gentle hymn to the continuity of life and connections beyond time.

As the midday sun cast its golden rays over the island, Ella stood on the deck of the boat, the gentle hum of the engine and the occasional cry of seabirds filling the air. The island, with its beautiful lighthouse, receded into the distance. The night before felt like a dream, its edges already blurring in her memory, yet the emotions it evoked were as vivid as ever.

Beside her, Benjamin was quiet, his gaze fixed on the shrinking silhouette of the lighthouse. The ritual had left an indelible mark on both their hearts. It was a shared experience, unique and profound, binding them in ways neither understood yet.

Ella's mind replayed the events of the previous night—the overwhelming sense of Nathaniel's love for Isabella, the sorrow of their unfulfilled lives, and the catharsis of their last goodbye. It was as if she had lived through a love story centuries old, feeling every moment of joy and heartache as her own.

The realization that she might share a bloodline with Isabella, as suggested by Ashlyn, added layers of complexity to her reflections. It wasn't just the psychic sensitivity that linked her to the past; it was the possibility of a familial connection spanning generations. This revelation made the island's history not just a curiosity but a part of her own story, a chapter of her ancestry that had been waiting to be uncovered.

Turning to Benjamin, she noticed the thoughtful expression on his face. "You're quiet," she said, breaking the silence between them.

He turned to her, a soft smile playing on his lips. "I was just thinking about Nathaniel and Isabella. About how, in the end, they found some semblance of peace. It's a powerful reminder of how love can transcend time, even in the face of tragedy."

Ella nodded, her eyes returning to the island. In her heart, she felt hope, a belief that the spirits of Nathaniel and Isabella were no longer bound by the sorrow that had tethered them to the lighthouse. Instead, she imagined them hand in hand, free to watch over the island together, their love a beacon as enduring as the lighthouse itself.

As the island faded from view, Ella felt a sense of closure, not just for the spirits, but for herself as well. The experience had changed her, deepening her understanding of her own abilities and opening her heart to the complexities of love and loss.

She turned to Benjamin, taking his hand in hers. "Let's promise to never forget this," she said, her voice steady and sure. "Let's keep the memory of Nathaniel and Isabella alive, as a reminder of what we've experienced and how it's brought us closer."

Benjamin squeezed her hand in response, his agreement silent but unequivocal. Together, they watched as the island disappeared on the horizon, a chapter closing behind them, leaving them to navigate the uncharted waters of their own future, strengthened by the past and the love that had revealed itself in the most unexpected of ways.

Ella stepped into the living room. The scent of pine and of sea salt lingered in the air and the gentle clink of her glass setting on the coffee table broke the silence. Benjamin, seated at the nearby desk, looked up from his laptop, his face breaking into a smile.

"Guess what Captain did today?" Ella began, a playful tone in her voice as she sank into the armchair.

Benjamin raised an eyebrow, closing his laptop. "What mischief has our fearless explorer gotten into now?"

"He decided that the neighbor's garden was the perfect place to bury his new toy. Mrs. Henderson was not amused." Ella chuckled, shaking her head. The Labrador in question, Captain, lay at her feet, offering a guilty but unrepentant wag of his tail.

"That dog has more adventure in him than most people," Benjamin laughed, standing up to join Ella, bending down to ruffle Captain's ears. "Speaking of adventures, today marks a year since our island journey."

Ella's eyes lit up, the memory sparking a warmth in her heart. "A year already? It feels like both a lifetime ago and just yesterday."

Benjamin nodded, his gaze softening. "It changed everything, didn't it? Speaking of changes," he shifted the topic, "the book's doing better than I could've dreamed. It's resonating with people, Ella. Our story, the history of the island, Nathaniel and Isabella's love... it's touching hearts."

Ella's smile widened. "I'm so proud of you, Ben. And... I have some news too. The gallery's ribbon-cutting is scheduled for next month. The invites went out today."

"Your own gallery," Benjamin mused, his voice filled with admiration. "Your art deserves this spotlight, Ella. Those beautiful scenes... they're a window to your soul."

Their eyes met, an acknowledgment of the journey they had shared, the love that had grown, and the future they were building together.

"You know," Benjamin began, a slight nervousness creeping into his voice, "I've been thinking a lot about our future, about us. And I can't imagine a day without you."

Ella's heart skipped a beat. Captain, perhaps sensing it too, lifted his head, his eyes darting between them.

Benjamin knelt down, not just to be closer to Captain, but to bridge the small space between him and Ella. From his pocket, he pulled out a small velvet box.

"Ella, will you marry me?"

Tears of joy welled in Ella's eyes, mirroring the sparkling diamond that lay nestled in the box. "Yes, Benjamin," she whispered, her voice steady despite the whirlwind of emotions. "Yes, I will."

As they embraced, Captain's joyful bark filled the room, a seal of approval from their furry family member. Outside, the setting sun cast a golden glow, a perfect backdrop to a new chapter in their story.

Their journey had begun with a dream, a vision that pulled Ella from the other side of the country to a destiny she could have never imagined. It was a call intertwined with spirits and past love, and to Benjamin. Now, as they looked toward the future, their path was lit not only by the experiences they shared but also by the spirits that first brought them together. The warmth of their home, the adventures that lay ahead, and the unbreakable bond of their love were all beacons of light shining on the journey that lay before them.

Afterword

Growing up, my dad was this amazing mix of historian and teacher, while my mom was all about cheering on my every wild idea. Childhood was this cool mash-up of creativity and diving deep into history. It wasn't the big, headline-grabbing events that grabbed me. The personal stories were the ones that caught my interest.

My family's open-mindedness lent itself to a curiosity about lesser-known lore. I couldn't get enough of the stories that simmered in the background, whispered rather than proclaimed.

That curiosity? It just grew with me. I found out that ghost tours are like this secret doorway into the parts of history that are a bit more... shadowy. They're this perfect mix of real historical facts and the supernatural stories that give you goosebumps. The best tour guides? They know exactly how to walk that fine line between what's real and what's just a great story.

So, the whole Kindred Spirits Mystery series idea? It hit me during one of those tours. Each book is going to pull from a ghost story. The way each story connects might change, but they all dive into these cool historical mysteries and the spirits that might still hang around.

I grew up in New England, which is a treasure trove of stories. Trying to pick just one is impossible. So, I dreamed up Misthaven Island. It's a bit like Egg Rock Island in Maine, and a bunch of other light house islands, all rolled into one. It's our fictional spot to explore bits and pieces from some of Maine's most haunted lighthouses.

I'm hoping that as you dive into the Kindred Spirits Mysteries, you'll get as excited as I am about exploring where history and the supernatural meet. These stories are your invitation to get curious, to explore, and maybe open your mind a bit to what might be out there. Thanks for coming along on this adventure with me.

Bridging the Heart

KINDRED SPIRITS MYSTERIES

BETH CONNOR

WOLF GROVE MEDIA, LLC

Contents

Whispers from the Past

Clara froze, the sound of laughter and whispers slicing the silence. There, Ethan was entwined with another woman, her face now burned into Clara's memory, shattering all trust.

Without a word, she turned, fleeing into the rain-drenched streets of Boston. Her heart pounded a frantic rhythm that matched her steps. She found herself poised at the threshold of a decision. Before her loomed a neon-lit entrance of a bar, its raucous laughter and the clink of glasses tempting her into oblivion. Yet something within her recoiled. She felt a silent plea for solitude over the solace found in the bottom of a glass. With a breath, she turned her back on the bar and made her way to the sanctuary that promised a different refuge—the Boston Public Library.

As she approached, its grandeur stood stark against the darkening sky. It was a beacon for lost souls seeking respite. Clara stepped into the embrace of the library, leaving behind the chaos that had torn through her existence only hours before. The image was a vision that scorched her insides, amplified because the apartment was *hers*—every bill had her name on it.

Inside the library, Clara wandered the endless shelves, but it was in the periodicals section she found her true escape. A magazine on New England Hauntings caught her eye, its pages whispering of mysteries and echoes from the past. In particular, the story of Anne of the Willows captivated her. It was as if Anne's tale mirrored her own—a story of love lost and betrayal that resonated with her soul.

She looked around to ensure she was alone, then did something she had never considered before. With a mix of desperation and defiance, she tore the page from the magazine. This act of rebellion was unlike Clara, yet the story of Anne of the Willows was a light in her storm, a connection she did not want to leave behind.

When she exited the library, the city of Boston lay transformed by the rain into a reflective maze. Back home, the apartment was silent. The woman and Ethan had gone, leaving behind only the faint trace of unfamiliar perfume and a careless note. Clara, with the torn page from the magazine clutched in her hand, stood amidst the remnants of her previous life and picked up the note.

The rain tapped on the window, each droplet a punctuation of the words that Clara couldn't seem to tear her gaze from. As the dim lighting of her apartment cast long shadows, emphasizing her solitude, Clara found herself surrounded by mementos of happier times — the ashtray she stole during their first vacation together, now holding the dying remnants of a burnt-out candle, and photos of shared laughs, kisses, and moments strewn across the coffee table.

The worn, blue rug beneath her feet, where they'd collapsed in giggles one evening, now felt cold and detached, much like the words from his letter and the echoing silence of the apartment. With each paragraph read and reread, the sorrow of her own story mingled with the intrigue of another's—Anne of the Willows. This would be her next novel, and with it she would rise like a phoenix.

Clara's heart ached for Anne. The tale of a woman waiting by the willow-lined bank for a lover who never came sparked a flame within Clara. It was a mystery wrapped in the soft veil of the past, yet it felt as urgent.

Drawing a deep breath, she set the letter aside, letting the pain it brought recede into the shadows. Her focus shifted, eyes landing her laptop. Clara felt a stir of excitement, a pull towards something beyond the confines of her sorrow. Here was a story that needed telling, a mystery that called to her with its silent whispers and unanswered questions.

Determined, Clara powered on the computer, the soft hum cutting through the rain's incessant patter. As Clara tapped the keys, she outlined Anne's story with her own, drawing closer to the mysteries shrouded around Willows Bridge. Yet, even as she delved into the realm of intrigue, her focus was hijacked by the biting contents of the letter lying beside her.

Taking a deep breath, she paused and gripped at the single sheet of paper. An affair laid bare. A conclusion without closure. Hollow apologies that resonated with the emptiness within her. The sharp sting of betrayal blurred her surroundings, pooling tears in her eyes. She pondered on the ruin that love had become.

They had charged the atmosphere in the room with electricity just weeks prior. The air had been thick with vanilla from the candles, the warm aroma intertwined with their breaths, creating a heady mix of sensation and emotion. As a sultry song played in the background, her fingers had grazed his cheek, pulling him close. They had been lost in heartbeats and rustling fabric, synchronized. Everything had felt so right, so perfect. Now, as Clara's gaze refocused on the present, the cruel irony was not lost on her. That deep connection, that undeniable passion, was gone.

The air in the room pressed down, making each breath a struggle. Clara's fingertips tightened around the edges of the paper, crumpling it. Her eyes darted over the words once more, each sentence, each confession, plunging her deeper into a whirlpool of emotions. A bitter taste formed in the back of her throat. Every "I love you," every stolen kiss, every promise—it all felt like a cruel mockery now.

She felt her heartbeat racing and a surge of anger boiling up inside. "How could he do this? Throw everything away?" she thought, glaring at the letter in her hand. It seemed to her that he was using those inked words as a shield, dodging the confrontation. She stood, the need to escape the moment pressing upon her. The letter slipped from her grasp, fluttering to the floor like a wounded bird.

"It's not you, it's me," she said, mimicking his words. The phrase seemed so trite, so insincere. A clichéd excuse for a clichéd betrayal.

She paused at the window, staring out at the city lights. The energy of the city, so full of promise and adventure, now felt alien. The shadows of the night echoed her own darkness, and the city's heartbeat felt out of sync.

As the reality of the situation sank in, her anger waned, giving way to an overwhelming sadness.

"Why?" The question, raw and heavy, hung in the air, unanswered.

Without thinking, she found herself in the kitchen, glass in hand. Pouring herself a drink. The old Clara would've let herself be consumed by the comfort the drink promised, especially when thinking of those nights with Ethan and their hot and cold relationship, the highs of love and music, the lows of fights and substances. But as she raised the glass to her lips, she felt the weight of the coin she carried in her pocket.

She remembered her journey to sobriety, her battles, her determination, and the promises she had made to herself. She thought of the times she had resisted, of the support she had gained, of the hope she held onto.

With an exhale, she moved to the window, looking out at the streets of Boston. She tilted the glass, letting the wine spill out, each drop symbolizing the choices she had made and the ones she was yet to make. As the wine pooled on the windowsill, the familiar sound of a key jingling sounded at the door.

Before she could process, the door creaked, revealing Ethan in all his glory. He pushed it open, looking as though he'd walked through a storm, perhaps expecting a tempest within as well. And he wasn't wrong. Without hesitation, she threw the letter at him, her voice raised in a torrent of emotion. "You couldn't even face me? A damn letter, really?!"

He winced, surprised by the storm in Clara's eyes. "Clara, I... I'm sorry."

"Sorry?" Her voice crackled with scorn, inches from his face. "You think a letter makes this easier?"

"I didn't know how else to say it," he confessed.

"So, you drop this bombshell in a letter? Coward," she spat, the letter crinkling in her clenched fist.

The air between them was electric, charged with a history too deep to sever. He reached out, a reflex from a time now past, but she stood her ground, her resolve a barrier between them.

"It was a mistake. Please, can we just forget about the letter, and..." Ethan's voice trailed off, the name of the other woman lingering unspoken between them.

"Forget?" Clara's voice was icy. "How can I forget?"

He looked at her, desperation etched across his face. "Wasn't it real? Everything we had?"

"It was real, too real. But it's over," she replied.

"So, that's it? You're just giving up on us?" Ethan narrowed his eyes.

"It's not giving up. It's moving forward. This," she waved the letter, "is about you figuring out who you are without me."

Ethan's stance stiffened, defiance flickering in his eyes. "I can't just walk away. We can't throw everything we had over a mistake. I know I can make things right."

Clara's gaze was unwavering. He wasn't lost without her, he was lost without her money. "A mistake? Ethan, your 'mistake' broke us. You decided it was over the moment you wrote this letter." She paused, the anger simmering in her veins. "And now you want to pretend it never happened?"

He took a step closer, desperation edging his voice. "Isn't what we had worth fighting for? I'm not giving up that easily."

"Fighting for? You chose this." Clara's hand dove into her purse, pulling out a handful of cash. With a swift movement, she flung it at him. "Here, for a hotel tonight. I'll be gone in the morning. And Ethan," her voice was cold, "you have one month to get your things out, then I'm changing the locks."

The money hit him with a soft thud, falling to the ground. Ethan's face was a mask of conflict.

"Clara, please—" he started, but the finality in her stance told him there was no room for negotiation.

"Goodbye, Ethan."

Ethan picked up the scattered bills. She watched him, the emptiness already settling in. He walked to the door, pausing, before stepping out into the night, leaving her alone in the aftermath.

These feelings weren't new to Clara. They were all too familiar.

She sat in the ruins of another failed relationship. Memories of her parents surged to the forefront. She remembered the whispered arguments late at night, the slammed doors, the icy silences that could stretch for days. Her mother's eyes, often red-rimmed and distant, her father's stoic face as he tried to pretend everything was alright.

The pain her mother felt, the cycle of hope and heartbreak, seemed to have imprinted on Clara. She'd promised herself she wouldn't end up like her mother, entrapped in a cycle of loving, trusting, and then getting hurt. And yet, here she was, feeling like history was playing a cruel joke, repeating itself with her at the center.

Clara hugged her knees, trying to find solace in her own embrace. She'd broken her own vow, become another casualty in the cyclical pattern of heartbreak that seemed to be her family's legacy.

After clearing the coffee table, she moved her laptop with a purpose in mind: to find a retreat. The story of Anne of the Willows was set in Stowe, Vermont—a location not even a half-day's drive away. Determined, she planned to get a place for the month, a sanctuary away from her heartache, where she could focus on her novel.

The allure of the little town, with its majestic mountains, rolling landscapes, and serene forests, captivated her. Anne's tale, mirroring Clara's own turbulent emotions, felt fitting. She saw Stowe's beauty as the perfect muse for her writing.

Without delay, Clara browsed for accommodations. She stumbled upon a listing for a cabin tucked away in the woods less then a half mile away from the bridge. The images revealed a warm, inviting interior with a stone fireplace, enveloped by towering trees. It seemed destined. With a few decisive clicks, she booked the place from May 14th to June 14th, hopeful that the coming month would offer the peace and clarity she sought.

The journey to Stowe was as much a voyage through Clara's inner self as it was through the hills and valleys of Vermont. As the car's tires hummed on the asphalt, Clara's mind played a slideshow of recent events, interspersed with fragments of memories both cherished and painful.

With every mile she covered, the city's cacophony grew fainter, replaced by the symphony of nature. Mountains stood tall, their peaks caressed by the early morning mist, while dense forests flanked the road, their canopies creating a serene green tunnel. The mirror-like lakes reflected the azure sky, offering her moments of tranquility and reflection.

As Clara's car meandered through the quaint towns and picturesque landscapes, she'd occasionally tune into local radio stations to break the solitude. Amid the casual chatter and local news, a segment on Vermont legends piqued her interest. The voice of the radio host introduced a series of local myths, but one stood out, echoing with resonance in her own life.

"... and of course, who can forget the haunting tale of Anne of the Willows? Legend has it that a young woman named Anne, heartbroken and betrayed by her lover, took her own life on that very bridge," the radio host began. The story was told in a somber tone, painting a vivid picture of a love that promised forever, only to shatter in the cruel hands of fate.

It was clear this story was following her. As Clara listened, every word seemed to strike a chord deep within. She could feel Anne's pain, her despair, the crushing weight of betrayal. The familiarity of it all was unsettling, yet comforting. It was as if the spirit spoke to anyone who's known heartbreak.

Clara was enthralled by the complex emotions and the dance between history and today, affection and sorrow. This concept blossomed into more than mere preoccupation—it was becoming a means for Clara to navigate and comprehend her experiences. She realized Anne's tale embodied the essence of love's resilience and its fragilities. Visiting the actual location propelled her to enrich the story further. There was an inexplicable pull, a magnetism that was hard to ignore.

The cabin Clara had rented was everything she had envisioned—a peaceful retreat, miles away from the chaotic remnants of her life. The sun hung low in the sky, casting its light over the landscape, painting the lush Vermont scenery with a touch of amber brilliance.

And then there was Willows Bridge.

Clara found herself drawn to it right away. The blend of heartache and mystery intertwined with her own emotions, compelling her to seek its roots firsthand. This wasn't just research—it was a personal quest, inviting her to step into the heart of the tale.

As she approached, the bridge seemed to materialize out of the fading daylight. The ancient wood, darkened by age and weather, created a backdrop against the evening sky. It was a structure frozen in time, its legacy written in every grain and groove. The setting sun made the shadows dance upon its wooden panels, making it appear the bridge breathed with memories of the past.

After parking her car at a distance, Clara walked the remaining stretch. With every step she took, a distinct chill crept over her. It was almost summer, and the evening was warm, but the cold she felt was deep, almost bone-chilling. The bridge seemed to exude an energy of its own.

The soft gurgle of the water beneath was like a muted lullaby, a counterpoint to the eerie ambiance. But as she ventured further onto the bridge, another sound emerged. The creaking of wood was expected, but the faint whispers that danced around her were not. These weren't the murmurs of visitors or the rustling of trees; they were something else, distant yet present. It was as if the very air around her was charged with the lingering echoes of Anne's lament.

She hugged her arms around herself, goosebumps prickling her skin. Clara tried to shake off the growing sense of unease. And just when she thought she might've imagined it all, out of the corner of her eye, she saw her.

A fleeting vision of a young woman, pale and ethereal, her silhouette undis-cernible in the dimming light. Her dress, though spectral, bore the marks of another era, and her face seemed etched with sorrow. But as quickly as the apparition appeared, it vanished, leaving Clara to question if it had been real.

She tried to make sense of the scene before her. The tales that had been distant, mere stories she had read or heard on the radio that she had forced into her own narrative. Yet, standing on the bridge now, they took on an undeniable reality.

With a shaky breath, Clara decided it was enough for one evening. The bridge, with its stories and spirits, would be there tomorrow. For now, she needed the solace of her cozy cabin, a warm cup of tea, and perhaps the comforting pages of her journal to make sense of the overwhelming emotions of the day.

The next morning, the sun filtered through the windows of Maple's Brew, a small cafe that seemed to be a hub for the locals in Stowe. The aroma of fresh pastries and roasted coffee lured Clara in from her morning walk. She chose a table by the window, hoping to find inspiration in the peaceful morning scenes of the town.

As she waited for her order, muted conversations filled the cafe, creating a comfortable background hum. As she was lost in her thoughts, a voice broke through.

"You're not from around here, are you?" a voice, seasoned with age, broke her reverie. She looked up to see an elderly man, with snowy hair and a face mapped with wrinkles.

"Just arrived yesterday. It's quite beautiful," Clara responded.

"Ah, drawn by the tales, then?" He nodded towards her journal on the table, while cradling Clara's last novel in his other hand, her portrait on the back cover smiling back at them.

Clara paused, her hand suspended in the air, clutching her coffee. "Yes, actually," she said, breaking into a smile and gesturing for him to join her.

The old man took the seat across from her and leaned in, a move Clara matched, captivated by his energy.

He began, "There's a legend, dear, woven into the fabric of this town. The tale of Anne of the Willows." His voice dipped, a solemn prelude. Clara chuckled. "I've heard bits and pieces," she confessed, eager not to overshadow his version of the story. Her mind wandered back to the encounter from the night before. The elderly man nodded, his voice taking on a reverent tone. "It's a sad story. A young woman, full of life and love, betrayed by the one she trusted most. Left waiting on that bridge for a lover who never came. And when her heart couldn't bear that pain, she took her own life, hanging from the very rafters of the bridge she'd hoped would be the start of her new life."

The cafe seemed to grow quieter, other conversations dimming as if out of respect for the tragic tale. Anne's pain and anguish echoed her own heartbreak, the sting of betrayal still raw.

He continued, "It's said her spirit still lingers, trapped between worlds. Many have seen her, especially on those misty evenings. She waits, hoping that maybe, just maybe, her lover will return." The tale continued. Anne's story, a poignant echo of Clara's recent wounds, left her with a lump in her throat.

"Thank you," Clara said.

The man nodded and held out the novel, her novel, Clara's face gazing up from the back cover. "Would you?" he asked, sliding the book towards her with a hopeful expectancy.

From one storyteller to another, Clara inscribed, her hand steady but her heart tumultuous.

With a sense of purpose, Clara thanked the man, leaving the cafe with more than just the taste of coffee on her lips. It was still strange when people recognized her. Success had come hard and fast. But now, the tragedy of Anne, and her own heartbreak was waiting to be penned.

That evening, Clara returned to the bridge, her heart aflutter with unease. Its wooden frame a portal to the past, stood bathed in the glow of twilight. Shadows nestled in its crevices, the structure arching over the murmuring river below. The lantern in her hand cast a light that battled the encroaching darkness, its light reflecting off the varnished wood and creating an eerie atmosphere. The silence was punctuated only by the distant call of an owl and the gentle whisper of the river.

Settling near the center, Clara placed her notebook on her lap, the light next to her provided just enough illumination to jot down her thoughts.

She wrote of love's ghosts, the echoes of those lost, their presence felt but unseen. "Love, when lost, leaves behind ghosts that never fade," she penned. A chilling gust swept across the bridge. Startled, Clara gripped her notebook, but the wind whipped the loose pages free, sending them dancing into the darkness. She watched, helpless, as her words vanished.

The bridge seemed to sigh, the air thick with tales of love and betrayal. Then, she saw her—a figure at the bridge's end, a wisp of history and heartache, her presence a fleeting glimpse into a bygone era.

Heart pounding, Clara was transfixed. The ghostly figure and she shared a moment of silent communion, an exchange of understanding.

A soft whisper floated through the air, so faint that Clara strained to catch it. Words of love, promises made, and dreams shattered echoed around her, tales of timeless betrayal that tugged at her very soul. "Wait for me," the voice pleaded, carrying with it centuries of hope and anguish.

The vision faded, but the presence lingered. Clara took a shaky breath, collecting her scattered thoughts and pages. What she'd witnessed was both haunting and heart-wrenching. Anne's spirit, still tethered to this world by the chains of her tragic past, sought solace, understanding, and perhaps, a voice. Still shaking, Clara wondered if it would be better to visit the bridge tommorow, in the daylight.

Nestled in the cabin, Clara leaned against the headboard, her legs cocooned in a quilt, with her notebook balanced on her legs. The faint chorus of crickets from outside softened the profound stillness that enveloped the room.

She wrote, letting the ink flow, guided by the raw emotions from the day's experiences. "Loneliness," she began, "isn't just the absence. It's the void left by their memories, the silent spaces that once echoed with laughter and whispered secrets." She felt those words, the pain of abandonment, the sting of betrayal—emotions she now shared with Anne.

Her hand faltered as memories rushed back. She could almost feel Ethan's warm hands and the shared moments of quiet affection. But interwoven with these recollections were the seeds of doubt, the overlooked signs, and the ultimate revelation of betrayal that had shattered everything. The line between joy and sorrow had become indistinct, each memory tainted by the knowledge of what was to come.

Drained from the rush of emotions, Clara set aside her notebook and lay down, pulling the quilt over her. The distant howl of the wind ushered her into a restless sleep.

In her dream, Clara was transported back to her old apartment, nestled in Ethan's embrace. As the comfort of their shared moments enveloped her, the scene shifted—the softness beneath her transformed into the unyielding expanse of Willows Bridge. In the distance, Anne's figure emerged.

As the dream unfolded, Anne's presence grew more menacing. With a sudden surge of anger, the ghostly apparition lunged towards Ethan, jolting Clara awake.

Clara, drenched in sweat and with her heart racing, grappled with the imagery of her nightmare. Anne's transformation from a passive figure to a wrathful ghost in her dream mirrored the unresolved anger and hurt that lingered within, painting a haunting picture.

CHAPTER TWO

The Engineer and the Novelist

A symphony of bird calls serenaded Clara on her morning walk toward Willows Bridge. The trail wound itself through the woods, and she breathed in the earthy perfume of pine and spruce. Dapples of sunlight played across the path, casting a magic that lifted her imagination into flight. She half-expected to glimpse a fairy, perhaps perched on a fern or on a rabbit's back. This place was full of magical tales with each tree and shadow a piece of the enchantment.

About a half mile into her walk, the dense curtain of foliage parted to unveil her destination. Yet, as she approached, it wasn't the bridge that captured her attention, but a figure. The man was engrossed in his task. Every gesture he made was a intriguing. Clara couldn't help but wonder if there was more to him than met the eye—perhaps a touch of the fey, a guardian of secrets old as the bridge itself.

Curiosity piqued, Clara took a few steps closer. The gentle crunch of gravel beneath her shoes marked her approach. She angled herself, attempting to get a glimpse over his shoulder. Her eyes traced the sweeping lines of his sketches and the meticulous notes he'd penned down. The drawings showcased the bridge's architecture, but there was an artistic flair to them, showing a deep appreciation of its beauty.

The light filtering through the trees illuminated his features. There he stood, a vision of confidence with a sprinkle of vulnerability that Clara found irresistible. She couldn't help but laugh at herself. Here she was again, painting strangers with the colors of her imagination, much like she had once colored Ethan in hues of unwarranted virtues. That ordeal had taught her a lesson—or so she thought. Ethan had been anything but the romantic hero she'd imagined him to be.

Determined not to repeat history, Clara had vowed to see the world as it was. But oh, how the sight of this man, engrossed in the bridge's aura, whisked her into a whimsy! She envisioned him as a seasoned traveler, a sage adorned with tales of love and loss, his wisdom woven into the very fabric of his being. And for a brief, indulgent moment, Clara allowed herself to be swept up in a fantasy where he was the protagonist.

In her daydream, they escaped to her hidden cabin, shrouded by the forest's embrace, a stone's throw from the bridge. Inside, the flicker of candlelight danced on the walls. They swayed in each other's arms, lost in a rhythm meant only for them, on the brink of a kiss that promised more. But reality, with its impeccable timing, had Clara tripping over her own feet, straight into the arms of the very man in her daydreams.

Their eyes locked, his lit with a spark of amusement, while Clara's cheeks blazed with mortification. Her heart pounded—not from the stumble, but from the revelation that her daydreams had crashed into reality. How utterly awkward. The man stepped back, radiating a rugged allure and tender fortitude.

Standing a little over six feet, his deep-set hazel eyes seemed to hold tales she couldn't quite read, but wanted to. The playful tousle in his chestnut hair and sun-kissed complexion spoke of outdoor hours, while the light stubble added a touch of masculinity. She drifted into another daydream where those very hands traced stories on her skin. Clara snapped herself back to the present. *Focus,* she thought with a smirk. Everything was looking like a romance novel.

"I'm so sorry," Clara mumbled, feeling her cheeks heat under his observant look. His laughter, deep and warm, eased the tension, sending an unexpected thrill through her.

"No harm done," he answered. "Seems we were both lost in thought. I'm Jack Thompson."

She grasped his hand, finding reassurance in its firmness. "Clara Mitchell. It's a pleasure."

Their handshake lingered for a moment longer than necessary before she let go. Then, trying to steer the conversation into less flustered waters, she ventured, "Do you come here often?."

Jack answered. "Actually, yes. Its history and architecture have always fascinated me."

That sparked Clara's enthusiasm, her earlier research bubbling to the surface. "You're interested in the legends, too? I'm working on a book and thought the tale of this bridge would be a perfect addition."

His eyebrows raised. "'This bridge' has a name, you know. But let me guess, you're thinking of including Willows Bridge?"

Clara was surprised. "Isn't that its name?"

He shook his head. "It's actually called the Gold Brook Bridge, built back in 1844. But I agree, 'Willows Bridge' has a pleasant sound to it."

She smiled. "It seems the local legends have more charm than the real name."

He laughed, nodding. "That's often the case. Sometimes the stories can be more compelling than the facts."

"That's what they pay me for," Clara grinned.

The conversation flowed from there, the initial awkwardness melting away as they found common ground in their shared interest. They talked about the history of the bridge, its architectural significance, and the tragic love story that gave it its infamous name. The more they chatted, the clearer it became that there was an undeniable chemistry between them. The universe, it seemed, had thrown them together at this moment, and neither was in a hurry to pull away.

As they stood side by side, overlooking the expanse, Jack described its architectural intricacies with genuine passion. "The way these beams intersect and hold the weight, it's a marvel. It's sturdy, designed to last decades, but even a minor flaw can lead to a collapse."

Clara's eyes lit up. "It sounds like relationships. Built to endure, but they can be so fragile, can't they?"

Jack looked at her with surprise. "That's an interesting analogy. You have a way with words. What sort of book are you working on? I would almost peg you as a poet."

She chuckled, her blue eyes dancing with mischief. "Close, but not quite. I'm a novelist. Mostly mysteries and paranormal stuff. And you? With your knowledge of bridges, I'd guess... an architect?"

Jack laughed, "Not quite, but you're in the ballpark. I'm a structural engineer. I work with structures, designs, the nitty-gritty details."

The revelation seemed to draw them even closer. Two individuals from opposite worlds, yet finding a connection.

"I bet this bridge has seen countless stories," Clara mused, leaning over the railing, her eyes dreamy. "Lovers meeting in secret, teary goodbyes, and ghosts..."

Jack raised an eyebrow, amused. "Ghosts? You're referring to Anne of the Willows, aren't you?"

"Absolutely!" Clara leaned forward. "A tragic love story ending in heartbreak on this very bridge. They say her spirit still lingers. You come here a lot. Have you ever seen it?"

"The spirit?" Jack shook his head, smiling. "I've been here many times, even late at night, and never once felt any presence. The tales are entertaining, but I'm a man of science. Ghosts are a bit out of my realm."

She tilted her head with a teasing smile. "You don't have even the slightest belief in the supernatural? The unexplained mysteries of the world?" Her eyes sparkled as she added, "It gives life a certain... mystique, don't you think?"

He chuckled, brushing a hand through his hair. "Mystique or not, I've always been the kind to trust facts over fantasies."

Clara leaned in, the playful glint still clear. "Well, while you were up late in college, lost in your equations and drafts, I wandered the world through my stories. Ever been to Morocco?"

Jack shook his head. "Never, but I bet you're going to tell me a story from there."

With a nod, she spun a tale of bustling markets and moonlit desert nights. He responded with an amusing recount of an engineering mishap during a project.

The sun had passed its zenith, marking the passage of time they seemed oblivious to.

Jack mused, "You know, a story set right here *would* be fascinating."

Clara chuckled. "I might just feature a skeptic engineer who ends up falling hopelessly in love with a ghost."

"That would be quite the story," Jack said with a wide grin. "Just make sure he's as charming as he is skeptical."

"Absolutely," Clara replied with a wink. "Imagine the tales this bridge could inspire on a day like this."

Jack's lowered as he touched Clara's shoulder, "With the way you tell stories, you'd have anyone believing in ghosts and hidden treasures by dinner."

Their laughter faded as they shared a moment. A spark kindled between them. Clara, caught up in the excitement, paused when she noticed a faint line on Jack's hand—a ring that had once been there.

The atmosphere shifted as reality seeped in. Clara's heart sank. "Are you married?"

Jack met her gaze, the lightness in his eyes giving way to a somber reflection. "Was. It's over now, though," he said. A slight edge hinted at a deeper story.

An awkward silence filled with a flurry of unasked questions and emotions—surprise, curiosity, and disappointment. Clara wondered about the significance of the ring mark. Did it represent a lingering attachment, or perhaps a difficulty in moving on?

Jack seemed to catch her look. He touched the spot where the ring had been, a thoughtful expression on his face. "It's been tough," he admitted. "But I'm being honest with you."

He changed the subject. "Ever looked into the history of this bridge? Or the town itself?"

Clara welcomed the shift in conversation. "Not really. I've been so wrapped up in the legends that I've missed the actual history."

His mood brightened as he launched into an explanation. "This bridge, this town, they're full of history. Way before any legend, this bridge was a marvel of its time. Stowe started in lumber and agriculture, but it was actually one of the first places to have alpine skiing!."

As Jack shared tales from the town's past, the sun shone brightly overhead, yet something unusual happened. A thick fog rose from the water, enveloping them in a cool mist that seemed out of place in the afternoon warmth.

Clara, caught between listening to Jack and observing the changing environment, couldn't ignore the bridge's transformation. "Is it strange," she asked, "for fog to roll in like this on such a clear day?"

Jack paused, glancing around at the creeping mist. "It adds mystery, doesn't it?" he remarked as the temperature dropped.

Visibility dwindled as the fog thickened. Jack's stories of the founding families and their enduring spirits seemed to breathe life into the mist. Clara's gaze was drawn to the bridge's edge, where she glimpsed what looked like a woman's silhouette within the fog.

"Did you see that?" Clara interrupted. "There, at the edge—it looked like someone was standing there."

Jack looked in the direction she pointed, squinting through the fog. "Maybe we're not the only ones interested in these stories."

Clara was sure she saw the same faint silhouette of a woman the day before. It wasn't solid, more like a wisp of smoke, yet human. Her heart raced, recalling the sensation she had felt. "Whatever or whoever it was... They're gone."

Jack offered a comforting smile. "This fog plays tricks on the eyes. And after the stories you've heard about Anne, it's only natural to think you're seeing things."

But Clara wasn't convinced. "It felt so real. Like she was right there, just out of reach."

Jack hesitated for a moment. "Let's head back," he suggested. "It's getting late, and this fog isn't helping."

Clara could still feel the coolness left behind by the bridge's chill, even as they moved away from it. The atmosphere felt charged, and there was an unspoken acknowledgment between them about the strangeness of the afternoon.

"Is your car parked nearby?" Jack asked, breaking the silence that had settled between them.

She shook her head, her eyes still taking him in. "I walked. I'm staying in a cabin not too far from here."

Something flickered in Jack's eyes. "Same here. Well, the walking part. Which way are you headed?"

She pointed down a path, her gaze drifting towards the bridge they'd just left. "That way."

Jack paused, his guarded for a split second, making her wonder what he hid more beneath the surface. "I'm headed the opposite way, but I've lived in Stowe all my life. Mind if I walk you home?"

She found comfort in his protective offer. "I'd like that. Thank you."

Best to shift the conversation away from the bridge and the unexpected pull she felt towards him. "Tell me more about your work."

Jack's face lit up, his guard dropping. "By day, I'm an engineer, but bridges, especially these historical ones, are my passion. Every bridge in New England tells a story, both of its construction and of the souls that have crossed them."

He handed her a sketchbook filled with detailed depictions of bridges. Clara was impressed. "These are incredible," she said.

Their fingers met as they turned the pages together, the connection between them undeniable. Lost in shared appreciation, the world around them faded away.

As the two journeyed deeper into the woods, an understanding seemed to form. Yet, with every step, Jack's walls seemed to grow taller, and Clara found herself more intrigued by the man beside her.

When they reached Clara's cabin, she posed a question to break the growing silence. "What do people around here do for fun?"

With a chuckle, Jack responded, "This is primarily a ski town. But there's a local bar nearby with live music on weekends. You might enjoy it."

The pause that followed was loaded, their respective pasts clear. Jack hesitated, then handed her a scribbled note. "In case you ever want to talk... about bridges or otherwise."

She hesitated and shook her head. "Jack...," she began, but the words seemed to elude her.

He nodded in understanding. "Just in case."

The sadness in his eyes spoke volumes, but he tried to lighten the mood. "Good luck, Clara Mitchell. I truly hope our paths cross again."

She offered a small, rueful smile. "Thank you, Jack."

Inside her cabin, Clara made her way to an armchair, letting the cushioned comfort envelop her. As she settled, the day replayed in her mind. Jack's confident stride, his uninhibited laughter, the way his eyes seemed to pierce right through her defenses. She couldn't deny the chemistry they shared. It had been intoxicating. In another life, she mused, she might've thrown caution to the wind and let the night take its course with him.

A soft sigh escaped her lips. She wanted an escape that might let her forget, even just the emotional baggage she carried. It would've been easy to let him in, to lose herself in a brief whirlwind of connection.

Yet, as inviting as the idea was, the reality lurked nearby. Jack's marriage, recent and raw, was a clear red flag. She herself was no stranger to heartbreak. Tenderness and scars mingled in her past, reminding her to tread carefully. And beyond all that personal history, Boston awaited her return, with its busy streets and bustling life.

She leaned back, squeezing her eyes shut. Hell, she hadn't been looking for some deep, soul-stirring connection. The intensity she felt with Jack was almost too much. She didn't need another romantic saga ending in tragedy. But of course, life didn't always play by the rules.

Ethan, with his erratic behaviors and moods, had brought both excitement and chaos into her life. That unpredictability, once exhilarating, had also been the root of their downfall. But Jack? His entire demeanor was different–grounded, mature, stable. It was as if he bore his experiences, but wore them like armor. That adult vibe about him, the composed facade with storms beneath. It hinted at depths and passions Clara wanted to explore. It made her wonder about the man behind those thoughtful eyes. What experiences had shaped him? How had they made him into who he was today? And, even if she wouldn't admit it aloud, it made her wonder what kind of lover he might be. Would he carry that same intensity, the same purpose and presence into more intimate situations?

After spending the afternoon engrossed in her work, Clara felt the day's efforts weigh on her. The evening's quietude pressed, signaling it was time to wind down. Yet, as she started her nighttime routine, a peculiar sensation interrupted the serenity of the cabin. An unsettling chill slithered through the rooms, insidious and unexpected. Her breath materialized as frosty puffs in the space. The room felt stripped of its coziness, overtaken by a cold malevolence that seemed to seep from the very walls. This abrupt shift from a day filled with productiveness to an evening charged with an eerie discomfort left Clara unnerved.

A book, which had rested on the shelf, now teetered at its edge. Without warning, it plummeted to the ground, landing with a thud that echoed in the stillness. Shadows contorted, their forms darkening and twisting as if animated by some unseen force.

Whispers then interrupted the oppressive silence. These soft murmurs amplified, yet never quite discernible. Like tendrils of smoke, they encircled Clara, faint cries hinting at old sorrows and betrayals. She shook her head, trying to scatter the sounds, chiding herself for letting her imagination take the reins. But her self-composure wavered when she felt a sharp sting on her arm. To her horror, a raw scratch stared back at her.

Clara's heart raced as she stumbled into the kitchen. The icy embrace of the freezer greeted her, revealing a bottle of vodka left by the last renter. Its surface was covered in a frosty sheen that seemed to glint mockingly at her. Memories of her struggles with alcohol surged forward, casting shadows over her recent victories.

In a moment of panic, her fingers sought the comforting weight of her AA coin in her pocket, only to find emptiness.

That coin was more than just a piece of metal. It was her anchor. The absence of this touchstone sent a chill through her, deeper than the cold air from the freezer. It left her feeling adrift, vulnerable to the whims of fate, or perhaps facing a critical test of her resilience.

Torn, Clara hesitated. Despite her inner turmoil, the allure proved irresistible. "Just this once," she murmured, succumbing to the temptation. She poured the drink, its chill a contrast to the warm burn as it slid down her throat.

She allowed herself another glass, the heavy silence of the house wrapping around her like a shroud. When she retreated to her bedroom, the atmosphere seemed charged with an eerie sensation, as if the shadows themselves were alive. Was it the spirit of Anne?

As Clara collapsed onto her bed, the room spinning, she felt enveloped by Anne's history and her escalating fears. Seeking refuge, she drew the covers close, yearning for protection from the unseen forces she sensed were at play. The bed seemed to confine her, intensifying the sensation of being watched.

Clara's mind raced. The presence of Anne's spirit, whether borne of jealousy or as a forewarning, seemed so close.

In this state of vulnerability, the line between reality and the supernatural blurred. Clara drifted into sleep, where the lives of her and Anne intertwined in a dream, their spirits connecting across centuries, bound by shared emotions and unspoken fears.

Chapter Three

Anne's Descent

The relentless rays of the morning sun wormed their way through the gaps in the curtains, illuminating the disarray of Clara's room and casting a harsh spotlight onto her weary face. She groaned, shielding her eyes with one hand, while attempting to prop herself up with the other. Her body felt heavy, laden with the sins of the previous night's excess. This feeling was a familiar foe, an echo of past regrets that Clara had hoped to leave behind. The brief escape provided by the alcohol now seemed a hollow victory.

In the cold light of day, the relief she sought only sharpened the edges of her reality. The vodka's embrace had turned into a reminder of her vulnerability to old habits, her struggle with the siren call of alcohol. The decision to drink, made in a moment of weakness, now weighed on her, a reminder of her ongoing battle with addiction..

This moment laid bare the incessant internal conflict between the desire to escape her reality and the need to confront it. She gave in and abandoned the arduous journey towards healing, tempted her with its simplicity. In this raw and unguarded state, Clara's resolve wavered, teetering on resignation. Yet, it was this very confrontation that ignited a spark of resilience within her. Despite the allure of surrender, a part of her clung to the belief that the fight for sobriety, however grueling, held meaning. This sliver of hope suggested that perhaps the true measure of strength lay not in never falling, but in the courage to rise.

She moved out to the living room, trying to shake off the weariness. The local books and magazines on the coffee table caught her blurry attention. She flipped through them. One particular title stood out — *Haunted Vermont*. Curiosity piqued, she opened it to a random page, and a headline: Willows Bridge captured her gaze. This seemed to be the same article she had found in the magazine in Boston. It appeared the universe still wanted her to tell Anne's story.

She settled more comfortably into the plush couch cushions and read:

The Mysterious Tale of Anne Wentworth: A Haunted Vermont Chronicle

In the landscapes of Vermont, where history seeps from the cobblestone streets and ghostly legends lurk in the shadows, the tragic story of Anne Wentworth remains a mystery, transcending time. Born on November 16, 1846, and tragically passing away on June 13, 1866, Anne's life and untimely death are woven into the state's haunted past.

A Love Story Shrouded in Mystery

The mid-19th century, a period marked by the glow of gaslights and the clip-clop of horse-drawn carriages, sets the stage for our tale. This period, characterized by its rigid adherence to tradition and the sanctity of family honor, serves as the backdrop to a tale of forbidden love that defies the era's stringent societal norms.

Anne Wentworth, born into a wealthy family renowned for its thriving lumber business, was the epitome of grace and ambition, her spirit unbound by the conventions of her time. Despite being nurtured in an environment where lineage and wealth dictated one's future, Anne's outlook remained untainted by cynicism. Her heart was a reservoir of dreams, brimming with optimism and a fervent passion for life that distinguished her from her contemporaries.

In the heart of this Vermont town, fate orchestrated Anne and Thomas's introduction. He was a young stable hand whose modest upbringing stood opposite to Anne's affluent background. This encounter ignited a flame of attraction that neither societal boundaries nor the dictates of class could extinguish. Their love, though forbidden, blossomed in the shadows, nurtured by the secrecy that enveloped their union. Beneath the watchful eyes of a society that would never approve, their bond deepened. Each clandestine rendezvous, each stolen kiss, and every tender whisper part of a shared dream—a dream of a life together, unshackled by the chains of social expectation.

Yet, the very essence of their connection—cast a long shadow over their hopes. This juxtaposition of worlds, one of privilege and the other of simplicity, set the stage for a love story that remains etched in the annals of Vermont's haunted history.

Tragedy at the Bridge

As is often the case, the brighter the flame, the darker the shadow it casts. Anne's joy soon turned to despair upon discovering she was with child, a development that threatened to bring disgrace to her family and ostracize her from society. Undeterred, the lovers hatched a daring plan: they would rendezvous at the old bridge at midnight, whence they would flee to a nearby town and start anew, free from the burdens of judgment and scorn.

The stage was set for their escape, but as the appointed hour approached, an eerie calm settled over the bridge. Anne, heart pounding with anticipation and fear, waited under the cover of darkness. Yet, as the night stretched on, it became clear that Thomas would not come. The dawn brought with it a devastating realization: Thomas had vanished, leaving Anne alone, vulnerable, and facing an uncertain future.

Overwhelmed by despair and a sense of betrayal, Anne found herself at a crossroads. The thought of returning home, to face the judgment of her family and the stifling constraints of a society that had never been her own, became unbearable. Her isolation and the shattered dreams of a future that would never come to pass engulfed her. In those darkest moments before the sun pierced the horizon, Anne made a heart-wrenching decision. Believing she had nothing left to hold on to and no one to turn to, she stepped off the bridge, seeking solace in the river's embrace rather than endure a life filled with the echoes of her lost love.

This tragic act marked the end of Anne Wentworth's story in the physical world, but it was just the beginning of her legend in the haunted annals of Vermont's history.

A Legacy of Haunting

Anne Wentworth's story is a reminder of the enduring power of love and the heartache of betrayal. Her spirit still haunts the old bridge, a sorrowful figure forever waiting for a lover who will never return. To this day, visitors report an inexplicable chill in the air and the faint sound of a woman's sigh carried on the breeze.

Clara felt a shiver crawl up her spine. The tale of Anne Wentworth was filled with a sorrow that seemed to transcend time, making her morning's hangover take a back seat. The story from "Haunted Vermont" lingered in Clara's mind, but it also sparked a surge of inspiration. She ventured out, back to the place it all happened, hoping the fresh air would invigorate her ideas.

As she approached, Clara's heart fluttered, half-hoping to see Jack. Yet, there was no sign of him. The bridge stood empty, surrounded by the chorus of nature.

Finding a secluded spot carpeted with wildflowers, Clara felt it was the perfect setting for her writing. She waited for inspiration, pen poised. But then, an uncanny sensation overtook her—a whisper of fabric, the soft rustle akin to a dress brushing against grass, and an invisible presence that felt like a perfume lingering in the air.

Emotions surged within Clara—anguish, hope, despair—as if she were channeling Anne Wentworth's sentiments from that fateful night. She wrote: "Heart pounding, anticipation sharp as a knife's edge, love and betrayal." Periodically, she paused, sensing an unseen touch or a whisper, yet finding nothing but nature's calm around her.

Her writing captured the yearning, waiting, and the profound sorrow of broken promises. It was as if Anne's spirit guided her hand, pouring the words into Clara from beyond.

As the sun hung in the sky, Clara noticed a glint by the water. Curiosity led her down the slope to the water's edge. A heart-shaped locket, tarnished by time, lay among the pebbles, its age and design giving it with an air of mystery.

With a moment of hesitation, Clara lifted the locket. Could this be Anne's? The idea appeared improbable, yet an undeniable connection lingered. Upon opening it, Clara discovered it was empty. The once-held treasures long faded away. She thought she detected a soft sigh, as if it echoed with whispers from the past. Tucking the locket into her pocket, she glanced at the sky; the afternoon was advancing, and she had no desire to find herself on the bridge after dark.

After Clara returned to her cabin, a sense of anticipation engulfed her. The retreat offered the perfect backdrop for introspection and creative work and she found herself compelled to explore the haunting saga of Anne Wentworth through this locket. There was an intrinsic connection between herself and the tangible piece of history she cradled in her hands.

Under the soft illumination of the cabin lights, Clara embarked on a delicate task. She prepared a simple cleaning solution, combining baking soda and salt, and placed the aged locket within it. With care, she scrubbed away years of tarnish, revealing a luster that had been obscured by time's relentless march. The act felt almost ceremonial, as if she were peeling back the layers of Anne's story. Once the locket regained its sheen, Clara threaded it onto a chain she often wore and put it around her neck.

As the evening shadows played along the walls, Clara's thoughts were adrift in a sea of memories that were not her own. She envisioned cobblestone streets alive with laughter, secret glances shared under the guise of night, and the unbearable pressure of societal expectations. The emotional turmoil of a young woman's heart, buoyed by hope and then shattered by betrayal, was something very real to Clara.

The locket's cold press against her chest seemed to beat in tandem with another's heart, bridging centuries. The sight of the empty vodka bottle, a reminder of her recent backslide, spurred a moment of introspection. Clara rationalized this lapse as a mere vacation misstep and promised to resume her sobriety when she returned to real life, yet considered the idea of allowing herself just one drink during her next visit to town.

Clara touched the locket, and it served as a conduit, whisking her away from the confines of the cabin and into the past. She found herself enveloped in a whirlwind of emotions, offering her a glimpse into the nuances of betrayal, love, and fleeting happiness—a scene that seemed to plead for a voice.

Suddenly, Clara was standing in a barn, the scent of hay mingling with the symphony of distant crickets. Before her, in the warm glow of a lantern, stood two figures caught in a clandestine rendezvous.

Anne's cheeks were tinged with excitement and trepidation. She stood beside a man whose presence was marked by a quiet intensity.

"Thomas," Anne whispered.

Thomas gazed into Anne's eyes and cradled her face in his hands. "Anne," he replied, his voice thick with feeling, "here and now, it's only us. Nothing else matters."

"I'm frightened. What if we're discovered?"

He soothed her, his thumb caressing her cheek. "Trust me, Anne, in this moment, we're all that exists. I wish for nothing more than to be by your side, always."

Hesitation flickered across Anne's face as she gripped his hand. "But if someone sees... The sin of it all..."

Thomas removed her bonnet, unleashing her hair to cascade. "My dear Anne," he murmured, tucking a strand behind her ear, "Forget the world outside."

Their connection deepened with a kiss. As they embraced, shedding the layers of societal expectations along with their outer garments, their passion was tangible.

Caught in the moment's intensity, Clara felt as though she was experiencing Anne's emotions firsthand. The memory was vivid, saturated with the longing and tenderness of their union.

Yet, as Clara remained a silent observer, a sense of foreboding encroached. The shadow of impending heartbreak that loomed over Anne's story pulled Clara back into her own reality, leaving her heart heavy.

She gasped for air, her heart pounding as she yanked the locket from around her neck. The moment it broke free, the vision of Anne's world released its hold on her. The locket, now disconnected, tumbled from her fingers and hit the drawer with a clatter.

As she settled back against the couch, her head throbbed from the experience. "I really need to unwind. Maybe find a little adventure." Her gaze drifted to the empty vodka bottle on the counter, taunting her with memories of the night before. The desire for another escape gnawed at her.

The shadows transformed ordinary corners and spaces into mysterious hideaways. Clara was terrified. With increasing desperation, she scoured every conceivable place where the owner might have hidden a bottle. She rummaged through the cabinets, the refrigerator, even the unlikeliest of spots.

After taking a steadying breath, Clara turned to her laptop for a solution. A quick search pointed her to the bar Jack had told her about. Relief was just a short stroll away. She threw on a sweatshirt and headed for the door, her thoughts already on escaping the confines of her temporary retreat.

As she headed toward the bar, she tried to push away the voices in her head.

This isn't you anymore. Remember the promises? The AA tokens? The late-night crying bouts swearing never again?

But another voice chimed in, louder, more insistent. *It's just a drink. You deserve a moment of reprieve. You're on vacation anyway, remember?*

As she walked, the fresh air seemed to clear her head. The streetlights painted an eerie glow on the path, and with each step, Anne's presence seemed to lighten.

It's just one drink to help with the stress, Clara reasoned. *The story, Ethan, this place, the memories from that damn locket. A drink, one drink, to calm the nerves, and then you can get to writing.*

By the time she reached the bar, her resolve had weakened. The door's chime as she entered was almost drowned out by her internal justifications. *It's different this time. Just one to take the edge off. I'll handle it.*

The bar radiated an old-world charm, its walls darkened by decades of memories. Antique bulbs lent the space a rich, golden glow. An acoustic band was setting up on the stage. As the lead guitarist adjusted his instrument, Clara's heart missed a beat. There was something in the way he moved, the tilt of his head, that reminded her of Ethan. The similarity wasn't exact, but the resemblance was uncanny.

A pang of longing coupled with an urgent desire to forget surged through her. She scanned the bar, her eyes darting from one face to another, searching for someone interesting, someone who might offer a momentary escape. The thrill of a diversion she felt she needed and deserved.

Clara signaled the bartender. "Whiskey, neat," she ordered. The first sip was sharp, a welcomed sting.

The bar's atmosphere buzzed with subdued conversations and anticipation of the evening's performance. As Clara's eyes locked onto the man a few stools away. Tall and with a lean build, there was a magnetic energy about him. The way the fabric of his shirt stretched across his well-defined arms, hinting at hours spent at the gym, sent her mind wandering. Perhaps he'd be the remedy for the evening's growing restlessness.

"Going with whiskey, huh?" The deep timbre of his voice sent a shiver down her spine.

She glanced back at her empty stool and quipped, "Is that a recommendation?"

With a smile that hinted at shared secrets, he replied, "From one connoisseur to another, it's a good choice."

She arched an eyebrow. "Is that so?"

He chuckled, a warm, infectious sound that drew her in even more. "Name's Leo."

"Clara."

As Clara was about to continue the playful banter, a cheerful voice from her other side interrupted her thoughts. "Hey there! Mind if I join you?" A girl with bright eyes and an even brighter smile introduced herself. "I'm Jess."

Surprised, Clara nodded and motioned for her to take the empty seat beside her. Just as Jess began sharing a story about her day, Leo's presence became more pronounced. Without a word, he handed her a glass filled with amber liquid.

"Top-shelf," he said with a wink, "on me."

As the second drink slid in front of her, Clara lifted it in acknowledgment. "Don't mind if I do," she murmured, letting the rich aroma of the whiskey tantalize her senses. She took a slow sip and let the smooth liquid roll over her tongue. Her gaze locked with Leo's, and with a seductive glint in her eyes, she gave a soft, "thank you."

As the third drink arrived, the night swayed and the edge of her vision blurred just enough to make her feel light and free. This was what she needed.

"Dance?" Leo asked, extending a hand.

"Why not?" She took Leo's outstretched hand and allowed him to lead her to the dance floor. As they moved in rhythm, the world around them seemed to sink into a hazy background. The feel of Leo's powerful hands on her waist sent a shiver up her spine. As he pulled her closer, the contours of her body molded against his, their movements synchronizing. This would do.

After the song, they headed back to the bar. "How about a shot to keep the rhythm going?" Leo suggested with a playful grin.

"Don't mind if I do," Clara replied.

All of a sudden, Jess was there, her presence exuding a unique energy that Clara hadn't noticed earlier. "Mind if I steal her?" Jess's voice was playful as she spoke over the music, wrapping an arm around Clara's waist. The unexpected touch sent a jolt of electricity through Clara, her skin tingling under Jess's fingers.

While Clara had been with mostly men in the past, she wasn't unfamiliar with the pull of attraction toward a woman. Her heart rate quickened, her mind racing to process the whirlwind of emotions. She hadn't entertained the idea of being with Jess tonight, but in that fleeting moment, the thought held a certain appeal.

Before long, Leo joined them. As the trio danced, their moves became more synchronized, their laughter blending into the music. The intimacy of the dance, combined with the alcohol coursing through her veins, made the world seem distant. Time seemed to lose its meaning, and all that mattered was the music and the electrifying connection.

Their playful rivalry for Clara's attention, the alternating warmth of Leo's touch and the soft caresses of Jess, left Clara elated. The push and pull, the ebb and flow of their interactions, heightened her senses. The closeness, the hot breaths, the shared laughter—all of it conspired to draw Clara deeper into the moment, her inhibitions melting away.

Jess took Clara's hand, her fingers intertwining, giving a tug. "Come with me," she said. The two made their way through the crowd, with Leo following close behind, and Jess pushed open the door to the bathroom, ushering Clara in.

The world seemed a little distant as the door shut and Jess clicked the lock. Sounds from the bar, the more immediate ambiance of water dripping, their synchronized breaths, and the occasional muffled laughter that penetrated the walls replaced the hum of conversation.

The bathroom's overhead lights painted the three in alternating shades of gold and shadow. As Leo removed his jacket, the contours of his muscular form became more pronounced. His woodsy fragrance filled the room. As Clara's vision wavered and the pain in her head became too much to bear, a flash of realization pierced the fog of confusion. This wasn't just alcohol. But the thought was fleeting. She was being swallowed by the overpowering sensations that held her captive.

"Maybe... maybe we should go back," she murmured.

Before Clara could take another step, Jess's hand captured hers. "Not yet," Jess whispered, her gaze locked onto Clara's.

The walls of the bathroom seemed to shift and spin, the dim lights appearing as hazy streaks in Clara's blurred vision. A sudden wave of lightheadedness washed over her, causing her legs to wobble and buckle beneath her. As the ground rushed up to meet her, she felt herself falling; the world turning dark around the edges.

In the fog, Jess and Leo exchanged a quick glance, their previous playfulness replaced with the precision of those familiar with such situations. They moved in tandem, their actions choreographed from experiences.

With a swift, well-rehearsed grace, Jess unzipped Clara's purse, her fingers searching its contents. "Wallet's on the left," Leo said.

Jess nodded, pulling out the wallet with ease. She handed it over to Leo, who slipped it into his pocket with a deftness that spoke of many repetitions.

As Clara's head lolled, her drugged state pulling her further into unconsciousness; she watched Jess and Leo shared one last glance. There was no guilt in their eyes, just a cool detachment.

Adjusting their clothes with practiced efficiency, they left the bathroom as silently as they had entered, merging into the bar's crowd, leaving a vulnerable Clara behind in their wake.

The bathroom seemed to pulsate, intensifying the throbbing in her head and the chilled tiles beneath her provided a jarring contrast to the growing warmth creeping up her face. All the scents—a mix of cleaning agents, spilled drinks, and an undercurrent of sweat—turned her stomach.

Every sound felt magnified, the knocking on the door sounding like thunderclaps in her ears. But above all, a voice, insistent and growing anxious, permeated her foggy senses. "Clara? Clara, are you in there?"

She tried to move, to respond, but her limbs felt like they were anchored. The weight of her eyelids was almost too much to bear, but she fought to keep them open, desperate for some tether to reality.

The door burst open, letting in a flood of ambient bar noise—the muffled beat of a song, distant laughter, the clinking of glasses. A figure stood in the doorway, backlit, casting a shadow over her. As her eyes adjusted, the familiar contours of a face came into focus.

"Jack..." she whispered, her voice sounding far away even to her own ears.

His eyes darted over her form. "Oh, Clara," Jack breathed out, rushing to her side. "What the hell happened?" She tried to answer, but before anything came out, the world went black.

The moon cast long shadows on the winding road that led to the bridge, painting a haunting silhouette of the girl as she walked. With every step, her secret grew heavier, a life growing inside her, the love that was supposed to be eternal, yet now tainted with betrayal.

She could hear the whispers of the villagers even in their absence, their judgmental voices forming a storm inside her head. The world seemed to blur and stretch, reality and her darkest fears becoming indistinguishable.

The bridge's truss seemed to beckon her and the girl hesitated for a moment, feeling the tiny flutter of life inside her. This reminder of her unborn child only intensified the shame and anguish she felt. She thought of the child growing within her, innocent yet already bearing her sins and society's judgment.

With rain beginning to fall, mirroring her tears, she approached the bridge. The water below roared, a tumultuous chorus to her internal storm. She leaned over the rail and whispered a soft apology to the life within her.

Clara, suspended between the realms of the conscious and unconscious, felt Anne's torment suffocating her. She could hear the faint heartbeat of Anne's unborn child, echoing the rhythm of her own pulse. The shared pain, the shame, the desperate acts of a soul tormented by love intertwined in Clara's mind, reminding her of the fragile threads that connect all human experiences.

Chapter Four

Distracting Desires

Clara's eyelids fluttered open, her headache pressing down like an anchor. A sharp sting pierced her temples, making the light that seeped through the curtains feel almost blinding. As she shifted beneath the covers, the textures and scents of her bedding felt uncomfortable. Confusion gnawed at her, intertwining with the remnants of a hazed intoxication. The room should have offered comfort, but it intensified her disorientation. How did she end up back in her own bed? She had no memory of returning home.

Clara forced herself to sit upright as she gritted her teeth against the throbbing in her head. Every movement sent fresh waves of nausea surging through her, making the room tilt. With a shaky hand, she brushed stray strands of hair from her face and swung her legs over the side of the bed.

The events of the previous night felt like distorted fragments of a dream — disconnected and surreal. Her clothes, creased and smelling of stale cigarettes and alcohol, clung to her skin. A flood of shame washed over her as the memory of drink after drink dominated her mind.

With a heavy sigh, she muttered, "Never again." It just wasn't worth it. She slipped out of her soiled outfit and reached for the nearest clean t-shirt. After pulling it over her head, she followed with a pair of sweatpants.

Then, steeling herself against the pounding in her head, Clara made her way to the kitchen. The thought of a strong cup of coffee became a singular focus, driving her forward, each step steadier than the last.

Just as she reached for the coffeepot, a shadowy movement in her peripheral vision sent her heart racing. Panic flared as the memory of the locket flooded her brain. In a split second of pure instinct, she scanned the countertops for anything she could use as a weapon. Her hand landed on a wooden spatula.

But as she whirled around, spatula raised and ready to strike, her eyes met a familiar, if unexpected, face: Jack.

"Whoa, hey! It's just me," he exclaimed, raising his hands in a placating gesture.

Clara's posture sagged with relief, the spatula now feeling absurd in her hand. She placed it back on the counter, her pulse still racing. Then she cleared her throat. "So, um... what are you doing in my house?"

Jack took a deep breath and leaned against the kitchen island, his gaze averted, as if searching for the right words. "I saw you last night at the bar," he began, his voice gentle.

She frowned, trying to recall. "You did?"

He nodded, his dark eyes searching hers. "I went over to say hello, but... you looked preoccupied. I didn't want to intrude."

Clara's cheeks flushed, embarrassment seeping in as fragmented memories attempted to piece together. "I... don't remember much after my third drink," she admitted.

Jack's expression turned serious. "Yeah, I noticed. That's why I kept an eye on you. That couple you were with, they acted... off."

"Off? How?"

He hesitated, choosing his words. "They seemed too familiar with you, considering you'd just met. They were constantly by your side, watching your every move. It made me uncomfortable." Jack paused, rubbing the back of his neck. "When I saw you go to the bathroom with them, I had a bad feeling. Then you never came back out."

Clara's eyes widened in shock, the implications of Jack's words dawning on her. "And then... what happened?"

Jack shifted, his cheeks tinged red. "When they came out, they seemed... oddly composed, given the situation. I watched them whisper to each other, and something about it didn't feel right." He coughed. "So, I checked the bathroom."

A lump formed in Clara's throat as realization dawned on her. "That's how you found me..."

He nodded. "You were out of it. I didn't want to leave you there, so I brought you home."

Clara took a shaky breath, her cheeks flushing a deeper shade of red. The mortification of being seen in such a state, especially by Jack, was almost unbearable. She was used to being the responsible one in her relationships, despite her occasional lapses into excess. And yet here she was, being cared for by someone who clearly had his life together far better than she did.

She looked at him. "I've been trying to control my drinking," she admitted. "Last night was a relapse. I just wanted to forget everything for a while."

Jack's gaze held understanding, perhaps even familiarity. "I've been there," he replied.

Clara perked up, a question forming on her lips. "You have?"

For a moment, a shadow passed over Jack's eyes, and he seemed to retreat within himself. "It's not something I talk about," he said, avoiding her gaze.

Jack cleared his throat and shifted on his feet. "Look, I don't want to be the bearer of bad news so early, but... they got away with your wallet."

Clara's heart sank, and her headache intensified. "Oh, shit!" She groaned. "I have to cancel all my cards. My driver's license was in there... everything."

Jack ran a hand through his disheveled hair. "I did my best. By the time I got to you, they'd vanished into the crowd. I made sure you were safe, though, and reported the theft to the police."

The ache in Clara's head dulled as she processed Jack's words. His rugged appearance was only made more captivating by his obvious concern.

"Oh no," she replied, shaking her head, her voice quivering. "It's not your fault, Jack. It's mine. I... I shouldn't have put myself in that position." She hesitated, meeting his gaze with vulnerable sincerity. "I appreciate everything you did for me. I can't thank you enough."

Jack shifted. "You don't have to thank me. I just did what felt right."

She winced, memories from the night attempting to resurface. The fragmented snippets played in her mind: dim bar lights, the press of bodies, the heady mix of alcohol, and a dizzying whirl of emotions. She drew in a shuddering breath. "God, I can't believe I let this happen," she said, pressing the heels of her hands into her temples, trying to wish away both the headache and the shame of the night.

"It's not your fault," Jack assured her. "People can be opportunistic. But I promise, we'll do everything we can to sort this out."

When she met his gaze, Clara felt a rush of gratitude, intertwined with the sting of her own self-imposed humiliation. She murmured a soft, "Thank you."

Jack hesitated. "Do you want me to leave?"

She bit her lip. "No, please stay. I mean, unless you have to be somewhere?"

Jack smiled. "Honestly, right now, there's no place I'd rather be than here, making sure you're okay."

His composure made her feel a little better as she went over how to get a new copy of her license and which cards she would need to cancel. A sudden knock on the door interrupted their process. Clara tensed up, and Jack moved in front of her, protective.

She opened the door and was met by a stern-looking man with a badge. "Morning, ma'am. I'm Sheriff Daniels. I believe this belongs to you?" He extended her wallet.

She grabbed the wallet, feeling a rush of relief as she flipped it open to ensure its contents were intact. "Oh my God, thank you!" she said, feeling tears prick her eyes.

Sheriff Daniels nodded, his eyes scanning the room and landing on Jack. "We pulled over a couple just outside Burlington last night. Found a bunch of stolen items, yours included. They've been at this for a while."

Clara gasped, "So, this wasn't just random?"

Jack scowled. "Those jerks."

The sheriff added, "If you wouldn't mind, ma'am, we'd like you to come by the station in the next few days to give a statement."

She nodded. "Of course, and thank you."

Jack stepped in closer, his hand finding a reassuring spot on her back. "Thanks, Sheriff. We really appreciate how quickly you're handling this."

As they watched the sheriff's car pull away, the dust swirling behind it on the gravel driveway seemed to pause time itself, bringing Clara back to the here and now. She tried to shift the conversation to lighter territory. "It's so cute here. You've always been in this town?"

Jack's face took on a faraway look. "Born and raised. Left for college, spent some years in Providence. But I found my way back after reconnecting with my high school sweetheart."

"Oh?" Clara wondered if this was his ex. "Is she still in town?"

Jack hesitated for a fraction of a second. "Lila... Yeah, she's still around."

"Lila... is she...?"

Jack, catching the hint, said, "Yes, she's the ex-wife."

A silence fell over them for a moment, and Clara, realizing she might have overstepped, mumbled, "I didn't mean to pry."

Jack tried to ease the tension with a half-smile. "It's a small town. If you are here long enough, you would hear it from someone."

The afternoon sun streamed through the kitchen windows, bathing the room in light. Clara, now feeling refreshed, began rummaging through her fridge. "Want a sandwich?" she asked, laying out various fillings.

"Sounds perfect," Jack replied, stepping beside her to assist. They moved around the kitchen in a coordinated dance, sometimes deliberately, sometimes accidentally grazing against each other. With every touch, a charge seemed to pass between them, adding to the electric atmosphere.

As they assembled their sandwiches, Clara thought about earlier. She could still feel the ghost of Jack's touch on her back and his warm breath when he'd leaned in to speak to her. She shook her head to clear her thoughts, focusing on spreading the mayo. He seemed to be lost in thought, glancing her way when he thought she wouldn't notice.

They sat opposite each other, their conversation touching on lighter topics, like favorite vacation spots and hobbies. But even as they chatted and laughed, there was an undeniable pull.

After finishing their lunch, Jack stretched, breaking the spell for a moment. "I should get going," he said, sounding somewhat hesitant.

Clara nodded, trying to keep her tone neutral. "Thanks for everything today."

His gaze met hers. "It was my pleasure."

He stood at the open door and turned to say his goodbyes. But as he looked down at Clara, the intensity in her eyes was unmistakable. The surrounding air grew heavy.

Jack took a half-step closer, the gap between them shrinking to a breath. Clara's chest heaved, the pulse at the base of her throat racing. Her skin felt like it was on fire, every nerve ending alive. As they held each other's gaze, Jack's breathing became heavier, and for a moment, Clara thought he might close the distance. But with restraint clear in his every move, he murmured a goodbye and stepped back, leaving her in the fading afternoon light.

The silence in the room seemed to amplify once Jack had left. Clara leaned against the door, feeling the coolness of the wood press into her back. She let out a sigh, realizing the strength of the pull between them. *Good thing one of us had some maturity.*

Even with Jack's departure, Clara's heartbeat refused to calm, a familiar pang of yearning echoing within her. Men and alcohol—her two main avenues of escape. She acknowledged the pattern she had sunk into. "I really need to break this cycle," she muttered, glancing in the direction Jack had vanished.

She needed to channel her energy into something productive, and couldn't spend the day pining over what could have been. A glimmer from her desk drawer caught her eye — the locket. It held so many questions, and perhaps the answers were the perfect distraction she needed, and she knew just the person who could help.

Ashlyn Alden.

Clara's debut novel had been a bestseller- landing her a lucrative five book deal with the publisher. Her second manuscript did not come as easily—a thriller entwined with elements of the supernatural—and was proved to be more challenging than she had expected. She needed authenticity, a way to breathe life into the paranormal aspects of her story without veering into overused tropes.

She had heard of Ashlyn through the grapevine of her writing circle—a psychic known not only for her abilities but also for her willingness to consult on creative projects. Taking a leap of faith, Clara reached out, and to her surprise, Ashlyn had been intrigued by her proposal.

The day they met, the air was dark and dreary with winter just giving way to spring. Clara entered the cozy, book-laden study where Ashlyn welcomed her clients. The walls were lined with shelves filled with old tomes and modern works on the supernatural and the aroma of sage lingered in the air. Ashlyn greeted her with a warm, knowing smile, as if she had been expecting Clara all along.

"Clara Mitchell, the suspense writer," Ashlyn had said, her voice tinged with amusement. "To what do I owe the pleasure?"

Clara explained her project—a novel centered on a protagonist who could communicate with the dead. She wanted to ensure her portrayal was respectful and grounded in some semblance of reality, or at least believability.

Ashlyn listened, nodding along as Clara outlined her vision. After a moment of contemplation, Ashlyn shared her insights, weaving tales of her experiences with the spiritual realm. She spoke of the delicate veil between the living and the dead, the energies that lingered in places of significance, and the emotional echoes that could sometimes breach the divide.

As Ashlyn described the sensation of connecting with a spirit—the chill that whispered across the skin, the electric tingle of presence, unseen emotions—Clara took fervent notes. The details were gold, the missing pieces she had been searching for to lend her narrative the authenticity it lacked.

"Remember, Clara," Ashlyn had cautioned, her eyes piercing, "the spirit world is not a parlor trick or a plot device. It's a dimension of existence, rich with emotion and a story. Approach it with respect."

That meeting had been a turning point for Clara. Not only did it provide her with the material she needed to break through her writer's block, but it also marked the beginning of an unexpected friendship. Ashlyn's perspectives on the supernatural had opened Clara's mind to possibilities she had never considered, enriching her storytelling in ways she couldn't have imagined.

Clara picked up her phone and scrolled through her contacts, stopping at Ashlyn's. After taking a deep breath, Clara pressed 'call'. She prepared herself for the conversation, hoping it might provide both a distraction and a clue about the locket's mysterious past.

The ring tone echoed through her ears until a calm, familiar voice answered, "Hello?"

"Hi, Ashlyn. It's Clara Mitchell," she began, her voice shaky. "I hope I'm not intruding. I just... I found something, and I need your expertise."

Ashlyn's tone changed to one of curiosity. "Ah, Clara, it's been some time. What seems to be the matter?"

Clara recounted her discovery of the locket and the initials engraved on it. She spoke of the legends of Anne, and the eerie events that had followed its discovery. The whispers, the dreams—everything spilled out in a rush.

Ashlyn listened, her silence punctuated only by occasional hums of interest. "Objects, especially personal ones, can carry strong residual energies. If it's hers and the legends hold any truth, it's entirely possible the locket keeps a part of her essence."

Clara's grip on the phone tightened. "I feel like I'm tapping into something, perhaps memories or emotions. I thought if anyone could help, it would be you."

"It sounds like more than just residual energy." Ashlyn's voice grew contemplative. "Perhaps an active spirit, one trying to communicate its unfinished business."

Silence hung between them for a moment until Clara broke it. "Are you able to help with this one?"

A soft sigh came from the other end. "It's a good thing I'm not too far from Stowe right now. How about I come into town, have a firsthand look at the locket, and see what I can sense?"

Relief washed over Clara. "That would mean a lot to me. Thank you."

"See you soon, Clara. Take care."

With that, Clara ended the call, anticipation and trepidation warring in her chest.

As twilight deepened, painting the room in shades of dusk, Clara sought refuge in her book, the reading lamp casting a cozy bubble of light in the encroaching darkness. Engrossed in a thrilling passage, she was startled by a cold draft that fluttered the pages and sent a shiver cascading down her spine. The room's temperature plummeted, surrounding her in a chilling embrace.

Unease prickled her skin. She rationalized it as the settling of an old house, yet the air felt dense, charged with an unseen presence. It was as if the very space around her was alive and watching her with unseen eyes. The back of her neck tingled, and she could swear she felt the faintest touch of fingers brushing against her skin.

When she scanned the room, Clara found nothing out of the ordinary. Yet, the oppressive atmosphere pressed on her, quickening her pulse. She summoned her bravery and called out, "Is someone there?" Silence followed, the room growing even colder, then suddenly, the feeling lifted, leaving her questioning reality.

As the evening progressed, shadows danced across the walls, and whispers filled the air. She suspected Anne. The presence felt insistent, almost suffocating, as if the walls themselves were trying to communicate. Suddenly, a book flew from the shelf, and a door slammed.

She felt a little less frightened this time, knowing she had Ashlyn to help. Was Anne attempting to convey a message? Clara recalled some of her friends' teachings and prepared to meditate and reach across the veil. But an electrical surge interrupted. The lights blinked.

Now she was feeling a little more fear. Clara abandoned the meditation and instead chanted a protective incantation. "Guardians of light, shield me tonight. Push away spirits, with all your might." She repeated the lines, each repetition more resolute than the last.

The tumult subsided, but a residual sadness lingered, reflecting the turmoil within Clara herself. Thoughts of Jack, their connection, and the unresolved tension of her life in Boston consumed her. She approached the window, where moonlight offered a serene counterpoint to her internal storm. Lost in thought, Clara stood at the crossroads of her past and the uncertain promise of the future, the night's beauty bittersweet as she pondered the cost of a love that might never be hers.

CHAPTER FIVE

Tales of the Spirits

The quaint cafe was Clara's chosen hideaway, a refuge from her relentless internal monologue. Tossing and turning the previous night, her mind had been full of thoughts about Jack. Did he distance himself because of her penchant for alcohol and wild nights? Was it the contrasting worlds they came from? The worst part? Realizing how deeply she cared about him. The act of admitting to herself that she was interested had been a harsh wake-up call. She wished she could switch off those feelings, make things simpler.

She hoped Ashlyn might be the distraction she needed. The ambience was comforting, filled with muted chatter and the inviting scent of coffee. Its eclectic furniture, each piece carrying a tale of its own, added to its charm. The day's sunlight wove through the windows, painting everything in a rainbow of colors. But even as she appreciated these details, Clara was aware of her purpose.

Then, a chime from the entrance pulled her from her reverie. Framed by the door stood a figure, illuminated and looking like she stepped out of a dream. Sunlight kissed her dark hair, making it gleam with a celestial sheen. The moment Ashlyn stepped into the room, the entire cafe fell into a hush, all eyes drawn to her. With an air that commanded attention, she seemed to eclipse everything else in the room. For Clara, the background chatter dimmed. All that mattered now was the conversation to come, and the truths it might unveil.

"Clara," Ashlyn greeted her with a smile, her voice soft yet carrying a playfulness and the knowledge that all were watching her. "It feels like forever."

Clara stood, embracing the woman. "It does. I can't believe it's only been a year."

"Time moves differently for people like me, I suppose." Ashlyns laughter filled the air. "Tell me, how have you been?"

"Better to see you," Clara replied with a grin. "And every time I come across 'Grave Secrets' in a bookstore or get a royalty check, I'm reminded of the magic we created together."

Ashlyn waved her hand but with a smile, "Oh, please! Your writing is extraordinary on its own. I just sprinkled stardust, that's all."

Clara leaned in, her tone conspiratorial. "That 'stardust' made all the difference. There is talk of a Netflix Series. The readers couldn't get enough of the paranormal elements you helped infuse. We made quite the team."

"I'm just glad it resonated with so many," Ashlyn replied, her eyes glinting. "But tell me about this thing that has been pulling you back to the realm of the supernatural."

With a sigh, Clara leaned back. "It started with a new story, inspired by a ghost story. It's one you'll find intriguing."

Ashlyn's gaze intensified, signaling her readiness to dive deep once more into the world of spirits and mysteries.

The aroma of baked bread and simmering soups wafted through the cafe. A young waiter approached them, menus in hand. Clara took a moment to peruse the list of hearty dishes before settling on her comfort food of choice, mac and cheese. Ashlyn opted for a creamy tomato basil soup with a side of garlic bread.

As the waiter left with their orders, Clara breathed, her fingers fidgeting with her napkin. "As you know, I didn't call you here just to catch up," she began. "There's been...an occurrence."

Ashlyns's violet eyes focused on Clara. "Go on," she coaxed.

Clara's shoulders dropped, her tension melting away. "I've been experiencing something... haunting. It's a spirit named Anne." She recounted the events that had transpired, the locket's discovery, the dreams, and the increasing sense of urgency and despair she felt.

Ashlynn listened, sipping her soup. Her eyes never left Clara's.

"I feel her pain, her desperation. But every time I try to connect, it just... gets worse." Clara continued.

Ashlyn reached over, covering Clara's hand with her own. The cool touch of her rings sent a calm through Clara. "This spirit, she's trying to convey something important. Something unresolved."

When the waiter dropped off their food, the smell of Clara's mac and cheese filled the air. She pulled up a gooey forkful, and it was like a hug in a bite, giving her normal in the middle of all this ghostly craziness.

Ashlyn broke her garlic bread. "A seance might be the key. To bridge the divide and give Anne a voice."

"I don't know..." Clara hesitated, picking at her mac and cheese. "I've never been involved in anything like that."

Ashlyn dabbed her mouth with a napkin. "You know, it will be more effective with many participants. Their energies can help bridge the realms. Do you have someone in mind? Your boyfriend, perhaps... what was his name?"

Clara's face darkened. "No, we broke up. It's just me here in Stowe. Well, mostly," she trailed off, a faint blush coloring her cheeks. "There is someone. Jack. We've become... friends. But I doubt he'd be into this sort of thing."

With a contemplative look, Ashlyn suggested, "Why don't we invite him?"

Clara hesitated, throwing Ashlyn a skeptical look. "Really? You think that's a good idea?"

In response, Ashlyn raised an eyebrow, her tone laced with dry amusement. "Would I suggest it if I didn't think it was a good idea?"

Despite the lingering doubt, Clara took a deep breath and dialed Jack's number, her fingers trembling as they hit the call button. She rehearsed her opening lines twice, attempting to smooth the nervous quiver in her voice. As the phone rang, anticipation knotted in her stomach. Then he picked up. His voice, deep and steady, resonated through the line, sending a fresh wave of uncertainty washing over her.

"Hey, Jack," she began, her voice shakier than she intended. "It's Clara. Remember when I told you about my consultant, Ashlyn Alden, for my last book?" She paused, trying to regain composure. "Well, she's here with me now. She believes a seance might help with my research for the novel, the one about Anne." Her words came out in a rushed stream, fueled by eagerness and apprehension. She swallowed hard, hoping her nerves weren't as transparent over the phone as they felt to her in that moment.

There was a pause, during which Clara looked at Ashlyn. "Look, I understand it's unorthodox, but if you're willing, it'd mean a lot to have you there. It's for the book, and maybe... to find some peace for Anne."

"Jack, you say?" Ashlyn's pendant, a crystal prism, caught the light as she leaned forward. "Would you mind if I spoke to him?"

Clara hesitated before nodding and handing it over to Ashlyn.

"Jack? This is Ashlyn Alden. Clara and I are planning a seance and she mentioned you. Would you be interested in joining? Your presence would be invaluable."

There was a pause, the muffled sound of Jack's voice emanating from the phone. Ashlyn's violet eyes sparkled with amusement. "Skeptics often make the best participants. Their grounded energy can be just what we need."

Another pause, longer this time, and then Ashlyn smiled, handing the phone back to Clara. "He'll join us."

After Jack's acquiescence, Clara let out a small laugh, relief flooding her system. "Thanks, Jack. I knew I could count on you. See you soon." She ended the call, her fingers lingering on the phone for a moment. Her heart raced, emotions churning inside. His willingness to step so far out of his comfort zone had to mean something, didn't it? Maybe he had a soft spot for her, even if it was just a tiny one.

Ashlyn, picking up on Clara's mixed emotions, leaned in with a smile. "You're brave to embark on this journey. Something tells me it's not just about Anne or your book."

Clara's cheeks tinged pink. "Is it that transparent?"

"You have a certain... spark when you talk about Jack." Ashlyns eyes twinkled. "You like him, don't you?"

A soft sigh escaped Clara's lips. "That obvious, huh?"

Ashlyn chuckled. "To those who've been around the block a few times." She paused, scanning the cafe menu. "How about a glass of wine to calm those nerves?"

The offer made Clara pause. She wanted to be back in a better place. "Mmm, no thank you. I appreciate the offer. Maybe some chamomile tea instead?"

Lorelei's eyebrows raised. "Chamomile it is." She signaled the waiter, who nodded in acknowledgment and moved to fetch their order.

The two women spent the next half hour engrossed in a light conversation, discussing everything from the latest books they'd read to their mutual admiration for small New England towns. As the waiter returned with their drinks, Clara took a moment to savor the aroma of her tea, letting the warm, calming scent wrap around her.

Ashlyn watched, her eyes softening. "Sometimes the smallest choices are the most defining. Choosing chamomile today might seem insignificant, but it's a step in the right direction."

After settling the bill, Clara caught Ashlyn's eyes and felt a shiver run down her spine. They seemed to harbor secrets from ages past, their depth uncanny. Ashlyn's knack for grasping Clara's unspoken challenges was perplexing. How could she know?

Then, the realization washed over her like a wave. Of course—Ashlyn was psychic, but not the kind who read palms at carnivals. She had a gift. Clara recalled tales of Ashlyn's guidance, her ability to perceive what lay beyond the visible, tangible world.

A subtle smile played on Ashlyn's lips, almost as if she were reading Clara's thoughts right then, reinforcing Clara's belief in her powers. Shaking her head, Clara was struck by the ways of the universe. "Thanks for getting it. I'm really hoping tonight clears things up, not just for Anne, but for me, too."

Ashlyn's nod carried wisdom. "Life has a way of weaving our paths with purpose. And remember, clarity often comes when we least expect it."

Rising from their seats, Clara felt a surge of confidence she hadn't possessed before.

As Ashlyn draped a lace shawl around her slender shoulders, the jewelry on her wrists glittered, capturing the sunlight streaming through the windows. They headed to the exit, side by side, the surrounding atmosphere charged with expectation.

After exchanging farewells, Clara wandered the streets of Stowe. Cobblestone pathways beneath her feet echoed with each step, a reminder of the town's history. She passed colonial-style buildings, each facade told a story, from ancient apothecaries to modern coffee shops. Baskets of vibrant flowers hung from lampposts, their petals swaying in the summer breeze.

Every corner seemed to hold a story or a secret, and for Clara, it served as the perfect distraction. She anchored herself in the present, pushing away the looming shadows of the upcoming seance.

Drawn to the inviting facade of a boutique, Clara stepped inside 'Lila's Closet.' The smell of fresh jasmine filled the air, mingling with the soft notes of a vintage record playing in the background. Clara browsed the curated selection of garments, admiring the material.

Then, the name of the store clicked in her mind. *Lila*. The connection was undeniable, given the size of Stowe. Clara's suspicions were confirmed as she locked eyes with a woman standing behind the counter.

It had to be her. Lila stood tall and graceful, her silhouette reminiscent of a delicate willow. Golden tresses flowed down her back, catching the ambient lighting.

Dressed in a silk blouse and high-waisted trousers, the woman moved with a confidence that dominated the surrounding space. Her presence was commanding, yet there was an underlying vulnerability in her posture.

Clara's heart twinged with insecurity, and she took a deep breath to find her ground. Lila radiated beauty and confidence, moving through her space with a grace that seemed almost daunting. Everything about her—the boutique, her aura, her effortless elegance—spoke of a self-assurance Clara found intimidating.

Her mind whirled, drawing comparisons and contrasts. Did Jack still have feelings for Lila? Were there remnants of emotion that could overshadow any connection Clara might build with him? It wasn't just about looks, either. It was the history the connections once shared that weighed on Clara.

A storm of doubt brewed inside her. How could she compare to Lila? These spiraling thoughts threatened to consume her, but Clara forced herself to breathe, to anchor in the moment. She was here for a purpose, not to drown in self-comparison. Yet, the seed of insecurity had taken root, and confronting it seemed inevitable.

Clara exhaled, attempting to steady her thoughts. She reminded herself that her daydreams of Jack, as vivid as they were, didn't signify something deep—it could just be a fleeting attraction. She was in Stowe for her book, not to find a relationship. Whatever was unfolding with Jack it shouldn't detract from her focus.

Closing her eyes, Clara conjured images of her Boston apartment, the city's skyline, her favorite coffee spot just around the corner—her life. A peace enveloped her. Jack was part of her Stowe experience, not the entirety of it.

With a refreshed resolve, Clara explored the boutique, setting aside the unsettling feelings and immersing herself in the moment. After all, finding beauty in the most unexpected places had always been her gift.

"Ah, you have an expert eye," Lila remarked as Clara picked up a vintage brooch, its design shimmering under the soft boutique lights.

"Thank you," Clara responded, her voice attempting a casual tone. "It reminds me of something my grandmother used to wear."

Lila leaned in, her green eyes assessing. "New to Stowe? I don't recall seeing you around."

"Just visiting," Clara admitted. "I am here for inspiration and research for my next book."

"A writer," Lila mused. "That's intriguing. I've always loved stories."

As Clara searched for her next words, Lila's voice dropped a shade cooler. "You know, stories can be deceiving. Just like people."

There was an undercurrent, a tension she hadn't expected. *Does she know?* She wondered. *That I know who she is? That I've been spending time with Jack?*

Lilas voice was dripping with insinuation. "Jack, for instance, is quite the raconteur, isn't he? He paints such vivid pictures with his words. Makes everyday occurrences seem almost... magical."

Clara felt a sting of unease, the pointedness of Lila's observation not lost on her. "Jack has been nothing but supportive since I got here. He's been a steady presence in an otherwise unfamiliar territory."

Lila's lips curled into a faint smirk. "All I'm saying is, be wary. People often showcase only the parts of their life that they're comfortable sharing."

The air between them grew tense. Clara revisited her interactions with Jack. Was Lila being spiteful, or had she missed something about Jack? Why was the woman pushing this so hard? Did she know something Clara didn't, or was this just some ploy to unnerve her?

"I hope Stowe gives you all the inspiration you need," Lila said.

Clara nodded. "Thank you. I believe it already has."

As Clara stepped out of Lila's Closet, she was blinded by the afternoon sun—like waking from a dream or a cautionary fable. The door chime's gentle ring behind her marked the end of a tumultuous visit.

The boutique's scented air clung to her, now feeling more like a burden than a perfume. Clara tried to shake it off. What just happened in there? Lila's parting words left a shadow of doubt about her fledgling connection with Jack. She massaged her temples and hoped to clear the haze of uncertainty. She reminded herself, not for the first time, that her purpose here was her book, not a dramatic love affair.

Walking on, the town soothed her—the quaint streets, the old-world charm of the buildings, the embrace of the natural surroundings. Yet, beneath Stowe's idyllic surface, Clara now perceived many layers. She filed away the day's events, to be revisited when she was ready to face them. For now, she sought refuge in the simpler joys, like ice cream. A respite from the tangled web of human connections.

A large table had been set up for the evening's seance. The room was dim, with only the soft glow of several ornate ivory candles illuminating the space. They flickered, casting shadows on the walls that seemed to play in time with the anticipatory energy in the room. The rich scent of sandalwood filled the air, mingling with the faint aroma of burning sage—Ashlyns's chosen blend to cleanse and protect the environment.

Ashlyn was a figure of focus and calm amidst the ambient energy. Her raven-black hair cascaded down her back, moving as she walked around the room, positioning cushions in a circle on the floor. Her delicate fingers traced patterns in the air, invoking unseen forces, her violet eyes intense and searching.

Next to the table in the corner stood her spiritual companion for the evening—Sebastian. His silver hair, short and coiffed, contrasted with his black suit. An air of flamboyance surrounded him, mirrored in the bold strokes of eyeliner stressing his expressive hazel eyes. He had a theatrical yet genuine air, someone who had embraced his spiritual gifts and wasn't afraid to show it.

"Darling, the energy in here is electric," Sebastian said, waving a hand. "Are we sure this isn't overkill?" He chuckled, revealing a row of white teeth.

Ashlyn smirked, her intense demeanor softening for a moment. "Full of opinions, aren't you, Seb? Just wait."

Sebastian approached the table, inspecting the array of crystals and trinkets. "Well, if there's one thing I've learned, it's to never doubt you," he mused.

Every detail of the room—from the circle of salt to the strategically placed crystals—was arranged, not just for effect, but with a genuine intent to connect with the beyond. As the preparations concluded, an energy of expectancy settled, readying for the souls and stories soon to unfold.

"Clara," Ashlyn began, her voice serene but purposeful, "for our seance to reach Anne, we need an object connected to her. Something that reverberates with her energy."

Clara's mind flashed to the locket. "The locket," she said. "It's on my nightstand."

Sebastian, with an intrigued look, responded, "Items with historical resonance, particularly those that have witnessed powerful emotion, can serve as powerful mediums to the spirit world."

Clara moved to her nightstand, drawing out the locket. It felt cold to the touch, its metalwork shimmering in the candlelight.

"I've felt its pull ever since I found it." Clara handed the locket to Ashlyn. "If Annes's spirit is tied to anything, it's this."

Ashlyn held the locket with a sense of reverence, feeling its weight and tracing the engraved patterns with her fingertips. "With this as our guide," she murmured, "we shall try to bridge the chasm separating us from Anne."

A knock at the front door announced Jack's entrance. The atmosphere, thick with incense and anticipation, seemed to shift with his assertive presence. He paused, taking in the myriad of candles, the intricate symbols, and the unfamiliar faces. His eyes settled on Clara, offering a reassuring nod, before shifting to Ashlyn and Sebastian.

"Quite the setup," he remarked, attempting to mask his unease. He then turned to Ashlyn, extending his hand in greeting. "Jack. I've heard a lot about you."

Ashlyn assessed him with a hint of amusement and accepted the handshake. "Ashlyn. Clara speaks highly of you." She gestured toward Sebastian, "And this is Sebastian, a dear friend and a guide on our spiritual journey tonight."

Sebastian, rising with an air of grace, greeted Jack with a soft, almost melodic voice, "Pleasure to meet you."

Jack offered a polite nod, his gaze still wandering around the room, trying to make sense of everything. To Clara, his attempt to navigate this unfamiliar territory made him seem more human, less the invulnerable figure she knew.

Yet, as Clara watched him, memories of her encounter with Lila clouded her thoughts. What had Lila meant with those veiled comments? Was there a side to Jack she was unaware of?

"I appreciate you coming, Jack," Clara said, her voice wavering.

Jack's eyes softened, meeting hers. "I said I would."

Ashlyn's voice began almost a whisper, its cadence rising and falling like a lullaby. "Spirit of the bridge, spirit of sorrow, Anne Wentworth, we call upon thee." The chant was repetitive, and with each iteration, her voice became firmer, more insistent.

Sebastian, eyes closed, his posture relaxed yet attentive, responded in kind, adding depth to the invocation. His voice melded with Ashlyn's, creating a duet of resonance that seemed to ripple through the very fabric of the room.

The atmosphere became denser. Clara felt a deep tug within her, like an old wound being reopened. She clutched Jack's hand tighter, seeking comfort from its reassuring warmth. The room seemed to pulsate, each throb echoing her mounting anxiety and anticipation.

Jack's thumb stroked Clara's hand, trying to offer solace, though his eyes, darting around the room, betrayed his own unease. His confident demeanor was now replaced by a subdued tension.

The aroma of the burning sage grew more potent, causing Clara's eyes to water. Her throat felt constricted, not from the scent, but from the rising emotions threatening to spill forth.

From the walls, or perhaps from a space beyond them, a soundless hum began, more of a feeling than an actual sound. The sensation snaked up Clara's spine, making her shiver. Jack looked down at her, his eyebrows furrowing with concern.

The locket, lying in the center, glowed, the metal gleaming with an intensity that drew Clara's gaze like a magnet. Soft chimes, their melody floating through the air like an ancient lullaby, accompanied its shimmer.

Ashlyn's chant persisted, her voice tinged with emotion. "Anne Wentworth, come forth. Share with us your story, your pain. We seek to understand, to bridge the divide."

The room's temperature plummeted. Each exhale produced puffs of frost, contrasting with the warmth of the summer night beyond the windows. A chilling draft enveloped them, making Clara pull closer to Jack, seeking his warmth. He responded by wrapping an arm around her, pulling her close, his own apprehension clear in his tightened grip.

A sudden, profound sadness weighed upon Clara's heart. She felt tears prickling at the back of her eyes, a cascade of emotions not her own.

Above the locket, a mist materialized, shaping into a recognizable form. Clara's heart thudded, knowing that they were on the verge of connecting with Anne's spirit.

Ashlyn's voice turned tender, almost caressing. "Anne, we are here with open hearts and open minds. Speak to us."

The waiting spirit of Anne Wentworth seemed to hover, hesitating on the precipice of communication. The seance had begun.

As the mist above the locket coalesced, Anne's form became more distinct. She wore flowing Victorian attire and had a mournful countenance. Her eyes, deep wells of sorrow, fixed upon Clara, while she displayed visible unease and perhaps even disdain when glancing at Jack.

Clara's heart raced, feeling an inexplicable kinship with the spirit before her. Their gazes locked, and in that silent exchange, she felt waves of shared experiences, heartaches, and deep, haunting regrets.

Anne's voice came through Ashlyn's mouth and carried an emotional weight that pressed down on everyone in the room. "Deception and betrayal. My heart was but a plaything to him," she said, casting a scornful look at Jack, as if he were a painful reminder of her past.

"I had loved with all my innocence," Anne continued, her voice shaky. "He promised to elope with me, to free me from the shackles of my life. But he left me, abandoned and shamed. I was ruined in the eyes of society, alone, knowing that my love had been a lie."

As Anne's tragic story unfolded, Clara felt a chill. The words, though belonging to another era, felt close to home. The promises of love, the impending heartbreak—Clara sensed that her own recent experiences resonated with Anne's tale.

Jack shifted, his gaze darting between Anne and Clara. He tightened his hold on Clara's hand, as if wanting to reassure her of his genuine feelings.

Sebastian, sensing the heightened tension, intervened. "We are here to listen and understand. We wish to aid in any way we can."

Anne's gaze returned to Clara, her eyes pleading. "Do not let history repeat itself, dear one. Protect your heart from hollow promises. I am bound to my regrets and sorrows. I do not wish the same fate upon you."

Clara felt tears streaming down her face, her emotions a tumultuous mix of sympathy for Anne's tormented past and the vulnerable rawness of her own recent experiences. "I...I understand," Clara answered, her voice shaking. "Thank you for your warning, for sharing your story."

Anne's form, which had wavered, regained its solidity for a moment. Her sad smile deepened with gratitude. "Remember my words. Trust your intuition."

Before she could fade again, Jack interjected, his voice desperate. "But what about the other side of the tale? Doesn't the man deserve to tell his side? History is always layered, filled with multiple perspectives."

Anne's form stiffened at the mention of the name. "Thomas," she spat, her spirit seething with palpable anger. The temperature in the room dropped. "He shattered my trust, toyed with my love, and then cast me aside like a discarded plaything. There's no redemption for such cruelty."

Jack, taken aback by her vehemence but undeterred, continued, "Every tale has two sides. Maybe he had his reasons, pains, and regrets, too."

Anne's form became threatening, her voice a chilling echo in the room. "Do not test me. My anguish is real. Do not dare diminish them with conjectures about him."

Ashlyn, sensing the escalating tension, stepped in, her voice firm yet soothing. "Enough! We are here to listen and to heal, not to instigate further unrest. Thank you, Anne, for sharing your pain and your message."

Anne's form disintegrated, her parting words lingering in the cold air. "Remember what I have said. Guard your heart."

"Why did you have to confront her like that?" Clara, unsettled, turned to Jack. "Tonight was supposed to be about uncovering Anne's story."

Jack looked into Clara's eyes, his expression earnest. "I just think... every story is seen differently depending on where you're standing." He paused. "Sometimes, we judge too quickly. I'm sorry if I messed anything up.."

Clara remembered how Jack had rescued her from the bar, free of judgment, filled instead with genuine care. A twinge of regret reminded her of her own insecurities.

"Let's just take a breather," Clara suggested. "It seems we both could use one."

As the seance wrapped up, Clara mulled over the tangle of unresolved feelings, the complex nature of love and judgment, and the myriad interpretations of truth.

In the soft glow of candlelight, doubt and uncertainty played across Jack's features. Ashlyn, halting her actions, caught his gaze. She moved to a small desk, scribbled something on a card, and offered it to Jack. "For those moments when words find their way."

Jack accepted the card, reading not just the message but also the intention behind it, and nodded in understanding.

Sebastian, approaching with a mischievous sparkle, teased, "For someone so grounded, you sure have a mysterious charm." He winked. "Or is it just your rugged good looks?"

A smile broke through Jack's contemplative mood. "Considering the source, I'll take that as a compliment."

Sebastian's laughter warmed the atmosphere. "Well played!"

As Ashlyn packed away her equipment, she observed, "Some nights leave a deeper imprint than others. Tonight's one of them."

Clara embraced Ashlyn, murmuring a heartfelt, "Thank you. Words just can't capture tonight."

"Sometimes, they don't have to," Ashlyn reassured her, patting her back.

Sebastian gave Clara an elaborate bow. "Till we meet again, dear Clara." He then turned to Jack, smirking, "And you keep dodging those spirits. The earthly ones, at least."

Jack's response came with a chuckle. "I'll do my best."

As the evening came to a close, Ashlyn and Sebastian's departure left Clara and Jack alone in the quiet aftermath.

The room, with its lingering traces of incense and spent candle wax, became a canvas for her reflections. Every shadowed corner seemed to hold a piece of Anne's tale, echoing with unresolved histories and pain.

Thoughts of Lila clouded Clara's thoughts, each one layered with uncertainty and an ever-growing sense of jealousy. Lila's vague comments, her cryptic insinuations, the glint in her eyes - it all made Clara's stomach churn with unease. Unbidden, an image of Jack and Lila together, arms and legs and cream-colored skin, making Clara's heart constrict, emotions threatening to overwhelm her.

Jack, rubbing the back of his neck, hesitated before speaking, "I don't know how much stock I put into... all of this." He gestured around the room. "But I can't deny what I saw, what we all experienced."

His words hung in the air, an attempt at understanding, at seeking common ground. Clara didn't respond, her gaze distant, lost in the maze of her own emotions.

He took a tentative step toward her, reaching out to touch her cheek to bridge the gulf that had opened between them. She flinched, pulling away from his hand. The walls she'd built, the defenses against hurt and betrayal, seemed more solid than ever.

"Clara..." Jack began, the pain of rejection in his voice.

But she cut him off, her voice a barely audible whisper. "I need time, Jack."

His eyes filled with confusion and a flicker of hurt. He searched her face for answers. For a moment, his jaw clenched, hinting at a suppressed anger or perhaps frustration. "I see..." he finally murmured, his voice colder than she had ever heard.

Without another word, he turned and made his way to the door. As it closed behind him, a tear trickled down Clara's cheek as regret overwhelmed her. She berated herself for allowing insecurities to overshadow her judgment, feeling both foolish and pained by the unexpected chasm that had formed.

CHAPTER SIX

A Love Rediscovered

The room felt cold and empty as Clara threw on a t-shirt and prepared for bed. Every noise seemed louder, every shadow deeper. Her conversation with Jack pressed down, filling her with regret. She toyed with calling him, to apologize, to explain, to just hear his voice. But what would she say? Maybe it was best to let things settle.

Her mind shifted to the bar. For a moment, she felt the familiar urge to go grab a drink and drown the maelstrom of feelings. That had gone poorly last time. She took a deep breath, reminding herself of the commitment she made earlier. Today *had* to be Day One.

Instead, Clara reached for the locket she had moved to the bedside table. She traced its carvings. The cool metal pulsed under her fingers, whispering secrets and stories.

As soon as her fingers made contact, a presence surrounded her: the haunting fragrance of roses filled the air, and a breeze rustled her curtains even though the window was shut. The world outside faded away as Clara lost herself in those tales that teased her senses and drew her deeper into Anne's memories and emotions.

In the secluded corners of Anne's world, Clara recognized the same desperate need to drown out the pain of reality. It wasn't alcohol for Anne, but the touch of a forbidden lover. There was a heady intoxication of sneaking glances and stolen kisses. Each era had its own form of escape, its own salves for the wounds of the heart and soul.

Anne's way of losing herself mirrored Clara's own struggles. Both women, separated by time, sought solace in something—or someone—that promised a brief respite from the pain. Just as Clara drowned her sorrows in a drink, Anne sought refuge in Thomas's embrace. Their love, though passionate, was also a dangerous diversion from the oppressive confines of her life.

As the memories flowed, Clara felt a strange kinship with Anne. They were both prisoners of their desires, struggling to find balance and control. They were women shaped by their times, by societal judgments, and by their own inner demons. It was a haunting realization: they were not so different. Tendrils of Anne's emotions wound their way around Clara, intertwining their yearnings and regrets. Past sins and the sweetness of forbidden pleasures fused with Clara's own heartbeat until she did not know which was her own and which where Anne's. She felt the unbridled rage at the fact that Thomas left her. Or was it Ethan? Jack would leave them both, too.

As morning came, Clara woke, her mind ablaze. The locket had shared its secrets, and she felt compelled to honor them. She would keep it near, drawing inspiration from its depths, and perhaps in doing so, offer Anne's spirit solace. The weight in her hand felt like more than just metal and stone. With each pulsation of its icy surface against her skin, she couldn't help but think of Anne and the suffocating world she was tethered to. A world where she had been constrained by the rigid bars of societal expectation.

In this age, Clara mused, Anne could've thrived, embracing her desires without the shame that once haunted her. An overwhelming sense of displacement swept over Clara, as if another presence sought to claim her. In a desperate bid to regain control, she hurled the locket across the room.

Feeling herself return, Clara grabbed her phone. Ashlyn would help. "The locket," she started, "I think it's trying to possess me!."

On the other end, sighed responded with a weighty sigh. "I was worried about that. It might be safer if I held onto it."

A sudden draft caused Clara's hair to dance around her face, and she could've sworn she felt the brush of fingertips on her wrist. A gentle yet desperate plea. She caught the flicker of a shadow, and its presence felt less threatening and more... imploring. She felt Anne's sadness, her loneliness and couldn't bring herself to dismiss the woman. Not yet.

"I...I'm not so sure I can give it up," Clara hesitated, the silent plea from the entity growing stronger, desperate. It seemed to beg her to hold on to the memories it safeguarded.

"Energies this powerful can be dangerous," Ashlyn warned over the phone. "If you're sure you want to keep it, be very careful." Clara could almost feel Ashlyn's worried gaze through the line.

She held the phone a little tighter and replied, "I know, I just... there's something about it. It feels important, like it's meant to be with me." She paused, considering Ashlyn's caution. "But I hear you. I'll be extra cautious, I promise."

The call ended, leaving Clara staring across the room at the locket. She picked it up, careful not to touch it for too long, and placed it on the edge of the desk where she wrote. Despite the warmth outside, an unyielding chill pervaded the room. Each keystroke echoed back to her, creating a duet with an unseen partner. The stories flowed not from her mind, but as if whispered directly into her.

The phone's chime broke the spell, causing her to jump. It was Jack. Clara's heart rate quickened, uncertainty making her fingers tremble over the device. Should she answer? Was he angry with her?

She took a deep breath and swiped to answer. "Hey," she began.

"Clara," Jack's voice came through, maintaining a careful lightness, "how about lunch?" Despite his attempt at casualness, Clara could detect strain, a concealed tension in his words.

She hesitated, a series of thoughts flashing through her mind. The morning's events, the ghostly whispers guiding her writing, the ever-present chill in her room despite the summer outside — it all swirled around her, creating a vortex of uncertainty.

"Clara?" Jack's voice cut through, bringing her back to the present.

She took a breath, feeling the locket's presence against her skin. "Yes, alright. Lunch sounds... nice," she finally responded, though the word seemed an inadequate description of the maelstrom of emotions she felt.

As Clara prepared to leave, the locket in her hand seemed to thrum with an unspoken yearning, almost as if urging her to take it along. Hesitating for a split second, she eventually placed it in her desk drawer, feeling an odd sense of parting. Dressed in a light summer dress, she began her short walk to the cafe to meet Jack, sensing a shift in the atmosphere with each step she took.

While she didn't know many in town by name, the stares were clear. The subtle pause in conversations, the slight turn of heads, and hushed tones made her aware of her surroundings. She took a deep breath, steeling herself as she approached the cafe. Somehow, she had become the other woman.

Jack stood outside, waiting. As she approached, their eyes locked—a silent understanding passing between them. They walked inside together, choosing a corner table. The atmosphere in the cafe was alive, but for them, the world seemed paused.

There was a long silence before Clara took a deep breath. "About last night... and the other night at the bar... I feel like there are things we haven't said, things I need you to know." She swallowed hard, avoiding direct eye contact. "I'm leaving in a few weeks, Jack. But it's more than that. After the bar incident, I started questioning how you see me. I don't want to be perceived as just... reckless."

She chanced a look at him, trying to gauge his reaction. "And I just got out of a relationship. Everything's still raw. I'm guarded, scared, and still figuring things out."

Jack's face remained inscrutable, though a muscle twitched in his jaw. "Clara," he began, his voice betraying his own vulnerability, "our time together has been... unexpected. But I'm not one to jump to conclusions or box someone into stereotypes. However, I do value clarity."

He paused, running a hand through his hair. "Look, I don't know what all this is. But I know I enjoy being around you. And if we only have a few weeks? I think it's worth making the most of it. Without... complications."

Clara frowned. "It's not about complications, Jack. It's about understanding. I don't want to mislead you, but I also don't want to regret not giving this—whatever this is—a chance."

Jack looked into her eyes, and for a moment, both of them allowed their defenses to drop. "Then let's take it one day at a time," he finally said. "No promises, no expectations. Just... us."

As they sat across from each other, the air was thick with tension. Clara took a deep breath and steadied herself. "There's something else," she started, her voice steady. "Ever since we first met, I've been getting these stares... and then bumping into Lila in town, her insinuations... I need to know the truth."

Jack winced, his eyes closing as if to shield himself from an unseen blow. When he looked up again, his features were set in a resigned expression. "It's complicated," he admitted. "After I left Stowe and went off to college, I started a new life in Providence. Lila and I had broken up. But then she appeared out of nowhere, and we gave it another go. For a while, everything seemed perfect."

Clara leaned back in her chair, listening.

He pressed on. "Lila dreamed of settling down in Stowe, closer to our roots. I chose her, my love for her overshadowing everything else. We made the move back, got married. But there was some resentment. I couldn't shake off the feeling that I had sacrificed my dreams for us."

"And then?" she urged.

Jack ran his fingers through his hair. "I won't lie to you, Clara. I struggled with anger. It was never directed at her, not in the way people think, but our home was filled with tension. Arguments became our new norm."

Clara saw a deep-seated regret. "And her...?"

With a whisper, Jack confessed, "She had an affair." His shoulders slumped. "When everything blew up, she didn't correct anyone. Just let the whole town spin a tale that made her out to be the victim, implying that it was my anger that pushed her away, into someone else's arms." Clara mulled over her thoughts, her mind replaying the conversation with Lila. "So, the town's convinced that..." she began, her voice trailing off as she sought the right words.

"That I was the aggressor," Jack cut in. "They think her infidelity was justified because of me. That I was a wife beater. But Clara, I swear, I never laid a hand on her."

There was an undeniable sadness in his eyes, a rawness that spoke volumes. Clara hesitated before she said, "In small towns, rumors have a way of becoming someone's unwanted reality. It's hard to know what's true."

He met her gaze, searching for belief. "Living under the shadow of these lies, feeling like you're constantly on trial—it's like you're gasping for air."

Clara felt a shift in the conversation was overdue. "Speaking of trials, last night's events... maybe we should look more into Thomas's actions, don't you think?"

Jack's features contorted. A fleeting look that was hard to decipher crossed his face before he could compose himself again. "Would seem even ghosts struggle with rumors."

They were slowly becoming the center of attention. "Maybe we should continue this somewhere less public?" Clara suggested.

He nodded. "There's a quiet spot by the lake. Away from the gossip."

With a cautious smile, Clara replied, "Let's go."

As they left the cafe, the cool air wrapped around them. Jack led the way through the town's winding streets, greeting a few familiar faces with a nod or a wave, but never stopping to chat. Now and then, he'd glance over at Clara, as if checking she was still there beside him.

They soon reached the edge of town, where the asphalt gave way to a dirt path lined with tall pine trees on either side. "It's just a bit further," Jack said.

The trees opened up to reveal a breathtaking view. They stood atop a hill overlooking a serene lake, its surface a mirror reflecting the soft pastel hues of the setting sun. Nearby, a lone bench sat facing the water, inviting them to rest.

"This is my sanctuary," Jack said, more to himself than to Clara. "Whenever the world becomes too much, I come here to clear my head."

They took a seat, and for a while, they just sat in silence, soaking in the natural beauty around them. The gentle lapping of the water against the shore, the distant call of a bird, Jack's hand as it brushed against Clara's—all of it painted a picture of peace.

"I can see why you love it here," Clara murmured.

He turned to her, their faces inches apart. "It's even better with company."

Their eyes locked, and something passed between them. The sorrow and understanding, the hope for a new beginning, the undeniable chemistry that had been building since their first meeting. There was a silent beckoning that neither could ignore. Her world fell away as Jack's gaze dropped. Time seemed to stretch as he hesitated for a heartbeat.

Their lips with a tenderness that caught them both off guard. As they leaned into each other, the soft caress deepened, pulling them into a vortex of emotions they had been skirting around.

When they finally pulled away, their breaths mingled in the cooling evening air. Clara felt a flutter in her chest, her heart trying to match rhythm with the emotions coursing through her.

Then the realization struck her like a bolt of lightning. Their relationship was living on borrowed time. Clara hadn't come to this town with intentions of permanence. Her visit was a brief interlude, a space for healing, creativity, and perhaps a dash of excitement. She never expected forging a bond, especially one with as complicated a history as Jack's.

She tried to shake off the thought, but it clung to her, the weight pressing on her chest. "Jack," she began, looking up at him, "what are we doing?"

He frowned, sensing her sudden shift. "What do you mean?"

"This," she gestured between them, "Us. I won't be here forever. I came here to escape, to write, and... and then I met you. And it's been wonderful, but..."

Jack placed a gentle finger on her lips, silencing her. "Clara, I know," he whispered. "Believe me, I've thought about it too. But didn't we agree to take this one day at a time? Can't you just be in the now?" He paused, his eyes searching hers. "Tomorrow is uncertain for everyone. What matters is this moment, and right now, I want to be with you."

Clara met his gaze, and a pang of hurt washed over her. Her need for reassurance about their future seemed dismissed by his plea for the present.

Clara looked out at the horizon. Could she even separate the present from the past and future? It was a dance she hadn't quite mastered, even in past relationships. Could she indulge in the now, in the connection she felt with Jack, without binding her heart to the future's uncertainties? Was it even fair to Jack or herself to attempt such a balance? It all made her head spin.

She took a deep breath, the crisp air filling her lungs, and turned to Jack. "I think I should go home," she murmured. "I need some time to think, to figure things out."

Jack's brows furrowed as a shadow of disappointment passed over his face. Yet, his expression softened almost immediately. He took a step closer, bridging the distance between them. "Alright," he whispered. Then, tilting her chin up, he pressed his lips to hers. It wasn't a long kiss, but one full of promise. As he pulled away, Clara was left breathless, even more conflicted than before.

When she returned to the cabin, Clara sensed an immediate change. The air was thick with a kind of melancholy, an intangible sadness that filled the space. Soft, sorrowful sobs seemed to drift through the rooms, serving as a constant reminder of the unseen presence dwelling alongside her. Now and then, a brief glimpse of white—a ghostly figure of a woman in a flowing dress—would appear just out of sight, disappearing the moment Clara tried to focus on it.

The occasional touch of cold, ghostly fingers against her skin still made Clara shiver, but the tremors were now mixed with a budding familiarity. Shadows around her seemed to pulse with unspoken emotions. "Living with a ghost mourning its own loss is more difficult than I ever imagined," Clara murmured to herself, feeling an odd sense of connection growing within her.

As she sought to narrow the distance between her world and the spectral realm, Clara reached for Anne's locket and clasped it. She lay down, the icy touch against her chest no longer felt cold but somehow grounding. It acted as a conduit to Anne's spirit, steadying Clara as she slipped into a trance, her senses intertwining with the ghost's sorrows.

The experience was far from serene. As soon as she closed her eyes, Clara found herself immersed in a sea of memories that weren't her own. She was transported to the barn, which, contrary to its usual mysterious shadows in her dreams, was now bathed in sunlight. The light seeped through the wooden slats, casting speckled shadows on the hay-strewn floor.

In this scene, Anne and Thomas were wrapped in an intimate embrace. Clara could almost touch the passion that radiated between them. The barn was their sanctuary, a place for tender moments, their love deepening with every furtive look and touch that lingered longer than it should.

But as the dreamscape continued to shift, Clara was outside the barn, under a vast expanse of inky sky speckled with stars. Thomas, with a nervous determination in his eyes, knelt before Anne, presenting a small box. As he opened it, the glint of a delicate ring caught the moonlight, the promise it held shining brighter than any jewel. The joy in Anne's eyes, the tears glistening on her cheeks, and the embrace they shared filled Clara's heart with warmth. The dreamscape encapsulated the purity and hope of their love — a life they dreamed of building together.

But dreams and memories are often unpredictable. The radiant landscape darkened, shifting to a scene of desolation. Anne stood at the bridge, her wedding dress flowing in the night breeze. She looked at the path, anticipation clear in her eyes. A small lantern by her side cast eerie shadows, flickering and revealing her face contorted with concern, then sadness. The hours seemed to stretch, and yet Thomas was nowhere in sight.

As midnight came and went, Anne's hope dwindled, replaced by the heartbreak of a love interrupted, promises unfulfilled. Clara awoke with a jolt, feeling the remnants of Anne's emotions—the soaring joy and the crushing despair—echoing in her own heart.

Clara had seen the love in Thomas' eyes. Something was wrong. Jack's intuition to hear the other side of the tale had been right. It was imperative they unearthed the reasons for Thomas's no-show. They owed it to Anne and Thomas, and maybe, in some strange way, they owed it to themselves. Restlessness consumed her, an urge that pulsed with every heartbeat, growing louder and impossible to ignore.

She placed the locket on the coffee table, its metallic surface catching the faint moonlight streaming through the window, and scrambled off the couch. As the cool night air kissed her skin, she moved instinctively, her thoughts a blur of urgency. Without realizing what she was doing, she had grabbed a hoodie, pulling it over her head, and slipped into her shoes. Every fiber of her being pulsated with a singular focus.

Compelled by this unshakable feeling, Clara began a frenzied search through the cabin. She rummaged through drawers, flipped through pages of books, and sifted through the small pile of receipts that had accumulated in the corner of the kitchen counter. Her hands moved of their own accord, driven by desperation. Then, amidst a stack of random paper, her fingers brushed against a small, unassuming card. There, in Jack's unmistakable handwriting, was an address.

She found herself in her car, the engine purring beneath the dashboard. The emotions, tangled and confusing, pressed on her chest. She needed clarity, an anchor amidst the emotional storm. Jack was that anchor. When she arrived at his place, she mustered her courage and knocked.

The door opened to reveal Jack's concerned gaze. "Clara? What are you—"

"I just needed to see you," she whispered.

He moved aside, letting her into the house. As she stepped through the entry, Jack closed the door behind her. Without a word, she leaned in. He backed away, his hands holding her shoulders.

"Clara, wait," he said. "You were the one that needed time to think."

Her hand touched his cheek. The air between them was filled with an awkwardness, a dance of emotions they hadn't quite learned the steps to.

"I'm sorry... I'm a mess," Clara said, her voice trailing off.

Jack smiled and replied, "It's okay, Clara. We're in a complicated spot, aren't we?"

There was a brief pause as they both considered their situation. The connection they shared was undeniable, but they were navigating a maze without a map.

Clara nodded. "Yeah, we are. I just... I guess I got carried away by the moment."

Jack's expression softened. "I understand. It's easy to do."

He led Clara into the living room, their footsteps quiet on the carpeted floor. They settled into the comfort of the couch, embarking on a journey through conversation. It spanned the mystery of Thomas' fate to the lighter moments that make life sweet. Laughter came easily, blending with more serious discussions. The night wrapped them in its embrace, passaging time marked only by the changing tones of their dialogue and the softening light.

Without realizing it, Clara's eyelids had grown heavy, the gentle cadence of their conversation weaving a lullaby that eased her into a deep, dreamless sleep. She awoke to the soft light of morning. The room was bathed in stillness, save for the comforting aroma of coffee brewing in the distance. A blanket lay over her, which she pushed aside as she sat up, startled. What had happened?

Jack appeared at the doorway, a grin on his face. "Good morning, sleepyhead."

Clara blinked, confusion clear in her eyes. "I... what?"

"Don't worry," he chuckled. "You just fell asleep. Nothing happened."

Relieved that she hadn't embarrassingly overindulged, Clara accepted the coffee he offered.

"Up for a hike today?" he asked, his smile inviting.

Still disoriented, Clara simply nodded.

Before long, Clara and Jack ascended a trail leading to a vantage point overlooking Stowe.

"You come up here yet?" Jack asked, breaking the silence.

"No," Clara responded. "It's breathtaking."

"That's the thing about Stowe. Everyone knows the town, but not everyone sees its true essence," he remarked, leading her to a venerable maple tree. Then, unexpectedly, he pulled out a small sketchbook and captured her silhouette in pencil.

"You draw more than engineering stuff?" Clara asked, eyes wide.

He just gave her a wink.

She couldn't help but smile back. "You're full of surprises, Jack Thompson." In the week that followed, Clara and Jack grew closer, even though the past continued to cast a long shadow over them. One chilly evening, as a sudden draft swept through the cabin's living room, the flicker of candle flames was accompanied by a soft sob.

Jack's expression shifted to alarm as he felt an unexpected sting on his back. He turned, questioning, "Did you...?"

With wide eyes, Clara shook her head in denial. The light revealed three fresh, red scratch marks on his skin. "She's... she's letting us know she's here," Clara said.

Jack swallowed. "Maybe, for now, we should spend time together at my place. I don't think your ghost likes me very much."

Clara agreed. She had grown accustomed to Anne's presence, but the woman clearly didn't like Jack.

The following morning found them poring over a microfiche machine in the local library. Clara's fingers flew over the controls, sifting through historical records until a headline snagged her attention. "Here," she breathed out.

"Mysterious Disappearance Shocks Stowe: Local Gentleman, Missing." They leaned closer, devouring the words, only to find the story was about another man, lost decades after Anne's death.

Disappointment settled on Clara. "It's not him," she murmured.

Jack's arm found its way around her waist. "We won't give up. We'll find what we're looking for," he assured her.

Their research was interrupted by Clara's phone. "Ashlyn?" she said, puzzled, putting the call on speaker. "You are on speaker with Jack and me."

Ashlyn's voice flowed through, light and full of purpose. "Perfect timing, then. I'm glad Jack is with you. You will both want to hear this. Jack, something you said during our session the other day struck a chord with me. I often guide the living, but your insight reminded me of our responsibility to the departed, ensuring they find peace."

Jack nodded in agreement, touched by the sentiment.

Ashlyn continued, "I spoke with someone familiar with local lore and Thomas's lineage. They've uncovered family journals, amongst other things that might shed light on that fateful night."

Clara's heart leapt. "What did you find?"

"It's too much for a call. Can we meet?" Ashlyn proposed.

Clara and Jack exchanged a glance, a silent agreement passing between them. "Jack's place would be best," Clara suggested. "My rental seems to be...occupied by Anne's spirit. Particularly around the locket. I'll text you the address."

"See you then," Ashlyn confirmed

The two of them walked to the parking lot together. Jack turned to Clara, his eyes searching hers. "You could...stay the night."

Clara felt a familiar heat rise in her. The temptation was undeniable, but she also felt the pull of her writer's obligation. She placed a hand on his cheek. "I need to get some writing done, Jack. But I promise I'll see you tomorrow."

He nodded, respecting her decision. They shared a lingering gaze before parting ways. That evening, Clara settled by the window, cradling the locket in her palm. The intricate designs felt cold against her skin, a direct contrast to the fervent emotions they encapsulated. The passionate love that Anne held for Thomas mirrored her own feelings for Jack.

A chill seemed to seep into the room. The locket, responding in kind, shimmered with a muted glow. Thoughts of her imminent departure from Stowe crowded her mind. While she looked forward to returning to her apartment in Boston, the thought was bittersweet. All traces of Ethan would be gone. She'd return to an emptiness, both in the apartment and in her heart, but it would be a fresh start.

She reached for her journal and wrote, letting her emotions flow. Every experience with Jack, every stolen moment, and their intense connection poured onto the pages. Amidst her scribbles, a few lines formed a spontaneous verse:

In Stowe's dark heart, I kindled a fire,

With you, Jack, my secret desire.

Yet we might break worlds, pulling us apart.

But your shadow, forever, haunts my heart.

Despite her deep yearning, Clara knew Stowe was just a detour in her life's journey. The energy of the city awaited her, though the thought of leaving Jack behind gnawed at her soul.

The room's chilliness retreated, replaced by a comforting warmth. It felt like a protective embrace, and Clara knew it was Anne. There was a sense of gratitude in the air, a silent thank you for shining a light on a story that had been shrouded in darkness for so long.

CHAPTER SEVEN

Old Flames

Clara's morning in town was filled with errands, culminating in a visit to the coffee shop for a well-deserved treat. As she lined up to order, she felt the atmosphere shift. Two older women, deep in conversation at a nearby table, shot Clara a look that was as quick as it was guilty. Then, their voices dropped to a whisper. Despite every instinct telling her she was the subject of their hushed tones, Clara attempted to focus on the pastries in front of her.

"...you know what he did last summer?" one of them whispered.

"Should we warn her?" the other muttered, her voice laden with concern.

The incessant whispering sent Clara's heart pounding. As someone who cherished her anonymity, she was outraged to suddenly become the subject of local gossip. Trying to keep her anger in check proved futile as she ordered a muffin and a small black coffee. When she caught another glimpse of the women, she saw not just pity but condescension in their eyes before they looked away. Fury surged through her. "If you have something to say, then have the guts to say it to my face!" she snapped as she stormed out of the store, slamming the door behind her.

As Clara walked down the street, she felt the pervasive gaze of the town's judgment, yet there was a part of her that hesitated. She questioned if perhaps there was a place for her in this small town. The community's warmth, though often overshadowed with scrutiny, hinted at a genuine connection. Jack, with his earnest efforts, was chipping away at her resolve. But the thought of returning to Boston lingered in her mind. It was and always would be home.

Back at her cabin, Clara unpacked her groceries, eager to write. A knock interrupted her solitude. She flung open the door to find Lila standing there, her hair perfectly styled and an unbearable air of sophistication around her. Clara felt an immediate and intense surge of dislike. This day had gone from bad to worse.

"Hello Clara." Lila's voice was soft with condescension.

Swallowing the lump in her throat, Clara responded, "Can I help you?"

Lila extended her hand. "We met at my store, but I felt a formal introduction was in order. I'm Lila." she began, her tone layered.

As Lila's eyes flitted past Clara's shoulder, Clara couldn't help but interject, "If you're wondering, Jack's not here." Lila's lips curled into a smirk.

Outside, the faint rustling of leaves provided a soundtrack to the awkward silence that filled the room. Clara's heart raced, sensing the storm brewing between them.

"Why are you here?" Clara felt no need for niceties.

"You seem to have made quite an impression on our little town," Lila began.

Clara straightened, refusing to let Lila's presence intimidate her. "Stowe has its charm. I've found reasons to like it here."

Lila's lips twitched. "And some of those reasons have dark hair and piercing eyes, I presume?"

Choosing her words, Clara replied, "Jack and I... We've become friends."

"Friends?" Lila chuckled, her laughter devoid mirth. "It's just... Jack and I have history, Clara. Deep, long history. You might be the talk of the town now, but you'll move on, and he'll be left behind, hurt."

Clara squinted her eyes. Was this woman trying to protect him? "Jack is a grown man. We know what we're getting into. And you don't get to dictate how he feels or who he spends time with."

"You're just a passing phase, a novelty." Lila's eyes flashed. "Once the thrill fades, where will that leave you? Do you think you are the first tourist he has fallen for?"

This was getting stranger by the minute., Now it seemed like this woman was trying to protect her. Maybe Lila was just crazy.

"I'm not here for games," Inside, Clara's heart twinged. But on the surface, she held strong. "What Jack and I have might be short-lived, but it's genuine and none of your business."

For a moment, Lila looked taken aback by Clara's boldness. Then, with a sigh, Lila relented. "Just remember, everything in this town has consequences. Jack's already been through a lot."

Clara's eyes softened. "I don't want to hurt him. But I also won't be scared off by town gossip or veiled threats. I'm here for the rest of this week, and I'm going back to Boston. Until then, how Jack and I choose to spend our time is our business."

Lila studied Clara for a heartbeat longer, then nodded. "Very well. Just... be careful."

With that, Lila turned and left, leaving Clara full of confusion. As the door closed, Clara's facade of strength wavered. *I'm not here for long... Do I need this small-town drama?* Shaking her head, Clara reminded herself to focus on the present and let the future take its course.

In the quiet of her rental, Clara watched as shadows lengthened around her, mirroring her thoughts. Lila's warning echoed in her mind, stirring a tension she couldn't dismiss. Did Jack's history with tourists matter? Clara considered herself far from perfect.

Her footsteps creaked on the wooden floorboards as she walked to the small table and rested her fingers on Anne's locket. Its chill sent a shiver through her, sparking feelings of anger, an emotion Anne must have known well. The locket encapsuled Anne's feelings about trust and love, particularly towards men.

Yet Clara knew her situation with Jack differed from Anne's tale. Theirs was a fleeting connection, not a doomed romance. However, But the thought of Jack's warm touch and his soft whispers left Clara torn. She needed to process her encounter with Lila, especially with her meeting Ashlyn at Jack's coming soon.

How would Jack react to hearing about Lila's confrontation? Would he be defensive? Concerned? Or dismissive? The more she thought about it, the more conflicted she felt. Part of her sought reassurance, but another part, influenced by Anne's spirit, nudged her towards self-preservation. She felt a strong need to divorce herself from this situation. Lila clearly still had some sort of feelings for Jack. Did he return them?

As the day progressed, Clara tried to shake off her doubts. As she prepared to meet Ashlyn, she questioned whether she was ignoring the potential red flags. She touched the locket once more and wondered if she was being blindly hopeful. With a heavy heart, she left for Jack's, the unresolved feelings and Anne's locket lingering in her mind.

At Jack's place, the scent of brewing tea greeted Clara. Ashlyn was already settled in the living room, a small box cradled in her lap.

She stood in greeting, her voice soft and knowing. "I've brought something I think might help. Or at least, it's another piece to our puzzle."

Upon opening the box, Clara was greeted by the sight of a plain ring. It featured a band, devoid of any stones, reflecting Thomas's humble means. The ring's beauty lay in its minimalism, telling a story of genuine commitment beyond material wealth.

"Are you proposing?" Clara giggled. Ashlyns lips curled into a small smile.

"If I thought you would say yes…" she joked. "It belonged to Thomas' family. They have passed it down through generations. And, like your locket, this ring has its own spirit attached."

Clara shifted, "Haunted?"

Ashlyn nodded. "Haunted, but intelligently so. Unlike residual hauntings where you might witness a repeated action or hear the same sounds over and over, like a tape stuck on replay, intelligent hauntings involve spirits that are aware. They can interact, respond, even show emotions. This ring... it knows."

Clara frowned, trying to process what this meant. Another haunted artifact added yet another layer to the mystery of the day Anne died.

"Why do you think it's connected to our situation?" Jack inquired, his brow furrowed.

Ashlyn met his gaze. "From what my contacts have relayed, this was the ring Thomas gave to Anne. It was found in his belongings when he passed. The restless energy suggests it's waiting for something... or someone."

Clara reached out to touch the ring. A distinct sensation washed over her. The metal felt cool against her skin, and she could feel the stories from the past.

"We're going to use a spirit box," Ashlyn began pulling out a small electronic device from her bag. She had explained its purpose to Clara when they first met: a tool designed to scan radio frequencies, capturing fragments of sound that spirits could manipulate to communicate. Clara glanced at Jack, aware that the paranormal wasn't exactly his cup of tea. He shrugged. The living room was dim, the heavy curtains blocking out the early evening light. Ashlyn set the stage, placing candles in a circle on the coffee table and lighting them one by one. The flames flickered, casting shadows on the walls.

Clara eyed the device, her heart racing. The idea of contacting Thomas was exciting. Another side to the story. She remembered Anne's turbulent emotions during the seance. Would this be similar? If they could reach out to Thomas, perhaps they could piece together the entire story and help the spirits find peace.

"I'm ready," Clara said.

Jack's fingers drummed a steady rhythm on the armrest, his eyes flitting from the spirit box to Clara and back again. Even after all the strange events they'd encountered together, a shadow of skepticism hung over him.

Ashlyn caught the hesitation in Jack's demeanor and addressed it directly. "Jack," she began, drawing his gaze with her measured tone, "it's not about embracing every aspect of the paranormal. It's about opening a channel for

Thomas to communicate." Jack paused, then nodded. A concession to the possibility.

As the spirit box cycled through frequencies, creating a static filled with snippets of sound, Clara and Jack shared a look. Clara could feel Jack's reservations lingering. She moved closer and offered him the ring. "Maybe it'll work better if you're the one holding it," she suggested. "Thomas might find it easier to connect with you."

Once Ashlyn paused the device, Jack grasped the ring, closing his hand around it. With the spirit box restarted, a static hum punctuated the room's silence.

"Focus on Thomas," she urged. "Remember his love for Anne. Let's bridge the years and hear what he's been longing to say."

Ashlyn adjusted the scan rate, ensuring that the white noise wasn't fast nor slow. The rhythmic shuffle of radio waves filled the room — snippets of songs, fragments of conversations, and static all merged into one continuous drone.

A few minutes in, amidst the white noise, a discernible pattern emerged — faint, but unmistakable. It was as if the white noise was punctuated by soft, drawn-out whispers.

"I... loved..." The voice was distant and static-laden, but there was an unmistakable emotion behind it.

Clara's heart raced, her eyes widening as she looked at Jack, who clutched the ring.

"...Anne..." the voice continued. Every time the name was mentioned, the electromagnetic sensor on the spirit box flickered, showing heightened activity.

"Thomas?" Ashlyn asked.

The answer came, not in words, but in an emotional surge through the radio waves, as though someone was trying to convey feelings more than specific messages. But among the feelings, two words were discernible, "...Held... back..."

Jack's grip on the ring intensified, as if trying to draw more from it. "What happened, Thomas? Why didn't you come?" He asked.

Amid the static and fleeting snatches of radio broadcasts, a clearer, more poignant message formed: "...Family... Anne's... Trapped..."

The trio sat in anticipation of more, only to be met with white noise. After they were sure Thomas had nothing more to say, Ashlyn retrieved some notes. "The family refused to release the old journals and documents, yet I discovered a journal detailing Thomas's confinement in a basement on the night he planned to elope with Anne. Anne's older brother uncovered their scheme, prompting the family to intervene."

"Did they know about the child?"

Ashlyn raised an eyebrow. "Child?"

"I... felt a connection to the locket and saw something..."

With a sigh, Ashlyn replied, "There's no record of a child anywhere. It's probable that Thomas was unaware himself."

"Why didn't you mention these journals earlier?" Jack asked.

"I wanted to avoid influencing our expectations of the spirit box responses," she explained. "Sometimes, our desires can shape the messages we receive from the spirits."

Tears formed in Clara's eyes as a painful realization dawned on her. Thomas had never abandoned Anne, and she died for nothing. He had been trapped by the very people she called family. The tragic nature of their love story, tangled in misunderstandings and outside interference, struck a chord. Jack's living room walls seemed to close in on Clara. Thomas's love for Anne had been pure, yet the constraints of societal expectations and family honor had torn them apart.

She drew unsettling parallels between their ill-fated romance and the gossipy nature of Stowe. She realized that, though centuries had passed, the underlying human tendencies had changed little. Families then, like the whispering towns- folk now, felt an intense pressure to maintain a facade of respectability. The ma- licious whispers she had encountered earlier in the day seemed trivial compared to the actions of Anne's family, yet the essence was the same. Both then and now, people were quick to judge, to stifle, and to manipulate in the name of societal standing.

It made Clara wonder about the true nature of human progress. Had society evolved? Or were we all just echoes of the past, doomed to repeat the same patterns, just with different faces and stories? The thought was haunting, and Clara felt a shiver run down her spine.

Clara felt the emotions running high. Each of them seemed lost in their own thoughts. As she looked up, she noticed a subtle change in Jack's demeanor. The man who had started off this journey as a skeptic, doubting the supernatural, was now affected. There was a spark of excitement, a light of belief in his eyes that hadn't been there before.

"It's heartbreaking," Clara said, "how society can twist the course of true love. The cruel lengths Anne's family went to, just to uphold their reputation. It mirrors the gossipy vibes of Stowe, even now."

Jack nodded, brushing his fingers over the ancient ring. "Their love story deserves closure. They deserve to be together."

Ashlyn met Clara's eyes, then shifted to Jack. "This bond between Anne and Thomas is still strong. The ring and locket need to be united. And where better than the bridge? It was their chosen rendezvous point."

A realization dawned on Clara. "Tomorrow's June 13th, the anniversary of the day Anne died," she murmured.

"The night they were supposed to get married." Recognition flared in Jack's eyes, and his initial skepticism seemed like a distant memory.

"It's more than just a date. We have a unique opportunity here." Ashlyn added, "The universe has its mysterious ways, and maybe it's led us to this moment."

Clara's spirits lifted. "Tomorrow night, then. We'll reunite them at the bridge, giving them the peace and union they were denied in life."

After Ashlyn agreed and headed home for the night, Jack and Clara shared a moment of closeness. She could feel the steady beat of his heart against hers, its rhythm a comforting anchor in the surrounding tumult. He pulled her closer, and in that embrace, the chaos of the world seemed to fade away. His touch, gentle and protective, promised to keep her safe. Clara's heart, though full, carried a tinge of sadness. She cherished the warmth of Jack's body against hers, the protective circle of his arms, but knew that these moments were fleeting. They were caught at the crossroads of past and future.

"You're distant," Jack spoke in her ear. His breath against her neck sent shivers down her spine, but the weight in her heart remained.

After taking a shaky breath, Clara's voice wavered. "I leave in two days." The raw pain in her words was an unmasked wound, exposed to the world, aching with the cruelty of fleeting moments and imminent goodbyes.

Jack's fingers brushed a stray lock of hair behind her ear, his touch lingering on her skin, cool against the warm flush of her cheeks. His eyes searched her face as if trying to commit every detail to memory. "I know," he murmured, his voice tinged with the same melancholy that shaded her own. "Time has never felt so cruel."

He cupped her face, his thumbs tracing her cheekbones. "These days with you, Clara, have been more real than entire years of my life. It's like I've been sleepwalking until now."

Clara swallowed hard, the lump in her throat stubborn and painful. "But what happens when I go back to Boston? When this...whatever this is... becomes just a memory? Another story in a life full of them? Will you come see me?"

Jack's gaze didn't waver. "Memories fade, but feelings? They stay. Even if time and distance try to dilute them, some remain forever." He sighed. "I won't pretend to know the future, but I know this—what we have isn't ordinary. It's something you remember, no matter where life takes you."

Their foreheads touched, an acknowledgment of the feelings that tied them together. It was the pain of impending separation, but also the beauty of having experienced something worth cherishing.

Clara's eyes dropped to the floor, gathering her thoughts. Lila's visit, her words and implied threats, pressed down on her. Honesty, she believed, was the only way forward, especially given their time-bound relationship.

She looked up into Jack's eyes. "Jack... Lila came to see me today."

His expression changed, surprise flaring before settling into something more complex. "She did?" his voice was tense.

She nodded, swallowing. "Lila had... things to say about you two, about your past. I think she was trying to warn me off, maybe out of jealousy or perhaps genuine concern. I don't know."

His fingers tensed around her, then relaxed. "Lila and I... our history is long and complicated. It was intense, passionate, but also volatile. We loved hard, and we fought harder. But that's all in the past." He steeled himself. "I won't deny that there was love between us. But we've both changed. We grew apart. What we had is over."

Clara nodded, absorbing his words. "I figured as much. And honestly, what I felt today wasn't jealousy, but more... sadness. I'm sad because our time is limited, and it seems like shadows from the past loom larger than they should. What we have feels special. And I don't want it to be overshadowed by drama."

Jack smiled, brushing a thumb across her lips. "Then let's not let it be. We can't change the past or predict the future, but we have now. Let's cherish it."

But as they clung to each other, the shadows of Anne and Thomas's story loomed, a haunting reminder of love lost and destinies changed. Clara looked out of the window, the silhouettes of trees stark against the evening sky, their branches swaying like restless spirits.

Her thoughts drifted to Boston, a life waiting for her return, now cleared of remnants of a failed relationship. But Stowe had gifted her a story, an intense connection, and a dilemma. As the night deepened, Clara wondered if, like Anne, she too was on the precipice of a bittersweet chapter in her life.

CHAPTER EIGHT

Confronting the Past

As the mid-morning sunlight crept through the curtains, Clara awoke alone. The imprint where Jack had been lay empty. Was he already up, perhaps making breakfast? The lack of coffee smell said otherwise.

She sat up, her thoughts a tangle of confusion. As memories of the night before flooded her, she smiled, thinking of how they had made plans for him to spend the following evening at her rental. Tomorrow would mark her last night in Stowe, and after their mission of reuniting Anne and Thomas, they both wanted to spend her last night in town together, holding onto the magic just a little while longer.

She slid the soft sheets away and pivoted towards the bedside table, where her eyes caught sight of a note. It rested there, its edges crumpled—evidence of Jack's haste. With a sigh of distaste for the all-too-familiar paper messenger, her fingertips grazed the note, unfolding it to reveal the message he had left.

Clara,

I hate to leave without saying goodbye, but something came up at the NYC office. They needed me there. It's complicated, but I promise it couldn't be avoided. Know that leaving you this morning was the last thing I wanted to do.

Once we're done at the bridge tonight, let's make some time for us — I owe you a night you won't forget, before you head back to Boston.

Jack

After reading the note, Clara's anger flared as she crumpled it in her hands. The warning bells echoed in her mind. She exhaled, allowing the note to fall onto the table. His abrupt departure and the promises in the note stirred a whirlwind of feelings. Anger bubbled up to the top, yet a flicker of hope persisted. They still had tonight. Clara's ride back to her rental was silent. The streets of Stowe seemed aloof and unyielding. The corners and landmarks that had once held the thrill of discovery together felt empty without Jack. She pulled into the driveway and shut off the engine. The quiet within the car echoed her own sense of solitude.

After lingering for a moment, she retrieved her phone.

A few agonizing seconds later, "Hey Clara," came Jack's familiar voice.

"I got your note," she began, striving for a calm tone, though her emotions threatened to spill over.

"Sorry Clara," Jack's voice crackled over the phone, the ambient noise of the city filtering through. "I didn't see this coming. They needed me."

"You mentioned that." She took a sharp inhale. "Jack, today was going to be ours."

"I know, I know. It's...complicated," he replied. "Look, once I'm done here, I promise to drive straight back. Even if it means flooring it the entire way."

Clara's voice trembled. "But will you make it by midnight?"

"I'll do everything in my power to be there. You have my word."

There was a brief silence, both grasping for the right words. Finally, Jack ventured, "You know, I could visit you in Boston."

Clara felt her walls rising. "Boston isn't Stowe, Jack. We are temporary, remember? You can't just come and go on a whim."

"I just thought... maybe we could spend more time together. Explore a new city, build some memories," he countered.

Her frustration broke through, her words more clipped. "Maybe you should've thought of that before running off to NYC on the last day I had here."

"Clara," Jack's voice held a plea, "I'm trying here."

"Just be at the bridge," she snapped.

"I promise," he replied.

After slamming the phone down, Clara paused, her breaths coming fast and uneven, the storm of anger, hurt, and confusion within her threatening to overflow. Her steps toward the cabin were sharp, each one a thud against the ground as if she were trying to stomp away the feelings inside her.

Upon entering, the quiet did not match the chaos in her heart. It was almost as if it were taunting her. Fueled by frustration and the need to do something—anything—she packed with a ferocity that had her clothes being thrown rather than placed into the suitcase. Each garment she handled was a trigger, unleashing flashes of memories with Jack—moments that twisted in her gut, turning sweet recollections bitter.

Something drew her eyes to the journal on the desk. It held so many memories, so many emotions, and she felt the need to pour her feelings into words. Taking a seat, she opened the book, the blank page before her, ready to accept her thoughts.

Two days ago, Jack and I shared an ice cream by the lake. The way the sunlight hit his face, the glint in his eyes as he tried to smear it on my nose... I felt seen, really seen, perhaps for the first time in years.

It's so different from how things were with Ethan. With Ethan, it was like dating a lost boy in a rockstar's body. His dreams, ambitions, and his constant need for attention overshadowed each moment with him. Every date, instead of being a moment between us, felt like another stage for him to perform, another crowd to win over. I often felt more like his manager or caretaker than his girlfriend, constantly picking up after his messes and making sure he was okay.

Yet, there was always a thrill with him. The high of being on his arm as we entered venues, the electric atmosphere of his shows, the late-night jam sessions and impromptu duets. The rush of living on the edge, never knowing what tomorrow might bring. With Ethan, life was a roller coaster—highs and lows. It was intoxicating, the way he'd pull me into his world, where passion and music blended, and every moment felt like a stolen scene.

Deep in her memories, the jarring ringtone shattered her thoughts, pulling her back into the present. Clara's heart fluttered, half-expecting Jack's voice, but the name on the screen froze her momentarily — Ethan. It was if her thoughts had summoned him.

She hesitated before answering. "Hello?"

"Clara? It's me."

His voice sounded disconnected. "Ethan... What do you want?"

"Just wanted to hear your voice," he began with a suggestive lilt. "You know, reminisce a little? Maybe see if you're up for hanging out?"

Clara's brow furrowed. "Isn't that a conversation you should have with your new girlfriend?"

He chuckled, a sound that once held charm, but now grated on her nerves. "She's not you. You know we always had that... spark."

As Ethan's voice droned on, a tidal wave of memories crashed over Clara. The panic when he overdosed, the dread-laden rush to the hospital, opposing against the electrifying sex they shared in the dim glow of their shared bedroom. Each moment, whether painful or intimate, played in her mind like an old film reel.

Clara realized that beneath the trials, there just wasn't an actual connection. Their relationship was an endless cycle of extremes, lacking the stability and depth that actual love brought.

"That 'spark' was just chaos," she told him, her voice cutting through the memories. "We mistook passion for intimacy. And I can't — won't — go back to that chaos."

There was a pause, and for a moment she thought he might argue. But he just sighed. "Had to try, right?"

Clara rolled her eyes. "Goodbye, Ethan."

After ending the call, Clara's pen hovered over her journal once more. This time, the thoughts flowed.

Today I'm hit with this realization—I've always had a thing for the love stories that are a bit... forbidden? Exciting? Definitely more 'ride or die' than 'happily ever after.' It's like how Anne fell hard for Thomas. Their thing was intense, all-consuming, but man, did it crash and burn. And Ethan? His wild unpredictability? Electrifying. But talk about a storm leaving behind its share of chaos. At the time, I was all in, not seeing the damage being done. Now? It's like I'm finding emotional bruises I never knew I had. The more she thought of Anne, the more she felt a kinship. *Anne's passion led her to make a final, irreversible choice in the face of despair. While my story with Ethan didn't have the same consequences, it taught me about decisions and the price of letting passion blind reason.*

And then there's Jack. Is it a story destined to repeat the same mistakes or an opportunity for an alternative path? Clara questioned, feeling histories intertwining with her present.

She sat back, her eyes lingering on the scribbles in her journal. The intertwining stories of Anne and her own life seemed to play out in parallel universes. Her pen was still poised above the paper as she continued to reflect on her own journey with Jack and Ethan.

Then it dawned on her. She remembered overhearing a snippet of conversation in town. Maybe Lila would have the insights she was missing. It felt like a light bulb moment—she realized she should speak with someone who had a relationship with him. Fueled by this thought, she shut her journal and grabbed her keys.

Clara parked outside Lila's shop, taking a moment to gather her courage before stepping out of the car. As she entered, the bell above the door announced her arrival. She found herself surrounded by the timeless elegance of antique dresses, lace gloves, and hats from yesteryears. Lila looked up. Her expression shifted to one of mild surprise upon seeing Clara.

"To what do I owe this unexpected visit?"

Clara hesitated for a moment. "I needed to talk, and I realized there's a lot I don't know. About you, Jack, this town... everything."

Lila's gaze softened, her posture relaxing. "Alright. Sit," she gestured towards a plush couch. "Would you like some tea?"

Clara nodded. As Lila prepared a pot of Earl Grey, Clara took a moment to collect her thoughts. The store, with its charm, felt like a portal to another era, a world where Anne and Thomas might have roamed.

When Lila returned, she poured the steaming liquid into dainty cups. "Speak your mind," she urged.

Taking a sip, Clara began. "I came to Stowe looking for an escape, a story, something... and I found all of that. But I also found Jack. And with him, an entire history, a past, and, honestly, a lot of confusion."

"Jack has that effect," Lila chuckled. "He's a good man, but life hasn't always been kind to him."

Clara paused, gathering her courage. "I'm not blind. I have seen the people in town talking... heard the things that were said."

Lila raised an eyebrow.

"Jack. Us. The stories that keep getting repeated. You're a part of his story, Lila, and I think understanding that could help me navigate mine."

For a moment, there was a heavy silence. "I shouldn't have gone to your place," Lila sighed. "Why dredge up old wounds?"

"But you did, and I see patterns," Clara responded, her voice soft but firm. "And maybe, just maybe, understanding them might prevent history from repeating itself."

Lila hesitated, then gestured towards a seating area, "Alright, but I won't promise you'll like what you hear."

As they took their seats, Clara's hands clasped together, betraying her nervousness. "Why did you hurt him?" she ventured.

Lila's eyes flashed. "Life... love... it's complicated. We were young, impulsive. I made mistakes. Big ones. But Jack wasn't perfect either."

"Everyone has their demons," Clara pressed, searching Lila's face for answers.

"He does," Lila admitted. "Jack used to drink. A lot. It clouded his judgment, made him angry. But it's been years since then. People change, grow. I had my role in our downfall."

Clara pondered on this. "So, why the rumors about him being abusive?"

Lila flinched, guilt clear in her eyes. "I was angry, hurt. I lashed out with words, let people believe things... things that weren't true. But by the time I realized the impact of those rumors, it was too late."

Clara's eyes widened, the implications clear. "So, he never..."

Lila looked away. "He has his flaws, anger among them. But he never raised a hand to me."

The moment hung between them. Clara nodded, grateful for the glimpse of truth, however veiled it was.

Clara hesitated for a moment, feeling vulnerable. "He left for a meeting in NYC," she shared. "Just when I thought we were connecting on a deeper level."

Lila gave a nod, her features softened by a rueful smile. "Jack and his commitment to work. It's always been his shield. When emotions threaten his logic, he often takes the easy way out. Runs, deflects, hides behind responsibilities."

Clara blinked away the sting of tears. "I thought... I thought maybe we could have something more."

Lila sighed. "He likes you, Clara. Quite a bit, I'd bet. But with Jack, sometimes that's a double-edged sword. Caring too much can make him push you away even harder."

Clara managed a weak smile. "I'm leaving tomorrow, anyway."

Lila seemed to take a moment to process this. When she spoke, there was a sense of relief in her voice, mixed with genuine concern. "Probably for the best. For both of you."

Clara nodded, absorbing the bittersweet reality of the moment. "Thanks, Lila."

After their conversation, the women exchanged a meaningful glance—a quiet recognition of the emotions and history they shared. As Clara stepped outside, her walk carried a feeling of closure she hadn't known she was seeking.

When she arrived back at the cabin, she settled down for the evening. Tonight presented a chance to revel in the memories of her time with Jack, to immerse herself in the sweetness of their connection. Yet Clara's pragmatic side whispered reminders of the inevitable march of time. With tomorrow's sunrise, she would press on, leaving behind the charming town and the shadows of a love story that was not to be hers to keep.

She grabbed her bag and moved to the writing nook by the window. Opening her laptop, she dove deep into the world of her novel, a world where Anne and Thomas lived, loved, and suffered. As she immersed herself in their story, it provided an escape from her own confusing reality.

Hours seemed to melt away as she poured her emotions, insights, and new-found clarity into the manuscript. The pain from Ethan, the moments shared with Jack, and the wisdom from her conversation with Lila all found their way into the intricacies of Anne and Thomas's tale.

But as the clock ticked on, the shadows growing longer, she hesitated, leaving the final chapter unwritten. That chapter, she decided, would be penned after re-uniting the spirits together, once she was back in Boston, drawing from whatever closure the night might offer her.

As she penned her thoughts, Clara was conscious of the time ticking away. The night promised more than just the hours ahead. It held the anticipation of Jack's return and their shared goal to bring the estranged lovers back together. Midnight was drawing near. With it, not only would Anne and Thomas's love story find its resolution, but so might Clara's own story with Jack.

Before leaving for the bridge, she picked up the locket from the bedside table. The once cold and inanimate object now held warmth and a story — one of love, betrayal, and longing.

As she clutched the locket, an unexpected chill raced down her spine. A fleeting feeling, as if Anne's spirit stood right next to her, urging her on, filled the room. Clara whispered, "We'll find closure tonight, Anne. For both of us."

Drawn by an inexplicable urge, she headed outside. The night sky stretched above her, speckled with countless stars, each one shimmering with its own story, its own secrets. She took a deep, steadying breath, taking in the crisp evening air. In this vast cosmic ballet, where did her own tale fit?

Clara picked out the brightest star, closed her eyes, and breathed out her wish, "I hope for clear skies in this storm of feelings, for the guts to make the choices that need making, and for everything to come together — for Anne, for Thomas, and... for me too."

With her fingers wrapped around the locket, Clara headed toward Willows Bridge.

CHAPTER NINE

A Bridge Between Worlds

Clara approached Willows Bridge, her heart pounding against her ribs. Each beat echoed the fleeting minutes before midnight. The headlights from Ashlyn's car illuminated the gnarled trees lining the road, their twisted limbs casting eerie shadows that tricked her eyes. A full moon hovered low, its shimmering reflections dancing on the water below, yet there was no sign of Jack. The bridge itself rose against the night, its wooden planks slick with dew. Clara could hear the river's gentle murmurs beneath her, its ripples gently kissing the shore. She felt that if she listened close enough, the night might whisper back.

She took a moment to soak it all in before approaching Ashlyn's car. It was haunting and beautiful, a scene straight out of a gothic novel. She could feel the history all around her. Excitement bubbled within her, but so did fear. Was she meddling in matters beyond her understanding? And then there was the gnawing void—still no Jack.

Clara knocked on the window of Ashlyn's car, her arms wrapped around herself to harness her emotions. She felt vulnerable, as if standing on the cusp of a pivotal chapter in her life—a chapter that risked remaining unwritten. The engine stopped and Ashlyn and stepped out.

She had an almost ethereal quality. Dark hair cascading down, and the fabric of her skirt that caught the light with every gentle sway. The air around them felt alive, vibrating with an energy that was mesmerizing.

When Ashlyn's eyes met Clara's, it was as if they held centuries of wisdom, sorrow, and patience. "I'm glad you're here. Jack?"

"Not yet," Clara swallowed. "I brought the locket. Do you have the ring?"

"Yes," Ashlyn nodded. "You ready?"

Clara's heart raced. "We need to wait for Jack," she asserted.

"We have little time," Ashlyn replied. "It's almost midnight. That is when they were supposed to meet."

"I'm aware," Clara snapped, then softened her voice. "I'm sorry. It's just this is as much Jack's journey as it is ours. He deserves to be here."

There was a beat of silence, the night seeming to hold its breath. Ashlyn answered, "Five minutes. I'll start preparing. Can I have the locket?"

Clara nodded, revealing the intricate piece, its engravings catching the moonlight. "Right here."

"Good." Ashlyn's expression shifted to one of deep concentration. "We'll be working with their energies, amplifying the connection between them. The locket and the ring. They serve as anchors, tethering the spirits of Anne and Thomas to this world. When we unite them, the bond becomes stronger."

As Clara listened, she realized the process was a delicate dance of energy. "How will we... facilitate their reunion?" she asked.

"We'll channel the energy of both artifacts, create a vortex of sorts." Ashlyn replied. "I will lead us in a series of incantations, drawing them closer. Your role is important. You must focus on their love story, envision their union, and urge them to find each other. You will hold the locket, and Jack will hold the ring."

A shiver ran down Clara's spine. She was ready. However, Jack, being late, was a persistent wound. They sat in silence, waiting.

"The window of opportunity is narrowing," Ashlyn warned.

Clara pulled out her phone and dialed Jack's number, the ringing tone echoing her growing impatience. After several rings, his voicemail chimed in. She hesitated for a split second, and then blurted out with a mix of annoyance and sarcasm, "Looks like 'communication' isn't exactly your forte, Jack. I thought our time together merited at least a callback. Or a text. Or even a carrier pigeon, if that's more your speed." After hanging up, she typed a text to accompany her voicemail, trying to keep it light yet pointed. "In case you missed my call–and I'm sure you did–just checking in- C"

She set her phone down and tried to distract herself from the gnawing sensation in her gut. She knew she had planned to move on, but she yearned for closure. A proper goodbye, even if it was over a simple call.

Ashlyn was right. With or without Jack, they had to act. "Let's begin," Clara said, determination seeping into her voice.

The stage was set. Under the vast night sky, two women readied themselves to bridge the divide between two lost souls, hopeful for a reunion that had been centuries in the making.

Willows Bridge became the backdrop to a world where reality and the supernatural danced on the knife-edge of midnight. A chill in the air intensified. The clear night gave way to an eerie mist, wrapping around the bridge like a ghostly shroud.

Ashlyn began, her voice a soft, lilting chant that seemed to meld with the murmurs of the water below and the rustling of the trees. In her hand, a ring sparkled, responding to her cadence, its glow merging with the ambient light that framed her.

Beside her, Clara clutched the locket close to her heart, urging Anne and Thomas towards reconciliation. The memories she had gathered, the stories she had heard, all flooded her mind, shining a hopeful light through the enveloping fog.

As Ashlyn's incantations grew in intensity, the atmosphere rippled. Two ghostly forms coalesced within the mist, their outlines shimmering and uncertain, but present. The translucent figure of Anne looked as if waiting for someone. A few paces away, the specter of Thomas formed, his posture reflecting a life of regret and an eternity of searching.

The air thrummed as Ashlyn's voice reached a crescendo, her words clear and powerful, willing the two spirits closer. Tears streamed down Clara's face as she whispered words of encouragement, guiding the lost lovers towards one another.

The distance between Anne and Thomas shrunk, their forms becoming clearer and more tangible with every passing second. They seemed to recognize each other, their movements hesitant yet filled with hope.

With midnight nearing, the bridge and its surroundings held a collective breath as if expecting a centuries-long awaited reunion.

In the dense mist, Anne and Thomas stood just a few feet apart. Though no words were exchanged, their emotions vibrated through the air — potent and raw.

Anne's form rippled with waves of anger and sadness. Her eyes bore into Thomas with a mix of accusation and pain. The anguish in her form was real, reminding Clara of the countless love stories cut short by societal constraints and misunderstandings. The heavy locket against Clara's chest echoed Anne's heartache. Clara felt her own anger. Ethan's infidelity, Jack's absence. But she had to shove those down deep. Thomas was here and now for Anne, and they could make things right.

Thomas's spirit emanated regret. He extended a hand, shimmering with regret, toward Anne, who initially recoiled.

Their story unfolded in the mist like a move, weaving itself into vivid scenes. These vignettes, strikingly clear, depicted the lovers' encounters — moments brimming with the exhilaration of newfound love, yet overshadowed by the strictures of their time. The laughter and tender touches shared in secret, and the looming shadows of societal condemnation and personal trials that followed. Moments of joy and intimacy — stolen glances at social gatherings, secret meetings under the cover of night, and handwritten letters exchanged in secrecy. But as their love story progressed, the scenes grew darker. Angry confrontations, not with each other, but with families who disapproved, with a society that forbade their union, with a world that couldn't understand the depth of their connection.

Anne's spirit showed her isolation, confined to her room, letters from Thomas being taken away, her pleas going unheard. The society had built walls around her, walls that even her love for Thomas couldn't penetrate.

Thomas's form portrayed his desperation. Efforts to convince her family. The devastating realization that these shackles were too strong to break.

For a moment, the two spirits were once again on the bridge, facing one another. Anne's anger subsided, replaced with an overwhelming sadness. Thomas once again reached out to her. This time, she moved closer, their forms merging, becoming a dance of light and shadow, love and loss.

Their emotions swirled around them, creating past regrets and unspoken words, but in that storm was an undeniable love, a bond that even death and time couldn't sever.

The mist continued to swirl, weaving another memory. Anne, in the solitude of her room, with her hands cradling her swollen belly. She was with child. Her heart, however, was heavy with the secret she carried.

Next, a stolen moment between Anne and Thomas appeared. Under the shelter of an ancient oak tree, they whispered sweet nothings, planning an elopement to escape the constraints of their time. Their love was filled with desperation.

But as the scene shifted, and their reality took its toll. Anne, isolated, her pregnancy becoming more apparent, faced the mounting pressure and judgment of a world that showed no mercy. There was no solace, as Thomas remained unaware of the child they had conceived together.

The next memory was of a lonely Anne in her wedding dress, standing at the edge of the very bridge they were now on, her figure silhouetted by the moon. The secret, and the isolation, proved too much.

As the spirits of Anne and Thomas lingered, their gazes met. In that connection, Thomas realized the child was his, and a profound sadness enveloped him. He hadn't just lost Anne; he had lost a future, a family he never knew existed.

Clara and Ashlyn, witnessing this heart-wrenching revelation, felt the depth of their tragedy and the bittersweetness of their love.

From the enshrouded mists, another scene unfolded. Thomas, held captive in the basement of Anne's family estate. The room was dank, cold, and unwelcoming. The chains around his wrists were as much a symbol of the chains that bound him to his place in the world as they were of the physical restraint imposed upon him.

Through the narrow window, the soft glow of the moon was the only light he could see, reminding him of their countless rendezvous under its gentle gaze. But that night, the moon was a cruel reminder of their missed meeting on the bridge.

Days turned into weeks. The walls of his confinement seemed to close in on him. The only thing that kept him going was the hope of seeing Anne again, of holding her close, of escaping together. But as the days went on, the reality of her absence became all too apparent. Whispers reached his ears, painting a tragic image of Anne's last moments.

Released by their own guilt, Anne's family let Thomas go, but it was too late. The world outside was no longer the same. Everywhere he went, shadows of his lost love followed him, every whisper of the wind sounding like Anne's voice, every shimmer of the moonlit water reminding him of that fateful night.

His heart, once full of love and hope, was now laden with guilt and sorrow. He wandered, searching for solace but finding none. His health deteriorated, and the sparkle in his eyes dimmed. It was clear to all who knew him: Thomas was dying of a broken heart.

In the last scene that the mist presented, Thomas was seen on the very bridge where he and Anne were to meet. He looked out at the horizon, perhaps searching for a sign of his love, a hope that had long evaded him. And as the first light of dawn broke, he took one last breath, his heart giving out, hoping to reunite with his love in the realm of spirits.

But it was not to be. In her anger, Anne could not see him there waiting all those years, right by her side. A transformation occurred within Anne's spirit. The realization that Thomas, too, had suffered, that he had remained tethered to her side through the veils of time and sorrow, dissolved her anger. His unwavering presence, invisible to her eyes but now undeniable, bridged the chasm of misunderstanding that had kept them apart.

In a moment of forgiveness, the specters of Anne and Thomas closed the gap. As they touched, a luminous energy enveloped them, and their forms merged. The surrounding light grew, pulsating with the power of their united spirits.

Clara and Ashlyn watched as Anne and Thomas, now a radiant entity braided together with a third strand, ascended toward a brighter realm. Their love, tested by time and tragedy, had not only endured, but had become the key to their transcendence.

In this ultimate act of union and forgiveness, they left behind the chains of earthly sorrow, moving into a place where love knows no bounds. Clara stood still, her emotions a mess. Willows bridge, though silent now, had seen countless stories unfold. It had borne witness to promises made and hearts broken. Tonight, it had seen two souls unite, but also witnessed Clara's heartbreak.

She stared into the distance, searching for a familiar silhouette, longing for Jack's presence. But all she saw was an empty path illuminated by the moon. Every tick of the clock was a sharp reminder of Jack's absence. His promise, their plans, the future they might have had - they all felt like distant memories now.

With a heavy sigh, Clara reflected on Anne and Thomas. Though separated by tragedy and time, had found their way back to each other. Their love story had crossed the barriers of life and death. But hers was a different story. One where love was a fleeting moment, a beautiful dream that disappeared with the morning light.

"I wanted to believe in us, Jack," she whispered, her voice almost lost in the wind.

She approached Ashlyn, who was still absorbing the surrounding energies. "Thank you," Clara began. "For everything. And, as always, send me the bill for our consult."

Ashlyn looked up, her sharp eyes softening. "Clara, I did this for Anne, not as a business transaction."

Clara smiled. "You can't always work for free. And besides," she glanced back at the bridge, the last traces of Anne and Thomas's spirits fading, "you have a unique gift. Perhaps you should consider a new venture—reuniting lost souls."

Ashlyn chuckled, the mood lightening a bit. "That has a nice ring to it, doesn't it?"

They both stood there for a moment, letting the night sink in. Ashlyn, sensing Clara's sadness, placed a comforting hand on her shoulder. "Every love story is different, Clara. Remember, sometimes the journey itself holds more beauty than the destination."

Clara nodded. "I know, and even if Jack isn't part of my final chapter, I'm grateful for the pages he filled."

With a final shared glance, the two women parted ways. Clara, while heartbroken, pushed forward.

The fire Jack had ignited within her—passion and a longing to love and be loved—would continue to guide her toward whatever adventures lay ahead.

She couldn't sleep that night, the silence in the house too pronounced. Accustomed to sharing the space with Anne's spirit, its absence was felt. Instead, she found solace in writing in her journal, capturing her thoughts until the first light of dawn graced the sky.

As sunlight brushed the horizon with hues of gold and pink, Clara finished packing her belongings, each item stirring memories of her time spent in Stowe. The aroma of her morning coffee blended with the musty scent of old wood, evoking a surge of unexpected emotions. The rented cabin had been a place of solace, creativity, and surprisingly love.

After closing her suitcase, she paused, eyes sweeping over the rental one last time. With her car packed, she drove toward the bridge. She took a moment to park and stepped out to a scene wrapped in magic. The gentle shimmer of the water below mirrored the dawn sky. She could almost imagine Thomas and Anne looking down at her.

Memories of Jack—of their first awkward meeting and the connection that blossomed—flooded her thoughts. It was ironic how this bridge, marking the beginning of their journey, now framed its end. With a bittersweet smile, Clara whispered into the breeze, hoping her words would find Jack, "Thank you for being a chapter in my story." Then she returned to her car, ready to follow the day and embrace the unknown.

The car's steady hum was her sole companion. The road ahead beckoned her towards Boston and the uncharted beyond, each mile a step from who she had been to who she was becoming.

She switched on the radio and a melody filled the air, capturing the moment—a song of heartbreak and starting over. Everything happens for a reason. It seemed the universe itself was affirming her belief in new beginnings.

A smile crept across Clara's face, her eyes glistening with tears not of sadness, but of recognition. Changed, evolved, and enriched by her experiences and the taste of fleeting love, she drove on. The promise of tomorrow called, and she was eager to answer.

CHAPTER TEN

Second Chances

Clara approached Boston, watching as the city's skyline cut a familiar silhouette against the sky. It was a change from Stowe's quiet nature. Gone were the soothing whispers of wind through the trees, now replaced by the urban symphony of honking cars and loud pedestrians. Starlit nights gave way to ever-lit evenings, constant city lights harsh compared to the peaceful skies she had grown accustomed to. Yet, for all its hustle and noise, Boston was home.

She navigated through the streets, readjusting to the angry drivers and finding her parking spot that cost almost as much as her rent. A piece of her heart had stayed in Vermont, with its quiet nights and the stories that seemed to flow like the river under that old bridge—especially those involving Jack. When she approached her building. A wave of nostalgia hit her. She made her way to her apartment, the keys heavier than she remembered. With a click, she unlocked the door and stepped into a realm of memories. The air smelled of the past — a mix of her favorite vanilla candles, the slight musk of old books, and the ghost of Ethan's aftershave.

This space, once brimming with shared dreams, now seemed too vast, its empty corners amplifying the quiet of her solitude. Yet, as she returned her belongings to their familiar spots, a sense of empowerment emerged.

The buzz of her phone snapped her out of her reverie. An incoming text displayed his name—her heart raced, but not with excitement, rather a pang of anxiety. The message read, "Saw you were home. Can we *talk*? I miss you."

Clara stared at the screen, memories of their last intense "talks", the undertones that overshadowed actual communication, and that they were on different paths, all resurfacing. A previous version of herself might've been lured into replying, but this was a new Clara. She had communed with spirits, unearthed age-old tales of love, and discovered the depths of her inner strength and tenacity.

Who needs Ethan or even Jack? The lightness of the thought was grounding, reminding her of her independence and the joys of self-reliance. Life was too short to be tied to anyone's games or whims, and Clara was ready to embrace every facet of her newfound freedom.

She swiped the notification away, choosing to leave the message unanswered. This was her story now, and she was determined to write it on her own terms.

Unfortunately, her determination wasn't as infallible as she had hoped. In the days that followed, navigating her apartment felt like she was the lead in a tragicomedy tailored to her life. Every corner, every shadow, seemed to dance with memories of Ethan. From the mismatched socks he left behind like a trail to those post-it notes scribbled with what appeared to be an alien script, decipherable to no one but him. She found herself on the verge of calling him more times than she cared to admit.

But the pièce de résistance was a bottle of tequila. Not just any tequila, but the one they'd used for 'make-up margaritas' after their many spats. It was their silly tradition: arguing, then reconciling over salt-rimmed glasses and regrettable decisions.

With the bottle in her hand, Clara entertained the idea of a solo margarita night. After all, tequila had a magical way of blurring reality, right? But then, a smirk forming on her lips, she had a better idea. Marching to the sink, she unscrewed the cap and poured it out.

"So long, liquid bad decisions," she chuckled, watching as the amber liquid swirled down the drain. This act wasn't about discarding memories, but asserting control. Her heart might still be on the mend, but Clara was calling the shots now. Well, not those kinds of shots, anyway.

The next day Clara sat down at her writing desk, pushing aside the remnants of her old life. The familiar feel of her keyboard beneath her fingers acted as an anchor, grounding her to her passion. As she pulled up her manuscript, images of the bridge, of Anne's form, and Thomas's lingering presence, filled her mind, as vivid as if she'd just experienced them.

Each word she typed was tinged with the past - the love she'd witnessed, the heartbreak, and the resolution she had helped bring about. There were moments of hesitation where she'd lean back and rub her temples, trying to find the right words. There were tears as memories, both beautiful and painful, made their way onto the pages. But there was also a profound sense of catharsis. Every sentence, every paragraph brought her closer to closure, not just for Anne and Thomas, but for herself as well.

Once the final chapter was complete, a sense of accomplishment washed over her. But one piece remained: the title. She wanted something that encapsulated the heart of the story, the love, the loss, and the undeniable power of Willows Bridge. After a few moments of contemplation, the perfect title came to her: "Bridging the Heart."

With a deep breath, Clara packaged the manuscript and sent it off to her publisher. The emotions she felt were dizzying - excitement at sharing her story with the world, apprehension about its reception, but above all, hope. Hope that her tale of enduring love would resonate with readers everywhere.

A few days later, there was an unexpected knock on Clara's door. She sighed, knowing that distinctive rhythm. Ethan always had a way of announcing his presence, even before she saw his face. After taking a moment to compose herself, Clara approached the door, rehearsing her boundaries.

"Ethan, I'm not letting you in," she called out, her hand on the door but not opening it.

"Clara, come on. We need to talk," came the pleading voice from the other side.

She closed her eyes, drawing in a deep breath. "We've talked enough, Ethan. It's over."

Silence reigned for a moment, broken only by a defeated sigh from the other side. Clara leaned her forehead against the door for a moment, willing herself not to open it.

She was just settling back with a book when another knock echoed in her apartment. Her irritation spiked. "Seriously, Ethan? I told you—" This time she flung open the door, ready to confront him, but stopped mid-sentence. It wasn't Ethan standing there.

The hallway seemed to stretch on forever between them. Clara, with a face etched in disbelief, eyed Jack. Her guard was up, emotions teetering between surprise and skepticism.

Jack looked worn. His eyes were a shade darker, maybe from sleepless nights or perhaps from regrets. He hesitated, then stepped forward, stopping when he sensed her need for distance. "Can we... talk?"

She eyed him for a moment longer before nodding and stepping aside. The door opened wider, but the emotional barrier remained. Once inside, Jack paused. The walls of the apartment bearing witness to another fragile moment between two souls.

"I know I owe you an explanation," he began, his voice hoarse. "And I'm hoping you'll hear me out."

She nodded again, folding her arms. "Start talking."

Jack rubbed the back of his neck, a gesture Clara recognized as his tell when he was nervous. "I should've been upfront with you. The trip to NYC? It wasn't for work. I was in Boston."

Her brow furrowed. "Boston? Why?"

He hesitated, the raw vulnerability clear in his gaze. "For us. Or at least the possibility of us. You see, I had an interview. I wanted to be closer, to see if... if there was a chance for something between us. But I didn't want to tell you right away. I didn't want you to feel trapped or obligated."

Clara's eyes flashed. "Why didn't you show up at the bridge, Jack? Why didn't you answer your phone?"

Jack looked down, struggling to find the right words. "I wanted to. God, Clara, more than you'll ever know."

She blinked, trying to process the revelation. "Then why didn't you?"

His eyes looked haunted when he locked them with her. "You know, everything changed on my way back from that interview, just a few miles outside of Boston. All it took was a moment. A truck swerved into my lane, and suddenly… I was caught in this pitch-black world. All I could hear was metal twisting and glass breaking." She looked more closely at him. He *did* look like he had been hit by a truck.

"Why didn't you reach out when you could? You have my number. It's been over a month!"

"I was in an induced coma for a week." His voice wavered. "When I woke up, I felt lost. I thought I'd ruined everything with you. That I'd lost any chance of being a part of your life."

He took a shaky breath, and continued, "When the job offer from Boston came in, it felt like the universe was offering me a way back. A sign that maybe, just maybe, I could make things right. Even if it meant laying my heart bare and risking rejection. I looked up your address and here I am."

She stared at him, and her heart raced, conflicting emotions waging a war within. She felt betrayed, the raw pain of the nights she spent wondering why he'd abandoned her at the bridge still fresh. But hearing about the accident, seeing the remorse in Jack's eyes, and the physical scars that marred his skin evoked a deep sympathy. And intertwined with all these feelings was that undeniable thread of hope that had always connected them.

Jack stepped forward. "Clara," he began, his voice thick with emotion, "I'm not here to offer excuses. I made decisions, and they had consequences. All I can offer you now is the truth. The truth about the accident, about the job, about how much I missed you, and how much I regretted not being able to tell you everything sooner."

She watched him, taking a moment to absorb his words, letting them sink in. The memories of their time together, the laughs, the shared moments, the chemistry, all came flooding back. But she also remembered the nights of doubt, the uncertainty that had clouded their relationship.

Jack's eyes lit up with hope, but he tempered it with caution, "Clara, things are going to be different. We can take it slow, get to know each other again. No pressures, no expectations." He paused. "No strings attached. I'll do anything you need."

She smirked, that playful glint in her eyes returning. "There is one thing you can do right now," she said. With that, she walked towards her kitchen, rummaged through a drawer, and returned holding a pair of bright pink rubber gloves.

"Time for you to become the dishwashing superhero you were always meant to be. First task: conquer Mount Dirty-dishes!" Her attempt at a stern look dissolved into giggles.

Jack blinked, taken aback for a split second, but then his own grin matched hers in mischief. "Well, let me see if I can be of any help."

"Where are you staying at?" Clara asked.

Elbow-deep in suds, Jack shot her a glance. "I'm in corporate housing while I hunt for a place. It's a bit like living in a fancy hotel, minus the room service. How's that for glamour?"

Clara handed him another dish, a smirk playing on her lips. "Oh, the luxury! So, you're basically on a prolonged vacation with chores?"

"Exactly," Jack chuckled, splashing water her way. "But without the beach and the Piña coladas. I'm living the dream, one lease application at a time."

"Sounds delightful," Clara laughed, dodging the water. "Need a local guide to navigate the treacherous waters of Boston real estate?"

"I might take you up on that," he said, placing a clean plate on the rack. "But only if you promise not to make me wear these pink gloves outside of dish duty."

"No promises," she quipped, and they both burst into laughter, the tension and distance of the past melting away.

"On a serious note," he began, his tone shifting, "can I take you out? A proper date? Just you and me, rediscover each other."

Clara nodded with a smile. "I'd like that."

Jack leaned over, placing a gentle kiss on her forehead. He sat up, making moves to get dressed. "I should head home, give you some space."

But as he headed to the door, Clara reached out, her fingers wrapping around his wrist. "Stay for a bit," she said.

Jack's eyes softened, transporting them back to Willows Bridge. The worn-out wood, the creaking sounds in the wind, the memories it cradled. It was a bridge that had witnessed countless sunrises and sunsets, alongside many stories of love and loss.

"Remember that day when we first bumped into each other?" Jack said. "The sunshine, the cool breeze... and us, caught up in the middle of it all. I knew then that I had stumbled into something extraordinary."

Clara nodded, a single tear rolling down her cheek, yet her smile remained firm. "I do. Willows Bridge... Annes Bridge..."

She leaned into him, closing her eyes. "Love is a lot like that bridge. It endures wear and tear, faces the harsh elements, but it stands strong, connecting one side to the other."

He wrapped his arms around her, their heartbeats synchronizing. "So, what do we do now?" Jack asked.

Looking up at him, Clara's eyes were hopeful. "We cross the bridge and move forward. Every story is unique, and ours is just beginning."

Outside, the city lights danced, casting the buildings into striking silhouettes against the evening sky. Far away in Vermont, the Willows Bridge remained steadfast, a symbol of their love, and heralding a fresh start for Clara and Jack.

CHAPTER ELEVEN

Afterword

When you grow up in New England, ghost stories are a part of life. They're told around campfires, during sleepovers, and on dark, snowy evenings. One story that always intrigued me was that of Emily's Bridge in Stowe, Vermont. Some say it's true, others just a tale made up to keep kids from jumping off the bridge. To me, as a fiction writer, the line between fact and fable isn't as important. What matters is the story's power to captivate, to chill, and to charm.

Writing "Bridging the Heart"and the entire "Kindred Spirit Mysteries" series has been like a journey back to my roots. It's funny how weaving these tales feels a bit like coming home. I get to walk the paths I did as a kid, and remember the thrill of thinking that maybe, just maybe, the shadows held something more.

Through these stories I've tried to create a little world where the spirits of New England might not just be real, but also have something to say. It's not about proving ghosts exist. It's about tapping into that sense of wonder and possibility that makes life a bit more interesting.

Even though I can't bring spirits together, I like to think that by sharing these stories, I'm putting something good into the world. Maybe these tales can be a bridge of their own—a way for readers to connect with the past, with each other, and with the places that I've loved all my life.

Thank you for joining me on this adventure. Every story is a piece of me, and I hope you find something in them that resonates with you, too.

The Curse at White Pines

Kindred Spirits Mysteries

Beth Connor

WOLF GROVE MEDIA, LLC

Contents

New Beginnings

Sienna Avery approached White Pine Resort and crossed into a realm where reality seemed to soften. As her green Toyota shuddered down the winding driveway, she clutched the steering wheel and muttered under her breath. "Just a bit further, don't quit on me now."

The morning sun bathed the resort's facade in a warm glow, unveiling its timeless architecture. Lush forests embraced the grounds, and she felt the trails calling out to her, inviting her to explore the wilderness beyond. There would be time for hikes, but for now, she would focus on the task at hand. Income.

Sienna's college was a mere 45-minute drive from White Pines. This job not only offered her the convenience of a place to live while campus was closed, but a much-needed escape. The winding mountain roads were her sanctuary. Every curve brought a sense of peace and each turn helped the pressures of paying for school melt away. It was summer break, and she relished the freedom to embark on an adventure. When she had steered through the scenic route, there was a thrill of discovery with each mile.

She wanted—no, needed—control. The open road, the guarantee that if things became too overwhelming or if she needed a respite, she could escape into the embrace of the nearby woods. The idea of relying on others for transportation, of being trapped or limited in her movements, dampened her spirit.

As she parked and stepped out, a sudden chill ran down her spine, unexpected given the summer warmth. The trees seemed to whisper secrets, and for a fleeting moment, she felt as if someone—or something—was watching her long before she arrived.

Her eyes darted around, seeking the source of her unease. There was an undercurrent of something... otherworldly?

As Sienna approached the entrance, her bag held close to her chest. She sensed the beginnings of an extraordinary summer. Romance and adventure beckoned, and as shadows danced across the walls of White Pine Resorts, she realized that the stories here were more than just tales—they were alive.

White Pine Resort was full of history and old stories. Whispers of legends, some lost and others just beginning. Star-crossed lovers, brave soldiers, and free spirits—all had found their lives interwoven within the walls and woods of the resort. Every brick, every leaf, every gust of wind carried that energy. The love that transcended time, and promises made beneath the same sky.

As the sun continued its ascent, the grounds came alive. Birds, perhaps the true custodians of its secrets, sang melodies old and new, their songs harmonizing with the rustle of leaves and the gentle gurgle of streams. Deer grazed upon dew-kissed meadows.

The resort seemed to grow from the land. Ivy draped the walls, flowers burst forth in vivid colors, and ancient trees stood sentinel, their boughs stretching over the heart of the resort. For those fortunate enough to witness the dawn at White Pine Resorts, the experience was nothing short of enchanting. It was a reminder that amidst luxury, the true magic lay in nature's embrace.

Sienna left the parking lot in awe of the lavishness that unfurled before her. Even at this hour, the place seemed to buzz with energy. She was struck by confusion and had expected clear signs to guide the summer help, but if there were any, she had missed them. Most of the newcomers arrived by shuttle, which probably had its own designated entrance and directions. With a soft sigh, she trusted her instincts and followed a path that looked more well-trodden than the others.

She passed a manicured garden, and observed gardeners at work, their hands moving with practiced ease as they pruned roses and arranged blooms. Their dedication was clear. Sienna could almost smell the fragrance of the earth and blossoms.

The sound of cleaning drew her attention next. Housekeepers were busy ensuring that every window gleamed, and every hallway echoed the resort's standard of perfection. Their meticulousness spoke volumes, and they moved with grace, their work a dance of precision.

Lost in her observations, she didn't realize she had wandered into a more private part of the resort until a voice startled her. "Miss! This area is off-limits." She turned to see a security guard gesturing her away from a set of double doors. Emblazoned on the entrance was the unmistakable crest of the Whitmores. The opulence visible through the doors was unlike anything Sienna had ever seen—ornate chandeliers, grand portraits, and a glimpse of what looked like a golden staircase.

Flushing with embarrassment, Sienna mumbled an apology. As she hurried away, her thoughts were a mix of awe and disdain. The Whitmores weren't just the owners; they were monarchs of their domain. Their wealth wasn't just from White Pine Resorts, but from an empire of luxury and old money. While the world around her sang of nature and hard work, the Whitmores' wing sang of excess and entitlement.

Sienna's heart rate steadied as she took in the sprawling expanse of the resort. She needed directions, and she needed them now. An elderly man that was tending to a patch of foxgloves nearby drew her attention. He had a wise, weathered face and an ease in his movements that suggested he'd known this place for years, maybe decades.

"Excuse me," Sienna began, "could you point me towards where the summer help shuttle arrives?"

The old man looked up, his eyes bright beneath bushy gray eyebrows. "Ah, Lot B, eh? Just follow this path," he pointed with a gnarled finger, "and turn left when you see the large oak. Can't miss it."

"Thank you," she murmured.

With renewed purpose, she made her way down the path. The sounds of laughter and excited chatter grew louder as she neared the designated spot. As she rounded the bend, she arrived just in time to see a large shuttle bus emblazoned with the White Pine Resorts logo pulling in. The door hissed open, and out stepped a wave of fresh-faced young people, a mix of excitement and nervous anticipation painted on their features.

Sienna stood a little apart from the arriving crowd. Her long, chestnut hair cascaded in soft waves down her back, catching the early sunlight and creating a warm halo around her. As she watched the new arrivals, a flutter of emotions danced within her. She felt a kinship with these newcomers, yet she felt a world apart, having driven herself here and already experienced a taste of White Pines Resort—its beauty and its opulence, its history and its present.

A sharp, professional voice interrupted her thoughts. "Good morning, everyone! I trust you all had a pleasant journey." The voice belonged to a tall, well-dressed woman with graying hair pulled into a bun. Her name tag read 'Clarice - HR Manager.'

She approached Sienna first, extending a manicured hand. "You must be Sienna Avery. They informed me you'd be coming in your own vehicle." Sienna nodded, taking the woman's hand and feeling the firm grip. "Yes, that's me."

"Very well. Let's not waste time. We have a lot to cover," Clarice announced, addressing the gathering. Her efficiency was clear, and Sienna sensed that beneath the veneer of professionalism, Clarice might have a warmer side.

Clarice ushered them through a grand set of double doors, revealing interiors as breathtaking as the exterior. Crystal chandeliers hung above, casting rainbows across the polished marble floors. Majestic fireplaces anchored the grand rooms, each adorned with paintings of the White Mountains.

As they explored, Sienna found herself drawn to the colors and textures of the sofas and drapes, her fingers tracing the plush fabrics. The meticulous attention to detail was everywhere, from the intricate woodwork to the ceiling frescoes. Each room seemed to have its own story, pulling Sienna deeper into the allure of White Pine.

Art the end of the tour, Clarice led them to a wing dedicated to the staff. "Here," she announced, "is where you'll collect your uniforms. Wear them with pride. These represent your identity as employees here at White Pine Resort."

Sienna picked up a folded set—crisp white shirts, tailored skirts for the ladies, trousers for the men, and a deep green velvet vest reflecting the hue of the surrounding pines. As they continued the orientation, Sienna's mind wandered—between the history in the hallways, the grandeur of her surroundings, and the adventure that awaited.

Her first few hours on the job were a flurry of activity. White Pine Resort was always buzzing with guests from various parts of the world, each with their unique set of expectations.

Amanda, a slender woman with a sparkle in her eyes, was Sienna's assigned mentor. Boasting five years of experience, Amanda was a wellspring of wisdom and practical advice. Flashing a smile, she shared her first rule: "Always wear comfortable shoes. We do a lot of walking and standing."

Sienna learned what Amanda had hinted at earlier. Their shifts were exhausting, packed with endless interactions, coordinating activities, and ensuring each guest felt valued. Sienna's first error occurred when she booked the same suite for two different families. The situation was tense, with both families upset. However, thanks to Amanda's diplomacy and seasoned approach, they upgraded one family to a superior suite and calmed the other with complimentary perks.

Throughout these trials, Sienna absorbed valuable lessons. The most crucial? People weren't just in pursuit of luxury—they craved meaningful experiences, memories, and connections.

Her shift concluded with a challenging encounter with a demanding guest. Once resolved, Sienna sought refuge on a secluded balcony of the resort. It offered a breathtaking view over expansive pines. A short while later, Amanda joined her, her eyes reflecting understanding.

"Sienna," Amanda started, her voice gentle yet seasoned, "this job is about more than just fulfilling requests or managing bookings. You're stepping into our guests' stories. Each one arrives here with their own personalities, some soft and some bold. If you really listen, you'll understand them. The better you understand, the better you can serve."

Sienna gazed out at the forest, its whispers of ancient tales floating through the air, older than any guest that had ever checked in. As she looked, her dream of becoming a travel writer stirred within her. She envisioned days filled not with serving at resorts like this one, but with reveling in them, capturing her adventures on paper, and inviting the world to share in the enchantment she felt now.

"See you tomorrow, Sienna," Amanda whispered, squeezing her shoulder before departing.

Left alone, the calm of the night enveloped Sienna. The play of the pool's reflection in the soft moonlight suggested that the stars had come down for a swim. The mountains, ever-present, stood guard, their peaks veiled in a dreamy mist.

A sudden drop in temperature made her shiver. Alongside the coolness, an aroma wafted around—a peculiar blend of lavender and old parchment. It was both comforting and eerie. A fleeting shadow, almost too quick to be real, passed by the corner of her vision.

She brushed it off as her tired mind playing tricks, but then another soft sound startled her. Pivoting, her gaze met that of a man she hadn't seen earlier. With his dark hair and deep blue eyes, he appeared to blend into the resort's atmosphere of mystery and charm.

He offered her a nod and their shared connection was a brief but intense, a wordless communication in the twilight quiet. Sienna felt an uncanny sense of familiarity, like an echo from a dream she couldn't quite remember.

With a tilt of his head and a small smile, he turned and left, leaving Sienna with a swirl of questions. She tried to follow his path with her eyes and noted he walked towards a corridor lined with portraits. One painting, in particular, drew her attention—a figure from a past era with a strong resemblance to the stranger.

A whisper of wind brought with it soft murmurs. Sienna shook her head, laughing at her own fanciful thoughts. Yet, the magnetic pull of the man remained, leaving her with the promise that this summer at White Pine would unveil more mysteries than she'd expected. *Time to snap back to reality,* she mused, pushing open the doors to the bustling heart of the resort's employee wing.

The noise of the staff cafeteria was a contrast to the expansive silence of the resort's balconies and hallways. Sienna, tray in hand, hesitated, scanning the room for a familiar face. Just as she was contemplating sitting alone, a cheerful voice broke her reverie.

"Hey! You're the new one, right? Over here!" A girl waved her over, her name tag shining: *Maya*.

Sienna made her way over. "Hi, yes, I'm Sienna. First day."

"You survived then? Good start!" Maya grinned. "How'd it go?"

They laughed, and as Sienna relaxed. "Actually..." she started, "I had this encounter on one of the balconies. A man, tall and very good looking. I'm worried he might be a guest. We're not supposed to—"

"Fraternize with the guests," Maya finished for her, nodding. "I know, they drum that rule for us from day one. Can you describe him?"

Her words painted an image of the stranger, and Maya looked thoughtful for a moment. "Doesn't ring a bell. But if you're that curious, the summer staff kick-off party is tomorrow night. It's the perfect chance to spot him, especially if he's part of the staff."

Sienna's heart fluttered at the possibility. "I just want to make sure I didn't break any rules on my first day," she said. A tiny part of her hoped to see him again.

Maya patted her hand. "Don't sweat it too much. Just enjoy your time here. And who knows? Maybe tomorrow's party will clear things up for you."

Boosted by her new friendship with Maya, Sienna left the cafeteria, feeling excited about the upcoming event. She traversed the resort's hallways, the echo of her footsteps on the marble floors amplified in the quiet. The grandeur took on an almost mystical quality, its windows shimmering like a constellation of stars brought down to earth.

With a sigh, she opened the door to her shared quarters, appreciating the thoughtful layout that offered each occupant some privacy. She moved toward her assigned area, where gauzy drapes around her bed created a private sanctuary within the room.

Sienna sank into her soft mattress, her mind buzzing as it replayed the day's happenings. The resort, the lively conversations in the staff cafeteria, and Amanda's wise counsel all mingled in her thoughts. But it was the fleeting encounter with the stranger that captivated her the most. That brief connection had sparked something inside her, stirring a flurry of emotions. Who was he? She wondered.

Boosted by Maya's friendship, Sienna left the cafeteria, feeling excited about the upcoming event.

As Sienna traversed the resort's hallways, the echo of her footsteps on the marble floors seemed amplified in the quiet. The grandeur of White Pine Resorts took on a mystical quality, its windows shimmering like a constellation of stars brought down to earth.

With a sigh, she opened the door to her shared quarters, appreciating the thoughtful layout that offered each occupant some privacy. She moved toward her assigned area, where gauzy drapes around her bed created a private sanctuary within the room.

Sienna sank into her soft mattress, her mind buzzing as it replayed the day's happenings. The elegant architecture of the resort, the lively conversations in the staff cafeteria, and Amanda's wise counsel all mingled in her thoughts. But it was the fleeting encounter with the stranger that captivated her the most. That brief connection had sparked something inside her, stirring a flurry of emotions. Who was he? She wondered, sensing that he was another piece in the intriguing puzzle that was White Pine Resorts.

The day's exertions weighed on her as she pulled the soft duvet around her and coaxed her eyelids to close. Yet, as she hovered on the edge of sleep, her heart fluttered with excitement for the days ahead. This summer promised a journey of discovery, adventure, and possibly, a romance. With these thoughts, Sienna drifted into a deep, dream-laden sleep.

CHAPTER TWO

A Party Under the Stars

The morning had been a gentler introduction than yesterday for Sienna. With most White Pine Resort closed for summer employee training day, the usual bustle of guests and activities was subdued. The owners dedicated most areas of the property to orientation sessions, training seminars, and team-building exercises. Only a select few areas remained open to cater to the minimal number of guests checked in; the seasoned, year-round employees managed these areas.

As a part of this training day, new and returning employees familiarized themselves with the vast property, not just in terms of their specific roles, but also to connect with the very essence of what made White Pine so special.

One highlight of the orientation was discovering a hike locals called Frozen Tears. It was part of the Appalachian Trail—which she hoped to conquer in its entirety someday. This trail was also steeped in lore, rumored to be haunted by the ghost of a jilted lover. Such tales of hauntings and tragic love merged her twin passions for the paranormal and hiking. She was determined to explore the trail herself.

Despite the reduced guest count, the resort radiated an air of excitement. The annual Employee Kick-Off Party was just hours away. To make sure every staff member, from managers to gardeners, could take part in the festivities, the Whitmores had hired outside caterers and temporary staff. This evening, hierarchies would blur, allowing every employee a taste of the luxury White Pine's guests reveled in daily.

A smirk played on her lips as Sienna processed the details of the evening's grand event. *Ah, the benevolence of the uber-rich,* she mused. *Giving us common folk a taste of their world for one magical night.* It felt like a theatrical performance that the Whitmores would elevate their staff to guest status, a charitable gesture to appease the masses. But for all her inner cynicism, Sienna couldn't suppress the flutter of excitement in her stomach. After all, who wouldn't be intrigued by a night of mingling in luxury, even if it was just a taste? The allure was undeniable, and Sienna couldn't wait for the festivities to begin.

As the sun began its descent, Sienna was ready for the night. The resort transformed under the waning light. Lanterns glowed, casting dancing shadows on the pathways. Distant sounds of a guitar tuning provided a soft backdrop to the murmur of eager conversations.

The guests of honor tonight, the employees themselves, emerged in their finest attire. Elegant dresses, sharp suits, and radiant smiles were the order of the evening. Sienna watched as tables laden with gourmet delights were set up, each dish looking more tantalizing than the last.

A little away, the promise of music and dance awaited under a canopy adorned with twinkling fairy lights. It beckoned everyone to forget their roles for a night and just lose themselves in the evening.

The Whitmores had orchestrated a night where barriers were forgotten. As Sienna looked around, taking it all in, she felt a deep sense of gratitude. She had a cushy, competitive summer job, a place to lay her head, and a fantastic party to attend. Summer was yet to kick into full gear, but tonight, Sienna felt right at home.

The cool evening air brushed against Sienna as she made her way to the heart of the party. Her outfit reflected her unique sense of style. She had chosen a flowy, knee-length dress in a subtle shade of olive, its simple cut enhanced by delicate embroidery at the neckline and hem. Strappy flat sandals and her signature messy bun completed the look. A pendant, gifted from her grandmother, hung against her collarbone, catching the soft light now and then.

Sienna's polished look was just the surface. Underneath, she was a mix of emotions: excitement for the evening, a touch of nervous energy, and a deep, persistent curiosity. She scanned the crowd more often than she'd like, searching for a particular face, unable to forget those piercing blue eyes and that captivating presence.

Making her way through the crowd of elegantly dressed guests, she spotted a familiar face. It was Maya who had quickly become a friend, their connection sparked by a shared sense of humor. Maya waved her over, beaming.

"Sienna!" Maya called out. "You clean up well! Who are you trying to impress?"

Sienna laughed, feeling a blush creep up her cheeks. "Oh, hush! I could say the same about you." She winked, taking in Maya's stunning crimson dress.

The two shared a light-hearted moment, trading observations about the evening and the surrounding extravagance. As they sipped on their drinks, they exchanged playful bets on which dish on the banquet table would be the first to run out, and chuckled at some of the more flamboyant dance moves on display.

Yet, even as Sienna reveled in the comfort of Maya's company, a part of her remained alert, her eyes drifting across the crowd. The mysterious stranger had left a mark on her mind, and the night was still young. She was mid-conversation with Maya when the atmosphere shifted. A tall figure, well dressed, stepped into the spotlight of the party.

Sienna's heart skipped a beat, recognizing those eyes that she had locked onto earlier that day. The memory of their fleeting encounter, so vivid, made her stomach flutter with excitement. Unable to contain herself, she nudged Maya, pointing in his direction. "That's him! That's the guy I was telling you about."

Maya's eyes widened, her playful demeanor overshadowed by a more dramatic tone. "Oh... oh no. That's Dylan. Dylan... Whitmore." Her voice rose with each repetition of his name.

Sienna blinked, a bit taken aback. "Dylan Whitmore? As in, the Whitmores who own this place?" An involuntary wrinkle of distaste formed on her forehead.

She had never been fond of the ultra-rich, finding their lifestyles excessive and often out of touch with reality.

Maya leaned closer, her voice thick with warning. "That very one. And honey, let me tell you, that man is trouble with a capital T. He's got the looks, the wealth, and the charm to draw anyone in. But he leaves a trail of broken hearts wherever he goes."

Sienna's lips pressed into a thin line. "Great. Just what I need. Thanks for the heads up, Maya."

Maya patted her hand. "Just watch your back around him. And maybe your heart, too." She winked, but her playful smile didn't quite reach her eyes.

Sienna mulled over Maya's words, a knot of disappointment forming in her stomach. Yet, despite the warning, every time her eyes settled on Dylan, her chest thrummed with an undeniable excitement. Damn it! She observed him weaving through the crowd, his magnetic aura undeniable. Every so often, his gaze would scan the room, seeming to search for something—or perhaps someone.

As the evening progressed, Sienna couldn't help but steal glances in Dylan's direction. And each time their eyes met, a silent spark passed between them. The warning echoed in her mind, but his allure was undeniable.

The music quickened, and Sienna caught the attention of a handsome man with chiseled features and sun-bronzed skin. His hazel eyes sparkled, and his wavy, sandy-blonde hair looked as though he'd just come from a day at the beach. "Care to dance?" he asked, grinning as he extended his hand.

Taken aback, Sienna's thoughts lingered on Dylan, but she welcomed the diversion. "I'd love to," she replied, smiling as she placed her hand in his.

The stranger introduced himself as Ben, a new lifeguard at the resort. As they danced, his athletic grace and easy way struck Sienna as he led her across the dance floor. He had a playful and light-hearted energy that was infectious. She laughed at his jokes and admired how his shirt hugged his toned torso.

Ben was her type: sporty, charming, and attractive. She tried to immerse herself in the moment, but her mind wandered.

As they spun around the dance floor, Sienna's gaze drifted back to Dylan. She wasn't alone. Many eyes seemed to be fixed on him, but one woman held his attention. She was stunning, with long, raven-black hair and red lips. She wore a figure-hugging dress that left little to the imagination. The two danced, their bodies merging. Sienna watched as the woman tilted her head back, allowing Dylan access to her neck, and his hand rested on the small of her back, pulling her even closer. Their dance was more than just intimate—it was a sultry grind.

A pang of something inexplicable — jealousy or longing, perhaps — surged through Sienna. She tried to focus on Ben, but the way she felt toward Dylan was undeniable.

Ben, sensing her distraction, leaned in. "You okay?"

She nodded and gave him a reassuring smile. "Yeah, just lost in thought. Let's keep dancing."

As the night wore on and the music transitioned into a slow, haunting melody, Sienna felt a shift in the atmosphere. She was drawn toward the bar area where Dylan was now standing. His previous dance partner was nowhere in sight.

Their eyes met across the room, recognition and intrigue clear. The world around Sienna blurred, the noise and the chatter fading into the background.

As they came face to face, Sienna's vivacity took charge. "Hey," she greeted him, "Seems like we keep running into each other."

Dylan's lips curved into a smile. "It would appear so," he replied, his voice deep and smooth. He took a moment to look her up and down. "You look incredible."

Sienna felt a blush creep up her neck. "Thank you," she responded. "Not so bad yourself, Mr. Whitmore."

The moment the words "Mr. Whitmore" slipped from Sienna's lips. Dylan's expression shifted. A slight downturn of his mouth and a flash of vulnerability she hadn't seen before overshadowed the playfulness in his eyes. It was as though a curtain had been drawn back, revealing a more complex character behind those confident blue eyes.

Sienna picked up on this subtle change. "Did I say something wrong?" she asked.

His eyes held a touch of surprise. "It's not about being wrong," he began, hesitating. "It's just... when people know who I am, all they see is my family and their money. I'd rather be seen for who I am."

Sienna's lips quirked, her gaze drifting over to where a cluster of women seemed to cast longing glances in Dylan's direction. "You don't seem to mind attention from the ladies though," she teased, gesturing towards his 'fan club'.

Dylan turned his head in the direction she showed, a wry smile curling his lips. "That's different. Momentary distractions," he said, his tone light but with a hint of underlying seriousness.

After taking a deep breath and bolstered by a surge of unexpected boldness, she chuckled, and continued. "Well, Mr. Whitmore," she emphasized the formal title again for effect, "how about we find a quieter place? Somewhere your... distractions," she borrowed his word, "won't reach?"

There was nothing left to lose, and sometimes, taking a chance made all the difference.

The moment Dylan's fingers wrapped around Sienna's, a current of warmth shot through her, making her heart race. They weaved through the party. Her thoughts were a whirlwind of emotions. The weight of his hand in hers, the texture of his skin against her fingers; it was intoxicating. The reality that he was a Whitmore, and the warnings of Maya, echoed in the background, but for now, she was captivated by the man leading her.

When they reached the secluded garden area, the cacophony of the party melted away. The evening's symphony of crickets and rustling leaves took its place, lending a more intimate ambiance to their escape. Lanterns hung low, illuminating the pathway with their soft, golden light, dancing with the gentle breeze.

They stood beneath a canopy of wisteria, its purple blossoms cascading around them. Dylan's fingers loosened, but rather than let go, he drew her against him. The surrounding atmosphere thickened with desire. She could feel the heat radiating from him, the solidness of his chest pressed against hers. His head lowered, lips a hair's breadth from her own, and for a dizzying moment, she was sure they would kiss.

The rapid rhythm of her heart echoed in her ears, and each shallow breath was laced with his scent—a beguiling mix of earthy musk and fresh pine. It intoxicated her, blurring the lines between caution and craving. The glint in his eyes suggested he was well-versed in this dance of seduction. Sienna's thoughts wandered, imagining the path this could take, the electrifying journey they might embark upon together in this hidden corner.

Just as the tension between them grew to an almost unbearable point, a sudden chill swept through the garden. Sienna felt it—a whisper of cold that didn't belong on this summer night, accompanied by a faint rustle that didn't come from the trees. She saw Dylan stiffen, his eyes darting around as if looking for the source of the disturbance.

"Did you feel that?" Sienna asked, her voice almost a whisper.

He nodded, breaking their intimate stance. "It felt... off, didn't it?"

A chuckle escaped her lips, and he joined her, the tension dissipating. "Perhaps the spirits of White Pine don't approve of our escapade," she teased.

Dylan grinned, but it didn't quite reach his eyes. "Or maybe they just want to join the party."

Sienna let out a hearty laugh. "You know," she began, tucking a stray strand of hair behind her ear, "I've always been fascinated by the paranormal. Ghosts, spirits, unexplained phenomena—it all draws me in."

"Really?" Dylan raised an eyebrow, his face unreadable. "You believe in all that?"

She nodded. "It's not so much about believing, but about being open to the mysteries of the world. There's so much we don't understand. Why not entertain the possibility?"

He paused, letting her words sink in. "White Pine has its share of tales," he began, his voice low and cryptic. "Many are steeped in history, and some... some bear the weight of the Whitmore name."

Sienna grinned, "See? Now you're getting it."

They continued to talk, the barriers between them lowered. "You know, being a Whitmore isn't all it's cracked up to be," Dylan confessed, his gaze focused on a distant point. "People often see the name, the legacy, and the wealth. But they don't see me—the real me."

She observed him for a moment. "You want to be seen for who you are, not just your last name."

Dylan met her gaze, his eyes sincere. "Exactly. Everyone assumes they know my life because of my family name. But there's so much more to me than just being a Whitmore."

Sienna tilted her head, studying him. "People often see only what's on the surface, but we all have depths waiting to be explored," she murmured.

"I'm not used to this," he admitted. "Being candid. It's... new."

Sienna looked up at him, her gaze steady. "Maybe it's time for some new experiences, Mr. Whitmore."

He chuckled, "Only if you promise to call me Dylan from now on."

The moonlight streamed through the leaves overhead, casting silvery patterns on the path, and they settled onto a stone bench.

Sienna hesitated for a moment, sensing a shift in the atmosphere. "I realized we haven't formally introduced ourselves," she began, extending a hand. "I'm Sienna Avery, college student, and nature lover."

Dylan chuckled, accepting her hand. His grip was firm, yet warm. "Dylan Whitmore."

Sienna raised an eyebrow. "Anything more to add, Dylan?"

He grinned, "Well, aside from the obvious 'rich guy' stereotype, I have aspirations, too."

She leaned in, curiosity piqued. "Do tell."

With a dramatic sigh, he replied, "Future eco-resort tycoon?" At her confused look, he continued, "Jokes aside, I genuinely want to transform White Pine. There's so much potential here. Instead of just being another luxury destination, I want it to be a sustainable haven. The resort will cater to eco-travelers, focusing on conservation. It's high time we tread lightly on this Earth, even in the world of opulence."

Her eyes lit up. "That sounds amazing. And from my future perspective as a travel writer," she said, emphasizing the word future, "that's a story I'd love to cover."

"A travel writer, eh?" Dylan looked pleased. "See? And here I was thinking our only common interest was sneaking around in dimly lit gardens."

After that, their conversation flowed. Sienna regaled him with her college escapades and her insatiable wanderlust, her dream of exploring every nook and cranny of the world. "Each place tells a story, you know? I want to be a part of that, even if it's just for a while."

Dylan listened, rapt. He then delved into his own life - a contrast of luxury, privilege, but also of heavy expectations and responsibilities. "Your world sounds so free," he remarked, a hint of longing in his voice. "Mine's...well, it's complicated."

She reached out and plucked some wisteria from a section marked as protected. With a triumphant grin, she tucked the flower behind her ear.

Dylan arched an eyebrow, amusement in his eyes. "Breaking the rules already, Miss Avery?"

She shot him a defiant look, her lips curling into a smile. "Sometimes, you need to bend the rules to truly experience life, Mr. Whitmore," she responded, emphasizing his formal title.

His laughter echoed in the quiet garden, the harmonious notes resonating in the stillness. Their eyes met and held, the world around them blurring into a hazy background. It was as if the universe conspired to draw them closer in that singular, magical moment.

The faint strains of music from the main event wafted over, a gentle reminder of the world outside their cocoon. Without breaking their gaze, Dylan rose and extended a hand toward Sienna, his fingers outstretched. "Care to dance?"

Sienna, surprised by the unexpected request, felt a rush of warmth spread from her cheeks to her toes. With a shy smile, she took his hand, and as their fingers intertwined. A jolt of electricity coursed through her. Those storybook descriptions of 'sparks' felt all too real.

He led her to an open space in the garden, and they moved to the soft rhythm of the distant music. Their dance begun with the formal steps of a waltz, their bodies maintaining a courteous distance. But as the minutes passed, and as they grew more attuned to each other's movements and emotions, the formality faded. The space between them shrank. Their steps became less structured, more intuitive, guided by the rhythm of their heartbeats and the melody that enveloped them.

Sienna felt the world receding. Dylan's hand was on the small of her back, and the firm yet gentle grip of his fingers, and the reassuring weight of his other hand holding hers, sent shivers down her spine.

The boundaries blurred. Was it the music guiding their movements or their shared pulse? Time seemed to stand still. With every turn, every sway, they drew closer, two souls entwined in a dance as old as time. And in that moment, beneath the canopy of stars and amidst the fragrant blossoms, Sienna felt alive, her heart dancing its own joyous rhythm.

Dylan's fingers traced delicate, mesmerizing circles on the small of her back, each swirl sending tiny ripples of sensation across her skin. Sienna's pulse quickened, every nerve ending alert and responsive. Meanwhile, his other hand cradled her face, his thumb tracing the soft outline of her cheek. Their faces inched closer.

Just as their lips were mere millimeters apart, a deliberate cough shattered the intimate bubble. Startled, they pulled apart to find an older gentleman standing a few paces away on the garden path. Sienna's eyes darted to the figure, recognizing in his features a refined, mature version of the man beside her.

His silvered hair was brushed back, revealing sharp, piercing eyes that held an uncanny resemblance to Dylan's. The same chiseled jaw, the same regal bearing, but with lines etched by time and responsibility. It was unmistakable; this was an elder Whitmore. The interruption pressed on the atmosphere, a palpable tension hanging in the air.

"Father," Dylan's voice took on a more formal tone.

"Dylan," the elder Whitmore began, his voice laced with an ice-cold calmness that only years of cultivated control could achieve, "This is the season's first major event, and it would be wise for you to remember your role here. You should be at the forefront, visible, not tucked away in some shadowy nook indulging in... distractions."

His gaze shifted to Sienna, sweeping her up and down in a brief, evaluative manner. "Miss," he nodded, a curt gesture of acknowledgment, but devoid of warmth, "I trust you'll continue to enjoy the evening's festivities." It wasn't a suggestion.

Sienna took in a deep breath, fighting the flush creeping up her cheeks. She gave a small nod. "Of course, Mr. Whitmore." Her voice maintained a respectful steadiness.

As the elder Whitmore turned to leave, Dylan caught Sienna's gaze. Unspoken words hung between them. Just before they were out of sight, Dylan mouthed, "Find me later."

Sienna watched as they retreated, their silhouettes fading into the grandeur of White Pine Resorts. She took a moment to regroup, her emotions a whirlwind. There was annoyance at Dylan's swift acquiescence to his father's demand, but a part of her understood. Their worlds, she realized, were vast galaxies apart. Yet, amidst the vastness, they'd found a shared star. She stood, lost in her thoughts, the surreal nature of the evening sinking in. The connection she had felt, that undeniable spark. Was it just a fleeting moment, or the start of something more profound? Only time would tell.

Sienna made her way back to the main event, the night air cooling the warmth in her cheeks. The soft sounds of the party grew louder, and as she approached, she was swallowed by the glow of lanterns and the hum of chatter.

"Where on earth have you been?!" Maya's voice cut through. She appeared beside Sienna, a champagne flute in hand.

Sienna laughed. "Exploring, I guess. And you? Enjoying the evening?"

Maya rolled her eyes. "Danced with a few cute guys. Had some drinks. You know, the usual party routine." She paused, taking a sip from her flute. "But you seem to have been busy with Whitmore royalty. Word travels fast, Sienna."

Sienna felt a small pang of discomfort. "It's not like that, Maya. We just talked."

Maya's demeanor shifted to a more serious tone. "Look, Si, I've seen enough summer flings come and go here. Dylan's... complicated. Just be careful, okay?"

Before Sienna could respond, a familiar voice resonated behind her. "May I have this dance?"

Both women turned to find Dylan, looking as handsome as ever, extending his hand towards Sienna. The urgency in his eyes was unmistakable. Maya shot Sienna a look and retreated, leaving the two of them in their own bubble once more.

Sienna hesitated for just a beat before accepting. As Dylan took her hand, he slipped a folded piece of paper into her palm. The unexpected gesture surprised her, and their eyes met with a shared secret. Without a word, she tucked the paper into her bra.

The music enveloped them as they moved together. This time, there was a tender familiarity in their dance, a mutual understanding that something deeper was unfolding between them.

No words were exchanged when their dance concluded. Throughout the rest of the night, Dylan mingled with other attendees, dancing and laughing, but his eyes often strayed back to Sienna, seeking her out amidst the crowd. Every glance felt like a secret shared between them, a connection they couldn't ignore.

Sienna stationed herself beside Maya, enjoying the rest of the evening with light chatter and soft laughter. They shared stories, observations, and the occasional playful gossip about the other party-goers.

As the night aged, the energy of the party waned. The live music dwindled to softer tunes, guests began their departures, and soon enough, Sienna and Maya made the walk back to their respective rooms.

Once inside her room, the buzz of excitement from the party still lingering in her veins, Sienna pulled the crinkled piece of paper from her bra. She unfolded it, revealing a number, Dylan's. Without overthinking it, she typed out a message: "It's Sienna. I had a wonderful time with you tonight." She pressed send and waited, but no response came.

Around her, the room was alive with her roommates' giggles and recounting of their own evening escapades. They were animated, their voices blending into a backdrop of chatter. Sienna tuned them out, her mind preoccupied with her own evening.

She crawled into her bed, the cool sheets enveloping her. As the soft murmurs of the night continued around her, she found herself deep in thought. The electric connection with Dylan, Maya's warning, the cryptic exchange of numbers — it was all so thrilling yet so perplexing. The potential of a summer romance was tantalizing, but the complexities it promised made her wonder: Was it worth it? With that thought lingering in her mind, Sienna's eyelids grew heavy, and she succumbed to a dream-filled sleep.

CHAPTER THREE

Rain-Kissed Revelations

White Pine Resort glistened in the early morning light, its beauty enhanced by the misty haze. As the days had gone by, Sienna had grown more comfortable in her role at the resort. Today, the scent of fresh linens mingled with the faint aroma of breakfast cooking somewhere in the distance. Nearby, the gentle clinking of dishes created a soft backdrop, setting the pace for the day ahead.

Sienna settled into the rhythm of the day, handling her tasks effortlessly. As she went about her duties, her eyes drifted, scanning the faces of guests and staff. She was looking for one person in particular. Dylan had been missing since the party, leaving her to wonder if their encounter had been nothing more than a mere distraction for him.

Friday had arrived with a sense of urgency. As soon as Sienna started her shift, she was swept up in the whirlwind of work, the resort alive with activity. The hours melded together in a hectic mix of tasks, guests, and brief moments of calm. Before she knew it, her shift supervisor signaled it was time for her break; lunchtime had crept up on her. The morning's frenzy had flown by in a flash.

In the bustling lunchroom, Sienna joined Maya and Jess, a fellow summer worker who served in the resort's upscale restaurant. Jess animatedly recounted tales of eccentric guest requests, her hands illustrating each story, drawing laughter from those around. After sharing a few of her own experiences, Maya leaned in, her voice dropping to a hush. "Have you heard? There's talk that the Whitmores might spend more time here this season. Rumor has it that someone in the family is sick, maybe with cancer. But nothing's confirmed yet."

Jess rolled her eyes, her voice laced with mock exasperation. "Just what we need—more Whitmores to entertain." As she said this, her gaze flickered toward Sienna, the unspoken words clear in her expression.

Sienna played coy. "Oh, speaking of Whitmores, is Dylan still around?"

Maya smirked, taking a sip of her drink. "Hoping for a little more quality time with Dylan?"

Before Sienna could even get a word out, Jess jumped in, rolling her eyes and saying in a grave tone, "Seriously? Why even bother? Word on the street is he's just here playing the rich boy role, waiting until he's called back to his fancy palace or whatever."

Sienna shrugged, trying to mask her curiosity. "We just had a... moment. I'm intrigued, that's all."

Jess leaned in closer, lowering her voice. "Look, I've been around this block a few times. Just watch yourself with the Whitmores, especially that Dylan guy. Guys like him? They pop in, stir things up and then jet. It's all fun and games for them, but it's the rest of us who end up dealing with the drama they leave behind."

Sienna looked back at Jess with a half-smile. "I hear you, Jess. But I can take care of myself, okay?"

Jess shrugged, "Whatever." She then quickly changed the subject, her eyes lighting up. "Anyway, did you hear about the new chef they're bringing in next week? I heard he's worked all over the world!"

Sienna savored the last bites of her sandwich, enjoying the brief respite her midday break provided from the morning's chaos. As she sat in the resort's sunlit cafeteria, the hum of conversations filled the air—employees discussing their tasks, guests, and the evening's upcoming events.

As she listened, Sienna picked up on a mix of stories about the Whitmores. Some people praised them for their smart business moves and charity work, while others dished about the family's more scandalous moments. Gossip spread about secret romances, shady business deals, and wild nights out, especially involving the younger Whitmores. And, of course, with Dylan being the heir and a bit of a mystery, he was often the star of these hushed conversations.

As she sipped her iced tea, lost in her thoughts, Maya pulled her back to the present moment.. "You look like you've run a marathon," Maya commented, noting Sienna's tired eyes.

"It feels like it," Sienna replied with a weary smile. "These Friday check-ins are no joke."

Maya nodded. "It's always a madhouse. But you're doing great. By midsummer, you'll be breezing through it."

Their chat moved on to everyday stuff, but Sienna didn't miss the quick look Maya shot Ben's way. Ah, Ben. He was funny, always had a witty comeback, and seemed to be everywhere. They'd danced at the party and bumped into each other a few times during the week. Sienna liked his straightforwardness, especially when he dropped obvious hints about Dylan. But dancing with Ben felt just... nice, lacking the electric connection she felt with Dylan.

Ben, sensing Sienna's gaze, looked up from his table across the room and sent a playful wink her way. She responded with a smile, noting the slight hint of hopefulness in his eyes.

As they started clearing their lunch trays and getting ready to head back to work, Sienna couldn't help but get caught up in her thoughts about Dylan. Was what she felt was just a one-off thing because of that night, or was there something real there?

After pushing the door open, she stepped back into the fray. The lobby buzzed with activity, the sound of rolling suitcases, and the constant chime of the reception bell. It was going to be a long day.

Fridays were always hectic at White Pine Resort, but this one topped the charts. A flood of check-ins had the place buzzing—families, couples, and solo adventurers all eager to soak up a weekend in the majestic mountains. Each guest brought not only their luggage, but a flurry of requests and tasks that Sienna and her team scrambled to handle.

She spent the day escorting guests to their rooms, fielding an endless stream of questions, and making sure every tiny detail upheld the resort's exacting standards. By evening, her feet throbbed, her voice rasped, and a dull ache pulsed in her temples. Toss in the emotional rollercoaster of dealing with Ben and Maya, not to mention her thoughts swirling around Dylan, and it felt like she'd lived a week in just one day.

Exhausted, Sienna trudged to her dorm, each step heavy with fatigue. See closed the door behind and collapsed onto her bed. A mix of excitement, doubt, and anticipation stirred inside her, leaving her to wonder if she was truly prepared for whatever lay ahead.

Pulling her laptop close, Sienna plunged into the shadowy lore of the frozen tears trail. Her screen flickered with accounts of chilling events and spectral figures that had been sighted weaving through the misty woods. As she absorbed an old tale, a sudden chill brushed against her, as if someone had settled next to her on the bed. She spun around, heart racing, only to find nothing there. A shiver ran down her spine as she shook off the feeling and refocused on the eerie stories before her. She had always let her imagination get the best of her.

As night deepened, thoughts of Dylan occasionally drifted through her mind—his intense gaze, the undeniable spark between them. It had felt almost otherworldly, and she half-expected him to appear, perhaps to join her on a nighttime adventure along the haunted trail. Yet, a week had passed without a glimpse of him. Sienna accepted that their encounter might have been just a fleeting thing.

Sienna leaned back into her bed and exhaled slowly. A fling with Dylan might not have been so bad, she pondered. No complications, just the pleasure of his company. But for now, the mysteries of the trail captured her intrigue. The allure of unraveling the unknown called to her. It pulled her thoughts away from what might have been and into the shadows of what awaited her in the haunted woods.

Tucked under her covers, the dim glow from her phone lit up. A notification flickered on the screen—it was a message from Dylan. He texted just as her thoughts had drifted away from him. Typical, that's just how the universe works.

"Hey Sienna. Hope you've been well. Been a bit caught up with family stuff recently."

She typed back, "Hey Dylan. I've noticed you've been MIA. Everything okay on the family front?"

He responded, "You could say it's the usual Whitmore family drama. Thanks for asking. How's the job treating you?"

Sienna's fingers danced over her phone's keyboard. "Busy, especially Fridays. But I'm getting the hang of it. Met some cool people too. Though I've heard a fair bit of... rumors about the Whitmores."

Dylan's reply came with a hint of humor. "Haha, we're kind of infamous in these parts. Not all of it's true, just so you know. How's your week looking ahead?"

She took a moment to frame her response. "Working straight through to Sunday. But I've got Monday and Tuesday off. I've made plans for Monday, but how about catching up on Tuesday?"

A few minutes of anticipation went by before his message came in. "Tuesday might be possible. Let me see how things pan out on my end. I'll get back to you."

Sienna smiled as she replied, "Sounds good. Let me know. And don't be a stranger."

His last message for the night was reassuring. "Promise I won't. Goodnight, Sienna."

She typed back with a soft sigh, "Goodnight, Dylan."

Sienna held her phone close, the glow from their conversation dimming. She felt a tug of conflicting emotions. Alone in her bed, amidst the occasional giggles and murmurs from her roommates, she wished for a space of her own. With a sigh, she turned to her side and wrapped herself around her pillow, seeking comfort and warmth as she drifted into a restless slumber.

It was Monday morning, and Sienna stood at the entrance of the Frozen Tears Trail. The days leading up to this had been a blur of activity—preparations, shifts at the resort, eager guests, and whispered rumors. Today, her backpack weighed on her shoulders as a thick mist swirled around her ankles, giving the trail an air of ancient mystery. The crisp morning air filled her lungs, invigorating and calming her at the same time.

The world of White Pine Resort had vanished behind her. Now, surrounded by the embrace of dense forest, Sienna stepped over roots and stones, her ears tuned to the chirps of birds and the murmur of a hidden stream. Each breath drew in the crisp air, mingling the scents of pine and earth. She paused, a shiver of excitement running through her as the forest whispered its ancient stories. The legends seemed to rise from the shadowed corners and thick undergrowth.

Sienna pressed on, the soft earth giving way under her boots. Each step intertwined her deeper with the natural world, every breath drawing in stories of love, betrayal, and restless spirits that had drawn her to this trail on her precious day off.

As she ventured further, ancient markers and symbols carved into rocks marked the haunting history of the trail. Each etching was like discovering a new chapter of the trail's saga, and Sienna delighted in piecing together its mysteries. From the tragic tale of a young woman named Eliza to the mysteries of those who disappeared without a trace. The stories were so vivid she could swear she saw shadows darting between the trees.

Meanwhile, thoughts of Dylan crept into her mind. Tentative plans had been made for Sienna and Dylan to meet for coffee at the resort the next day. They had only exchanged a few texts, and Sienna couldn't help but wonder if he would even show up.

Before long, the path led her into a dreamy clearing. Golden sunlight filtered through the trees, casting dappled patterns on the ground. She paused, captivated by the serenity and the nearby stream. It was a snapshot moment, one she wished she could hold on to a little longer.

As she sipped from her water bottle, a rustle from the bushes caused her to freeze in place. Her pulse quickened, and for a split second, the ghostly legends associated with the trail flashed through her mind. Could it be? She turned her head toward the sound, bracing herself. Instead, as the foliage parted, a familiar pair of blue eyes met hers, reflecting an equal measure of surprise.

"Dylan?" Sienna stammered, incredulous.

He stepped out, looking disarmed. "Sienna? What are you doing here?" He laughed, brushing a hand through his tousled hair. "Not that I'm complaining."

She chuckled, shaking her head. "I could ask you the same thing. I thought you'd be busy with... whatever it is the Whitmores do."

He grinned. "Needed a break from the world. You?"

"Same." She smiled. "Plus, I've wanted to hike this trail since I got here. Heard a lot about its legends."

"That's right, you had an interest in the supernatural." Dylan's gaze swept across the clearing, landing on Sienna. He held her eyes and murmured, "It's beautiful."

A faint blush tinged Sienna's cheeks, uncertain if he was talking about the trail or something more. The intensity of his stare made her heart flutter. A comfortable silence settled between them, punctuated only by the babbling of the stream and the occasional chirp of a bird. Then, with a playful smirk, Sienna broke the silence. "So, did you follow me here?"

He raised an eyebrow, feigning indignation. "Now, why would I do that? Maybe it's you who followed me."

Sienna laughed, the sound echoing in the clearing. "Oh, so it's like that, is it?"

Dylan's face softened, and he took a step closer, his voice dropping to a whisper. "Honestly, this feels like one of those cosmic jokes. Of all the trails, at all the times..."

She looked up into his eyes, the depth of their blue even more pronounced in the daylight. "It does feel like the universe is playing some sort of game with us, doesn't it?"

He nodded, and for a moment, they stood there, lost in each other's gaze, the weight of the past days and their unspoken words hanging between them.

Sienna cleared her throat, the spell breaking. "Well, since you're here, and I'm here, fancy joining me for the rest of the hike?"

Dylan's smile was genuine, lighting up his face. "I thought you'd never ask."

Together, they continued along the trail, the barriers that had existed between them seeming to melt away with each step. The easy banter, the shared laughter. It all felt like they were picking up from where they'd left off. The universe might play games, but in that clearing, on that day, it felt like it was rooting for them.

The trail twisted and turned, revealing hidden gems like cascading waterfalls or panoramic viewpoints. With every step, Sienna and Dylan seemed to shed layers of their initial apprehensions and hesitations, finding comfort in the shared journey.

Dylan paused near the edge of a brook, his gaze distant, as if remembering a tale from long ago. "See that brook over there? It's named after Eliza Goodwin. The story is pretty tragic."

Sienna's eyebrows furrowed in curiosity, her attention piqued. "Tell me more about Eliza. I read about her in the brochure, but it only gave a brief mention."

"Ah," Dylan started. "Back in 1788, right here in Crawford Notch, there were two young people—Eliza, a servant, and John Swanson, a loyal farmhand. They both worked for my ancestor, Colonel Joseph Whitmore. They dreamed of running away and building a life together. Eliza managed to save up a dowry and even went back to Portsmouth to plan their wedding."

Sienna leaned in, captivated. She had read the story, but it felt like it was alive when Dylan told it. "So, what happened?"

"Colonel Whitmore persuaded John to give up his plans with Eliza and join the revolutionary forces, and took Eliza's hard-earned dowry to help fund their efforts." Dylan said, his voice growing heavier. "When Eliza found out, she rushed back from Portsmouth, intent on confronting John. In her haste, she tried to cross an icy brook and, tragically, she never made it to the other side."

"Hence the Frozen Tears…" Sienna's eyes widened in shock. "That's heartbreaking."

"There's more," Dylan whispered. "When John found out about Eliza's fate, guilt consumed him. The burden of what he had done drove him to madness."

Sienna sighed, her heart heavy. "And now, they say her spirit still lingers here?"

Dylan nodded. "Especially on cold winter nights. Some claim they hear a young woman's laughter, turning to sobs of despair." His eyes darkened. For a moment, it looked like he was going to divulge more, but then he just shut his mouth, as if catching himself. The weight of a deeper story hung in the air between them. Sienna studied his expression, sensing there was more he wasn't saying.

The story lingered in the air, and for a moment, the natural sounds of the forest seemed to hush. Bird chirps ceased, the rustle of leaves stilled, and even the water seemed to quieten. The sudden stillness was palpable, the world around them holding its breath.

Then a gentle breeze wafted through, sending a shiver down Sienna's spine. The sensation intensified, and it felt like someone was watching her. She wrapped her arms around herself, as if to ward off the sudden chill, but it wasn't just the cold that affected her. It felt as though the essence of Eliza Goodwin was present, mourning her lost love.

Dylan, too, sensed the shift. He glanced around, his eyes searching the surroundings before settling back on Sienna. "It's said that sometimes, when her story is told, she makes her presence felt," he whispered.

Sienna gulped. "It feels like she's right here with us, doesn't it?"

He nodded and stepped closer to Sienna. "You know, sometimes the past doesn't just stay in the past, especially in places like this where emotions are so deep."

The two stood close, wrapped up in the place's ambiance. After what seemed like an eternity, the forest stirred once again. Birds resumed their songs, and the gentle gurgle of the brook filled the air, bringing with it a sense of normalcy.

Sienna took a deep breath. "That was... surreal."

Dylan smiled, his eyes still reflecting the depth of the moment.

As they progressed down the trail, they found a serene spot beside a moss-draped rock near the water's edge. The streams refreshing mist cast upon their faces created a calming ambiance. Here, Dylan opened up, sharing more about his life. With every story, Sienna glimpsed a side of Dylan that was worlds away from grand events or the expectations tied to the Whitmore name.

They shared sandwiches, chuckling at the quirks of guests they'd encountered at the resort. Sienna playfully mimicked a demanding guest, causing Dylan to burst into laughter. Amid their camaraderie, sometimes their hands would accidentally brush. Each fleeting touch left her wanting more. Their eyes would meet, holding onto that shared moment a second longer than necessary.

The world around them seemed to blur. It wasn't just about the trail's mysteries anymore; it was about them, discovering each other amidst nature's embrace. At one particularly breathtaking viewpoint, they stood side by side, looking out at the expanse below. The sun's rays painted the sky in hues of gold and crimson, casting a warm glow on their faces.

Dylan broke the silence, his voice barely above a whisper, "I often come here when I need a break from... well, everything. It's like a sanctuary."

Sienna glanced sideways at him. "The resort, the parties, the expectations... It's a lot, isn't it?"

He sighed, nodding. "More than you can imagine. But out here, it all fades away."

She felt a pang of sympathy. Maybe the player rumors were just that—rumors. Perhaps beneath the facade was a soul yearning for simplicity, just like her.

As the afternoon progressed, the forest canopy and the fading sunlight wrapped them in their own secluded world. The sky, once clear and blue, gradually darkened with gathering clouds. Suddenly, a lone raindrop landed on Sienna's nose, followed by more that pattered against the surrounding leaves. What started as a few sporadic drops quickly escalated into a steady downpour, and in no time, they were caught in a full-blown storm.

Dylan glanced up, cursing softly under his breath. "Didn't think it'd rain today."

Sienna laughed, feeling the water soak through her clothes. "Neither did I. We need to find shelter."

Driven by the urgency of the situation, they scanned their surroundings. It was Dylan who spotted it first — a small cave-like alcove tucked away between massive boulders, offering a semblance of refuge from the relentless rain.

"Over there!" he pointed, and without wasting a moment, the two of them sprinted towards it. They stumbled into the shelter, gasping and dripping, their bodies pressed close together in the confined space. The sudden proximity caused Sienna's heart to race — or perhaps it was the sprint; she couldn't quite tell.

Outside, the rain continued its symphony; the sound amplified in their shelter. Each drop seemed to beat in time with Sienna's heart. Dylan's body felt warm against hers, and she turned to look at him. Their eyes locked, and for a moment, the rain, the alcove, and the world outside ceased to exist. It was just the two of them, their breaths mingling in the cool, damp air.

"I, uh…" Dylan started, his voice betraying a hint of nervousness. "I didn't expect our day to turn out quite like this."

Sienna chuckled softly, "Neither did I." She paused, her gaze dropping to his lips for a split second, then returning to his eyes. "You think Eliza's trying to tell us something?"

Dylan smirked. "Maybe she's playing matchmaker from beyond?"

Their shared laughter echoed, but beneath it, an unspoken tension simmered. As the rain continued its serenade, Sienna wondered if Dylan was feeling the same pull she was experiencing. She ventured a guess. "You know, I've always found the rain… romantic."

Dylan, with a playful tilt of his head, replied, "Is that so? Perhaps we should thank the rain then, for this unexpected moment."

In the close quarters, their shared laughter gradually faded, leaving behind a silence charged with anticipation. The dim light filtering through the curtain of rain outside cast a gentle glow on their faces, highlighting the drops of water that clung to their skin.

Dylan's look, usually playful, took on a serious intensity. He paused for just a moment before closing the gap between them.

Their lips barely touched when Sienna, swept up in the moment, shifted her stance. Unfortunately, her head collided with a low-hanging rock, abruptly ending their kiss. A surprised yelp escaped her as they both pulled back, trying not to laugh at the sudden turn of events.

Dylan pulled back, concern in his eyes. "Are you okay?"

Sienna rubbed the spot where she'd bumped her head and chuckled. "I'm fine. Just the universe's way of keeping me grounded, literally."

Dylan's laughter joined hers, easing the moment. "Seems like nature always has a knack for reminding us it's here, usually when we least expect it."

Then Dylan took her hand, intertwining their fingers, and together they shifted. They settled side by side, their shoulders touching, leaning back against the cool stone of the alcove. The silence wasn't uncomfortable; it was a shared moment of contentment and understanding. The steady rhythm of the rain became their soundtrack, each drop telling stories of moments like this—fleeting, yet unforgettable.

"You know, I've always had this privilege, this cushioned life as a Whitmore, but with it comes a cage. Walls of expectations." Dylan's eyes held a sadness, the weight of a gilded cage pressing down. "It's why I'm here, working different roles at the resort. To understand the real essence of our business, and to, well, find a bit of freedom. My grandfather... he always told me about his adventures, and I guess that's what inspired me."

Sienna nodded, the longing for freedom in his voice resonating with her own aspirations. "I grew up on my grandmother's tales. Stories of love, adventures, the beauty of nature. It's why I'm so drawn to the outdoors. My parents taught me the values of hard work and integrity. They've given up so much for me to attend college, and every day, I juggle classes with part-time jobs. But when I'm out here," she gestured at the surrounding expanse, "it feels like I can breathe. I dream of seeing the world, maybe writing about it or making documentaries."

"Documentaries?" Dylan's eyebrows lifted in genuine interest, his hand brushing a droplet from her cheek, his touch lingering longer than necessary. "That's amazing. The world needs more authentic storytellers, people who can capture that raw essence of life."

Sienna blushed at his touch, her heart rate picking up. "It's just a dream for now," she admitted. "But every time I'm out here, it feels like a step closer to that reality."

Dylan's fingers brushed against hers. "You know, our dreams might not be so different," he mused. "I want the resort to be a place that tells stories, too. Stories of nature, of sustainability, of connection."

Their faces were close now, their breaths mingling. Sienna's eyes flickered down to his lips and then back up, a challenge and invitation all in one. "Sometimes, dreams have a way of becoming reality when we least expect them to."

With that, Dylan leaned in, capturing her lips once again, this time with a soft, lingering kiss.

As minutes passed, the intensity of the rain diminished. What started as a torrential downpour eased into a soft drizzle, then mere droplets falling from the trees.

"Seems like the storm's passing," Dylan remarked, peering out of the alcove.

She nodded, taking a deep breath, inhaling the fresh scent that always follows a rainstorm. "Let's get going," she said.

Together, they stepped out onto the damp earth, drawn by the beckoning end of the trail. The world around shimmered with droplets on leaves, and distant birdsong filled the air as they journeyed side by side.

Chapter Four

Whispers of the Past

The forest seemed alive with ancient memories, each rustling leaf and distant bird call echoing the rhythms of long-past eras. As Sienna and Dylan ventured deeper, they came upon a fork in their path—a divergence where beams of dappled sunlight broke through the thick canopy, beckoning them to explore.

However, as they approached, a sudden silence enveloped them, halting the forest sounds. It was as though time itself paused, paying homage. At the end of the side trail, there was a brook. Next to it stood an old marker, entangled in nature's grasp, its story veiled by moss and time.

Dylan, a flicker of unease in his eyes, stepped forward. He brushed aside the debris to reveal the cracked inscriptions beneath. Words like *love* and *betrayal* emerged, causing him to swallow hard, a shadow passing over his face. "I've never been here," he whispered. "This is where she died... Eliza Goodwin."

Sienna followed his gaze to the marker when suddenly, Dylan staggered back, clutching his cheek where a vivid red mark flared.

His eyes widened, a flash of recognition crossing his face, but he quickly covered it with a forced casualness. "Must've been a stray branch or something," he muttered, dismissing the incident, although the mark on his cheek suggested otherwise.

Sienna looked around, noting the absence of any trees close enough to have hit him. Then, the air grew heavy, making each breath a struggle. Wordlessly, Sienna reached for Dylan's hand. Did he feel it too? It was if time itself had grown dense. A barely noticeable breeze stirred, making Sienna shiver. She thought she felt a light touch on her hair, like a caress. Startled, she looked around, but nothing was out of place.

She hesitated a moment, her eyes searching Dylan's, then whispered, "Let's keep going."

Dylan nodded. Together, they went back to the main path; the marker continuing its silent watch over the brook, waiting for the next souls brave enough to approach.

As they distanced themselves from the scene, the forest stirred back to life. The suffocating stillness gave way to nature's chorus: leaves rustling in the breeze, the lively calls of birds overhead, and the harmonious hum of insects. Yet Sienna couldn't shake a nagging sense of unease. Now and then, she thought she heard an extra footstep or a whisper uncomfortably close.

Meanwhile, Dylan seemed captivated by the beauty, unaware of her discomfort. "Every time I come here, it feels like the first time," he said, his voice taking on a distant tone.

Sienna nodded, but her senses were on high alert. When she tried to reach out and touch Dylan, a heavy sense of foreboding gripped her heart. It was as if an unseen force was warning her, urging her to maintain her distance. She tried shaking off the feeling, attributing it to the strange marker.

"You okay?" Dylan asked.

"Yeah, just... thought I felt something," Sienna replied, trying to sound casual.

The odd sensation intensified. Sienna was almost certain she heard muted whispers, but each time she tried to locate where they were coming from, they faded away. Despite the eerie atmosphere, being near Dylan provided a measure of comfort, even though he seemed oblivious to the ghostly undertones enveloping them.

Sienna pushed her discomfort aside. "Let's keep going."

For the rest of their hike, an unspoken tension lingered, with Sienna on edge and Dylan none the wiser. As they neared the parking lot, the dense canopy thinned, giving way to the open sky. A familiar crunch of gravel under their feet announced their arrival. The area, once bustling, had quieted down, with only two cars remaining in the lot. Long shadows stretched across the ground, dancing in the soft glow of the early evening sun.

Sienna walked towards her trusty Toyota and patted its roof. "This is me," she said with a hint of pride in her voice, always valuing her self-reliance.

Her eyes darted between the cars—her older, worn-out vehicle and Dylan's shiny BMW parked just a few spaces away. The contrast was a silent reminder of the different worlds they came from. A tight knot formed in her stomach as she caught a brief shadow of discomfort cross Dylan's face before he masked it. Did he regret bringing his fancy car? Was he judging her?

Dylan's voice broke through her spiraling thoughts. "You know, there's a diner not too far from here. Ever tried it?"

Sienna, grateful for the change in topic, shook her head. "Can't say I have."

"It's a classic. Let's grab a bite? You can follow me."

As Sienna drove behind Dylan, her mind was a whirlwind of thoughts. Growing up, she had always been the one hustling—picking up extra shifts, saving for everything, wearing her independence like a badge of honor. She took pride in managing on her own, driving an older car, and skipping nights out to make ends meet.

In stark contrast, Dylan's world seemed steeped in privilege. The allure of his lifestyle was undeniable—sleek cars, sophistication, and doors that were always open. Yet, it also brewed a mix of intimidation and insecurity within her. She wondered if he could ever understand the struggle of not having everything handed to him. Would she always feel a twinge of inadequacy around him? The pressures of 'having it all' already consumed her thoughts, and being near Dylan seemed to amplify these feelings tenfold.

The drive to the diner was short but tense. Dylan's BMW took each turn while Sienna followed in her older car, her headlights occasionally catching his image in the rearview mirror. She adjusted the radio and tried to shake off the heavy thoughts about their contrasting worlds.

Soon, the diner's glowing neon sign appeared, bathing the parking lot in a warm red glow. The place had a vintage vibe, which felt comforting. Dylan parked near the entrance, and Sienna pulled in beside him, pausing a moment to collect her thoughts before getting out.

As they walked side by side to the diner, the nostalgic sounds of a classic jukebox tune welcomed them. They stepped inside, and were wrapped in the hum of sizzling grills, lively chatter, and the smell of diner classics. Dylan gestured for Sienna to choose their seats. She picked two stools at the counter, their shiny chrome reflecting the diner's charm.

"These fries are the best," Dylan said, a hint of pride in his voice. "This place is my favorite."

Sienna looked at him. "You really prefer this to the upscale places you're used to?"

Dylan laughed, brushing a hand through his hair. "Yes! Growing up, I went to boarding schools, and our main house is in New York. But I've always loved it here. I didn't come every summer, but when I did..." He swept an affectionate hand around the diner. "The mountains, the atmosphere—it's grounding. Coming here feels like reconnecting with a piece of my heart."

Sienna leaned closer. "Why is that? If it's so special, wouldn't you want to come more often?"

Dylan paused and tilted his head before speaking. "Every summer, I could choose one place to spend my vacation. Despite having tons of options, I always picked here. It was a break from the pressures of school and high expectations. One summer, after a tough term, I found this diner while sulking around town. The smell of grilled burgers pulled me in. For a few hours, I wasn't the heir to a business empire or the kid who had to be perfect; I was just a teenager enjoying a burger."

Sienna smiled. "It's amazing how places tie us to memories, isn't it? My family camped up north every summer. Not here, but the feel is the same. Story Land, hiking, campfire nights with hotdogs on sticks." She smiled, a trace of nostalgia in her voice. "One summer, when I was seven, we stayed at a campground the entire season after losing our apartment. It was tough, but those memories are precious." She paused, her eyes wandering over the diner. "I've never been here before, yet it feels linked to all those moments from my past."

Dylan met her gaze, his expression softening with understanding. "That's the magic of places like this—they're timeless. Whether it's our hundredth visit or our first, they stir up memories and help us make new ones." He grinned. "Speaking of making memories, shall we start with those famous fries?"

The fries, golden and gleaming in a red plastic basket, beckoned. Sienna bit into one, its crispy shell giving way to the soft, flavorful potato inside. The perfect blend of salt and earthiness exploded in her mouth. She couldn't help but moan in delight. Dylan chuckled, "That good, huh?" Blushing, Sienna nodded and reached for another.

Their easy banter continued as they shared the meal, but Sienna's thoughts lingered, pondering her place in Dylan's world. Could their different paths merge, or would the contrasts always stand out?

Then she caught sight of an older woman a few booths away, observing them. Her face, etched with lines that spoke of many years, was focused. To Sienna, there was something unsettling about her stare. She couldn't help but wonder if the woman recognized something in their interaction, or if she was lost in her own memories from long ago.

It felt almost as if she was taking part in their conversation, piecing together his own narrative from their interactions. The old woman seemed to sense her observation. She approached, steps deliberate but unhurried. Sienna's heartbeat quickened, curiosity piqued.

"You two were at the old Eliza Goodwin monument earlier today, weren't you?" she inquired.

Sienna's brows knit together. "How did you know?" she asked, a touch of disbelief in her voice.

The woman smiled. "I heard you two talking about it earlier. Plus, folks who venture there always have a certain... look about them afterward."

Dylan raised an eyebrow. "We were, indeed. It's quite a spot. Have you always known about it?"

"Always?" The woman laughed. "Well, that might be stretching it a bit, but let's just say the story of that place has been a part of my family's lore for many years. I'm Mrs. Caldwell, and I've spent a fair bit of my life digging into our town's history."

Sienna's voice carried a hint of anticipation. "We sensed something... peculiar there. If you have time, we'd love to hear more about it."

Mrs. Caldwell settled onto a stool beside them. After taking a moment to collect her thoughts, she began, "You see, Eliza Goodwin wasn't just any young woman. She was fiercely independent and had dreams much larger than the constraints of her station."

Dylan and Sienna exchanged a glance as Mrs. Caldwell continued, "Working on the estate of the ambitious Colonel Joseph Whitmore, she fell in love with John Swansonl, a farmhand with eyes as deep as the Notch's valleys. They both dreamt of a future away from the watchful eyes of the Colonel."

Her voice took on a softer, mournful tone. "To secure this dream, Eliza handed over her saved dowry to John and left for Portsmouth to plan for their new life. However, Colonel Whitmore, sensing an opportunity, convinced John to abandon Eliza and join the forces for independence, with her dowry as finance."

Sienna nodded, remembering the story.

Mr. Caldwell continued, "When Eliza found out, her heartbreak was immense. Driven by both love and a sense of betrayal, she raced back through the winter terrains. But near an icy brook, overcome by cold and despair, she made the fateful decision to cross it. She didn't survive the chilling waters."

A silence hung in the air, only broken by the low hum of the jukebox in the background.

"But that's not where the tale ends," Mrs. Caldwell added. "Learning of Eliza's tragic end, Jim was shattered. The guilt of his betrayal and her death led him to madness, and he died, tormented, in an asylum."

Dylan's voice, soft and full of emotion, broke the silence. "And the Colonel?"

Mrs. Caldwell's eyes darkened. "He might've escaped man-made justice, but they say nature has its own ways. His life, thereafter, was filled with misfortune and tragedy. Some believe it was Eliza's spirit ensuring he paid for his treachery."

Her voice dropped to a near whisper, causing Sienna and Dylan to lean in. "Some say that Eliza's spirit, in her sorrow and anger, cursed the Whitmore lineage. They say that no Whitmore shall ever find a true love that lasts, that every romance is doomed to end in heartbreak."

Sienna shot a sidelong glance at Dylan, whose face had turned a shade paler, the playful light in his eyes replaced by a shadowed darkness. He looked lost in thought, haunted by his family's past. However, he masked it, offering a tight-lipped smile to Mrs. Caldwell.

The old woman, sensing the shift, said, "But legends, they change and evolve. Curses can be broken, and destinies can be rewritten."

Sienna sighed and broke the silence, remarking, "You have a gift, Mrs. Caldwell. Ever considered being a tour guide? Your storytelling is...captivating."

"Perhaps in another life, dear." The woman chuckled, "For now, I'm content with occasional listeners like you."

Sienna's eyes were wide as she watched Mrs. Caldwell shuffle back to his booth. "That was... intense," she began. "A curse? Dylan, do you think she knew who you are? About you being a Whitmore?"

Dylan's lips pressed into a thin line, an uncharacteristic unease flitting across his features. "It's hard to say. Maybe she just wanted to spook the city folks who wandered into her territory. The Whitmores are well known in these parts." He took a deep breath, then admitted, "But there is talk of a curse within the family. I've always taken it with a grain of salt, considering it is just a strange tale spun by the older generations."

Sienna leaned forward, intrigued. "A family curse? That's... fascinating, and kind of scary."

Dylan chuckled, trying to lighten the mood. "Every illustrious family has its skeletons, right? Perhaps ours is more... mythical. But honestly, I wouldn't worry too much about it. Mrs. Caldwell probably just has a flair for theatrics."

Sienna played with the straw in her drink, deep in thought. "It's strange," she began, "how some stories seem to transcend time. That story of Eliza and John... it felt personal, as if we've lived it before."

Dylan looked thoughtful. "You mean like... destiny?"

She nodded. "Maybe. It's as if our paths, like theirs, are intertwined by something larger than just chance. A cosmic pull, maybe."

Dylan studied her. "That's a heavy thought, Sienna. But it's beautiful, too. Do you believe in fate?"

She hesitated, then whispered, "I didn't use to. But with everything that's happened, I'm wondering if there are forces at play beyond our understanding. I just... I hope our story has a different ending than Eliza's and John's. And it's one filled with happiness, not heartbreak."

Dylan reached across the table and squeezed her hand. "Me too, Sienna. And if there's one thing I've learned, it's that we have the power to write our own story, no matter the family curses or old tales we've heard."

Sienna smiled, feeling lighter from his words, though the stories and omens of the past still echoed quietly in the back of her mind.

As they left the diner, the rain from earlier had given way to a clear sky. Stars peppered across the inky black night and Sienna took a deep breath, the crispness of the air filling her lungs. However, amid the peace, a sudden chill enveloped her, as if an icy finger had traced the length of her spine.

She stopped and glanced around, attempting to source the cause of the feeling. At the edge of the diner's parking lot, a shadow darted — so quick and indistinct that she questioned if it was a trick of the light or her imagination playing games with her. She remembered the tale from earlier and her experience on the trail, and couldn't help but wonder if it was Eliza's spirit. Was she being warned? Protected?

Or was the spirit curious, seeking a connection in their shared experiences of love's intoxicating pull?

Sienna turned to find Dylan watching her, a hint of concern in his eyes. "You okay?" he asked.

She hesitated before answering, choosing not to voice her unsettling thoughts. "Yeah, just lost in thought. The tale from earlier was... a lot."

Dylan stepped closer, his proximity offering warmth and a sense of security. "Legends have a way of lingering, especially when they're tied to real emotions," he murmured, his voice a soothing balm to her jumbled nerves.

The intensity of his gaze drew her in, the world narrowing to just the two of them. They gravitated closer, their lips inching toward one another. Their kiss was soft, holding the promise of many more shared moments.

Dylan pulled away and brushed a stray strand of hair behind Sienna's ear. "Goodnight, Sienna," he whispered, leaving the words unsaid but understood — there was more to come between them.

With a last lingering glance, Sienna made her way to her car. As she drove away, the shadows and uncertainties of the evening faded, replaced by the warmth of that kiss and the promise of the days to come. But deep down, the chill she'd felt outside the diner remained, a quiet reminder of the mysteries that surrounded them.

After the eerie vibe of the evening and the nostalgic feel of the diner, her dorm room seemed both comforting and strange at the same time.

She shrugged off her jacket and kicked off her shoes before crawling into bed. Outside, the world was peaceful, bathed in soft moonlight—a sharp contrast to the whirlwind of emotions swirling inside her.

She had just settled under her covers, the cool sheets enveloping her tired body, when the soft ping of a text message broke the silence. Sienna grabbed her phone from the bedside table and opened it to find a message from Dylan.

Hey, just wanted to make sure you got home safe.

The warmth that spread through her was immediate and comforting.

Home and all tucked in. Thanks for checking.

There was a brief pause before another message from Dylan popped up.

So... heard of the Lost Pond Trail?

She raised an eyebrow, intrigued. *Another trail? You're full of surprises.*

His response came quick. *Wait till you hear the legends surrounding this one. Thought it might be our next adventure?*

She grinned, typing back, *You trying to scare me with another ghost story?*

Maybe. Or maybe just looking for another excuse to spend time with you, he replied.

The fluttering in her stomach intensified. After taking a breath, she typed, *Will I see you during the week at the resort?*

Dylan's reply took a little longer this time. *Things are hectic, but we're still on for coffee tomorrow, right?*

Definitely, she responded, heart pounding.

Goodnight, Sienna, he texted.

Goodnight, Dylan, she replied, placing her phone back on the bedside table.

After turning off her lamp, Sienna settled deeper into her pillows. While the shadows of Eliza's legend and the unexpected encounters of the day played in her mind, the most persistent thought was the developing bond between her and Dylan. The summer had presented her with mysteries and adventures, but the most tantalizing prospect of all was the deepening connection she felt with him.

CHAPTER FIVE

Promises in Twilight

Sienna woke up refreshed, her mind still replaying the delightful moments of her adventure. Eager to start the day, she laced up her shoes for a morning walk around the grounds. The crisp air and quiet paths provided a perfect backdrop for her thoughts, which were filled with the anticipation of meeting Dylan again.

Birdsongs filled the air, creating a natural melody while dewdrops sparkled on the leaves, painting the scene with a touch of early morning magic. Sienna inhaled, relishing the crisp, cool air and the peaceful solitude around her.

Her tranquility was interrupted by the buzz of her phone, but seeing Dylan's name flash across the screen quickened her pulse and brought a flush to her cheeks. The message that followed chilled her excitement to dismay. "Sienna, I'm truly sorry. I can't meet this morning. Family obligations. I hope you can understand."

She froze for a moment, surprised by the sudden shift in her emotions. Anger bubbled up inside. Was his wealthy background allowing him to set the terms of their relationship? Was she just a passing fancy in his privileged life?

Trying to keep her composure, she typed back, "Of course. Just let me know when you're available."

His reply was quick and non-committal. "Thank you for understanding. We'll reconnect soon."

This did little to calm her swirling thoughts. As Sienna reflected on the exchange, a whisper brushed past her ears—a sigh that seemed to echo with sorrows. The momentary pause left her shivering, prompting her to continue walking. The sun, which had seemed so welcoming earlier, now felt cold, mirroring the sudden gap that had opened up between Dylan and herself. Could she really find a place in his world, or was she destined to always feel just out of reach?

This emotional churning only intensified her sense of dislocation since the hike. Though the resort maintained its daily cadence, an uncanny haze consumed her nights. The legends of Eliza Goodwin seemed to resonate within her, echoes of the past clamoring for attention.

Since the day Dylan canceled their morning plans, Sienna's fascination with the Eliza Goodwin legend had deepened into a full-blown obsession. As days turned into weeks, she spent her free time hunched over a computer in the resort's business center. She dove into the mysteries of New Hampshire's history circa 1778. Under the harsh glow of the computer screens, Sienna sifted through articles, historical records, and any references she could find.

Her focus soon shifted towards understanding the experiences of women during the Revolutionary War. The stories she discovered highlighted their resilience and fortitude amidst great hardship. Women of that era were often confined within rigid societal roles—caring for families, maintaining homes, and tending to wounded soldiers. These examples of survival and courage moved Sienna, fueling her determination to uncover more about Eliza's life.

However, the more she delved into the past, the more it intertwined with her present. Sleepless nights became the norm as the history she had read infiltrated her dreams. She envisioned women in period attire, heard the march of soldiers' boots, and the distant beat of war drums. These dreams often left her waking up with a racing heart, overwhelmed by desperation, as though she had experienced those turbulent times herself.

Her relentless pursuit was taking a toll on her. Dark circles formed under her eyes, and her usual energy dimmed. Concerned comments from resort staff and her new friends became frequent, noting her worn-out appearance. But Sienna was too captivated by the past to heed them. She felt an unbreakable connection to Eliza's story, a bond that pulled her deeper into history, unable to detach even if she wanted to.

One evening, after they had finished their dinner, Sienna and Maya took a stroll along the winding pathways. They chatted, enjoying the cool night air and the crunch of gravel beneath their feet. Their conversation reflected the strong connection they had developed over the past few weeks.

"You seem distant," Maya remarked.

Sienna hesitated, her eyes lingering on the path ahead. "It's just this place. Adjusting to everything is... challenging."

Not convinced, Maya nudged, "It's not something about Dylan, is it?"

"No, it's not about Dylan," Sienna responded, her tone betraying a touch of fatigue. "He's complicated, yes, but I've let him go."

Maya looked at Sienna. "You haven't been sleeping well. I can tell."

A weary smile played on Sienna's lips. "Is it that obvious?" she sighed. "I'm just caught up in something, I think. But thank you, Maya. It's kind of you to be concerned."

As the pair continued along the resort's walkways, a sudden, unseasonably cold gust of wind seemed to sweep through the area. Out of the corner of her eye, Sienna glimpsed a shadowy figure near an old oak tree. But just as quickly as it had appeared, it vanished.

Sienna stopped to tie her shoelace, attempting to hide her startled reaction and using the moment to collect herself.

Maya, waiting and oblivious to the ghostly presence, remarked, "That was cold! Odd for a summer evening."

Sienna forced a light laugh. "Yeah, probably just a freak New England weather thing."

Her heart raced, but she tried to play it cool. Despite her effort, she couldn't stop herself from casting quick glances around, half-expecting to see the apparition again. Everything around them, however, remained peaceful, bathed in the soft twilight. She kept her concerns to herself, trying not to worry Maya.

Sienna's nights were filled with restlessness. In her dreams, a haunting lullaby—melancholic and ancient—wove tales of deep love and loss. When she woke, she'd scan for the source of the music, only to find the quiet room.

During the day, she felt an unseen presence accompany her near water features like fountains or brooks. Sometimes, she'd feel a gentle touch on her arm or hear a sigh carried on the breeze, as if a spirit was trying to share its sorrow with her.

These supernatural encounters blurred her sense of reality. Sipping morning coffee, she'd half expect to see her cup shrouded in mist. The gardens now seemed to host shifting shadows that flickered at the edge of her vision.

"Is this all in my head?" Sienna whispered to herself, looking into a mirror for answers. Her reflection showed weary eyes filled with confusion. And as she voiced her fears, a mournful sigh seemed to fill the room, echoing her inner turmoil.

The next day, as Sienna walked down the corridor to begin her shift, her footsteps rang out on the polished stone. Her thoughts were elsewhere when an unexpected grip encircled her waist. Her breath hitched, a scream bubbling up but never escaping, as she was quickly whisked sideways into the shadows of an empty banquet hall.

The glow from the ornate chandeliers cast a soft light on Dylan's face as he gazed into Sienna's eyes and drew her closer. She had all but written him off, but as he kissed her, the surprise gave way to a rush of emotions. For a brief instant, everything else blurred away, their connection becoming the only thing that mattered.

As his hands touched the small of her back, Sienna felt a shiver run through her, torn between the thrill of his touch and annoyance at herself for letting him get to her again. Just as she lost herself in the moment, he pulled away. Regret, perhaps even a hint of pain, flickered in his eyes before he turned and disappeared through a side door.

Sienna stood there, trying to catch her breath, her hand touching her lips. The encounter left her in a daze as she slowly made her way to start her shift.

Throughout the day, Sienna moved mechanically, serving guests and managing her tasks. Her mind kept drifting back. She was annoyed with herself for being so affected by him.

Every hallway, every doorway, every hidden corner of the resort became a place of possibility. She glanced over her shoulder at the slightest hint of a footstep, hoping and dreading in equal measure Dylan would appear. She could almost feel the pull of his presence, imagining his fingers brushing against her, or his gaze as he watched her from afar. Every unexpected touch or shadowed figure had her heart racing.

It kept her in an almost perpetual state of distraction. The war within her was tumultuous—she couldn't decide if she wanted to confront him or never see him again.

Her inattentiveness did not go unnoticed. "Sienna," the day manager said, pulling her aside mid-shift, "This isn't like you. Is everything okay? You've been off all day."

The reprimand snapped her back to reality. The fog she had been in cleared, replaced by responsibilities and the repercussions of her distraction. She murmured an apology, trying to ground herself and focus on the job. But no matter how hard she tried, she couldn't get Dylan out of her head.

After her shift, Sienna headed to the cafeteria. The room was bustling with activity. Groups of her colleagues gathered together, chatting in lively tones. But as Sienna approached, the atmosphere changed. Conversations turned into hushed whispers. She could feel the eyes on her..

"Sienna! Over here!" Maya called. Sienna made her way to where her friend sat, relieved to see a friendly face.

Maya's gaze probed her face. "You okay?" she asked, nudging a cup of tea toward Sienna.

After taking a deep breath, Sienna nodded. "I'm fine. Just another day, I guess."

There was a pause, one filled with the unspoken, before Maya ventured further. "People have been talking... about you and Dylan. Someone saw you two together." Her voice trailed off, her eyes full of questions. "And given the Whitmores' reputation, well... they're all wondering how it's going to play out."

Sienna's heart skipped a beat. She had hoped the stolen moment would remain theirs alone, but in a place like this, there were no secrets. She met Maya's eyes. "It was just... a kiss. Nothing more." But even as she said it, she wondered if she was trying to convince Maya or herself.

Before Sienna could process this, Ben sauntered over. "Sienna," he began, fixing her with a meaningful look, "is it true? Are you and Dylan...you know?"

She met his gaze. "Why does it matter, Ben? Why is everyone so interested?"

Ben sighed, glancing away, "Because, Sienna, Dylan's a Whitmore. There are expectations, stories, history..."

"You know we care about you." Maya intervened. "We just don't want to see you hurt."

The raw wound of their hike together throbbed in Sienna's consciousness. It jarred that, aside from today, she had not seen Dylan at all. They'd made plans, which he canceled, a fact she'd concealed from even Maya. That slight felt personal, and she harbored the sting, tucking it away behind a facade of indifference even as it gnawed at her.

"The Whitmore family is...complicated," Maya remarked.

Sienna smiled. "Aren't all families?"

Maya and Ben exchanged glances, the unspoken agreement to drop the topic clear between them. The trio continued with lighter banter for a while longer, but Sienna's thoughts kept drifting back to Dylan.

After her friends had left, Sienna pulled out her phone, her fingers hovering over the screen before she typed out a message: "Hey Dylan, hope all's well. Will I see you again?"

She hit send and the familiar anxiety of waiting for a reply settled in her stomach. Minutes passed, feeling more like hours, and then she saw it—the read receipt. But those minutes turned into more minutes, and no reply came. The uncertainty gnawed at her.

Sienna felt the urge to drown her unease with some distraction. Instead of heading straight to her room, she detoured to the resort's business center, eager to delve deeper into the legend of Eliza Goodwin.

Once engrossed in her research, hours slipped away, and by the time she left the business center, the resort was blanketed in the cool embrace of night. Sienna chose the scenic route back, hoping the beauty of the gardens under the moonlit sky would clear her head.

At night, the gardens transformed into a serene, almost otherworldly space. Moonlight streamed through the branches, casting silvery pools of light along the pathways while crickets chirped a soothing nocturnal melody. For a moment, Sienna felt a sense of peace, the stresses of the day melting away.

But as she continued, the shadows lengthened, and the air grew chillier. An eerie feeling crept up her spine, giving her the unsettling impression that she was being watched. Her heart beat faster, and she picked up her pace. When she glanced over her shoulder—nothing but the deepening darkness met her eyes.

She hurried back to the building that housed her room. As she turned the corner to her hallway, she saw a familiar silhouette leaning against the door to her room.

Dylan.

He looked up as she approached, his blue eyes intense in the dim light. Without a word, he stepped forward, bridging the gap between them. She took a step back.

He raised his hands in a gesture of peace. "I didn't mean to startle you."

After taking the time to gather herself, she managed a weak smile. "It's okay. Just been one of those days." She motioned for him to follow her inside. But as the door opened wider, the animated chatter of her roommates ceased. Three sets of eyes darting between Sienna and the handsome figure behind her. The weight of their stares was palpable.

Dylan cleared his throat, breaking the tense silence. "Maybe we could go somewhere else?"

She hesitated for just a moment, then agreed, and they made their way to the parking lot. The roar of the engine from Dylan's sleek BMW coupe seemed to symbolize the vast difference in their worlds. As they drove away from the resorts grounds, Sienna glanced at Dylan's profile, noticing the tension in his jaw and the worry lines that seemed more pronounced tonight.

Finally, he broke the silence.

"I'm sorry," Dylan began, his eyes still fixed on the road but his tone sincere. "For earlier. I saw you, and I just... I couldn't help myself."

Sienna's gaze shifted from the window to him. She was torn between anger and desire. "You ignore my texts, vanish without explanation, and then think you can just pull me into a corner to make out?" Her voice trembled.

Dylan sighed, running a hand through his hair. "I know. It's complicated, Sienna."

She turned to face him, her frustration clear. "Isn't everything with you? One minute you're the charming guy who swept me off my feet on our hike, and the next, you're distant and elusive, always hiding behind vague excuses."

He pulled into an overlook and turned off the engine. Then he faced her, taking a deep breath. "Sienna, you have every right to be angry. And I promise I'll explain everything.... But none of that excuses how I've been acting. You deserve better."

Sienna took a moment, trying to calm the storm inside her. "Dylan, I'm not some plaything you can pick up and drop when you feel like it. I thought we had something real, something special. But now, I just feel like I'm caught in this whirlwind that is Dylan Whitmore, and I don't know how to find my footing."

He reached out, taking her hand.

Sienna took a deep breath. "Look, Dylan, I can handle whispers and sidelong glances. But I need you to be honest with me. What's really going on?"

Dylan turned away for a moment, collecting himself. "My stepmom... she's been very sick. It's been hard on all of us." He admitted, his voice quivering.

Sienna's gaze softened. "I've heard the rumors. They talk at the resort, you know?"

He nodded. "I figured as much. What they don't know is that she's been more than just a stepmother to me. My mom passed away when I was just a baby. She stepped in, raising me as her own. We're close, incredibly close. And watching her suffer... it's tearing me apart."

Sienna reached out, placing a comforting hand on his. "I'm sorry, Dylan. I did not know."

He smiled, "Thank you. And on top of all that, the family dynamics... they're not normal... it's all a bit much."

She raised an eyebrow.

Dylan hesitated, his voice lowering. "There's something else," he sighed. "Remember the old woman at the diner? She mentioned Eliza's curse. My family avoids the topic, but whispers of it linger—they all believe in it. It's like an old family legend, the curse of the Whitmores."

A chill ran down Sienna's spine. "The same curse?" she asked.

He nodded. "Actually, the real reason I was on that hike the day we met was to see if connecting with Eliza might help my mom get better. But I found nothing."

"Nothing?" Sienna arched an eyebrow, her curiosity piqued. "I'm not so sure about that."

Dylan cracked a smile, and he brushed her cheek. "There was you, and you're definitely not nothing."

Sienna leaned in, her face flushing. "I've been looking into Eliza Goodwin's legend. The story has... captivated me," she confessed.

"It's a big part of our family history," Dylan acknowledged. "A tragic story of love, betrayal, and heartbreak. But the curse—it's believed to bring misfortune to any Whitmore who falls in love. Most the men in our family choose not to fall in love. My father was different- he did it twice."

Sienna, piecing everything together, suddenly realized the complexity of their relationship. Dylan's hesitance wasn't just about his stepmother's illness or his responsibilities at the resort. He was grappling with the fear of a curse, worried about what their growing closeness could mean for both of them.

Dylan let out a long breath. "It sounds crazy, right? But when I think about my family's past, I can't help but wonder. I've tried to talk about it with my dad and grandfather, but they shut it down quickly. My grandfather just warns, 'Don't fall in love,' and my dad... he doesn't want to believe it's real. To them, it's just a tale, but I've experienced things, felt things that make me think there's more to it."

Dylan paused, his gaze shifting to the dark road beyond the windshield. He swallowed hard, his Adam's apple bobbing. "There's something else I haven't shared, something I should have."

Sienna placed a comforting hand on his arm. "You can tell me, Dylan."

He took a deep breath, the grip on the steering wheel tightening before he relaxed. "Ever since that day in the woods, I haven't been sleeping well. At first, I thought it was just the stress of everything with my family. But then... every time I close my eyes, I see you."

Sienna's heart raced at his words, unsure of where he was going with this. She remained silent.

"In my dreams, it's always you," he continued, his voice shaky. "At first, it's beautiful—scenes of us laughing, walking together, or sharing moments. But then, they take a dark turn. I see all these terrible things happening to you—accidents, dangers, shadows closing in. I can't explain it, but it feels so real, as if they're premonitions."

Sienna's breath caught. "Premonitions?"

Dylan shook his head, frustration clear. "I don't know. It feels different, more vivid than regular nightmares. And the worst part is, I'm helpless in those dreams. I try reaching out to you, but something always stops me. It's like a constant reminder of the Whitmore curse, and I can't shake the feeling that by bringing you closer to me, I'm putting you in harm's way."

Sienna processed his words. She thought of her own experiences, the whispers she heard, the mysterious encounters at the resort. But looking at Dylan, the raw vulnerability in his eyes, she felt a rush of protectiveness.

"I've felt something too since our hike." Sienna's voice was gentle. "Whispers when no one's around, cold gusts on warm nights. I didn't want to believe, but after what's been happening..."

They shared a moment, both lost in the legends and the strange events surrounding them.

Dylan broke the silence, "Being with you this summer, it's been unexpected, and it feels different from anything I've known. But with these rumors, the family tales, and now your experiences... it scares me."

Sienna paused, keeping her gaze fixed on Dylan. "Dylan, these legends... they're stories. They are echoes of the past. We're here, in the present. And while I respect them, we can't let them overshadow us." She reached out, touching his hand. "Whatever we face, we face together."

His eyes met hers. "Thank you, Sienna. That means more than you know."

They sat in silence, enveloped by the night's stillness at the overlook—only the distant chirping of crickets and the occasional rustle of leaves breaking the quiet. Above, the stars twinkled, their soft, silvery light filtering through the car's sunroof.

Sienna turned to Dylan. "You know, it's weird," she whispered, "everything about this place, this moment... it feels like it's out of time."

He smiled, tucking a stray lock of her hair behind her ear. "Feels like the universe just paused everything for us, doesn't it? Just to let us be here, together."

They drifted from casual childhood stories to more revealing conversations. As they delved deeper, the space between them seemed to close, leaving them in a comfort of shared truths and raw emotion.

After another bout of quiet, Dylan took a deep breath and asked, "About all the ghost stories... Can you tell me more?"

She was relieved to share her concerns. "It's been really bizarre. I keep waking up to what sounds like lullabies. I see shadows flickering just beyond direct sight, and there's this weird chill that seems to linger around me."

Dylan's expression grew serious. "Eliza's history isn't just a tale. I can't shake the feeling that she's at the heart of the curse."

"You really think it's all real? Eliza and the curse?" Sienna asked.

He nodded. "I have a plan, a way we might figure this out. Are you free Monday?"

Sienna hesitated, memories of past disappointments clouding her expression. "Dylan, just promise me you won't bail this time."

"I can't change the past," Dylan said, his voice firm. "But I promise, this time I'll be there. No more letdowns."

Sienna paused, considering. Finally, she nodded. "Alright, I trust you. Monday it is."

Their moment was shattered by the ring of Dylan's phone. His hand tightened around hers before he pulled away. As he answered, his casual confidence shifted to concern.

"It's my stepmom," he murmured, anxiety threading through his voice as he tried to stay composed. "They've taken her to the hospital. I have to go."

Sienna felt a pang of sympathy for him. The vulnerability that had enveloped them earlier was now overshadowed by the urgent reality crashing in.

"I'm so sorry," she whispered.

He nodded, his face tense as he fought to maintain control. "Thanks. It's just... it's been tough, watching her fade and feeling so helpless."

They sat together for a minute before Dylan started the car, breaking the silence with its steady hum. The drive back to the resort was quiet, each lost in their thoughts. When they arrived, he parked and turned to her, his face lined with strain.

"I'm sorry our evening ended like this," he breathed.

She leaned in and kissed him. "It's okay. Life throws us curveballs. Just focus on your family right now. And when you're ready, I'll be here."

With one last look, he stepped out of the car and watched her walk into the resort. The night had been a rollercoaster of emotions, but as Sienna lay in bed later, one thing was clear: her bond with Dylan was just beginning, and whatever challenges lay ahead, they would face them together.

Chapter Six

Gifts of the Heart

Sienna had grown accustomed to the familiar hum of the White Pine Resort staff lounge, a refuge from her duties, always alive with chatter and camaraderie. Yet, something had shifted this evening.

Golden light washed over the patterned carpets lining the hallways, its warm glow stark against the cool undercurrents of tension Sienna felt as she approached the employee lounge. Words, snippets of hushed conversations, reached her ears and halted abruptly as she reached the threshold.

"... Dylan and her, alone at the—"

"...you'd think she'd have more sense, getting involved with—"

"... the Whitmore name and a mere—"

Each broken fragment pricked at her consciousness like a thorn. Sienna took a deep breath and entered. The room, with its melange of overstuffed chairs and dark woods bathed in soft ambient lighting, seemed to pause. A few heads turned, eyes meeting hers briefly before darting away. Conversations that had been lively seconds ago fell mute, replaced by artificial smiles and furtive glances among her colleagues.

She tried to dispel the unease, reminding herself she had done nothing wrong. Her relationship with Dylan was unexpected, but undeniably genuine. Yet, each step she took intensified the gnawing sensation in her stomach, like tendrils of smoke curling around her insides, planting seeds of doubt.

Was their connection fodder for every whispered rumor? Had their private moments turned into a public spectacle? Each shadowy glance and unspoken insinuation deepened her sense of violation.

She attempted to maintain her routine, exchanging casual pleasantries and making sure not to linger in one place too long. But even as she immersed herself in tasks, the undercurrents of gossip persisted. A colleague brushed past her, releasing an almost imperceptible sigh. Their fingers grazed, and the woman whispered, "Be careful, love. Not everyone wishes you well."

Sienna paused, stunned. The boundary between her professional life and personal feelings for Dylan blurred. How had something so pure become so corrupted in the mouths of others?

As the evening progressed, Sienna felt like an outsider. The resort seemed a labyrinth of mirrors, each reflection distorting her image. The real Sienna, the one who laughed and loved, seemed lost amid these warped perceptions.

She leaned against the balcony railing and took a deep breath of the night air. The complexity of her relationship with Dylan made her question the depth and authenticity of their connection. What was real, and how much had been tainted by the judgments of others?

The soft rustle of leaves and distant chatter from below provided a backdrop to her contemplation. But it was the quiet approach of footsteps that drew her out of her thoughts. Turning, she saw Dylan, the usual spark in his eyes replaced with weariness. However, his presence, even during uncertainty, was comforting, grounding her amidst the chaos.

Without a word, he stepped closer, enveloping her in his embrace. The world seemed to shrink, their shared heartbeats the only sound that mattered. She felt the slight tremble in his frame and tightened her grip, wanting to offer whatever solace she could.

"She's stable," Dylan whispered, his voice carrying a mix of relief and exhaustion. "They're letting her come home tomorrow."

Sienna could feel the emotion behind his words. "Tell me about her," she prompted.

Dylan leaned back against the railing, looking out into the night. "She's been everything to me. My mom passed when I was a baby, but when my dad remarried, my stepmother stepped in and never made me feel any less loved. She's kind, generous…"

He paused, the pain clear in his down-turned eyes. "My father, he's never been the same since he lost my mom. Something inside him broke. And he doesn't always treat my stepmother the way she deserves. It's complicated. My grandmother also passed away young, so she's the only consistent female figure I've had."

Tears welled in Sienna's eyes, spurred by the pain of Dylan's revelations and the relief of his stepmother's recovery. She reached out, cradling his face in her hands. "Dylan, that's wonderful news about her coming home." Overcome with emotion, she pressed her lips to his in a deep, comforting kiss.

Time seemed to stand still as they savored the moment. Yet their bubble of intimacy was shattered by a flicker at the edge of Sienna's vision. They pulled apart and turned towards the shadows at the balcony's fringe. There, caught in the interplay of moonlight and darkness, was a fleeting movement—too swift to decipher. Was it merely the echoes of the Whitmore curse or someone with intentions far more tangible?

Sienna's heart raced, her hand reaching for Dylan's. "Did you see that?" she whispered.

He nodded, scanning the area. "I did."

Silence surrounded them once more. Dylan squeezed Sienna's hand. "I should go," he murmured.

She nodded, understanding his need to be with his family and away from the prying eyes that seemed to be everywhere. "Be safe, Dylan," she said.

He smiled, pressing a soft kiss to her forehead. "Always."

With that, he disappeared into the night, leaving Sienna with a growing sense of unease. Whether they were being watched by someone from this realm or another, the challenges they faced were only growing.

Sienna's footsteps echoed on the polished floors of the resort as she clocked out, the residual stress of her shift dissipating. The familiar sight of Maya waiting by the lockers brought a much-needed smile to her face.

"Finally!" Maya exclaimed, looping her arm around Sienna's. "I was thinking we'd need a search party! How about the cafe?"

Sienna nodded, grateful for Maya's attempt to keep things light. Together, they made their way through the resort's corridors to the cafe next to the main lounge.

As Sienna sipped her latte and Maya chatted animatedly, the peace was shattered by Lila and Monica's abrupt arrival. Their confidence was palpable, and their intrusion was no accident.

"We saw you two from across the room and just had to join," Monica said, her tone veiling her true intentions. Without waiting for an invitation, both women slid into the booth beside them.

Lila's gaze swept over Sienna, her lips twisting into a smirk. "Spending a lot of time with Dylan, I hear. Reminds me of last summer when he couldn't look away from me."

Monica's laugh rang hollow. "Those Whitmore men—always on to the next best thing."

Maya rolled her eyes. "What do you want? If you're here to stir up old stories, find another table."

Lila ignored Maya and leaned closer. "Just thought you should know what you're getting into with Dylan. His little... adventures never last."

Monica's smirk widened. "Be careful, dear. You wouldn't want to be just another Whitmore conquest."

Though Maya tensed, ready to confront them, Sienna took a deep breath and responded with composure, "Thank you for the advice, but my relationship with Dylan is none of your business."

As the duo left with a final smug glance, Maya exhaled. "Why must they meddle in everything?"

Sienna's lips curled into a mischievous smile, her fingers tracing the rim of her coffee mug. "You know, Maya, Dylan and I... we kissed. And it was magical."

Maya's eyes lit up, her initial surprise turning into a beaming smile. "Really? Oh, Si! That's wonderful!"

But as her excitement surged, her protective side emerged. "I'm thrilled for you, Sienna. Just promise me you'll be careful? I want the best for you, especially in love."

Sienna met Maya's earnest gaze. "I promise, Maya. And thank you for always having my back."

Whispers, insinuations, and sidelong glances had spun a story in Sienna's mind she hadn't considered before. What had Dylan done to earn such a notorious reputation? Doubts loomed large, yet amid the voices in her head, reason prevailed. It reminded her of the toxic nature of gossip and how easily distorted stories could skew perception. Sienna resolved to find the truth from Dylan.

Sienna replayed Lila's and Monica's veiled warnings and overt insinuations. Determined to understand the truth from Dylan himself, she pulled out her phone and sent him a message. His almost immediate reply told her he was in the offices.

Despite the possibility of waiting for a more appropriate moment, the urgency to confront him propelled her forward. She approached one of the resort's grand halls, reserved for formal events. The unmistakable deep resonance of Dylan's voice reached her ears, piquing her curiosity.

Sienna tucked herself behind an ornate marble pillar and listened. The familiar, authoritative tones of Dylan's father and grandfather carried through their hushed but intense conversation, sending a thrill of urgency through her veins.

"Understand, Dylan," his father's voice was authoritative, "the Whitmore reputation is paramount. It's not just about us, it's generations of hard work and legacy. We can't afford another scandal."

Dylan's voice carried a note of frustration. "I understand, Dad. But what does that have to do with—"

"The last one," his grandfather cut in, his voice dripping with disdain. "Remember? How we had to clean up after? We won't let that happen again."

Sienna's heart sank, her mind racing. What were they talking about? What "last one"?

"I know what happened," Dylan responded, tension clear in his tone. "But Sienna is different—"

"Like the others said they were?" his father countered, his voice dripping with sarcasm. "Or have you forgotten so quickly?"

The room went silent for a moment, the tension palpable. "Alright," Dylan conceded, his voice a whisper. "I'll end it. I'll do what's best for the family."

Sienna's heart felt like it was being squeezed in a vise. She'd expected Dylan to stand up for her, to counter his family's apparent disapproval. But he seemed to fold under their pressure, leaving her feeling betrayed.

Tears pricked Sienna's eyes as she backed away. Had Dylan discussed their private moments with his family? Or was she being judged based on unknown past events? The weight of her insecurities, compounded by the sting of perceived betrayal, made it hard to breathe.

She needed space to think. Sienna vowed to uncover the truth, but the glimpse into a world she wasn't prepared for left her reeling.

The fading echoes of Dylan's conversation with his father and grandfather reverberated in the hallway. Pressed against the cold wall, hidden by a tapestry depicting some historic event, Sienna felt the oppressive weight of the overheard words. Each heartbeat seemed to echo the painful revelations.

She risked a glance around the corner and caught Dylan's eye. His usually confident gaze was now clouded with desperation. He stepped towards her, his mouth parting as if to speak, but Sienna, driven by instinct, turned and fled.

As she hurried out, Dylan attempted to follow, but was obstructed by his imposing grandfather.

"Dylan!" the elder Whitmore's voice boomed. "Where do you think you're going?"

Twilight cast a silvery glow over the sprawling estate as Sienna's steps quickened, each one in sync with the frantic beating of her heart. Dylan's voice echoed behind her.

"Sienna! Wait!"

His tone carried a raw edge of pain. Yet, driven by a tumult of betrayal, shock, and pain, Sienna increased her pace, desperate to distance herself from Dylan and the confining legacy of the Whitmore family.

She didn't look back. With every fiber urging her on, she sprinted through the gardens, past the blurred faces of staff and guests, towards the sanctuary of the staff quarters.

Once safe, she darted to her workstation. Settling in, a suffocating weight descended upon her chest. Every corner of the space, filled with memories of her moments with Dylan, seemed to echo a haunting web of deception.

She needed a break from this place.

As she approached her supervisor, she blurted, "I need some time off," her voice strained. "A family emergency."

The woman raised an eyebrow. But seeing the raw pain in Sienna's eyes, nodded in understanding. "Very well. But not for too long. We're nearing peak season."

With a brisk nod, Sienna rushed back to her quarters. She started gathering essentials: a hiking backpack, a small tent, and enough food for a few days. As she moved about, the familiar process of preparing for a solo hike brought calm. The repetitive act of rolling, folding, and packing grounded her amidst the emotional storm she found herself in.

However, as she zipped up her backpack, a sudden chill swept the room. The soft, unmistakable whisper of a ghostly voice sent shivers down her spine, its message clear, "Good. Get far away from here." The voice seemed to emanate from the very walls, wrapping around her like a spectral embrace. It was as if the spirits of White Pines were urging her onward, pushing her away from the looming danger and heartbreak.

Maya's face flashed in her mind, but she hesitated, deciding against telling her. She couldn't bear another conversation, another round of advice or sympathy.

The shroud of night had already cloaked the Frozen Tears trailhead by the time Sienna arrived. Darkness engulfed her, the dense canopy above smothering the few stubborn stars trying to pierce through. She clicked her headlamp to life, its pale beam cutting a path through the gloom, stretching shadows into eerie figures that mimicked her ascent.

The path was both familiar and alien, transformed under the nocturnal veil. Daytime sounds lay subdued, while the night amplified whispers of the wilderness: leaves fluttering in a breeze, an owl's distant lament, the ceaseless dirge of crickets and frogs.

She was drawn toward the cave that had protected her and Dylan from the rain. As she got closer, the burdens of Dylan's mysteries and her own chaotic emotions lifted, muted by the forest's age-old whispers. The cave's entrance loomed, resembling the gaping maw of a benevolent giant, offering her a strange solace in its dark embrace.

A cold blast greeted Sienna as she neared, forcing her to wrap her sweatshirt tighter. The cave's chill contradicted the balmy evening, sending shivers through her as if warning her of the foreboding within.

She stepped inside and the light from her headlamp flickered across the damp walls, casting unsettling shadows. As she settled into the cave's embrace, a tension thickened the air, intensifying the unease that clung to her like a second skin.

A soft whisper floated towards her, like the gentle hum of a distant song. She halted, trying to discern the source, but the sound vanished as quickly as it came. A quiet giggle echoed in the confines of the cave, a girlish laugh tinged with a shade of melancholy.

"Hello?" Sienna called out, her voice trembling. The giggle intensified, transforming into a series of heart-wrenching sobs. An icy chill enveloped her, and she felt an unseen presence, its pain palpable, its sorrow tangible.

With a bravery she didn't know she had, Sienna whispered, "Eliza?"

The noise ceased, replaced by silence. Then, as if summoned from the very walls of the cave, a figure materialized before Sienna's eyes. The ghostly apparition of a young woman stood before her, dressed in period clothing, her eyes sorrowful yet intense.

"Eliza," Sienna whispered again, a strange connection drawing her to the spirit.

The ghostly figure nodded. "Betrayed by love, betrayed by trust. He took all, left me in the dust."

Sienna's heart ached for the lost soul before her. "I'm here, Eliza. I'm listening," she whispered.

A single tear slid down Eliza's cheek. "John, he promised forever, but his words were but lies. Left with the Colonel, chasing false skies."

Sienna, thinking of her own heartbreak with Dylan, felt a deep kinship with the spirit. "I know what betrayal feels like," she murmured, reaching out a hand towards Eliza.

The temperature in the cave seemed to drop an oppressive cold emanating from the ethereal form of Eliza. Her sorrowful eyes darkened with rage, her voice taking on a sharp, chilling edge. "The Whitmores have taken much from me. They've sown seeds of deception, and now they shall reap what they've sown."

Sienna took a step back, sensing the shift in Eliza's energy. The spectral figure continued, her voice dripping with malice, "They think they can continue their games. That time would have dulled my vengeance. But every Whitmore who betrays will know my wrath."

Sienna's heart raced. The thought of Dylan in danger took precedence over every other emotion. "Eliza, please," she pleaded with urgency, her voice thick with apprehension, "don't harm Dylan. Regardless of his family's past actions, he should not be the one to endure your anger."

A wicked smile curled the edges of Eliza's lips. "We shall see," she hissed, her eyes glinting with a malevolent light.

The form dissipated, and the cave grew darker. Sienna's heart pounded in her chest. The threat felt imminent. Time seemed to stand still as she fumbled with her phone, tried to find a signal to call or warn Dylan. Panic set in when she realized she was cut off from the outside world.

The night air seemed to press against her as Sienna scrambled through the dense woods. Every rustle seemed amplified. The path she once found serene now felt ominous. In her haste, she stumbled over an exposed tree root, her knee slamming into the hard ground. Pain shot through her, but she pushed herself up, her need to warn Dylan fueling her movements.

She made it to the parking lot, her chest heaving. Her hand shook as she retrieved her phone, dialing Dylan's number. He answered almost immediately, but his voice sounded strained, sending a fresh wave of anxiety through her.

Panic surged through Sienna's veins as she heard Dylan's voice on the other end, strained but alive. "Sienna, I'm okay," he began, his breaths coming out ragged. "There was this woman, standing right in the middle of the road. I had no time, and I just... I swerved. The next thing I knew, the car was spinning out of control. I could feel the drop just inches away. It's a miracle I didn't go over."

Sienna pressed a hand to her chest, feeling her heart hammering against her ribcage. The haunting words of Eliza echoed in her mind. "Oh my God, Dylan! You could have been..." She couldn't even finish the thought.

He continued, "The car's in bad shape, maybe totaled. But by some luck, I escaped with just some scrapes." There was a pause, and when he spoke again, his voice held a hint of vulnerability. "Sienna, it was close."

The swell of emotions threatening to overwhelm her as she responded, "Where are you? Just tell me. I'll come get you. We'll figure everything out together."

After Dylan relayed his location, Sienna sped in that direction. Upon finding him, she slowed the car to a stop, and he got in. The quiet hum of the engine filled the space between them as Sienna then pulled over to a more secluded spot under the wash of orange streetlights. The dim light inside the car cast long shadows, accentuating the raw emotions flickering across their faces.

Dylan's fingers trembled as he undid his seatbelt, turning to face Sienna. In a moment of mutual need, they reached for each other, their embrace serving as an anchor amidst the emotional storm swirling around them. The warmth they shared spoke volumes, offering silent comfort and reassurance.

Still reeling from her intense encounter in the cave, Sienna felt an urgent need to share everything. As she recounted her brush with the spectral Eliza Goodwin, Dylan's face, already pale, blanched further. Her story seemed to mirror the threats and challenges that had been haunting their relationship from the start.

Dylan ran his hands through his disheveled hair. "Sienna," he began, his voice hoarse, "I've been meaning to tell you something, to clear the air between us. But I never knew how."

Her eyes urged him to continue.

"That girl," he started, "the one everyone talks about? We had a few dates, nothing serious. But then she came to me with the pregnancy claim. I was shocked." His eyes held a mix of anger and vulnerability. "It couldn't have been mine. We never... we never did that.."

He looked away, lost in the memories of that tumultuous period. "But it was her word against mine. My family, with their obsession with our image, took matters into their hands. They believed paying her off was the best way to protect both me and the Whitmore name."

Sienna felt a wave of empathy wash over her. The burden of carrying an ancient family name, with its limitless expectations and relentless scrutiny, was something she could only imagine.

Dylan met her gaze once more, his eyes searching hers for understanding. "It's not just the scandal. There have been too many people who've gotten close to me with ulterior motives, looking to capitalize on the Whitmore legacy. My family wanted to protect me. But in doing so, they ended up isolating me behind walls."

Sienna absorbed his words, her thoughts racing. She recalled Eliza's warnings—the vengeful spirit determined to haunt the Whitmores. Was it all connected? The past and present tangled in a complex web of love, betrayal, and secrets?

Turning to face Dylan, she searched his eyes for sincerity. "We're both being tested in different ways. But if we stand together, if we stay honest with each other, we can overcome this."

Dylan nodded, squeezing her hand. "I want that. More than anything." He rubbed the back of his neck and added, "I really don't want to go home right now. Could you drop me off at a motel or something?"

Sienna nodded in understanding, feeling his need for distance from the White Pines Resort. "Of course, Dylan. I know a quiet place not too far from here."

He looked at her, vulnerability in his eyes. "Would you... stay with me? Just for the night? I could use the company."

Sienna, recognizing the genuine plea in his voice, replied, "Of course."

The dim light from a neon "Vacancy" sign led them to a modest motel, with rows of doors opening to the parking lot. The surrounding area was quiet, with only the faint chirp of crickets breaking the stillness. Dylan glanced at Sienna, a wordless question in his eyes. She nodded, and they made their way to the front office.

They registered under Sienna's name for discretion and out of an unspoken agreement that, for now, they needed to keep things as low-key as possible.

The motel room was a stark contrast to the opulent halls of the Whitmore resort. A faded floral bedspread covered the queen-sized bed, matched by patterned curtains. The carpet, showing signs of wear, had seen better days. A small television perched on a dresser, its blank screen mirroring back at them. The air held a faint mix of old cigarette smoke and cleaning agents.

For Sienna, the room was familiar. It was reminiscent of the countless nights she'd spent in such places during her childhood travels with her parents. They couldn't afford fancy hotels, so these budget motels had been their temporary havens. Memories flooded back—her parents' whispered conversations late at night, the comforting touch of threadbare motel blankets, and the thrill of exploring a new place, even if it was just another nondescript motel.

She glanced at Dylan, curious about his reaction to the room. There was no hint of disdain or discomfort on his face. Instead, he surveyed the room with a quiet curiosity, as if exploring a chapter of life he had never known.

After settling in, the day's burdens seemed to weigh heavier on them. Dylan broke the silence first. "You know, there's something comforting about this place. It's simple, without pretense. It's just... real."

Sienna smiled, touched by his insight. "It's quite a shift from what you're used to."

He nodded, "It is. But right now, there's nowhere else I'd rather be."

The room's lone lamp cast a soft amber glow, illuminating the inviting bed. Its worn sheets, though far from luxurious, promised a comfort that the pristine beds of White Pines could never offer.

Dylan glanced at the couch, then back at Sienna. "I can take the couch tonight, if you'd prefer the bed to yourself," he offered.

Sienna smiled, touched by his consideration. "I don't mind sharing. Just to sleep, though."

Dylan nodded, understanding her need for closeness without crossing boundaries. He turned down the covers, gesturing for Sienna to climb in first. She hesitated for a moment, appreciating his respect for her space, then slid under the sheets. Dylan joined her, settling into the mattress at a respectful distance.

They lay side by side, their fingers interlocking in a gesture of silent understanding and support. Sienna turned to face him, her expression soft. "It's been a long day," she murmured.

"Yes, but it's better now," Dylan replied, his voice low and reassuring.

As they talked about their experiences and the mysteries they were unraveling, their connection felt more genuine. Their conversation tapered off into a comfortable silence. Surrounded by the simple peace of the room, the day's tensions dissolved and Sienna drifted off to sleep.

Echos of the Past

Sienna awoke to the comforting aroma of coffee. Her eyelids fluttered open, and memories of the previous night flooded back. Dylan stood there with a gentle smile, offering a steaming cup. "Thought you might like this," he murmured.

The simple gesture warmed her heart. The coffee, likely from the motel lobby, felt like the most thoughtful gift in that moment. "Thank you," she whispered.

As they sipped their coffee, the warm liquid mingling with the soft glow inside them, Dylan broke the silence. "Remember, I planned a day for us. Seems even more fitting now." His soft baritone carried a hint of mystery, piquing her curiosity.

"What are we doing?" she asked, her eyes alight with anticipation.

He shook his head. "It's a surprise."

With a chuckle, Sienna let the mystery engulf her, basking in the joy it brought. They set off, her car humming as Dylan guided it along winding roads. Outside, the landscape was a tapestry of nature's rich hues, where greens and blues merged in a dance that seemed to whisper ancient secrets of earth and sky.

The car came to a halt in front of a white building adorned with grand pillars, a beacon of knowledge in the quaint town of Bartlett, NH. Sienna's heart fluttered with confusion as she gazed at the public library. "A library?" she murmured, puzzled.

They stepped inside and were greeted by the scents of aged paper and bound leather, each carrying tales of old, eager to be discovered. A gentleman with a warm, welcoming demeanor stood waiting, an open book in his hand.

The library's intimate space radiated a hushed reverence, its corners alive with the echoes of ancient stories and past readers. Drawn by curiosity, Sienna's steps were tentative as she followed Dylan toward the back of the room, where a tall, lean figure awaited among the shelves.

Mr. Richardson, a silver-haired man with spectacles resting on his hawkish nose, looked up as they approached. His sharp, discerning eyes met Sienna's, their intensity catching her off guard.

"Dylan," Mr. Richardson greeted, nodding at the younger man before turning his piercing gaze back to Sienna. "And you must be Sienna. A pleasure to meet you."

Sienna smiled, trying to quell the trepidation rising within her. "Mr. Richardson," she replied. "Thank you for seeing us."

The elderly archivist smiled, a soft, reassuring expression that put Sienna at ease. "Ah, my dear, when Dylan contacted me regarding your interest in the history of Eliza Goodwin, I couldn't resist. Our town's history is full of fascinating tales, and that of Eliza and the Whitmores are among its most poignant."

Dylan squeezed Sienna's hand, guiding her to a large oak table laden with materials. There were yellowed letters tied in faded ribbons, paintings whose colors had withstood the test of time, and newspaper clippings that told tales of love, betrayal, and mystery.

Sienna's fingers traced the words on the page, feeling the textured grooves of the dried ink, each stroke heavy with emotion. The letter revealed a heart full of longing, a soul grappling with forbidden desires and societal constraints. Each note, signed with Eliza's distinct flourish, was a declaration of a love that transcended time and boundaries.

Beside the letters there lay a series of detailed sketches. One sketch depicted Eliza, her hair flowing down her back, her eyes a complex mix of sorrow and hope. Next to her stood a man, John, his posture protective, his eyes filled with love and resolve.

As Sienna studied Eliza's portrait, a realization dawned on her. The resemblance was striking; this was the same figure that had appeared before her, the same face that had haunted her dreams and materialized on the road. A shiver traveled down her spine.

Dylan leaned in, his voice a whisper. "That's her, Sienna. The woman I almost hit on the road."

What gripped Sienna's attention were the aged newspaper clippings. Yellowed with time, they whispered tales of the notorious Whitmore curse. They detailed heart-wrenching stories of those who defied it, their lives cut short, leaving behind dreams that never saw the light of day.

As Sienna absorbed each word, a weight seemed to settle deeper within her. The tragic romance of Eliza and John mirrored her growing feelings for Dylan, stirring a chilling thought: Was history doomed to repeat itself?

Mr. Richardson, observing her concern, said, "The past is filled with stories, some unsettling. But remember, history records what was, not what must be. You and Dylan shape your own futures."

The atmosphere in the library thickened when Mr. Richardson presented a detailed genealogical chart. Its delicate branches of family connections sprawled like a web, each name and date meticulously noted. He unrolled it, exposing the intricate network of lives intertwined.

"There's something you should see, Miss Avery," he murmured, directing Sienna's gaze to a specific branch of the chart. Her eyes traced from Eliza Goodwin's name to her sister's, spanning generations, until landing on a familiar name—Sienna Avery.

Her breath caught, a mix of awe and shock. "This... this means I'm descended from Eliza Goodwin's family?"

Mr. Richardson nodded with understanding. "Yes, through her sister."

Sienna turned to Dylan, emotions swirling. "How did you find this?"

Dylan looked away, his expression tinged with sheepishness. "I had help from HR. I wanted to understand more about our history, our connection."

Dylan's access hinted at resources beyond mere wealth, suggesting he might use the resort's HR department to delve into her past. The potential power dynamics were unsettling, as she considered the implications of his actions.

Mr. Richardson then introduced another item—a box bearing the Avery family crest. Inside, a worn, leather-bound journal with 'Avery' embossed in faded gold caught her attention. As Sienna flipped through its pages, recounting interactions with the Whitmores across centuries, the weight of their shared history settled in.

She looked up to meet Dylan's gaze, and a question hung in the air: How much did he know about her life now?

A soft chime from Dylan's wristwatch cut through the tension. He checked it, then met her eyes with a grave look. "We have one more appointment to make, Sienna."

Mr. Richardson began gathering the historical artifacts, placing them back into their respective boxes. "It's been a pleasure sharing this history with both of you," he commented, handing Sienna his card. "Should you have any more questions, don't hesitate to reach out."

Sienna clasped the card, her voice warm with gratitude. "Thank you, Mr. Richardson. I never realized how deeply our lives are intertwined with the threads of the past."

Outside, the sun streamed down. As Sienna and Dylan made their way to her Toyota, she could feel a myriad of emotions swirling within her — a mix of shock, fascination, and anticipation.

As she settled into the driver's seat, Dylan turned to her, taking a deep breath. "Before we go any further, I thought I'd tell you where we're heading next. It's a bit... unconventional, but I remembered how you said the paranormal intrigued you."

Sienna's eyes went wide, her heartbeat kicking up a notch. "Go on," she encouraged, leaning forward.

He paused, his eyes locked on hers. "We're meeting a psychic medium who deals with ghosts of unrequited love and star-crossed lovers. Given everything we've dug up today, it seems like the perfect fit. Her name's Ashlyn."

"Ashlyn Alden? The psychic from that ghost hunter show?"

A grin spread across Dylan's face. "Yeah, that's her. I figured someone with her clout could really shed some light on things."

Excitement surged through Sienna. "No way, I've seen all her episodes! She's unreal! This is gonna be epic, Dylan." She paused, catching her breath, her mind racing with the possibilities of what they might discover with Ashlyn.

She started the car and said, "Alright, lead the way. Let's find out what the spirits are dying to tell us."

The car slid into a parking spot of another grand resort, different from the Whitmore estate, yet equally opulent. As Dylan adjusted the rearview mirror, he reached into his backpack and pulled out a baseball cap, placing it on his head. A playful smirk danced on his lips.

"Don't want the competition spotting a Whitmore dining in their territory," he joked, winking at Sienna.

Sienna chuckled, shaking her head. "Your secret's safe with me," she teased.

They approached the resort's pub, named "The Tap House." It had a rustic charm to it, with dark wooden beams and low lighting. Before they even entered, Sienna felt the charged atmosphere that seemed to hint at both history and mystery.

The door chime announced their entrance, and almost immediately, Sienna's gaze was drawn to a table near the window. There, bathed in the gentle glow of the afternoon sun, sat a woman who could only be described as enchanting.

Ashlyn Alden had an aura of mystique about her that was undeniable. Even without the captivating violet eyes or the luxurious black waves of her hair, she would have commanded attention. The way she moved, the way she spoke, every action seemed deliberate and powerful. Sienna had watched her countless times on TV, analyzing haunted locations and communicating with spirits, but seeing her in person was unreal.

"Dylan," Ashlyn greeted him with a warm voice. The crystal pendant around her neck shimmered as it caught the ambient light, drawing Sienna's eyes.

As the two spoke, Sienna tried not to gawk. The paranormal had always fascinated her, and here she was, standing in front of a celebrity in that very field.

"And you must be Sienna." Ashlyn turned to her, a smile lighting up her face. Her gaze was intense, making Sienna feel both scrutinized and seen. As Ashlyn clasped her hand, a chill shot up Sienna's arm—an unexpected sensation.

Sienna swallowed her initial nervousness and smiled. "It's an honor to meet you. I've followed your work for years."

Ashlyn's laughter was light. "Thank you, dear. And while I haven't known of you for years, the spirits, it seems, have been eager for our paths to cross."

The admission sent a thrill through Sienna. She pulled out a chair and sat down, feeling the reassuring touch of Dylan's hand on her shoulder. The air in the room grew heavy as Sienna locked eyes with Ashlyn. The intense violet seemed to pierce right through her, as if reading her soul.

"I've felt her," Sienna whispered, her voice shaky. "Eliza. Following me, watching me."

Ashlyn fixed on Sienna with a penetrating gaze. "You, dear, have an undeniable connection with Eliza, something that goes beyond mere coincidence. Perhaps it's a shared emotion or experience that makes you particularly receptive to her energy. Spirits are drawn to those with whom they share deep resonances. It's as if your souls echo similar tunes."

Sienna blinked. "Are you saying that Eliza is... reaching out to me because she sees a part of herself in me?"

Ashlyn nodded. "Exactly. And this connection might make you sensitive to her presence and emotions. It could be why you've been feeling her so intensely."

Dylan cleared his throat, drawing their attention back to the apparition he'd encountered. "And the woman on the road? Was that Eliza's doing?"

Ashlyn's expression darkened. "Yes, that was indeed Eliza, but her intentions weren't benign. Her pain and anger have muddled her perceptions, making it hard for her to see past her rage. She might view you as a threat, or perhaps as someone akin to those who wronged her in the past."

Dylan swallowed hard. "So, she was trying to...?"

"Harm you," Ashlyn finished. "You need to be cautious, both of you. Eliza's emotions are tumultuous, and her actions are unpredictable."

Dylan's grip on his glass tightened, his knuckles whitening. "But why? Why now? Why through Sienna?"

Ashlyn continued, her voice soft but with a steel edge, "Because of your connection, and because of Sienna's. Eliza sees in Sienna both an ally and a weapon. She's using Sienna's ties to the past, her very blood, as a conduit to reach you. Manifestations, especially ones as powerful as this, thrive on unresolved emotions. It's what gives them strength, what binds them to the realm of the living."

Ashlyn leaned forward, her fingers playing with the rim of her teacup, her violet eyes sharp yet understanding. "You see, curses, in their truest essence, are about grief, anger, and vengeance. And when powerful emotions remain unsettled, they bind spirits to the realm of the living."

Dylan shifted, eyes flitting around the room before settling back on Ashlyn as she continued.

"Eliza is very much tethered to this world. Her anger, her sense of betrayal, it's what keeps her anchored. And John," her eyes flitted towards Sienna, "he's trapped in her shadow. His love for her is still profound, but he's hesitant, conflicted. He wants to reach out, but her overpowering rage keeps him at bay."

Sienna found her voice. "So, what does this mean for us, for Dylan and me? Is there a way to... I don't know, appease Eliza's spirit?"

"Eliza's anger is directed at the Whitmore lineage, and Dylan, you are in the line of fire." Ashlyn took a deep breath. "As for you, Sienna, being tied to the Goodwin line, she will see you as a tool, a means to inflict pain upon a Whitmore."

Dylan's fingers tightened around Sienna's, his face paling. "How do we stop it? There has to be a way."

Sienna added, "Is there a way to free both Eliza and John, to let them find peace?"

Ashlyn pursed her lips. "It's complex. To break a curse, especially one so deeply ingrained, one must first understand its origins, its true essence. It's not just about pacifying a spirit; it's about resolving the root of that intense emotion."

She paused, taking a sip of her tea. "There might be a way, but it will require delving deep into the past, confronting truths, and possibly facing dangers. Are you both prepared for that?"

Dylan's jaw set. "Whatever it takes. I can't—I won't let this curse continue to harm those I care about."

Sienna squeezed his hand. "We'll face it together."

"Then let the journey of unravelling begin. The spirits have spoken, and they are waiting." Ashlyn smiled. "To confront and find resolution, both of you need to face Eliza at the site of her heartbreak on the Frozen Tears Trail. The tether binding her spirit to this realm is strongest there. Together, you both must be present and unified."

Sienna's heart felt like a stone sinking into the chilling depths of a brook. Images of Eliza danced in her mind, accompanied by the haunting silhouette of John, her star-crossed lover. Sienna couldn't shake off the eerie sense of connection to Eliza, maybe because of their shared lineage or the echoing patterns of fate. The burden of history and intertwined destinies pressed on her.

Dylan squeezed her hand. "We'll face it together," he promised, then turned to Ashlyn. "What should we expect? And what about John?"

"Ah, John. He's bound by the same emotions but hidden, overshadowed by Eliza's raging spirit. If we reach out to Eliza, calm her turmoil and guide her towards understanding, then John will naturally gravitate towards her." Ashlyn tilted her head and smiled. "The hope is for them to find solace in each other and be united in peace."

"So, there's a chance they can be together in the end?" Sienna asked. "After all this time?"

Ashlyn nodded. "Indeed. Spirits, like living beings, seek resolution. And John has been waiting, silently, for his beloved. If all goes well tomorrow, they'll find each other."

Sienna took in a breath, her eyes watery. "Then we have to do it. Not just for us, but for them, too."

Ashlyn leaned forward, her voice dropping to a whisper. "Prepare your hearts. This journey you're embarking on is not just about ending a curse; it's about mending broken souls. Remember that."

As they made their way out of the pub and back to Sienna's car, the weight of the impending evening settled between them. The atmosphere in the car was thick, filled with a silent understanding of what was at stake.

Dylan broke the silence, his voice low and steady. "I've got some things to handle tomorrow during the day, but I'll pick you up in the evening. We'll drive together to The Frozen Tears Trail."

Sienna cast him a sidelong glance. "What about your car?" she asked.

He gave a sheepish grin. "I've got another one."

They drove back in silence. Once they reached Sienna's place, Dylan leaned over, placing a gentle kiss on her forehead. "Rest up. Tomorrow will be... intense."

Sienna nodded, watching him go, then made her way inside.

In the quiet of her room, with only the soft hum of the ceiling fan broke the silence, Sienna laid on her bed, moonlight casting gentle shadows across the walls.

The revelations of the day weighed on her. Her connection to Eliza, Dylan's family curse, the looming showdown—all wove together into a complex tapestry of history, destiny, and emotions. And her feelings for Dylan? They added yet another layer to the mix. Were they just replaying an ancient love story, or was it a new, dangerous entanglement in their own right?

She mulled over Eliza and John, the tragic lovers. The possibility that her and Dylan's fates might be linked with theirs was both haunting and oddly romantic. Could they change the course of their histories and carve out a future for themselves?

Meeting Ashlyn Alden added an exhilarating edge to everything. Sienna had been following Ashlyn's shows for years, and now to meet her in person? It was surreal. Ashlyn was a part of the puzzle in this intricate web of past and present, and Sienna was eager to see what insights she would bring.

CHAPTER EIGHT

Whispers of Deception

The gentle rhythm of rain against her window lulled Sienna into a reflective state. In the muted light of her room, she let her thoughts wander, the glow from a lavender-scented candle casting dancing shadows on her walls.

Eliza Goodwin. The name echoed in her mind. It felt so surreal, being connected to someone from a different era. Sienna wondered what Eliza had been like, how she dressed, the songs she liked, and the dreams she had for herself. It felt like they were kindred spirits in some bizarre way, and Sienna couldn't shake off the feeling that she needed to help Eliza find peace. Was this her new life now? Channeling spirits, decoding age-old mysteries?

And then there was Dylan. A rush of butterflies took flight in her stomach at the mere thought of him. This wasn't like her past flings or those college dates that ended in awkward goodbyes. With Dylan, everything felt amplified—the chemistry, the emotional roller-coaster, the intrigue. Plus, he was just... different, complex, and fascinating, even if his family history was a tad more than she'd bargained for.

The reverberation of a firm knock echoed through the room, wrenching Sienna from her reverie. When she opened the door, there stood Dylan's grandfather, his gaze piercing and familiar—it mirrored Dylan's own striking blue eyes. Eyes that had borne witness to decades of hardships, now fixed on her with a disconcerting intensity. His presence carried the weight of a lifetime's guardedness, a hardness forged by trials, that rendered her at once humbled and intimidated.

"Sienna," he announced, stepping past the threshold without waiting for her consent.

Her breath caught as the room seemed to close in with his entrance. "Mr. Whitmore," she responded, her voice a mask over her rising apprehension.

He surveyed her small quarters, his eyes pausing just a beat too long on the lone candle flickering by her bed—an unsettling reminder of her vulnerability. "My grandson holds you in high regard," he started, his voice a chilled timbre, seasoned with years of skepticism. "But does he truly see who you are?"

Tension coiled within her. "I've been nothing but honest with him."

A cynical smirk twisted his lips, devoid of warmth. "Is that so? Or are you merely spinning yarns to ensnare his heart? Because if so, it will end poorly for you."

Her heart thudded, taken aback by his blunt accusation. "I've done nothing to deserve that."

He stepped closer, his presence looming like a storm. "You tread dangerous ground, young lady. The Whitmore legacy is steeped in burdens and old blood—not tales for the faint-hearted." His expression softened, revealing a glimmer of the anguish beneath his stern exterior. "I once lost someone dear to me, a casualty of the very shadows you and Dylan flirt with. The ruin it leaves in its wake is profound."

There was sincerity in her voice when she spoke. "I'm truly sorry for your loss."

He dismissed her with a wave. "Spare me your pity. I need you to grasp the weight of your actions. The repercussions." He drew a deep breath and presented an envelope from his coat. "Consider this a lesson. Take it, leave Dylan be, and spend your summer elsewhere. You'll receive your pay, regardless."

"And if I don't?"

His eyes, icy and unyielding, met hers. "Then you'll find yourself without a job. I'll see that you leave with nothing. As for Dylan? I'll inform him you sought to leverage our family for money. It will hurt him, but he'll move on, recognizing you for the opportunist you are."

Tears threatened her resolve, but she fought them back. "Why are you doing this?"

A shadow of deep sorrow flickered across his face before it was masked by resolution. "I've seen too many drawn to our family with false pretenses, seduced by our wealth. I've suffered enough heartbreak, and I refuse to let Dylan endure the same fate, not at the hands of someone like you. Loyalty to the Whitmores runs deep; betray that, and the fallout is severe."

Sienna straightened as she met his challenging stare. "I care about Dylan," she declared, her tone unwavering. "I'm not here for your money or your name. My feelings for him are genuine, and I will not betray him."

He studied her for a tense moment, his scrutiny heavy. "Perhaps you believe that now," he conceded, weariness seeping into his voice. "But life's winds shift swiftly. Today's certainties can evaporate by tomorrow."

He placed the envelope on a nearby table, a symbolic gesture laden with temptation. For Sienna, it wasn't just paper; it was an escape from debt, a gateway to a future free from financial worry.

Yet, as she considered it, her thoughts returned to the many nights spent with Dylan under the stars, dreaming of a different future together. She remembered his passion, his vision for a different path for his family's resort—a vision not bound by old money but by new ideals.

Her decision made, Sienna extended the envelope back to him. "I can't accept this," she stated, her voice steady despite the storm inside.

His eyebrows arched, surprise flickering across his features before his expression shuttered once again. "You're rejecting a secure future."

"I'm choosing a chance at something real," she countered, her chin lifted in defiance.

A tense silence fell, heavy with unspoken threats. William exhaled, a sound of reluctant respect or perhaps resignation. "Very well. You've made your choice," he said as he turned toward the door. Pausing, he added without a backward glance, "Remember this decision. Whatever comes next is on your head."

Sienna watched him leave, her heart racing. She felt a mix of fear and determination, but above all, clarity. Dylan deserved to know the truth, and together, they would face the storm that was coming their way.

Her feet carried her to the parking lot, the gravel crunching beneath her boots. She had envisioned the evening to unite forces - herself, Dylan, and Ashlyn, coming together to lie to rest spirits that had roamed for too long. But when she arrived, the space where Dylan's car should be waiting greeted her, sending a pang of unease.

Her hand slipped into her bag, pulling out her phone. She scanned the messages, hoping for a late notification, an explanation. But none came. Her fingers began typing out a message to Dylan. *"Where are you? We're supposed to meet now."*

Seconds that felt like eons passed. The dimming sky, painted with strokes of twilight, seemed to grow darker with her mounting anxiety. The phone buzzed. A message from Dylan.

"I can't believe you'd try to extort money from my family. Was all of this just a play for my family's fortune?"

The message felt like a punch to her gut. Sienna's eyes blurred with tears. How could he think so low of her? After the moments they shared, the dreams they weaved, the connection they felt. She felt the weight of William Whitmore's manipulation, the depth of the trap she had walked into.

Desperation fueled her response, fingers trembling over the keys. *"Dylan, how could you believe that? After everything, after all our conversations, the time we spent... I'd never... How could you?"*

She sent the message, waiting for a reassuring reply, a call, something. But as minutes stretched on, and the cold, indifferent parking lot lights blinked to life around her, she felt the sting of isolation and betrayal. The silence of the evening was broken only by the distant murmurs of the resort, and inside, Sienna's heart wrestled with the painful twist of events.

With heavy steps and a heavier heart, Sienna trudged back to her quarters. The once comforting trees and paths of the resort now seemed oppressive, their looming shadows reflecting her turmoil. She needed the sanctuary of her room, a few moments to process the whirlwind of accusations and emotions.

But as she rounded the corner, the sight that met her was far from welcoming. Two burly figures in resort security uniforms stood outside her door, looking grim.

"Miss Avery," one of them, a tall man with a graying beard, addressed her with a mixture of pity and formality. "We've been instructed to inform you that your employment at Whitmore Resort has been terminated, effective immediately."

Sienna's heart raced. "What? On what grounds?"

The second officer, younger and more uncomfortable, shuffled his feet. "Orders from the top. You have 24 hours to vacate the premises."

Sienna's eyes widened in shock. The reality of her situation sank in, amplifying her sense of betrayal. "So I'm just being thrown out like some... criminal?"

The older officer sighed. "Miss Avery, we're just following orders. This comes from Mr. William Whitmore himself."

She felt her cheeks burning, tears threatening to spill. "Does he even know the reason?"

The younger guard shifted. "We're not privy to those details. We've just been told to carry out these instructions."

Sienna steadied herself. "Alright," she said, voice shaking but defiant. "Give me a few minutes to grab some things. I'll come back tomorrow for the rest."

The older officer nodded, a hint of sympathy in his eyes. "We'll wait out here. Stop by the security office when you are ready for the rest."

As Sienna stepped inside her room, anger and confusion engulfed her. With each item she threw into her bag, she replayed the events of the day, wondering how everything had unraveled. It wasn't just about the job or the accusations; it was the shattered trust, the hurt of being misunderstood and falsely accused.

She folded her clothes and stuffed them into her suitcase as memories of hushed conversations and sideways glances from other employees flooded back. They had whispered words of caution about getting too close to the Whitmores. She had brushed off such warnings as mere workplace gossip, perhaps even jealousy. But now, she saw those warnings in a different light.

William Whitmore's stern admonition echoed in her mind. *"Cross the Whitmores, especially when it comes to family, and you'll regret it."* She realized his words weren't just a threat; they were a promise.

Yet, amid the shadows cast by the Whitmores' power and influence, what wounded her heart most deeply was Dylan's silence.

Sienna zipped up her bag. She had to see Dylan and look into his eyes so he could see the pain and confusion that his family's actions had wrought. If, after that, he still sided with his family's unfounded accusations, she would know where she stood.

One thing was clear: Sienna would not leave without a fight. The Whitmores might have their legacy, their sprawling estate, and their deep-rooted power, but she had truth, grit, and determination on her side. And she was not one to be silenced.

Navigating the hallways of the resort wasn't a simple task for Sienna. With each step she took, unspoken judgments bore down on her. The sidelong glances, some full of pity and others laden with scorn, stung like a slap. While being the epicenter of a scandal was both unfamiliar and unsettling.

Suddenly, she spotted Maya, a friendly face among the throng of unfamiliar and judgmental ones.

"Sienna, wait!" Maya rushed towards her, concern in her eyes. "I heard... I mean, everyone's talking about..."

Sienna raised a hand to stop her. "I know what they're saying. But it's not true, Maya."

Maya nodded, her lips set in a tight line. "I believe you. But you know how it is here—the Whitmores are untouchable. Everyone just believes whatever they're told."

Sienna sighed, feeling the weight of the situation. "I thought I could change things, maybe even break the cycle."

The two women shared a moment of understanding. It was clear that the family's influence had long tentacles, touching everything and everyone associated with the resort.

"Be careful, Sienna. Not just with the family, but... with everything."

Sienna smiled. "I will."

Maya took Sienna's hands and squeezed them. "Whatever you decide to do, just know you've got friends here, okay?"

With a grateful nod, Sienna moved past the crowd and towards the exit, her head held high. She might have lost her job and the budding relationship she had with Dylan, but she was leaving with her integrity intact.

After the harrowing exchange with Maya, Sienna trudged to the parking lot and hurled her suitcase into the trunk of her car. Closing her eyes, she drew upon every shred of courage remaining within her. One last task lay ahead before she could contemplate her future moves.

Cool marble from the family wing corridor chilled Sienna's hastened steps. In her turmoil, the hushed ambiance of the space felt almost mocking. The grandeur of the Whitmore estate loomed intimidating and hostile.

As she approached the ornate double doors leading to the heart of the residential wing, her resolve intensified. But before her hand could even rise to knock, a stern-faced staff member stepped in her path.

"Miss Avery," he began, his tone rigid, "you're not permitted here."

Sienna's desperation was clear in her voice. "Please, I just need to see Dylan. I have to explain."

But the man was unyielding. "I'm sorry, but Mr. Whitmore has given strict instructions. The family is not to be disturbed tonight."

The weight of rejection and the reality of her isolation from Dylan's world pressed on her. She was on the outside, and those imposing doors were ensuring she stayed there.

Sienna squared her shoulders, her voice unwavering, "I'm not leaving until I see Dylan."

The employee shifted, his face showing traces of sympathy but bound by his role. "Miss Avery, I understand how you feel, but if you don't leave, I'll have to call the police."

Before Sienna could respond, the shrill ring of her phone sliced through the thick air of tension. Recognizing Ashlyn's name on the display, she answered.

"I am so sorry we are not there yet!"

The mystic's voice carried a note of concern. "Where are you both? I was expecting you two by now."

Sienna hesitated, then recounted the evening's events. She could hear Ashlyn's soft sigh on the other end.

"Oh, Sienna... this is a difficult situation."

Sienna felt her heart pounding. "I don't know what to do, Ashlyn. I need to see Dylan to clear things up. But I also understand the urgency of what we have planned."

There was a pause before Ashlyn responded. "Sometimes, we have to make choices that aren't easy. The spirits are important, but so is setting things right. You will make the right decision."

Sienna took a deep breath, her mind racing. "I'll come by myself. If I stay here and get arrested, it won't help anyone. And maybe, just maybe, once this curse is lifted, everything else will fall into place."

Ashlyn's voice was gentle. "Very well. I will see you soon."

Sienna, still smarting from the abruptness of her recent confrontations, was just about to succumb to a tearful retreat when a feeble but clear voice interrupted her.

"Miss Avery, is it?"

Pausing, Sienna looked up and saw a woman whose body bore the undeniable marks of chemotherapy but whose eyes sparkled with sharp intelligence. Mrs. Whitmore, Dylan's stepmother, looked Sienna over with a discerning glance.

"Mrs. Whitmore, rest," the employee admonished, stepping forward with a protective stance.

She waved him off, her voice keeping its clarity. "Rest? I've been resting all day. Had a little fall earlier." She gestured to a nearby room. "Come, Dylan is in my sitting room. He wouldn't leave my side, even when I assured him I was alright."

Sienna's heart swelled with relief and continued confusion. The pieces weren't aligning.

Mrs. Whitmore continued, "Dylan mentioned he had plans tonight, and he's been searching for his phone. I suspect he wanted to tell you he'd be running late. These things happen when you're watching over a clumsy woman." Her wry smile hinted at many stories untold.

Sienna blinked away the moisture in her eyes, words failing her. Mrs. Whitmore gestured towards the entrance to the family wing. "Come, let's get this sorted. There's no reason a misplaced phone should lead to so much drama."

Gratitude welled up inside Sienna as she followed, more hopeful about the evening's prospects and her relationship with Dylan.

The opulence of the Whitmore family wing was undeniable. Antique portraits of stoic ancestors adorned the walls, and plush carpets softened their steps. Mrs. Whitmore led Sienna to a comfortable sitting area, where a tray of tea sat ready, its steam curling up like fragile wraiths.

"You must wonder why my son stood you up," she began, her fingers wrapping around a porcelain teacup. "I had a minor fall today. Nothing serious, mind you, but enough to cause a fuss." She rolled her eyes, smiling. "Dylan... he has a heart as big as the ocean. He refused to leave my side until he was certain I was alright."

Sienna's heartstrings tightened. She'd known Dylan's warmth, his deep sense of care, but this...

Mrs. Whitmore continued, "I've been in your shoes, dear. Marrying into this family wasn't... smooth. William has always had his ways. He protects the family name, its reputation, often came before everything. Even happiness."

Sienna took a shaky breath, feeling the weight of William Whitmore's manipulations. "He offered me money to leave," she confessed, her voice a mere whisper.

Mrs. Whitmore sighed, nodding. "It's not the first time, and it likely won't be the last. But you, my dear, you've given Dylan something precious—hope, joy, a glimpse of a life beyond these gilded walls. I've seen the way he looks at you. The way you light up his world."

The door burst open, catching everyone off guard. Dylan stood there, looking disheveled with worry marking his features. Yet, when his gaze settled on Sienna, the worry transformed into surprise and relief.

"Sienna," he exhaled, bridging the distance between them to envelop her in a heartfelt embrace. In that single touch, amidst the surrounding chaos, their worlds seemed to find their balance again.

"I'm so sorry for not being at the lot. After the fall," he looked into her eyes, regret etching every line of his face. "I was so focused on Mom and then... I couldn't find my damn phone to call you."

Sienna touched his cheek, trying to calm the self-blame she saw there. "It's not just about the phone, Dylan. Your grandfather..."

Dylan's expression hardened, a storm brewing behind his eyes. "What did he do?"

She took a deep breath. "We'll talk, but for now, just know it's not your fault."

The floors echoed their footsteps as Mrs. Whitmore ushered them to the exit. Her eyes sparkled with mischief. "Now, you two better hurry," she murmured, the corners of her lips curling into a knowing smile. "This family has waited long enough for a change."

Outside, the evening had deepened into shades of dark purple and blue, with stars lighting up the sky. A cool breeze carried with it whispers of love, betrayal, and a curse that had lingered far too long.

Dylan looked down at Sienna, tightening his grip on her hand. "It's hard to believe all that's happened," he said, his voice filled with awe and a touch of regret. "But we're in this together, all the way to the end."

Sienna nodded, buoyed by his commitment. "Every twist and turn today has brought us here. It feels like the universe is steering us to correct a mistake."

The expanse of the estate lay before them, a land rich with memories of joy and pain. The surrounding trees seemed to be cheering them on, their leaves rustling in encouragement.

Approaching their destination, Sienna stopped and looked up at the vast night sky. "Despite everything, I have faith in us," she whispered, her voice steady with resolve. "Tonight, we'll alter the course of Whitmore history."

CHAPTER NINE

Frozen Tears

The luxury of Dylan's backup car unsettled Sienna. Knowing about Dylan's affluence was one thing; seeing it in such stark display was another. She couldn't help but ponder the extent of the Whitmore family's possessions.

Her fingers traced patterns on the plush leather seat. Although the overt wealth made her uncomfortable, thoughts of Dylan's stepmother brought relief. The woman's genuine warmth seemed out of place in a world brimming with privilege. Sienna found comfort in the notion that not all money corrupts, hoping she might eventually accept this facet of Dylan's life.

As the car wound along the road, Sienna tried to dismiss these thoughts, instead taking in the scenic beauty. Trees lined the road, their branches interlocking above like a secret handshake from the past. The world outside was draped in muted blues and silvers, the moon playing peek-a-boo through the leaves. Every splash of moonlight on the ground seemed to dance, lighting the path to The Frozen Tears Trail.

Sienna turned to Dylan. The dashboard's soft glow cast his features in gentle contrasts, highlighting a furrow of concern on his brow. Their eyes met, and their hands came together, fingers entwining, mirroring the trees above.

The winding road ahead seemed to stretch, both of them cocooned in their own thoughts. Dylan broke the silence. "What did my grandfather do?"

Sienna took a deep breath, turning to Dylan. "Your grandfather offered me money—a lot. He wanted me to leave and never come back. He even offered to cover my college expenses, just like that."

Dylan's grip on the wheel tightened. "What did you say to him?"

Her voice wavered as she replied, "I won't lie. The thought of being debt-free and starting fresh was tempting, even if just for a second. But then I thought about us, all our moments, everything we've been through. I couldn't walk away without telling you."

He exhaled. "I know it's been hard for you, Sienna. Grandfather can be persuasive, making offers that seem too good to turn down."

Looking away, she gathered herself before continuing. "After I refused, he changed. He threatened to make it look like I was after the family fortune." A tear escaped down her cheek. "And when I tried to message you, the replies... they didn't sound like you."

Dylan glanced at her. "I saw him watching you earlier and felt uneasy, but I didn't imagine he'd go to such lengths."

Sienna intertwined her fingers with his. "It's clear he wields a lot of influence, even over you, to some extent. Family dynamics are complicated."

He met her gaze, his expression conflicted. "I should've seen through his tactics. I should've been there for you."

She leaned back. "It's uncanny, isn't it? How our situation mirrors Eliza and John's. It feels like we're caught in a repeating pattern."

Dylan nodded. "It does, but this is now. We don't have to repeat the past. We can make our own way."

She smiled. "Exactly. We have what they didn't: hindsight. We can use that to our advantage."

"You're right," Dylan squeezed her hand. "They didn't get to fight for their love. We do. We can make our own ending."

A comfortable silence fell over them, punctuated only by the hum of the engine and the whisper of the trees outside. Both were acutely aware of the challenges ahead—not just with appeasing restless spirits, but in carving their own path into a world strewn with obstacles.

Dylan glanced over. "I hate to see you hurt by my family's schemes. Let me help. I could use my influence to get your job back. It's the least I can do."

Sienna turned to him. "This isn't about the job. It's about principle. I value your support, but I'm not a damsel in distress you can rescue with money. I've always stood on my own two feet and I don't want that to change now, even if we are together."

He parted his lips to argue, but she cut him off. "This isn't about pride. It's about my identity, my self-respect. I refuse to let your grandfather's actions define me."

Dylan sighed. "I get it. I just wish I could do more."

Her smile softened. "Being here, understanding and supporting me—that's enough. I'll figure the rest out."

As they neared the trailhead, the surrounding air seemed to grow heavier. "Your stepmother... she's truly remarkable, isn't she? Like a ray of sunshine."

Dylan nodded, his smile genuine. "She's always been a guiding light through the chaos of my family."

After parking, they retrieved flashlights from the glove compartment and faced a narrow dirt trail concealed by overgrown foliage. There was only one other car in the lot, likely Ashlyn's. Sienna shivered, admiring that woman's bravery for venturing into the dark to appease the spirits. Then she remembered her own nighttime hike.

Stepping onto the trail, they began their trek through the woods, illuminated by the moon's pale glow. The rustling leaves and the distant calls of an owl composed a natural symphony around them. With each step, the atmosphere thickened, charged with what was to come.

Sienna felt the damp, cold ground beneath her, her senses sharpening in the night's embrace. Thoughts of Eliza played in her mind, imagining what she might have felt on her fateful walk through this same place.

The soft murmur of water grew clearer, guiding them onward. After navigating a slight incline and maneuvering around twisted roots that seemed to emerge from the earth's very core, they reached the clearing that cradled the small brook where they had first found the post.

Under the moonlight, the water shimmered, casting playful reflections on the surrounding trees. The serene yet melancholic sound of the flowing water wrapped around them.

Emerging from the shadows near the brook was Ashlyn, her flowing robes merging with the essence of the night. Their meeting at this charged location was intentional; tonight marked a turning point in the long, intertwined histories of the living and the dead.

The clearing felt different now—not just a picturesque spot beside a brook, but an arena where the boundaries between the seen and the unseen were thin. Three figures stood at the water's edge, their shadows stretching out long and wavering. The torches Ashlyn had placed in a protective circle around them casting a warm, orange hue. The flames wavered and danced as if touched by an unseen force, their movements mirroring the chaotic whirlwind of emotions enveloping the trio.

Ashlyn, her posture erect and commanding, motioned for Sienna and Dylan to join hands with her. Their fingers intertwined, the shared warmth a contrast to the cool night air. Ashlyn chanted, her voice resonating, the words unfamiliar yet evocative. Each syllable seemed to pull at the very fabric of the world, reaching out to those who existed just beyond the veil.

The brook seemed to respond to her call, the gentle murmur of the water growing louder, as if the spirits of the water itself were listening. Sienna's heart raced, feeling the energy of the place seeping into her, grounding her and heightening her senses. Every sound became acute.

Dylan's grip tightened around Sienna's hand. She could feel his apprehension, but there was also a determination, a resolve to see this through. Their shared experiences, culminating in this very moment, made their bond feel unbreakable.

Minutes felt like hours as Ashlyn continued her incantations. The temperature dropped. A cold mist rolled in, blanketing the surroundings and sending shivers down their spines. The still waters of the brook began to roil and churn, icy tendrils snaking out onto the bank.

Out of the freezing mist, a spectral form took shape. Eliza materialized, her visage clear against the warm glow of the torch flames. Her ghostly attire, reminiscent of her time, was encrusted with frost. Her eyes bore anger and resentment from the decades of torment.

Just outside the silvery glow of the clearing, John's spectral form stood alone, a sorrowful guardian watching over the scene. He tried to communicate, but Eliza, consumed by anger, couldn't perceive him.

Spotting the ghost, Sienna gasped in surprise, her eyes widening. "John's here!" she whispered, pointing toward the spectral figure. Realizing he had been observing them all this time added an extra layer of complexity to their mission.

"Why have you summoned me?" Eliza's voice was laced with bitterness.

"We're here to help," Ashlyn replied, "to end the suffering that's bound you to this place."

Eliza's icy stare fixed on Sienna and Dylan. "More Whitmores? The very root of my pain?"

Sienna stepped closer. "We've seen the toll of this curse. We're here to offer peace."

Eliza's laughter hung in the air. "Peace? After all that I suffered? Each Whitmore generation pays for what they did to us."

"We know your pain," Dylan intervened. "We're familiar with your love story with John, and want to set things right."

John's spectral form strained, his mouth opening, trying to speak, but no sound emerged.

Eliza's tone was filled with heartbreak. "Every night, I yearn for him. But we remain separated, our souls forever reaching but never touching."

Sienna replied, "John's still here. Please see him and let us help you break this tragic loop."

Doubt danced in Eliza's eyes. "But John's moved on, hasn't he? My only solace has been vengeance against the Whitmores."

John tried to move closer, his eyes desperate, begging her to recognize his presence.

"It has to end. For both the living and the departed," Dylan pleaded. "Sienna and I, we feel your pain. We're living it."

"John and you, you had love," Sienna added. "Help us. Let us help you find the peace you deserve."

Eliza seemed conflicted, her form flickering. "Seeing you both, willing to risk so much for love... Reminds me of what John and I had."

Ashlyn intervened. "John's love was genuine. It's time you both find peace."

"Please. Let's end this torment." Sienna approached the ghost.

Eliza hesitated. "I want to believe there's hope."

A gust of wind rustled through the trees, carrying faint, haunting whispers with it—echoes of old accusations and betrayals. The voices fed Eliza's doubts, stirring memories of past deceits.

Suddenly, the air turned icy cold. Eliza's anger flared again, her form growing darker. "Whitmores, always deceiving! How can I trust any of you?" she hissed.

Before Dylan could respond, an icy grip clutched his throat, lifting him off the ground. Panic surged as he struggled for air.

Sienna screamed, "Eliza, no! Please!"

Consumed by fury, Eliza seemed beyond reach. Dylan's face turned a dangerous shade of blue. Beside her, John's form brightened, his mouth moving in a silent, desperate plea. Despite his efforts, the chains of Eliza's wrath rendered him invisible to her. His expression was one of deep anguish as he witnessed the unfolding scene.

Ashlyn, summoning all her strength, chanted a potent incantation, attempting to counter the overwhelming energy Eliza radiated. The torch flames flickered wildly, casting eerie shadows that moved in sync with the escalating clash between the living and the dead.

John's gestures became more frantic, his pleading eyes filled with urgency.

The atmosphere around the brook darkened as Eliza's wrath intensified, her focus narrowing on Dylan. Her eyes, burning with a supernatural glow, fixed on him as she declared, "The blood of the Whitmores! They're the root of my suffering!"

A chilling wind enveloped Dylan, draining his warmth and turning his skin a ghastly pale. As frost crept up his neck and face, Sienna watched in horror, realizing he was close to succumbing to the same fate that had befallen Eliza. His eyes showed his torment as his breaths grew shallower and more infrequent.

Then a cry cut through the clearing. It wasn't from any of the living, but from John, his spirit stirred by the cruel replay of his own past. With desperation and love, he broke the silence, calling out, "Eliza... please."

The fierce spirit halted, her focus momentarily shattered. From the deeper shadows by the brook, John's spirit emerged, his face full of pain and regret. "It wasn't the boy. It was me. Don't blame him for my actions."

Eliza's gaze flicked between John and Dylan. "John?" her voice wavered. "Why did you leave me? I trusted you with everything!"

John's spectral form approached her. "I was weak. Promises tempted me. By the time I realized the consequence of my choices, it was too late. But please, don't continue this cycle of pain and revenge."

Dylan, weakened by the attack, murmured, "I'm... I'm so sorry for what my ancestor did. But please, let us help you find peace."

"This cycle of pain and revenge won't bring you happiness." Sienna approached a shivering Dylan, clutching him close to her, and added, "Let us help you both find each other, find love once again, and rest."

Eliza's spirit looked torn, her gaze shifting between Sienna, Dylan, and John, who reached out a translucent hand towards her. "Come to me. Let us find peace together."

But Eliza cried out, "He's gone! He left me to freeze, to die alone and heartbroken!"

"I never left you, my dearest." John's voice, filled with raw emotion, echoed through the night. "I've been here, tormented by my decisions, wishing I could change the past. Let's not let another generation bear our pain."

Eliza looked at John as she released Dylan, tears of frost forming in her eyes. "Is it really you?"

John nodded, reaching out to her.

Sienna watched with relief as color crept back into Dylan's cheeks. His breathing grew steadier, the frost retreating from his skin. He coughed and opened his eyes, meeting Sienna's concerned gaze. She pulled him close, feeling the returning warmth of his body and the strong beat of his heart against her chest.

Around them, the brook's waters calmed, the restless ambiance giving way to deep silence, broken only by the gentle crackle of the torches. The world held its breath in anticipation.

Eliza hesitated for a moment. The years of betrayal and sorrow still lingered. John reached out to touch her ethereal cheek. "My love. I am so sorry. I should have been there for you."

She responded, her voice trembling, "You left me. Alone in the cold, betrayed by love."

John nodded, his spectral eyes filled with tears. "I know, and that guilt has tormented me every moment since. I wish I could turn back time, do things differently. But now, we have a chance, here, together."

The two spirits moved closer to each other, their forms intertwining, hands reaching out to hold one another. Eliza rested her head on Jim's shoulder, her anger melting away in the warmth of their reconnection.

Sienna whispered to Dylan, "They deserve this moment, after all they've been through."

Dylan nodded and squeezed her hand. "It's time for healing."

Ashlyn's eyes sparkled under the torchlight as she started another chant, her voice blending themes of reconciliation, forgiveness, and new beginnings. The surrounding energy shifted, becoming lighter.

As her chant reached its peak, John and Eliza, now fainter, shared a tender, lingering kiss—a symbol of everlasting love that transcended life and death.

The brook, reflecting their reunion, shimmered under the moonlight, mirroring the two spirits as they dissolved into countless motes of light that rose and danced in the night sky.

Overwhelmed by the beauty of the moment, Sienna felt tears well up. She turned to Ashlyn, her eyes questioning. "Is it over? Has the curse truly been lifted?"

Ashlyn surveyed the now peaceful surroundings and took a deep breath, soaking in the renewed energies. "Yes," she said. "Their spirits have found peace and are finally at rest."

Dylan turned to Sienna. "It feels like a weight's been lifted, doesn't it? Like we've been holding our breath, and now..." He inhaled deeply and exhaled.

Sienna nodded. "Maybe, just maybe, we can start to move forward."

Dylan looked into her eyes. "Their story has ended, but ours is just beginning."

Ashlyn's eyes shimmered with wisdom as she smiled at Sienna and Dylan. "The spirits are reunited," she said. "Being part of your journey has been a privilege beyond words. Remember, the essence of love is to bridge souls and mend what was once broken." She glanced around and her words echoed through the clearing as if meant for more than just those present.

Her robes rustled as she gathered her belongings and moved towards the forest's edge. Bathed in the silver light, she paused and looked back. "Cherish these moments and let this sacred ground strengthen the bond you're building."

With an effortless grace, Ashlyn disappeared into the depths of the forest, leaving Sienna and Dylan alone in the clearing.

As the past's remnants dissipated, Sienna felt a surge of sensations. The ambient energy of the clearing, tinged with the centuries-old feelings of Eliza and John, enveloped her. She almost believed she could hear Eliza's voice, echoing the ache of long separations.

Dylan caught her gaze with a deep, understanding look. He reached out and touched her cheek. "You feel it too, don't you?"

Their faces drew closer, and their lips met in a kiss. It was gentle yet profound, bridging centuries of longing with the freshness of new affection.

As they parted, Sienna breathed deeply, feeling overwhelmed by the intensity of the moment. "It's like we're not just us. We're them too—Eliza and John, somehow," she whispered.

Dylan nodded. "It's powerful, isn't it? To feel so connected to the past, yet right here, right now, it's just you and me."

The cool night air seemed to echo their realization. A gentle breeze rustled the leaves, and the moonlight cast a soft glow that enveloped them.

"Look at the brook," Sienna said, pointing towards the gently flowing water that shimmered under the moonlight. "Even it seems calmer, like it knows."

Dylan squeezed her hand, his smile tender. "Maybe it does. And maybe we can find our own peace, too."

"Tonight feels like a new beginning," Sienna said, her voice filled with hope.

Dylan agreed, his eyes bright. "A new beginning for us, free from the past but enriched by it. Let's see where this journey takes us."

Hand in hand, they turned away from the brook, each step forging a new path in their story, under the vast, starlit sky.

CHAPTER TEN

Rooted in Love

In the dim glow of the motel's aging lights, Sienna climbed into the bed she once shared with Dylan. The room was charged with echoes of their past intimacy, casting a patchwork of shadows and muted reflections. Outside, the chirp of crickets blended with the steady hum of the air conditioner, a lullaby both eerie and comforting.

As sleep tugged at her eyelids, Sienna's mind drifted—to the brook, to Eliza and John, and inevitably, to Dylan. The weight of the past few days pressed on her, as if the spirits of old lingered, whispering their stories and sorrows.

But tonight, as Sienna sank into sleep, an unexpected figure appeared in her dreams. It was Eliza, no longer a vengeful ghost, but a vision of timeless beauty. Her gown, flowing and iridescent, shimmered like dawn's first light. Her eyes sparkled with calm wisdom, transcending time itself.

"Sienna." Eliza's voice was a gentle whisper, like a breeze through autumn leaves. "I've come to thank you."

Caught in the dream's surreal embrace, Sienna responded, curiosity coloring her tone. "Why now, when you can finally be with John?"

Eliza drifted closer, her presence soothing. "Because of you, I'm free from centuries of torment. You bridged what seemed impossible. Now, before I become a mere echo of a forgotten tale, I want to share some wisdom."

A flicker of uncertainty crossed Sienna's face. "What do you want to tell me?"

Eliza locked eyes with Sienna. "Love fiercely, against all reason. Cherish it, for it is the purest magic. Don't let past mistakes bind you. Walk forward with Dylan. Let your light together outshine our dark past."

Tears welled in Sienna's eyes, her fears surfacing. "But how can I be sure it's real? How do we avoid heartbreak?"

Eliza touched Sienna's cheek as lightly as a snowflake. "You can never be certain, Sienna. But that's the beauty of love—it's a leap of faith, a commitment of courage. Follow your heart's rhythm; it will guide you, as mine did, on a perilous journey. Let love be your compass, even when the path is clouded."

A profound peace enveloped Sienna, comforting her as dawn's light began to seep through the curtains. Her connection with Eliza, forged through shared trials, would remain a part of her forever.

As she awoke to the new day, Sienna's heart felt lighter, blessed by Eliza's spirit and filled with a new resolve. With every heartbeat, she felt an irresistible draw to Dylan. Their intertwined destinies, once shadowed by history, were now ready to forge a new future.

She stretched, the cool sheets whispering against her skin. It was a truth she could no longer deny, a new dream in her heart. True, she wanted to travel unknown terrains, to pen down tales from ancient towns and bustling metropolis. Sienna aspired to be a travel writer, a blogger who'd capture the very essence of places and people. Yet, amid this yearning, was another—she craved to have Dylan beside her, as both her muse and confidant.

Sienna stretched under the cool sheets, a new dream blossoming in her heart. She envisioned herself traversing unknown terrains, capturing the soul of ancient towns and vibrant cities through her writing. The notebook on her bedside table, filled with blank pages, seemed to beckon her, ready to absorb tales of adventure and romance. In her mind's eye, she traveled through bustling markets, serene mountaintops, and down cobblestone streets of charming villages. Dylan was there in each scene, his insights adding depth to every experience.

Compelled to share these dreams, Sienna grabbed her phone to message Dylan. She poured her heart and ambitions into the text.

Just as she hesitated over the 'send' button, a knock at the door caused her to pause. The insistent sound pulled her back to reality, and with a flutter of anticipation, she opened the door. Dylan stood there, his eyes brimming with hope.

"I know we agreed on a day apart, but I couldn't wait," Dylan admitted, his voice shaking. He seemed to search for the right words, his gaze flitting away, then back to hers.

Moved by his presence, Sienna reached out, her hand touching his cheek, and then pulled him into a gentle kiss. It was a kiss that spoke of reunions and resolutions, sealing their understanding in a moment of quiet intensity.

Dylan's initial surprise melted, his arms eventually coming around to hold her close. When they finally parted, their bond felt renewed, more solid than ever.

"Let's start the day together," Sienna suggested, stepping aside to let him in. They moved to the small table by the window, where the morning light cast a hopeful glow. Together, they planned out a day of simple joys—visiting the local bookshop, walking through the nearby park, discussing her travel ideas and how he could be part of that journey.

As they talked, the notebook lay open between them, its pages filling with notes and sketches, plans for future adventures that they would document together. Dylan's laughter and enthusiasm enriched every plan, making Sienna's dreams feel even more possible. Whatever challenges they might face with others, like Dylan's family, they were ready to face them together.

"Let's make it official and introduce you to my family," Dylan proposed later, his tone light. Sienna smiled, a touch of nervous excitement in her expression. She agreed, knowing that facing his family was the next step.

As they arrived at the family wing of the resort, Sienna's heart raced a touch faster. As the great doors opened, a wave of warmth enveloped her from Dylan's stepmother. The gentle crinkle around her eyes and her inviting smile hinted at an unspoken understanding.

As the aroma of a lavish feast filled the dining room, Sienna couldn't help but feel a twinge of discomfort. The wooden table at the center was laden with an extravagant spread, mirroring a grand festivity that seemed at odds with her simpler tastes. Conversation flowed around her, shifting from light anecdotes to deeper discussions about the future.

Dylan's grandfather showed a surprising change. His demeanor had softened, the hard lines around his eyes replaced by a semblance of peace. Still, the grandeur of the setting was hard for Sienna to reconcile with the man she remembered—one who had openly doubted her intentions because of her modest background.

Dylan's grandfather was a man of formidable presence and strict traditional values and had not changed overnight. His acceptance of Sienna was reluctant, shaped more by resignation than genuine approval. After dinner, he summoned Sienna with a nod, his voice carrying a rare tremor as he addressed her.

"Miss Avery," he began formally, his tone lacking its usual harshness but still far from warm. "I've lived a life deeply rooted in our family's legacy, a legacy I see now that Dylan is ready to redefine. The strength of your commitment... it is undeniable."

He paused, his eyes searching Sienna's. "Our past is a stubborn beast, yet the future—your future with Dylan—is yours to shape. I see that now. And while old habits die hard, your place here... it is acknowledged."

Sienna felt a surge of emotion, her eyes brimming with tears at the unexpected affirmation, however grudging it might be. It wasn't the warm embrace she might have hoped for, but it was a step—a nod to her potential role in Dylan's life.

As they rejoined the group, Sienna sensed a subtle shift in the atmosphere. The oppressive cloud that had loomed over the Whitmores seemed lighter. Dylan's grandfather's stern gaze met hers again, and this time, there was a glint of something that might pass for respect. Dylan and his father bridged the gap with small talk that, for the first time, didn't feel entirely forced.

Dylan, brimming with energy, began sharing his ambitious plans for the resort. "We owe it to this place," he began, "to not only preserve its heritage but also its environment. Eco-tourism and sustainability are the way forward."

Sienna watched as Dylan's father and grandfather leaned in, intrigued. "Eco-tourism?" His father raised an eyebrow. "What sort of changes are you envisioning?"

Before Dylan could answer, his stepmother jumped in, her eyes sparkling with pride. "He's been researching and making plans for months now. You'd be amazed at what he's come up with."

Dylan shot her a glance. "It's about balance. Making the resort a place of sustainable luxury while ensuring it doesn't harm the very beauty it showcases."

His grandfather drummed his fingers, contemplating. "And the business implications?"

Dylan's eyes gleamed. "Imagine guests coming to White Pines, not just for the luxury, but for a unique experience. We'll integrate the natural beauty of the surroundings into every facet of their stay."

His father quirked an eyebrow, intrigued. "Go on."

"We can have guided eco-tours, showcasing the native flora and fauna, and perhaps collaborate with local environmentalists to educate our guests." With enthusiasm in his voice, Dylan described this place as a hub for both relaxation and personal development.

His stepmother nodded. "The land here is full of potential. It's a brilliant way to make use of it."

Dylan's grandfather steepled his fingers, his eyes assessing. "And the accommodations?"

Dylan grinned, "Eco-friendly cabins. Solar-powered, built with sustainable materials. Minimizing our carbon footprint while offering a unique, luxurious experience. The spa can use organic, locally sourced products. The restaurants can shift towards farm-to-table dining."

His father looked thoughtful. "And what about the long-term profitability?"

Dylan responded, "By branding White Pines as an eco-luxury resort, we'd be targeting a niche but rapidly growing market. Time is about more than just profit, but legacy. We'll be setting a standard, drawing discerning guests who will pay a premium for ethical, sustainable luxury."

Sienna squeezed Dylan's hand under the table. She loved how his vision wasn't just about revenue, but about making a lasting positive impact on the environment and the community.

As Dylan finished, there was an appreciative hum around the table. His stepmother beamed with pride, but it was his father who broke the silence, turning his gaze to Sienna. "And what about you, Sienna? Apart from working at the resort, what are your other pursuits??"

Sienna hesitated for a moment, the attention on her. "Well, I've been working my way through college. I've always had a love for words and stories, so I'm majoring in literature."

Dylan's stepmother smiled. "Ah, a storyteller. That's wonderful."

Sienna's face lit up, her initial hesitation fading. "Yes, and my dream is to combine that with my love for travel. I aspire to be a travel writer, capturing the essence of places and cultures, the hidden stories waiting to be told."

Dylan's father stroked his chin, eyes narrowing. "That's an interesting combination. Travel and literature. With White Pines moving toward an eco-luxury brand, having authentic stories and experiences documented could be beneficial. And considering the Whitmore Group has resorts and hotels around the world..."

Dylan caught on. "Sienna could document her experiences, offering an authentic perspective on each location. It would be fantastic branding, connecting with audiences on a personal level."

His grandfather, not one to be easily impressed, nodded. "It's not a bad idea. People resonate with stories, with genuine experiences. It could set our brand apart."

Dylan's stepmother added, "And it's always wonderful to support young talent, especially when it aligns with our vision."

Sienna hesitated, processing the sudden turn of events. She was wary of wealth and its trappings, and being thrust into the Whitmore family's world was both overwhelming and a tad suspicious. However, the prospect of earning her place, on her own terms, was enticing. "I appreciate the sentiment," she began, "but I would like to finish college before making any major decisions. Education has always been important to me."

Dylan's father raised his hands in a placating gesture, his eyes twinkling with mischief. It was clear where Dylan got that grin. "We're just speculating right now, young lady." He winked at her. "The door is always open. Take your time."

After their heartwarming conversation at lunch, Dylan took Sienna by the hand, leading her toward a gardener. With a brief exchange and a knowing smile, the gardener handed Dylan a small sapling.

As they approached his car, Sienna's eyes were filled with questions. "Where are we going?" she asked.

Dylan just smiled, a glint of mischief in his eyes. "You'll see."

They drove in companionable silence, the world outside shifting from the manicured beauty of the Whitmore estate to the wilder, untamed landscapes. They arrived at The Frozen Tears trailhead.

"This place," Dylan started, "will always be ours. It's intertwined with pain and tragedy, but I want us to change its narrative. I want this place to be a symbol of beauty, joy, and our love."

They walked to the brook, a young sapling cradled between them. Together, they planted it at the water's edge.

"This tree," Dylan said, holding the sapling, "will grow alongside our love. Strong, enduring, always reaching for the sun."

Sienna brushed her fingers over the young leaves and smiled. "Every time we come here, we'll see its growth."

Together, they stepped back to admire their handiwork. Under the canopy of trees, with the gentle babble of the brook in the background, they envisioned a future brimming with hope, love, and growth. The haunting legacy of Eliza's curse was now reborn as a living testament to enduring love.

The Last Act

Kindred Spirits Mysteries

Beth Connor

Wolf Grove Media, LLC

Contents

CHAPTER ONE

Setting the Stage

Nora Sinclair was out of her element, and she knew it. As she stood in the doorway of the Majestic Theatre, she felt like she'd wandered into a dragon's lair armed with nothing but the clothes on her back. Dance had always been her armor, something she could rely on to win over any audience. But acting? That was a different beast..

She grew up believing she would become a Rockette. There was never any doubt in her mind that she could attain this goal. That is until the paperwork read that she had to be 5'5. So now, here she was, on the brink of a new career, about to step onto the stage with nothing but her wits. She wondered if she was about to take a giant leap—or land flat on her face.

Inside the theater's grand lobby, she thought of her childhood, when she first fell in love with dance. Sports never suited her. She remembered the feeling of the spotlight, the thrill of the music, and the way the world melted away when she was on stage. But acting? Acting made her feel vulnerable, like it put a big target on her back.

She sighed. There had been so many dance auditions where each panel member seemed to look past her, focusing instead on the taller dancers. It wasn't easy being short and curvy while dreaming of a career that demanded a tall, lithe body. Despite training and dedicating her teenage years to ballet, tap, and jazz classes,

Nora had remained a steadfast 5 foot 2 and three-quarters. For the Rockettes, those missing inches mattered.

As she reminisced, Nora's thoughts drifted back to how she ended up in Boston. She had grown up in central New Hampshire and back home, people knew her name. When the Radio City Music Hall dream didn't pan out. Her love for the arts led her to Boston, where she studied performing arts and dance at Emerson College. During those years, she fell in love with the city.

After graduating, Nora landed a job teaching dance just outside the city and tried out for as many opportunities as she could find. The *Chicago* audition was on a whim—never in a million years did she think she would get an actual role. She felt hopeful for a part in the dance ensemble, and if she was lucky, one of the "Cell Block Tango" gals. But Roxie Hart? It was an opportunity she couldn't pass up, one that promised to push her harder than she had ever been pushed. But now, as she stood alone, she felt like a sheep in wolf's clothing.

Somehow, Nora Sinclair had landed the lead in a Boston Stage Ensemble's production of *Chicago*. Roxie Hart was a character who owned the stage and charmed everyone around her. And Nora? She was a dancer who had stumbled into a role that required a world of swagger and confidence she wasn't sure she had. Yet here she was, about to tackle the impossible.

The read-through had been manageable, even though her nerves seemed determined to make a spectacle of themselves. The other actors were friendly, offering nods and smiles when she fumbled her lines. But that was just reading words on a page.

Tonight was different. Tonight was the first rehearsal at the theater. Here, she would try to convince everyone—including herself—that she could do this. The prospect was terrifying.

The Majestic Theatre was a relic of another era, with its grand arches, opulent chandeliers, and velvet curtains. Its walls held stories of triumphs and tragedies, laughter, and tears. The air itself seemed to hum with the echoes of past audiences, as if they were waiting to see what stories would unfold.

She took a deep breath and stepped inside, hoping that somewhere within its walls, she'd find the courage to carry her through the night. As Nora moved deeper into the theater, she paused in front of a framed photograph of an actress who had performed there decades ago. The woman's eyes seemed to follow Nora, her knowing smile almost unsettling. A shiver ran down Nora's spine.

She had heard stories about the theater's ghosts, but something about this picture felt different. As she stared at the actress's face, she swore she heard a soft whisper brush past her ear, though the words were too faint to understand. A sudden chill swept over her, sending goosebumps racing up her arms.

Nora leaned in closer, noticing something odd about the photograph. The nameplate was blank, almost as if it had been erased. Who was this woman? Was she one spirit rumored to linger here?

Maybe the ghosts would lend a hand tonight. Or maybe, like everyone else, they'd find her performance as awful as she feared. It didn't matter. She was here now, and there was no turning back. She would channel Roxie Hart—or at least bluff her way through it with the best of them.

The silence was reverent, as if the very walls held their breath. Her footsteps echoed on the polished floor and she looked around, hoping to find another actor to follow. Maybe then she could imitate their rehearsal etiquette. But the lobby was empty, save for the strange shadows cast by the chandeliers.

"Hello?" she called out. Her voice bounced back to her, lingering in the air, reminding her she was very much alone.

The butterflies in her stomach were relentless, doing what felt like a full tap routine. A sudden wave of nausea swept over her. What if this was all some elaborate joke? Maybe she was being punked, and any moment now, someone would leap out from behind a curtain with a camera crew in tow.

Then she heard it—a soft rustling, like fabric brushing against the wall, though no one else was there. The scent of roses lingered in the air. Nora paused, trying to figure out where the noise was coming from. Just as quickly as it began, the sensation vanished, leaving the lobby still and silent once more.

Before she could dwell on it, the door to the house swung open, and the director, Martin Holloway, stepped out.

"Nora," he said, his brow furrowing in mild confusion.

She felt close to tears, her mind racing. "Did I miss rehearsal?"

Martin chuckled, his expression softening. "No, sweetie," he said, patting her on the shoulder. "You're an hour early!"

Nora's face paled to a shade whiter than she already was, and her freckles turned a bright red.

Martin put his arm around her shoulders in a comforting gesture. "It happens to the best of us—and better early than late! Let me show you around, then you can explore a bit before the others get here."

He led Nora through the winding corridors of the Majestic Theatre. The building seemed to have more personality than most people. It wasn't just grand; it was grand with a capital G, and it knew it. The walls were covered in intricate gold leaf patterns, like some sort of ornate wedding cake, and the velvet curtains looked so thick that they could stop a bullet—or at least muffle a sneeze.

"This theater's seen its fair share of drama," Martin said, his voice echoing in the cavernous space. "From its earliest days, it's been a home to actors, musicians, and even a ghost or two."

Nora clutched at her script. The corners crumpled from nervous fidgeting. Martin glanced at the paper and raised an eyebrow, his expression somewhere between amused and fatherly.

"You know," he said, "Roxie's lines are supposed to be memorized by now."

Nora's heart sank like a stone in a pond. Memorized? Nobody told her that! She felt as though she had shown up to the wrong party, wearing a clown costume instead of a ball gown.

"Memorized?" she repeated, her voice squeaked.

Martin chuckled. "Don't worry, Nora. You've got some time before the others arrive. Use it well."

He smiled and continued the tour, showing her the backstage chaos. Then the green room with its ancient couches that had seen more drama than Shakespeare, and the orchestra pit that looked as though it could swallow the entire string section whole.

After Martin's tour, Nora wandered down a narrow corridor lined with posters from past productions. Her fingers brushed against the faded paper. She felt drawn to the past, as if the theater was urging her to uncover its secrets.

The Majestic was a maze of hidden doors and winding staircases, each turn revealing another layer of its character. She felt as if she were inside a giant clock, all gears and pulleys, ticking away as the minutes slipped by.

In the shadows of one hallway, she discovered a small wooden door. She opened it and peered inside, seeing shelves filled with old props and costumes. As she stepped inside, the floorboards creaked underfoot. A sense of history wrapped itself around her. There was something magical about this place.

"This'll do," Nora muttered to herself, brushing off a chair and settling in. The room was dim and smelled like old costumes and varnish, but it was quiet. A perfect place for a bit of last-minute cramming.

She perched on the chair, surrounded by the ghosts of performances past. With only thirty minutes left, she opened her script and read, her voice mingling with the faint noises of the theater, and the building itself leaned in to listen.

Nora was surprised that she had memorized most of her lines and she allowed her attention to drift. Across the room, she noticed a seam in the wall with a curious little indent that almost looked like a handle. She wandered over, deciding to give it a closer inspection. When she pressed her hand into the indent, the panel popped open with a soft click.

Inside was a small, tarnished tin box, its surface weathered and streaked with age. The faint outline of an engraved pattern, now softened by time, caught the light. She traced a finger over the etching before prying the lid open with a soft creak. A familiar scent. Roses—old, dried, and faint—rose from the box, wrapping around her senses like a distant memory.

Nestled inside was a bundle of letters, yellowed with age and tied together with a faded ribbon that looked like it might disintegrate if she so much as breathed on it wrong. On the top letter, the name "Helen" was scrawled in a bold, masculine hand, the ink dark and smudged in places. Helen. The name tugged at something in the back of her mind, but it was like trying to catch smoke.

Nora's fingers hovered over the letters, itching to untie the ribbon and dive into their contents. Who was this Helen? And who had written these letters to her with such careful strokes? Her imagination wandered—old lovers, tragic endings, secrets never meant to be uncovered. It all felt like the opening chapter to a gothic romance, the kind where she'd soon be fending off cursed paintings or unraveling ghostly mysteries.

She was just about to slide one letter free when her watch buzzed. Nora jumped, startled, out of her reverie. Rehearsal. Of course. She sighed, casting one last glance at the letters. Time had a way of slipping by when you were on the verge of uncovering forgotten stories.

After a minute, she blinked herself back into the present. Careful not to crumple the fragile paper, she tucked the letters back into the tin, fastened the lid, and slipped the whole thing into her backpack.

As she made her way back to the stage, her mind was still half-lost in the past, wondering about this mysterious Z and Helen, and what happened to them. Did they get married? Were they famous actors of the time?

The theater was buzzing with activity now, people milling about, waiting for rehearsal to start. There was a familiar tightening in Nora's chest.. It was like getting ready to leap from a great height, and hoping a net would appear before you hit the ground.

As she waited in the wings, she caught snippets of conversation from the other actors arriving for rehearsal. There was talk of a strange noise backstage, and someone mentioned seeing a shadow flit across the balcony.

"Do you believe in the ghosts?" one whispered to another.

Nora leaned closer, her curiosity piqued.

"Of course," the other replied with a grin. "This place is full of them. But don't worry—they're friendly... mostly."

Nora wobbled. She was relieved to see a few others glancing over their shoulders. Maybe she wasn't the only one who felt the theater's energy humming just beneath the surface.

Martin Holloway was in the wings, deep in discussion with a crew member who was making adjustments to the fly system. Martin's voice was warm and carried across the lobby, mingling with the murmur of other preparations. He had a way of making everyone feel included and capable. This made him not just respected, but cherished among the theater folk.

Nora's gaze drifted to the person Martin was talking to. With an easy familiarity, this individual served as a calm port amid the storm of pre-rehearsal chaos. Their presence eased Nora's frayed nerves. With a gentle smile, a brief, quiet moment of understanding passed between the two of them.

She felt a delightful tug at her heart—like the first page of a story she couldn't wait to read. Their eyes sparkled beneath cropped curls, and a halo seemed to form in the light. Adorned with an array of piercings, they oozed charisma. Something about that smile, simple yet reassuring, helped settle the nerves in Nora's stomach.

"Ready to jump in?" Martin called out, his voice a lifeline.

"Yes, I think I am," Nora said, though the words felt hollow in her throat. Her hands trembled as she lowered her backpack in the wing, fingers fumbling over the straps. Each step toward the stage made her knees wobble, a slow, creeping weakness spreading through her legs until it felt like the ground itself might give way beneath her.

Today's rehearsal focused on blocking—no choreography, no music—just the actors finding their place and navigating the bare bones of the performance. It should have been simple. Yet, as Martin called for silence, a tension settled, and Nora's nerves twisted into tighter and tighter knots.

The rehearsal began with Ciera, who played Velma, entering. Ciera was all sharp edges and commanding presence. Her voice filled the theater with an effortless authority that Nora envied.

Then it was her turn. As she stepped forward to embody Roxie Hart confronting Fred, the stage lights blazed down, harsh and unforgiving. She reached for her lines, but instead of words, her mind served up an image of the letters she'd found earlier.

Nora hesitated. "Um…" she stammered, her mind flipping between Roxie and the mysterious letters, and finding neither. The lines were right there, buried under her growing distraction, but she couldn't pull them free. "Line?"

Martin sighed, the tapping of his script against his leg picking up a deliberate, tired rhythm. "Hey, why the hurry? Again, Nora. Focus"

Focus. Right. She blinked, trying to push away the questions gnawing at her brain. Her heart raced as frustration bubbled up—she wasn't just forgetting her lines, she wasn't *present*.

Martin cleared his throat, louder this time.

Nora swallowed hard, casting a quick glance toward the wings. The crew member from earlier caught her eye, offering a slight, encouraging nod. She took a deep breath and her pulse slowed as she exhaled, pushing the thoughts of the letters to the back of her mind. They could wait—*they had to*. She straightened her shoulders and rolled her hands into steady fists at her sides. Roxie needed her attention, not the past.

With a small, determined smile, she stepped forward to attempt her lines again.

"Hey, why the hurry?" Nora began, but her voice wavered, shaky and unconvincing. Her eyes darted to Fred—portrayed by Lucas, whose confidence on stage felt as natural as breathing.

"Stop," Martin's voice cut through the air, sharp and impatient. "Again, without the nerves, Nora. Please."

She shifted her weight, trying to steady herself, when something caught her eye—a young boy, no older than ten, darting between the seats in the back row, grinning as he weaved in and out of the aisles. Who brings a kid to rehearsal? Wasn't this supposed to be professional? She blinked, thrown off. It seemed odd, but maybe someone on the crew had brought him along.

She opened her mouth to try again, but couldn't shake the distraction. The boy now climbed onto a seat, his slight frame almost bouncing with energy. She furrowed her brow. No one else seemed to notice, which only deepened her unease.

"Nora?" Martin's voice cut through the silence, his frustration barely concealed. "What's going on? You seem a million miles away."

"Sorry, I just—" She hesitated, glancing back toward the boy, who was now perched on the edge of a seat, watching her with that same mischievous grin. "There's a kid running around in the audience."

The room fell still for a beat before a ripple of quiet chuckles spread through the cast. Martin didn't even glance toward the seats, just raised an eyebrow as he sighed. "Kids are not welcome in my rehearsals unless they are cast."

Nora's stomach flipped. She looked again, but the boy was gone. The seats were empty, as if no one had been there at all. A prickle ran up the back of her neck. Had she imagined it?

"I—" She swallowed, her throat dry. "Never mind."

The crew exchanged glances, their smirks not even hidden, and someone muffled a laugh. Nora's face flushed hot, the uneasy feeling gnawing at her insides. Did they think she was losing it?

Martin rubbed his temple, exasperated but resigned. "Let's take it from the top," he muttered, as though he had dealt with this before.

This time, her delivery was smoother. "Hey, why the hurry? Amos ain't gonna be home until midnight." The lines weren't perfect, but they felt more authentic, more hers.

The scene unfolded with Nora's confidence building. By the end of the scene, though far from flawless, Nora found her stride. She wasn't Roxie yet, but she was no longer just Nora. She had moved somewhere in between, finding her footing in a role that seemed as unreachable as the stars.

When the rehearsal concluded, Martin nodded, letting out a long breath. His lips twitched—not quite a grin, but close enough—and his eyes crinkled, suggesting things had gone as he intended.

"Better," he grunted, scribbling notes in his script.

Nora exhaled, the tension in her shoulders easing. *Better* was something, at least. She glanced toward the wings, where the crew member who had been watching earlier gave her a thumbs-up before disappearing behind the curtains.

As the cast began to scatter, Nora lingered, replaying the awkward moment with the boy and the laughter. She was about to head outside when the same crew member approached, offering her a friendly smile.

"Hey, new girl," they said, sticking out a hand. "I'm Alex, by the way. I handle most of the tech stuff around here."

"Nora," she replied, shaking their hand, trying to match their easygoing vibe. There was something about Alex's calm, warm energy that put her at ease, more than she expected.

"You did great up there," Alex said, their smile genuine.

Nora let out a breathy laugh, shifting on her feet. "Not really. It felt like everyone was laughing at me."

Alex shook their head, grinning. "Nah, that wasn't about you. That was because of Ollie."

Nora blinked. "Ollie?" She furrowed her brow, the name not ringing any bells.

Alex glanced around, leaning in, as if letting her in on a secret. "Yeah, the kid you saw in the audience?"

Nora's stomach dropped. "How did you know I saw—" She hesitated, not wanting to sound crazy. "Yeah, I thought I saw a kid running around. No one else seemed to notice, though."

Alex chuckled, their eyes bright with amusement. "That's because most of us are used to him by now. Ollie's one of the theater ghosts."

Nora's heart skipped a beat, and she stared at Alex, waiting for the punchline. "Wait, what? You're telling me that boy was a ghost?"

Alex nodded, their expression casual, as though this was normal. "Yup. Shows up now and then during rehearsals, messes with the new folks. It's kind of his thing."

Nora's mind spun, trying to process this. "So... everyone knew?"

Alex shrugged, a sympathetic smile tugging at their lips. "Pretty much. Martin just ignores it—he's not big on acknowledging the weird stuff. But the rest of us? We're used to Ollie by now. The laughter? That wasn't at you. It's just part of the ritual when someone new sees him for the first time. Call it a theater hazing tradition, I guess. Welcome to the club."

Nora let out a long breath she didn't realize she was holding. "So I wasn't imagining it?" The knot in her stomach loosened, though she still felt a bit rattled.

"Nope, you really saw him. Don't worry, he's harmless. Likes to play pranks, but he's never caused any trouble. More mischievous than anything."

Nora managed a smile, a strange sense of relief washing over her. "Well, thanks for letting me know. I thought I was losing it."

Alex chuckled. "Nope, you're good. See you tomorrow, Nora."

The streets of Boston were still alive, though the late hour had finally begun to quiet the hum of the city. There was something comforting about it—the way the world slowed, as if it, too, needed a moment to breathe. The streetlights cast a soft, golden glow over the sidewalks, their light guiding her steps as she made her way back to Washington Street.

This was her favorite time of day. The city winding down, the air cool and sharp, and the streets almost hers alone. She let the rhythm of her walk settle into her bones, but her mind, as usual, was elsewhere. Rehearsal. Had she done enough? Could she ever become Roxie Hart, that brash, fearless woman who seemed to inhabit a world so far removed from her own? Doubts curled around her thoughts like stubborn cobwebs she couldn't quite shake off.

But then she remembered the smile—the one that had cut through her nerves like a beam of sunlight. *Alex.* Their quiet confidence in her had meant more than Martin's half-smile ever could. Maybe she wasn't as terrible as she'd feared. Maybe, just maybe, she was good enough.

Her pace slowed as her thoughts drifted to the letters she'd found. The tin box. She hadn't read a word yet, but her fingers itched to pull the letters from her bag. There was a strange excitement bubbling up, like she was teetering on something important—something bigger than herself. The city may have been winding down, but her mind was just starting to stir, full of possibilities.

When she reached her building, the lobby was quiet, save for the soft hum of the elevator that accompanied her ascent. The day had been long, but there was something comforting about the silence here.

Her apartment was a kind of sanctuary. She shared it with two other introverts, roommates who, like her, cherished silence as if it were something rare and precious. They rarely saw each other, and when they did, it was usually in passing—an exchange of nods, maybe a muttered "hey" over a cup of tea. But it worked. There was a rhythm to it all. The quiet companionship of people who understood that sometimes, the best way to live together was to simply not talk too much.

The living room was a delightful mess of mismatched furniture, the kind that seemed to have come together by accident. An armchair slouched in the corner, looking like it had given up on life years ago, while the couch sagged in the middle, as if it had seen one too many people collapse into it after a long day. The shelves were overflowing with books—some precariously stacked, others wedged in at odd angles, as though they'd been read so many times they now demanded to live wherever they pleased. It wasn't elegant by any means, but it had a well-worn charm that made it feel more like home than any magazine-worthy living room ever could.

Her bedroom, though, was the real haven. The walls were a patchwork of posters from past performances, each one a little window into a memory. A small, cluttered desk sat by the window. Dance shoes and leotards lay in a heap on the floor, creating a kind of organized chaos. But it was *her* chaos, the kind that made sense in a way nothing else did. Here, in this little corner of the world, she could breathe. She could dream. It wasn't much, but it was enough.

Nora sat in bed, legs tucked beneath her. The lamp beside her cast a warm light over the mess scattered across the floor. She promised herself she'd clean up tomorrow. Tomorrow was always good for that kind of thing. Right now, she had something far more interesting to deal with.

She reached over to her backpack and pulled out the tarnished tin box. It sat in her lap, heavier than it looked, The metal was cool under her fingers, its engraved design faded with time and handling. There was something old about it, like it had been waiting for her in the theater, gathering dust for decades until she came along.

It felt almost like a treasure chest.

Who didn't love a good mystery? Especially one that involved secret letters tucked away in an old tin box found in a haunted theater. The whole thing was begging for a dramatic reveal—maybe there'd be a tragic love story, or a scandalous affair, or... well, something interesting, anyway. It had to be better than whatever the newest reality TV show on Netflix was.

Nora tilted the box, listening to the soft rustle of paper inside. She hesitated for just a second—what if the letters were just grocery lists?

But that was the thing about mysteries: you didn't know until you looked.

With a little sigh, she popped open the box. The hinges creaked, naturally, like they'd been practicing for this exact dramatic moment. Inside were the bundle of letters. The faint scent of dried roses wafted up, like someone had pressed a bouquet between the pages long ago.

She blinked. That was... poetic.

"Okay," she murmured, reading the name scrawled across the top letter in thick, dark ink. "Let's see what you've got for me."

My Dearest Helen,

I must confess, seeing you on stage today was nothing short of a revelation. You have a presence that commands attention and a voice that lingers long after the last note has faded. It is in those moments that I am reminded of how extraordinary you truly are.

Our rehearsals are the brightest part of my day. Running songs with you, even in the quiet of an empty theater, fills me with a joy that I find hard to express. I hope you will allow me to do so whenever you wish, for there is no greater pleasure than sharing those moments with you.

Please do not doubt your talent or your place on that stage. You are not a fraud, my dear. You possess a gift that is all your own, and I have no doubt that the world will one day come to see it as I do.

Until we meet again in the shadows of the wings, know that my thoughts are with you.

Yours truly, Z.

Nora sat back, the words settling over her like an old, well-worn blanket—familiar, but not in the way she'd expected. It was strange, really, how something written so long ago could feel like it was meant for her. Whoever Helen was, she'd wrestled with the same gnawing self-doubt, the same aching need to belong. Some things, apparently, didn't care about time. Nora folded the letter carefully, her mind buzzing with questions and possibilities as she pulled out the next letter.

Dearest Zeke,

Tonight, as the curtain fell, and the applause roared like a storm, I thought of you, and how your presence fills the empty spaces between the notes. Your faith in me is a light in the dark, a beacon that guides me through the chaos of this world we call the stage.

The world beyond the theater is vast and uncertain, yet with you, I find a place of belonging. Our moments together, though brief, are precious beyond words. It seems the world would prefer our paths not to cross, but in you, I have found a kindred spirit.

Let us face whatever comes with courage and a shared smile, even if they whisper otherwise.

Until our next encounter, know that you are in my thoughts.

Yours affectionately,

Helen

Nora paused, her eyes lingering on the name *Zeke*. She knew their names now. Zeke and Helen. A little thrill ran through her, like she'd just unlocked the first clue in some grand, forgotten puzzle. There was something about a name that made it all feel more real—more tangible. Two people tied together through time, their story tucked away in these hidden letters, waiting for who knows how long.

She frowned, wondering why all the letters had been kept together. It seemed odd—something so private, stashed away in a dusty old theater. Maybe someone had needed them close, a quiet comfort in the shadows. Or maybe the letters had just been patient, waiting decades for the right person to stumble upon them, like some forgotten relic that didn't mind being lost.

With a satisfied nod, Nora refolded the paper, careful not to crease it more than it already was. These letters were a treasure—secret, tucked-away pieces of someone's life, and she could savor them, bit by bit, when the time felt right. She placed the tin box on her desk, feeling an odd sense of contentment. It was there, waiting for her, a quiet little mystery to return to whenever she was ready.

CHAPTER TWO

Cast and Crew

Nora felt like she'd been trampled by a herd of elephants. Every muscle groaned in protest. What made it even stranger was that she hadn't danced at all yesterday—just spent hours obsessively going over the rehearsal in her mind. Apparently, mental gymnastics was just as punishing as the physical kind.

Her body creaked as she got out of bed, each movement reminding her of the awkward tangle of thoughts she'd been stuck in the night before. She'd replayed every flubbed line until Martin's critiques became a symphony of disappointment. Stress, she told herself. It's just stress. It had better be, because she could not afford to get sick right now. Not with rehearsals intensifying.

If she had to be honest, last night's practice had been rough, but it wasn't catastrophic. Still, the little nagging voice in her head was making sure she remembered every mistake in excruciating detail.

She pulled her hair back into a ponytail, her fingers moving on autopilot while her brain went galloping ahead into the day. She hummed, flipping through lesson plans in her mind, trying to convince herself she was organized. The soft morning light trickled through the window, casting gentle, comforting shadows across the walls. This was her space—she should have felt at ease here, but something kept gnawing at the back of her mind, a persistent, uncomfortable feeling.

She glanced around the room, her eyes sweeping over the familiar clutter—scripts piled haphazardly on the desk, dance shoes peeking out from under the bed, and the letter tin sitting on the desk. It was the same space she woke up to each morning. A comfortable chaos that reflected her busy life. Yet today, it felt different. As if the very air around her was charged. She shook off the feeling, telling herself it was just nerves. But the sensation lingered.

Nora opened the tin and lifted a letter, treating it like it might crumble under her touch. As she unfolded the fragile paper, she could almost feel the past pressing against her fingertips. A sudden creak from the floor made her heart leap into her throat. Her eyes shot up, half-expecting to find someone lurking in the shadows. But the room was still, as it had been. She let out a weak laugh, trying to shake off the creeping unease that clung to her.

Still, as she packed the tin back into her bag, she couldn't shake the feeling of being watched. The play of shadows on the walls seemed to deepen, as though the room itself was watching her every move. Was it possible that Helen was there, somehow aware of her intentions to uncover her secrets? She shrugged off the thought, steeling herself for the day ahead. With one last glance around, she grabbed her things and headed out the door.

Today was not a day to think about the letters (at least not until she was back home). She needed to stay grounded and focused. It was the first day of the summer dance session, and she had rehearsal right after classes. While she wasn't able to teach any of this summer's intensives, Linda, the studio owner, had given her all the morning preschool classes.

The little kid's unbridled enthusiasm was contagious, but she was going to miss the challenge of refining technique with older students. Also, the *Chicago* gig paid well. But it would be over in October, and she couldn't afford to give up her teaching job just yet. Balancing both roles was important, even if it meant sacrificing her own training time for the stability she needed.

Fortunately, Linda was incredible. She supported Nora and was rooting for her to succeed. Linda's faith in her was a steadying force, a reminder someone other than her parents believed in her potential. In reality, Linda was nice, but having a big name working for her brought in more business. Nora appreciated Linda saw the mutual benefit and was thankful for her understanding and flexibility.

Nora stepped out of her apartment and was enveloped by the sticky humidity that signaled summer in Boston. The heat clung to her skin, making her hair frizz in the moisture-laden air. She adjusted her backpack and made her way to the nearby station, hoping the train would offer some relief from the morning heat. As she descended the stairs, the air became cooler, offering a brief respite from the oppressive humidity outside. Nora swiped her card at the turnstile and pushed through, joining the crowd of commuters waiting for the next train.

The platform was bustling with the typical morning rush, filled with commuters who seemed to be in a race against time. Nora found herself caught amid it all, trying to focus on her lines for Roxie Hart. Her eyes skimmed the script, but her mind was distracted, flitting between thoughts of her upcoming rehearsal and the letters she'd found in the theater.

The train was running late, and the growing crowd pressed in from all sides. She shifted her weight and glanced down the tunnel, willing the train to arrive. Her attention caught on a familiar figure across the way, a person whose cropped curls and easy smile she recognized—the mysterious crew member from the theater.

Her heart skipped a beat. There was something about their presence that had given her reassurance the previous day. They stood still amidst the bustling crowd, their gaze meeting hers. Nora's eyes caught on a familiar face, and something flickered inside her—almost a smile. Her hand twitched, ready to lift in greeting, but then the train roared into the station. The blast of noise and wind hit her all at once, rattling through her bones. She blinked, disoriented, her thoughts scattering with the rush of air.

As the doors slid open with a mechanical whine, the crowd surged forward, sweeping the mysterious figure into the throng of passengers boarding the train. Nora craned her neck, trying to catch another glimpse of them, but it was as if they had vanished. She stood there, staring at the spot where they had been, feeling a mix of curiosity and disappointment. Questions whirled in her mind. Who were they? Why did their presence feel so significant? Nora boarded the train herself, feeling the pressure of the crowd as she squeezed into a small space by the door.

As she ran her lines in her head, the train approached her stop before she knew it. She glanced at her watch, hoping she wasn't running late, and sighed with relief—it was all in her head. When the train came to a halt, she stepped off and joined the stream of commuters heading toward the exits. The walk from the station to the studio was quick, but the heavy humidity made it feel longer today. As she weaved through the crowd, her mind shifted to the lessons she would teach that morning.

Nora arrived at the dance studio, greeted by the familiar sounds of laughter and chatter. The children's eager faces reminded her why she loved teaching. Their eyes lit up, wide with curiosity and bursting with energy, tiny feet bouncing with every step. As they spun and stumbled, giggling through their wobbly twirls, Nora's heart skipped along with them. Every laugh, every clumsy leap sent a quiet thrill through her, like she was handing down a secret—one of rhythm and grace—wrapped up in their joy.

Even though teaching wasn't her ultimate dream, it was rewarding in its own right. Here, she could nurture their love for dance and see immediate results. She felt a sense of purpose as she helped shape their experiences with dance, knowing she was creating a foundation that might inspire some of them to pursue it further.

After class, Nora moved through the studio, gathering the scattered props and bits of ribbon left behind by the little dancers. The faint scent of sweat and rosin clung to the air, but her smile lingered, her chest still light from the laughter and twirling excitement that had filled the room. The soft patter of tiny feet and the murmur of parents chatting in the hallway faded, leaving the space bathed in a gentle, peaceful quiet. As the last echoes disappeared, Nora felt the floor beneath her cool and steady, the stillness almost soothing. Linda appeared in the doorway, her warm smile as bright as ever. Just seeing her standing there made something in Nora's chest relax—a constant reminder that, here in the studio, she was always surrounded by support and understanding.

"That was a great class," Linda said, stepping inside. "The kids love you."

"Thanks," Nora replied, beaming. "The kids make it easy."

Linda smiled, but her expression shifted, growing more thoughtful as she leaned against the barre. "Actually, I wanted to run something by you. I'm planning a musical theater workshop for November, and I'd love for you to teach it."

Nora's eyes widened, surprise and excitement bubbling up. "Seriously? That sounds incredible! I'd love to."

"I had a feeling you'd be on board," Linda said with a knowing nod. "You've got so much energy and experience to bring, especially with you doing *Chicago* now. Which reminds me—how would you feel about choreographing 'Cell Block Tango' for our competition team?"

Nora's heart leapt, the prospect sending a thrill down her spine. "Are you kidding? I'd *love* to work on that! It would be amazing!" She could feel the choreography already taking shape in her mind, a delicious glimpse into the career she was hungry for.

Linda's grin widened, pleased by her enthusiasm. "I knew you'd be the perfect fit. Once the team's finalized, we can work out the schedule."

"I can't wait," Nora said, her thoughts already racing with ideas and possibilities.

"Great," Linda replied, pushing off the barre. "Let's catch up later this week to go over the details. Friday work for you?"

"Absolutely," Nora agreed. "Thanks, Linda. This really means a lot."

As Linda left, Nora stood there, a surge of excitement coursing through her. The workshop, the choreography—everything she had been hoping for was finally within reach. She felt lighter, more confident, as if the future she'd been working toward was finally starting to take shape. Roxie Hart wasn't the only one going places.

Nora glanced at her watch as she pushed through the doors of the Majestic Theatre—4:30 PM. Just enough time. She hurried down the hall, the click of her shoes echoing against the old walls, and headed straight for the storage room.

Inside, the familiar scent of old costumes and varnish hit her, thick and musty, like a well-worn blanket wrapping around her shoulders. She shut the door behind her with a soft thud, the noise from the theater fading into a dull hum. The rickety chair creaked as she dropped into it, one leg wobbling.

Nora took a slow, steady breath, eyes drifting to the piles of forgotten props and dusty fabric. The theater's chaotic energy couldn't reach her here—not the rush of rehearsals, not the ghostly whispers brushing past her ear. This was her space now, carved out for a few quiet moments before she'd have to step back onto the stage.

A wave of hunger reminded her she hadn't eaten since breakfast. With rehearsal stretching until 9 PM, she needed something to tide her over. She rummaged through her bag and found a squished snack bar, tearing it open. Its crinkled wrapper was a lifeline, promising at least a temporary reprieve from the hunger pangs. She unwrapped the snack bar and took a large bite, the wrapper crinkling in the quiet room. Chocolate and oats, a poor substitute for a proper meal, but better than nothing. The crumbly mess was sticky, and she could feel the sugar coursing through her veins, providing a much-needed energy boost.

Then she started her vocal warm-ups, humming scales and enunciating phrases with her mouth half-full. Halfway through a particularly tricky tongue twister, she realized she must look ridiculous. Bits of the oat bar stuck to her cheek. She wiped the crumbs from her face, laughing at herself. Before she could restart, the temperature in the room dropped. It was as if someone had opened a window to a frigid winter night. Her thoughts went back to the muscle aches she felt that morning, and a sense of dread washed over her. *I will not get sick, I will not get sick,* she repeated as a mantra.

Determined to focus, Nora shifted her posture, standing taller and full of the confidence Roxie Hart would exude. She narrowed her eyes and practiced Roxie's smirk, letting the character's swagger seep into her bones. Just as she began to feel like Roxie, a loud whisper interrupted her concentration. The voice seemed to come from nowhere and everywhere at once, and it was angry. Nora paused, curious, as she strained her ears to listen. The whispering grew louder, yet the words remained elusive. A gust of wind brushed past, leaving the lingering scent of roses in its wake. It was unsettling, as if someone had rushed by her in a hurry—but there was no one there.

A crash sounded from the corner of the room, and her heart lurched. She twisted her head, her mind racing with possibilities. *What was going on?* The whispers intensified, seeming to hiss right by her ear, crescendoing to an almost deafening volume. Whoever or whatever this was, it was angry.

Her fingers dug into the arm of the wobbly chair. The entire room seemed to hum with a strange energy. Whoever—or whatever—was here, it didn't seem happy.

"Who's there?" she squeaked out, her breath tight.

The door creaked open behind her, the sound cutting through the tension. "Hello? Someone in here?"

And just like that, the room stilled. The whispers vanished, leaving only the soft thrum of her pulse in her ears. Nora's grip loosened on the chair. Slowly, she stood, glancing toward the door. The hallway was empty, but as she stepped closer, she caught a glimpse of Alex just rounding the corner.

"Alex?" she called, her voice a little shaky.

They turned, their face lighting up as they spotted her. "Hey, Nora," Alex greeted, walking toward her.

Alex raised an eyebrow. "You alright?"

Nora let out a shaky breath, trying to steady her voice. "Yeah, I—" She swallowed, her words feeling stuck in her throat. "I think so." She glanced around the now quiet room, the sudden warmth of it unsettling after the chill that had run through her moments before. "I just thought... I... heard something."

Alex leaned against the doorframe, a half-grin playing on their lips. "Weird as in 'crash and whispering ghosts' weird?"

Nora's stomach twisted. "You heard that?"

"Didn't have to." Alex stepped inside, brushing past her as if they'd been through this a hundred times. "It's this room. They like to stir things up in here. Ghosts have a sense of humor, I guess."

Nora's pulse quickened, but her fear was giving way to curiosity. "The whispers... are they dangerous?"

Alex shook their head, a spark of amusement in their eyes. "Nah. They're harmless. They like to make noise, throw things around, maybe mess with you if you're new, but they've never hurt anyone. We'd all be in trouble if they were dangerous."

Nora frowned, still eyeing the corners of the room where the crash had come from. "But what was that crash?"

Alex shrugged, like it was no big deal. "Could've been anything. Props shifting, old junk falling over—half the time it's the ghosts just getting bored. This used to be a dressing room back in the early 1900s. Lots of energy trapped here. People who never quite left, you know?"

Nora wasn't sure if she wanted to be relieved or more freaked out. "Has anyone ever tried, I don't know, to get rid of them?"

Alex chuckled. "Oh yeah, a couple of times. Even had one of those ghost-hunter TV shows come in. You know the type—night vision cameras, dramatic voiceovers, the whole deal. They claimed the place was haunted for sure. Pretty sure it got us more ticket sales, though, so Martin didn't mind."

Nora's mouth twitched in a reluctant smile. "So, they're just... here? Doing their thing? Watching us?"

"Pretty much." Alex nodded, crossing their arms. "But they're not dangerous. Well, maybe Ollie's pranks will freak you out, but other than that, it's just noise. Energy. And a lot of history."

Nora let her eyes wander back to the spot where the crash had sounded. The room, now calm, seemed almost normal again, though the thought of ghosts lingering in the shadows still made her uneasy. Yet, at the same time, something about it intrigued her.

"Do they mind if I keep warming up in here?" She asked.

"Mind? Nah. If anything, they'll probably appreciate the company." Alex shot her a wink. "Besides, it's not like they're going anywhere."

Relief washed over Nora. "Thanks, Alex. I think I needed that."

"Anytime," Alex said, giving her a quick, reassuring squeeze on the shoulder. "Now, come on. Martin's getting things moving. You ready?"

Nora glanced around the room. "Yeah," she said, her voice steadier now. "I think I am."

Chapter Three

CHAPTER THREE

Overture

Last night's rehearsal had been better than the first, but that wasn't saying much. Nora still felt like the greenest actor on the stage, sticking out like a sore thumb—or maybe a sore everything. The number of times Martin had swapped her out for Lexi was… alarming, to say the least. Every time he called Lexi forward, Nora felt her stomach twist into a tighter knot. But what could she do? She just had to keep pushing through.

Lexi, of course, made it all look so easy. She glided across the stage with the confidence that made Nora feel like she was wearing someone else's shoes—too big. Lexi had been at this for years, and Nora? Well, she was still learning how to keep her knees from locking up when the lights hit her.

But she wasn't about to give up. Not now. She'd come in early today, hoping to steal some quiet practice time before everyone else showed up. Maybe, if she was lucky, she could catch Martin and talk through her progress, prove she was serious about the role. That knot in her stomach had settled into a hard, determined lump. She'd prove herself.

The room seemed to welcome her today. No chilly air, just the faint, comforting smell of roses. As she began some vocal warm-ups, her eyes kept wandering to her backpack. She took the tin everywhere with her now, but she had not rewarded herself with the chance to read another letter. Perhaps today was the day. Perhaps Zeke's letters would remind her that perseverance was key and that, like Helen, she needed to trust in her abilities.

She finished her warm-ups, feeling her voice grow stronger and more assured with each note. The tin continued to beckon to her, promising secrets and encouragement from those who had faced their own trials.

Nora couldn't help herself, so she reached for the tin and pried it open. She unfolded the next letter, half-expecting it to crumble in her hands. Helen's words flowed across the page, and Nora hoped something she read might lend her the same grit that had carried Helen through her struggles. Maybe it could give her a nudge to believe in her own. Heaven knew she could use it today.

My Dearest Zeke,

I scarcely know where to begin, for my heart is so full after our last meeting. How fortunate was the day when our paths first crossed at the Majestic Theatre! Your music, so vibrant and true, has been a balm to my soul and has filled my days with a joy I had long thought lost. In your presence, the world seems to shine with a new light, one that has given me hope in the darkest of times.

We stand, my dear Zeke, against the tides of convention and expectation. Society, with its relentless gaze, seeks to confine us within its rigid walls, yet my heart remains steadfast and unwavering in its affection for you. There are whispers of disapproval, eyes that linger too long, but know that my love is resolute and boundless, transcending the barriers that seek to divide us.

I must confess my concerns about Catherine, my understudy. She watches me with eyes sharp as daggers, her ambition palpable in every glance. She covets the role I hold, and there are moments when I ponder whether it would be wise to relinquish it to her. Yet, my passion for the stage and my belief in our shared dream urges me to persevere. Still, her presence is a shadow upon my thoughts.

Let us not surrender to fear, for in you I have found a kindred spirit, a love that defies all conventions. Together, we shall face whatever trials may come, hand in hand.

Yours devotedly,

Helen

Nora refolded the letter and tucked it back into the tin. The actress's worries about Catherine felt familiar, like they had jumped through time and landed right in Nora's lap. She could feel Catherine's sharp stares, the same way she sometimes caught Lexi eyeing her during rehearsals. It wasn't overt, but there was no mistaking the quiet ambition behind Lexi's glances, and honestly, it unsettled Nora more than she cared to admit.

But Helen had dealt with this same tension over a hundred years ago, and she hadn't let it stop her. That thought settled Nora's nerves a bit. If Helen could push through understudy drama and stay in the spotlight, then Nora could do the same with Lexi.

Challenges weren't meant to be roadblocks, but large boulders on a path you had to clamber over. Helen seemed to say as much, and though Nora despised scrambling over obstacles, the thought of tackling them was far more appealing than retreating. After all, mountains could be climbed, provided you had sturdy shoes and were willing to get a little dirty.

Nora checked her watch to see how much time she had left before rehearsal. To her relief, she had plenty. Perfect. She could spend a few more minutes with her newfound friends from the past. She smiled to herself and unfolded the letter, eager to see what wisdom it might contain.

My Dearest Helen,

Your words are a treasure that I hold close to my heart. Your courage and grace inspire me daily, and I am in awe of the strength you possess. Never, my beloved, should you entertain the notion of relinquishing your role to Catherine, for it is you who brings life to the stage. Fear must never be given the power to dictate your path.

In my dreams, I envision a world where our love is not shadowed by prejudice and judgment. I believe fervently that music and love possess the power to transcend these barriers, uniting us in a future of harmony and peace.

Though the world outside may be harsh, let us cling to our dreams. Our bond, forged in the fires of adversity, is unbreakable. Together, we shall find our place where we are free to be as we truly are.

With all my love and admiration,

Zeke

Zeke's words were filled with love and longing, but there was something else woven into the lines—an undercurrent of fear and defiance. He spoke of prejudice and judgment as if they were tangible enemies to be battled every day.

Sitting there in the dim light, Nora wondered what it must have been like for them. Why did they face so much disapproval? What was it about their relationship that drew such ire? Was it merely the era they lived in, or something more insidious?

She frowned, tapping the tin with her fingers. Relationships back then must have been so different. The theater had been built in 1903, so these letters had to be written after that. Had Helen been expected to marry someone her family chose for her? Did they still do that sort of thing at the turn of the century? Nora had read enough Victorian novels to know that arranged marriages were common, but this was America, not some European court. Surely people could choose for themselves by then... right?

Zeke and Helen had a bond that defied the norms of their time. It was a reminder of how many things had changed and yet, in some ways, stayed the same.

She tried to imagine what it would be like to have her life planned out for her, her choices constrained by expectations and propriety. It made her a little queasy to think about. Nora had never been one to follow rules just for the sake of it, and the thought of being forced into a mold by society made her itch to run the other way.

Setting the tin aside, she resolved to learn more about the era they lived in and what might have stood in their way. Perhaps there were answers buried in the theater's dusty archives—or maybe even within the letters themselves. Whatever the case, she felt an urge to uncover the truth about Zeke and Helen, driven by a desire to honor their courage and perhaps learn from their struggle.

Her curiosity burned, and she couldn't help herself. The questions demanded answers, and the next letter was waiting for her. Anticipation was electric, like the moment just before stepping onto the stage. What secrets might this one reveal? As she unfolded the paper, she devoured each word, hoping to learn more about the lives and loves of these two kindred spirits.

My Dearest Zeke,

I write to you with a heavy heart, for there are matters that weigh upon my soul. Edward Pritchard's attentions grow ever more intrusive and unsettling. His presence at the theater is like a dark cloud, casting shadows over the joy I find in our craft. He has made his interest in me abundantly clear, yet he remains unaware of the true object of my affections. Were he to discover the truth, I fear the consequences would be dire.

The world seems to close in around us, and yet my thoughts remain fixed on a future where we might be free of these chains. Once the curtain falls on our performance, my dearest wish is to leave this life behind and find a haven where we can live without fear. But where might such a sanctuary exist? My heart longs to flee with you, yet I tremble at the uncertainty of our path.

Still, I draw strength from your presence, and I am emboldened by the love that binds us. Together, we shall find our way through this darkness.

With all my love and hope,

Helen

Nora sat back. A new player had entered the scene—Edward Pritchard. The name sent a shiver down her spine and Helen's descriptions of him conveyed his presence was more than just bothersome; it was downright ominous.

Pritchard. Where had she heard that name before? Nora chewed her lip, racking her brain. Of course! The Pritchard family name was practically etched into the very walls of the theater. They were the sort of benefactors who funded art and culture, probably to make up for a past of unsettling dalliances in dark corners.

This was an opportunity to learn more about Helen and Zeke. The Pritchard family was prominent. There had to be clues scattered throughout the archives. Old newspapers, dusty playbills, and perhaps even a gossip column or two might offer glimpses into the time and place Zeke and Helen were from. She was like a detective!

Nora refolded the letter, determination settling into her bones. Uncovering the story of Helen and Zeke had become more than a passing fancy. It had become a mission!

Her fingers itched to read just one more letter. After all, she was on a roll, and there was no time like the present. Nora smiled to herself and reached for the next letter, eager to dive back into the lives of these long-gone lovers.

My Dearest Helen,

The winds of change are upon us, and I have made arrangements that I hope will lead us to a brighter future. My cousin in the Barbary Coast has written to me of a place where cultures mingle freely, and the constraints of society hold less sway. It is there, in the vibrant heart of San Francisco, that I believe we can begin anew.

The journey will not be without its challenges, but I am resolute in my desire to protect you from Edward and his insidious threats. He has begun to encroach upon my life as well, but I stand firm in my resolve to shield you from harm. His influence may be vast, but our love is greater still.

I shall secure passage for us both, and when the time is right, we shall depart this place and seek our refuge. Know that I am with you always, in spirit and in heart, and that no force on this earth shall keep us apart.

With all my love and determination,

Zeke

The mention of the Barbary Coast intrigued her. It sounded like a place full of possibilities, where people of all kinds might gather without the usual fuss and bother.

Then it struck her, the realization that had been hovering just out of reach: Zeke might have been black. The way he wrote about a place where "cultures mingle freely" and the mention of "constraints of society" suggested that their love crossed not just social boundaries but racial ones, too.

It was obvious why they faced such fierce disapproval and why Edward's threats felt so ominous. In those days, a relationship like theirs wasn't just frowned upon;

it was dangerous. Their love was a bold act in a time when the world was not accepting of such unions.

Nora leaned back, her chest aching. This wasn't just a love story—it was a quiet rebellion. The kind that takes a lot more courage than anyone ever gives it credit for. She tried to picture what it must have been like, living in a world where society seemed determined to trip you up at every step. Exhausting, probably. Maddening, definitely. It made her feel oddly grateful for how much had changed, but also annoyed, because somehow, it wasn't enough. The world had inched forward, sure, but not nearly as far as it liked to pretend.

The room seemed to hold its breath, the air thick with silence, like even the walls had paused to listen. Nora took a sharp breath—somewhere between a sigh and a laugh, though neither felt quite right. Zeke and Helen's story stuck to her like a stubborn melody, bittersweet and impossible to shake. What had happened to them? Had they escaped, or had their plans fallen apart right here, in the very dust she was kicking up now? She pictured the theater—its creaky floors and lurking shadows—watching it all unfold with cold indifference, just like it always had.

Just then, Alex's head appeared in the doorway. "Hey, Nora, Martin's looking for you."

Nora blinked, shaking off the fog of the past. "Oh. Thanks, Alex," she replied, folding the letter with care and tucking it back into the tin.

She stood up, brushing imaginary dust off her pants, and took a moment to gather herself. The echoes of Zeke and Helen's story were in the forefront of her mind, a reminder that courage could be found in the unlikeliest of places—even in old letters hidden away in a dusty corner. Nora paused for a moment, then pushed the stage door open. The light spilled out into the hallway, beckoning her forward. Whatever Martin had to say, she was ready to hear it.

Nora found Martin leaning against the backstage wall, flipping through a script. She took a moment to steady herself before approaching him.

"Hey, Martin, you wanted to talk?" she asked, trying to keep her voice casual even though her nerves felt like a troupe of hyperactive squirrels.

Martin looked up from his script as Nora approached, his sharp eyes softened. He tucked the pencil behind his ear and nodded for her to sit beside him. "Nora," he started, his tone gentle but direct. "I've been watching your rehearsals, and I think we should talk about where things are at."

Nora's stomach flipped, her nerves jangling like a bad cymbal crash. She sat down, gripping the chair as if it might steady her. "I know I'm still pretty green," she said, forcing her voice to sound steadier than she felt. "But I'm working on it."

Martin leaned back, crossing his arms as his gaze lingered on her, not judging, but searching. "You've got a lot of raw energy, and that's great. You have something real in there. But sometimes it's like you're holding back. You hesitate, and I can see it."

She dropped her eyes, a sigh slipping out as her shoulders sagged under the truth. He wasn't being harsh, and that was the hardest part. He was right. "Why did you pick me for this role?" The question came out quieter than she intended, like it had been hiding at the back of her mind, waiting for the right moment to escape.

Martin's chuckle was soft, almost affectionate, and it echoed through the empty theater. "Because you remind me of Roxie. She's trying to make it in a world that doesn't feel like hers, through sheer grit and determination. She's crafty, ambitious—hell, maybe a little ruthless when she needs to be. But underneath all that, she's just trying to survive, to find her place. I see pieces of that in you."

Nora blinked, her breath catching in her throat. His words hit deeper than she'd expected, unearthing a part of herself she wasn't sure she was ready to look at. "I guess... yeah, there's some of that in me," she admitted, her voice thick with something she didn't understand.

Martin leaned forward, his gaze softening as he looked her in the eye. "You just need to commit, Nora. Let Roxie take over—no half measures. Dive in, give her everything you've got, or the audience will know you're holding back. And you don't want them to see that, right?"

She swallowed hard, the truth of it settling into her like a stubborn cat finding the coziest spot in her soul. "I will," she promised, the words almost a whisper. "I'll give her everything."

His hand found her shoulder, firm but kind. "I believe you will. Now go out there and show them the Roxie you've got inside. Make them remember."

As she stood to leave, Nora felt something shift between them—a quiet understanding, like Martin wasn't just her director, but someone who saw her, really saw her. And that, maybe more than anything, was what gave her the strength to believe in herself.

Chapter Four

Act I

On Saturday morning, Nora awoke to the low rumble of thunder, the sound reverberating through the thick, humid air. The heat was oppressive, even this early, clinging to her skin like a damp second layer. Outside, the clouds hung low and heavy. They were the kind that promised a storm but seemed in no hurry to deliver it. It was the weather that made the city feel restless, as if it, too, was waiting for something to break.

Rehearsals had improved since her talk with Martin. Something had shifted. His belief in her had sparked something she hadn't even realized she was missing. But, if she was honest, there was something else at play. Something that gnawed at her—a strange obsession she couldn't shake.

Helen and Zeke. Characters out of a love story, only this wasn't fiction. Their letters had sunk their claws into her. Zeke's words were full of encouragement. If he could believe in Helen, maybe she could believe in herself, too. At least on stage, when she lost herself in Roxie's brash confidence. It felt good—like slipping on someone else's skin and leaving her own doubts behind.

Off stage, the letters wouldn't leave her mind. Zeke and Helen lingered, their story haunting her thoughts. Secret glances, whispered promises, the way they clung to each other in a world bent on tearing them apart—she imagined it all.

The decision to dig deeper had already been made. Their story deserved more than to be forgotten.

Last night, she'd stayed up too late reading, her only company the flicker of a single lamp. She swore she could smell roses coming off the old pages, even though she knew that was just her brain being overdramatic. The letters hadn't given her all the answers she wanted, but they made one thing clear: she needed to dig deeper.

The last few letters had been a whirlwind. Zeke and Helen plotting to escape Boston, clinging to desperate hope. But just when she thought she was getting somewhere, the tone of their writing shifted, their words twisting into riddles. Caution crept in, like they were speaking in code.

As she lay there now, listening to the storm gathering strength, she felt that same pull. The library was waiting for her. Today, she would dig deeper. She would find out who they were, these two lovers who had reached across time to touch her life.

With a sigh, Nora pushed herself out of bed, the wooden floor cool against her bare feet. She threw some clothes on, the humid air making them stick to her skin. Outside, the thunder grumbled again, louder this time, as if the sky was finally ready to let loose. She grabbed her bag, tucking the tin inside as if they were a talisman, and headed out into the morning, determined to beat the rain.

It was only a fifteen-minute walk to the library, and she almost made it. But just as she was passing through Copley Square, the skies opened with a sudden, deafening roar, releasing a deluge that soaked her within seconds. The muggy air turned cool and sharp as the rain pelted down.

With a gasp, Nora made a mad dash for Trinity Church, her shoes splashing through the puddles as she raced across the slick pavement. The towering church loomed ahead, its dark stone and red sandstone contrasting with the stormy sky. She reached the sanctuary, ducking beneath the arches.

Nora's heart pounded, the sound drowned out by the hammering of the rain against the cobblestones. In a panic, she yanked her bag open and pulled out the tin, her fingers trembling as she fumbled with the latch. She held her breath, praying the seal had held, that the sudden onslaught had n't ruined the precious letters inside.

With an exhale of relief, she found the tin dry and the letters safe. Nora sagged against the cool stone behind her, letting the tension drain from her shoulders as the rain continued to pour just inches away.

She stayed huddled under the archway; the rain drumming on the stone steps in front of her, creating a misty spray that drifted toward her like a fine veil. But the storm raged on, the sky a churning mass of dark clouds that crackled with the occasional flash of lightning, followed by a growling rumble of thunder. The square, usually bustling with people, was deserted, transformed into a shimmering, rain-soaked landscape.

After what felt like an eternity, The rain eased and the downpour softening to a steady patter. The sky was still overcast, but the worst of it had passed. Nora tucked the tin back into her bag and stepped out into the square.

The library wasn't far, and once inside, the imposing marble lions flanking the entrance seeming to watch her approach with a stern gaze. She hurried up the wide steps, grateful to be out of the rain, and made her way through the maze of rooms and corridors.

Nora's pulse quickened as she made her way to one of the library's most tucked-away treasures—the microfiche room. There was something about the room that held a magic no one else seemed to understand, like an old secret only she was in on. She knew it was an odd hobby—most people would have clicked through a website and called it a day—but for her, this was where the past felt most alive.

As a kid, she'd spent entire afternoons at the Concord Public Library, sitting in the same hunched-over posture, her fingers sliding across the yellowed film strips. Births, deaths, lives boiled down to a few stark words—so impersonal, and yet so intimate. It was like wandering through a graveyard made of stories, the beginning and end of someone's world crammed into a few lines of faded newsprint. She wasn't sure what had drawn her to it back then, but even now, the thrill hadn't worn off.

The familiar dim lighting of the microfiche room greeted her, as did the musty, metallic smell of old film. The walls were lined with drawers, each containing years of forgotten stories waiting to be rediscovered. She found an empty station and slid into the chair, her fingers tracing the edges of the machine before powering it on. The soft whir and click brought a smile to her lips, a comforting sound from a time when she could lose herself in the quiet, slow work of digging through the past.

Sure, the records were digitized now—just a few clicks away—but that was too easy. It felt distant, detached. Here, with the flicker of film and the hum of the machine, she could *feel* the history between her fingers. She selected a reel of playbills from the Majestic Theatre; the film crinkling as she loaded it into the machine. There was a ritual to it—the click of the reel locking into place, the faint glow of the screen, the delicate art of scrolling at just the right speed so you missed nothing.

The first images flickered to life on the screen, a flicker of black-and-white that felt more alive than anything on the internet ever could. It wasn't just research. It was like opening a window into another world, one that whispered secrets only she could hear.

She turned the dial, images flashing across the screen in grainy black and white. It wasn't long before a name leapt out at her—Helen O'Donnell. Her pulse quickened as she adjusted the focus, centering the playbill on the screen. *The Storks*, a musical comedy, had graced the Majestic in the summer of 1905.

As she leaned in closer, a faint whiff of roses drifted by, startling her. The scent was so out of place, yet so familiar, that it made her pause. This had to be it—the connection she had been searching for.

She scrutinized the program, her eyes scanning each line for any sign of Zeke. But there was nothing. If Zeke had been a black musician, would he have even been credited? The thought of his name lost to history filled her with a deep sadness. Yet, despite the absence of his name, something inside her whispered that this was the right trail.

Knowing the play had run in the summer of 1905, she turned to the Boston Globe headlines for June, July, and August of that year. She scrolled through the dates, hope flickering alongside a growing frustration as each page revealed nothing of note.

Then, just as she was about to give up, a headline blazed across the screen: "Local Actress Murdered!" Nora's breath caught in her throat. Hands trembling, she brought the article into focus.

Local Actress Found Murdered in Her Dressing Room

Boston, August 18, 1905—The theater community was rocked yesterday by the tragic news of the untimely death of Miss Helen O'Donnell, a beloved actress known for her recent performances at the Majestic Theatre. Miss O'Donnell, just 24 years of age, was discovered in her dressing room late Monday evening following a performance of *The Storks*, a popular musical comedy in which she played a leading role.

Authorities were called to the scene after Miss O'Donnell failed to emerge from her curtain call. Upon investigation, they found the young actress lifeless, the apparent victim of foul play. Early reports suggest that Miss O'Donnell had been strangled, though the exact details are still under investigation.

In a shocking turn of events, Mr. Ezekial Turner, a musician employed at the Majestic Theatre, was arrested after Miss O'Donnell's body was discovered. Mr. Turner had been working with the theater's orchestra for several months and was reportedly seen leaving the vicinity of Miss O'Donnell's dressing room just moments before her death.

Witnesses claim to have overheard exchanges between the two in the days leading up to the tragedy, leading to speculation that a personal dispute may have been the motive. Police have stated that evidence found at the scene, including a vial of poison, points to Mr. Turner's involvement in the crime.

The trial, which concluded with remarkable swiftness, saw Mr. Turner convicted of murder in the first degree. Despite his protestations of innocence, the jury returned a guilty verdict after just three hours of deliberation. The conviction has sparked controversy, with some questioning the fairness of the proceedings.

Miss O'Donnell's untimely death has left a void in Boston's artistic circles, where she was known for her talent and charm both on and off the stage. Friends and colleagues describe her as a rising star, destined for greatness in the world of theater. Her loss will be deeply felt by all who knew her.

Ezekial Turner now faces the harshest penalty under the law for his crimes. Meanwhile, the city mourns the loss of a promising young talent, whose life was tragically cut short by a crime that has left many unanswered questions.

Oh, Zeke—it can't be.

Nora stared at the article, her eyes moving over the words again and again as if they might somehow change on the third or fourth reading. *Helen O'Donnell murdered in her dressing room. Ezekial Turner, convicted.* She rubbed her temples, trying to force it all into some kind of shape that made sense.

But it didn't.

The Zeke from the letters, the one who had written to Helen with such tenderness, who had believed in her so fiercely—how could that Zeke have done this? How could he have killed the woman he adored? The two pieces didn't fit together, no matter how hard she pushed.

Nora's breath hitched, and she glanced up, half-expecting to find the ghosts of Helen and Zeke staring back at her from the dim corners of the library. But the room was just as it had been, empty except for the low hum of the microfiche machine.

The kind, gentle man from the letters—*her* Zeke—couldn't be the same man who was convicted of murder. She knew it. But the more she tried to hold on to that certainty, the more it slipped away, like trying to grip water. What if she was wrong? What if the letters had just been Zeke's way of covering up guilt, or worse—manipulating Helen? She shook her head. No. That didn't feel right either.

Her hands clenched into fists. It *wasn't* right.

She took a shaky breath. It didn't matter what the article said. This was the same man who had called Helen a kindred spirit, who had written about her voice lighting up his day. *There had to be more to the story.* She could feel it in her gut, like the strange brief twinge you get when you know you've left something behind, but can't quite remember what it is.

But how was she supposed to prove the innocence of a man who had been dead for over a century? She let out a bitter laugh. "Yeah, Nora, just a casual afternoon hobby—proving a ghost didn't commit murder."

Still, she couldn't let it go. He couldn't have done it, and if no one else was going to clear his name, then maybe it had to be her.

But where the hell do you start with something like that?

She sat back in her chair, the cool metal biting into her back as she stared at the microfiche machine. It wasn't like she could just stroll into the local courthouse and request a century-old trial transcript. Did they even keep records that far back? What if there was nothing to find?

Her eyes narrowed. Well, there had to be *something*.

At the very least, she had a name. Ezekial Turner. There had to be something on him in the records, some thread she could pull. She tucked the microfilm away, her movements sharper now, more purposeful. She had no clue where this path might lead, but she knew one thing for sure: she couldn't stop now.

Gathering her things, she headed for the main desk, the idea of the genealogy department ticking at the back of her mind. She'd always heard they were good at finding old records and tracking down family histories. It was a long shot, but maybe it was the first step toward untangling this mess.

As she approached the librarian, her mind buzzed with a nervous energy. Zeke's face, or at least the version she'd built from his letters, flashed in her head. She wasn't sure if she was about to make the biggest mistake of her life, chasing ghosts and riddles, or if she was on the verge of something huge. Either way, she was committed now.

The librarian looked up from behind the desk, his round glasses slipping down his nose. He smiled, a little too eagerly. Probably bored out of his mind, Nora thought. Well, at least one of them was having a good day.

"Hi," Nora began with a tentative smile. "I was wondering where I could find the genealogy department? And what do I need to access the information there?"

The librarian's eyes lit up with interest. "Genealogy, huh? That's always exciting. You're in luck—our specialist is available today. Let me show you where it is." He stood up with enthusiasm, motioning for her to follow him. "Do you have a particular ancestor or family line you're researching?"

"Not exactly," Nora replied, her voice steady despite the uncertainty gnawing at her. "I'm trying to find more information about a man named Ezekial Turner. He lived in Boston around 1905."

"Ah, historical research! Even better." The librarian's excitement was contagious. "We have plenty of resources for that. Census records, city directories, old newspaper archives—those can all be goldmines for this kind of thing. And if there's anything specific you're after, the specialist can help guide your search."

As they walked, the librarian explained that the genealogy department was one of the library's hidden gems, filled with tools for tracing family histories and uncovering long-forgotten stories. Maybe this was the help she needed.

They reached a door marked "Genealogy and Local History," and the librarian pushed it open, revealing a room lined with shelves full of thick volumes and computers dedicated to genealogical research. The air smelled of the promise of discovery.

"Here we are," the librarian said, gesturing around the room. "I'll introduce you to the specialist—she's brilliant with historical mysteries. If there's something to find about Ezekial Turner, she'll help you uncover it."

Behind the oak desk sat a woman with steel-gray hair pulled back into an immaculate bun, her sharp eyes focused on the computer screen in front of her like she was on the verge of uncovering some great mystery. The click of keys stopped as she looked up, a quick, assessing glance that made Nora feel like she was the mystery.

"Dr. Harris, we've got someone here who could use your expertise," the librarian said, a note of excitement in his voice, like he was handing over a treasure map. "I'll leave you in good hands."

The woman stood, offering her hand with a smile that was both kind and no-nonsense. "I'm Dr. Lydia Harris, but please, call me Lydia."

"Nora," she replied, shaking the woman's hand, feeling a little awkward under that sharp gaze. "Nora Sinclair. I'm trying to find information about a man named Ezekial Turner. He lived in Boston around 1905, and..." She hesitated, unsure how to condense the storm of emotions into something that wouldn't make her sound like she was chasing ghosts. "Well, I think he was involved in a tragic event. I've found some things, but I need to dig deeper. Especially if there's anything about his family."

Lydia's eyes sharpened, not with suspicion but with the same curiosity that had led Nora here. That hungry need to know, to find the thread and pull until the entire story unraveled. "Well, that sounds interesting," she said, sitting back down with a little hum of approval. "Let's start with court records. If he was convicted of anything, we should be able to track him down."

Nora watched as Lydia's fingers flew across the keyboard, navigating the tangled web of history with the ease of someone who had spent years learning to speak its language. The clack of keys filled the room as the seconds stretched, heavy with anticipation.

Lydia's eyes flicked back to the screen. "Ah. Here we go." Her voice softened, but it had a finality. "Ezekial Turner. Convicted of murder in 1905. Executed later that year—November 3rd."

The words hit Nora like cold water, and for a moment, she forgot how to breathe. She had known, of course. The article had practically screamed it. But seeing it there in the dry language of the records—just a date and a crime, as if that was all a person was—made it feel more real. Too real.

"Executed," she repeated, the word tasting bitter on her tongue. Poor Zeke.

Lydia glanced at her, and her expression softened, becoming something almost motherly. "Let's not stop here. Sometimes the official story isn't the real one." She turned back to the screen. "Let's see if we can trace his family line. Sometimes they hold pieces of the puzzle the records can't show us."

Nora nodded, feeling the tightness in her chest ease a little. The hope, however faint, flickered back to life.

After a few more taps on the keyboard, Lydia's mouth curved into a small smile. "Ah, here's something. It looks like Ezekial had a brother. And his direct descendant—a man named Calvin Turner—is still in Boston. In fact, it looks like he's recently done one of those genealogy DNA tests and made the results public."

Nora's pulse picked up. "Calvin Turner? Do you have an address?"

Lydia scribbled the details onto a slip of paper and handed it to her. "Here you go. If he's interested enough to make his history public, he's probably got more than the bare facts. Families like his have stories, traditions. The kind of things that get passed down but never make it into the official records. He might have exactly what you need."

Nora stared at the paper in her hand, her fingers curling around it like it was a lifeline. "Thank you, Lydia. This is more than I could have hoped for."

Lydia smiled, the sharpness in her eyes now replaced with something kinder. "You're welcome, Nora. I hope it helps. And if you find anything particularly interesting—well, I'd love to hear about it." She winked, the curiosity still bright in her gaze.

Nora nodded, her mind already racing ahead to Calvin Turner, to Zeke, to the pieces of the past she hadn't even uncovered yet. There was a weight to it all, but for the first time, it felt like she might be able to carry it.

The rain outside had slowed to a drizzle, but the sky still threatened more. Walking would have been nice, giving her time to gather her thoughts, but the risk of getting drenched again wasn't worth it. She tucked the paper safely into her pocket and made her way to the nearest T station.

The train ride felt like it took forever. As they emerged from the tunnel, the view opened up to quieter neighborhoods, where the chaos of downtown dissipated. Forest Hills was a neighborhood with its own rhythm, slower and steadier, with streets lined by old trees whose branches hung low.

The houses here were sturdy and unpretentious, their porches adorned with flower pots and wind chimes that tinkled in the breeze. Nora's tension eased as she walked, the calmness of the place seeping into her bones.

She followed the winding streets, her heart picking up speed with each step as she approached the address Lydia had given her. The house was small and neat, with a pale green exterior and a front yard dotted with bright, cheerful marigolds. The windows were framed with dark shutters, and a weathered welcome mat lay in front of the door.

Nora hesitated for a moment at the foot of the porch steps. This was her chance to learn more about Zeke, and she did not know what she would find—or if Calvin Turner would even be willing to talk. She shook off her nerves, climbed the steps, and knocked on the door.

For a long moment, nothing happened. The neighborhood was so quiet that she could hear the rustle of leaves and the distant chirp of a bird. Nora's heart sank thinking she'd come all this way for nothing. But then, from inside, she heard a thud followed by quick, heavy footsteps. Someone was coming.

The door swung open, and Nora stared straight into the eyes of Alex, the stage manager from the Majestic Theatre.

CHAPTER FIVE

A Chorus Line

"Hi," Nora squeaked.

Alex flashed a wide smile, the kind that could melt ice in the dead of winter. "Well, look at this! Is this your new method for rehearsals—popping up at people's houses unannounced?"

Nora's cheeks burned a bright crimson, and she stumbled over her words. "No! I—um—"

"Relax," Alex said, their voice like honey. "I'm just teasing. No harm done. Besides, you clearly didn't expect to find me here, did you?"

"No..." Nora giggled, the sound a bit too breathy as if she were trying to laugh off the butterflies in her stomach. She steeled herself. "I'm actually looking for a Calvin Turner."

"Ah," Alex replied, their smile shifting. "That would be my grandfather. You've come to the right place. Let me grab him for you. Please, come on in."

They swung the door open wider, revealing a small living room. Every available surface was crammed with books, magazines, and what looked like half-finished craft projects. A large, worn sofa sagged in the middle, covered in an eclectic assortment of crocheted blankets that seemed to clash with each other in a way that somehow worked.

Alex wove through the chaos of the living room with a casual grace that spoke of long practice—probably the kind that comes from growing up around a grandparent with a love for both hoarding and storytelling. Nora, stuck in the doorway, felt a bit like she'd wandered into a colorful storm. Somewhere down the hall, a low conversation carried over, punctuated by a chuckle that was amused or surprised, hard to tell. She caught snatches—something about "unexpected visitors" and "rehearsals"—before Alex reappeared, their grandfather trailing behind with a look that was equal parts curiosity and suspicion.

Calvin Turner was small, but he carried himself with the energy of someone twice his size. The family resemblance to Alex was obvious—those sharp cheekbones and the kind of bright, sharp eyes that missed nothing.

"Well, well," Calvin said, his voice a smooth drawl that sounded an awful lot like Alex's, only with more history behind it. He gave Nora a long once-over, eyes narrowing in a way that was both friendly and suspicious, like he was trying to figure out if she was going to pull a rabbit out of her hat. "You related to us? 'Cause I can't say folks usually show up claiming to be interested in the Turner family without some blood ties. Feels a little... odd, doesn't it?"

Nora's cheeks went red. "Oh, no! I'm not related at all," she blurted, a little too fast, and definitely a little too high-pitched.

Calvin's eyes flicked from her to Alex, his eyebrows creeping upward as a grin spread slowly across his face like a cat who'd just discovered the canary was missing from its cage. "Ahhh," he said, dragging the word out. "I get it now. You've got a soft spot for my grandchild, huh? That's what this is about."

Nora's face turned from red to tomato, full-on glowing with the heat of a thousand suns. "No! It's not like that!" she yelped, and somewhere, deep down, wished the floor might just swallow her whole. She glanced at Alex, who was watching the entire scene unfold with an amused, lazy smile, not helping at all. "I mean, Alex is great, but that's really not why I'm here."

Calvin chuckled, a sound that was all good-natured mischief. "Alright, alright," he said, waving his hand in a dismissive but not unfriendly way, like he was brushing off a stray leaf. "Just pulling your leg. But seriously, what's got you poking around in the Turner family history, if it's not romance?"

Nora took a deep breath, trying to regain some semblance of dignity. "I found some old letters at the Majestic Theatre," she said, and once she got going, the words spilled out in a rush, like they'd been waiting for this moment. "They were written by Zeke Turner, and I thought maybe you'd have more letters or something that could help me understand his story."

At the mention of Zeke's name, Calvin's eyes widened, and he broke into a broad smile that made him look twenty years younger. "Zeke Turner, huh? Well now, that's a name I haven't heard in a while. You've got my attention, that's for sure. Come on in, come on in!" He waved them both further into the living room.

Nora, feeling less like an intruder and more like a guest, stepped inside and perched on a well-worn armchair Alex flopped down onto a patchwork-covered couch, still grinning, their body language as easy as someone who had long ago given up on trying to control the chaos of family gatherings. "Grandpa's always been a sucker for a good mystery," Alex said, giving Nora an encouraging nod.

Calvin settled into his own chair. "You're in the right place for family history. Let's see what old Zeke left behind, shall we?"

Nora handed over the letters. She watched as Calvin's face shifted with every passing word—his brow furrowing, his lips twitching, his eyes squinting at the faded handwriting like it was an old friend speaking in code. When he finished, he passed the letters to Alex, who read them with the same intensity.

When the last letter was done, Calvin sat back with a satisfied grin, waving the papers in the air like they were a winning lottery ticket. "Well now, young lady, this is something else! You've hit the goldmine with these letters, no doubt about it. If you've been talking to that librarian, I'm guessing you know what happened to Zeke?"

"Yeah, I found out," she mumbled. "It's awful. He never got the chance to prove he was innocent, and I'm certain he was."

Calvin leaned back, arms folding across his chest as he looked her over again. "Most people would just accept the story they're handed and move on. But you, you're like a dog with a bone, aren't you? I like that."

He leaned forward, dropping his voice into a conspiratorial whisper. "You know, I got interested in all this family history because of a woman at my church. She was doing a podcast series on the histories of black and indigenous people around here. Mighty fine lady, sharp as a tack. If I were thirty years younger... well, I'd be front row at every one of her lectures, that's all I'm saying."

Alex, clearly used to this kind of talk, rolled their eyes and gave their grandfather a light smack on the arm. "Grandpa, behave."

Calvin just chuckled. "What? A man can dream." He turned back to Nora. "Anyway, I dug up some old family letters to help her out, and that's when I found out more about our Zeke. Let's just say the history books only tell half the story."

His tone grew serious now, the playfulness giving way to something more solemn. "There's more to what happened to Zeke than what the newspapers printed. My great-grandfather wrote some things that didn't make it into the official records. I've been keeping them safe for the right time."

With a knowing smile, Calvin reached under his chair and pulled out a small, battered wooden box, the surface scratched and worn from years of use. He opened it carefully, revealing a few yellowed pieces of paper, folded neatly as if they'd been tucked away just yesterday. "Here," he said, handing them over to Nora. "These might fill in some of the blanks. Letters from Zeke's brother, written right around the trial. Not everything made it into the papers, you know."

Nora took the fragile pages from Calvin's hands, the paper crinkling softly beneath her fingers. As she unfolded one letter, the room seemed to hold its breath, a cool breeze brushing past her cheek even though the air was still.

She blinked and shook off the strange sensation, focusing on the letter in her hands. As her eyes moved over the careful handwriting, she felt a slight pressure, almost like a gentle nudge, urging her to continue. Her heart beat a little faster, the room around her seeming to hold its breath.

Dear Brother Zeke,

I pray this letter finds you well. I'm glad to tell you that everything's been arranged for your trip out to the Barbary Coast. Our cousin Elijah has lined up a good spot for you—playing piano at a fine place where folks know good music. He said you're welcome to stay with him and his family when you get there until you get settled on your own. Elijah's word is solid, and I trust you'll find a home out there.

But, brother, I gotta say, it might be best for you and Miss Helen to marry here in Boston before you go. We don't know what California is like for folks like us, and it's better to have things right before heading out. I found a deacon willing to marry you quietly, without much fuss. I know Miss Helen wanted a Catholic priest, and maybe you can find one in California to do it proper in her church, but this way, you'll be man and wife in the eyes of the Lord.

The deacon is willing to marry you two after the closing night of your show at our church. It'll be quiet, just a few of us, and then you can leave here knowing you've done right by each other.

I want nothing but the best for you, Zeke. You and Helen deserve a chance to build a good life together. Take care, and may God bless this new path you're on.

Your brother,

Samuel

"They never made it that far," Nora sighed, her voice heavy with regret. "She died on opening night."

Calvin nodded, his expression grim. "The letter was in Zeke's personal effects when he was arrested. After he was executed, it went to his next of kin, Samuel. It was never used as evidence in the trial."

"Of course not," Alex scoffed, rolling their eyes. "Why would they bother with evidence when they'd already made up their minds?"

Nora frowned, her fingers tracing the edges of the letter. "How would we even prove he was innocent after so many years?" she wondered aloud.

Calvin leaned back in his chair, stroking his chin. "Well, I suppose we'd have to figure out who actually did it—and gather some kind of evidence."

Nora let out a short, humorless laugh. "That's next to impossible! This all happened over a hundred years ago. Most of the people involved are long gone, and any evidence that existed is probably dust by now."

"I have an idea," Alex interrupted, a spark of excitement in their eyes. "A few months ago, there was a ghost hunting show that did a segment on the Majestic Theatre..."

Nora's eyes widened, her heart skipping a beat. "I saw that! I was so excited when I got the role of Roxie and realized I'd be working in the Majestic!"

Alex nodded. "The medium, Ashlyn Alden, gave me her card. She seemed pretty genuine, as far as mediums go. Maybe she could help us connect with Helen's spirit—or even Zeke's."

"That's brilliant!" Nora exclaimed, leaning forward, her earlier frustration giving way to renewed hope.

Calvin, however, narrowed his eyes. "I don't know about all this ghost stuff. I've never been one to believe in things that go bump in the night. And it's not really proof, anyway."

Alex grinned, patting his arm. "Come on, Grandpa. You've always loved a good mystery. Besides, what have we got to lose? At the very least, it might point us in the right direction."

Calvin huffed. "Well, I suppose it can't hurt to hear what she has to say. But don't expect me to go chasing after ghosts or anything."

Nora smiled, her resolve strengthening. "Alex and I can take care of that. It's settled, then. We'll reach out to Ashlyn and see if she can help us uncover the truth. With her help, maybe we can finally clear Zeke's name and give Helen some peace."

Calvin glanced at Alex, an eyebrow raised. "Since when did you get interested in all this ancestry business?"

"I guess the excitement is just... contagious."

Calvin chuckled and turned back to Nora. "They never cared when it was just me digging around. But a pretty girl shows up, and wham—"

Alex rolled their eyes, but there was a smile tugging at the corners of their mouth.

"Do you have anything else from Samuel or that time period?" Nora asked, knowing that even the smallest piece of information might be helpful.

Calvin shuffled through the papers for a moment before pulling out a small stack of yellowed sheets. "Just these." He handed them to Nora, and she realized it was sheet music—a song titled *My Boston Rose*. As she took the music from him, an overwhelming sense of sadness fell over her, heavy and suffocating, like a damp fog wrapping around her heart. The scent of roses, the one she now associated with Helen, filled her senses. Nora couldn't tell if it was all in her head or if Helen's spirit was there with them, watching over her shoulder.

Nora's knowledge of music was rudimentary, but she recognized the 3/4 time signature on the pages. She could almost see Zeke and Helen waltzing together, lost in a world where their love didn't need to be hidden. As she read through the music, she felt the heart Zeke had put into it and wondered if he had ever had the chance to play it for Helen.

"My Boston Rose" *E. Turner*

(Verse 1) In a theater, bright with splendor, On the stage, she takes her place, With a voice that charms the heavens, And a light that fills the space.

(Chorus) Oh, my Boston Rose, enchanting, How you steal the night away, But our love must stay in shadows, hidden from the light of day.

(Verse 2) When she sings, the world is silent. Every note a whispered plea, But in secret, we find solace, In the love she gives to me.

(Chorus) Oh, my Boston Rose, enchanting, How you steal the night away, But our love must stay in shadows, hidden from the light of day.

(Bridge) Behind the curtain, hearts are racing, In the wings, I watch her shine, Though the world can never see us, Still, I wish that she were mine.

(Verse 3) With each act, she weaves a story, Of a love that cannot be, But beneath her mask of sorrow, Lives the heart she saves for me.

(Chorus) Oh, my Boston Rose, enchanting, How you steal the night away, But our love must stay in shadows, hidden from the light of day.

(Outro) In the glow of footlights burning, And the final curtain's fall, I will wait there in the darkness, Till she hears my silent call.

Nora put the pages down, blinking back tears. "It's beautiful," she whispered.

Alex moved closer and placed a hand on her shoulder. Nora felt a jolt, like the tiniest spark of static. She bit her lip and looked away, unable to meet their eyes. Alex was so sure of themself, so steady—how could they ever be interested in someone as tangled and awkward as her?

"I can play it," Alex said, their voice low.

"Alex is a brilliant musician and performer," Calvin interjected. He sprang up and began shoving stacks of books and papers off an old table. Except, of course, it wasn't a table at all—it was a piano, buried under the detritus of a thousand forgotten afternoons.

Once the piano was revealed, Calvin gave a theatrical bow and gestured for Alex to take a seat. Alex accepted the sheet music from Nora, their fingers brushing hers, sending another jolt up her arm. They sat down at the piano and then began to play.

The music filled the room, and Nora felt it wrap around her, soft and insistent. Alex's voice joined the melody, deep and smoky, each note tugging at something deep inside her chest. She wondered, not for the first time, what it would be like to be Helen, and if Alex was anything like Zeke. She shook her head, clearing the silly thoughts away, but her heart wouldn't quite let go of the idea.

When the last notes faded into silence, Nora realized she had been holding her breath. She let it out in a rush, then stammered, "I think it's you who should be on the stage."

Alex gave her a small, crooked smile. "Thank you," they said, but their voice was wistful. "There was a time when I wanted that more than anything. I love the theater, but the roles... well, there aren't a lot of them for someone like me. Like when people ask my vocal range. Do I say contralto? Countertenor? It's all a bit much sometimes." They laughed, but it was a brittle sound.

Nora had never seen Alex like this—so uncertain, so... *unguarded.* They seemed like the calm in any storm, the one who never flinched, no matter what chaos surrounded them. But standing here now, she could see the cracks, the places where their usual confidence didn't quite reach. It was a strange, quiet reminder that even the most self-assured people weren't as invincible as they seemed. It made her think about herself—how many times had she thrown on a smile or some forced bravado when, inside; she felt anything but steady? How much of Alex's confidence was real, and how much was armor?

She stepped closer, her heart doing a little flip as she hesitated before laying her hand over theirs. The contact was solid but trembling beneath the surface, like a string pulled too tight. Their fingers stiffened under her touch, and for a moment, she wasn't sure if it was helping or just making it worse. The vulnerability in that moment sent a shiver through her.

Alex looked up at her, their eyes searching hers, and for a moment, they just sat there, hand in hand, connected by the quiet understanding that sometimes, being strong meant showing the places where you weren't.

Just as the silence wrapped around them, Calvin clapped his hands, jolting them both back to reality.

"Well! That was a heart-wrenching display of vulnerability," he declared with a dramatic flourish. "If I had a heart, it'd be weeping right now. But let's save the theatrics for later—there's a mystery afoot!"

"Right," Alex said, clearing their throat and sitting up straighter. "We need to focus. There has to be evidence somewhere, and we need to prove Zeke's innocence. I'll reach out to Ashlyn."

"What should I do?" Nora asked, standing up, her mind snapping back to the task at hand.

"One letter mentioned a Pritchard and another actress," Alex said. "Maybe you can dig up more about them?"

Nora nodded, making a mental note. "Will you let me know what the medium says?"

"Of course." Alex held out their hand. "Give me your phone."

Nora blinked, but handed her phone over. Alex typed in their number and texted themself. "There—we've got each other's numbers now."

Nora blushed. "See you at rehearsal on Monday?" she asked.

Alex nodded with a smile. "Can't wait!"

CHAPTER SIX

Intermission

Nora opened the door to her apartment with gusto, the handle rattling in protest as she threw herself inside. She was on cloud nine! Her class today had been a blast—the preschool kids were growing on her. Sure, they were a little loud and had the attention spans of hummingbirds, but they were sweet and enthusiastic, and their excitement for dance was infectious.

And Linda had solidified her plans for the Musical Theater intensive—Fosse-themed, no less! It was a dream come true for Nora, who was a big fan of the legendary choreographer's sultry, stylized moves. Alex had called yesterday, and just thinking about their voice made Nora's heart flutter all over again. They'd confirmed that Ashlyn Alden would come to the Majestic Theatre after rehearsal. Tonight!

She still couldn't quite believe it—*the* Ashlyn Alden, who was a guest on all the best paranormal shows, was going to help them connect with the spirits in the theater. The real Ashlyn Alden! She glanced over at the tin of letters on her desk, the ones she'd discovered hidden in the theater. "We'll figure out what happened, Helen," she whispered, her fingers brushing the cool metal of the tin. The room seemed to hold its breath in response, as if the very walls were listening.

She didn't even bother changing out of her leotard and leggings. Instead, she just threw on a T-shirt over them. Tonight's rehearsal was a small one, just her and Ciera, focusing on "Nowadays/Hot Honey Rag." They would dance—really dance, with all the flair and finesse that the number required.

She bounced on her toes, feeling like she might burst from happiness. Mondays usually had a reputation for being the worst day of the week, but whoever came up with that hadn't had a day like hers. Today was shaping up to be perfect, and she couldn't wait to see what else it had in store.

As she headed toward the Majestic, Nora's mind drifted to Alex and the strange, fluttery feelings that seemed to take over whenever she thought of them. She'd always put her dance career first—everything else came second, including relationships. Sure, she'd gone on a few dates here and there, but they usually ended with some guy who was more interested in how flexible she was than in who she was as a person.

But Alex was different. They weren't anything like those men, who only pretended to be charming until they slipped up and said something gross. No, Alex was kind and funny and—Nora's cheeks flushed hot, and she ducked her head, trying to hide her smile from no one in particular—smooth. That voice of theirs could melt butter, and they had this way of making her feel like she was the only person in the room. She was looking forward to seeing them more than she cared to admit, even to herself.

Her cheeks were still red as she walked into the theater, and lo-and-behold—there was Alex, standing right by the entrance, waiting for her.

"Hey," they said, flashing a smile that could break her heart into a million tiny pieces and still leave her wanting more.

"Hi yourself," she replied, aiming for flirty but landing somewhere between awkward and tongue-tied. Her blush deepened, spreading all the way to her ears, but if Alex noticed, they didn't show it.

Instead, they stepped forward and wrapped her in a hug. "I just wanted to say hi before you got caught up in rehearsal. I'm excited about ghost hunting with you tonight."

"Me too," Nora said, hugging them back and wishing she didn't have to let go. It was a wonderful hug, the kind that made her feel like she belonged there, safe and sound. But then, of course, her brain ruined it with that pesky inner voice. *What if they don't really like you? What if they're just this nice to everyone?*

She took a step back, trying to shake off her doubts. Alex, thankfully, didn't seem to notice the turmoil brewing inside her. They both stood there in silence for a moment, and just when it got a little too quiet, Nora found her voice. "I'll see you after rehearsal?"

Alex nodded, still smiling. "I'll see you during!" they said with a grin.

Today's rehearsal was being led by the choreographer. The only performers in the building were herself, Ciera, and Lexi, which should have made things easier, but somehow only made everything worse. Lexi was now understudying both Velma and Roxie, and from the way her feet kept tangling up under her, she was having a terrible time of it. They had already learned the music, but translating notes into steps was proving more difficult than any of them had expected.

Lexi fumbled her way through the routine, her movements awkward and off-beat. Nora felt a twinge of sympathy watching her, but it was hard to hold on to with that small, sneaky flicker of relief creeping in. Martin's sigh of frustration echoed across the stage, but this time, it wasn't aimed at her. For once, she wasn't the one under the spotlight, messing up. She didn't want to smile, but there it was—just a tiny one, barely noticeable.

Nora hovered near the back, doing her best to stay out of the line of fire, while Lexi tried to juggle two sets of choreography at once. It was like watching a duck try to waltz—her legs tangled up beneath her as she fumbled through the steps. Poor Lexi, Nora thought, feeling guilty for enjoying the chaos. She knew how it felt to be the one in the spotlight, tripping over her own feet and Martin's constant corrections.

Ciera, who was usually perfect, seemed to wrestle with the choreography too. Her brow furrowed, and her face twisted in confusion, as if someone had swapped out her feet when she wasn't looking. This was new—Ciera was normally unflappable, gliding through every step with the grace of a swan. Today, though, she looked lost.

Martin, meanwhile, looked like he was about to combust as he watched the choreographer clapping her hands and barking out counts like a drill sergeant. He paced back and forth, muttering under his breath about timing and technique, his face growing redder by the second. Nora couldn't help the little bubble of satisfaction that rose. It was a rare day when she wasn't the one making Martin's eyebrows do that dangerous twitching thing. She kept her head down, steps precise. It was a minor victory, but in a sea of rehearsals where she usually felt like a floundering fish, it felt downright triumphant.

She glanced over to see Alex marking the movements well—too well, in fact. That sneaky little performer. They were a dancer too! Effortlessly moving with a kind of casual grace suggested they were having no trouble at all. Even adding extra flair to their steps that were almost obnoxious in its smoothness. They looked up and noticed Nora watching, but instead of being embarrassed, they gave her a wink and threw in a cheeky little spin.

Nora giggled, which drew Martin's exasperated gaze. "Nora, honey," he said, rolling his eyes, "it's gonna be a bit. Why don't you take a quick break so I don't murder you..."

She gave him a sheepish smile and nodded, slipping off to the side to catch her breath. For once, it wasn't her fault things were going awry, and she intended to savor every minute.

Alex sauntered over with a bottle of water and handed it to Nora, their smile easy and warm. She took the bottle, sucking down half of it in one go and wiping her mouth with the back of her hand, trying not to think about how sweaty she must look. "Thanks," she said, smiling back, trying to ignore the way her pulse quickened whenever Alex was around.

"Anytime," they replied. "You're in your element tonight." They reached out and brushed a stray piece of hair from her eyes. The subtle, lingering contact sent a shiver down her spine, and Nora's heart did a funny little flip. She knew she was grinning like an idiot, but she couldn't help it. There was something about Alex—something that made the universe tilt sideways and turn bright and strange.

"Do you think we'll connect Helen, or any spirits, tonight?" she blurted out, regretting it. It wasn't the smoothest line, but it was something. After all, everyone knew the theater had its fair share of ghost stories.

The Majestic was infamous for them. There were tales of cold spots and strange noises, of props that moved on their own and mirrors that showed reflections of people who weren't there. Once, someone had even claimed to see a figure on the balcony, watching with dark, hollow eyes.

Alex didn't laugh, though. Instead, they seemed to consider the question, tilting their head to the side in that way they did when they were deep in thought. "Hmm," they murmured. "Well, if not Helen or Zeke, there's always the rumor about the old stagehand who still haunts the place, looking for his lost toolbox. And then there's the story about the actor who never quite left her dressing room. They say he still paces back and forth, muttering his lines. Sometimes, if you're quiet, you can hear whispering in the walls."

Nora shivered, but not from the thought of ghosts. There was something enchanting about the way Alex spoke, like they were weaving a spell with their words. She leaned in closer, drawn to them and hanging on every word. She was about to ask them for more ghostly gossip when Martin's voice cut through the air like a knife.

"Nora—break's up! Let's run this thing!" he called from across the stage.

Nora gave Alex one last lingering look, her stomach doing another little flip. "Guess I better get back to it," she said, pulling away. Alex's smile was soft, almost knowing, as if they could see right through her.

"Break a leg," they said, their voice low and warm, and Nora felt her cheeks heat as she turned back toward the stage. She tried to shake off the silly, fluttery feeling and focus. But as she headed back to her spot, she couldn't help but glance over her shoulder, just in time to see Alex watching back, and her heart skipped a beat all over again.

After everyone else had gone and the echoes of footsteps had faded into silence, Martin approached them. "You good to lock up, kiddo?" he asked Alex, his voice gruff. Alex gave a nod, and Martin gathered his things, turning back one more time with a crooked smile. "You crazy kids have fun tonight. And don't do anything I wouldn't do!"

"So, do whatever we want?" Alex shot back.

Martin just grunted in response and shuffled out the door, leaving the theater for the two of them.

Nora couldn't help but feel a little jealous of the straightforward relationship Alex had with Martin. The older man still terrified her a bit, with his barked orders and his furrowed brow. "How are you able to talk to him like that?" she asked as they sat alone in the empty theater, the vastness of the space making her voice sound smaller than usual. Ashlyn had yet to arrive, and the quiet was almost eerie, like the building was holding its breath.

Alex leaned back in their chair, a small smile playing on their lips. "I practically grew up here," they said. "My dad was a lighting tech, and I loved the theater from the moment I first set foot in it. He'd drag me along to work with him, let me watch the shows from the spot booth. Eventually, I got to work the spotlight myself."

"That sounds amazing! Does your dad still do lights?" Nora asked.

Alex's smile faltered, a hint of sadness creeping into their eyes. "He died when I was thirteen."

"Oh, I'm so sorry," Nora said, reaching out without thinking and touching their face. She froze, realizing what she'd done, but Alex just placed a hand over hers, holding it there. She felt a warmth spread through her, a soft, comforting heat that settled, making her feel all warm and gooey inside.

"Thanks," Alex murmured, squeezing her hand before letting go. "It was right in the middle of a rough spot in my life. My dad always got me, you know? My mom, not so much. Martin was a lifesaver back then. He always said that theater folk take care of their own. I started working as a grip around that time, and I've been at the Majestic ever since."

Nora smiled, touched by the story. "That's beautiful. Your mom, is she..." she trailed off, realizing she was venturing into dangerous territory.

Alex laughed, a soft sound that eased some of the tension in the room. "She's alive and well. Grandpa Calvin is her dad. We don't talk much these days, though." Their lips thinned, and Nora noted the flicker of pain in their eyes. This was not a subject they wanted to dwell on.

Nora let it go, sensing that some things were better left unsaid. Instead, she reached out and gave Alex's hand a gentle squeeze. The theater was still and quiet around them, and for a moment, it felt like they were the only two people in the world.

"Tell me more about the theater ghosts," Nora said, breaking the silence.

Alex's face lit up. "Calvin doesn't think I like history, but that's not true." They grinned, their excitement contagious. "I just like the little bits no one ever hears about. The *human* stuff, you know?"

Nora leaned in, smiling. She could tell this was going to be good.

"When Ashlyn's crew came in to film that documentary," Alex continued, warming to the topic, "I was *so* excited to be the tech on site. They had historians digging up all kinds of stuff about this place. Like Edward Pritchard—one of the suspected haunts. His family were major benefactors when the theater was built."

"Oh, I did some research on him on Sunday," Nora said, glancing at Alex.

"Yeah? What did you find?"

Nora leaned in, her voice lowering. "Turns out, he was known for his predatory behavior—specifically around the theater. His family poured a lot of money into this place, and he expected people to worship him for it."

"That tracks. You can still feel the creepiness lingering here," Alex said. "It's like his influence left a stain. He had this... reputation. Not just for getting what he wanted, but for making sure people feared him."

"Did you find anything on the understudy?" Alex prompted.

"Catherine Mayfield," Nora said. "I came across a few mentions of her. Let's just say, she might've had a similar... dynamic with Pritchard as Helen did."

"Interesting," Alex replied, frowning in thought. "I don't remember anything about her from Ashlyn's crew, but there were a lot of names to sift through. They focused on the spirits that manifested."

Nora's voice softened. "Helen and Zeke?"

"Helen's tied to this place," Alex said, their tone more thoughtful now. "But Zeke... not so much. Records for black musicians back then were often incomplete, or missing altogether, especially if they weren't famous. The system didn't care enough to remember them. He didn't die here, either, so there's less connection."

"Oh," Nora replied. Zeke had come to life for her through the letters—passionate, full of humanity. It felt wrong that his legacy could be lost while Helen's remained intact.

Alex gave her a sympathetic look, sensing her thoughts. "Yeah," they said. "It's messed up how easily people like Zeke got erased. But Calvin's done his best to keep our family story alive."

Alex must've sensed the shift because they changed gears. "There's also Ollie, you met him. He likes to scream during performances. It's hilarious."

Nora's eyebrows shot up. "During a production?"

"Yup," Alex said, grinning. "Throws a lot of the actors. The audience always thinks it's just someone's kid, so they get all annoyed. We usually leave a stuffed toy on an empty seat just to keep the little guy entertained."

Nora giggled. "Thanks for the heads up!"

"Of course," Alex replied, leaning forward to brush a stray piece of hair from Nora's face. Her heart raced at the gesture, a flutter of nerves and excitement.

Their eyes met again, and this time, Nora couldn't help but inhale. She leaned forward, her pulse quickening as Alex's lips parted—

"Hello?" Ashlyn Alden's voice echoed through the theater, carrying with it a kind of warm authority that caught Nora's attention.

A woman with dark hair and a long, flowing skirt wandered down the aisle, moving with a casual grace that made it hard to look away. At first glance, there was nothing out of the ordinary about her—just dark hair that spilled over her shoulders and striking eyes. But there was something more to Ashlyn Alden. It wasn't her beauty, though she had a unique, almost otherworldly elegance. It was her *presence*. She radiated warmth and strength in a way that made you feel you'd been wrapped in your favorite old blanket, the kind you keep because it smells like home. No wonder the ghosts were drawn to her.

Ashlyn embraced Alex with an easy familiarity, kissing them on both cheeks. On anyone else, it might have looked pretentious, the gesture you see people do at fancy parties where no one really knows each other. But with Ashlyn, it was as natural as breathing, like she'd been doing it her whole life and everyone loved her for it.

"This is Nora Sinclair," Alex said, turning to introduce her. "And Nora, this is Ashlyn Alden."

Nora froze, her heart stumbling like it had tripped over its own feet. *Ashlyn Alden*. The Ashlyn Alden. The one from all those ghost-hunting shows she binge-watched on rainy afternoons, wrapped in a blanket with a mug of tea. She'd imagined meeting her a hundred times, and now here she was. Of course, in her head, she'd been witty and charming, saying something clever that Ashlyn would laugh at, maybe even nod approvingly. But in reality? She could only manage a nervous smile, the kind that said, *Hi, I'm completely overwhelmed and possibly about to embarrass myself.*

Ashlyn didn't seem to notice Nora's internal panic. She stepped forward with that same welcoming energy and pulled Nora into a hug. Normally, Nora would have cringed at the unexpected closeness—physical affection from strangers was not her thing—but with Ashlyn, it was... fine. More than fine. It felt almost comforting.

"And now," Ashlyn said, stepping back and clapping her hands, "tell me what we know, and what we're hoping to learn."

Nora glanced at Alex, who gave her an encouraging nod, and together they explained everything: the love letters between Helen and Zeke, Zeke's trial and conviction for Helen's murder, and that Zeke was one of Alex's ancestors.

Ashlyn listened, her head tilted as if she were absorbing not just the facts but the emotions woven through them. When Nora mentioned Zeke's conviction, Ashlyn's brow furrowed in thought, but when Alex revealed their family connection to him, Ashlyn's eyes lit up with sudden interest.

"Oh, that could be helpful," she mused, her voice low and thoughtful. "Do you have the letters?"

Nora reached into her bag and pulled out the box of letters. As she handed them to Ashlyn, the psychic's fingers brushed hers, and a shiver ran down Nora's spine. It wasn't an unpleasant feeling, but it left her oddly exposed, like Ashlyn could see straight through her.

Ashlyn paused, her gaze lingering on Nora for just a moment longer than expected. "You have a gift, you know," she breathed.

Nora blinked, surprised. "A gift?"

Ashlyn nodded. "You're more receptive to spirits than most people. You may not realize it, but you can feel things others can't—see things they overlook. It's almost more of an empathic ability."

Nora's heart skipped a beat. "What does that mean? Is it... safe?"

Ashlyn smiled, her eyes softening with reassurance. "Oh, it's perfectly safe. What you're experiencing is a natural sensitivity. Spirits—especially ones with unfinished business—are drawn to people like you because you can understand them in ways others can't. It might explain why you feel such a strong connection to Helen."

Ashlyn reached out and squeezed Nora's hand. "If you ever feel like it's a burden, or if it overwhelms you, you can reach out to me. I'll help you manage it."

Nora exhaled. "Okay," she whispered. "Thank you."

Ashlyn acknowledged her with a gentle smile and opened the tin as if it were something sacred. She sifted through the letters.

"What's our goal?" Ashlyn asked, her fingers pausing over the fragile edges of a letter.

"We want to prove Zeke's innocence," Alex said. "If it's possible."

Ashlyn nodded, her expression shifting to something more serious, more focused. "All right," she said. "Let's see what we can do."

"Where do you want to start?" Alex asked as they walked toward the stage.

"Up here is good," Ashlyn replied.

"I'll go get the lights."

Alex bounded off as Nora watched. They had such a beautiful love for life. The stage lights came. Alex dragged a few folding of chairs to the stage, placing them in the center. As Ashlyn prepared to commune with the spirits, the stage was quiet, save for the soft rustle of fabric as she moved. Alex and Nora sat in folding chairs positioned near the center of the stage, each waiting in silence. A third chair sat empty, ready for Ashlyn when the time came.

Ashlyn moved almost reverently across the stage, her steps soft and deliberate. She wasn't in a rush—this wasn't something to be hurried. She was feeling the space, testing the energy. Now and then, she would pause, closing her eyes for a moment, as if listening to something no one else could hear.

The dim theater lights cast long shadows that seemed to stretch across the stage, adding a weight to the air. The room, already vast and echoing, seemed to grow more still. Ashlyn walked to the far end of the stage and stood for a long moment, facing out toward the empty seats. Her hands rested at her sides, but her posture was calm, grounded. Everything about her said *presence*. She was waiting, but for what? Nora wasn't sure.

Without warning, a chill swept through the room, sharp and sudden. The temperature dropped in an instant, the cool air raising goosebumps on Nora's arms. She inhaled, her body tensing. It wasn't just cold—it was a cold that seemed to seep into her bones, bringing with it an overwhelming sense of dread. She didn't move, didn't speak, but her heart hammered, an icy trickle of fear crawling up her spine. The stage, which had felt like a sanctuary moments before, now seemed like a place she didn't want to be.

Out of instinct, Nora turned her head toward Alex, seeking comfort in their presence. To her surprise, Alex was already looking at her, their eyes wide with something that mirrored what she was feeling. The fear. The *knowing* that something was here. Alex's usual calm had vanished, replaced by a flicker of unease that they were trying—and failing—to hide.

Neither of them said a word. They both just sat there, gripping the edges of their chairs, as the cold pressed down on them like an invisible weight.

Ashlyn seemed unfazed by the change, or perhaps she had expected it. She approached the empty chair, the stage floor creaking beneath her feet, and took her place in the center of the two. The temperature had already shifted, the air around them thick with tension. Ashlyn sat straight, eyes closed for a moment, hands resting on her lap, composed despite the atmosphere that had changed.

Nora bit her lip, keeping quiet, though her mind raced. Her fear was almost tangible now, but something in her trusted Ashlyn—this was part of the process, wasn't it? She glanced at Alex again, who gave her the smallest of nods, as if to say, *Stay steady*. They were both holding it together, but only just.

Ashlyn opened her eyes and spoke out loud. "If there are any spirits present, we're here to listen." Her voice carried through the stillness, calm and welcoming. "We come with respect."

The silence that followed felt deep, like the theater itself was holding its breath. The air was thick, as if time had slowed to a crawl, every creak of the old stage and faint shuffle of feet amplified in the stillness. Ashlyn sat still, eyes closed, her brow furrowing with concentration. She seemed... strained, like she was trying to tune into something just out of reach.

"There are so many voices," she murmured. "All trying to speak... reaching for Helen."

The words sent a shiver down Nora's spine, and she swallowed hard, her eyes darting around the stage. The shadows felt heavier now, stretching long, as if the theater itself was shifting under unseen forces. Nora shifted in her chair, very aware of how exposed they were in the middle of the stage.

Ashlyn's eyes snapped open, darting around the space, scanning it as if she could *see* something—something neither Nora nor Alex could.

The lights overhead flickered, casting the stage in a stuttering, eerie glow. A faint buzz filled the air, like the hum of electricity straining against the theater's old wiring. The hum grew louder, a high-pitched whine that made the back of Nora's teeth ache.

Nora glanced at Alex. "Is this... normal?"

Alex shook their head, eyes wide, lips pressed into a tight line. "No," they whispered.

Before Nora could ask another question, the theater itself seemed to answer. A deep, guttural groan rumbled through the walls, so low it felt like it came from the foundation—like the very bones of the place were protesting under some unseen weight. It was the sound that made your teeth ache, the sound that warned of things shifting in the dark.

Then came the screech.

Metal, twisting, slow and deliberate, like nails dragging across a chalkboard, but far worse. It scraped through the air, and Nora's breath hitched, her heart stuttering. She tilted her head back, eyes wide, just in time to see it—the massive lighting rig overhead shifting. Not by much, just a whisper of movement, but enough to make the lights sway, as if something unseen had given them a nudge.

"Alex..." Nora whispered.

The groaning grew louder, more insistent, vibrating through the floor beneath their feet. Alex shot to their feet, eyes wide with alarm. "Nora, MOVE!"

The shout cut through the air. but Nora was frozen, rooted to the spot. Then Alex was moving, crossing the space in a heartbeat, their hands gripping Nora's shoulders in a bruising grip as they yanked her sideways. The world tilted, her feet scrambling to keep up, when—

CRACK.

A stage light broke free, crashing down with a thunderous bang, smashing into the chair where Nora had been sitting. Shards of metal and glass exploded outward, the sound reverberating through the empty theater like a gunshot. The force of it sent a shudder up through the floor, rattling Nora's bones as she staggered back, gasping for breath.

But before she could process the narrow escape, something else groaned—a deeper, more ominous noise. This time, it wasn't coming from the rig.

It was coming from the walls.

CHAPTER SEVEN

Act 2

"What *is* that?" Nora breathed. The ringing in her ears was fading, and she realized it wasn't real—just the echo of her pulse pounding in her head. Her gaze was still locked on the shattered remains of the chair, now a mangled mess of splinters and crushed metal. The stage light that had crashed down was sprawled out like some twisted, broken beast, its cables curling across the floor like dead serpents.

Alex was already pulling Nora to her feet, eyes darting toward the ceiling, checking to make sure nothing else was about to fall. "Are you okay?" they asked, voice tight, sharp with adrenaline.

Nora nodded, though her heart was still hammering. "Yeah. I think so." She glanced at the wreckage again, her skin crawling with the realization of how close it had been. If Alex hadn't moved her, if they'd been just a second slower—

"Everyone in one piece?" Alex's voice cut through her spiraling thoughts, steadying her. They turned, eyes scanning the room until they landed on Ashlyn, who was still sitting, serene amid the chaos.

Ashlyn's gaze was distant, her eyes following something none of them could see. "That was a warning," she murmured, her voice as cold as a winter draft. The calm way she said it, like she'd been expecting it, made a shiver trace down Nora's spine. It was as if the crash was the exclamation point at the end of some unseen conversation.

"A warning?" Alex repeated, incredulous. "Ashlyn, that light nearly *killed* someone!"

Ashlyn blinked, finally shifting her gaze to the others. "Helen wants to speak," she said, her tone unwavering. "But someone—or something—doesn't want her to."

Nora swallowed hard, her mind racing. The scent of roses still hung in the air, as though the theater itself was breathing around them, alive and full of secrets. "Helen is here?"

Ashlyn nodded, her face pale but composed. "She's trying to reach out. There's something she needs to say, something unfinished." Her gaze flicked toward the crumpled stage light, lips pressed into a thin line. "But she's not the only one here."

The silence that followed was thick and suffocating, broken only by the faint creak of the theater settling around them. Nora's skin prickled as if something—or someone—was watching, waiting in the wings, just out of sight.

Alex let out a breath, running a hand through their hair. "Alright, so what do we do? If the lights are going to start dropping, we can't just—"

Before they could finish, a soft sound echoed through the space—a sigh, low and mournful. It seemed to come from nowhere and everywhere all at once. The three of them froze, listening, hearts pounding in unison.

"What was that?" Nora whispered.

Ashlyn stood, her eyes scanning the dim corners of the room. "It's Helen," she said, her tone matter-of-fact, as if she'd been expecting this all along. "But she's not alone." She stepped forward, her presence somehow grounding, even in the eerie quiet.

Alex's eyes darted toward the darkened backstage, their body tense. "We need to get out of here," they muttered. "Or at least figure out who—or *what*—is trying to kill us before it drops the whole stage on our heads."

Nora's breath caught as a cold breeze swept through the theater, carrying with it the unmistakable scent of roses. The lights overhead flickered once, twice, casting long shadows that seemed to stretch and writhe across the walls like living things. They dimmed, and this time, the shadow of a woman appeared on the far side of the stage, barely there, as if made of smoke and whispers. It lingered for a moment, watching, waiting—and then it vanished.

Ashlyn's gaze locked with Nora's, her expression sharper than it had been moments before. "Helen wants to tell her story," she said, voice low, "but we need somewhere safe."

Alex shot her a look, eyebrows raised. "Somewhere *safe*? What does that even mean?"

Ashlyn gave them a glance that was somewhere between patient and exasperated, like she was explaining to a child why fire is hot. She turned back to Nora. "Where did you first find her?"

Nora shifted on her feet. "I never really *met* her," she admitted. "But I found her journal. I can show you."

Ashlyn tilted her head, considering. "Lead the way."

They moved through the winding corridors, the air thick with the smell of dust and time. Alex kept pace, mentioning that the storage room had once been a dressing room, though the walls held more than just mirrors and costumes now.

Nora stopped in front of a faded seam in the wall, her hand brushing over the rough surface. "It was here," she said softly, her voice almost swallowed by the shadows. "This is where I found it."

Ashlyn's eyes followed Nora's hand, but her focus was elsewhere—her head tilted, as if listening to something just out of reach.

"I could always smell roses," Nora added. "Whenever I read the journal."

Ashlyn pulled the cushy chair over to the far wall, and for a moment, it was as though the room remembered itself. The dusty corners softened, and Nora could almost see it as it had been—glamorous in a faded way. A mirror with a row of lights flickering above it, a makeup table cluttered with powders and brushes. It was easy to picture Helen sitting there, preparing for her performance, oblivious to the tragedy that was to come.

Ashlyn sat down, shutting her eyes, her body swaying. The air in the room felt thicker somehow, like it was waiting.

"What's happening?" Nora whispered, the hairs on the back of her neck rising.

Ashlyn's hand shot up, palm outward, a silent plea for quiet. The swaying grew more pronounced, her breath coming in sharp, shallow gasps. Then her entire body went rigid. A low, guttural sound escaped her—a grunt, full of anger and pain, followed by a soft, pitiful whimper that made Nora's skin crawl.

Nora glanced at Alex, panic flashing in her eyes. *Should they help her?* She didn't know what was happening, didn't know what to do. Alex looked just as uncertain, their fingers twitching like they wanted to intervene but weren't sure how. So they both stood, frozen, as the temperature in the room dipped, their breath coming out in faint puffs of mist.

And then, as quickly as it began, it was over. Ashlyn slumped forward in the chair, her body shaking off the tension like a bird ruffling its feathers. She stood, her face pale and drawn, but her eyes clear.

"I'm so sorry," she said. "I should've explained better. Helen wanted to show me what happened, and I—I didn't prepare you." She took a step toward them, arms open. "It's kind of like... reliving her death. It's terrifying, but you get used to it. I've done it enough times that I can shed the trauma afterward. I didn't mean to scare you."

Before either of them could respond, she pulled them into a tight hug, warm despite the cold that still lingered in the air. Nora felt herself relax against Ashlyn, though her mind still raced.

Nora's chest tightened as Alex pulled back, rubbing the back of their neck in that awkward, nervous way that made them seem both relatable and, for some reason, reassuring. "Did you..." Alex trailed off, the unspoken question hanging between them.

"...see what happened?" Nora finished, her voice quieter, as if speaking too loud might make the moment unravel.

Their eyes met, and for a brief, absurd second, they both giggled. It wasn't the kind of laugh that came from humor, more the kind that bursts out when tension coils so tight inside you that it has to find an escape somewhere. The kind of laugh that says, *we're still alive, right?*

Ashlyn raised an eyebrow, the corner of her mouth twitching into a knowing grin, like she'd seen this all before—people, shaken by something unspeakable, trying to patch themselves back together with nervous smiles. She'd seen enough, no doubt, to know what that felt like.

"I did," she said, her voice steady, but her eyes... her eyes were somewhere else.

Nora felt her stomach drop. Something about the way her face clouded, as if she were dragging herself through the memory, made Nora's skin prickle with dread.

"It's like being inside someone else's skin," Ashlyn began, her tone soft but clear. "Helen was getting ready for the evening's performance. You could feel her excitement—like an electric hum just beneath the surface. She thought it was going to be a good night."

The room seemed to darken, not literally, but in that way where the air thickens and every little noise fades into the background. The sound of traffic outside, the distant hum of the building, all of it receded, leaving only Ashlyn's voice to fill the space.

"She was brushing her hair, humming to herself," Ashlyn continued, and Nora could almost see it—the soft glow of a vanity mirror, Helen's reflection looking back with that quiet smile people wear when they're thinking of someone they love. "Then there was a knock at the door. She thought it was him—Zeke. Her heart jumped. You could feel it, the way everything in her lit up with anticipation."

Nora's pulse quickened, and she glanced at Alex, who was leaning in, just as caught in Ashlyn's words as she was.

"But when she opened the door..." Ashlyn's voice dipped lower, more haunted. "...it wasn't Zeke. It was a man—tall, thin, with skin stretched too tight over his bones. His eyes were dark, hollow, like he was already halfway to something terrible. He smiled and handed her flowers."

Nora's mouth went dry, a creeping unease snaking up her spine. Ashlyn's description painted the scene, Nora could almost smell the musty, overripe scent of the flowers in the man's hands.

"Something about the way he did it," Ashlyn's voice faltered for a moment, "made her skin crawl. But she accepted them. What else could she do?"

Nora's breath hitched as Ashlyn's fingers curled into her palms, tension rippling through the room like a sudden gust of cold air.

"Then... he stepped closer. Too close." Ashlyn's face tightened, her voice carrying what was coming next. "He grabbed her, put his mouth on hers, and she shoved him back. She was scared—*really* scared now. But he didn't stop. His smile twisted, turned ugly. He wanted more."

The words hung in the air like a terrible fog. Nora's stomach churned, her hands balling into fists at her sides. The room seemed colder, heavier. She could feel Helen's fear like a cold hand on her shoulder, like it was seeping through the walls of the theater, wrapping around her.

"They struggled," Ashlyn's voice shook, but she kept going. "She scratched at his arms, tried to scream, but he slammed her against the table. The corner hit her head. Hard."

Nora felt her breath catch, her mind conjuring the image before she could stop it—Helen crumpling to the floor, the brutal, hollow sound of her body hitting wood.

"Not dead," Ashlyn said "Just... unconscious."

Nora's heart was racing now, her eyes wide, waiting for the next horrible thing that she already knew was coming. But hearing it... *hearing* it from Ashlyn made it feel like it was happening right in front of her.

"The man panicked," Ashlyn continued, her voice growing tight. "He turned to leave, but then—" she hesitated, her brow furrowing as if pushing through the memory herself "—he came back. He couldn't help himself. His hands wrapped around her throat. He squeezed, tighter and tighter."

Nora's throat felt like it was closing up, her breath shallow as she listened, her hands trembling in her lap.

"And then—" Ashlyn's fingers twitched, mimicking the sound of a sharp crack. Her own voice trembled, just a little. "Her neck snapped."

A shiver ran through the room, cold and sharp. Nora swallowed hard, her heart pounding so loud she was sure Alex could hear it. The air was too thick, too cold. She felt sick, like the world had tilted just a bit too far off its axis.

"And then?" Alex's voice was a whisper, but somehow it cut through the dense silence like a knife.

Ashlyn's face paled, her eyes hollow as she spoke. "He scurried away, like a rat in the dark, but before he could escape, someone came down the hall." She paused, her voice tightening with disgust. "He ran right into Zeke. And that's when his fear turned... cruel. He pointed back at the room, right at Helen's body, and screamed, 'Murder most foul!' He tried to frame Zeke for what he had done."

Nora gasped, her hands shaking now. Everything about the story clawed at her, the injustice, the horror, the sheer wrongness of it all.

With fumbling fingers, she pulled out her phone. Her stomach flipped as she scrolled to a picture she'd snapped in the lobby earlier that week. *It couldn't be.* But it had to be.

She turned the screen toward Ashlyn. "Did the man... look like this?" Her voice was shaking as she showed the image: a portrait of Edward Pritchard, the theater's benefactor.

Ashlyn's breath hitched, her face going pale. Her hand trembled as she reached for the phone, her eyes locking onto the image. She didn't speak at first, but the look on her face said it all.

"Yes," she breathed, her face ashen. "That's him."

Nora felt the world sway beneath her, her stomach lurching as if she were falling through the floor. Everything made sense now, and yet none of it did.

Before any of them could speak, a soft sound broke the silence—a slow, deliberate *footstep* in the hallway. Then another. The air seemed to freeze in place, the shadows stretching and deepening as the sound grew closer, each footfall echoing through the old walls like a distant drumbeat.

Nora's pulse quickened, her eyes darting to Alex, then to Ashlyn.

The footsteps stopped just outside the door.

The temperature dropped, sharp and sudden, like stepping into a winter's breath. It wasn't just cold—it was the kind of chill that crept under your skin, burrowed into your bones. Nora shivered, her breath coming out in small puffs of mist. The air thickened, pressing against them, making it hard to breathe.

Ashlyn stiffened, her eyes wide as if she could see something none of them could—a shadow moving just beyond the edge of the light, circling them. The room felt tight, the walls too close, the space shrinking behind something unseen.

Then it hit. A force, raw and invisible, slammed into them like a wave. Alex moved without thinking, stepping between Nora and the assault, but the air itself seemed to coil around them, twisting, tightening. The cold deepened, and the lights flickered, casting jagged shadows that crawled up the walls like broken fingers.

Nora's skin crawled with a prickling dread. She didn't need to see it to know—it was there. *He* was there. Something old, something wrong, like the feeling you get when you stumble on a house that's been abandoned too long, but worse. The surrounding air hummed, thick with it, a low vibration that carried a kind of malice that made her stomach twist.

Alex grunted, their jaw clenched as they braced against whatever it was. But the pressure was too much. It pushed back hard, like a wave of ice crashing against them, and Nora didn't have time to register the look of strain on Alex's face before they were both knocked off their feet.

They hit the floor together, the impact forcing the breath from their lungs as the cold bit into their skin like sharp, invisible teeth. The presence pressed down on them, heavy and suffocating, and for a split second, Nora wondered if this was what it felt like to drown—airless, helpless, pinned beneath something far too big to fight.

Ashlyn didn't move. Her hands trembled, but her feet were rooted to the floor, her eyes squeezed shut like she was listening to something distant, something awful. A spike of fear twisted in Nora's gut. This wasn't the confident ghost-hunter from the TV shows—the one who made banishing spirits look as easy as making toast. This was different. Ashlyn looked... vulnerable. Like she was balancing on a knife's edge.

Nora's breath caught in her throat. She didn't want to watch, but she couldn't look away. Ashlyn swayed, like she might topple over at any second, but then—just as Nora thought about calling out—Ashlyn's shoulders squared. There was a subtle shift, the kind you feel in the air right before a storm breaks. Her arms lifted, fingers curling toward the unseen force like she was reaching for something fragile and dangerous at the same time.

Nora's skin prickled, a cold sweat running down her spine. *What was she doing?* Every instinct screamed at her to grab Ashlyn, to yank her back from whatever invisible thing she was challenging. But something in the back of her mind, the part that still whispered that Ashlyn knew what she was doing, kept her rooted in place.

Still, Nora couldn't shake the feeling that they were teetering on something that, if they weren't careful, would tip them all into the abyss.

The room buckled under the strain, the walls groaning as if they might collapse, the cold so sharp it stung with every breath. Then, with a sudden crack, Ashlyn fought back. Air shimmering, and warmth rippling faintly from her hands.

The lights flickered once more, but this time they held steady. Shadows hesitated, slowly withdrawing as if tugged by an unseen force. Ashlyn exhaled, her breath misting in the air, her eyes still closed. Though pale, her expression remained resolute. Her hands, now firm, pushed the presence back, inch by inch.

The room loosened its grip, the tight, suffocating weight lifting as the shadows slunk back into the corners. The cold ebbed away, leaving only a faint, lingering chill—a ghost of what had just pressed in around them.

Ashlyn lowered her arms, her breath still unsteady but controlled, like some-one who had just weathered a storm. The tension in the air snapped, like a bowstring finally released after being drawn too tight for too long.

"It's probably time to be done for the night," she said, voice soft and worn. "I've calmed him for now, but I don't want to risk it again."

She turned to Alex, brow furrowed. "Are you going to get in trouble for the light?"

"Nah, it'll be fine. I'll report it," Alex replied with a shrug. "The theater's insured through the teeth, and Martin knows how careful I am."

Ashlyn nodded, satisfied. "Good."

There was a beat of silence, thick and uneasy, before Alex broke it with a suggestion. "We should get a drink—calm the nerves."

Ashlyn gave a tight smile. "I need to get back to my hotel," she said, glancing between Nora and Alex. "But call me once the spirits settle. I'd like to see if I can reach Zeke."

"Deal," Alex said, then turned to Nora, eyebrows raised. "How about you? Drinks?"

Nora's face warmed. Was this... like a date? She tried to keep her cool, but the blush creeping up her neck betrayed her. She nodded, feeling her heart stumble over itself. "Yeah, okay."

Ashlyn waited as Alex powered down the lights and locked up the theater. When they finally stepped through the heavy double doors at the front, she handed the letters back to Nora. "Keep these. They're tied to both Helen and Zeke. If we try to reach out to them again, they'll help. But first, we need to calm Pritchard."

Nora took the tin and tucked it into her backpack with a nod.

"Want us to walk you to your car?" Alex offered, glancing at Ashlyn.

"I'm good," she replied, turning down the road. "I'm this way."

"Thank you," Alex called after her, their voice softer now. "Seriously. This means more than you know."

Ashlyn just smiled and waved before disappearing into the evening.

Alex turned back to Nora, an easy grin playing at the corners of their mouth. "There's a great spot around the corner where we go after shows. Want to check it out?"

"Sounds perfect," Nora said, a warmth rising in her body.

They led her down Tremont to a quirky little pub called The Crossroads. It was a strange mishmash of Irish pub vibes, theater memorabilia, and a dash of new-age decor thrown in for good measure. The whole place felt like it couldn't quite decide on an identity—and that made Nora love it all the more.

They slid into a booth and ordered a couple of beers, along with a plate of fries to share.

"You okay?" Alex asked, studying Nora's face.

"I will be," she said, exhaling. "Just trying to balance my relief that Zeke didn't do it with the fear of what comes next."

"Yes!" Alex agreed, their voice filled with conviction. "I didn't realize how important it was to know he was innocent until it was clear."

"Do you think there's any way to prove it?" Nora asked, her fingers tracing the rim of her glass.

Alex paused, their expression growing thoughtful. "I'm pretty sure he didn't get a fair trial... and it was so long ago. It might be easier to prove Pritchard's guilt."

"Yes!" Nora leaned forward. "It's not like the family's hard to track down. Anthony Pritchard is a big politician, and when I was doing research, I confirmed it's the same family line."

"Think you could get a meeting? Maybe they have something useful?"

Nora hesitated "I could try... but honestly, it feels like a long shot. I doubt a rich political family's going to want to admit their ancestor was a murderer."

"It's worth a try," Alex said with a lopsided grin. "Worst they can do is say no. And in the meantime, we can look into getting Zeke a posthumous pardon."

"I love that idea."

The conversation drifted into easier territory, the heavy tension easing away. Alex shared stories about their father and growing up in the city, while Nora talked about her childhood in New Hampshire, her early obsession with dance, and the feeling of freedom it gave her. The more they talked, the more the surrounding world faded into the background—just two people in a strange little corner of the world, sharing pieces of their lives over cold beers and hot fries. The air between them softened, and it felt like the rest of the world had fallen away.

Nora glanced at her watch and gasped. "Oh no! We need to go or you'll miss the last train!"

Alex's face fell, a flicker of disappointment. "I didn't realize it was so late."

Nora's heart tugged—she didn't want the night to end, either. The warmth of the pub felt like a bubble that had held them apart from the world, safe from everything waiting outside. Tomorrow, the bubble would burst, bringing back the stress of pulling off Roxie Hart, with opening night looming like a storm on the horizon.

Outside, the air was crisp, the kind that hinted at coming autumn and made you pull your jacket just a little tighter. As they walked, Alex's fingers brushed against Nora's, hesitant at first, then curling around her hand. The simple gesture sent a warmth through her, and she squeezed back, feeling a spark she wasn't ready to let go of.

When they reached the station, the looming sense of goodbye hung between them. Alex stopped, glancing down at their joined hands, then back at Nora, as if weighing a decision. They leaned in, brushing their lips gently against hers—a soft, tentative kiss.

"I really like you," Alex whispered.

CHAPTER EIGHT

In the Spotlight

When Nora arrived back at her apartment, she hovered somewhere between cloud nine and her own personal hell. Her emotions were doing a chaotic little dance, pirouetting from panic to euphoria, and occasionally taking a spin through simmering rage. She was falling for Alex. Hard. The falling where you thought, *This is fine. Everything is fine,* as you plummeted toward the ground with no parachute in sight.

Her debut in *Chicago* was looming on the horizon, a monstrous thing, full of bright lights and the potential for utter disaster. What if she flopped? What if the entire show flopped *because* of her? That was the stuff of nightmares.

Then, there was the anger—a slow, building fury at the world for ripping Helen and Zeke apart. She could almost hear the injustice humming in the back of her mind, a low, angry buzz that refused to be quieted.

She needed a distraction. Something other than her terrifying emotions and the ghosts of the past that had taken up residence in her head.

Nora opened her laptop and typed "Senator Pritchard" into the search bar. The senator's website appeared with the all-too-friendly face of a politician who wanted your vote, your donation, and—your patience with his slow website.

There it was: a contact form. Right there, waiting for her to write a letter to a man whose ancestor may or may not have been complicit in the murder of someone she'd grown far too invested in.

What exactly does one say in a letter like that? She thought, her fingers hovering over the keyboard. *Dear Senator, I'm trying to prove your great-great-grandfather was a murderer. Any help would be appreciated!*

No, that would not work.

She sighed, steeled herself, and typed.

Dear Senator Pritchard,

I hope this message finds you well. I am conducting research on my family history and have come across a connection to your ancestor, Edward Pritchard. As part of my study, I am hoping to find more detailed information regarding Mr. Pritchard's time in Boston, particularly any records or personal documents he may have left behind.

If you or your office have any archival materials or recommendations on where I might look for additional resources, I would greatly appreciate your guidance.

Thank you in advance for your time.

Sincerely,

Nora Sinclair

Nora sat back, feeling satisfied. It wasn't a perfect plan, but it was a start. And sometimes, in the middle of all this emotional chaos, a start was all she could hope for.

***

Nora woke the next morning with a knot in her stomach the size of a grapefruit. Dress rehearsal was tonight. *Dress Rehearsal.* All the work, all the stammering line readings, all the embarrassing false starts—it all came down to this. Martin had been patient so far, but if tonight didn't go well, she didn't know what he'd do. She wasn't sure what she would do either, except perhaps melt into a puddle of shame.

Unlikely though it was, Nora reached for her laptop. The senator wouldn't have replied—not so quickly, not after the vague little form letter she'd received from the website submission. Still, she found herself clicking into her email with that small, irrational hope gnawing at her gut.

And there it was.

From the office of Senator Pritchard.

Her heart leapt and dropped a strange little plummet of excitement and dread. With shaky fingers, she opened the email.

Dear Miss Sinclair,

Thank you for your recent correspondence. Senator Pritchard acknowledges your inquiry regarding shared ancestry and appreciates your interest. Unfortunately, after a thorough review of our records, we have found no relevant personal documents.

We regret to inform you that we are unable to assist with your request at this time. We extend our best wishes for your research and endeavors moving forward.

Sincerely,

The Office of Senator Pritchard

P.S. We hope to have your support this November!

Nora's lips pressed into a tight, thin line, the words blurring as her frustration bubbled up. The whole thing was as polite and empty as the politician himself—shiny on the surface but hollow underneath. There was no way they'd even bothered to look, not in the short time since she'd sent her inquiry.

She let out a long breath through her nose, willing herself not to scream into the laptop screen. What had she expected? A senator to hand over family secrets because she'd sent a nice email? A box of old letters and records tied up with a neat little bow?

It was clear now. She and Alex were on their own. She slammed the laptop shut, trying to ignore the fact that her hands were shaking. The senator's email had at least distracted her from the looming rehearsal for a few minutes, though the dread of it returned in full force now, slithering back into her thoughts like a vengeful snake.

Still, that cold brush-off stuck in her mind, swirling around with the rest of her worries. "Best wishes," they'd said. As if she were just another voter, they hoped to pacify before election day.

She pushed her laptop away with more force than necessary. The day was only just starting, and she was already wrapped in gloom.

***

The last week of rehearsals had passed in a blur. Helen and Zeke were pushed to the back burner. Each day, the cast sharpened their timing, refined their choreography, and smoothed over the rough edges. But for Nora, the pressure mounted in a way she hadn't expected. She had pushed through her self-doubt before, but this was something else.

Martin had pushed them hard. "Roxie's lines need to *snap*, Nora!" he called from the front row. "I need fire, I need attitude, I need you to *own* it."

Nora nodded, doing her best to channel the confident swagger of Roxie Hart, but she wasn't owning it. She was still pretending. But in the back of her mind, the doubts kept creeping in: *Am I good enough? What if I ruin this? What if everyone sees through me?*

The last notes of "All That Jazz," rang out, and Martin clapped his hands. "That's a wrap for today. You've got a day to breathe before dress rehearsal."

Nora forced a smile as the cast trickled out, their voices fading like the last echoes of a song. She lingered, letting the empty theater press in around her. The energy that had filled the space moments ago evaporated, leaving only a heavy, hollow quiet. The walls seemed to creep closer, swallowing every scrap of laughter and conversation. Her stomach churned, sharp and heavy, like she'd swallowed a fistful of gravel.

"Nora, can I see you?" Martin's voice cut through the quiet, pulling her attention. He stood waiting, arms folded across his chest like he was bracing for something unpleasant.

She swallowed hard and made her way toward him, already feeling the sting of impending disappointment. Maybe it was the way he looked at her—eyes narrowed, lips pressed together in a thin line. Not good.

"Sweetheart, you are too nice," he said, his tone so matter-of-fact it felt like a slap.

Nora blinked, surprised by the bluntness. She opened her mouth, but no words came. Too nice? She'd been told that before—by strangers, by friends, by an ex who once said it like it was an apology. But hearing it from Martin, someone who was supposed to believe in her, hit different.

"And I can tell," he added, his lips still tight, as if he'd been holding back the critique for a while.

"There are worse things to be," Nora said, forcing a crooked smile that even she didn't believe. It was an olive branch, a flimsy one, expecting some reassurance or at least a little sympathy. A laugh, maybe.

But Martin's expression didn't budge. "I just don't believe it." He shook his head, his disappointment hanging between them. "Your performance is hollow. Roxie is not nice, Nora. She's calculating, and—" He waved a hand, searching for the right word. "She's selfish. There's nothing about her that says 'nice.'"

He trailed off, and the silence felt like it was settling into her bones.

Nora's throat tightened. She could feel the tears pricking at the back of her eyes, but she blinked them away. Where was the Martin who had believed in her? The one who had picked her, who had seen something in her that even she couldn't see? She wanted to ask him, wanted to grab onto that moment and shake it until it came back.

Instead, she nodded, trying to swallow the lump in her throat, even though it felt like it might choke her.

Martin sighed, the sound heavy with exhaustion, or maybe frustration. "Look," he said, rubbing the back of his neck like the conversation had worn him out. "You've got potential, Nora. But Roxie? I need more from you. More grit. More... something. Because right now, I just don't buy it."

She nodded again, though every word felt like another nail in the coffin of her confidence. "I can do better," she said, the words leaving her mouth before she even realized she was saying them. It was a promise she wasn't sure she could keep.

He gave her a long, unreadable look, then sighed again, his gaze drifting somewhere over her shoulder. "I've got a lot to think about."

That didn't sound good. Nora's stomach churned, and she felt like she might be sick this time.

Martin turned away, already moving toward the wings. "Lexi!" he called out, his voice bouncing off the theater walls. The name echoed in the hollow space, leaving Nora standing alone as his words settled in.

And just like that, he disappeared, running after her understudy.

At that moment, something inside her snapped. A cold, sharp crack, like ice breaking underfoot. He didn't believe in her. Of course he didn't. No one ever did. And no one ever would, would they? She could feel it—the years of frustration, of trying to prove herself, of being just *not enough*—all of it boiling up, ready to explode.

If she was going to do anything, it would have to be on her own.

"Not tall enough, my ass," she muttered under her breath, the words sharp, like they'd been burning inside her for far too long. "Not good enough? Not Roxie enough? What a joke." Her hands trembled, and she shoved them into her pockets, her breath coming fast and shallow.

She swayed for a moment, unsteady, as if every rejection she'd ever felt was finally pressing down on her. The auditions, the cutthroat competition, the constant reminder that she was never *quite* right. Just a little off, a little less than what everyone else wanted. But she would not crumble. Not today.

The theater felt suffocating, the walls too close, the air too thick. Her heart pounded, but it wasn't from nerves. It was anger—hot, consuming, and, for the first time in a long time, productive. If they didn't believe in her, then screw them. She'd prove them wrong. She'd show them all.

Alex's voice called her name in the distance, soft and filled with concern. Nora didn't care. Sympathy wasn't what she wanted, nor did she need anyone's coddling or reassurance. What she needed was action—and she needed it now.

Without a second glance, she stormed toward the door, her footsteps heavy and purposeful, stomping out every shred of self-doubt that had been planted in her. She shoved the door open with more force than necessary, the cool evening air hitting her like a slap to the face, but it barely registered. Her mind was already racing, already deciding what to do next.

Nora hardly registered getting on the Blue Line. The train clattered along, its noise blending into the steady hum of her thoughts, all sharp edges and rising fury. Before she even realized it, she was standing at the front door of Senator Pritchard's house, her heart pounding more from anger than anything else. How had she ended up here? The details were fuzzy, but the goal was clear. She was done waiting for people to believe in her. If she was going to make a difference, if she was going to exonerate Zeke, she'd have to take matters into her own hands.

The house loomed in front of her, all rich, dark stone and ironwork, like it had been plucked straight from a Gothic novel. The tall windows reflected the night, giving it an air of cold indifference. She approached and knocked, her knuckles smarting from the force of it. The door creaked open with the heavy, old-world sound that made her think of ancient castles and the sort of places that had hidden dungeons.

An older man answered—tall, stiff, and dressed in black. A butler. She almost laughed, a harsh little noise stuck in the back of her throat. Did rich people *actually* still have butlers? Of course, Senator Pritchard would. It suited the level of pompous she'd imagined.

"I'm looking for Senator Pritchard," she said, her tone hard enough to cut glass. Her head buzzed with the fury still thrumming beneath her skin. "My name is Roxane Hartman, and I have an appointment."

The butler's face shifted as he looked her up and down, eyes scanning her with the disapproving scrutiny that made her skin itch. He was judging her. Of course he was. She didn't belong in a place like this. To him, she was some nobody off the street.

"I'm sorry," he said after a pause, his voice smooth and polite in the most condescending way possible. "There are no appointments on the schedule."

Nora felt her patience fray, like a thread being pulled too tight. "Check again," she snapped, stepping halfway into the doorway before he could even react.

His eyes widened just a fraction, but it was enough. He wasn't expecting a confrontation—not from her. The rush of power that followed surprised her. Maybe she was more like Roxie Hart than she thought.

The butler hesitated, weighing his options. After a tense moment, he dipped his head and disappeared around the corner, presumably to check the schedule or to tell Pritchard there was a crazy woman at the door. Either way, he was gone.

Perfect.

Without a second thought, Nora slipped inside. The entryway was grand, of course—tall ceilings, intricate molding, polished floors that gleamed under the dim light of a chandelier that looked like it belonged in a ballroom. She glanced around, her gaze falling on a door to her left that led to what looked like a library. The bookshelves were tall and stuffed with volumes that hadn't been touched in years. Rich people's bookshelves were never for reading, were they?

But if she was going to find anything useful—anything that could exonerate Zeke—it would be somewhere in that office. Her anger fueled her as she crossed the room, her footsteps too loud in the quiet space, but she didn't care. She scanned the shelves, her hands itching to pull books down, to tear the place apart if she had to.

But then... the heat cooled. The farther she got into the room, the more the anger drained away, like water slipping through her fingers. What had she been thinking? She wasn't some mastermind spy. She was Nora Sinclair, a dancer who got tongue-tied on stage and had never even *sneaked* into a movie without paying, much less a senator's house.

Her hand paused over the spine of an old leather-bound book, something important-looking and weathered. Without thinking, she pulled it from the shelf and cracked it open, expecting secret codes or some dusty old ledger. Instead, she stared at the title page of a first edition of Robert Frost's poems.

The words "First edition" caught her eye. Wow. Her fingers lightly traced the pages, lingering over the poetry she adored. For a moment, she stood still, the scent of old paper filling the air. Her heart quieted, and the earlier storm of anger gave way to a slow, creeping sadness.

With a sigh, she closed the book and slid it back onto the shelf. The world was right; she really was too nice.

A soft cough sounded behind her, and her stomach plummeted. She turned, half-expecting to see the butler ready to throw her out or maybe even call the police. Instead, there he was, standing just behind her. His face was unreadable, though his eyes flickered with something—surprise, maybe. Amusement?

"Miss Hartman," the butler said, his voice low and calm, as if the situation wasn't weird at all. Maybe this *was* just what happened in rich people's houses all the time. He didn't look shocked or angry, just inconvenienced, like someone who had found a stray cat in the parlor. "I have the police on hold. You should leave."

Nora's face went hot, her blush so fierce it felt like her skin might catch fire. She stammered, "Ss-sorry," the words barely escaping her throat, and before she could think of anything else, she turned and bolted. Her boots echoed on the polished floors as she fled, every step screaming failure, failure, failure.

She yanked the door open and stumbled out into the night, the heavy wooden door closing with a solid thud behind her. The cool air hit her like a shock, but she didn't stop. She crossed the street, not noticing the world around her—cars, the faint hum of city life—until she found herself at a pedestrian walkway lined with trees and benches.

There, beneath the canopy of branches and surrounded by the muffled quiet of the city park, she collapsed onto a bench. Her hands flew to her face, and she buried her head in them, humiliation burning through her. She'd done it this time. Broken into a senator's house, stammered like an idiot in front of an actual butler, and then nearly gotten the cops called on her. All in the name of some half-baked plan to find evidence. What was she even thinking?

She wasn't thinking. That was the problem.

Nora let out a shaky breath and wiped her eyes, which had stung with the threat of tears. What now? Who was she supposed to call? It wasn't like she had a lot of options. Her boss? Linda would be kind, of course, but she wouldn't understand. Linda would pat her on the head and tell her to take a hot bath and meditate on her chakras or something. Martin? Yeah, right. Martin already thought she was a disaster.

With a sigh, she pulled out her phone and stared at the screen, her thumb hovering over the contacts list. After a long pause, she dialed Alex. It took less than a minute for them to answer. And within twenty, Alex was sitting next to her on the bench, their presence a warm and comforting.

They said nothing at first, just sat there, the park's streetlights casting soft shadows on the grass. Alex was good at that—knowing when to speak and when to just... be.

Finally, after a long stretch of silence, Alex glanced at her. "What were you thinking?" they asked, their tone gentle but not without a hint of you did this, didn't-you?

Nora let out a dry laugh. "That's the thing," she said, running a hand through her tangled hair. "I wasn't thinking. I just..." she trailed off, feeling her throat tighten. How could she explain it? The frustration, the endless feeling of not being good enough, the desperate need to do *something* right for once.

Alex didn't push, just slid an arm around her shoulders, and Nora leaned into them. She rested her head against Alex's shoulder and closed her eyes, willing the world to stop spinning for just a minute.

"I just wanted to do something right," she whispered. "I wanted to prove Zeke innocent. I thought—if I could just find something, anything—it would make all this worth it. Like I could actually... matter."

Alex's arm tightened around her, their hand giving her shoulder a reassuring squeeze. "Nora," they said, "you're enough

***

The day of the dress rehearsal arrived far too soon for Nora's liking. The Majestic Theatre buzzed with the familiar, chaotic energy of last-minute preparations—crew members shouting instructions, props being shuffled into place, and the constant hum of nervous excitement. But as Nora stood backstage in her Roxie costume, all that movement felt distant, like a storm rolling in from miles away.

Her heart pounded. At first, it was just a flutter, something small and ignorable. But then it grew, swelling into a full-on stampede. Her breaths came shallow, sharp. Too sharp. Her hands trembled at her sides, the sensation alien, like they weren't even hers. Was this a heart attack? Oh god, she was too young to die!

What's happening?

Nora leaned back against the wall, trying to steady herself, but it only made things worse. The harder she tried to control it, the more it spiraled out of her reach. Her vision blurred, and the familiar sights of the theater—the velvet curtains, the wooden boards—wobbled and stretched like something out of a bad dream. She could hear her own heartbeat pounding in her ears, drowning out everything else.

She gasped for air, but no matter how much she pulled in, it wasn't enough.

I can't breathe. Oh god. What's wrong with me?

Panic crashed over her like a wave, stealing the breath from her lungs and the ground from under her feet. The dread that had been building all week pulled her down, sinking her deeper and deeper. She wasn't Roxie; she was just Nora—the too-nice, too-small girl who didn't belong here.

Roxie Hart... The thought of her character clawed its way into her mind. Roxie, the conniving, manipulative woman who shoots her lover and walks away scot-free, acquitted and adored. How was it that someone like Roxie—a murderer—could charm her way out of a death sentence while someone like Zeke, who didn't hurt anyone, was convicted and executed for murder? It wasn't fair. None of it was.

Her pulse raced even faster as her thoughts spiraled. *Roxie gets to walk free.* But Zeke... Zeke never stood a chance. He'd been convicted, his life taken, for a crime Nora was sure he didn't commit. How many Roxies had the world let off the hook? How many real-life Roxies used charm, luck, and privilege to escape the consequences of their actions, while innocent people like Zeke were punished?

The realization hit her like a train, and the floor didn't feel real anymore. *Roxie's fictional, she's fictional,* she chanted to herself. But it didn't stop the world from spinning. There were too many Roxies out there—too much injustice. And Zeke? Zeke was real. He never got to plead his case.

Her breath stuttered. Her lungs seemed to shrink, folding in on themselves like someone was squeezing them with both hands. She blinked, but her vision was blurry, as though the world had been smeared with fog. Roxie's swagger felt like a sick joke now, something she could never hold on to. How was she supposed to play a woman everyone loved, when Zeke's story—his truth—was all wrong?

"Nora?"

Martin's voice snapped through the haze like a twig breaking underfoot, harsh and loud. Too loud. She couldn't stand it. His words grated against her thoughts, dragging her back to the present, but not in the way she needed. *I can't do this.* He stood a few feet away, brows furrowed in that familiar "what now?" look.

"You look... pale," he said, eyeing her like a ticking bomb. "Are you alright?"

She tried to answer, but her throat was dry, and her tongue felt like lead. She opened her mouth, but all that came out was a ragged, shallow breath. *This isn't happening. Please, not now.*

Her pulse hammered—roaring in her ears like the ocean was crashing down on her. Everything else was fading, blurring, *vanishing.* The world was spinning too fast, and she wasn't part of it anymore.

"Lexi!" Martin barked, a sound like nails on glass. The words crashed into her like a punch, knocking the breath out of her again.

Lexi appeared, looking every bit the Roxie Nora couldn't be—polished, smug, *ready*. Nora's stomach twisted. She was slipping. She was losing everything, and she couldn't even speak to stop it.

Her chest was so tight now, every breath scraping like broken glass, and just when she thought she might crumble into pieces on the floor, a hand touched her shoulder. It was gentle but firm, like an anchor yanking her out of the storm. She flinched at the contact but didn't pull away.

"Nora, hey." Alex's voice was soft but solid, cutting through the noise. "Look at me."

She blinked, struggling to focus on their face through the haze. Their presence felt... real. Something to cling to.

"Breathe with me, okay? In through the nose, out through the mouth."

Her breath hitched again, shallow and painful. "I don't—" she rasped, her voice strangled. "I don't know what's happening." She wasn't sure she could breathe at all anymore. She wasn't sure of anything except that she was falling apart, right there in front of everyone.

Alex's hand stayed on her shoulder, grounding her. "You're having a panic attack," they said, matter-of-fact, like it was something as normal as rain.

A panic attack. That's what this was? But she didn't have panic attacks. Not like this. She tried to explain, to say something, but her throat was tight, and the words didn't come.

Alex inhaled, showing her, slow and steady. "In through the nose. Hold it. Now out through the mouth."

Nora tried to copy them, but her lungs felt like they were stuck in a vise. Still, she followed, even though each breath felt too thin, too shallow. But Alex kept going, guiding her.

"That's it," they murmured, and somehow, their voice was calming—like a rhythm she could cling to. "Just keep going. You're doing fine."

Gradually, the world came back into focus. The tightness eased just a fraction, enough that she could feel the floor beneath her feet again, real. She wasn't floating away anymore.

She squeezed her eyes shut, then opened them, gasping. "I'm… I'm sorry," she whispered, her voice trembling. "I don't know what—"

"You don't have to apologize," Alex said, and their voice was so gentle it made her want to cry all over again. "It happens. But you're okay. You're going to be okay."

Martin was still there, arms crossed and looking like he wanted to say something, but Alex raised their hand, keeping him back. They turned back to Nora.

"You've been rehearsing for weeks," they said, meeting her eyes. "You know this, Nora. Your body knows what to do. Let it take over."

Nora's breathing was still shaky, and her legs were like jelly, but she wasn't drowning anymore, and the fog was lifting. "I don't know if I can do this," she admitted.

Alex stood and offered her their hand. "You've got this. You've earned this role. The only thing standing in your way is the fear. You're stronger than that."

The words hit her like a challenge, echoing inside her. *Fear.* Maybe that's what this all was, at the heart of it. Fear. And hadn't Roxie thrived on fear? Turned it into power?

She took a breath, still shaky, still unsure, but deeper this time. Steadier. Hesitantly, she reached out and took Alex's hand, pulling herself to her feet.

"Lexi, stay ready," Martin called, still hovering, but Nora barely heard him now. He wasn't the point. The stage was.

Her legs wobbled as she stood, but she stayed upright. Alex's hand, warm and steady, gave her balance.

"One breath at a time," they reminded her, squeezing her hand before letting go. "You've got this. I'll be right here in the wings."

Nora took another breath, shaky but real, and the spark of determination inside her flared just enough to feel possible. She wasn't Roxie yet, but maybe, maybe she could be.

She stepped into the spotlight.

CHAPTER NINE

Curtain Call

Backstage was its usual charming disaster. People were running around, set pieces were being wrestled into place, and someone was muttering about a missing prop. The doors were opening soon, but no one looked like they believed that. It was the good chaos—the kind that usually meant things were going to turn out fine, even if it didn't look that way right now.

Nora stood with the others onstage, waiting. Martin called over the crew, and Alex slipped in beside her, giving her hand a quick, reassuring squeeze. She squeezed back, grateful for the moment of calm in all the noise. But even in the buzz of pre-show excitement, there was something else. The faint sensation that someone—or something—was watching. She felt it like a soft touch on the back of her neck; the hairs rising.

She scanned the wings and the back of the theater, half-expecting to glimpse someone. Was it just nerves? She thought about what Ashlyn had said. Receptive. Empathic. The word had settled in her mind like a key turning in a lock she hadn't known was there. It had given her something to hold on to, an explanation for why she felt so connected to Helen, why she couldn't shake the story of Zeke's conviction.

Now, standing under the dim backstage lights, it felt real. She imagined Zeke in the back row, watching from the shadows, his eyes fixed on her, waiting.

Martin cleared his throat, the way he always did before one of his little speeches. "Okay, everyone—my job's done. Now it's all on you. I trust you to do your jobs, own the stage, and shine. Break a leg!"

As Martin spoke, Nora half-listened, her thoughts drifting. Somewhere in the back of her mind, she could almost hear Helen's voice—soft, steady, and ready to step into the spotlight. Did Helen ever feel like this? That strange cocktail of excitement and dread, like her heart, was trying to dance and hide at the same time? Maybe she had, just before stepping on stage, with a crowd waiting and everything on the line. Or maybe Helen had been braver, stronger—someone who didn't unravel when the pressure hit.

Martin started for the house, then paused just long enough to lean in close to Nora. "You've got this, girl. Knock 'em dead."

The crew scattered to their places, and Nora felt it—the familiar tingle of adrenaline. But this time, it wasn't panic. This was the good kind, the kind that used to hit her right before a dance performance. Something clicked into place, like sliding on an old, comfortable pair of shoes. She could do this. It did not differ from letting her body take over and do what it knew how to do.

Everyone was set. The audience hushed. Somewhere, a child squealed, and Nora smiled. *You're gonna love this one, Ollie.* Her breath steadied, her heart slowing into a familiar rhythm.

One last glance toward the wings, and she could have sworn she saw a figure there—a fleeting, ghostly shadow, the outline of a woman, watching her.

The lights dimmed, the curtain rose, and Nora stepped into the spotlight.

**

The next three weeks passed in a blur of sequins, stage lights, and breathless applause. It was an odd sensation—so much work, so many long rehearsals, all for the briefest whirlwind of performances. But every minute had been worth it. Nora felt like she was eating, sleeping, and breathing Roxie Hart. (And there had been a lot of sleeping, too. Even Roxie needed her beauty rest.)

The hunt for Zeke's story, the mystery she and Alex had become so wrapped up in, had been shoved to the back burner. She didn't have time to think about anything other than stage cues and costume changes. But on that final night, as the audience's applause faded, and they took their last bows, Zeke and Helen crept back into her thoughts, as persistent as ever.

As the cast and crew packed up and started trickling out of the theater, Nora hung around, loitering like a shadow in the corner. She wasn't quite ready to leave the stage just yet.

Alex was still there, of course. They were in their element, directing the crew to dismantle the set and making sure the theater was shut down, their voice carrying over the sound of footsteps and packing crates.

"Hey!" they called when they finally noticed Nora lurking. "Martin throws a mad post-production party—you should be there. You earned it."

"Are you going?" Nora asked.

"Yeah, but I've got to finish up here first."

"I'll wait," Nora smiled. "We can head over together."

Alex smiled back. "May as well put you to work, then." They nodded toward the dust mop leaning in the corner. "Want to get the stage?"

"Of course!" Nora grinned.

She grabbed the mop and pushed it across the stage, sweeping up bits of glitter, confetti, and the odd prop piece. As she swung back toward Alex, she said, "I think I saw Zeke tonight, you know..."

That got Alex's attention. They stopped mid-task, looking over at her. "He was watching from the back of the house," she continued, making another pass with the mop. "He seemed sad."

Another pass. "And Helen was with me, too."

When Nora finished sweeping, Alex joined her at center stage. "We need to finish what we started, don't we?"

Nora nodded. The performances had been amazing, but this felt just as important.

"I think I have an idea..." Alex said.

Nora's curiosity flared. "What is it?" she asked.

"Let me smooth it out first, okay? Don't want to jump the gun."

"Alright, but don't leave me in the dark too long!"

As they spoke, Nora's gaze drifted toward the balcony, where she saw a lone figure—a man—sitting in the shadows at the back. He wasn't part of the crew. She knew, without a doubt, who he was. Zeke. Watching, waiting.

She nudged Alex, and when they followed her gaze, they gave a small, solemn nod. No one else noticed, but Nora didn't need anyone else to see. She knew.

Then, without another word, she and Alex headed offstage and through the backstage hallway, leaving behind the ghostly image of Helen, standing near the wings, still watching the empty theater with eyes full of longing.

"We'll fix this," Nora whispered as the door clicked shut behind them.

***

The next night, Nora and Alex were back at the theater, this time with Ashlyn Alden joining them. The party had been a blast. While Nora felt closest to Martin and Alex, there was still a sense of camaraderie with the rest of the cast—a shared pride in what they'd accomplished. No matter their backgrounds, they had all been on the same team. Nora had too much to drink, though, and she'd spent the entire day sleeping it off. Luckily, she lived within walking distance.

"Before we try to contact Zeke," Ashlyn said as they entered the lobby, "we need to make sure Pritchard isn't a threat."

"How do we do that?" Alex asked.

"By confining him to his own space." Ashlyn grinned. "From what we've uncovered, he was a man of immense pride. He's angry because he doesn't want to be blamed for Helen's death. But he killed her in a fit of rage—like a toddler smashing another kid's toy because he couldn't play with it."

Ashlyn wandered over to the giant painting of Edward Pritchard hanging in the lobby. "We need to show him that he's still revered, and then we'll build a barrier to keep him confined to this space."

"Is it too much to ask to just banish him?" Nora asked, frowning.

Ashlyn smiled. "You can only banish spirits who agree to leave, and I don't think we'll be convincing Pritchard of that. But we can make him feel adored, secure in his pride."

"So, trick him?" Alex asked.

Ashlyn held a finger to her lips. "Careful, he could be listening. Based on our previous sessions here, I've never detected a powerful presence in the foyer. It's a suitable space. Let's get started."

The air in the theater lobby was thick enough to chew. Nora, Alex, and Ashlyn stood in a loose triangle near the towering portrait of Edward Pritchard. Even from within the frame, his eyes seemed to follow them.

Ashlyn closed her eyes, exhaling, like she was listening for something just out of reach. Her hands hovered at her sides, fingers twitching once or twice, before she stilled.

"We need to make him feel at home," Ashlyn said. "Pritchard was all about pride. We can use that. Pride anchors spirits like him—it keeps them from flying off in a rage or, you know, haunting toilets."

Alex raised an eyebrow. "Toilets?"

"Some have a flair for drama," Ashlyn replied, deadpan. "We don't want him haunting the ladies' room. Trust me."

She turned and made her way toward Pritchard's portrait, resting her hands on the frame. "This is where he will feel the strongest connection—the foyer, the entrance to his domain. It's like... a king at the gates of his castle. He needs to feel respected."

Alex looked skeptical, but kept quiet. Nora shifted, her gaze darting between Ashlyn and the portrait, as though expecting the ghost to pop out at any second.

Ashlyn knelt and pulled a small bag of herbs and salt from her coat pocket. With a practiced flick of her wrist, she started sprinkling the mixture in a neat circle around the base of the portrait. "We're building him a little sanctuary," she explained, muttering something that might have been in Latin—or possibly just gibberish. Nora wasn't sure.

"What's the salt for?" Nora asked, her voice soft.

"To create a boundary," Ashlyn said, looking up. "This isn't about banishing him. You can't banish someone unless they want to go and let's face it—Pritchard's not the 'willing to be exiled' type. But we can make this space feel important to him, a place where he'll want to stay."

Alex crossed their arms, half amused, half concerned.

Ashlyn gave a faint smile. "We're giving him what he thinks he deserves. To him, this will feel like an offering." She finished the circle and stood up, brushing her hands off. "He's getting a fancy little velvet rope to keep him happy. And inside that rope, he'll feel like the king of the world."

Alex glanced at the portrait. "Not sure he needs any help with that."

Once the circle was complete, Ashlyn lit a small candle and placed it in front of the painting. The flame flickered and danced, casting odd, jittery shadows that made Pritchard's already unnerving face seem to glower even harder.

Ashlyn took another deep breath, holding her palms up toward the portrait. "Edward Pritchard," she called, her voice as smooth as silk, "we invite you into this space. This is your domain. You are honored here, remembered here."

Nora felt the temperature drop. Not dramatically, but enough that the hair on her arms stood up. The candle flame wavered, shrinking for a moment before flaring brighter. She exchanged a glance with Alex, whose wide eyes suggested they weren't as comfortable with this as they were trying to seem.

"He's here," Ashlyn said, as if she were commenting on the weather. She opened her eyes, now fixed on the empty space in front of the painting.

"Edward," she began, her voice taking on a gentle, coaxing tone, "we know your story. We know you don't want to be blamed for what happened to Helen. You were angry. But that anger wasn't meant to destroy her, was it? You were frustrated, not... cruel."

A shiver rolled through the room, like the theater itself had taken a breath. The candle's flame guttered again, then steadied.

"You don't need to haunt this place in anger anymore," Ashlyn continued, her tone soothing, like she was trying to coax a spooked animal out of hiding. "Your legacy is here, Edward. This foyer is your space. You are powerful here. Respected. Revered."

Nora squinted at the shadows near the painting. Had they always been so... deep? Something was there, listening, deciding.

"You belong here, Edward," Ashlyn continued. "This is where you will stay. You will not interfere with the others. You will not go beyond this boundary."

For a long moment, the room was as still as a graveyard at midnight. Nora held her breath without realizing it. Then, the heavy pressure in the air lifted, like someone had opened a window and let out a long-held sigh.

Ashlyn exhaled, the tension draining from her posture. "He's agreed. As long as we respect this space, he'll stay confined to the foyer."

"Just like that?" Alex's voice was a little higher than usual, glancing at the painting.

Ashlyn gave a small, satisfied smile. "Spirits are a lot like people. They want to feel important. And if you give them what they think they deserve, they're usually happy."

Nora felt her chest lighten. There was more work to do, more spirits to deal with, but for now, at least, Edward Pritchard was no longer a problem. They could finally focus on Zeke.

"Now," Ashlyn said, dusting her hands off, "let's go talk to someone who wants to be helped."

"I saw him on the balcony," Nora said, her voice quiet but certain, leading them toward the stairs.

They climbed the narrow staircase, each step making the air feel a little cooler, a little heavier. By the time they reached the top, Nora couldn't shake the feeling that the theater was holding its breath, waiting for something. The old balcony seats stretched out in the dim light, their worn red cushions contrasting the shadows. The whole place felt... watchful, but not in a bad way. It was eerie, sure, but there was something peaceful about it too, like the ghosts here had already settled in for the night.

Ashlyn stood at the balcony, her gaze sweeping over the rows of chairs. Nora could feel the tension in the air—the kind that prickled at your skin, like you were being watched, even if no one was there.

Ashlyn closed her eyes and inhaled. "Zeke," she called, her voice calm but firm, "we're here for you. We know you've been waiting."

Nothing happened. No sudden chill, no flicker of shadows—just the silence of an empty theater.

Alex glanced around, eyebrows raised. "So much for someone who wants to be helped."

Ashlyn sighed. "He's here," she said under her breath, eyes still closed. "He's just... reluctant." She opened her eyes, her gaze now fixed on the far corner of the balcony. "Zeke, we're here to help. We know what happened."

Still, the air was thick with silence.

Ashlyn's face tightened with concentration. "He's... upset," she said slowly. "Wary."

Alex shifted their weight, uncomfortable with the invisible conversation happening in front of them. "Can't blame him," they muttered. "But how do we get him to listen?"

Ashlyn turned, her eyes locking on Alex. "You," she said. "You're his family. That's what he needs to hear."

Alex blinked, surprised. "Uh, what?"

Ashlyn nodded toward the shadowy end of the balcony. "You're from his brother's line. He knows that."

Alex glanced at the darkness and then back to Ashlyn. "You sure he knows? Because it feels like I'm about to give a speech to the floor."

Ashlyn gave them a look, her patience running thin. "Trust me."

Alex sighed but stepped forward, clearing their throat. "Zeke," they began, "I'm Alex Turner. My family—your family—came from your brother's side. We're... connected."

For a moment, nothing happened. Then, there was a noticeable shift—a chill in the air, like a door had opened somewhere far off. Ashlyn straightened, eyes widening. "He's listening."

Nora couldn't help but shiver. She couldn't see Zeke, but she could feel something, a presence hanging back in the shadows. It wasn't menacing, just... sad. Heavy with regret.

Ashlyn's voice softened, as though speaking to someone fragile. "Zeke," she said, "Alex is your family. They've come here to help. We want to reunite you with Helen. She's been waiting for you all this time."

Nora held her breath, waiting. The shadows seemed to shift, deepen. It was as if Zeke was there, just out of sight, but not quite willing to step forward.

Ashlyn tilted her head, her expression becoming more focused, as if she were hearing something the rest of them couldn't. "He's... not ready."

Alex let out a frustrated huff. "What do you mean, he's not ready? Helen's been waiting for him. We've been working to clear his name. This is what he's been stuck here for, isn't it?"

Ashlyn winced, as if absorbing a hard truth. "He thinks he doesn't deserve it," she murmured. "He believes Helen deserves better."

Nora's chest tightened. "But he didn't kill her," she said, her voice almost pleading. "He wasn't a murderer. We can fix this."

Ashlyn nodded, eyes still distant, as if half of her mind was elsewhere, communing with the spirit. "He's not listening to that. It's not about the truth—it's about what everyone believed. He's been carrying that weight, and now..." She paused, then added, "He doesn't want her to be stuck with him."

The air around them felt thick with sorrow. Nora glanced toward the shadows where Zeke's presence hovered, feeling a pang of frustration. "But Helen's been waiting for him," she whispered. "Doesn't he know that?"

Ashlyn's lips tightened. "He knows. But he doesn't think he deserves her. Not anymore."

A deep, quiet silence fell over them, the kind that felt like the end of a conversation, whether or not they wanted it to be.

Alex sighed, running a hand through their hair. "So... what now? We just leave him?"

Ashlyn took a slow breath, lowering her hands. "Sometimes... spirits have to come to terms with things on their own time. We can't force him to move on."

Nora stared at the space where Zeke lingered, her heart heavy with disappointment. She had wanted this to work—to help him, to bring him back to Helen. But as she looked at the dark corners of the balcony, she knew there was nothing more they could do tonight.

"We'll come back," Ashlyn said, as though speaking to Zeke himself. "We're not giving up. But for now... rest."

The chill in the air lightened, the strange heaviness beginning to lift. Whatever connection Ashlyn had been holding faded, and the theater felt like just a theater again—no ghostly presence, no lingering regret. Just silence.

Ashlyn turned to Nora and Alex. "There's nothing more we can do today."

Nora gave one last glance toward the darkened balcony, feeling the unfinished business hanging in the air. Zeke wasn't ready, and that hurt more than she expected. But maybe... maybe one day, he would be.

"We'll fix this," Nora whispered, more to herself than to anyone else, as they made their way down the stairs and out into the cool night air.

The theater door clicked shut behind them, leaving the balcony—and Zeke—alone in the quiet.

The three of them headed to The Crossroads. Nora slumped into her chair, feeling defeated. "I can't get proof to exonerate him, and Zeke doesn't seem to want to act without it."

Alex gave one of their lopsided grins, the kind that usually meant they were about to drop something big. "I think I'm ready to share my idea..."

They pulled a stack of printed papers from their bag and set it on the table.

"What is it?" Nora asked, eyeing the stack.

"It's a play," Alex said, leaning back. "A tragedy. Telling Helen and Zeke's story."

Nora blinked, not sure if they were serious. "A play?"

"Yeah. We tell their actual story—everything we've learned. Zeke's version, the truth. People love tragic love stories, especially with a murder mystery twist. We get people talking, revisiting the case, and it might even reach the folks who can do something about clearing Zeke's name."

Ashlyn, who had been quiet, raised an eyebrow. "And you think a play is going to convince people that a century-old ghost story is real?"

"Why not," Alex shrugged. "You do it on T.V. shows. People believe what you make them feel. We can't get Zeke exonerated through facts alone, but if we turn his story into something that tugs at the heartstrings? That can change how people see him."

Ashlyn looked at the script. "It's not a bad idea," she admitted. "If we can't change public opinion with hard evidence, we change it with emotion. People love a good ghost story. And this one is full of heartbreak."

Nora leaned back, considering it. It was crazy. But then, everything about this situation was crazy. "So we rewrite history as a tragedy?"

"No," Alex corrected, their grin widening, "we set the record straight."

Nora felt a flicker of hope. "And we're doing this for Zeke and Helen? To clear their names?"

"For them. For the theater. And maybe, a little, for us," Alex said. "I have enough pull that I think we can get the production funded."

"I may be able to help, too," Ashlyn added.

Nora shook her head but couldn't help smiling. Leave it to Alex to turn tragedy into something hopeful. "Alright. Let's do it."

CHAPTER TEN

Finale

Alex worked tirelessly on the play, and Nora was right there by their side, day in and day out. It was a modest production, a labor of love. The cast was so small that everyone did everything—props, costumes, even painting the set. Alex, with their quiet focus, directed the production with a kind of relentless, joyful determination that left Nora breathless. And, of course, who better to play Zeke and Helen than the two of them?

History clung to them during every rehearsal, heavy and undeniable. There were moments when Nora could almost feel Helen's presence hovering in the wings, her spirit watching, waiting for her story to be told. And Zeke—well, Nora suspected Alex could feel him, too. Sometimes they'd exchange a look during rehearsal, and Alex would give her that small, secret smile as if to say, *They're still here with us, aren't they?*

It was a one-night-only performance, gifted by the theater association with a reluctant nod to Alex's persistence. One night. The entire production hinged on a single chance, like a high-wire act without a net. And yet, it was all they needed.

The moment Linda got wind of it, she plastered the city with flyers, tapping into her dance studio connections, and Martin—ever the subtle mastermind—spoke in low tones to the right people in Boston's theater scene. Word spread. Calvin Turner, Zeke's great-nephew, turned out to be the play's most devoted advocate, charming anyone who would listen with stories about Zeke and Helen, their doomed love, and the injustice of their story.

By the time the day of the performance arrived, even the cast of *Chicago*—Nora's old crew—had rallied behind them, their voices echoing through the city's coffee shops and social media channels.

Senator Pritchard, sitting in the audience, was perhaps the only question mark of the evening. Nora had spotted him as soon as he entered, moving through the seats with all the ease of someone used to controlling rooms much bigger than this one. His ancestor's portrayal was hardly flattering, and Nora's stomach twisted at the thought of what he might say afterward. She hoped, prayed, that the man had enough of a care to see the performance for what it was—a story, a reckoning. But if he didn't, well...he'd have to deal with it. The truth had been buried long enough.

And then there was Ashlyn. Oh, Ashlyn. Ever the opportunist, she had mentioned the show in one of her ghost-hunting episodes. Nora had seen the gleam in her eye when she'd said it — "Ghosts, history, romance," she'd grinned. "Who could resist?" The mention worked. That evening, a good chunk of the audience was there just as much, hoping to see one of the Majestic's infamous spirits as in the story itself. Some had come with cameras, whispering about orbs and temperature changes. *Let them hunt their ghosts,* Nora thought, as long as the message got across.

The house lights dimmed, and Nora's heart thundered, a pulsing rhythm in time with the scuff of feet settling into seats. She stood in the wings, her breath held, waiting. The air was thick with anticipation, the kind that felt like it might spark into a storm at any moment. She glanced at Alex, standing just a few feet away, their head bowed, eyes closed as if they were centering themselves. When they looked up, they gave her a small nod, calm and reassuring, the sort of gesture that said, *We're ready. We've got this.*

Nora exhaled, feeling the floor beneath her feet as she grounded herself. She wasn't Nora Sinclair tonight; she was Helen O'Donnell, a rising star from a forgotten era. Helen's legacy draped over her shoulders, settling her nerves with an odd sense of calm.

The curtains began their slow ascent, revealing a hauntingly simple set—a grand piano tucked into the corner, a few chosen props hinting at the early 1900s, and a chandelier casting long, wavering shadows over the worn stage floor.

It was perfect. The Majestic Theatre felt alive tonight, like a living entity that was as much a part of the story as she was. Nora stepped into the glow of the stage lights, her body falling into Helen's movements. The hum of nerves still buzzed under her skin, but her voice found its rhythm, her lines slipping from her mouth like they'd always been a part of her.

Across the stage, Alex sat at the piano, fingers poised just above the keys. In that moment, they weren't Alex—they were Zeke Turner, the quiet, intense pianist who had stolen Helen's heart. Nora felt herself drawn to them before they even played a note. Then the music started, soft and melodic, filling the theater with its delicate notes. Her voice followed, weaving through the melody.

Just the two of them were on stage now, exchanging glances as their characters met for the first time.

"You're rushing it!" Nora said as Helen.

Alex—*Zeke* grinned. "Maybe I was waiting to see if you'd catch up."

Something shifted between the characters, pulling the audience into their world. Helen and Zeke's connection grew, their friendship transforming into something deeper, even as the world around them darkened. Nora could feel it as Helen—the pull, the intensity, the unspoken bond forming.

Shadows had a way of creeping in. Catherine, Helen's understudy, slid onto the stage, her every movement sharp and deliberate, her smile thin and cold. She was the embodiment of ambition, her venomous presence. The audience could feel the malice lurking beneath Catherine's every word, a storm waiting to break.

Nora stood center stage, rehearsing Helen's lines, when Catherine's voice sliced through the air like a knife.

"If I were you, Helen, I'd be careful," Catherine said, her tone laced with warning. "There's only so much attention one can draw before people notice."

Helen—no, *Nora*—gave a tight smile, brushing off the veiled threat with practiced ease. But the tension simmered. Catherine's jealousy was festering, twisting into something darker, something dangerous. In a later scene, Catherine appeared alone, clutching a small vial in her trembling hand, her eyes fixed on it with grim intent.

"She doesn't have to die," Catherine whispered to herself, her voice soft. "Just a little something to keep her offstage. Just enough for me to take her place."

The theater seemed to close in around them; the walls pressing in as Catherine's sinister plan took shape in the shadows.

Then came Edward Pritchard.

Nora couldn't see the senator, but she could feel his presence in the audience. His ancestor, Edward, was everything Helen had learned to navigate with care—a charming patron with far too much power and a streak of danger running just beneath the surface. Onstage, Edward's advances toward Helen were polite at first, but with each scene, they grew more insistent, more menacing. Every lingering touch of his hand, every whisper, twisted the tension tighter, making the audience shift in their seats.

"Why fight it, Helen?" Edward growled, his voice a rumble in the intimacy of her dressing room. "I could give you everything you've ever wanted."

Nora—*Helen*—held her ground, her voice steady but cautious. "What I want, you cannot give me," she replied, each word measured. It wasn't just rejection; it was survival. Edward Pritchard's money funded the theater, kept her career alive. But when his patience finally snapped, so did his charm.

In the dim light of Helen's dressing room, Edward's shadow loomed large, his hands closing around her throat. Nora's pulse quickened, a chill running down her spine as Edward's voice rose in fury.

"I've given you everything," Edward hissed, his grip tightening. "And you throw it away for *him*?"

The struggle was swift, but brutal. Helen's hands clawed at Edward's, her breath slipping away. The audience held its breath. The theater plunged into an uneasy silence as the lights dimmed and Helen's body crumpled to the floor. Nora felt it—the finality, the horror. Helen's life had been snuffed out, and with it, something shifted in the air, like the quiet before a storm.

Then came Zeke's trial.

The courtroom scene was stark, the air heavy with injustice. Zeke stood alone, accused of Helen's murder, and Alex—*Zeke's* voice cracked with emotion as they pleaded their case.

"I loved her," Zeke cried, raw grief spilling into every word. "I would never—*I couldn't*. I can prove it."

But no evidence was called for. The gavel came down, sealing Zeke's fate, and in that moment, the world collapsed around him.

Then, something unexpected happened. The actors turned, breaking the fourth wall, facing the audience with solemn expressions. The judge's voice rang out, not to the characters, but to the crowd.

"The court asks you: Who here believes Ezekial Turner is innocent?"

For a long moment, there was silence. Then, one by one, hands rose. A murmur rippled through the crowd, a collective shifting in their seats, and soon, every hand was in the air. It was a moment of redemption, too late for Helen, but not for Zeke. The audience had done what the court had failed to do—they had restored his honor.

As the lights dimmed once more, Alex knelt beside Nora—beside *Helen's*—body, their hand brushing her cheek with a tenderness that made Nora's heart ache. The same soft piano melody from the opening scene played again, but now it was mournful, a lament for what had been lost. The audience was quiet, reverent, as Zeke mourned for Helen in the final, heartbreaking scene.

And then, just as the cast gathered for the curtain call, Nora's eyes flicked to the wings. There they were—Zeke and Helen, hand in hand, watching from the shadows. Nora's breath caught in her throat. No one else seemed to notice, but she saw them as clear as day.

They stood there, smiling, and then they clapped. A small, simple gesture, but it made Nora's heart sing. After everything, they were at peace—together, at last.

As the applause roared around her and the cast took their bows, Zeke and Helen faded into the shadows, their hands still entwined. The stage lights dimmed, the curtain descended. The ghosts were gone. But something had changed. The theater would never feel quite the same again.

When the lights rose again and the curtain lifted for the final bow, the audience erupted into a standing ovation, their cheers filling every corner of the space. Nora blinked, her heart racing, her body still humming with the energy of the night. The cast bowed again, but her eyes found Alex's.

Their gaze met, something unspoken passing between them. Before Nora could second-guess herself, she stepped forward, and Alex moved toward her.

And then they kissed.

Right there, in front of everyone, the applause swelling to a fever pitch. The kiss was unexpected, yes, but it felt right—like the final note of a symphony, perfectly timed and inevitable. It wasn't just an onstage kiss; it was the start of something real. Something that had been building all along.

When they finally broke apart, Nora glanced out at the cheering crowd, her heart full. This wasn't just about Zeke and Helen anymore. This was about second chances, about love that defied time and expectations, about love that found a way through even the darkest of moments.

As Nora looked at Alex, smiling in the glow of the lights, she knew her story was only just beginning.

CHAPTER ELEVEN

Afterword

Thank you for taking the time to read *The Last Act*. While all my stories are special to me, this one holds pieces that are particularly close to my heart, as many elements touch on different aspects of my life. Originally, I included a scene where the senator, moved by the play, decides to dig deeper into Zeke's past, with the hope of securing him a posthumous pardon.

Ultimately, I chose to remove that scene. I wanted my story to focus on love prevailing, hope, and a happy ending—even if it's not the one Nora and Alex originally envisioned. *The Last Act* touches on some darker chapters of our history, and while I never want to overlook those moments, that wasn't the primary aim of this narrative.

In my research, I came across some invaluable resources I'd like to credit, including a podcast episode titled "Illuminating the Unseen" (https://www.oldnorth.com/itu/) and the New England Innocence Project (https://www.newenglandinnocence.org/).

About the Author

B eth Connor is a weaver of tales, captivated by writing and fueled by a love for storytelling.

Beth's creative pursuits are a reflection of her life philosophy, and she is always searching for new ways to expand her knowledge and understanding of the world. She has a keen eye for detail and a remarkable ability to create vivid, dynamic settings that resonate with her audience.

Beth's talent has earned her recognition as the author of several published works, including the novel "Hollow City" The Isdralan Chronicles Series, and the Kindred Spirits Mysteries, as well as a contributor to many anthologies. Beth is also an accomplished audiobook narrator and the host of the popular podcast, "Crossroads Cantina."

Despite her many endeavors, Beth remains down-to-earth and dedicated to living authentically, true to her passions and values. She resides in the Pacific Northwest with her husband, two children, and canine companions, who bring her boundless inspiration and delight.

Also by

ALSO BY BETH CONNOR:

Hollow City

The Isdralan Chronicles:
Micah and the Candles of Time
Prodigy of Flame
Bridge of Blood and Thornes

Kindred Spirit Mysteries:
The Secret of Misthaven Island
Bridging the Heart
The Curse at White Pines
The Last Act

I'll be Home for Christmas

Kindred Spirits Mysteries

Beth Connor

WOLF GROVE MEDIA, LLC

Contents

Do You Hear What I Fear?

"Help me," There was a womans voice on the other end of the line.

The urgency of the request did not surprise Ashlyn Alden. It wasn't the first time someone had opened with a plea, and it wouldn't be the last. Still, she had answered the phone on a whim—usually; she let these calls go to voicemail, filtering out the pranksters, skeptics and the ones who weren't ready for help.

But today, something had nudged her to pick up. Maybe she'd been feeling bold. Maybe even adventurous. If she were honest, she had just been feeling lonely.

"Okay," Ashlyn said, her tone steady. "Start from the beginning."

"I have a ghost. She gets angry sometimes." The woman paused, her breath hitching. "I run a bed-and-breakfast, and... I'm afraid she might hurt someone."

"I'm sorry," Ashlyn began, "I don't banish ghosts. You'll probably want to call—"

"No!" the woman interrupted, her voice sharp. "Why would I want to banish her?"

Now, that was interesting. Most people wanted their ghosts gone, exorcised like yesterday's bad luck. Plenty of folks out there offered that kind of service—some genuine, others complete frauds. But Ashlyn had never been like most people.

She'd known she was different from a young age. While other little girls were dreaming of fairy tales and imaginary friends, Ashlyn was having full-blown conversations with spirits—philosophical ones, even. And not just ghosts. Ghosts were only part of the picture. There were things out there—spirits of the land, whispers of memory, old gods—that most people never noticed.

But ghosts? Ghosts were her favorite.

"How can I help?" she asked in the tone she'd perfected for these situations. Calm, kind, the voice that made people believe things would be okay.

"Vera's very sweet. I just don't know what's making her so angry."

Well. That was an unexpected twist.

Ashlyn leaned back in her chair, intrigued. "Alright. Let's go back a bit. Tell me everything."

"Well, we bought the place about five years ago when John retired," the woman began, her voice a little breathless. "John is my husband."

"Hold up," Ashlyn interrupted, balancing the phone between her ear and shoulder. "What's your name?"

"Oh! I'm sorry, dear. I'm Delores Miller. I own Lilac Grove B&B up in Laconia, New Hampshire."

"Nice to meet you, Delores. I'm Ashlyn Alden."

"Thank you, sweetie. I'm all flustered. This whole situation has me feeling like I've lost my marbles."

"Don't worry about it," Ashlyn said. "Take your time."

Delores took a moment, then started again. "Like I said, John and I bought Lilac Grove after we retired. We don't have kids, so we thought a little bed-and-breakfast would keep us busy, keep us part of the community. He does all the handyman work, and I do the cooking, cleaning, decorating—you know, the usual."

"Makes sense," Ashlyn replied, already picturing it. A cozy inn, lilacs in bloom, a perfect place for a haunting.

"We named it Lilac Grove because of the flower garden out back. There's a whole grove of lilacs—just beautiful in the spring," Delores added, her pride evident. "Anyway, we found out it was haunted almost right away."

Ashlyn straightened up. "Haunted? From day one?"

"Oh yes. The very first day. We were walking through, dreaming up our little projects, and when we stepped out into the garden. And there she was."

"Who?"

"A woman," she said, her voice dropping to a conspiratorial tone. "She was out there, tending to the lilacs in this long fur coat. Now, that didn't seem too odd at first, considering how chilly it's been that May. But then—" she paused, "she turned around, and I saw she wasn't wearing a single thing under that coat. Not one stitch."

Ashlyn stifled a laugh. "You're kidding. Your husband must have loved that."

Delores snorted into the receiver. "Oh, honey, let me tell you, he didn't know where to look. I swear, the man's eyes nearly popped out of his head. And here I am, thinking maybe I needed stronger glasses."

"That's one way to may an impression."

"We thought she might be confused, maybe one of the previous owners. But before we could say anything, she just... faded. Like smoke."

Ashlyn nodded to herself. "That's a classic one."

"Yes. After that, we'd see her now and then. She putters around and rocks in the old chair in the parlor. She's always been quiet—friendly, even. Guests love her. She's part of the charm."

"But something changed?"

Delores hesitated. "That first December, she started tearing down the Christmas decorations, knocking things over, even pushing guests. We tried talking to her, but I don't think she can hear us."

Ashlyn raised an eyebrow. "Only around the holidays?"

"Exactly! And after Christmas, she calms down. The next December, it was worse. She started a fire in one room, and a poor man almost got shoved down the stairs. We had to shut down for the season."

Ashlyn frowned. "And now?"

"We've closed for the holidays the last two years. Figured it was safest. But we can't afford to keep doing that. December's a busy month, and with everything getting more expensive..." Her voice trailed off, dropping to a worried whisper. "I'm scared of what she'll do if we stay open."

Ghosts had personalities—quirks, just like the living. Some stuck around for sentimental reasons, others for unfinished business. But this kind of pattern, escalating during the same season every year? That was interesting.

"How do you want me to help?"

"Well," Delores hesitated again. "We were hoping maybe you could talk to her? See what she wants? We don't want her gone. She's part of the place now, you know?"

Ashlyn thought it over. Spirits weren't the sort to just spill their secrets, and this would not be a simple chat. Building trust with the dead took time. Effort.

"This isn't the kind of thing that'll be fixed overnight," Ashlyn warned.

"Oh, no, no," Delores agreed. "We don't expect that. I know we probably can't afford your usual rates, but the place is empty in December. Maybe you could stay with us for the month? We'll feed you, take care of everything. I promise we'll be excellent hosts."

Ashlyn paused, considering. A cozy B&B, tucked away in New Hampshire, surrounded by snow and a temperamental ghost to figure out? She had no family to spend Christmas with, and her spirit friends weren't the caroling type. The idea of a month-long holiday away, with a supernatural mystery to solve, was... tempting.

"All right," she said, the decision made. "I'll come."

Delores' exhaled. "Oh, thank you, Ashlyn! You have no idea how much this means to us."

"I'll have my business manager get in touch to work out the details of the contract. We'll get everything squared away before I head up."

"Of course," Delores replied, her excitement clear. "Thank you. We've been at our wits' end."

"Not a problem. I'm looking forward to meeting you and seeing the Lilac Grove for myself. It sounds lovely."

"It is," Delores said. "We're proud of it. And... well, we're proud of Vera, too. She's part of the family in her own way."

Ashlyn's smile widened. "Vera, huh? I can't wait to meet her as well."

Delores chuckled, the tension easing. "Let's hope she's on her best behavior."

"We'll see," Ashlyn replied. "I'll see you soon. Take care."

"You too, sweetie."

When the call ended, Ashlyn sat back, tapping her fingers on the desk. A haunted bed-and-breakfast, a ghost with a holiday grudge, and an entire month to sort it all out?

Ashlyn had sent off an email to her business manager mid-conversation, her thumb tapping out details while Delores rambled on about lilacs and holiday décor disasters. By the time they ended the call, Ashlyn already had one foot out the door.

Ashlyn sat at her desk, the phone still in her hand. The universe had a way of arranging things, weaving events together in patterns she didn't always recognize until later. Sometimes, it knew what she needed before she did.

Her phone buzzed, pulling her from her thoughts. It was a reply from Caroline, her business manager—quicker than usual.

Details sorted. Lilac Grove B&B, starting tomorrow. Looks like you'll be there by noon if you leave on time. They're covering meals, so don't scare them with your snack habits. C.

Ashlyn smiled at the screen. Leave it to Caroline to handle things faster than she could even plan. It was comforting, really. Caroline was a force of nature, the kind of person who could wrangle chaos with a cup of tea and a clipboard.

If she packed tonight, she'd be ready to hit the road by morning. The drive wasn't long—just a few hours—but it would give her time to think. Lilac Grove was waiting, and with it, whatever mess was brewing beneath the surface. She'd learned long ago that small towns always had trouble simmering, like a pot on a stove left too long.

Her gaze drifted to the framed photo on her desk. A little girl, five or six, standing between her parents. It was the last picture they'd taken together. Sometimes it felt like a relic from another world, proof they'd been real, because her memories were fraying at the edges. Her dad's big, warm hugs, her mom's smile—things she used to be able to recall so vividly—were growing harder to hold on to.

They'd always accepted her. Never questioning her odd little gifts, the way she'd talk about things no one else could see. And when they'd been taken from her, she'd half expected them to come back. Not alive, but... present. Lingering. Watching over her. Spirits, after all, were supposed to stick around, weren't they? The ones with unfinished business?

But they never had.

Maybe they'd moved on. That's what people said when they wanted to offer comfort. "They've found peace," they'd tell her. "They're in a better place." And maybe that was true. But it wasn't comforting. Not to her.

She exhaled, leaning back in her chair. After they'd passed, it had been foster home after foster home. Each one was more interested in her oddities than in her as a person. Some feared her abilities, whispering about devils and curses. Others saw them as something to exploit, a party trick or worse. She'd learned to keep quiet. It was easier that way.

At least her ghost friends had been more understanding. But even they didn't have answers. Not about her parents. Not about why they hadn't stayed. Ghosts didn't have all the answers. Being dead didn't make you wise, just... well, dead.

She pushed the thoughts aside. It hurt less now, in a distant, quiet sort of way—like anyone else who had lost their parents, except her holidays always had an extra twist of loneliness.

She stood, stretching her arms and glancing around her small apartment. Relationships had never been her strong suit, and she preferred to keep her friends at a comfortable distance. Alone wasn't so bad. She had her routine, her work and her friend Sebastian when she needed a distraction. That was about as close as she got to companionship. He wasn't looking for anything more, which worked for her.

Dating? Well, that was always a temporary affair. A few dates, nothing serious. She liked to keep things casual, before things got to the point where explaining the ghosts became necessary. That was usually the deal-breaker.

It didn't bother her. Some people had pets; she had a handful of spirits who dropped by for a chat.

Ashlyn gave a small shrug, shaking off the melancholic thoughts before they could settle. She had a trip to prepare for. She flicked on her laptop and opened a browser, pulling up articles about Lilac Grove. Most were puff pieces—*Charming B&B in Laconia*—filled with reviews about the delightful décor and the infamous ghost, who was known for moving guests' shoes or knocking over a teacup. But then she found an old local legend buried in the archives: Vera Beaumont had once been a woman of high society in the late 1800s, known for her hospitality.

Ashlyn would have to see what information the Millers had already dug up on her. Obviously something, as they had named her. The timeline of her life was murky—rumors of a lost child, a conspiracy with her husband, murder or worse—but nothing concrete.

"Classic," Ashlyn muttered to herself. Tragic backstory? Check. Holiday tantrum? Double check.

She leaned back, thinking through the details. It wasn't like spirits to get angry without reason, and Vera had been a benign presence for years—cheeky, sure, with her pranks and shoe-misplacing, but nothing violent. The sudden change in behavior, and its predictable recurrence, meant something had triggered the shift.

But what?

Ghosts usually had a reason for everything they did. Unfinished business, unresolved trauma, or even an emotional connection to a specific time of year. If Vera was throwing a seasonal tantrum, then something about Christmas—or maybe winter itself—had to be a factor. Maybe it had been the anniversary of her death, or the date of some event that had left her unsettled in the afterlife.

Ashlyn frowned, running a hand through her hair as she mulled it over. Perhaps it was something that happened at the Bed and Breakfast itself?

She'd seen it before—an unintentional stirring by guests, renovations, or even emotional energy from living people passing through. Could someone staying at Lilac Grove have unknowingly sparked something? A guest with ties to Vera's past? Or maybe a family tradition that reminded Vera of something she'd lost?

Ashlyn crossed her arms, staring at the holiday lights outside. It wasn't just the usual haunting that interested her—it was the transformation itself. Harmless pranks turning into fire-starting rages. It was too much like other cases, ones that hadn't ended well. A ghost that suddenly gets violent is often a ghost that's about to unravel.

"Whatever it is, I'll find out soon enough," she muttered, feeling the hum of anticipation that came before every case.

She snapped her laptop shut, her mind buzzing with half-formed theories. Crossing the room to her closet, she pulled out a stack of sweaters. New Hampshire in December demanded layers, and she wasn't about to face restless spirits without some cozy knits.

As she tossed sweaters, jeans, and wool socks onto the bed, a sudden chill brushed past her. She didn't even flinch.

"Hello, Hank," she said, reaching for her duffel bag. "Decided to pop in, did you?"

The air shifted near her, tingling with the presence of her old friend. Hank had been hanging around since she'd first moved in. He wasn't much for conversation, just a presence she found comforting—like a lazy cat who liked to watch her pack. He'd never said why he stayed, and she'd stopped asking years ago.

"Going somewhere cold," she added, folding a sweater. "Got a spirit need of some ghost therapy."

The curtain by the window fluttered, though the window was closed. Hank's version of a sarcastic eyebrow raise. She smiled. "I know. Nothing says 'happy holidays' like an angry spirit lighting things on fire."

Ashlyn grinned as she tucked a bundle of sage into the corner of her bag, followed by a pendulum and a few crystals. Some people would roll their eyes at her "essentials," but she'd found they worked just as well as any high-tech gadget. Still, she tossed in an EMF meter and a digital recorder. She liked to balance the mystical with the tech-savvy—it was part of her charm.

As she continued packing, her eye caught a holiday card on the table from Ella Hawthorne—one of her clients with a hint of the gift, someone she kept in touch with. The cheery scene of snowmen and carolers reminded her of how distant she was from most people. She spent her life reuniting spirits with unfinished business, yet she hadn't worked hard on her own relationships.

Her thoughts wandered back to her parents. They'd been gone for so long now. Then she sighed and shook her head, forcing herself to focus on the task at hand. Dwelling on the past wouldn't pack her bag. She zipped up the last compartment and glanced around the room to make sure she hadn't forgotten anything.

Then she crossed the room and set the alarm on her phone for an early morning start. It would be an easy drive, only a few hours assuming she beat the snowstorm, but the sooner she got there, the better. Something about Vera's unpredictable holiday behavior had her on edge.

She tossed the phone onto her nightstand, feeling Hank's presence nearby.

"Well, Hank, I guess this is it," she said, turning toward the window where the air seemed to shimmer, the subtle sign that he was listening. "Off to another haunt. Try not to get bored while I'm gone, alright?"

The curtain stirred, despite the fact that the window was shut tight.

She padded over to the window, her breath fogging the glass as she gazed out at the scene below. Snow coated the streets in a perfect holiday postcard way—lights twinkling along rooftops, wreaths hanging on doors. The warmth of it all felt far away, like a scene she could see but never quite touch.

"Merry Christmas to me," she whispered, her voice tinged with irony. Spending the holidays with a moody ghost, a bed-and-breakfast in danger, and whatever secrets the past was about to dig up? Typical.

But even with the loneliness pressing in at the edges, there was a tiny flicker of excitement in it all. Something new. Something interesting. She didn't mind the ghosts—they were more reliable than most living people. But there was still a part of her, buried deep, that hoped maybe this time, she'd learn something she didn't expect. Maybe Vera's unfinished business would bring answers she hadn't even known she needed.

Ashlyn glanced once more at the snow-covered street before climbing into bed. "Goodnight, Hank."

A faint rustling at the curtain was his only reply.

With that, she pulled the blankets up to her chin. Tomorrow, the road to New Hampshire would unfold before her, and with it, whatever mysteries awaited at Lilac Grove.

CHAPTER TWO

O Come, All Ye Restless

The drive to Laconia was uneventful. Ashlyn had beaten the storm, though the news had made it sound like the blizzard of the century was about to descend. Instead, snowflakes drifted from the sky as she pulled up to the inn, a soft blanket already forming on the ground.

A weathered sign by the road read "Lilac Grove B&B," with a long driveway leading to a grand Victorian home that loomed ahead. The house stood like something out of time, its peaked roof and intricate trim framed against the snow. Delores had decorated the place with simple, tasteful lights—warm, golden twinkles along the edges of the porch and roofline. It was beautiful, like driving straight into a Thomas Kinkade painting.

Ashlyn questioned the point of decorating just for her. Electricity wasn't cheap, and no one could see the lights from the road. But who was she to question what brought someone else joy? If hanging lights made Delores happy, that was reason enough. Ashlyn had learned long ago that small acts of beauty—no matter how unnecessary they seemed—had their own value.

As she stepped out of the car, the crisp air biting at her cheeks, Delores and John were already making their way down the steps of the front porch to greet her. They looked like the quintessential New England couple, bundled in flannel-lined jackets and practical boots. Delores was sturdy and soft all at once, her graying hair pulled back in a neat bun, while John had the quiet, weathered face of someone used to hard winters and long hours.

"You must be Ashlyn Alden!" Delores called, her voice warm and bright, matching the glow of the house. Without hesitation, she wrapped Ashlyn in a hug. "I'm a hugger. I hope you don't mind."

It wasn't the polite, surface-level embrace Ashlyn often tolerated from strangers. Delores hugged like she meant it, her sincerity radiating from the moment her arms wrapped around Ashlyn. For a second, Ashlyn froze, not because she didn't like the contact, but because it was so *genuine*. She could sense when people were faking, their emotions layered with awkwardness or obligation. But this wasn't that. Delores was the real deal, and her warmth eased some of the tension Ashlyn didn't realize she'd been carrying.

John, standing a few feet back, extended his hand in a more restrained but friendly greeting. "Good to meet you," he said, his voice a quiet rumble.

Ashlyn smiled, taking his hand in hers. "Likewise." His handshake was firm but gentle, a perfect complement to Delores' exuberance.

As she stepped back and took in the couple before her, Ashlyn felt a surprising sense of ease. She didn't meet people like this often—people who were exactly what they appeared to be, no pretense, no hidden agendas. Delores and John weren't trying to impress anyone; they cared. About their inn, about the spirits in it, and about the people who passed through. It was clear in their smiles, in the way they stood close together, and in the simple joy they took in greeting her.

Ashlyn loved them already. They were good people—solid, grounded, and real. People you could trust to look out for you, whether you were alive or a wandering spirit.

With all its beauty, the place evoked a strange, sorrowful energy that Ashlyn couldn't quite put her finger on. It certainly didn't come from the Millers—those two were practically made of sunshine and warm cookies. No, this was something else. Something darker. It felt like frustration, like the house itself was holding its breath, ready to burst with whatever it was keeping bottled up.

It made her feel uneasy, though not afraid. Could it be Vera? Perhaps.

"We're so glad you're here!" Delores said, beaming, as John hefted Ashlyn's suitcase up the stairs. They made their way inside to a grand entryway that was, frankly, ridiculous in the best possible way. A Christmas tree dominated the space, soaring at least twenty feet into the air, covered in ornaments that looked like they'd been chosen with great care. There were delicate glass birds, twinkling lights, and ribbons that spiraled down the tree like soft whispers of snow.

"Did you do all this?" Ashlyn asked, impressed. The place could have graced a magazine cover.

"Oh, I picked out the decorations," Delores admitted with a modest wave of her hand, "but John did the lights and the heavy lifting. I get dizzy just thinking about ladders."

John gave a shy smile, a man proud of his handiwork and even more clearly still head-over-heels for his wife.

"Well, it's gorgeous," Ashlyn said with a grin. "Way more than I need."

"Nonsense, honey! You just take care of our Vera," Delores said, her voice warm as fresh-baked pie.

They moved into the heart of the house, and Ashlyn took in the grand tour. The place was a textbook Victorian, all elegance and charm, but with the cozy touches that made it feel like a home rather than a museum. The kitchen was a sprawling affair with wooden cabinets, gleaming copper pots hanging above the island, and the faint smell of something sweet, like cinnamon and apples, lingering in the air.

They passed a library that had Ashlyn slowing her pace, drawn to the towering shelves crammed with old, leather-bound books and a pair of wingback chairs just begging for someone to curl up in them with a cup of tea. A sitting room off to the side boasted heavy drapes, deep armchairs, and a piano in the corner.

"All the bedrooms are upstairs," Delores continued, leading the way up a creaky but solid staircase. "There's also a back stairwell down to the kitchen if you feel like sneaking a midnight snack."

They reached the landing, where the hallway branched out to reveal four doors on either side. "We've got four double rooms, four king-and-queen rooms, and one suite." Delores shot Ashlyn a wink. "Naturally, we're putting you in the suite."

Ashlyn couldn't help but smile as they reached her door. Each room had a small plaque outside with a name engraved on it. "The Lilac Suite," hers read. The others were named after local flora and fauna.

"Small touches make a house a home," Delores said, noticing Ashlyn's gaze.

Ashlyn stepped into her room, where everything from the quilt on the bed to the faint scent of lavender in the air made her feel both welcomed and on edge. That same uneasy energy lingered, tucked just under the surface.

"I'm sure she wants to get settled in, dear," John said, cutting through Delores' well-meaning chatter with the gentle authority that only comes with years of practice.

"Oh, yes, of course." Delores straightened the already perfect bedspread, her hands smoothing out non-existent wrinkles. "I left some lunch meat, cheese, and bread in the kitchen if you'd like to make yourself a sandwich. And I'll bring muffins and breakfast things in the morning. Tonight, we'd love to have you over for dinner, if you're willing. I've got a lasagna all ready to pop in the oven. We can tell you more about Vera, and—"

"Let's give her some peace, dear," John interrupted again, his voice as calm as ever.

"Oh, yes, of course." Delores flashed a quick, apologetic smile. "Ah! I do the shopping on Mondays, so just give me a list of anything you need, and I'll make sure you're all stocked up."

John took her hand and guided her toward the door, his touch full of affection rather than urgency. "We're just down the drive, about a quarter mile. Follow the path along the lake, and you'll find us. Dinner's at six."

"Thank you," Ashlyn said, touched by their warmth. She already liked them both—Delores with her constant bustling, so eager to make everything just right, and John, the quiet, stoic counterbalance. He radiated calm, a deep-rooted steadiness that seemed to ground Delores in the best way. Ashlyn could see what a good team they were. Where Delores fussed, John reassured. Where she flitted, he steadied.

As the door clicked shut behind them, the room fell into a comfortable silence. Ashlyn exhaled, feeling the tension she hadn't realized she was holding unwind. She wandered over to the window, pushing aside the lace curtain to peer out. From her view, she could see the lake shimmering through the trees, a glint of silver against the deep green of the pines.

She shivered, though the room wasn't cold. That unsettled feeling still lingered, a whisper of something just out of reach. Not malevolent—just *watchful*.

"Vera," she murmured to herself. Whoever Vera was, her presence was in every corner of this place, from the creak of the floorboards to the shadows that stretched long in the afternoon light.

With a sigh, Ashlyn turned back to the room, noting again the little touches that made the Lilac Suite feel both cozy and—well, if she was honest — eerie.

She shook off the thought and headed downstairs to make herself that sandwich. Maybe a little food would help ease the tension. Besides, a house this big deserved to be explored, and she wasn't about to miss out on what had to be an over-the-top Victorian kitchen.

As she passed the sitting room, something flickered in the corner of her vision. She stopped. Turned. A woman was sitting in the rocking chair near the window, swaying back and forth, the wood creaking in the quiet room. Ashlyn's heart jumped in her chest, but not with surprise. It was almost a relief. She'd expected a haunting, and there it was, like a guest who'd arrived a little early to the party.

The woman in the chair wasn't a shadow or a mist or some vague impression of a person. No, this ghost was as solid as if she'd walked in off the street. She was dressed in an old-fashioned gown; her graying hair pulled up in a tight bun, the kind of look that said she wouldn't stand for any nonsense. She narrowed her eyes at Ashlyn like a strict schoolmarm. Then she tutted, a soft, disapproving cluck, shaking her head before fading away as quickly as she'd appeared.

Ashlyn sighed. One might think that seeing a ghost would inspire terror or at least mild alarm, but she'd been dealing with spirits for so long that it barely registered as more than a curious inconvenience. Still, she wasn't expecting *this* ghost to pop up so soon. Usually, the house took a few days before throwing its spectral residents at her.

"I'm just here as a guest," Ashlyn said aloud to the now-empty room, her tone light but respectful. If Vera—or whoever the rocking-chair woman had been—was nearby, it was best to start things off on the right foot. "My name's Ashlyn Alden. Pleased to make your acquaintance. I hope we can be friends."

The room remained silent, but Ashlyn could feel the air shift, as if someone was contemplating her words.

With a small shrug, she turned back toward the kitchen. The smell of cedar lingered in the hallway, mixing with something floral that hadn't been there before. Whether it was Vera's perfume or just the house, she couldn't say.

The kitchen, when she reached it, was enormous. It sprawled out with long counters, a farmhouse sink that could double as a small boat, and an island that looked like it could seat half a dozen people. Copper pots hung from hooks above the island, gleaming in the soft light, and a collection of mason jars lined the shelves, filled with spices and dried herbs. There was a comforting warmth in the space, the kind that made you want to stay and bake something from scratch, even if you did not know what you were doing.

Ashlyn made herself a simple sandwich and ate standing at the counter. The uneasy energy from before had settled into something calmer, though she could still sense that watchful presence lingering in the background. If Vera—or whatever spirits lived here—wanted to talk, they could take their time. She wasn't in a rush.

After finishing her meal, Ashlyn wandered back through the house, finally making her way to the library. It was the coziest room she'd seen yet, with bookshelves that stretched up to the ceiling, filled with all manner of old, well-loved volumes. A small fireplace sat in the corner, and she couldn't resist lighting it. The flames crackled to life, casting a warm glow over the room.

Settling into one of the deep, overstuffed chairs, Ashlyn pulled a book off the nearest shelf—something old and musty, perfect for a quiet winter's afternoon.

As she flipped through the pages, the tension in her shoulders eased. The house might be haunted, but it was also lovely. A perfect spot for the holiday season.

Later that evening, Ashlyn bundled up in her down coat, knit hat, and scarf, taking the path along the lake to the Millers' house. The driveway wound around too, but it seemed ridiculous to drive such a short distance—even if it was freezing. And it *was* freezing. A cold that sinks into your bones and makes every breath sharp, your lungs tight with the crisp bite of winter air. As she stepped onto the path, the snow crunched underfoot, that squeaky sound that only comes when it's dry and packed hard by the chill.

The lake, dark and still, stretched out beside her, a smooth pane of ice that mirrored the twilight sky. Occasionally, the wind skimmed across it, whistling through the bare branches of the trees, and she swore she could feel it trying to sneak under her scarf. Her cheeks prickled with cold, and her gloved fingers were already numbing. She picked up the pace, her breath coming in little clouds that disappeared into the night.

When she reached the Millers' house, a small red manufactured home that stood out against the snow, she sighed with relief. Simple, comfortable, and welcoming. It was a house that didn't try too hard to impress, but made you feel you'd just come home from a long day. She knocked, and as soon as the door opened, a wave of warmth washed over her. It wasn't just the heat—it was the smell. The savory aroma of lasagna hit her like a soft punch to the stomach, and it growled in response.

John greeted her with his usual quiet smile, stepping aside so she could step into the glow of the house. The door opened into the dining room, and Ashlyn couldn't help but notice the table was already set.

"Let me take your coat, dear," Delores said, bustling over to help Ashlyn out of her winter layers. She could feel her face thawing, the prickling sensation of blood returning to her fingertips.

Once her coat and scarf were whisked away, Ashlyn settled at the table. The food was delicious. The lasagna was rich and cheesy, perfectly seasoned, and the homemade garlic bread had just the right amount of crunch. As they ate, Ashlyn shared stories about some of her past cases, ghosts she had met, and the work she did with spirits. To her relief, the Millers weren't put off by it at all—in fact, they seemed interested. John listened with quiet attention while Delores peppered her with questions. By far, they were some of the easiest people she'd ever worked with.

Over dinner, the conversation drifted to Vera.

"So, when did you realize Vera was going to be a permanent guest?" Ashlyn asked.

Delores exchanged a glance with John. "Well, we first saw her in the garden, of course—just standing there, clear as day. But after that, she started making herself known in... smaller ways. Little things around the house."

John nodded, leaning back in his chair.

"It started with the flowers in the parlor," Delores continued. "We'd just brought in a new bouquet, and I'd arranged them in this vase on the mantel. Thought they looked quite nice, honestly. But Vera? Well, she didn't agree."

Ashlyn raised an eyebrow. "Oh? How could you tell?"

Delores chuckled. "We went out for groceries that afternoon—gone for maybe an hour or so—and when we came back, the entire arrangement had been scattered, The flowers were everywhere. It was like she was saying, 'No, no, this won't do at all.'"

John added, "I just looked at them and said, 'Guess Vera doesn't like your taste.'"

Delores swatted him with her napkin. "He acted like it was the most normal thing in the world! Me? I nearly jumped out of my skin." She shook her head, a smile still playing on her lips. "But that wasn't the end. Next morning, I found the candlesticks on the mantle had been rearranged. Moved just a few inches over, but it was clear—she had her own ideas about where things belonged."

Ashlyn grinned. "Sounds like she's got a knack for interior design."

Delores laughed. "That's one way to put it. And it wasn't just the parlor. Over the weeks, little things started happening all over the house—picture frames tilted, curtains pulled back just so. It took me a while to realize it wasn't random at all. She's got an eye for detail, our Vera."

"She definitely prefers things her way," John added. "Once we started calling her by name, things calmed down a bit. I think she appreciated the respect."

"Does that mean you did some research?"

"We did," Delores replied. "She seemed to be dressed in late 1800s clothing, so we dug around in the house records and town archives. Turns out, the house once belonged to a couple named Vera and Andrew Beaumont. When Andrew passed, Vera stayed on for a few years, but we couldn't find much about her after that. No solid death record, no mention of whether she moved away or died here."

"She seemed pleased when we started using her name, so we think we got it right." John said.

"The moment we called her Vera, the house just felt... lighter. Like she'd finally gotten what she wanted. No more rearranging the furniture or turning the pictures upside down—well, not as often, anyway."

John chuckled, "I think she still likes to remind us who's in charge now and then."

"Sounds like you've found a way to live in harmony with her," Ashlyn said, smiling. "A bit of give and take."

"Exactly. We treat her like a part of the family." Delores said. "I leave out fresh flowers for her sometimes, and in return, she lets us be. It's her home as much as it is ours."

There was a brief pause as Ashlyn absorbed that. The way the Millers spoke about Vera wasn't just with the detached curiosity of people living in a haunted house—they spoke about her with genuine warmth, like she was a quirky but beloved relative.

"Do you ever feel like she's trying to communicate anything?" Ashlyn asked after a moment. "Beyond just rearranging the décor?"

John thought for a second, then said, "I think she wants the house kept in good order. It was hers, and she loved it. As long as we look after it, she looks after us."

Ashlyn smiled. "It sounds like you've built a good relationship with her."

"Mostly," John replied.

Delores sighed, glancing at John before folding her hands in her lap. "The reason you are here..." she said. "Things change around this time of year."

Ashlyn's brow furrowed. "Cany you give me more details?"

Delores glanced toward the window, where the moon had slipped behind a veil of clouds. "Something about the season stirs her up. We noticed it the first year we stayed open through the holidays. Vera gets... more active. And not in a good way."

John's expression hardened. "It starts small. Lights flickering, doors refusing to stay shut—or refusing to open. But as the month progresses, it's like there's this pressure. She gets restless, sometimes angry."

"What does she do?"

Delores answered. "One year, we had a guest locked in her room. The door wouldn't budge. John had to force it open, and when he did, the windows were frosted over—on the inside."

"And another time," John added, "the Christmas tree tipped over in the middle of the night. I'd put it up myself, and it was solid. But it came down, smashed half the ornaments, and scared the guests half to death."

"And the fire..." Delores started, but did not continue.

Ashlyn shivered. "Has anyone been hurt?"

"Not yet," John said. "But it's like she doesn't know her own strength during the holidays. She becomes... unpredictable."

Ashlyn leaned forward, using her most comforting voice. "This is exactly what I'm here for. You don't need to worry. I've handled spirits that react to anniversaries, holidays, even certain scents. It's always tied to something unresolved. If Vera's growing restless around Christmas, there's a reason behind it. We just have to figure out what it is, and help her deal with it."

Delores relaxed a little. "We've tried asking her, but she never answers. At least, not in any way we can understand."

"It sounds like it could be tied to a memory. Something about Christmas has a deeper significance for her—possibly something painful." Ashlyn pondered out loud. "I'm confident we can figure this out."

Delores gave a small smile. "Just don't get hurt, dear. She doesn't mean to lash out."

"I understand," Ashlyn said. "But this is my job. I'm here to help Vera, and I won't let things get out of hand."

The room fell into a thoughtful silence. Ashlyn could feel their concerns. She broke the silence with a practical tone, steering the conversation back to her task. "If I want to dig into Vera's past, where's the best place to start?"

John, grateful for the shift, answered. "The public library on Main Street. They've got records going back to when the town was founded. That's where we found her name in the property records. And there's a cemetery nearby—though we never found a death record for her. Still, it might be worth checking again."

Delores perked up. "And the historical society. They've got old photographs, documents—if Vera was active in the community, there could be something there. I've been meaning to go myself, but—" she trailed off, looking almost sheepish. "I've been a little too afraid to dig deeper."

Ashlyn gave her a smile. "That's what I'm here for. I'll see what I can uncover."

"Thank you. I know it's a lot, and I—well, we—really appreciate you coming to help."

John stood, beginning to gather the plates from the table. "We're lucky to have you here."

The night wound down with warm conversation and the comforting weight of a good meal. By the time Ashlyn made her way back to her room, exhaustion had settled deep in her bones. When she reached the door to the Lilac Suite, she was more than ready to collapse into bed and let sleep claim her.

But as soon as she stepped inside, she froze.

Her suitcase lay open in the middle of the floor, its contents flung in every direction. Clothes, books, her journal—everything had been tossed about like someone, or something, had rifled through it in a frenzy. Even her toothbrush was lying on the bed, far from where she had left it.

A chill that had nothing to do with the cold crept up her spine.

"Thanks for the welcome, Vera," she muttered under her breath, forcing a wry smile. This was one way to unpack.

Silent Fright

3 AM. The witching hour.

Some people say it's just a phrase, a bit of folklore to describe the stage of sleep where your body's deep in REM—heart rate slow, temperature dropped, breathing uneven. But there's another theory. One that says when you wake in that dark stretch of night, it's because something woke you.

Ashlyn's eyes snapped open.

At first, she thought she should be relieved. There were no eerie footsteps, no ghostly whispers, no clang of unseen hands tossing pots around in the kitchen. No, this quiet wasn't peaceful. It was too thick, too *intentional*.

Fear crawled up her spine, slow and ice-cold. She wasn't the type to scare easily, but this—this was different. Her heart beat out of sync with the silence, faster and faster, until it pounded so loudly in her chest she was sure something would hear it. She tried to sit up, tried to move, but her limbs refused to obey. Her body was frozen, stiff.

The families she'd lived with as a child had always brushed these moments off as "night terrors." But Ashlyn knew better. This wasn't a dream.

Panic tightened its grip. She tried to scream, to shout for help, but her voice was as paralyzed as her body. Nothing. Not a sound. Not even a gasp.

It felt like hours trapped in that void of silence, with her pulse the only evidence that she was still alive. And then, just as suddenly as it had seized her, the paralysis shattered. The invisible weight lifted, leaving her trembling, her breath shaky and ragged as she pushed herself upright.

She swung her legs off the bed, the cool floor grounding her as she moved to the window. Outside, a fresh layer of snow blanketed the earth.

The clouds had scattered, leaving a bright, full moon hanging in the sky, its silver light so bright it almost looked like dawn.

Ashlyn exhaled, letting the tension bleed out of her muscles. But even as she stared at the serene, moonlit snow, a part of her couldn't shake the feeling that something had just left. Something she couldn't see—but that had been watching her, waiting for that exact moment of stillness.

She turned to crawl back into bed, but something flickered in the corner of her eye.

Her breath caught. There, in the large, overstuffed chair that sat against the far wall, was the woman from the sitting room.

Ashlyn's heart thudded in her chest. The woman sat still, her back straight as a ruler, hands folded in her lap. Her hair, a pale gray that bordered on silver, was pulled into a severe bun at the nape of her neck, not a strand out of place. The high collar of her gown—a somber, old-fashioned thing in deep, dusty black—brushed her jawline, emphasizing the rigid Victorian propriety etched into every line of her posture. Her face was pale, almost translucent in the moonlight, with deep-set eyes that seemed too sharp for the world she no longer inhabited.

Those eyes, hollow but alert, locked onto Ashlyn, studying her in silence.

"Vera?" Ashlyn whispered, her voice only a breath.

The woman didn't move. Didn't blink. Just *watched*, like she was waiting for something.

Ashlyn swallowed, trying to steady her nerves. "I'm Ashlyn," she said, introducing herself to the woman who may or may not even know she was sitting there. The ghost didn't move, just kept watching her with those sharp, glassy eyes.

Her gift had always been unpredictable. Most of the time, hearing ghosts felt like trying to tune into a weak radio signal. The voices faded in and out like distant whispers on a breeze. She could pick up fragments, stray thoughts that slipped through the veil between worlds.

Every once in a while, when a spirit wanted to make itself known, the connection became crystal clear. In those moments, she could hear them as plainly as if they were standing right beside her, flesh and bone, speaking directly into her ear. These were like her childhood friends. The ones that were easier to say were imaginary. Clear as day to Ashlyn.

They could have full conversations, the kind that made her forget they weren't alive anymore.

Most ghosts had their own minds, their own unfinished business, and they didn't always choose to speak. Some didn't even know they could.

Ashlyn waited for that clarity, but Vera's face darkened, her features twisting into an angry scowl. Her sharp gaze, still focused on Ashlyn, seemed to flicker, as if she wasn't seeing her at all.

"You!" Vera spat, her voice trembling. But it wasn't directed at Ashlyn. "Annie! What are you doing in here?"

Vera's expression grew harsher, her back rigid with indignation.

"This is *my* room," she hissed, her voice rising with an old authority that brooked no argument. "You belong in the servants' quarters! Don't think you can just waltz in here and do as you please!"

Ashlyn could almost feel the shift in the room.

"And you've been in here before, haven't you?" Vera's face twisted. "Rifling through my things, stealing what doesn't belong to you. I'll see you punished for this, Annie. Mark my words."

Then Vera blinked, her expression softening as if the fog in her mind had lifted, and for the first time, she seemed to truly *see* Ashlyn standing there. The anger melted into something confused, almost fragile.

"Where... where am I?" Vera asked, her voice wavering. She looked around the room as if seeing it for the first time.

Ashlyn stepped forward, her tone gentle. "You're in your home. My name is Ashlyn." She paused, giving Vera a moment to orient herself. "I'm here to help."

Vera's eyes darted to the window, then back to Ashlyn, wide and lost. "Ashlyn …" she repeated, the name unfamiliar on her lips. "Where is Andrew?" she asked. "He promised… He promised he would be back. Why hasn't he come back yet?"

Ashlyn's heart clenched. She opened her mouth to speak, but before she could find the words, Vera's figure blurred around the edges, like a painting smeared by an invisible hand. Her form grew faint, the lines of her once-sharp face dissolving into the dim light of the room.

Ashlyn let out a shaky breath, her pulse still racing. There was no way she could go back to bed—not after that. The air in the room felt too thick, too charged. Sleep would have to wait.

Ashlyn threw on her robe and grabbed her notebook, her mind restless. The encounter with Vera had rattled her more than she cared to admit, and there was no way she'd find any peace until she figured out what Vera wanted. She headed down to the library and start drafting a plan, something that might give her a sense of control over the chaos swirling around the house.

As she stepped into the kitchen to brew a pot of coffee, her breath hitched. For a split second, she thought she was seeing Vera again, sitting there like a shadow from another time, hunched over in the moonlit glow. But it wasn't Vera.

It was Delores—standing in the middle of the kitchen, dressed only in a robe and slippers, looking dazed.

"Delores!" Ashlyn exclaimed, her voice half-caught between surprise and concern. "What are you doing here? It's not even 4 AM!"

Delores blinked at her, eyes cloudy with confusion. She didn't seem to recognize where she was—or who Ashlyn was, for that matter. Then she sighed, a deep, weary sigh that seemed to collapse her entire frame. "Oh, my... I've done it again, haven't I?" Her voice was soft, filled with embarrassment. "I must have been sleepwalking."

Ashlyn frowned, her heart sinking a little. Delores looked so small, standing there in her thin robe, shivering in the kitchen light. "It's freezing out, and you're in a robe and slippers. Does John know where you are?"

"I'm... I'm not sure," Delores murmured, her cheeks flushing pink. "I didn't mean to—"

"It's alright," Ashlyn interrupted. "Let's get you warm, and I'll call him."

Even though the house was already heated, Ashlyn stoked the fire in the library. The flames crackled to life in the hearth as she grabbed a large woolen blanket from one of the upstairs rooms. She wrapped it around Delores, who seemed more subdued than usual, the faint tremor in her hands betraying her embarrassment.

With Delores settled, Ashlyn picked up the phone and dialed John. She winced as his groggy voice answered on the third ring. "I'm so sorry to wake you, John. Delores is here. She seems to have been sleepwalking."

There was a beat of silence on the other end, followed by a heavy sigh. "I'll be right over," John said, his voice full of concern.

Ashlyn hung up the phone and glanced over at Delores, who was gazing into the fire. Her eyes were distant, as if the flames might reveal an answer she couldn't quite grasp. She shifted in her chair, pulling the blanket tighter around her shoulders, as though it could shield her from more than just the chill.

After a long stretch of quiet, Delores spoke, her voice barely more than a whisper. "Things have been a bit... off lately."

Ashlyn tilted her head, staying quiet, letting Delores take her time.

"I haven't been sleeping right," Delores continued. "Not just tonight. It's been happening more and more. John... well, I think he's worried, but I've been brushing it off. You know me." She gave a weak chuckle, but there was no humor in it. "I keep telling myself it's nothing, that it's just a phase. Maybe stress. But I keep waking up in strange places... like tonight."

Ashlyn's heart tightened at the vulnerability in her voice. She leaned forward, resting her elbows on her knees. "Delores, it's okay to be scared," she breathed.

"But if things feel off, it's worth talking to someone. A doctor could help—maybe it's something small, something fixable. It doesn't have to be scary."

Delores looked at her, her eyes watery in the firelight, the flickering flames casting long shadows over her face. "I've been meaning to make an appointment," she admitted, her fingers twisting the edges of the blanket. "But... what if it's not something small? What if it's... something I can't come back from?"

Ashlyn reached out. "You don't have to face it alone. You've got John, and I'm here now. No matter what, knowing is better than wondering. You're stronger than you think."

Delores let out a breath she seemed to have been holding. "You're right. I know you're right. It's just... terrifying."

Ashlyn gave her hand a gentle squeeze. "I get it. But sometimes, facing the unknown is less terrifying than letting it live in your head. And if you need someone to go with you, I'm here."

Before Delores could respond, a knock echoed through the room.

"John doesn't need to knock to get into his own house," Ashlyn said with a smile.

"He's always been so polite. I sure love that about him."

Ashlyn made her way to the entrance and opened the door to find John standing there with a smile of relief.

"She's fine, and cozy in the library," Ashlyn reassured, stepping aside to let him in. "Just a little cold and a bit embarrassed. But we've got her warmed up now."

When they got to the library, John's eyes found Delores. "You gave me quite a scare, love," he said, his voice low but tender.

"I'm sorry, John," Delores whispered, "I didn't mean to."

"You never do," John replied, walking over to her and draping an arm around her shoulders.

Ashlyn gave them a soft smile, though uncertainty nagged at the back of her mind. She wasn't sure what was going on. The sleepwalking, the confusion—it felt like more than just a rough night. Still, she didn't want to jump to conclusions. All she knew was that a warm fire, and a blanket didn't seem like enough to fix whatever this was.

"It's early," Ashlyn said, eyeing the clock. "But since you're both here, how about some breakfast? I've got bread and cheese, and I think I saw a few eggs in the fridge."

"That would be lovely," Delores replied, her voice still a little shaky from the morning's events.

Delores attempted to help with breakfast, but Ashlyn waved her off with a grin. "You just relax and let me handle this."

They shared a simple breakfast of toast and eggs. The quiet clatter of forks against plates seemed to fill the silence, making the house feel almost normal again. Almost.

"So, I met Vera," Ashlyn said, breaking the stillness.

Delores glanced up. "I know it's only been one night, but... Vera's been quieter since you arrived. Maybe you're having a good effect on her."

Ashlyn paused, then shared the story of the suitcase and the eerie 3 AM incident. As she finished, John leaned forward, looking thoughtful.

"That's why you knew Dolly was here," he said, nodding as if a puzzle piece had just clicked into place.

"It's been quiet this last hour, though," Ashlyn started, but the words barely left her mouth when a loud crash echoed from upstairs.

"I might've spoken too soon!" she said, standing up just as the temperature in the room plummeted. Doors began slamming upstairs, one after another, in a rapid, rhythmic sequence that felt anything but random.

Ashlyn grinned, but her smile was more a mask for her alertness than amusement. "Let me go see what's going on."

At first, it seemed like Vera was having fun. A gust of wind swept through the house, even though the windows were all tightly shut. Holiday decorations fluttered—Christmas baubles rolled off the tree, lights flickered, and the wreath twisted until it was hanging upside down. Ashlyn watched the spectacle, feeling

Vera's presence. There was a mischievous energy to it, like a child testing boundaries.

Ashlyn caught sight of Vera's faint, flickering form near the tree. Silver bulbs clustered at the bottom, a lone red one dangled from a branch that couldn't hold its weight, and garlands were draped haphazardly across the tree like a child had gotten into the decorations and called it art.

"I think the star goes on top, Vera," Ashlyn called out, trying to be funny.

Vera paused, her head tilting, as if considering the suggestion. Then, with a grin, she flung a string of lights across the room, letting them sail through the air before they tangled themselves around a lamp. Ashlyn couldn't help but wince. *Okay, then.*

For a moment, the whole thing almost felt lighthearted, like Vera was just having a bit of fun, but as soon as Ashlyn relaxed, the surrounding air shifted.

Ashlyn took a deep breath, knowing this was the part where things could spiral if she wasn't careful. "I think you and I should talk," she said, keeping her voice steady but firm. "I know this is your home, and I respect that. But it's not just you here anymore. There has to be some compromise. Why are you angry?"

Vera's form solidified, her face twisting in a sort of amused disdain. "Angry?" she quipped. "Who says I'm angry?"

Ashlyn raised an eyebrow, glancing at the tangle of lights now draped over the couch. "Well, normal people don't throw lights around..."

From the doorway, John and Delores were watching, their expressions hovering somewhere between confusion and fascination. Ashlyn felt awkward. She was standing in the middle of their house, talking to someone only *she* could see, and they were witnessing the entire thing. *Great first impression.*

"Is she there?" John asked, his voice a little hesitant, like he wasn't sure if he really wanted to know the answer.

"Yep," Ashlyn replied, her tone a little too casual, given the circumstances. She shot them a quick smile, hoping they weren't regretting having her around. *I wonder what they think of me now,* she thought, picturing their conversation once she left. Something like, *'You remember that time we invited a psychic to stay, and she started chatting with our Christmas tree?'*

Vera, meanwhile, hovered by the tree, watching the exchange with mild amusement, as if she found Ashlyn's attempts at negotiating entertaining. The tension in the air remained, though, and Ashlyn knew she had to keep the situation from tipping into something worse.

"Look, Vera," Ashlyn said, turning back to the ghost. "I'm not here to make things harder for you. But we need to figure out how to live together. So, are we going to have a conversation about this, or are you just going to keep redecorating?"

Vera let out a small, almost mischievous laugh. "We'll see," she said, her form flickering as she hovered near the ornaments. Then she was gone.

Ashlyn let out a breath she hadn't realized she was holding. "Well, that could've gone worse," she muttered.

"Did it... work?" Delores asked from the doorway.

Ashlyn shrugged, eyeing the now-untangled string of lights. "She's thinking about it."

"This was a bad idea," Delores said, her voice shaky, her hands twisting together. She looked distraught, her eyes filled with concern that seemed to weigh her down. "You're such a sweet girl. What if Vera hurts you?"

Ashlyn forced a reassuring smile, even as her stomach knotted. "It's okay," she said, the words feeling sharper than she meant them to. "This is what I do—everything's going to be alright."

I hope I'm telling the truth. The thought whispered in the back of her mind, and she shoved it down. Delores was already teetering on the edge of worry, and the last thing Ashlyn needed was for her to see how rattled she felt. She could handle this. It wasn't her first haunted house, after all—but something about this place, about Vera, gnawed at her in a way she couldn't quite shake. Still, she had to keep her calm, if only for their sake.

Delores stood there looking so tired, fragile even, with John standing next to her, his hand resting on her arm. The older couple seemed out of their depth, and Ashlyn couldn't help but feel a pang of guilt.

"Now," Ashlyn said with a gentle but firm tone, "you go make that doctor's appointment, and I'm going to get down to work."

John and Delores exchanged a glance and gave her a reluctant smile. As they headed toward the door, John turned back and offered a kind but weary grin. "Remember, you're always welcome at our place, anytime you need a break from... well, the ghost."

Ashlyn smiled back, grateful for the offer, even though she had no intention of leaving Vera unsupervised. "Thank you. I'll keep that in mind."

Then, almost as an afterthought, she added, "Hey, I've got a colleague who doesn't live too far from here. Is it okay if I reach out to him for help? Maybe let him stay a night or two?"

Sebastian would get a kick out of this, and she'd feel safer knowing she wasn't alone.

John raised an eyebrow and then glanced at Delores, who gave him a playful swat on the arm.

"It's not like that!" Ashlyn blurted, her cheeks flushing. "We're just friends."

John chuckled, and Delores gave her a knowing smile. "Of course, dear," she said, trying not to giggle. "Whatever you need. We trust you."

As the door clicked shut behind them, the house fell into a thick, oppressive silence, leaving Ashlyn alone with her thoughts—and Vera. She stood in the empty kitchen, staring at the last wisps of steam curling from the coffeepot. Her nerves hummed in the quiet, and it felt as if the very walls absorbed Vera's presence.

Ashlyn exhaled, a shaky breath that did little to ease the cold grip of unease settling over her She'd promised Delores that everything would be fine, but the truth was, she didn't have a clue what Vera wanted—or worse, what she might do next.

Spirits could induce fear, sure, but not always out of malice. Sometimes, they just wanted to be left alone, their emotions tangled up with the living in ways that felt like an attack but were more akin to a plea. Yet... was that what this was? Did Vera just want peace, or was there something darker lurking behind those sudden bursts of rage?

There was a certain Jekyll-and-Hyde quality about Vera that Ashlyn couldn't ignore. One moment, she was quiet, almost pitiable in her isolation. The next, she was slamming doors and making her presence impossible to ignore. It made Ashlyn wonder: Was Vera angry because she was trapped here—or because she had no intention of leaving?

A loud thud echoed from upstairs, the sound that made your heart skip a beat even though you weren't sure why. It was followed by deliberate, heavy footsteps.

Ashlyn froze, her pulse quickening. Her body wanted to stay put, but she forced herself to move, turning toward the stairs even as her stomach twisted.

"Well," she muttered under her breath, her voice thin in the quiet, "here we go."

With a deep breath, Ashlyn placed one foot on the first step. The wood groaned beneath her, the creak unnervingly loud. She hesitated, listening. The footsteps above her stopped, too—pausing as if whatever was up there was waiting.

Her hand gripped the banister so tightly her knuckles ached, as though the thin rail could somehow protect her. Maybe Vera wasn't done with her redecorating spree. Or maybe—Vera was done with her.

Ashlyn's skin prickled as she took another step. The temperature seemed to plummet, the cold not just seeping in but clawing at her bones, biting in a way that wasn't playful this time. It felt angry. Dangerous.

Something was watching her.

Waiting.

"Please don't push me down the stairs," she whispered, as if saying it any louder would provoke the very thing she feared. Spirits could be unpredictable, their moods mercurial, especially when they were cornered. Or scared.

But was Vera scared—or something else?

"We don't want to banish you," Ashlyn said, her voice shaky as she tried to reassure Vera.

The whisper came, like an icy gust curling down the staircase, low and venomous.

"You won't take me alive…"

Ashlyn's breath caught in her throat. Her heart pounded, and for a moment, she stood frozen, her blood running cold. This wasn't just a restless spirit trying to make its presence known. This was fury. Real, unfiltered fury.

A door creaked open above her. The sound was slow and deliberate, as if to punctuate the ghost's words. A warning.

Ashlyn had promised Delores that everything would be alright. She had said it with a confidence that now felt naïve. As she stood there, on the brink of something far darker than she'd expected, she could only hope she'd be able to keep that promise.

CHAPTER FOUR

Have Yourself a Scary Little Christmas

Ashlyn's pulse hammered in her ears as she stared up the staircase. *Was that in the Lilac suite?* The door above had stopped creaking, leaving the house in silence.

You won't take me alive...

Her mind latched onto the whisper, puzzling over it. *What does that even mean?* The fear she'd felt in the moment had already evaporated, like morning mist under a rising sun. Dealing with Vera was like riding a rollercoaster: all fun and games on the climb, but just when you thought things might be safe, your stomach dropped, and suddenly everything was chaos.

She swallowed, her throat dry as dust. *Water. I should start carrying a water bottle. Wouldn't that make me look professional— "Ashlyn Alden, ghost whisperer and hydration enthusiast."* An icy breeze snaked down the stairs, lifting the hair on the back of her neck, as if someone—or something—was brushing by.

And then it was gone.

Ashlyn froze. *Wait... what?* Had Vera fled? Some spirits were shy—skittish things that hid in dark corners, or wanted to be left alone. But not Vera. No, her antics practically *begged* for attention. Most of the ghosts Ashlyn delt with either clung to their space like territorial barn cats or threw temper tantrums loud enough to rattle windows. But this... this was something else entirely. *Vera didn't seem like the type to just disappear.*

The whisper now replayed in her mind, softer this time. Less like a threat, more like a plea, shot through with raw, exhausted desperation.

Okay... so, what scares a ghost?

If Vera was worried about being taken, that begged two questions: where had she run to? And, more importantly—*what* was she running from?

Ashlyn's stomach tightened, and before she could think twice, she hurried up the stairs. "Vera? Vera, are you still here?" she called, her voice echoing into the stillness.

The hallway stretched out before her, with doorways leading into shadows. She peeked into one room, then another, half-expecting Vera to pop out, arms folded, wearing a scowl and ready to chastise her for being nosy.

Nothing.

"Where the hell did you go?" Ashlyn muttered, rubbing the back of her neck.

This was feeling less like an investigation and more like a round of hide-and-seek. *Not exactly my specialty...*

She moved from room to room, her boots making soft, deliberate thuds on the worn floorboards. "Vera, come on," she called, exasperation creeping into her voice. "I'm not here to hurt you... unless you're planning on the whole pushing-me-down-the-stairs thing again, in which case, I'd *really* like to renegotiate."

Still no response.

The house had been buzzing with Vera's presence earlier—now, it just felt... *abandoned.*

Ashlyn paused at the top of the stairs, chewing her lip. What was she missing? Her thoughts drifted back to what the Millers had told her. Their first encounter with Vera hadn't been in the house.

It had been in the garden.

Ashlyn groaned. *Of course. The garden. Why wouldn't the ghost hang out somewhere freezing and miserable?* The dead didn't care about seasonal blooms—or frostbite.

She gave the house one last look before heading toward the stairs. *Okay, garden it is. Vera, you better be out there. Because if I freeze to death searching for you, I swear I will come back and haunt you.*

She bundled up, pulling on her coat and scarf, the wool scratching at her neck as she braced herself for the bite of the chilly December afternoon.

The air outside was biting at her cheeks and coming out in small puffs as she stepped onto the porch. She followed the narrow path around the house. It was lined with stone that peeked through patches of snow and made its way toward what must have been a stunning garden in the warmer months.

Now, bare lilac bushes stood like skeletons along the edge of the garden beds, their branches tangled against the pale winter sky. Even in the winter, Ashlyn could almost smell the soft, heady sweetness of their blossoms, the memory of it lingering in the cold air.

To her left, a trellis stood, woven with the dormant tendrils of a climbing vine—honeysuckle, maybe. In the spring, she imagined it would be alive with tiny flowers, their sweet scent drawing bees and butterflies. For now, the vines were stiff, clinging to the wooden structure, refusing to let go and waiting for warmer days to return.

There was a strange stillness here. It was beautiful, yes, even in its barren state, but it felt... watched.

She pulled her coat tighter and followed the path deeper into the garden. The snow crunched beneath her boots, each step echoing in the otherwise quiet air.

"Vera?" she called out. "I know you're here. Or, at least, you've been here before."

The wind stirred, rattling the dry branches of the lilac bushes, but there was no answer.

As Ashlyn rounded the corner, she saw it—a small alcove nestled between two bare lilac bushes, sheltered by a trellis that looked like it might once have held a cascade of flowers. Two stone benches flanked the space, their surfaces frosted over. And there, on one of them, sat Vera, arms wrapped around herself like she was trying to hold her form together.

Ashlyn approached with caution, her footsteps slow and deliberate.

Vera's eyes lifted to meet hers, filled with a quiet, aching sadness that made Ashlyn's heart squeeze in her chest. The woman's form, once an angry, swirling mist of rage and grief, was now opaque. No longer the vengeful, flickering figure from before. Ashlyn could feel it—Vera had shifted. The fury had drained out of her like the last traces of a storm, leaving only a heavy, hollow silence in its wake.

Ashlyn hesitated, the cold gnawing at her fingers and biting at her nose, but she didn't turn away. "Vera?" she whispered, softer than she meant.

The ghost didn't move. She just sat there, her expression distant and lost.

Ashlyn slowly lowered herself onto the opposite bench, the stone so cold it seemed to seep right through her coat. "Hi," she said gently. "Do you remember me? I'm Ashlyn."

Vera blinked, her gaze flickering back to her, as if she had to reassemble herself piece by piece from wherever her thoughts had drifted. "Yes," Vera answered, her voice thin. She glanced around, as though expecting someone to appear from the shadows. "Where is Andrew? He was supposed to come back."

Ashlyn had learned not to lie to the spirits. It never went well. But there was such a raw, hopeless edge to Vera's voice, she didn't want to crush it. Bits and pieces of the past were spilling out now, offering Ashlyn a place to start.

"I don't know," she said, gently. "But I'll find out."

Vera looked so fragile, as if the slightest breeze might blow her away.

"Where did Andrew go?" Ashlyn asked, keeping her voice steady.

"I..." Vera's face clouded, her brow knitting together as if she were sifting through a long-buried thought. "I don't remember. But he promised to be back by Christmas." Her voice wavered. "He left Annie to take care of me."

"Annie?" Ashlyn repeated, filing the name away for later.

"My nurse," Vera said, her tone shifting to something softer, almost nostalgic. "And our serving girl. She was my helper."

Helper. That explained a lot. Vera must have been ill. The pieces of her story were falling into place, though there were still plenty of jagged edges left to fit together.

Ashlyn opened her mouth to ask another question, but the change came fast—too fast. Vera's expression twisted, going sharp and bitter like a sudden frost. The warmth drained from her voice as she shot to her feet with a startling abruptness, sending the frost-laden branches around her shivering in protest.

"She stole my money," Vera hissed, her voice low and venomous. "I *know* it."

And just like that, she was gone—vanishing into the shadows as if carried off by the wind, leaving only the faint rattle of dead leaves in her wake.

Ashlyn let out a slow breath, feeling the sudden stillness settle over the garden again. "Well," she muttered, brushing a stray lock of hair from her face. "That's a start."

She replayed Vera's words in her mind, sorting through what she knew so far. *Vera and Andrew Beaumont.* The Millers had confirmed that much. Andrew had gone away at some point, and Annie—the nurse, or perhaps a servant—had been left to care for Vera in his absence.

It was a promising lead. Household records might mention Annie, and if Ashlyn could track those down, she'd have something solid to work with. But this case was already shaping up to be more complicated than she'd expected, and Vera's erratic nature was becoming... concerning. This wasn't the kind of ghost she wanted to handle on her own—and the last thing she needed was to drag the Millers any deeper into it.

No. She needed backup. And she knew just the person for the job.

Sebastian LaRue.

Another medium, though *medium,* didn't quite capture the full extent of Sebastian's energy. Where Ashlyn preferred to keep her abilities discreet, Sebastian was about as subtle as a neon sign in the dead of night. Flashy, dramatic, occasionally ridiculous—and absolutely effective. Beneath all the theater, the man had genuine talent. And, more importantly, he *loved* what he did.

Ashlyn could already hear his voice in her head: *"Honey, spirits want attention, and I am here to give it to them."* She could see the exaggerated wink, the flair of a brightly patterned scarf, and the playful way he'd strike a pose, as if every conversation was a photoshoot waiting to happen.

His parents had been real flower-power types—free-spirited, metaphysical hippies who'd raised him to embrace the mystical without shame. While Ashlyn had spent her childhood keeping her abilities hidden like a guilty secret, Sebastian had thrown himself into his gift with open arms and unshakable confidence.

Yeah. He'd be perfect for this. And, as a bonus, they'd have some fun along the way.

Ashlyn pulled out her phone, already scrolling through her contacts.

***

Vera stayed unusually quiet for the rest of the day and well into the night. It was as if the haunting had sapped whatever energy she possessed, leaving her no choice but to drift off into some unseen corner to recoup. For once, Ashlyn had the place to herself. She should've felt relieved, but instead, it left her on edge. Quiet ghosts were rarely harmless; they were simply reloading.

By the time Sebastian arrived the next day, the stillness was pressing on Ashlyn's nerves. And, of course, Sebastian's entrance shattered it completely. He swept into the B&B with all the energy of a gale-force wind.

His knock was followed immediately by the door swinging open. He wore a long black coat, and a bright scarlet scarf trailed around his neck like a living thing. A fedora sat at an angle atop his silver hair.

"Darling, it's so good to see you!" Sebastian sang, throwing his arms wide as Ashlyn came to greet him at the door. He pulled her into a warm, exaggerated hug, somehow managing not to wrinkle a single seam of his meticulously tailored coat. "This place! Absolutely charming. So quaint, my dear—how positively adorable."

Ashlyn couldn't help but grin at the way he said "adorable," as though it were both a compliment and an insult.

"Come on, you big show-off," she said, shaking her head fondly. "Let me show you the rooms, and you can pick your favorite. And fair warning—Vera is our resident ghost. She's not shy, so don't be surprised if she introduces herself before dinner."

Sebastian arched one elegant brow, handing her his hat. "Oh, thank you, dear. I've always enjoyed a bit of ghostly company—far better than most living people, wouldn't you say?" He winked.

They climbed the narrow staircase; the wood creaking underfoot, and Ashlyn thought back to the first time she met Sebastian. He'd swept into her life the way he approached everything—dramatic and charming. She'd been young and lost, fumbling her way through the spirit world, and he'd taken her under his wing. Now, she had her own wings. He was a bit of a father figure, though she'd never tell him that.

As they reached the landing, a gust of cold air gusted down the hallway. Sebastian gave an exaggerated shiver. "Ooh, yes. There's something unresolved here," he murmured, eyes narrowing as he scanned the dim hallway. "Vera, you said? She's not just angry—she's confused. I can feel it. There's a lot of pain buried under all that flair."

Ashlyn nodded. It was what she'd been sensing, too—though Sebastian always seemed to put things into words before she could. It was one reason she respected him, despite his antics.

"Come on," she said. "Let's see if you like any of the rooms."

The first stop was the Violet Room, where soft purples and grays wrapped the space in a calm, understated elegance.

"My favorite, aside from my suite," Ashlyn said, opening the door with a gentle creak. The quilt on the bed was hand-stitched, the furniture simple but cozy. "It's peaceful."

Sebastian took one glance inside and let out a snort so exaggerated it bordered on theatrical. "Darling, you know I'm no shy violet." He didn't even bother to step inside, already sashaying down the hall with a flick of his scarf.

Ashlyn shook her head, grinning despite herself. Some things never changed.

Further down the hall, they stopped at two more doors: the Peony Room and the Iris Room. The little brass nameplates gleamed under the soft glow of the hallway sconces.

Sebastian paused, inspecting the nameplates as if weighing the merits of each flower with deadly seriousness.

"The Iris," he murmured. "A showstopper, no doubt—elegant, but bold. Refined, yet a little wild. They command attention. Like a performer wearing silk and feathers. Mmmm, tempting."

He trailed his fingers along the brass plate before turning to the Peony Room.

"But peonies," he continued, "oh, darling, peonies are lush drama queens. Unapologetically dramatic. They're divas—stealing the spotlight wherever they're planted. A peony doesn't just exist; it demands to be adored."

He turned the knob with a flourish; the door creaking open. Inside, the Peony Room was a riot of blush pinks and velvety reds, soft gold accents catching the light. The scent of rosewater drifted faintly from a porcelain dish on the dresser. It was the sort of room that expected admiration.

Sebastian stepped inside, surveyed the space with a satisfied smile, and spun on his heel to face Ashlyn.

"There's no question," he declared. "I am a peony."

Ashlyn leaned against the doorframe, arms crossed. "You realize you just compared yourself to a flower, right?"

Sebastian raised one hand, regal as a monarch granting an audience. "It is not mere comparison, my dear. It's destiny."

Ashlyn laughed, the tension easing from her shoulders. "You are impossible," she said, still chuckling as she turned to leave.

"And you," Sebastian called after her, "need to spend more time with the living. Honestly, Ashlyn, you can't let ghosts be your only social circle."

She glanced over her shoulder. "Why not? They're usually quieter."

Sebastian grinned. "Get ready, darling. I'll unpack, and then you and I are having a night on the town!"

His bright, uninhibited laughter echoed down the hall as she walked away, a sound that warmed the old house. It was good to have him here; she thought—not just for his insight, but for the way he pulled her back to the surface whenever she started drifting too far into the spirit realm.

When they left the B&B, Ashlyn drove toward town, stopping at a gas station to fill up and grab a few flyers from a rack by the door.

"Ooh! Ice skating at Opechee Park!" she squealed, pointing at a poster. "We should do that!"

Sebastian made a face, his nose crinkling as though she'd suggested ice fishing. "Darling, that sounds dreadful. Cold and physical? No, thank you. But," he added with a dramatic sigh, "I'm here for you, honey. Lead on."

While the pump clicked away, Ashlyn stepped up to the counter with a snack and the gas payment. The cashier, a young guy with long stringy hair, glanced up with all the enthusiasm of a bored sloth.

"So," Ashlyn asked, "what's fun to do around here?"

The kid blinked, then shrugged. "Uh... bars. Drinking. That kinda thing." He handed her the change without making eye contact.

Ashlyn gave him a thin-lipped smile. Sebastian had been sober for ten years, and taking him to a bar wasn't happening. She leaned on the counter. "Anything that doesn't involve drinking?"

The cashier blinked again, like the concept had never crossed his mind, then shrugged. "You could go to Funspot."

Ashlyn tilted her head. "Funspot?"

"Oh..." Sebastian drawled, already unimpressed. "That sounds... fun."

Ashlyn snorted, tucking the change into her coat pocket. "Come on, grumpy. First, we're going ice skating. Then we can check out this mysterious Funspot."

Sebastian sighed dramatically, but he followed her back to the car without complaint, scarf trailing like a bright banner of resignation.

They headed out as the afternoon sun cast a golden glow over the snow-covered town. Opechee Park looked like it had been plucked straight from a holiday postcard, with skaters gliding across the frozen cove and the distant sound of holiday music drifting from hidden speakers.

Sebastian, naturally, looked like he'd just stepped off the cover of a winter fashion catalog. His black coat swirled behind him as he adjusted his fedora, bright scarf tucked just so. They rented skates from a grumpy man in a parka, who gave them a suspicious glance.

"This," Sebastian muttered, eyeing the scuffed rental skates, "is going to end badly."

Ashlyn waggled her brows. "Confidence, darling." She said, mocking him. "Confidence and momentum—that's all skating is."

"Momentum is what worries me," he muttered, lacing up his boots.

Once on the ice, Ashlyn took to it with effortless grace, gliding in easy loops like she'd been born skating. Sebatian, on the other hand, looked more like a baby deer encountering ice for the first time. He wobbled, arms pinwheeling as she fought for balance.

"Use your legs!" Ashlyn called.

Sebastian shot her a mock glare. "Helpful advice. Truly."

She barked a laugh, the sound clear and unexpected. Despite the cold air stinging her cheeks, a warmth spread through her chest. Sebastian had a way of making everything seem lighter.

After a few more wobbly laps—and only one near-catastrophic fall—Sebastian finally gave up, shuffling to the edge of the rink and leaning on the wooden railing to catch his breath. Ashlyn glided up beside him, not the least bit winded, a triumphant grin on her face.

"See? This is what you need," he said, nudging her with his elbow. "More skating. Meanwhile, I'll be right here, on the sidelines, where it's safe and sensible."

Ashlyn snorted, her breath puffing in the cold air. "You? Sit on the sidelines? Not a chance."

Sebastian chuckled, adjusting his hat. "I'd make it look good, though." He gave her a sideways glance. "I'm telling you, darling. You've got to find more things like this. With the living."

They took a break at the concession stand by the rink, cupping their hands around steaming mugs of hot cocoa, piled high with whipped cream. Ashlyn sipped hers slowly, letting the warmth chase away the cold that had settled in her bones.

The arcade was a few miles away and a lucky discovery, even if most of the machines were older than Ashlyn. They took turns at an ancient pinball machine with chipped paint and flickering lights. Sebastian was a showoff, dramatically tilting the machine just enough to win without setting off the alarms. Ashlyn's attempts ended with flippers flailing uselessly and her score somewhere in the gutter.

"You are the absolute worst," she told him after he racked up his second high score.

Sebastian grinned. "I prefer to think of it as charmingly competitive. Again?"

He didn't wait for her answer, already plunking another quarter into the slot. The machine sat there, lifeless, as if it had given up on entertaining them.

Sebastian's brow furrowed. He gave the machine a stern look, then kicked it with the heel of his boot. "Give me back my money, you rusting monstrosity!"

A kid standing nearby—couldn't have been more than seventeen—strolled over, hands in the pockets of his oversized hoodie. Without a word, he gave the side of the machine a casual slap, followed by three sharp punches on the opposite panel. With a flicker and a groan, the machine whirred back to life, lights blinking as if it had never stopped working at all.

Sebastian's face lit up, his previous frustration forgotten. "Amazing! You're like the pinball whisperer!"

The kid just shrugged, heading back to another machine.

"Hey!" Sebastian called after him. "Do you work here?"

"Yeah," the boy replied. "I keep these babies running." He gave the pinball machine an affectionate pat, then glanced back at them—really looking this time. His eyes narrowed.

"Wait a minute," he said. "You guys are on that ghost hunting team, aren't you?"

Sebastian, sensing an opportunity, straightened up a little taller, as if sitting on a throne rather than a sticky arcade stool. Ashlyn winced. She'd done a few TV shows with Sebastian—and a few solo projects of her own—but she preferred to slip through crowds unnoticed. Not Sebastian. Sebastian thrived on recognition like a plant in sunlight.

"I am," Sebastian announced with a grin.

The boy's face brightened. "You doing a show around here?"

"Nothing for TV," Ashlyn answered before Sebastian could start making promises. "We're investigating the Lilac Grove B&B."

The kid's expression shifted, his brows lifting. "Nice. That's the place where they tried to take that lady to the asylum, right?"

Ashlyn blinked. That was new. Ghost stories did not come with neat little summaries, and sometimes locals had the missing pieces she didn't even know she needed.

"What do you know about the story?" she asked, trying to sound casual.

"Not much," the boy admitted with a shrug. "My girlfriend's more into that stuff. But I think, way back when they used to lock people up in asylums, they wanted to take this rich lady. She didn't wanna go, though. Put up a fight, from what I hear."

Ashlyn leaned forward. "Did they take her?"

The boy shrugged again, unfazed. "Not sure. Never heard what happened after that."

Ashlyn exchanged a quick glance with Sebastian. This wasn't just another ghost with unfinished business—this was a woman who might have fought tooth and nail against being erased. And now, decades later, that fight had somehow carried over into the spirit world.

Sebastian gave a brief hum, the corner of his mouth twitching in thought. "Well, that complicates things."

Ashlyn nodded, already piecing together what this new thread could mean.

As they walked back to the car, the night air crisp and starlit, Ashlyn realized just how much she'd needed this—a break from ghosts and mysteries, a reminder that life could still hold joy. Sebastian had always known that.

And the truth was, she didn't mind. It was good advice.

CHAPTER FIVE

Oh Haunted Night

Ashlyn had always felt invisible. Like the moment she left a room, everyone forgot she'd ever been there. She wondered if Vera felt the same way—trapped in a house full of people, yet unseen.

It had been that way for as long as she could remember, bouncing from one foster home to the next. Not the worst off—not by a long shot. Some of the other kids had horror stories, living in places that never should've been called homes. She'd been lucky, she supposed. The families she'd stayed with were mostly safe, if not warm. Sure, there were the ones who tried to pray the demons out of her, or worse, trotted her out in front of their friends like some parlor trick. But they didn't mean harm. Compared to what she'd seen others go through, well, that was nothing.

But the loneliness—that had been the hardest part. The way no one seemed to care about the little things, like what her favorite cereal was. Or that she hated mushrooms. None of them ever asked, just as no one had asked why Vera was throwing such violent tantrums around Christmas.

She stopped expecting people to notice after a while. Learned to blend in. Just another fixture in the house until it was time to leave. Always have a bag packed, waiting by the door. She knew she'd be forgotten soon enough. Even here, in Lilac

Grove, she hadn't fully unpacked (although Vera had helped by throwing her stuff everywhere.) It just made things easier.

She was grateful, she supposed. Really, she was. But sometimes she wondered what it would feel like if someone remembered her. Maybe that's why she kept doing the psychic shows. As "Ashlyn Alden, Psychic Medium," people at least recognized her. Or, more accurately, they knew her face. It was something.

Sebastian had been the closest thing she had to a friend, always reminding her, "Darling, you need to spend more time with the living." He meant well, but it wasn't that easy. The living were exhausting—judgmental, dismissive, too busy with their own lives to notice her. Ghosts, on the other hand, were honest in their misery. They didn't pretend to care. They didn't smile politely, only to forget her moments later.

That's why she kept going back to the dead, wasn't it? Misery loves company, and Ashlyn had found plenty of it among the dead. In some ways, they were the only ones who saw her—just as she saw them. While the rest of the world forgot she existed, Vera was proof that the forgotten would always find a way to make themselves known.

Still, every time Sebastian suggested mingling with the living, she couldn't help but think, *That's easy for you to say. They all love you.* People and spirits alike were drawn to him. He was the life of every room he entered, while Ashlyn felt more like wallpaper. She had spent her life slipping through the cracks, unseen and overlooked.

Today, Sebastian was back at the B&B, seeing if he could connect with Vera while Ashlyn did some research. She had put in a request with the Lake Winnipesaukee Historical Society and was headed there to meet with someone.

One thing she loved about New England was its history. There was never a shortage of historians eager to share what they knew. They got lost in old stories the way she got lost in the past herself. Most of them didn't care that her research wasn't for academic purposes. *History is history*, right?

Her father had been a history teacher before he passed. Sometimes, when she met with these historians, she liked to imagine him sitting there with them. Would he have been like them if he were still alive? Would he have that same glint in his eyes when he talked about some long-dead general or a historic building?

Maybe, in a way, this was why she did what she did—why she sought the dead, trying to pull their stories from the shadows and bring them into the light. Because, deep down, she wanted to believe that just as she remembered her father, someone—*anyone*—would remember her, too.

The Lake Winnipesaukee Historical Society was housed in a yellow building that looked more like a roadside motel than a museum. It was the kind of place you could drive by a dozen times and never notice, tucked away, content to be forgotten.

Ashlyn bypassed the main entrance and headed for a side door marked Historical Society. It creaked open, revealing a room cluttered with desks, old filing cabinets, and the musty smell of well-aged paper. A man with wild, white hair and wire-rimmed glasses looked up from a sea of documents and smiled.

"You must be Ashlyn Alden. My one o'clock," he said, standing up and offering a firm handshake.

"That's me," she replied, smiling back as she shook his hand.

"Glad you're here," he said, waving her toward a chair across from his paper-strewn desk. "Digging into these old records is always fun for me, but sharing what I find? That's the best part. Let's dive in."

Ashlyn settled into the chair as he shuffled through stacks of paper.

"I'm Henry Erickson, by the way—though most folks just call me Hank," he said. "Now, about Vera and Andrew Beaumont. Fascinating couple."

Ashlyn leaned in, eager to hear what he'd uncovered.

"Vera was born in 1827, Andrew in 1822. They married in 1868—late in life, especially for the time. Vera was already in her forties. No children."

Ashlyn's mind raced ahead. "Why do you think that is?"

"Well," Hank said, leaning back in his chair, "Vera inherited quite a fortune when her parents passed away in her early twenties. Back then, if she'd married younger, all of it would've gone straight to her husband, as was the custom. Could be she didn't want to hand over control of her money." He chuckled.

"Just speculation, of course, but it seems like Vera wasn't too keen on playing by society's rules."

Ashlyn smiled at that. She liked Vera more and more. "And what about Andrew?"

"Dr. Beaumont," Hank began, pulling out another sheet, "was a well-respected physician. He had strong ties to the New Hampshire State Hospital in Concord. In fact, both Andrew and Vera made a substantial donation to help start their nursing school."

"Tell me about the nursing school." She said.

"It was one of the first of its kind," Hank continued, "established in 1888 with free tuition, room, and board for students. The idea was revolutionary for the time—trained nurses instead of untrained caretakers. The Beaumonts funded part of it. But then their lives took a tragic turn."

Ashlyn leaned in, sensing the shift. "What happened?"

Hank's face turned solemn as he pulled out a faded newspaper clipping. "Andrew died in a train accident in December 1892. He was on a southbound train, heading to Concord. It collided head-on with a northbound freight train just above The Weirs."

Ashlyn felt a knot form in her stomach. She could picture it—the screech of brakes, the deafening crash, the metal tearing apart like paper. She'd seen enough death to know that the end could come suddenly, without mercy.

"The wreckage was catastrophic. Both engines were destroyed, and Andrew was one of several passengers killed. His body wasn't found right away—it was trapped in the debris. From the reports, it sounded like chaos. Two trains, head-on, right by the lake."

Ashlyn stared at the clipping, trying to process it. Andrew's violent death made everything about Vera's grief and anger so much clearer. "And Vera?" she asked. "What happened to her after that?"

Hank shuffled through more papers. "Vera died a year later, in 1893. The cause of death was listed as 'atrophy,' which back then meant she simply wasted away—stopped eating, stopped living. Grief can do that to people."

"Atrophy," Ashlyn echoed. "So, she just... gave up."

"That's what it sounds like. She didn't have anyone left—no children, no family. She likely couldn't find a reason to keep going after losing Andrew."

Ashlyn's mind raced, piecing together what she'd learned so far. Andrew's sudden, violent death. Vera's slow decline into nothingness. And then there was the mystery of Annie. Vera had seemed convinced that someone had taken her money, and that they had tried to take her away. "Did you find anything about an 'Annie' in your research?"

Hank frowned, flipping through his notes. "Nothing concrete about that name, but Vera and Andrew had hired help. Perhaps a maid, or even a nurse. She could've had a caretaker toward the end. The records are murky."

Ashlyn sat back, her thoughts swirling. There was more than Andrew's death and Vera's grief. Something else had happened. Vera had thought someone was after her money—someone she trusted. And if the inheritance had stayed with her after Andrew's death, why would she think it was stolen? And who would have tried to take her away?

"What would have happened to Vera after Andrew died?" Ashlyn asked. "Would she have lost her money?"

Hank shook his head. "No, it would have reverted to her. She was still a wealthy woman."

Ashlyn nodded. The money was still there. So why had Vera felt so threatened?

"Would anyone have tried to... take her away?" she asked.

Hank raised an eyebrow. "It's possible, though she would've had the means to afford care at home. But..."

Ashlyn leaned in. "But?"

Hank's expression darkened. "Do you know what the New Hampshire State Hospital was originally called?"

Ashlyn's heart skipped a beat. She knew exactly what it was called. What kind of ghost hunter would she be if she didn't? But she wanted to hear him say it without bias. "No, tell me."

"It was the New Hampshire Asylum for the Insane," he whispered. "Back in the 19th century, the hospital was one of the few places in the state that offered organized care for the mentally ill. But it wasn't... ideal. It started as a compassionate institution, but over time, like many of these asylums, it gained a darker reputation. Treatments were primitive—things like restraints, cold-water immersion, isolation. Those old buildings have seen more misery than most cemeteries."

"And like most asylums of the time, it wasn't a place you wanted to end up. If someone decided Vera was mentally unfit—grieving too hard, perhaps—they could have pushed to have her committed. And in those days, you didn't need much of an excuse to put someone away."

Ashlyn's blood ran cold. The image of Vera alone in that big house, scared and grieving, haunted her. What if Vera hadn't just been afraid of losing her money? What if she'd been afraid of being locked away, her life controlled by someone she didn't trust? Would this Annie have tried to put her away? It made little sense.

"Thank you, Hank," Ashlyn said, "This is more than I expected."

Hank leaned back in his chair. "It's always a pleasure to help someone who appreciates history. If you find anything else in your, uh, investigations,"—his tone danced around the word — "be sure to come back. I'd love to hear about it."

He handed her a thick manila folder. "Here, I made photocopies of all the important stuff for you. Easier to pin to your murder board that way."

"You're a gem." She smiled, though her thoughts were already slipping away, miles down the road toward the B&B. She stepped outside, and the cold air hit her like a slap. Who had Vera been running from?

When Ashlyn arrived back at the B&B, Sebastian was in the sitting room, fanning himself dramatically with a magazine.

"You okay?" she asked, raising an eyebrow.

"Darling, poor Vera needs a therapist," Sebastian replied with a sigh, his voice dripping with mock tragedy. "She's all hot and cold—one moment she's as angry as a hornet, the next she's frightened out of her wits. I swear, the woman could start a weather pattern with her mood swings. I hope you've found something useful."

Ashlyn smiled, her lips twitching at his flair. "I think I've got a lead."

She gave him a quick rundown of Andrew's death and the few details she'd dug up about their past, watching as his expressive eyebrows rose with interest.

"And what about you?" she asked, leaning forward. "Did you get anything out of her?"

"Well," Sebastian began, setting down his imaginary fan and sitting up straighter, "I had just poured myself a nice cup of tea and was getting ready to commune when she appeared, clear as day, and sat right down like we were old friends. Charming, really. She spoke about her husband, Andrew, and her nurse, Annie."

"That tracks," Ashlyn murmured, nodding.

"But when I asked why she's been acting like a banshee, she just... blinked at me, as if I'd asked her to solve a riddle." He shook his head. "She said she hadn't been feeling well, and that Andrew would be back soon to help sort things out. I pressed her on what he was supposed to help with, but she got all confused. Then, just like that—" he snapped his fingers, "—the mood flipped. She demanded to know what I was doing in *her* house, accused me of trying to take her away, and said Andrew wouldn't allow it. The next thing I know, she's throwing books off the shelves at me like they were frisbees."

Ashlyn winced. "Ouch. She's stronger than she looks."

Sebastian fanned himself again, with real gusto this time. "Darling, 'strong' doesn't quite cover it. If I hadn't ducked, I'd be buried under a pile of Dickens right now."

Ashlyn laughed, but her expression sobered. "I think we need to find Andrew."

"Yes," Sebastian agreed, casting a wary glance at the bookshelves. "Before she turns this cozy little place into a ghostly war zone."

Sebastian leaned back in his chair, eyes narrowing. "Andrew... everything seems to come back to him, doesn't it?"

Ashlyn nodded. "Vera's mood swings seem to center on him—whether he's coming back, or supposed to help her. But there's no sign of him."

"So, Andrew died in a train wreck..." Ashlyn glanced over at Sebastian, who was sprawled elegantly on the armchair. "I think it's time to go full-on investigation mode. If we do not find him here, we can check out that scene next."

Sebastian gave a quick nod, his sharp eyes flicking between the papers scattered on the coffee table. "Agreed." He leaned forward, all business now. "Do you have the details on the wreck?"

Ashlyn fumbled through the stack of papers Hank had given her. After a moment of shuffling, she pulled out a copy of the article, smoothing it out on the table between them. "Right here."

The headline stared back at them: *Local Tragedy: Train Derails Near Laconia, Beaumont Estate Mourns Loss.*

Ashlyn swallowed. The article felt too neat. Too tidy. Andrew was supposed to be the answer to Vera's haunting, but somehow... he still felt like a ghost himself.

They didn't rush. Ghosts didn't care what time of day it was, but the house felt different at night—quieter, with fewer distractions. It made focusing easier. The snow outside added an extra hush to the already still evening, muffling every sound until it felt like the world beyond Lilac Grove had disappeared.

Sebastian was lounging in the library, feet kicked up on a footstool as he fiddled with his spirit box, a faint crackle of static filling the room. "I know you hate this thing," he said, glancing at Ashlyn, who was seated nearby, her hands wrapped around a mug of tea.

Ashlyn shrugged. "I don't hate it. I just like hearing what ghosts have to say without the '80s radio station cutting in."

He flashed a grin, waggling the spirit box. "You're just jealous because it's dramatic."

"You're dramatic," she shot back, unable to resist a smirk. She'd already laid out her own equipment—an EMF meter, pendulum, digital recorder, and a stack of crystals for good measure. She liked having all the bases covered.

Outside the window, snowflakes fell in a slow, steady drift. The entire scene felt almost too peaceful, considering they were about to wander around looking for dead people.

"I think it's time," Ashlyn said after a while, setting down her mug and stretching.

Sebastian hopped up with the enthusiasm of someone who had been waiting to put on a show. "Let's gather our toys and see who's home."

Vera was nearby, even if she wasn't visible. She'd been trailing them for the past hour, silent but curious, as if trying to figure out what they were up to. Ashlyn had felt her presence—just a light tug on the edges of her awareness.

"She's watching us again," Ashlyn murmured.

"Of course she is." Sebastian didn't even glance over his shoulder. "She's probably admiring my scarf." He adjusted the bright scarlet fabric draped around his neck with a flourish. "Good taste, Vera, if I do say so myself."

They started in the Lilac Suite. Ashlyn always liked to begin methodically, moving from room to room with careful steps, like peeling away layers of the house's energy.

Ashlyn stood by the bed, running her hand along the faded quilt. "Do you think this was their bedroom?"

Sebastian was about to respond when a soft voice, clear and disembodied, answered: "Yes."

Both of them froze, and then Sebastian, never one to miss a beat, turned toward the air as if Vera herself had appeared in front of him. "Thank you, darling. Always nice to have confirmation."

If this *was* Vera and Andrew's bedroom, then it made sense why Vera hovered here so often.

They swept the room, moving from corner to corner. No sign of Andrew. Vera followed them, flitting from spot to spot, watching with a sort of detached curiosity, as if the investigation was a show and she was waiting for the big reveal.

They moved on to the kitchen. Sebastian, ever dramatic, cranked the spirit box a little higher, the static louder now as it scanned the frequencies. The occasional burst of a distant voice broke through—random, disconnected words that meant nothing.

"Well," Ashlyn said, "no signs of anyone else. Just Vera."

It stayed that way as they moved from room to room. The library, with its towering bookshelves and fireplace, felt like it should have held something—some hidden energy. But the only presence was Vera, trailing after them with the quiet persistence of someone waiting for them to figure out something they hadn't quite grasped yet.

"Nothing," Sebastian said, his voice edging toward disappointment as they passed through the sitting room. The rocking chair by the window sat still. Not even a flicker of energy from the EMF meter.

"I'm thinking Andrew's playing hard to get," Sebastian quipped.

It wasn't until they reached the door to the attic that everything changed. Vera, who had been floating nearby like a curious bystander, shifted. Her form solidified, and a sharp chill swept through the air as she moved in front of the door.

Her expression hardened, her eyes narrowing with a fierceness Ashlyn hadn't seen all night.

"It's mine!" she hissed, her voice no longer soft or curious, but sharp, possessive.

Ashlyn felt a prickle of unease at the intensity. "Vera, it's just the attic. We're not taking anything from you."

"She doesn't want us up there." Sebastien stated the obvious.

Vera's figure flickered, her translucent form twisting and distorting as though she were burning through every shred of energy to keep them from opening the attic door.

Then the chaos began.

A door down the hall slammed shut, rattling the walls. Another followed, and then another, as if Vera's rage was shaking the very bones of the house. The lights flickered overhead, dimming and brightening in rapid succession. The spirit box in Sebastian's hand erupted into a burst of static, screeching as if the radio frequencies had come alive, feeding on the raw energy pouring from Vera.

"Vera, stop!" Ashlyn called out. But Vera wasn't listening.

The attic door shook in its frame, rattling violently as if it were going to explode. Every inch of the house seemed to vibrate with Vera's frenzied energy.

And then, just as suddenly as it started, everything stopped. The doors ceased their slamming, the lights steadied, and the spirit box fell silent.

Ashlyn exhaled, the tension in her body refusing to release. "She did this before,. It's like she has to recharge after she throws a fit."

Sebastian gave her a sidelong glance, his hand already reaching for the doorknob. "Well, now that she's taken a little break... shall we?"

Ashlyn grinned. "Naturally."

With Vera's anger still fresh in their minds, they made their way upstairs. The house creaked around them, but Vera stayed absent. No gust of cold air, no disembodied voice protesting their ascent.

It was unsettling to have her gone, especially now that they were inching toward what seemed like the heart of the mystery.

The attic door creaked open with little resistance, and the dusty air hit them like a wall. Ashlyn half-expected some other spirit to be there—after all, attics were infamous for hauntings—but there was nothing. No lingering ghosts, no flickers of movement in the shadows. Just a stillness that felt more like neglect than a supernatural presence.

The attic stretched out before them, its slanted roof cutting the space into uneven angles. Dusty beams crisscrossed above, and cobwebs hung in the corners like forgotten curtains. Old trunks and furniture covered with white sheets sat haphazardly. In the center, a single window let in a sliver of moonlight, casting pale shadows across the floorboards.

"Attics like this are supposed to be crawling with ghosts," Sebastian muttered, glancing around. "It feels... underwhelming."

Ashlyn nodded, frowning. "Yeah, this is almost disappointing."

They searched the room, moving past piles of moth-eaten drapes and crates filled with who-knew-what. Every corner was checked, but the further they went, the more anticlimactic it felt. No eerie voices, no cold spots. If Vera was hiding something, she wasn't here to stop them from finding it.

It wasn't until they reached the far end of the attic, behind an old armoire, that Ashlyn spotted something. "Sebastian," she called, nudging a crate aside with her foot. There, nestled between the armoire and a stack of old ledgers, was a small metal box.

"Well, well," Sebastian said, crouching down to inspect it. "What do we have here?"

The box was old but solid, its lock covered in a thin layer of grime. Ashlyn knelt beside him, running her hand over the surface. "Looks like it's from the right period. Could this be what Vera was so protective of?"

Sebastian didn't answer right away. He pulled a small lock-picking kit from his pocket—because of course he had one—and got to work. The lock was resistant at first, but within moments, there was a soft click, and the lid popped open with a faint creak.

Inside the box was a single brass key that looked as though it would fit this very lock. It was old-fashioned, with a thick, ornate bow and a long shaft.

Ashlyn picked it up, holding it between her fingers, and tried it without luck. "It doesn't fit this one."

Sebastian's eyebrows arched. "Curious," he said, leaning in to inspect the key. "Why would someone hide a key inside this box?"

Ashlyn frowned, the pieces of the puzzle swirling in her mind. She turned the key over in her hand. "So Vera was worried about her money. But if someone stole it, why was a key left behind? What does it even open?"

Sebastian stood, his usual dramatic flair tempered by genuine curiosity. "That," he said, dusting off his hands, "is what we need to find out. But whatever it is, it's not here."

They had uncovered a clue, but it only raised more questions. What had happened to Vera's money? Did she even have money? Who had taken it? And why had she been so protective of a key that didn't even fit the box it hid in?

Whatever the answer, this mystery was far from over.

CHAPTER SIX

Wreck the Halls

It had been a few days since Ashlyn had touched base with the Millers, though she'd meant to check in sooner. Delores had called the night before, inviting her for coffee in the morning. A nice surprise, though Ashlyn sensed the meeting wasn't entirely casual.

John had been called away to a board meeting—something about Granite State Precision Manufacturing needing his attention—which left just her and Delores. So much for retirement. Despite how in sync the couple seemed, it didn't take a psychic to know Delores had something on her mind.

That suited Ashlyn just fine. Something had been off about Delores that night she'd wandered in half-asleep, and it gnawed at the back of Ashlyn's mind. She hadn't heard how the doctor's visit had gone, and a quiet coffee seemed like the perfect opportunity to check in without pushing too hard.

The past couple of days had been a blur of frustration, with her and Sebastian searching high and low for the box the mysterious key was supposed to open. Despite their best efforts, they'd had no luck. Tonight, the plan was to investigate the train wreck in the hope that Andrew's spirit might finally show himself. Maybe he would have some answers about the key or, at the very least, point them in the right direction. She wasn't holding her breath.

Meanwhile, Vera had been... well, Vera. Running hot and cold, as was her fashion. One moment she'd be calm and almost sweet, the next, she'd be knocking ornaments off the Christmas tree like a disgruntled cat. Sebastian had taken to referring to her as "a doll" when she was in a good mood, followed quickly by, "... when she wants to be." Ashlyn had to agree. There were times when Vera's presence was almost pleasant, like having a stern but protective grandmother hovering nearby. And then there were the tantrums.

They'd both learned the hard way to keep the Christmas lights—and the tree—unplugged. After the third near-miss with a fire, Ashlyn had made it a firm rule. Vera had a thing about the decorations, and while Ashlyn couldn't fault her for being particular, she also wasn't keen on burning the place down over some tangled tinsel.

This morning, as sunlight peeked through the edges of her curtains, Ashlyn stirred, blinking against the winter glow. The air had that crisp, clean bite that only came with fresh snow, and she could feel the cold radiating from the windows. Outside, the world gleamed, and she winced at the thought of stepping out without sunglasses.

Still, it was a beautiful day, and Ashlyn bundled up, bracing herself against the cold as she made the short walk to the Millers' house. Her boots crunched through the fresh powder, the sound satisfying in the morning quiet. The air smelled sharp and clean, tinged with pine, while the world felt muffled, its usual sounds dulled by the blanket of white covering everything in sight.

"It's so good to see you, sweetie!" Delores greeted Ashlyn at the door with a warm hug, her usual energy a bit dimmer today. "How are things going with Vera?"

"Slow," Ashlyn admitted, stepping inside. "But we've got some great leads."

They moved into the dining room, where the scent of fresh coffee greeted them. It was already set out on the table, steam rising from the mugs in the cool air. It felt welcoming, but something was off. Delores was usually a whirlwind of energy, but today, she seemed more subdued.

"Cream and sugar?" Delores asked, her hand hovering over the tray.

"Just cream, thanks." Ashlyn smiled, trying to lift the mood as she settled into her seat. She recapped their recent discoveries for Delores—how the train wreck had killed Andrew, their investigation of the key, the Beaumont connection to the Asylum, and Vera's atrophy death. Each piece of the puzzle seemed to lead them in a new, darker direction, but Ashlyn was used to that by now.

"Poor woman," Delores sighed, her eyes lingering on her coffee cup like it held answers.

Ashlyn studied her for a moment. "You okay?" she asked. It wasn't like Delores to seem so distant.

Delores took a deep breath. "Just feeling my mortality is all."

There was a long pause, the words hanging between them like the snow outside—cold, inevitable.

"Speaking of that," Ashlyn ventured, "did you ever make it to the doctor?"

Delores hesitated, her expression shifting from embarrassed to something more vulnerable. "I have an appointment today, but I'm thinking of canceling. John got called away, and... I've been feeling much better."

The way Delores' voice lifted at the end made it clear she was trying to convince herself more than anyone else. Ashlyn could see through it—the same way she could sense spirits. She knew when someone was skirting around the truth.

Delores frowned, her honesty breaking through. "John says he thinks I'm fine, but I think we're both just skirting around our fear. What if it's bad news?"

Ashlyn's heart tightened. She understood that fear—how it gnawed at you, made you want to turn away from answers that might hurt. But she also knew how much worse it could be to live in the dark. "What if it's not?" she countered, leaning forward. "What if it's something you can deal with?"

Delores just shrugged, her gaze dropping back to her cup, the uncertainty on her face.

"It's better to know," Ashlyn said. She waited for Delores to meet her eyes. "Tell you what. What if I take you? You shouldn't have to do this alone."

Delores blinked. "You'd do that for me?"

"Of course," Ashlyn replied. "You don't have to face it by yourself."

Delores brightened, a bit of her usual spark returning. "Thank you, sweetie. Really, I don't know what I'd do without you."

Ashlyn gave her a warm smile. "What time's your appointment?"

"11:30," Delores answered.

"Perfect," Ashlyn said, taking a sip of her coffee. "We'll leave from here. It's going to be alright."

Delores drove them to the clinic on Main Street, a small-town medical office shared by several doctors. The place had the usual hum of a busy practice, but the wait wasn't as long as Ashlyn had dreaded. After the nurse took Delores's vitals and asked about her symptoms, they sat together in the quiet exam room.

Delores looked small, folded into herself like a wilted flower, her usual bright energy dimmed by fear. Ashlyn felt a pang of sympathy and filled the silence with something light.

"So," she said, her voice cheerful, "you want to hear about my favorite ghost encounters?"

Delores's eyes brightened. "I suppose I could use the distraction."

"My favorites are the cases where I help not just the people, but the spirits, too," Ashlyn continued, leaning back in her chair. "It's extra special when I reunite lost loves."

"That sounds beautiful." Delores smiled. "What was your last case?"

"Old theater in Boston," Ashlyn said. "Love, murder, mystery—the whole package. And a happy ending, believe it or not!" She winked, earning a soft chuckle from Delores.

Before they could dive into more stories, there was a gentle knock on the door, and the doctor entered. He was an older man, his hair snow-white, with a face that seemed to have been shaped by smiles.

"Dolly! How are we today?" he greeted Delores.

Delores straightened. "Dr. Albee has been treating me since I was in my twenties!" she told Ashlyn, her voice fond.

The doctor extended his hand to Ashlyn, who shook it. "And who might you be?" he asked.

"Ashlyn Alden," she replied.

"She's a friend," Delores added. "John had work, something about the share buyouts, and I didn't want to come alone."

"Still working?" Dr. Albee raised an amused eyebrow. "I thought he was supposed to be retired!"

"I know, right?" Delores chuckled. "He's on the board now—keeps him busy and feeling important."

Dr. Albee gave a knowing nod. "I've seen that happen before." He turned his attention back to Delores. "And how's the B&B these days?"

"Oh, it's marvelous!" Delores beamed. But when her gaze flickered to Ashlyn, she hesitated. "Ashlyn's here, to uh, help us out..." She trailed off, sharing the whole ghost situation. Not everyone believed in spirits, and Ashlyn knew when to keep her mouth shut.

"Well, that's great!" Dr. Albee said, unaware of the unspoken detail. He sat down on the rolling stool and leaned forward. "So, what's going on? What brings you in today?"

"Well, I've been having some memory problems lately," Delores began, her voice wavering. She cleared her throat and continued, "Insomnia. And, um... I've been sleepwalking. When I manage to sleep, that is. I ended up in the B&B the other night, in my robe and slippers."

Dr. Albee frowned. "That must have been frightening for you."

"Thankfully, Ashlyn was there," Delores said. "She called John. He hasn't been sleeping much either because of me."

Ashlyn shifted in her seat, feeling a twinge of discomfort. She didn't know Delores well, but she felt a protective urge toward her. "You don't need to feel bad about that, Delores," she offered. "John loves you. He just wants you to be okay."

Delores nodded, but there was sadness in her eyes that made Ashlyn's heart ache. The woman sitting next to her was so different from the one she'd met only days ago—the one who had shown off the B&B's holiday decorations and talked about lilacs like they were old friends. Now she looked fragile, like her own mind was becoming too much to carry.

Dr. Albee had begun his examination, moving through the usual steps with quiet professionalism. He asked a series of questions, the kind that Ashlyn knew assessed Delores's memory, cognitive function, and overall health.

"Have you had any trouble remembering recent events, Delores?" he asked as he listened to her heart, his tone calm and reassuring.

"Sometimes," she admitted. "I'll forget where I put something or what I was going to do next. But isn't that normal?" She forced a nervous laugh. "I mean, I'm not as young as I used to be."

Ashlyn's mind wandered as Delores answered more questions. She was starting to wonder if Vera might have had similar issues. The way she lashed out, her sudden mood swings, and her erratic behavior... could it be that Vera had been suffering from dementia when she was alive? Could that explain her confusion, her anger? Ashlyn tucked the thought away for later.

Dr. Albee straightened up, pulling his stool closer to where Delores sat. "Here's my concern," he said. "Your symptoms... they're pointing toward the early stages of dementia. But before we go down that road, I'd like to rule out other things—like a vitamin deficiency or thyroid issues. We will get you a blood draw. We'll also make you an appointment to visit a specialist to get a clearer picture."

He paused, glancing at Ashlyn. "John should really be there for that appointment," he added, with a small apologetic smile. "No offense, Ashlyn."

Delores swallowed hard. "What does this mean, Doctor? Am I... am I going to forget who I am?"

Ashlyn's heart clenched. It was such a raw, terrifying question—one that Ashlyn didn't have an answer to, and one she wished no one ever had to ask.

Dr. Albee leaned forward, his expression gentle but serious. "It's a good thing you came in as soon as you started noticing changes, Delores. If this is dementia, catching it early is important. It gives us time to educate you about treatment options and coping strategies. There are medications that can slow the progression, and we can help you manage the symptoms so that you can maintain your quality of life for as long as possible."

Delores sat for a moment, her hands clasped in her lap. "Why me?" she whispered, her voice trembling. "Could I have done something better?"

Ashlyn felt a pang of helplessness. She wished she had something comforting to say, but what could anyone say in the face of something like this? She reached out and squeezed Delores's hand, hoping the gesture would be enough to let her know she wasn't alone.

"It happens to the best of us," Dr. Albee said. "As we get older, these things can creep up on us. But you're not alone in this, Delores. We're going to work together to figure out what's going on, and you'll have your family—and your friends—to help you along the way."

Delores nodded, though Ashlyn could see the unshed tears glistening in her eyes. She wanted to ask more, but she didn't know how to push without making things worse.

Then Ashlyn asked, "Doctor, can dementia... sometimes make people... angry? Like, confused about where they are and... lash out at others?"

Dr. Albee looked at her with a curious expression, his eyebrows raising. "It can," he replied. "In the early stages, some people do experience mood swings, agitation, or even aggression. They might get confused about their surroundings or misinterpret situations. Has Dolly shown these symptoms?"

"Oh no," Ashlyn answered and hesitated before continuing. She couldn't very well explain that she was wondering if a ghost might have had dementia. "I've just... seen it before," she said vaguely. "Someone close to me."

Dr. Albee nodded, satisfied with the explanation. "Yes, it's not uncommon. But again, we don't know for sure what's going on yet. Let's focus on getting Delores the tests she needs and take it one step at a time."

Ashlyn forced a smile, but inside, her brain was spinning. If Vera had dementia when she died... if that confusion and anger had carried over into death... what would it take to help her find peace? And what did that mean for Delores, if she was starting down a similar path? The ride home was silent. Delores looked lost in her own personal hell, and Ashlyn could only imagine the whirlwind of thoughts running through her mind. The woman looked like she was trying to hold the world together with sheer willpower, and it was unraveling right in front of her.

When they arrived at the bed-and-breakfast, they entered together. Ashlyn braced herself the moment they stepped inside.

The sitting room was a disaster zone.

It looked like Vera had hosted a brawl with the Christmas decorations. The tree was half-toppled, lights strewn across the room like discarded party streamers. Broken ornaments littered the floor, glinting in the afternoon light like shards of misplaced hope. Dirt from an overturned poinsettia plant was scattered across the rug, mingling with torn garlands, and picture frames—once hanging neatly on the walls—now lay shattered in a heap. It was as if the room itself had given up.

Sebastian sat in the middle of the chaos, looking absolutely done. He had a rag in one hand and a dustpan in the other. His normally impeccable appearance was disheveled—hair tousled and his scarf askew.

"Darling, I am a wreck," he declared dramatically, as if he were the one suffering the most. "Our lovely Vera was on the warpath again. First, she accused Annie of stealing her money, then Andrew, and—brace yourself—she even blamed you, sweetie," he said, looking at Ashlyn with wide eyes.

Then, spotting Delores, Sebastian shot up from the floor, smoothing his hair and offering his hand. "Oh, my stars, I'm so sorry. Sebastian LaRue, charmed to meet you."

Delores blinked, as though only now registering the world around her. She didn't take his hand. Her gaze swept over the chaos, and her face crumpled.

"Oh my..." Her voice broke as she sighed. "This... this is bad."

Without another word, she made a beeline to the small closet in the corner and retrieved a broom. Her hands shook as she started sweeping up the shattered frames, the delicate glass crunching under the bristles. She moved mechanically, as if cleaning would somehow fix it all—the mess, the haunting, the fear that was building inside her.

Ashlyn watched her heart sinking. The dam was breaking. Delores crouched to gather the dirt from the destroyed poinsettia, tears welling in her eyes, her breath coming out in short, jagged bursts.

"It's too much," she whispered, her voice trembling. "It's all too much!"

Sebastian, sensing the breakdown, stepped in. "Darling," he said softly, prying the broom from her hands with a gentle tug. "Let us take care of this. Ashlyn, please, make this poor woman some tea before she keels over."

Ashlyn nodded, ushering the shell-shocked Delores into the kitchen, her arm a steady presence at her back.

Once they were alone, Ashlyn guided her into a chair, boiling water for the tea. "Has it ever been this bad before?" she asked.

Delores had her head in her hands, her fingers trembling. "It's not just this," she whispered, her voice barely holding together. "It's... it's me. I'll never be able to keep up with this place if I have... D..." She choked on the word, unable to finish. "Dementia," her eyes filled with a raw, quiet terror. "We never should have bought this place. What was I thinking?"

"Honey, we don't know anything for sure yet. Don't give up so fast," she said, keeping her tone light. "Seb and I are going to help Vera, and worst-case scenario, you hire someone to help you keep up with the inn. You don't have to do it all alone."

Delores didn't answer. Her gaze had drifted to something on the table, her attention caught by a small object.

It was the lockbox. Beside it sat the key.

"Oh, what a beautiful key!" she said as she picked it up. "It's... it's a lilac!" Her fingers traced the delicate engraving, the lilac motif wrapping around the handle.

Ashlyn blinked, looking at the key as if seeing it for the first time. How had she not noticed that before? She picked it up, feeling its cool weight in her palm, the strange pull of something old and unsolved.

"Could this be for something in the garden?" she murmured, turning the key over in her hand. For the first time that day, a spark of hope flickered in the gloom.

"Sebastian!" Ashlyn called, "Come here!"

The kettle was boiling, steam curling up into the kitchen air. She poured three cups of chamomile tea, the soothing scent filling the room as Sebastian joined them at the table.

"Look at this key," she said, sliding a cup toward him. "What do you see?"

Delores handed him the key, now looking more alert, a little embarrassed. The emotional storm from earlier had passed, but there was still a flicker of uncertainty in her eyes.

"I'm so sorry," she gushed, her voice regaining its usual warmth. "I'm not usually like that. As you already know, I'm Delores." She smiled, soft but genuine. "Thank you so much for helping Ashlyn. She's a doll, and so are you."

Sebastian placed a hand on his chest. "Oh, darling, thank you. The pleasure is all mine." He examined the key with a raised brow, turning it over in his fingers. "Hmmm, it is a lovely old key," he said, giving a slight shrug. "Got some strong vibes coming off it."

Ashlyn leaned in, watching his expression. "If I tell you it's a flower, what do you see?"

Sebastian narrowed his eyes, squinting at the key as if it might bloom in his hands. Then his eyes went wide. "Oooooh!"

"What's the big deal?" Delores asked, curiosity sparking in her voice.

"I think you found a clue!" Ashlyn said with a grin. She pointed to the delicate lilac motif etched into the metal. "This would make a perfect garden key."

"But the garden doesn't have any locks," Delores said, tilting her head.

"Not that we know of," Sebastian chimed in, his voice conspiratorial.

"I didn't mention the key this morning," Ashlyn continued, her voice dropping into a hush, "because we got a little distracted. But Seb and I found it up in the attic. It was locked in a strongbox. And trust me—Vera really didn't want us to find it. She's been pretty touchy ever since, which explains today's... um... episode." She gestured toward the chaotic mess in the next room. "I think it's important. Maybe it has something to do with the money she thinks was stolen."

Delores frowned, her forehead creasing. "Do you think her money is in the garden? Like buried treasure?"

Ashlyn laughed. "I doubt we need to start digging through the frozen ground with shovels. But maybe, if we can figure out what this key unlocks, we can help Vera settle down." She paused, thoughtful. "Kind of like how we can't treat a problem until we know what it is. Once there's a diagnosis, there's a way forward—even if it's not a cure."

Sebastian nodded, sipping his tea with a flourish. "Ah, like therapy for spirits. We just need to find the root of her troubles."

Their conversation was interrupted by a knock at the door. A familiar voice called out, "You here, Dolly?"

"In the kitchen!" Delores called back.

John stepped in, his face creased with concern. "I saw your car and thought you might be here..." His gaze shifted to Delores, and his expression softened. "Have you been crying?"

Delores blinked. Reality seemed to crash back over her, and she stood up, smoothing her hands over her clothes. "Let's go home," she said quietly. "We've got some things to talk about."

John looked from her to Ashlyn, his brow furrowed with confusion. "What's going on?" he asked.

Ashlyn waved them off with a reassuring smile. "Don't worry, we'll catch up later. Seb and I are doing an investigation tonight—at the site of the train wreck. We're hoping to find Andrew."

"Train wreck?" John echoed, glancing back at Delores.

"I'll explain everything," Delores said, steering him toward the door. "Let's go."

As they left, Ashlyn's eyes lingered on the key, still resting on the table, a quiet mystery waiting to be unlocked.

Chapter Seven

We Wish You a Scary Christmas

They had planned their investigation of the train wreck carefully. Tonight was the Cold Moon—the December full moon that lingered longer than others. Ashlyn knew that lunar phases, especially during the changing seasons, often heightened paranormal activity. With the solstice just around the corner, this felt like the perfect night to make a connection.

Sebastian drove, squinting at the dark road ahead. Ashlyn navigated as they wound through a sleepy neighborhood.

"Take the next right on Watson," Ashlyn instructed, glancing at the map on her phone.

He turned, focused on the road ahead.

"Now, another right onto Scenic. Look for house number 215," she added as Sebastian slowed. "Here. Park in front of this one. I've arranged with the owners to let us cut through their backyard. There's a path that leads down to the old tracks by the lake."

The car rolled to a stop in front of a cozy little house. A wreath hung on the front door, and the glow of Christmas lights lined the windows. Ashlyn imagined the family inside fast asleep, probably with visions of sugarplums dancing on their heads. At least the owners were kind enough to let them cut through their yard.

Moonlight bathed the snow in a silvery glow, transforming the world into a quiet, glittering wonderland. As they made their way through the yard, the soft light made their flashlights seem almost unnecessary, though Ashlyn kept hers on—just in case something jumped out from the shadows. With so much paranormal energy in the air, you could never be too careful.

The path was narrow and cold, and their boots crunched through the snow as they navigated around branches that clawed at their sleeves. Ashlyn could feel the familiar excitement bubbling in her chest, even if her toes were losing feeling.

Sebastian, however, was not bubbling. "Are we going to get stuck on these tracks and, I don't know, die horribly? Just checking."

Before Ashlyn could answer, a distant whistle cut through the night air. Low and mournful, it sent a shiver down her spine.

"These tracks are mostly for the scenic line now," she said. "Nothing runs at night."

"Except for the ghost trains," Sebastian muttered.

They reached the tracks, a pair of long, frost-covered lines stretching out under the night sky. Sebastian kept a wide berth from them, eyeing the metal rails like they might spring to life and wrap around his ankles. Ashlyn had to admit, with the cold and the moonlight and that whistle still echoing in her head, she wasn't feeling too confident about the tracks either.

"Let's get across and head for the pier," she said. "We'll set up there."

The pier jutted out over the frozen lake. Every step they took made the wood groan beneath their boots, as if the structure itself was debating how much longer it wanted to hold up. At the end, they set their gear.

The frozen lake stretched out in front of them, and behind them, the faint outline of the woods swallowed the world in shadow. Somewhere out there, over a hundred years ago, a train had derailed on a night like this.

"The passenger car is supposedly still down there," Ashlyn pointed out toward the darkness. "It's a historical scuba spot now."

"Is that even a thing?"

"I don't know," she laughed. "I found it mentioned on a scuba forum while researching. Just trying to lighten the mood."

Sebastian set down a battery-powered lantern and began unpacking their supplies. He pulled out a manila folder and opened it.

"This one's my favorite," he said, smoothing the top sheet. "I love the way the journalist described it: 'So great was the force of the collision that the locomotives were welded together. The forward cars, driven by momentum, leapt over them in a wild game of leapfrog.' The writer should've been a novelist."

"Maybe they were," Ashlyn quipped, smiling at the grim poetry of it.

Sebastian continued reading. "The train derailed, slid down the embankment, and skidded out onto the ice before breaking through and sinking." He paused. "Can you imagine that?"

Ashlyn nodded, her gaze drifting toward the lake; the story playing out in her mind.

Suddenly, the wail of a train whistle sounded again, louder this time. It was followed by the screech of metal grinding against the tracks. Ashlyn's breath caught, and in an instant, she was no longer on the pier but right in the middle of the wreck. The deafening crunch of metal echoed around her as the cars collided. She felt the shock as the train broke through the ice, the freezing water rushing in, pulling everything down.

And then she was back. Ashlyn blinked, meeting Sebastian's eyes. Neither of them said a word—they didn't need to. That was the beauty of another medium for a friend. They both understood. You couldn't rush through fear like this; you just had to ride it out like a wave and hope you didn't drown. Being an empath to the dead wasn't a job for the faint-hearted.

They sat in silence, hands clasped, grounding each other until their breathing slowed and the sharp edges of panic dulled enough for them to think straight.

Finally, Ashlyn broke the quiet, her voice steady. "We're looking for Andrew Beaumont."

The wind answered, a faint whisper in the frozen air. "Vera..."

Sebastian straightened. "He's here," he said, a confident note in his voice. "I can feel it."

Ashlyn could feel it too—Andrew's presence, weak and distant. He was there, but just barely, like a man pounding on a door no one could hear. His fear crashed over her in waves, raw and unfiltered, as if he were still beating against the ice, desperate to escape. Panic rolled off him in suffocating bursts, choking. No more whispers now, just blind, primal terror.

Sebastian already had the recorder out. He recorded the empty air, then played it back. The voice crackled through, thin and desperate. "Help... help... help..." The same plea, looping over and over, trapped in his last moments.

Ashlyn's heart broke. It wasn't just fear—it was hopelessness. He'd been stuck in that same moment for far too long, his mind frozen in the instant everything ended. She reached out with her senses, searching for any other spirits to latch onto, but there was nothing. Andrew was alone in this.

"Andrew," she said, her voice dropping into the soothing tone she reserved for anxious spirits and people alike, "it's okay. You're safe now. You're not trapped in the ice anymore."

The air stilled, just for a second—like the tiniest crack. A pause in the panic. But it didn't hold. The fear snapped back, like a beast that couldn't be caged. It was as if Andrew didn't know how to stop, like he'd been terrified for so long, he'd forgotten how to feel anything else.

"Andrew," she tried again. "We're here to help. But I need you to stop—relax. You're safe. We can't help you if you're still freaking out."

Another pause, longer this time. She could almost feel him listening, like he was hovering on the edge of understanding.

"We're going to get you out of this," she added. "But you've got to calm down. Panic won't break the ice—it'll only make it worse."

Her words settled into the air, like the first warm breath of air after a long, cold winter.

"Hello, Andrew," Ashlyn said. "Try the EVP again. I think he's just finding his feet."

Sebastian nodded and clicked on the recorder. They sat, waiting for any sign of response. When he played it back, Andrew's voice crackled through the static. "Help... Vera..."

Ashlyn tilted her head thoughtfully. "Interesting," she murmured. "He's not asking for help from the ice. He's asking for her."

Her thoughts were cut off by a sudden shift in the air.

"Oh—hello!" Sebastian blurted out, his hand moving to his throat. His voice carried an unfamiliar edge, like someone else was nudging their way through. Ashlyn's eyes widened as she realized what was happening.

Andrew was reaching out—trying to connect.

"That's it, Andrew," Ashlyn encouraged. "You can use Sebastian's voice if you need to. Just... share it."

Sebastian opened himself to the spirit. "I'm here," he whispered. "I'm ready. We can do this together."

There was a brief pause, and then a change.

"I need to get home," Andrew's voice said.

Ashlyn glanced at Sebastian, who gave a quick nod, signaling he was fine—though his eyes were a little wider than usual. Sharing a voice with a ghost was no small feat.

"We can help you get home," Ashlyn said, keeping her tone gentle. "But why does Vera need help?"

"She's..." Andrew paused, like someone trying to remember a dream after waking. "She's unwell. And Christmas is her favorite time. I promised I'd be home for Christmas."

Ashlyn's stomach twisted. Andrew Beaumont didn't realize how much time had passed. She could almost feel his confusion hovering just beneath the surface. If she wasn't careful, she'd lose him to it.

"Andrew," she asked, keeping her voice calm, "do you know where you are?"

Another long pause, then: "The hospital," he said, but the uncertainty was creeping in. "I must be. It's cold, but it's always cold in hospitals, isn't it?"

Ashlyn exchanged a glance with Sebastian, who raised an eyebrow. Spirits often latched onto places that made sense to them—hospitals, old homes, anywhere that could explain their current state of confusion.

"It's not a hospital, Andrew," she said. "It's... a little more complicated than that."

The air rippled. "What do you mean?" His voice was tighter now, bracing for bad news. "I was on my way home. The train was late. Vera—she's waiting for me. I promised I'd be home by Christmas."

Ashlyn took a deep breath, choosing her words. "Andrew, listen to me. That train ride... it was a long time ago. The train... didn't make it. It derailed."

There was a beat of silence. "Derailed?" Andrew's voice was strained now. "No. That's not right. I would've... I'm going home. I promised."

"I know," Ashlyn soothed. "But the accident... it happened over a hundred years ago. You didn't make it home, Andrew. Not in the way you think."

Another long pause, and then Andrew's voice wavered. "But I can't be... I'm not..." His words trailed off as the reality of it sank in. "I'm dead."

"Yes. You died in the train crash, Andrew. But you've been stuck here ever since."

The air turned colder, sharp enough that Ashlyn could feel it cutting through her coat. His presence wavered, a flicker on the edge of panic.

"No," he said, his voice breaking. "No, that can't be right. I promised Vera. I promised I'd come home."

"You didn't let her down," Ashlyn said quickly. "You couldn't have known what would happen. It wasn't your fault."

"She needed me," he whispered, the guilt heavy in every word. "I let her down."

"No, Andrew," Ashlyn said. "She's been waiting for you, but she's not angry. She's just... been lost without you. Just like you've been lost without her."

"I was supposed to protect her," he murmured, more to himself than to them. "I was supposed to come home..."

"And you can still keep your promise," Ashlyn said. "You're not stuck anymore. We're here to help you get home, but you need to let go of this... of the guilt. You did everything you could."

There was a long, aching silence. The cold pressed in on them, deeper and sharper, but Ashlyn felt the change—small, like a breath catching in the wind. Andrew was listening.

"How?" he finally asked, his voice only a thread. "How can I get to Vera?"

Ashlyn gave a smile, even though he couldn't see it. "You just have to let go, Andrew. We'll guide you. You can go where you're meant to be. You don't need to stay at the scene of the crash anymore."

The wind seemed to hold its breath. Ashlyn did the same. For a moment, nothing moved, and then Sebastian's shoulders slumped.

"He's gone," Sebastian whispered, his voice almost as quiet as Andrew's had been.

Ashlyn felt her chest tighten. There was that strange, hollow feeling when a spirit left—like something in the air had lifted, leaving it lighter but a little sadder too. Andrew's presence drifted away like a sigh on the night wind.

"He was a quick learner," Sebastian murmured, rubbing the back of his neck with a grimace. "Most spirits take a lot longer to figure it out."

Ashlyn nodded, her breath fogging in the cold air. "Do you think he'll be back here or at the house?" She stared out over the frozen lake, where the moonlight made the ice gleam like glass. "Or do you think he's crossed over?"

Sebastian frowned, staring into the distance as if he could still sense Andrew somewhere just out of reach. "I don't know. It's like he's retreated into a place we can't reach him. He hasn't passed over yet, but he's not here either."

Ashlyn blew out a long breath, watching it curl into the night before vanishing. "I guess that's all we can do for now." She sighed, then gave a half-hearted shrug. "Let's pack up. It's cold enough out here to freeze my eyelashes off."

Sebastian gave her a tired smile, already reaching for the lantern. "That would be a look."

The drive back to Lilac Grove was quiet, the road ahead winding through the snow-dusted trees like a path into a frozen, forgotten world. Ashlyn was in processing mode, sorting through the puzzle of Vera and Andrew. She loved that Sebastian understood this about her, letting the silence settle between them without feeling the need to fill it.

"Thank you, Seb," she said, breaking the stillness. "For understanding my quiet."

"Far be it from me to interrupt the ghost therapist's thoughts," he replied. "Hmmm, maybe you should add that to your title."

Ashlyn smirked. "I think I'd need a therapy license first."

"Mmhmm." He shot her a sidelong glance. He wasn't wrong, though. There was something about her—whether it was her energy or just how the universe seemed to work—that drew these kindred spirits to her. Or maybe it was the other way around.

Andrew and Vera were no different from many of the cases she'd taken on before. Most of the time, the ghosts were separated for one reason or another: evil entities, confusion, guilt. And more often than not, they just needed to get out of their own way. Unfinished business was the term everyone used, but it went deeper than that. People spent their lives fighting the obstacles of society, but after death? The only thing left holding them back were their own notions of what was important.

Her job was to either clear up their unfinished business—or teach them it didn't matter anymore.

Reuniting lovers was her favorite, though. There was something so satisfying about helping souls find their way back to each other after death. Andrew felt like he needed to protect Vera, and Vera? She just needed her love. There was always the chance Andrew had moved on once they freed him from the ice—but in Ashlyn's experience, that wasn't the case. They would see him again.

She felt a strange kinship with him. Maybe Andrew had gone away to process everything, to find the next logical step. It had to be a shock to realize you'd been dead for over a hundred years. That sort of thing took a minute.

Before she knew it, they were pulling back into the driveway of Lilac Grove. The B&B stood quiet, bathed in the soft glow of moonlight. It was close to 1AM, and the house had that peaceful, sleepy look to it—except for the figure on the porch.

Ashlyn squinted, recognizing Delores standing at the front door. She was fumbling with the handle, her movements clumsy and hurried.

"Is that Delores?" Sebastian asked, leaning forward in his seat.

"Yeah," Ashlyn replied, already unbuckling her seatbelt. "Come on."

They hurried out of the car and up the porch steps, finding Delores muttering to herself. At least this time she was wearing her heavy winter coat, but her hair was mussed as if she'd just woken up—or hadn't really gone to bed at all.

"Delores?" Ashlyn said, trying not to startle her. "What are you doing out here?"

Delores jumped a little, turning to face them. There was a distant, confused look in her eyes, as though she couldn't quite place where she was. "Oh, I need to get the room ready," she said, her voice a bit breathless. "There are guests arriving, and I—I can't seem to find the keys..."

Ashlyn's heart sank. She stepped forward, placing a hand on Delores' arm. "It's okay, Delores. There aren't any guests right now. You don't need to prepare anything."

Delores blinked, her brow furrowing. "No guests? But... I could've sworn I..."

"You're just a little turned around," Ashlyn said, keeping her voice soothing. "Let's get you inside where it's warm, okay?"

Sebastian moved to open the door, and they guided Delores in, the warmth of the house enveloping them as they crossed the threshold. Once inside, Delores seemed to deflate, the confusion giving way to recognition.

"Oh no," she murmured, her shoulders slumping. "I did it again, didn't I?"

Ashlyn exchanged a quick glance with Sebastian. "Let's get you comfortable," she said, helping Delores out of her coat.

Delores gave a tired, self-conscious chuckle, shaking her head. "I keep telling John we should strap me into bed, so I stop wandering around in the middle of the night."

Sebastian gave her a kind smile and Ashlyn stepped into the next room and pulled out her phone, dialing John's number. After a few rings, his groggy voice answered.

"John? It's Ashlyn," she said. "I think you need to come over. Delores is here."

There was a pause on the other end before John sighed, the exhaustion clear in his voice. "I'll be right there."

As she hung up the phone, Ashlyn returned to Delores, who was now sitting in the armchair, looking small and vulnerable. "John's on his way."

Delores nodded, her gaze distant once again. "I'm sorry," she whispered, almost to herself. "I didn't mean to cause any trouble."

Ashlyn gave her shoulder a gentle squeeze. "You're not causing trouble, De-lores. We've got you."

Ashlyn made her way into the kitchen, the quiet hum of the house settling around her. There was still a plate of cookies on the counter, the store-bought kind she'd picked up earlier. They looked a little sad in the pale light, but they'd do. As she reached for them, she felt a familiar presence—cool, but not unsettling—hovering near her shoulder.

"Hi, Vera," she said, smiling softly, as if speaking to an old friend.

The spirit's energy was gentle tonight, a far cry from the agitation that had filled the house earlier. Ashlyn felt a wave of gratitude wash over her.

"We found Andrew," she said, glancing over her shoulder. "He's on his way."

Vera's form, barely more than a shimmer, seemed to brighten at the mention of his name. Her outline flickered, as if her essence was responding to the hope. Ashlyn wasn't sure if a spirit's eyes could truly brighten, but something in Vera's energy shifted—lighter, more eager. Ashlyn only hoped she wasn't giving her false hope.

She turned to warm some cocoa, pouring the rich liquid into mugs as the smell of chocolate filled the air. Vera drifted near her, the calm presence swirling like a gentle breeze, watching Ashlyn's every move. It felt... domestic, in a way. As if Vera was waiting for the familiar rhythms of a holiday gathering she used to know. Ashlyn arranged the cookies on a tray, adding the mugs of cocoa.

"You always loved Christmas, didn't you?" she asked, glancing at the ghost.

Vera didn't speak, but her form twirled, as if the very memory of it set her dancing. Ashlyn smiled and carried the tray into the sitting room, Vera floating behind her, swaying as though moved by some invisible melody only she could hear.

"I brought treats," Ashlyn announced with a grin, stepping into the room.

Delores blinked, bleary-eyed, and a little confused, as John entered behind her, having just arrived. "But... it's the middle of the night."

"What better time to celebrate?" Ashlyn replied, handing them both mugs of cocoa. John gave her a tired but grateful smile as he took his seat next to Delores.

Sebastian, who had been sitting by the fire, caught Ashlyn's eye. He, too, could feel it—the atmosphere was different now, charged with something gentle and sacred. He rose and made his way to the piano in the corner of the room. His fingers hovered over the keys for a moment before he played, the notes soft and slow, like a memory unfolding.

The melody was faint at first, but Ashlyn recognized it immediately. Her heart swelled as Sebastian sang in a low, reverent voice.

Silent night, holy night.

All is calm, all is bright.

Ashlyn's voice joined his, the words falling from her lips. Outside, the snow continued to fall, the moon casting a pale glow through the windows. In her mind, she could almost picture that night—the one from so long ago. A mother and child, meeting each other's eyes for the first time in that stillness, in that peace.

Round yon Virgin, Mother and Child.

Holy infant, so tender and mild.

The room seemed to glow with the song, as if the spirit of Christmas itself had settled into the old bed-and-breakfast. Delores and John, sitting side by side, sang as well, their voices soft but full of warmth. Even the air seemed to still in reverence.

Sleep in heavenly peace,
Sleep in heavenly peace.

As the last note lingered in the air, Ashlyn looked up—and there, standing in the doorway, was Andrew.

CHAPTER EIGHT

Grim Tidings We Bring

They had finally gone to bed just after 3 a.m. The Christmas carols soothed Vera enough to settle her, and John had taken Delores home. Tomorrow, she had an appointment for a brain scan, which was scheduled for the afternoon.

Ashlyn hoped they'd get some rest. John had said little after the carols ended, but it didn't take an empath to know he was terrified. His hand trembled when he wrapped Delores' scarf around her shoulders, as though he feared even the most basic task was slipping from his control.

When Ashlyn had pulled him aside in the hallway, his eyes had been dark with fear. He stared at the floor when he whispered, What if I'm not enough? The words felt like a punch. John was a man made of quiet strength and seeing him unravel like this tugged at something deep.

She knew that love, no matter how strong, couldn't always keep you from feeling helpless. In fact, it did quite the opposite. Ashlyn had reassured him—but the words felt hollow. She'd seen that same fear in Andrew. And if love was all that was needed, Vera wouldn't still be here. Love is powerful, but fear can make the road feel long and lonely.

Ashlyn watched them leave, John's hand resting on Delores' back, guiding her through the falling snow. They didn't speak, but there was comfort in the silence. She knew that kind of silence, the kind that came from years of understanding.

But now, alone in the quiet house, her mind started spinning again. That Vera might have suffered from some form of dementia in life had been nagging at her for a while, but now it felt undeniable. Vera wasn't just a restless spirit, she was stuck in her own confusion, trapped in the loops of her fading memories.

And Andrew... His guilt, his connection to the state hospital... It all clicked into place. He hadn't just been Vera's husband. He had been her caretaker. Maybe that's why his spirit lingered, tangled up in the same unresolved guilt and helplessness John was feeling now. If Andrew had worked in what was considered mental health back then, he would've known how terrifying it was to watch someone you love to slip away, and the dark place they may end up.

Ashlyn sighed, rubbing her temples. Spirits didn't get better just because they died. Death didn't erase always unfinished business. It just... froze it. Vera had been lost in her mind before she passed, and now she was stuck in that same fog.

It all started making sense, but her brain felt too tangled to untangle it. She had to bring them together—Vera and Andrew—but how? And what did that even mean? Ashlyn did not know what "finishing" their business would look like.

Her mind wouldn't stop racing, and even though it was late, sleep refused to come. When it finally did, a deep, low chime shattered the silence.

Gong...

Ashlyn blinked awake, her body heavy with exhaustion. Did the house have a grandfather clock? She couldn't remember seeing one.

Gong...

She'd barely drifted off when the noise started again. She growled in frustration, pulling a pillow over her head.

But Vera was there, pacing back and forth. *He's supposed to be here. Where is he?* Ashlyn didn't so much hear the words as she felt them—frantic, fragmented thoughts spilling over in waves.

Gong...

The annual party... our friends... Vera's thoughts raced, tangled up in panic. *He left me.*

Gong...

Ashlyn winced, feeling the sharp edge of Vera's fear cut through her. *How am I going to take care of myself? They're going to take me away... they're going to make me leave!*

Gong...

Ashlyn's heart pounded as Vera's confusion overwhelmed her. *I can pay them off... they won't take me...*

Gong...

It's gone... the money's gone... Annie took it...no—Andrew... Andrew took it... Vera's thoughts spiraled, each more erratic than the last. *I'm all alone...*

The relentless tolling of the clock reverberated through Ashlyn's skull, drowning out her own thoughts. She couldn't think straight. The clock, Vera's voice, the thoughts—they wouldn't stop. It was driving her mad.

The thoughts crashed over her in waves—Vera's panic, her confusion, and that ever-present fear that twisted around Ashlyn's own mind like vines, choking her. She could feel it, so real it was suffocating. He left me... they're going to take me away. Ashlyn's breath hitched as her vision blurred. She stumbled, the sensation of waiting, of fear, of abandonment clawed at her chest. Gone... everything's gone... Vera's thoughts fragmented, pulling Ashlyn deeper into a fog so thick it was like drowning. And somewhere, beyond that crushing despair, the chime of the clock—counting down...

Gong...

And then it started again. *He's supposed to be here...*

A soft rapping caught Ashlyn's attention, pulling her from the swirling haze of half-dreams and confusion.

What was that? Where was she? Who was she?

The door creaked open, and Sebastian slipped in. Concern softened his usual swagger as he rushed to her side, hands gently gripping her shoulders. The contact grounded her.

"I'm here," he murmured, voice soothing.

Ashlyn inhaled, the haze lifting just enough for her mind to clear.

"I felt it too," Sebastian said, his brow furrowed. "I was worried about you. You are closer to this—closer to Vera—than I am."

A shiver ran through Ashlyn. "That was… a powerful manifestation. It's been a long time since I nearly lost myself like that."

Sebastian nodded, his expression serious. "It was intense. But you're safe now. I'm right here."

For a few moments, they sat in the quiet, the only sound the faint ticking of the clock. Ashlyn stared at the window, where the night outside was still thick, the garden cloaked in darkness.

Finally, she spoke. "It all felt so real. But—it's good. I realized something."

She explained the breakthrough, the understanding of Vera's torment. The confusion, the anger—it wasn't just the frustration of a spirit clinging to the past. Vera had been suffering in life. "Dementia," Ashlyn said. "She was already losing herself when Andrew died. And after that, it only got worse."

Sebastian's eyes darkened. "Oh no. Those turn-of-the-century hospitals…" His voice dripped with disdain. "Horror houses, really. I've seen too much pain in places like that."

"Andrew was involved with one in Concord," Ashlyn continued, her mind piecing it all together. "He was a doctor. I don't think he was an evil man… I think he was trying to protect her. To keep her from being institutionalized."

Sebastian gave a slow nod. "You're probably right."

Ashlyn rubbed her eyes. "What time is it?"

"Just before six," Sebastian answered after glancing at his watch. "We've got a couple hours until sunrise."

"Well, we're up." Ashlyn shrugged. "And I'm definitely not going back to sleep. Want to check out the garden while she's quiet?"

Sebastian's expression lightened. "I'm with you."

As they stood to leave, Ashlyn glanced back at the window, where a faint shimmer of frost clung to the glass. "Christmas had always been a strange season for Ashlyn. For other people, it was full of warmth and family. For her, it was something different—a reminder of the homes she'd passed through, of the brief glimmers of happiness that were always too fleeting.

Vera had loved Christmas too, once. Ashlyn could feel that love, the remnants of it clinging to Vera's spirit like old tinsel. But now, that joy was tangled in grief. The holiday had turned into a cruel ghost of itself, much like Vera had. And Ashlyn? Well, she understood that better than she cared to admit.

"Come on," Sebastian said, nudging her. "Let's go see what the garden has to say."

Ashlyn followed him out, her mind still turning over thoughts of Vera, of loss, and the quiet ache that seemed to haunt both the living and the dead during the holidays.

The moonlight had dimmed, but it was still bright enough for them to make out the shadowy shapes of bushes and trees as they trudged toward the garden. Sebastian had grabbed the lilac key from the table, and Ashlyn stuffed it in the backpack with their usual ghost-hunting gear.

Cold air wrapped around them as they stepped outside, sharp and bracing. The garden stretched out before them, a snowy blanket covering everything, and the moon hung low, painting inky shadows that stretched long as they walked.

An unsettling quiet filled the space between the brittle lilac bushes, which stood like bony fingers reaching for the sky. The stillness was almost too perfect.

"What exactly are we looking for out here? And where do we even start?" Ashlyn asked, frowning as she scanned the bare branches and path winding through the snow.

"It would be helpful if Andrew showed his face," Sebastian replied.

"Speaking of," Ashlyn began, giving him a sidelong glance. "Did you see him last night?"

Sebastian froze mid-step, turning, eyes wide. "What? You saw him and didn't mention it?"

A sheepish grin tugged at Ashlyn's lips. "I was tired! It slipped my mind."

"Slipped your mind?" Sebastian let out a dramatic sigh, hands flaring briefly. "Ashlyn, rookie mistake. You should have told me!"

She blushed, the cold hiding most of her embarrassment. "You're right. I was just caught up in the moment."

Shaking his head with exaggerated disappointment, Sebastian reached into the backpack for a small tape recorder. "Andrew, if you're here, we'd really appreciate a conversation," he said, addressing the empty space around them before pressing record. After a few seconds, he rewound the tape and held it to his ear.

A pause. He frowned. "Nothing. Too quiet, if you ask me."

Ashlyn cast her gaze across the snowy expanse. The lilac bushes, bowed under the weight of snow, seemed almost sad. The feeling tugged at her, pulling her attention toward a small alcove hidden in shadow, where Vera's presence seemed to lurk just out of reach.

"We should probably split up," Ashlyn suggested, her eyes lingering on the alcove. "You look for Andrew, and I'll try to coax Vera back."

Sebastian raised an eyebrow, skepticism written across his face, but eventually shrugged. "Sure, I guess," he said, muttering to himself as he head down a winding path deeper into the garden.

Alone, Ashlyn's thoughts drifted—Christmas always did this to her. She couldn't remember much about holidays with her parents; it was a blur of warmth and vague images, nothing substantial. Foster care Christmases had been bleaker—a reminder she didn't have anyone waiting for her. Vera had loved Christmas once, too. The grand balls, the lights, the joy. Now, it was nothing but a tangled mess of grief and confusion festering in her spirit like an old wound.

The flood of memories hit Ashlyn without warning, so sudden and powerful she couldn't tell where her own thoughts ended and Vera's began. She could feel Vera's joy from those long-ago winters, the grand Christmas parties in the very house behind them—music, laughter, warmth. And Andrew. Oh, the way her heart soared when she danced with him, the way the world had felt whole in those moments. It was too much.

Ashlyn doubled over, clutching her head as the memories threatened to drown her. She was waiting again, just like before. But waiting for what? Why was she in the garden? Andrew was gone, and they were going to send her away—they were going to take her. The fear, the helplessness, it all surged through her, raw and unbearable.

The snow under Ashlyn's knees might as well have been miles away. She could feel it, sure, but only in that distant, numbed way you feel things when your mind is spiraling into someone else's despair. Vera's emotions were like a heavy fog, dragging her down, making it hard to think clearly.

Then, suddenly, there was Sebastian, and his hand landed firmly on her shoulder. "Okay," he said, his tone flat, like he was already over this entire situation. "Splitting up? Terrible idea."

The steadiness of his voice yanked her out of Vera's head long enough to take a shaky breath. Ashlyn nodded, still a bit wobbly from it all, but feeling her own thoughts start to separate from Vera's again. Vera was still there, though, lingering at the back of her mind, fractured and confused.

Sebastian looked around the garden and spoke to the air in the most casual way, like he was inviting Vera over for tea. "Alright, Vera. What are we looking for?"

But there was no answer. Ashlyn could still feel Vera's presence, but it was like trying to hold on to water. Her thoughts were slipping away, barely there.

"She doesn't know," Ashlyn said, her voice unsteady. "She... can't remember."

Sebastian squinted into the dark, scanning the area again. His eyes landed on something—a small, shallow dip in the snow, just a little too neat to be natural. "Wait. Look there."

Ashlyn followed his gaze and saw it too. It wasn't much, just a patch where the snow didn't sit quite right. But it was enough. They scrambled over, dropping to their knees, digging into the frozen ground with their gloved hands. It was slow going, frustratingly slow, and the cold seeped in deeper with each passing second.

"We're never getting through this," Ashlyn muttered, her breath coming out in sharp puffs of frustration.

And then the air shifted. This wasn't just the winter chill. This was something sharper, colder—unnatural. It crawled down Ashlyn's spine, and when she looked up, she saw him.

Andrew.

At first, he was barely there, just a flicker, a whisper of a figure in the moonlight. But then he took shape, solidifying bit by bit. He stood at the edge of the bushes, and he wasn't anything like the man Vera had been waiting for. His shoulders sagged, his face gaunt and worn down with the weight of everything he'd carried—or failed to carry. The regret hung around him like a heavy coat, and even in the faint light, Ashlyn could see it, clear as day.

Vera saw it too. Her lips parted, and for a moment, there was something soft in her expression, something broken. Her hands hovered in the space between them, trembling just enough to show that deep down, part of her still wanted to reach for him, even after everything.

"You said you'd come back," she whispered, her voice tight with years of waiting. "You promised me... and I waited."

Her voice cracked, and it was like the fog of confusion that had kept her here all these years suddenly lifted, replaced with something rawer. The weight of it all—the waiting, the hurt, the abandonment—settled over her, and Ashlyn could feel the sharp sting of it.

Vera's fingers twitched, curling inward as her face hardened. Whatever tenderness had been there a moment ago was gone, replaced by the anger she'd held onto for so long.

Andrew stepped forward, just a little, like he wanted to close the distance, to fix it. But Vera's eyes darkened, and that fury that had kept her tethered here for so long rose up again, burning hot and cold all at once. Her hands dropped to her sides, fists clenched.

She didn't say another word. She just turned and vanished into the shadows, gone as quickly as she had come.

Andrew's form flickered, his hand still outstretched, his voice thin and broken as he called after her. "Wait..."

But she was already gone.

Chapter Nine

All I Want for Christmas is Boo

"Oh, my Vera," Andrew whispered.

Andrew's manifestation was stronger than before, almost solid. Ashlyn heard him clear as day, and it seemed Sebastian did too, judging by his curious expression.

"It's to be expected, I'm afraid," Andrew said as his features relaxed, touched with sorrow. "This... this softening of the brain. I counted each month, watching for it to settle in fully, but I hoped the promise of our annual party would keep her spirits bright a while longer."

"She was not losing her mind, you know," Sebastian huffed.

"If she was so unwell, why on earth did you leave her alone?" Ashlyn added.

Andrew's back stiffened. "Alone?" he repeated, affronted. "No, I would never have left Vera alone. Annie was with her—my own cousin, and one of the very first to graduate from the nursing school! She was prepared for this, emotionally and practically."

Ashlyn pondered his words, but the puzzle still nagged at her. "Then why is Vera convinced Annie stole her money?"

Andrew's brows knitted in genuine confusion. "Annie? Never! When Vera's memory began to fail her, we were the ones who sponsored Annie through nursing school. We knew we'd need her help, and she was family. When we passed, the money would have gone to her anyway—no need for thievery."

Ashlyn could see the sincerity in Andrew's eyes, but he continued, almost as if speaking to himself. "No, Annie loved Vera, even as her mind unraveled... still, I knew what people might try to do if I couldn't come back. We hid our valuables, Vera and I, locked them away and buried them in the lilac garden. It was our way of keeping her safe if I didn't return in time, safe from the greedy sort who would take her away for their own gain."

"The asylum," Sebastian murmured.

Andrew nodded. "Precisely. That act was meant to protect her from the worst of what might come. Annie knew of it, of course. She would have been Vera's keeper. But if we truly have been dead these hundred years..." He trailed off, his face shadowed with loss.

Ashlyn watched as Andrew moved to the edge of the lilac bushes, reaching toward a spot he seemed to remember with absolute certainty. His hand wavered above the soil, fingers stretched as if he might feel the cold metal of the box beneath the earth. Ashlyn sensed that he was caught halfway between memory and reality.

"Aye, the strongbox," he murmured. "We buried it together, Vera and I. There's a key—a small, silver one with a lilac etched on the bow. I didn't want anyone else to find it, save Annie, who knew where to look if it came to that." He glanced at Ashlyn. "Vera's safety, her dignity... those were the things I valued more than gold."

Ashlyn could almost see him there, in another time, huddled over the turned soil, Vera beside him.

Andrew continued, almost speaking to himself. "I thought I would return by Christmas, you know. I only left to improve the curriculum, to make sure nurses knew what kindness looked like, how it felt in the hand." His gaze grew distant, fixed somewhere far away. "Our party was waiting. Our traditions..."

"Oh, my Vera," he whispered. "I never meant for this. I was the one to be alone. It was my cross to bear."

A silence followed, stretching long and thin. Ashlyn felt it, the loneliness of love bound by memory but broken by time.

Sebastian cleared his throat, glancing between Andrew and Ashlyn, his voice quieter than usual. "And without you, she passed, left to drift through the years, trapped in a Christmas that never came."

Andrew flinched, as if the memory itself had struck him. "Our Christmas—once filled with light—became nothing but fog and shadows for her."

Words tumbled around in Ashlyn's mind, but none seemed enough to touch the ache woven into Andrew's voice. She felt a pang herself, understanding that Vera—poor, stubborn, lost Vera—had clung to Christmas and to Andrew's promise as though they were her lifeline. But instead of saving her, they'd only served as an anchor, pulling her deeper into the darkness.

A flicker of resolve pierced through the grief in Andrew's eyes as he turned to Ashlyn. "Bring her here, to the garden," he said. "It was her joy, her haven. If anything can reach her, this place will."

Ashlyn exchanged a glance with Sebastian before they stepped away, leaving Andrew standing alone. As they walked back toward the house, his figure blended into the shadows of the garden, a solitary silhouette swallowed by the day.

"That was a little harsh, don't you think?" Ashlyn murmured, glancing sidelong at Sebastian. "Making him feel like Vera's heartbreak was his fault?"

Sebastian gave a noncommittal shrug. "It wasn't my intent to hurt his feelings," he replied. "But any path to resolution starts with the truth—and whether he knows it or not, I did him a service."

"Maybe you're right. But Vera... she's going to be a much harder nut to crack."

They scoured the house, weaving through Vera's usual haunts—the sitting room, the entryway, even the Lilac suite. Not a trace. At last, they found her in the attic, crouched in a shadowed corner like a wounded animal. Her rage hummed through the room as she tore into old clothing and furniture, her touch leaving a mess in her wake. To anyone who didn't know her sadness, the scene might have been terrifying.

"Vera," Ashlyn called. "Andrew never meant to leave you. He wanted to come home."

With a hollow gasp, Vera's face appeared inches from Ashlyn's own, her eyes dark with something almost feral. "He's dead to me," she spat, the words sharp as broken glass. Then she vanished back into the corner, ripping at the attic's contents, lost in her relentless loop.

Sebastian placed a gentle hand on her arm. "Unlike Andrew, she needs a softer touch. Let's give her a moment."

They retreated back downstairs, leaving the attic behind, and settled into the sitting room to gather their thoughts.

The house stayed quiet that morning. Ashlyn found herself lost in a book, and Sebastian settled in at the piano, fingers drifting over the keys. It was peaceful, a rare calm before the inevitable storm.

But when Delores and John arrived, the music faded, and Sebastian stood to greet them. They looked calm but quiet, a settled sort of acceptance in their eyes.

"How was the appointment?" Ashlyn asked.

Delores sighed. "As expected. Its confirmed, but I'm in the early stages. We've got a plan to slow things down, but..." She gave a shrug, her eyes meeting Ashlyn's. "It's a road I'll be traveling, like it or not."

"I'm so sorry." Ashlyn crossed the room and pulled Delores into a hug.

"Oh, don't worry about me, dear." Delores managed a small smile. "I'm all right, at least for now. How's our Vera?"

Ashlyn couldn't help but smile. "Quite a big step forward today."

She filled them in on Andrew's manifestation and Vera's own struggle with dementia.

"They called it a softening of the brain, or sometimes madness," she murmured.

"Well, I certainly feel a bit mad myself when I find I've wandered into strange places," Delores said, chuckling.

Sebastian turned to John. "How are you holding up?"

John was quiet, his brow furrowing. "If I could trade places, I would," he said. "Dolly's always been the one with the gentle touch. The natural caretaker…"

"Oh, nonsense," Delores interrupted, giving him a reassuring squeeze. "Think of it as a role reversal! You'll do just fine."

Then her gaze shifted to Ashlyn, thoughtful. "Do you think…Vera would talk to me?"

Ashlyn looked over at Sebastian, who nodded. "She's had sometime to calm herself," he said. "It would be lovely to try."

They climbed to the attic in a quiet line, John helping Delores up the narrow stairs. Ashlyn brought the spirit box, figuring it was the easiest way to facilitate a conversation. If Vera was as loud as she'd been earlier, the box might not be necessary—but for those who couldn't hear the ghost, it made things simpler.

Setting up the box, Ashlyn tuned it to a low, steady static so Delores and John could hear. She explained how it worked, watching Delores's face shift with wonder.

"Vera," Sebastian called out. "This is Delores and John. They're the homeowners now. I believe you've met them?"

Vera's figure, still crouched in the far corner, lifted her head. Her gaze lingered on Delores and John, curiosity breaking through her sulking. She straightened, studying them.

"Is she here?" Delores asked.

Ashlyn gestured toward the corner, and Delores turned, her hand instinctively reaching out. John pulled a chair closer, guiding his wife to sit down.

"Thank you, John," Delores murmured as she settled in. The spirit box crackled, and Vera's voice came through, soft but distinct.

"Andrew was a gentleman."

Delores's eyes lit up. "She's here!" Her voice trembled, and for a moment, all of them fell silent.

Then Delores took a deep breath and began. "Hello, Vera. We've always loved having you here as part of our home. I hope you feel the same, sharing it with us and with our guests." She paused, glancing at Ashlyn and then back at the faint outline of Vera. "Today, I learned something that I think you and I share. I found out that I, too, have this... condition, this softening of the mind. And yes, I am scared. I don't want to fade away, to lose myself."

Vera watched her, the anger in her expression dimming to something more vulnerable.

Delores reached into her purse and pulled out a neatly folded piece of paper. "This is my care plan, Vera. I'm still well, and being with people I love, doing the things that bring me joy, that will slow the process." She smiled. "I want you to know that, even if they didn't understand it in your time, the work you and Andrew did—the kindness you showed—has helped people. And it will keep helping people."

Vera's figure seemed to flicker, the anger loosening around the edges. She drifted closer, and her voice whispered through the box.

"I don't want to slip away," Vera said, her words laced with longing. "I just... sometimes I don't know where I am anymore."

A tear slipped down Delores's cheek. "I know that feeling," she murmured. "But I've found a way to keep my feet grounded in the here and now, even if it's just one day at a time." She looked down at her plan. "And I hear you love Christmas and gardening. If you're around, I'd love to share those things with you—I love them too."

Vera's image grew clearer, the years of confusion lifting just a little. The walls she'd built to protect herself had begun to crumble. "I don't have to stay?"

As she spoke the words, a clarity washed over her face.

Delores smiled through her tears. "No, you don't. But if you do, know that we'd love to have you here. And if you go, know that we'll be happy for you, too."

For a moment, Vera looked around the room, truly seeing it—seeing all of them. Her shoulders relaxed, and a peace settled over her. "Thank you." The radio crackled.

"Will you come talk to Andrew?" Ashlyn asked.

Vera looked at Delores, then inclined her head.

Outside, the garden stood still and bare, frost clinging to the branches like delicate lace. Ashlyn, Sebastian, Delores, and John made their way into the clearing, moving through the brittle air. It felt heavy, almost expectant, as if the space itself was holding its breath, waiting for something to unfold.

Then Vera appeared. She was almost as clear as any of them; her form was steady in the winter light, her face softened in a way that seemed new. But her gaze went beyond, to where a figure waited under the frost-laden bushes.

Andrew stood, half in shadow, his eyes fixed on Vera as though he could hardly believe she was there. Vera drew closer, a little hesitantly, but then her hand reached out, curling around his. Her shoulders eased, the last of her anger falling away like autumn leaves.

"Andrew, you're—oh, you're here." Her voice sounded as if she were remembering herself for the first time in ages.

"Yes, my Vera." Andrew wrapped his arms around her, pulling her close, his face pressing into her hair. "I promised I'd come home for Christmas, didn't I?"

He leaned back and met her eyes, then looked toward the sky. "Shall we go, my love?"

Vera looked up, her gaze following his, the faintest shimmer of something just beyond their reach. The edges of her spirit seeming almost to blur in the cold air. But then she shook her head.

"One last Christmas, Andrew. With you," she whispered. She took his hand, her fingers lacing through his. "Let's stay and see it together."

Andrew touched her cheek. "Then one last Christmas it shall be." He looked over her shoulder, as if inviting everyone else into the thought. "We'll make it one to remember."

Ashlyn felt the ache settle deep in her chest—a bittersweet pang, realizing how much this strange, found family had come to mean to her. She wasn't ready to let them go, not Vera or Andrew, or even the Millers with their quiet strength. There was something here, in this old garden and old house, something that bigger than herself. She wanted to keep it, even if it was just for a little longer.

Sebastian, sensing the thought in her gaze, laid a hand on her shoulder. "They'll stay through the holiday," he said, a smile in his voice as he looked over at John and Delores. "For one last celebration."

"Oh!" Delores clutched her hands together, her eyes wide with delight. "Vera will join us for Christmas! Isn't that something, John?"

John grinned, his face softening with relief. "Seems fitting, doesn't it?" He looked over at the garden, though he couldn't see what Ashlyn and Sebastian could. "She ought to have her Christmas."

Sebastian's eyes gleamed with a familiar spark, the one that meant he was about to cause trouble. "Well, then," he said, rubbing his hands together with an enthusiasm that felt almost contagious, "let's make it official. A Christmas party at Lilac Grove!" He paused, looking pointedly at Ashlyn. "All of us. Together. With living, breathing people."

Delores lit up, clapping her hands. "Oh, yes! We'll bring in holly, ivy—maybe some candles! And mulled wine! And music!" She spun to John, eyes sparkling. "And maybe even a few guests?"

Ashlyn hesitated, surprised by the sudden enthusiasm. "Well, that all sounds lovely, but... I'm not sure who we'd even invite." She looked down, half-hoping the idea would fade if she didn't sound too interested. "I mean, most of my friends are, well, ghosts."

John's brow furrowed as he considered it, glancing at Delores as though she might have the answer. "Well, I suppose we'd want folks with, you know... an open mind." "Exactly!" Delores nodded, warming to the idea. "People who would appreciate Lilac Grove's... unique charms."

"Unique charms?" Ashlyn repeated, giving a weak laugh. "You mean people who wouldn't run screaming if they met a ghost in the hall?"

"Oh, nonsense," Delores said, waving a hand. "We have plenty of friends who'd enjoy something a little unconventional! Don't we, John?"

John looked panicked, but nodded. "Certainly..."

Ashlyn shook her head. "I don't know, Delores. I'm not exactly the holiday hostess type."

"Oh, you'll be wonderful, dear," Delores said, dismissing Ashlyn's reluctance with a wave of her hand. "You don't have to do anything. Just leave it to us."

At that, Sebastian leaned in with a wicked grin. "I'll handle the invites." His eyes sparkled with a mischief that made Ashlyn nervous.

Ashlyn raised a wary eyebrow. "Sebastian, who exactly do you have in mind?"

"Oh, I have a few people," he said, his voice smooth, almost too innocent. "Consider it a surprise. You'll love them."

Delores gave a little gasp, clasping her hands. "Oh, I do love a surprise! And Ashlyn, just think—friends to help celebrate!."

Ashlyn bit her lip, realizing the warm feeling in her chest was, indeed, creeping up again. Friends who understood. Family, even, in a way that was unexpected but no less real. She tried to brush it off with a small shrug. "Fine," she muttered, half-smiling.

Sebastian chuckled. "Oh, just you wait. I guarantee this will be a Christmas to remember."

Chapter Ten

Auld Lang Syne

I t was Christmas Eve, and the night of the party. Ashlyn stood in front of the mirror, tugging at the hem of a dress she hadn't worn in years. It was a deep burgundy, with just enough shimmer to catch the light, but not so much that it screamed holiday office party. She had tucked it into her suitcase just in case, and was glad she did.

She adjusted the neckline, tilting her head to one side as she inspected her reflection. If this didn't make her look like a responsible adult who was going to a real grown-up party, she didn't know what would. The sleeves felt restrictive, as if the dress could sense she usually lived in flowy skirts and long shirts. There, all set, she thought, giving herself one last once-over. Now she just needed a glass of something festive, and she will be ready to pretend she was having the time of her life.

Normally, she'd be at home. The past couple of years, that meant sharing the evening with Hank, her silent housemate. Part of her liked it that way—no holiday stress, no big dinners to cook or clean up after, just her, a warm blanket, and a few Christmas movies playing on loop. She could skip all the obligatory cheer and keep her holiday spirit at a low simmer, which was about as festive as she ever felt comfortable being.

Sebastian, on the other hand, had a sister with two little girls who adored him. Every year, he'd spend the season with them, spoiling them with gifts and, according to him, instigating a little chaos. In fact, he was leaving early tomorrow morning to make it to Christmas dinner with his nieces.

Ashlyn sometimes received invitations from clients or people she'd worked with, usually phrased in that polite, cautious way that suggested they were more curious about her than genuinely interested. "Do you have plans for the holidays, Ashlyn? You're more than welcome to join us." She could hear the unspoken questions behind their words, and she always politely declined. She wasn't sure if they thought she was lonely, or if they were just trying to learn more about her home life, but it never felt quite right to accept.

On a typical Christmas Day, she'd make herself a quiet breakfast, sit by the window, and reflect. She wondered how many other people spent the holidays alone. Were they lonely, or was it a choice? Society had placed such a heavy weight on this season, and she had learned to embrace the quiet moments, to find comfort in them.

There was always a little sadness for what could have been. What might have been. Who would she be if her parents were still around? If she hadn't been shuffled from one foster home to another? She liked who she was now. She really did. She'd built a life, a strange and sometimes transient one, but hers all the same. And she wouldn't change it.

But, the thought of an alternate version of herself, one who had a family that wasn't made up of ghosts, was... intriguing. Would she pity the version of herself who spent Christmas alone, or would she be envious of the peace and freedom that came with it?

Ashlyn shook her head, smiling at her reflection. "Alright, enough of that," she said, smoothing the front of her dress one last time. "Let's go do this." She gave herself a wink in the mirror. "Happy Christmas to me."

The Millers and Sebastian were already gathered downstairs. Ashlyn hesitated at the top step, taking a deep breath before making her way down. She could smell warm cider and freshly baked gingerbread, mingling with the faint hint of pine. As she descended, she heard Sebastian's voice, teasing.

"Fashionably late, darling," he called, flashing her a grin as she appeared. "I love it."

"How can I be late if no one else has arrived?" she shot back, lifting an eyebrow as she took in the scene.

"You're the last one to our party," he replied as he handed her a glass of merlot. "Which, technically, still makes you late."

Ashlyn accepted the glass. "At least I'm worth the wait."

Sebastian laughed. "Always."

He looked spectacular tonight, dressed in a midnight blue suit that complimented his silver hair. He'd added a crimson pocket square that matched his signature scarf, and the whole effect was striking—like he'd stepped out of a magazine ad for expensive cologne.

Ashlyn turned her attention to the rest of the room, and her breath caught. Delores and John had outdone themselves. The large tree in the entryway, already impressive, now seemed to glow from within, strung with hundreds of tiny white lights that winked like stars. Ornaments in shades of gold and red hung from every branch, catching the light and casting a kaleidoscope of colors across the room.

Vera had been quiet over the past week, no tantrums or outbursts. Ashlyn suspected that having Andrew's spirit by her side had calmed her. Still, she had made her presence known, poking her head around now and then to supervise.

The Millers were standing by the fireplace, their hands intertwined. Delores looked radiant in a red, sparkly dress that shimmered every time she moved. John was wearing a deep red tie that matched her dress, his dark suit a subtle, classic counterpoint to Delores's shine. It was perfect—he was her grounding force.

"This place looks spectacular," Ashlyn said, her voice full of awe. "I mean, it was already gorgeous, but now it's... it's like a magazine spread come to life."

Delores beamed. "Oh, thank you, dear. We wanted it to feel special, you know? Like a proper celebration."

"And here's to you, Ashlyn." Sebastian clinked his glass against hers. "You've been a busy little elf this month, keeping the peace and solving mysteries. I think we can all agree. We wouldn't be here without you."

Ashlyn blushed. "I didn't do that much."

"Oh, hush," Delores said, stepping forward to pull Ashlyn into a hug, her sequins catching the light and sparkling even more. "You did more than you know. This whole place feels... lighter. Happier. That's because of you."

Ashlyn felt a lump form in her throat, and she took a sip of her wine to swallow it down. "Well, if I'm going to keep getting compliments, I'm going to need more of this," she said, raising her glass with a grin.

John chuckled and nodded toward the bar. "Plenty more where that came from. Help yourself."

They were interrupted by the chime of the doorbell. Okay, game face, Ashlyn told herself, setting down her glass and straightening her dress. She glanced up at the banister as John moved to answer the door.

There, at the top of the stairs, stood Andrew and Vera, side by side, like royalty, looking down on their subjects. They were radiant, their faces alight with a joy that seemed to belong to a different time, a different world.

Andrew was dressed in a tailored black tailcoat, his white shirt crisp with a high, starched collar. Beneath, a deep green vest embroidered with gold filigree glimmered in the light. He looked every inch the gentleman.

It was Vera who dazzled. Her gown, a rich burgundy velvet with black lace that traced delicate patterns along the bodice and sleeves. The modest neckline framed a string of pearls that rested against her throat. The dress cinched at her waist, flaring out into a sweeping skirt that seemed to float as she moved. Long satin gloves reached past her elbows, and her hair was styled in a loose, elegant chignon, with a few soft curls framing her face.

They looked as if they had stepped out of a vintage portrait, composed and timeless. For a moment, Ashlyn could hardly believe they were spirits—there was such vitality in the way they stood, shoulders almost touching, like a couple who had spent a lifetime together. It was hard to imagine the sadness and restlessness that had haunted Vera, seeing her now, so poised and graceful.

Ashlyn turned back to the door, squinting at the couple standing on the threshold. The man was tall with sandy blond hair, and the woman beside him had chestnut hair that framed her face—and a very noticeable baby bump.

"Oh my goodness!" Ashlyn squealed, her usual composure slipping. "The Hartley's!"

She had worked with Benjamin years ago, back when she was consulting for a TV show investigating paranormal sites. Misthaven Light had been one of her earliest mysteries, and it was during that case that Benjamin had met his wife, Ella. Ashlyn liked to think she had played a small part in bringing them together.

She rushed forward to greet them, her arms already outstretched. "Ella! Benjamin! It's been ages! Look at you—glowing, both of you!"

Ella beamed, her cheeks flushed with happiness, and she patted her rounded belly. "We're doing great, Ashlyn. I'm still painting, and people are buying my postcards like crazy."

"They've clearly got excellent taste," Ashlyn said, grinning. "And you, Benjamin? Still neck-deep in dusty old records?"

Benjamin chuckled. "Guilty as charged. I've actually been promoted—head of the Maine Historical Society. And I published that book on lighthouse history. It's even got a chapter about Misthaven Light."

"Oh, that's wonderful!" Ashlyn clapped her hands together.

"Turns out there's a whole world of people out there who want to know the gruesome details of shipwrecks and haunted beacons," Benjamin said. "Who knew?"

"And the baby?" Ashlyn asked as she glanced at Ella's belly. "Do we have a name picked out yet?"

Ella and Benjamin exchanged a look, a silent conversation passing between them. "We're thinking of 'Margot,'" she said. "It was the name of Benjamin's favorite great-aunt. She was a bit of a legend in the family, so it just... feels right."

Ashlyn's eyes softened. "I'm so happy for both of you."

They chatted a little longer, catching up on old times, and Ashlyn marveled at how life had changed for the Hartley's. They were both thriving, with a family of their own on the way.

While Ashlyn had been catching up, the room had filled. She glanced around, her eyes scanning the crowd and taking in so many familiar faces, each one bright with holiday cheer. It felt like a reunion of sorts, a gathering of people who had, in one way or another, become part of her life.

"Did you organize all this, Seb?" she asked, turning to Sebastian, who was sipping a glass of something festive.

"It was easy," he replied, grinning. "Everyone loves you so much."

Ashlyn's heart gave a happy flutter at that. Before she could respond, her eyes landed on another couple she recognized.

Clara and Jack stood nearby, and Clara's face lit up the moment she spotted Ashlyn. In her hands, she held a neatly wrapped book, tied with a ribbon that had a tiny sprig of holly tucked into it.

"Ashlyn!" Clara beamed. "I have something for you." She held out the package, and Ashlyn took it. "It's a signed copy of my latest! I couldn't have finished it without your help on all the spooky details, so... Merry Christmas."

"You didn't have to do that—but thank you! I'm so proud of you. Another bestseller on the way, I'm sure."

Clara blushed, waving off the praise. "Well, let's hope. We're still living with those Boston rents, so I'd better keep writing."

Ashlyn laughed, but then her eyes flicked to Jack, who seemed a little more fidgety than usual. His hand kept slipping into his pocket, as though he were double-checking something important. Curious, she tilted her head, but before she could ask if everything was alright, Sebastian nudged her.

Ashlyn followed his gaze, watching as Jack lead Clara toward the hearth. A few others gathered around, sensing that something special was unfolding. Jack, looking slightly nervous, took a deep breath and then, without another word, dropped to one knee.

"Clara," Jack began, his voice a little shaky, "you make every day brighter and more chaotic and... well, wonderful. I can't imagine life without you, and I don't want to." He pulled a small velvet box from his pocket and opened it, revealing a simple yet elegant ring that sparkled in the firelight. "Will you marry me?"

For a heartbeat, the room was silent. Then Clara gasped, and she threw her arms around Jack, nearly knocking him over in her eagerness. "Yes! Of course, yes!" she managed.

The room erupted into applause and cheers. Ashlyn clapped along.

"Looks like it's not just ghosts finding happiness tonight," Sebastian whispered, leaning close so only she could hear. "There's some love for the living, too."

The applause for Clara and Jack's engagement settled, though Ashlyn could still hear bursts of laughter and excited chatter echoing through the room. She backed away from the cluster of well-wishers, feeling a pleasant hum of happiness that wasn't her own. It was nice, this kind of joy—she wasn't used to it, but she found she didn't mind.

Her stomach growled, reminding her she had skipped lunch. She turned to head towards the refreshment table, intent on locating whatever remained of the cheese platter, when she caught sight of a pair of familiar faces huddled together near the fireplace. Sienna Avery and Nora Sinclar were leaning in close, talking. Ashlyn's curiosity sparked; she hadn't known they even knew each other.

As she got closer, she caught the tail end of their conversation.

"—since high school, can you believe it?" Sienna was saying, her eyes wide with excitement. "I still can't get over it. You look exactly the same!"

Nora laughed, tossing her head back. She caught sight of Ashlyn approaching and grinned. "And look who it is—the woman who seems to know everyone, everywhere."

Ashlyn smiled back, slipping between them. "Hey, I didn't realize this was a reunion. Do I need to break out the yearbooks?"

Sienna gave a little hop, still glowing. "We went to high school together! And we haven't seen each other since... well, graduation, I think. This is so wild."

"Small world, isn't it?" She glanced between them. "So, what have you been catching up on? I need updates too!"

"Oh, all the usual things," Nora said, waving a hand. "School, work, how life makes no sense, but we're all trying to pretend it does. Sienna's about to graduate from Plymouth State. Can you believe it?"

"It's true!" Sienna said. "I'm finally finishing my degree this spring. And I've been working with Dylan on the rebrand of White Pines Resort."

"That's brilliant, Sienna. I knew the two of you make it happen."

"He's been amazing," Sienna said. "Handling all the business-y stuff, which is great because I'm terrible at it. I am doing marketing, blogs articles and such. It's nice, you know? Working together is so special."

Nora arched an eyebrow. "You're not alone there. I've been in a similar boat—except my boat has more drama and people forgetting their lines." She turned to Ashlyn. "Alex's play is getting a second run."

"No way! That's fantastic. They are so talented. You both are. "

"Yep," Nora said, sounding equal parts proud and amused. "Alex has been so supportive. We've got this weird, lovely little creative partnership going on."

"Just creative?" Ashlyn teased. "I'm sure it's a little more than just a creative partnership. You two were pretty close. Last I checked."

Nora blushed.. "We just… fit. Anyway, we'd love to have you come to the show. You were there for the first one; it feels right that you're there for this one, too."

"I wouldn't miss it," Ashlyn said, and meant it.

"Well," Sienna said, glancing around, "I should probably find Dylan before he gets himself in trouble. But I'm so glad we got to do this, Nora. We need to catch up more often."

"We will," Nora said. "And you, Ashlyn—don't disappear before I have time to corner you about the show dates. Plus, Alex will want to say hi."

Ashlyn smiled, feeling something small and warm nestle itself in her heart. "I'll be here."

As Ashlyn stood surveying the crowd, she spotted Vera near the fireplace, her form mingling almost naturally among the living guests. The ghost's presence was subtle—a flicker at the edge of the twinkling lights, a faint wisp of breath that misted the air. Vera seemed content, watching the festivities with an air of nostalgia.

"Having fun?" came a voice beside her.

Ashlyn turned to see Sebastian.

"More than expected," she replied.

The evening wound down, and the room settled into that cozy, sleepy calm that comes after too much wine and just the right amount of merriment. Conversations softened into murmurs, and the last of the guests began pulling on their coats, clutching leftover cookies wrapped in napkins, and making all the vague, well-meaning promises people make at the end of a party.

It was well past midnight by the time the last guests trickled out, leaving the house quiet and warm. Over by the fireplace, the Millers were engaged in a playful debate about whether John would need to shovel the walk again in the morning. Delores, hands on her hips, informed him that if it snowed tonight, she'd drag him back inside by his ear. "No work tomorrow," she declared, a mock sternness in her tone. Ashlyn smiled, feeling a familiar warmth settle over her.

From across the room, Sebastian caught her eye, his shoes clicking softly on the floor as he made his way over. "Happy Christmas, all!" he announced, glancing at his watch with a playful flourish.

"And to you," Ashlyn replied, her voice light. Delores added a more enthusiastic, "Merry Christmas, Sebastian!" as she beamed at him.

"Well, darlings," he said, his grin softer than usual, "I think it's time I made my exit to bed. I need to leave absurdly early tomorrow if I want to make it home for Christmas morning with my nieces. They'd have my head if I missed it. And probably try to put tinsel on it."

Ashlyn sighed, wishing he could stay up a bit longer, but she managed a smile. "I wouldn't dream of getting between you and your tiny, tinsel-wielding tyrants. Besides, you've got a long trip ahead. You'll need your beauty rest."

"Is that code for, 'You need to go to bed, old man?'" he teased, narrowing his eyes. Then he pulled her into a hug, squeezing just a bit tighter than usual. "Thank you, Ashlyn. For everything. This was… a strange and lovely kind of Christmas."

As he spoke, Ashlyn's gaze drifted to the staircase, where she saw them—Vera and Andrew, standing side by side at the banister, looking down at the quiet room below. They were almost glowing, their forms shimmering with a soft, ethereal light that seemed to pulse gently, like a heartbeat. The glow brightened, intensifying until it was almost blinding. Then, just as quickly, it began to break apart, dispersing into a million tiny stars that drifted upward, fading like embers on a dark night.

"That was beautiful," Sebastian whispered.

Ashlyn blinked away a tear that had stubbornly formed at the corner of her eye. "I don't think we'll see them again," she said.

Sebastian nodded, his expression tender. "I'm glad they found peace." He slipped an arm around her shoulders and gave a comforting squeeze. "Thank you for inviting me, darling. This has been a Christmas miracle."

Ashlyn hugged him back, holding on just a little longer than usual. "I'm glad I got to share this moment with you, my dear friend."

"Likewise," he said. "Now, I really must get a good night's sleep before I'm buried under a pile of Christmas bows and overexcited children."

He gave a final, exaggerated salute to John and Delores, who waved back like they were seeing off royalty. Then, with a swirl of his scarf, he was gone.

Without Sebastian, the room felt emptier. As the fire crackled and the lights blinked, she could hear the creak of the old house settling, like it was sighing into sleep.

"Well," Delores said, breaking the silence, "I suppose we should turn in too. I've got to make a feast tomorrow, and John's going to need all his strength if he plans on finishing the last of the pies."

"I'm saving room," John said with a sage nod, then gave Ashlyn a serious look. "We're planning on having a proper hunt for that old strongbox come spring when the ground melts."

"It's more curiosity than anything, really." Delores added. "Just a little mystery left over, like a puzzle piece." Then she reached out and took Ashlyn's hands in hers. "You'll have to come back in the spring and see if we find it."

"Oh, I'll be back," Ashlyn replied. "I'm far too curious to stay away."

John chuckled, gave her a firm handshake, then turned toward the door.

"Goodnight, Ashlyn," Delores said, letting go of her hands. "Merry Christmas. And thank you for everything you've done."

Ashlyn followed them and watched from the porch as John and Delores made their way home, arm in arm, their laughter drifting through the still night. She felt a quiet contentment settle over her. The night had been perfect—not because she loved parties, but because of the wonderful people that had touched her life over the years.

Then she stepped back inside. The fire had burned low, leaving just a few glowing embers that pulsed like stars that weren't quite ready to fade. She stood there for a moment and let herself savor the peace. She had spent years on her own, drifting through towns, solving mysteries that no one else could see, but something was different now. For the first time in a long while, she didn't feel like a visitor passing through. Maybe that was what finding your place was—realizing that home could be a collection of mismatched moments, with people who didn't need to be asked to stay.

She let her voice drift into the stillness, a simple blessing, before turning to go upstairs. "Merry Christmas."

Also by

ALSO BY BETH CONNOR:

Hollow City

<u>The Isdralan Chronicles:</u>
Micah and the Candles of Time
Prodigy of Flame
Bridge of Blood and Thornes

<u>Kindred Spirit Mysteries:</u>
The Secret of Misthaven Island
Bridging the Heart
The Curse at White Pines
The Last Act
I'll Be Home for Christmas

About the Author

Beth Connor is a weaver of tales, captivated by writing and fueled by a love for storytelling.

Beth's creative pursuits are a reflection of her life philosophy, and she is always searching for new ways to expand her knowledge and understanding of the world. She has a keen eye for detail and a remarkable ability to create vivid, dynamic settings that resonate with her audience.

Beth's talent has earned her recognition as the author of several published works, including the novel "Hollow City" The Isdralan Chronicles Series, and the Kindred Spirits Mysteries, as well as a contributor to many anthologies. Beth is also an accomplished audiobook narrator and the host of the popular podcast, "Crossroads Cantina."

Despite her many endeavors, Beth remains down-to-earth and dedicated to living authentically, true to her passions and values. She resides in the Pacific Northwest with her husband, two children, and canine companions, who bring her boundless inspiration and delight.

www.ingramcontent.com/pod-product-compliance
Lightning Source LLC
Chambersburg PA
CBHW011436200726
48289CB00009BA/2739